"A truly engaging novel!"

– Tracy Hickman, NY Times Bestselling Author and Creator of the Dragonlance Series

"Wolf has created a richly detailed, complex fantasy universe populated by intriguing characters who will continually surprise readers throughout the briskly paced tale. Gray is a particularly well-developed protagonist, and [the novel] refreshingly allows the villainous characters to change... A strong, confident fantasy novel [and] an impressive, page-turning adventure for fans of the series."

– Kirkus Review (Citadel of Fire)

"This an entertaining quest fantasy with a fascinating twist... Gray brings freshness as a sort of Frodo struggling with what is going on to him with the changes in his life. The support cast... enhances the exciting story line as we want to know why people strongly fear the Return and why just about everyone believes the Ronin are malevolent."

– Harriet Klausner, #1 *Hall of Fame Reviewer*

"Amazing, I am so happy when I find books that keep me up all night. This is a tome of light among darkness."

– Tor Ole-Hansen, Goodreads Reviewer

"... Wolf continues to grow as a writer, to develop his own distinct style and to separate himself from the rest of the genre. If he continues his rapid growth, I would not be surprised to see him become one of the best fantasy writers of his generation."

– Eduardo Aduna, (Five Stars) READERS' FAVORITE REVIEW

"This is strong mythic fantasy with good characterizations, plenty of action, and an interesting - and complex - world. It reads quite a lot like the Inheritance Cycle Books, but a bit more mature - more like the last book than the first. I recommend it for fans of that series, younger Tolkien fans, and anyone who likes elemental match ups. I believe that my son, who tore through the Inheritance Cycle and who, at thirteen...will enjoy this quite a bit.

– OneMoreThing – Top 500 Amazon Reviewer

"A worthy epic treat to continue after *The Knife's Edge* for those, like me, who revel in drawn out worlds of high adventure and vast plots. A strong recommendation for teens (and older)."

– Tinfoot, Top 50 Amazon Reviewer

Bastion of Sun

Bastion of Sun

Book Three of The Ronin Saga

To Eva –

Enjoy!

Vaster Waits...

Matthew Wolf

Cover Art & Map Art – Flavio Bolla
Book Design – Emily Christensen
Author Photo – Sherry Phillips

To my fans. When busy roads grow quiet (and books take too long to come out), they still travel with me, seeing greatness around the bend.

The Abyss
FARHAVEN
Death's Gates
Burai Mountains
The White Plains
DE'GHAEL
Sobeku Plains
The Green Valley
Woodshire
The Silvas River
Burmen's Bank
Lakewood

DRERVRL

Dol

ty

Kimdel

The Gold Road

Werkal Desert

EASTERN KINGDOMS

The Crags

ower

The Wastelands

Maiden's Mane

DMS

Other novels by Matthew Wolf

The Ronin Saga
The Knife's Edge
Citadel of Fire
Bastion of Sun

Contents

THE THREE RULES

One

Only nine of the twelve kingdoms will be chosen and deemed "The Great Kingdoms", those who bear the eternal elements as their sigil: wind, sun, leaf, fire, moon, water, stone, flesh and metal.

Two

The warriors known as the Ronin, with nine magical swords, will be bound to the kingdoms—each matched to their elemental power in turn. Baro for metal - the Ambassador of the Great Kingdom of Metal, Seth for fire, Hiron for water, Aundevoriä for stone, Aurelious for flesh, Dared for moon, Maris for leaf, Omni for sun, and lastly, their leader, Kail for wind. They will be the peacemakers of the land, the arbitrators of justice.

Three

A prophecy will be forever engraved upon the walls of each Great Kingdom, words to spell the future of the world.

The Ronin's Return

Together—
They'll heave the seas,
Set fire to old bonds,
Unearth lost secrets,
Shed light upon the shadows,
Unveil the half-truths,
Give backbone to the damned,
Sprout new alliances,
And shift the wind to change its course.

— *Anonymous, song entitled "Ode to the Nine Elements"*

* * *

Sunroad

Brightness lightness – the road of Sun!
Glowing, flowing – it feeds us fun!
Never *stopping*, never *ending* –
But if it fails, it is said:
'Sickness, sickness - we all fall *dead*!'

—*A Children's Rhyme of Vaster, Great Kingdom of Sun*
Heard and written down by Devari Horus, in the 12th age during the celebration and construction of the Macambriel

A Missing Sword

Prologue

Nolan walked through the mist of morning, his thoughts churning. His white robes whisked at his side, brushing the immaculate stone beneath him, but his mind was set inward, thinking on the piece of paper he held in his white-gloved hand.

A note that would be Vaster's salvation or its doom.

He stopped abruptly at a crossroads, placing his hands on the stone and looking out over Vaster, the Great Kingdom of Sun. He attempted a steadying breath while taking in the sights below, hoping the familiar scene of the beautiful city would set his racing mind at ease. Though all the Great Kingdoms were visions to behold, to Nolan there was no city the equal of Vaster.

Around him like a field were spiraling towers born of crystal, glass, and white stone. Below, streets ran like narrow rivers of gold, winding their way through the high city, flowing all the way to its base far below. The whole of it sat on a rise as if propped up to graze the sun—its spires the golden fingers scraping the clouds.

Yet the true spectacle of Vaster was still an hour away.

When the sun crested the skyline, gracing the kingdom with its presence, the thousands of mirrors positioned all over the city, the glass statues in the courtyards, the golden turrets, and all else—the whole kingdom would burst with brilliant gold light, showing its namesake as the "shining jewel" of Farhaven.

Some thought the City of Sun was built using the sun to reveal its splendor, but Nolan knew the truth. Vaster was a city of unparalleled beauty—as were many of the Great Kingdoms—but it was only ever meant to highlight the magnificence of the sun, never to surpass it.

Nolan grew restless and turned.

He couldn't sit still and think. He needed to move. And when his mind was racing, as it was now, there was only one place he could go that made sense, one place where he found solace. Nolan headed to the very pinnacle of it all—the center tower called the Apex, and a clear, crystal room that sat upon its crown.

He made his way through the winding corridors until he found himself before a large door made of pure gold, the weight of a hundred men. Upon its surface, two flame-tailed phoenixes were embossed into the metal, as if caught in mid-flight. In the center of the doors was the image of the rising sun.

With a breath, Nolan freed the leather thong from around his neck, holding the heavy key before him. He inserted it into the keyhole and it clicked open.

Only the dozen Council members, the ruling government of Vaster, along with the Steward of the City of Sun were gifted a key to the Chamber of Sun.

Nolan entered, walking toward the glass case in the center. The room was circular and the far walls weren't stone, but glass. The morning fog pressed against the glass, suffusing the room in a moody dull-gray light, which gave the impression of walking amid quiet storm clouds. His soft-booted steps echoed loudly off the walls. As he approached, Nolan felt the hollowness inside him grow. He stopped an arm's length away.

Before him was a glass case as tall as a man, standing on a small marble pedestal. The pedestal was engraved with the words: *Here lies the light of Vaster, the Sword of Sun.*

Inside, it was hollow. He reached out, his hand grazing the tempered glass—forged by Reavers of old, strong enough to take a hundred hammer blows. Despite its emptiness and the strange feeling it gave him, something about it was comforting.

"Trying to fill that void?"

Nolan smiled, knowing that gravelly voice well. "Good morning, Councilor."

"Is it?" Godfrey asked.

Nolan turned, eyeing his compatriot. Godfrey was, by all accounts, an older looking gentleman. He looked exactly how Nolan thought a wise councilor should look. His hair and curly beard were nearly the same length, both a sun-bleached white. His face reminded him of stories of wise men Nolan used to read to his daughter. Heavily lined, kind, and with knowing eyes, Godfrey exuded a presence of virtue and sagacity. In a world gone mad, he was a saving grace. Nolan smiled. "It is a good morning when you're around."

Godfrey arched a noble brow. "Flattery? So early in the morning?"

"Early or late, it wouldn't change its veracity."

Godfrey chuckled. "Come now, you'll make an old man blush. Alas, I didn't make the trek up those thousand light-cursed stairs to be showered in praise. At least, not only for that." The old man's trailing brows lowered, suddenly serious. "You've been coming to the Chamber of Sun often, haven't you?"

Nolan turned away so as not to face the man and reveal his troubled thoughts.

"What's bothering you, my son?"

Any other would take offense at the title. Nolan was nearly sixty summers in age, young for a denizen of the magical Farhaven—the vast amount of spark in the land aging its inhabitants slower—but not *that* young. More than that, Nolan was the Steward of Vaster. None outranked him within the City of Sun, not even Godfrey. Yet Godfrey was different. He'd even had his chance at the position of steward, but when Nolan was suggested, Godfrey had backed him instead. "Sometimes…" Nolan began. "Sometimes I wonder if it was you that should have been Steward and not I."

Godfrey placed both hands in his voluminous sleeves and nodded as if what Nolan said was wise—but Nolan had the feeling that he was humoring him. "All great men have moments of doubt, Nolan. Do not think you are alone in that, nor are you alone otherwise. Steward is just a silly title that makes other men bow to you, like Councilor, or like having this beard," he said, stroking his long white beard, making Nolan smile. "But always their novelty wears off, when it does, you understand the truth."

Nolan realized he was still gripping the note in his hand. Surreptitiously he stuffed it in his vambraces and asked, "And what truth is that?"

"That we're never really alone. Even now wouldn't you agree?"

But Nolan was staring into the glass case. "What's that?" he asked, realizing he was lost in his thoughts again. "I... I'm sorry. My mind was elsewhere... It seems I've not been myself lately."

"Not yourself? What an odd thing—who else would you be?" Godfrey jested.

Nolan couldn't dredge a smile.

Godfrey seemed to notice. "What's changed?"

"The world," he answered, gazing out into the gray abyss. "It feels off-kilter—nothing feels quite as it should. The mantle of a leader, the unity of the kingdoms that feels so distant, the darkness that's rising... I remember being young and gazing out over the kingdom, the sun upon my face, and looking upon the Apex gleaming in the morning light, full of strength, and knowing, not feeling that it all would be right. Now—" he laughed softly, "—I'm not so sure."

Gathering his white robes behind him, Godfrey circled the glass case slowly and spoke. "The missing Sword of Sun. Did you ever hear its name?"

Nolan shook his head. "No... I can't say I have. I've read nearly every story of the Great War of the Lieon, and yet I don't remember it." He found that odd, and the man's sudden change of topic should have been equally odd, but he knew that's how Godfrey taught—like a maze, bewildering until one looked at it from above and saw where the paths led.

Godfrey smiled a grandfatherly smile. "Interesting, isn't it? The most important, defining moment in all our history—for good or ill—"

"For good?" Nolan interrupted.

Godfrey continued, unperturbed. "For good or ill, and yet we don't even know the sword's name."

"It means the act itself was the true abomination," Nolan said, feeling foolish explaining the details of an event that all knew, especially to a man like Godfrey. "The only fact that mattered was that the sword went missing, and as a result was the catalyst for the Lieon."

"And the Ronin and Vaster took the blame," Godfrey finished. "Yes, yes. It's the weight that all Vasterians feel—that of the unknown culprit of a war that cost tens of thousands of lives and nearly brought Farhaven to its knees, all because of a missing sword." He smiled as he continued to walk, his steps soft and deliberate like his words. "And yet... I wonder... Guilt of the war aside, for I feel it too, sometimes I wonder if it is simply engrained in our blood at birth now rather than inherited by word of mouth—I wonder *why* we've forgotten the blade's name. You say it was because the sword's theft was the only relevant fact to remember, but shouldn't such an important artifact be immortalized in the annals of time?" He paused in his steps then shrugged as if perhaps it were a trivial question, but Nolan knew it was anything but—such was the way Godfrey debated. Posing a simple question and allowing others to slowly draw out its greater ramifications—ramifications that always won him the heart and mind of the Council. But Nolan was tired, and his head hurt from concentrating, his thoughts turning again to the letter tucked up his sleeve.

Trust them, it had said. *Trust them or all will fall.*

He smiled, but his sigh outweighed the gesture. "I'm too tired, I'm afraid, for your puzzles, my friend. Too tired, and perhaps too witless. Mind telling me what you're getting at?"

The man showed no ill will toward Nolan's impatience. The back of his fingers grazed the glass, almost an intimate caress. "Perhaps the ramblings of an old man, but my guess is, dear Steward, if the Sword of Sun's name is forgotten… perhaps there is a reason. We remember Morrowil, do we not? Kail's sword—the legendary Sword of Wind. I remember hearing of Masamune, the leaf-shaped blade that the Ronin, Maris of Eldas wielded. But my memory seems absent when it comes to Omni's blade, the Sword of Sun… I wonder why."

"Enough suspense," Nolan pressed, but his curiosity had piqued. "You wouldn't have brought it up if you didn't have a clever theory. I know you too well. Tell me—why can we not remember?"

But Godfrey was transfixed, gazing into the glass as if something were there—as if the sword sat before his eyes and Nolan were blind. Godfrey gave his familiar, knowing smile as if the answer were so simple and he spoke, his voice distant, "I wonder if the reason we cannot remember the blade of light's name is because it was never meant to have a name… not yet, at least." The words settled, bouncing softly off the chamber's ceiling.

Nolan squinted as if staring into the sun, now truly baffled, and yet curious beyond all measure. "What… what does that mean?"

"What does what mean?" a voice boomed.

Both men turned to face the newcomer, but Nolan knew whom it was immediately—he felt his heart darken with the words.

Logan strode into the room with the presence of a king, his scarlet robes whisking along the ground as he joined their circle. His face was classically handsome with dark brown hair that fell to a strong and broad jaw, not sharp and angular like Nolan's. The Reaver's skin was tanned

5

dark from the Farbian sun—his homeland—and he had an odd characteristic of running his tongue across his teeth when he was thinking. But most notably, upon his cuffs were four stripes, black like night.

Reavers were men and women who could extract the elements from the land and conjure them to life by *threading* water, fire, stone, metal, flesh, moon, sun and leaf. Reavers were a rare breed, and some rarer still. Nolan wasn't very familiar with their ranks, but from what'd he'd gleaned over the years, a one stripe Reaver could only do simple things: lift metal pots and pans, make thick branches snap or light a campfire from thin air.

A four-stripe Reaver, however, was nearly an Arbiter—the highest ranks of threaders in all of Farhaven. Only a handful existed, and from the little Nolan surmised of Farbian politics, each was considered a figurehead much like the Council of Sun. And while Reavers' reputations were less glorious than the days of old, they were still highly respected and welcome in most lands.

Logan's arrival had come on the back of a recent, momentous meeting conducted by the Patriarch in order to decide the fate of the lands with the onset of the rising darkness. Nolan still felt his stomach churn in memory. Unfortunately, the meeting had resulted mostly in the squabbling of monarchs, gnawing and bickering over a thousand years of bad blood and old rivalries. It made sense, naturally, for historically sovereign nations to hold friction when the topic of uniting was revisited. In the end, the meeting had served its purpose: it opened the lines of communication once more, and set a future date to cement definitive plans of allegiance. All had signed the treaty to reconvene to establish lines of communication and each agreed to provide portions of their armies to conquer the rising evil plaguing the lands, an evil seeming to originate behind the twisted metal gates of the Great Kingdom of Metal. Of course, there were those who failed to cooperate. The thief-lord of moon, the Shadow King, was a growing stain on Nolan's already worried mind. It didn't help that two of the Great Kingdoms were lost during the war—Stone and Wind, destroyed by the ancient conflict of the Lieon. That put five united Great Kingdoms: Water, Fire, Leaf, Flesh and Sun. These were all that remained of the nine now.

The day after the meeting to decide the fate of Farhaven, Logan had arrived. The Patriarch sent him as an ambassador to oversee any affairs between the two Kingdoms, as an example to the other Great Kingdoms of what trust and camaraderie should look like. That had been a fortnight ago. It had only taken a day before Nolan wanted to strangle the man.

As per usual, he paid Nolan little mind, his words addressing the wiser, older Godfrey. "What does *what* mean?" he repeated.

Godfrey looked up as if broken from a spell. The man was wise, but sometimes he seemed to be a daydreaming youth trapped in an old man's body. "Greetings, our magical denizen."

Logan grunted.

"We were discussing the Lieon and the missing sword," Nolan said, diplomatically and honestly.

The Reaver snorted. "You people of light are so open about everything." He looked around the room with a wrinkled nose, eyeing the mirrors, the glass walls and especially the glass casement as if it were tainted. "Even about your horrible misdeeds. If I were you, I would bury that incident in the past where it belongs, along with this *relic* of a room. After all, a stain can only be removed if cut from the fabric, and a stain such as yours requires much cutting."

Nolan bristled, feeling his face flush in anger.

But Godfrey stepped in, saving Nolan from his rising temper. "Surely, my wise friend, you don't believe that. The deeds of one's ancestors are not the fault of their descendants, are they?"

Logan approached with confident strides, his red robes skimming smoothly along the marble. "How are they not? If your family is noble, you follow in its line—do you not? My father was a great threader of the spark, a four-stripe as well and nearly an Arbiter—if it wasn't for the promotion of another who now holds the second rank, an injustice I remember to this day." He spat the words then shook himself, remembering the topic at hand and raising his head. "But his legacy lives on through me and my two brothers, just as your legacy lives on through you."

"Perhaps," Godfrey said, "But how we embrace that legacy is up to us, is it not?"

Logan hesitated.

"Furthermore," Godfrey continued, gaining force, seizing upon the man's rare moment of rationality, a skill Nolan was accustomed to seeing him do. "You must remember the past in order to prevent the same mistakes in the future, wouldn't you agree? For instance, if your father, may the light bless his memory forever, performed an abominable deed— would it not be your duty to remember that and make sure not to repeat the same misdeed?"

Logan snarled. "Repeat the same misdeed? You and your people misplaced the greatest artifact this world has ever known." Logan laughed, but there was no mirth in it. "The day the Sword of Sun was stolen, Vaster became a dark stain upon Farhaven. A disgrace to all of the world. My father would never make a mistake like you. He would never be tarnished so. The very reason you are remembered that way is because of your carelessness. You let the sword out of your grasp and thousands died, thousands upon thousands and—"

Nolan stepped forward, interrupting the man. "—And if your beloved father loved the Ronin?"

The words were like a dagger to Logan's rant. Nolan knew where Logan's allegiances lay when it came to the Ronin. All men of zealotry believed the Ronin a plague that had brought Farhaven to its near ruin, but Nolan knew the truth was much more convoluted for he'd read the ancient stories and seen the unspoken truth. The Ronin were not evil— something else had been the downfall of Farhaven those millennia ago. But it didn't matter. To Logan, Nolan had just accused his father to be a lover of the dark lord, or worse.

Logan's face turned red with blood, a vein throbbing in the man's forehead. Nolan felt the air turn crisp. He knew Logan was threading the spark, and yet part of him didn't care. He hated Logan to his core, and part of him welcomed whatever came... If the fool roasted him to the ground where he stood, the Council would have his head and—

"Come, come," Godfrey said loudly, his voice ringing through the room like a bronze bell, attempting to diffuse the tension. "Let's not get so heated over such silly theories. Besides, it's too early in the morning for such talk." He grabbed the Reaver's shoulders but the man shrugged him off.

"Yes," said Logan, his shoulders slowly falling, rage slipping from his face like a mask—there one moment, gone the next. "Too early indeed. Besides, the Ronin are legends that had their time. Now is a new age— and the Patriarch will guide us to it." He held Nolan's gaze, at last turning.

As the two neared the golden door, Nolan saw a woman. He'd nearly forgotten that Logan had come with a two-stripe Reaver. She was beautiful, with a long fall of chestnut colored hair framing her proud, noble features, and most notably her eyes. One was gray and the other a startling green. Logan had never seen two different colored eyes before. He'd heard tales of it from the folk of Cloudfell Lake, but the most he'd been

8

told was of slightly different dark eyes, one tan and one brown or some such thing. He felt strange memories, rumors of another city whose people had different colored light eyes, but they disappeared as he focused his skittering thoughts on her fully. A brief flash of emotion passed over her face that bespoke of sadness, but then it was gone as she dipped her head servilely as if burying it away like a cold gem beneath the sands.

"Come, Miriam," Logan ordered, striding past.

The woman caught Nolan's gaze—lingering. She looked as if she wanted to speak. He felt something touch the back of his mind, like an itch inside his skull... He shook his head, and when he looked up the door was shutting, Godfrey guiding the two Reavers away with diversions and talk of inane matters of state.

Nolan was left standing in the room alone.

Slowly, he unfurled the paper tucked in his vambrace and read:

The Ronin have come again. Be ready, for they will arrive on your doorstep upon the new moon. You must welcome them, trust them... or all will fall to ruin.

The note itself had been slipped beneath his door—that was all he knew.

That and he trusted it. He didn't know why, but he did.

As he finished the words, in the corner of his vision Nolan saw the sun slowly peak over the horizon, shedding its first brilliant rays upon the room—hinting at the majesty of the kingdom at his back. Miraculously, as the sun touched the thousands of mirrors in the room, like a brilliant show of light, the air began to hum.

It was a song enchanted within the glass, triggered *by* the sun—an ancient, ethereal tune that took the chill out of the cold air. Normally it warmed his heart, and made him feel connected and at peace. Yet today, under the weight of his thoughts, staring at the empty glass case, it simply provided a chilling chorus to Godfrey's words echoing in his mind.

It was never meant to have a name... not yet, at least.

9

THE SHIFTING SANDS

A mist appeared, rising from the ground, curling and moving with dark purpose. Gray pulled on his reins, stopping short. The others slowed at his side, tense and wary. Their destination loomed in the distance: Vaster, the city of sun with its golden turrets and glassy spires, but then the mist rolled in and shrouded it from sight.

"What's happening?" Darius asked, his bay charger dancing nervously beneath him. Darius rode at Gray's side. His brown hair was its usual matted mess, though his discerning, tan-colored eyes flicked from left to right, as if creatures were about to leap from their ashen surroundings. The rogue's cloak wavered behind him, its shade of green matching the sword on his back: Masamune—the leaf blade and sword of the Ronin of Leaf. Though sheathed in a dull brown scabbard, the steel within pulsed, issuing a soft emerald glow. Ayva was to Gray's left, riding a cormac, and Hannah and Zane—brother and sister—rode close by, near one another as usual.

Luckily the cormacs—elven mounts with silken hair, long necks and sloping backs—that Gray and Ayva rode, merely stamped lightly at the ground with cloven translucent hooves, calm as their elven kin.

Gray reached into his memories as Kirin—his old self.

Heaviness in the air.

Black, anvil-shaped clouds in the sky.

Then he rolled back his sleeve, reaching out. The mist curled about his arm, and he watched as goosebumps trickled up his skin and his hairs stood on end, confirming his fears.

"A storm is coming," Gray announced.

"A sparkstorm?" Darius asked, gulping.

He was rightfully fearful. Sparkstorms were fierce thunderstorms of lightning, rain and lashing wind that lasted for days. They were fueled by the magic of Farhaven, the land itself. In their journey thus far, they'd already been waylaid by them twice. Gray shook his head. Something felt different this time. Each time he'd felt a sparkstorm in their journey, despite the charge in the air, and the heaviness, he'd felt alive with magic—a vibrant sense of urgency, life and power filling his veins. This time, however, he felt a gnawing hole in his chest, as if his energy were being drained, carved away by merely standing in the thickening mist. This time, instead of life, he felt death.

"Something tells me this is different," Gray said simply, making his voice even, not wanting to worry the others.

"Whatever it is, it's magic," Zane said, lip curling in disdain. For a man who threaded the flow, the essence of all magic, Zane had an odd contempt for it, though Gray doubted his spirited friend would see the irony.

"If it's not a sparkstorm, what is it?" Darius asked.

"I'm not sure."

Hannah ushered her steed closer, her shy white mare whinnying as the mist crept closer. "Um, can we talk later and move now? I don't like this place."

Gray nodded. "Best we do."

They continued, Ayva at his side, the others close behind. They rode in silence, Gray watching the mist, his skin prickling at its touch. It wasn't wet or cold, but oddly warm. The mist reminded him far too much of the battle upon the sands. Of Faye. Of Darkwalkers and of death.

Gray glimpsed a gleaming turret of glass in the distance, peaking above the mist, and found a sliver of comfort. *At least it's still there.* They'd been so close... If he squinted before he almost felt as if he could see guards walking the lacy bridges that spanned between towers. But now? The Great Kingdom of Sun seemed a thousand leagues away.

Through the ki, Gray's ability to empathetically feel another's emotions, he sensed Ayva's wariness and some other emotion he couldn't quite identify, like a gnawing uncertainty. Gray edged closer to Ayva.

11

"Do you know what's happening? Do your books or Faye's knowledge say anything about this?" It felt odd to hear his voice, muffled by the wall of fog on all sides, but he was glad to fill the silence.

Ayva shook her head, her short-cropped blonde hair swaying. "Farhaven is like a book with no beginning or end whose words can be amended at any point. There's no predicting it."

"I've heard of this," Hannah said.

"You have?" Zane, her brother, asked. Broad, but not tall, Zane looked like he was built out of brick and mortar. His face was bluff, his brows thick and heavy over his hooded eyes. His blond hair was kept short and spikey, and he moved with a surprising amount of slyness for one so heavily muscled—perhaps a trait gained from his life as a charitable thief. As it turned out, Zane's past life had involved robbing from the rich and giving to the poor, and that life had seemed to ingrain a sort of burning anger, Gray had noticed, in his friend's soul. He always bore a residual ire behind his eyes, except when looking at his sister as he did now.

"It's just a story," Hannah said, but her eyes said differently. She looked afraid.

"Even stories have merit," Gray said, wiping the mist that clung to his arm. Did it just *slither?* No, just his mind playing tricks. "Go on."

They continued to ride as Hannah spoke.

"It was a tale from this group of traders. They were a wretched-looking lot. Four men, older than us, with silver rings and gold threading on their cloaks, merchants I guessed, but they had this look in their eyes... that look someone gets when they've seen too much, you know?"

Gray knew that look well.

"Anyway, after a bit of prodding and a lot of silence, they told me what happened to them." Her smile faltered and Hannah looked away.

"What happened?" Gray asked.

Hannah explained how the merchants had been traveling for weeks when they got caught in a terrible Farhaven sparkstorm. They'd survived, but they'd been at the brink of death, starved and half-mad from dehydration. So when the merchants stumbled upon a Node—a magical oasis that Farhaven spawned for those in need, often providing water, food and shelter for the wayward traveler—they said they could scarcely believe their luck.

"They saw it in the dead of night. Glowing blue, 'like an omen from the Messiah himself'," Hannah recounted. "I'll never forget the way they described it: crackling, violent, but utterly silent, like lightning without thunder." She went on, describing how inside they discovered skeleton trees, scorched, cracked earth, rotting vegetation, and…" Hannah swallowed, looking about, "Clinging fog. Like it was death's breath."

Gray shivered, and he noticed Darius and Ayva did too, itching in their clothes as they skirted a particularly dense batch of mist, but it seemed to swirl and follow.

"What happened then?" Darius asked as they rode.

Hannah shook her head. "I only got bits and pieces, but over and over again, when they had the courage to speak at least, I realized the merchants said 'us five'. But there were only four of them. I… I didn't have the stomach to ask any more and I don't think they had the stomach to answer. But they did call the place something," Hannah said. "Among a dozen other curse words, they called it one thing above all else — a Void."

Voids… Gray distantly remembered that name.

"Places without magic." Ayva scratched her arm as if her skin crawled. "I can sense a lack of magic within these mists, something draining and pulling at my soul."

Again, Gray felt it too, and sensed it in the others with the ki.

The ki was an ability Gray possessed to sift into another's body and sense their emotions. Whether it was fear or anger, love or hate, Gray could feel nearby persons' feelings. The more powerful the ki, the more intricate the emotion Gray could detect and decipher. The ki had its limits, of course: he still had trouble sensing certain people's emotions. In some people Gray could only sense their basest emotion. Those who'd been trained could block his ki altogether. But right now, in his friends, Gray felt their fear and a profound emptiness at losing touch with their magic.

Ahead, Gray saw something.

Stone, he realized. It looked like a white stone wall, shrouded in mist.

"It's a little hard to see. Someone mind clearing this damned fog?" Darius asked.

Gray raised his hand, trying to touch his *nexus*—an imagined swirling ball of air that sat in his mind. It was the source of his flow, his power. But as Gray reached for it, his nexus flickered, a pale imitation of its usual self. "It seems it goes for the flow, my power is next to useless here," he confessed.

"Together then," Ayva said, and fits of fire, sparks of light and erratic

13

wind laid into the mist. Gray suddenly felt completely exhausted, as if he'd run a dozen miles, but luckily their work cleared some of the fog to show sand and ruins. Stone walls of an ancient city crumbling around them. The land directly under their feet was cracked. A gnarled tree hung over him, the only sign of life, but it was dead, withered and crooked and reminded Gray of a wizard's finger casting a nefarious spell. The land itself was dark and the clouds above looked stormy and angry. Silver lightning forked through the roiling thunderheads. Bits of orange shone through, however, indicating daytime beyond the mist.

Unexpectedly, Ayva dismounted.

"Ayva…"

She ignored Gray.

He kneed his cormac closer and saw what she was looking at. Her hand played over symbols scratched in one of the larger shattered walls. Moss and vines crawled over the stone, but where the words lay it was bare, as if exposed by magic.

14

"What's it say?" Hannah asked.

Zane grunted. "It's not the common tongue. Old Language? Or Sand Tongue?"

"It's Elvish," said Ayva before Gray could. "But my Elvish is…*rough* at best. I can't read it."

"Nor I," Gray admitted. He knew a few words in Elvish, but reading the strange, sharp glyphs was something altogether different.

All turned to Darius, and the rogue grudgingly dismounted. "I'm the scribe now, am I?" he joked half-heartedly, then squinted at the strange text. "It's old. It feels familiar."

"What's it say?" Gray asked.

"Beware. Magic holds no sway here, and all who enter the realm of the Void will die."

"A Void," Ayva echoed.

"I don't like this…" Zane said. "We should leave."

At Zane's words, the sand shifted all around them.

"Algasi!" Gray shouted.

The sands broke and two dozen warriors leapt from beneath. Gray reached out with his nexus, readying blows. A pitiful sphere of fire burst forth and crashed into a wall—stone littered the air, creating a cloud of dust. The Algasi warriors wore sand-colored rags, their faces covered in midnight black shrouds save for their dark eyes, each wielding spears and bladed staves. As the fire burst, several Algasi were blown back, but a dozen more took their place, sand sloughing from their dark clothing. Their eyes, the only distinguishable feature on their face, blazed with fury, and their cries cut the silence.

As two more Algasi sprang from the sand, Gray's cormac reared up as spears jabbed toward its chest. Gray unsheathed Morrowil, the legendary Sword of Wind with a ring, cutting the first spear from the air. But the second came down, aiming for his cormac's throat.

Gray cried out, grabbing his nexus, and power rushed forth. Gray summoned a gust of wind and knocked the man from his feet. But as the man fell, his spear veered to the side and cut Gray's saddle. Gray was upended and thrown to the sands. His head struck something hard, ringing dully, but he managed to find his feet. Rage and power roared through him like a tempest, lifting his hands, white wind swirling at his fingertips, ready to level anything that stood in his way.

There was a strangled cry, and the fighting stopped as suddenly as it had started. Gray's breath caught when he saw why. Hannah's hair was in the grip of an Algasi. Another held a spear to her throat, ready to kill her.

Zane growled, taking a step forward. As his foot fell, the Algasi's spear pressed closer to Hannah's throat, drawing a pinpoint of blood. Hannah made a small moan of pain and Zane's eyes went wide with rage.

Gray's blood ran cold. No... He called out for his friend, but it was too late.

Zane roared and leapt towards Hannah. His fist connected, smashing an Algasi in the face—one of the two holding Hannah. The Algasi crumpled beneath Zane's blow. The other Algasi holding Hannah watched his compatriot collapse in disbelief. Zane, looming over the Algasi, reached for the hilt of his blade. Metal rung, but before the blade was free of its scabbard, a half-dozen Algasi leapt upon him. Zane struggled, growling, kicking and roaring with primal fury, trying to wrestle free. But Gray knew it was a losing fight—and he watched, teeth grit, as an Algasi slammed his fist into Zane's jaw, dazing the muscled youth. Another Algasi stripped

15

Zane free of his blade, while two more pinned Zane's arm's behind his back and the last few placed spears to the hollow of Zane's throat.

It all happened in a matter of moments. Gray wouldn't have been able to help had he wanted to, and he knew if he had, it would have been a useless fight. There were twenty Algasi and only five of them. Still, his grip tightened on Morrowil.

"Drop your blades," a voice thundered.

Gray turned to see a familiar white shroud and cunning blue eyes. Another Algasi stalked forward, appearing out of the dark ruins, but this one was different: tall, broad-shouldered, and foreboding as ever. His banded spear was gripped loosely in one hand. Four Algasi flanked him.

No, Gray realized, not just Algasi—Mundasi as well. Algasi was a race—a nomadic desert tribe that much of the world feared. That sentiment, as a Ronin, Gray empathized with *deeply*. But to be an Algasi was also, he'd discovered, a name attributed to a rank within the tribe. And while Algasi-ranked members seemed to be sufficiently skilled with various weapons, from knives to spears to nunsais, to be a *Mundasi* was an echelon all of its own. Gray knew little about Mundasi aside from the fact they bore a single blue band on their spears as testament to their superior rank. And an even sharper fear burned into his brain was the memory of what this particular Mundasi had done to Faye—making the highly skilled woman look like a toddler with a sword during the pair's duel to the death. The Mundasi had nearly killed her without breaking a sweat. Gray knew a single-banded Mundasi was every bit a match for a Devari.

And the speaker's spear bore not one stripe, but two.

"Dalic," Gray said.

"Greetings, liars and betrayers," Dalic, the Algasi leader replied. He stopped and rolled his broad, heavy shoulders as if preparing to fight while his cold blue eyes, like icy daggers, scanned Gray's party with brooding intensity.

Dalic was the same Mundasi who'd fought Faye. Faye was danger incarnate, only wrapped in leather and topped off with a sly smile and haunted eyes. She'd easily bested Gray during their first encounter, but Dalic? The Algasi leader had somehow made Faye look tame and weak. The two-striped Mundasi had almost killed Faye, running her through with his spear until Gray had broken their Honor Duel, grabbed Faye from Dalic's killing blow, and fled in order to survive.

Gray had worried they'd cross paths with Dalic and his Algasi eventu-

16

ally. He'd heard rumors of the desert warriors roaming closer and closer during their journey, but he hadn't imagined it'd be here, so near to their goal. He eyed the glimmer of Vaster's translucent towers, pillars of light rising out of the darkness, and felt as if he could almost shout and attract the guards. It was just wishful thinking—they were still hours from Vaster, and it felt like leagues.

"Let my sister go and I promise not to kill all of you," Zane growled, still pinned by multiple Algasi, but Gray saw his eyes—they burned with fire.

Dalic approached Zane. The Algasi leader put his spear to Zane's throat, lifting his chin. "There's fire in your eyes. The fire of anger and pain. You are a man who wishes to die, aren't you?"

Zane said nothing, but his eyes smoldered with anger.

"What do you want with us?" Hannah asked, eyes wide, watching the spear to her throat.

"Your friends have not told you, have they? You've chosen poor travel-ing companions, girl, for you journey with liars."

"We never lied," Darius snapped.

"What's going on? What's he's talking about?" Hannah asked.

"This is not our first meeting," Dalic said. "Your friends promised a duel of honor the last we met, a sacred thing among my people, only to break it and flee. An act unheard of by my kind, and by the laws of an Algasi, punishable by death. For if there is no honor in this world, then we are nothing more than beasts."

"You wanted to kill us all!" Darius exclaimed. "Why would we follow your laws, your supposed holy path?"

Dalic snorted as sand blew across the stalemate, catching in Gray's lashes. "Our path *is* holy. It is the way of balance. We seek the sword and the sword will restore order to Farhaven. It will bring balance to a world cast in shadows. There is no greater reason than that."

Gray spoke, drawing eyes at last. "Let her go."

"Why should I, Windspeaker?"

Dalic was furious, but there was something else. Gray reached out with the ki again, hoping the warrior couldn't sense it. He felt Dalic's terrible anger. No, there had to be more to this man. And Gray searched and... he felt it. *Guilt. Hesitation.* He smiled. Now he could play on it.

But before he could, Gray saw Zane begin to rise, subtly reaching for his sword nearby. The fire in Zane's eyes grew and it danced at his fin-

17

gertips. Gray knew what he was planning to do. His own will like a heated blade, Gray slammed his thoughts into Zane's. *Enough, Zane,* he commanded. *If you do that, they'll kill her. We'll all die for your rage. It isn't worth it.*

Zane seethed in reply. *What does it matter? They will kill her and us anyway. Algasi murderer without conscience. All the world knows it, and I'd rather die fighting than have my throat slit while on my knees.*

No, a reply came, sharp and confident. It wasn't Gray. They both turned to see Ayva, standing calmly. She sheathed her translucent dagger. *I've a plan, Zane. Trust me.*

Zane sighed but fortunately, he remained where he was.

He hesitates, Gray told Ayva. *Dalic's not a bad man. He just doesn't know if he can trust us yet, and he fears for something. If you can discover his fear and make him trust us—*

Make him trust us? We betrayed him, at least in his mind, Darius replied. *If you remember, we trounced his men and ran away from his sacred Honor Duel.*

Ayva can do it, Gray said. He looked to her. *I trust you.*

Ayva nodded. *First, lower your sword, Darius.*

Lower my what? You're kidding, right? That's the only thing keeping us alive at the moment.

There's two dozen of them and five of us. If they wish to kill us, they can do so at any moment. Your sword would do us little good. If you drop it, it will show a sign of faith. You too, Gray—don't fight. They may still kill us, but I can promise you your swords won't save us.

Grudgingly, Darius obeyed. Masamune fell and the Algasi he was holding slowly pulled away, puzzled. Gray saw Dalic watching. It *was* working. But then Dalic looked to Ayva, as if recognizing her at last.

"You…" Dalic flicked two fingers, and the waiting dozen Algasi flowed in at them from all directions, raising spears, brandishing steel to their throats. Two Mundasi approached Gray. Dalic raised his hands and they kicked, buckling Gray's knees, and he fell with a grimace. Another backhanded him hard; pain and blackness blotted out his vision. His mouth stung and he tasted blood. His vision slowly returned. Despite his rage, Gray knew a losing battle when he saw one. He had one last idea: Morrowil. The blade, like all of the Ronin's swords, would cause excruciating pain to any but its destined wielder. Gray dropped Morrowil, feigning reluctance. A door-wide Mundasi sheathed his spear and reached for the blade, but then noticed the look in Gray's eyes, his hand a breath away from Morrowil, and froze. The big Mundasi snorted contemptuously, rising, ignoring the fallen blade. Gray cursed himself, realizing he'd been too attentive, too eager-looking.

Zane laughed. "What're you waiting for?"

"A valid question," Dalic answered, then waved his hand. "Finish it."

"Wait," Ayva shouted, stalling them. "You don't want to kill us."

Dalic's eyes never shifted, but he did raise three fingers on his right hand. The spears remained where they were. "Why should I listen to you? I named you Lightspeaker. I name you again. *False-tongued, Breaker of Words.* You led me to an Honor Duel and then broke your oath and fled. Tell me now, why would I not want to kill oathbreakers such as yourself?"

"Because," Ayva replied, "I know how to get your sword."

Dalic's white cloth shroud tilted inquisitively.

Even Gray felt a stab of curiosity, but he remained silent, spear pressed to the hollow of his throat.

"What do you mean?" Dalic asked. "And if you lie to me I will kill you myself."

"The Sword of Sun is what you seek, is it not? I can retrieve it for you." She turned to Darius, then Gray. "You explained recently how you found your sword, Darius—tucked in the folds of a tree. But how did you find yours, Gray?"

He shook his head, baffled. "Ayva—is this really the time?"

"*How, Gray?*"

Gray sighed. The memory was still painful, but he could recount it. "I..." The words nearly followed: *I walked in on my sister impaled with a sword in her gut and dark wings sprouting from her body. That sword was Morrowil.* But he knew now wasn't the time for the full truth. Instead he answered, "I found it in Farbs long ago. I stumbled upon it, much like Darius."

Ayva nodded, excited. Did she realize that they were surrounded by a dozen ruthless warriors who were moments from cutting their throats? "Precisely," she exclaimed. "That's just it." She grabbed Dalic's dusty sleeve, sand falling away. Surprisingly, the fearsome warrior eyed her hand but made no move. "I know how to get your sword."

"Speak," said the two-banded warrior.

"You see, we're..." she began then stopped, seeing Gray's eyes. He

19

shook his head slightly, feeling the spear on his throat scratch, but he suffered the pain. *No, Ayva. They're not ready to hear that.* "We're more than we seem."

"How so?"

She shook her head. "For now it doesn't matter. But I know what you're looking for. You're seeking the Riddle of Sun, aren't you? The prophecy."

Dalic's eyes hardened, the only feature not covered by his white shroud. "Who told you of the prophecy?"

"No one told us," Darius said, "We found one already, a riddle, that is, and—"

A Mundasi jabbed him in the arm and Darius cried out in pain. "Silence, dog," growled the one-banded Mundasi who held Darius. "You were not told to speak."

"Stop," Ayva called, adding quickly, "he's right. We found the Riddle of Fire. It led us to what we needed. In the same way you're looking for this Riddle of Sun because you believe it will lead you to the Sword of Sun." Dalic said nothing. His blue eyes narrowed to dagger-like slits, and Gray could only assume that was Dalic's version of curious and rapt. Ayva continued. "More than that, we can find your sword because... I'm not sure how to make you believe this, but we're meant to find it. I'm *meant* to find it. You see my friend's sword?" She pointed to Darius' Masamune. "And his?" She pointed to Gray, to Morrowil glowing silver upon the ground. "They are not normal weapons. My friends were pulled to their blades, and their blades were pulled to them. I believe the missing Sword of Sun will be the same for me."

"The Sword of Sun is beholden to no man or woman," an Algasi said in his clipped speech. "Not even the Lightspeaker."

Dalic raised two fingers, silencing his brethren. He tilted his head, a customary trait of his, Gray was beginning to realize. "Why you?" he asked. "What is so special about you that the Sword of Sun is bound to you, girl?"

Other Algasi grunted like beasts, as if supporting his words.

"Because," Ayva began, taking a nervous breath.

Gray shook his head. *Please, Ayva, no. The world is not ready.* He knew even if they believed her, they very well may blame her as Omni's successor, and Omni's failure to secure the blade would be Ayva's as well. And all the guilt and pain that the Algasi bore would fall upon her head.

20

"I…" Ayva swallowed, then said more firmly, "I can't tell you, but you'll just have to trust that I'm not lying. Trust the truth in my voice. Besides, how do you plan to enter that, anyway?" She pointed to the gleaming bastion of sun, built upon a green rise, gilded walls, pillars, gold-capped domes and spires like glass flutes. It sat above the mist like a dream. "If I'm not mistaken, if you step foot inside that city you will be surrounded by a thousand Vasterian guards and slaughtered quicker than a hen in a den of foxes."

"Your words make no sense. Phoxes? They are beings of wind who do not kill unless it is a Darkwalker. And what is this *hen* you speak of?" Dalic questioned.

Gray winced, realizing while Farhaven had thousands of magical creatures, they did not have some of the creatures Daerval had.

"She means you will all die," Darius answered, earning another sharp jab and a snarl.

"Algasi do not die so easily," Dalic replied angrily.

"No, they do not," Ayva agreed, "but they will. And what then? Your death serves no one. Most importantly, it gets you no closer to your goal, and only enforces the claim that you and your people are wild, that you deserve death. And we both know that's not true."

"A good death in search of the Sword of Sun is all any Algasi can wish for."

Ayva sighed. "Don't be the blind savage they try to label you as, Dalic—"

Dalic moved so quickly that Gray's eyes could barely follow. The Algasi leader backhanded Ayva hard, spraying blood. Gray lunged forward but a spear stopped him, pressing to his throat. He didn't care. Despite the void sapping his flow, he felt his power swirl around his palm, eddies of wind curling at his fingertips and—

Ayva raised a hand. Her words resonated in his mind. *No, Gray. If you fight here, we all die. Let me handle this. Please.*

He glanced over. Darius and Zane had witnessed Dalic's blow as well. He saw they had tried to fight their captors, but Zane was on his knees pressed to the ground. They'd heard as well. At Ayva's words, Darius and Zane settled slightly. Zane still growled fiercely, spitting at the feet of his captor.

Ayva lifted her head. She put a hand to the corner of her mouth, wiping away a small trickle of blood. "Forgive my rudeness," she whispered,

21

her voice tight with pain, but her eyes blazed. "The simple truth is this—you *will* die if you enter Vaster, and then you, your men, and your quest will fail, and the sword will remain lost for all time."

Dalic lifted his chin, looking down on her warily. "And what do you propose, wise one?"

"You can never enter the City of Sun, but we *can*. We'll enter Vaster, find the Riddle of Sun, decipher its contents, and return. Then, as promised, we'll retrieve the Sword of Sun and set all in its proper place."

"Proper place?"

"The Algasi are not evil and never were. You aren't the wandering murderers the world believes. I know this. I—*we*," she corrected and pointed to Gray and the others, "can help you prove that."

"Truly a bold and wise plan," Dalic said, musing. He rubbed at his jaw through his white shroud then shook his head. "But it will never work. The Riddle of Sun is guarded, restricted to only those blind fools who call themselves leaders of the fallen city, placed high inside their precious Apex, a turret so tall and well-defended it is said to be..." He squinted, as if searching for a word. "Un-sailable."

"Unassailable?" Ayva asked.

Dalic nodded, unperturbed by the correction. His thick forearm pointed to the highest gleaming tower, peaking above the mist. "Even a wandering murderer like me, as you say, knows this. You will never get close enough to the riddle. Not like we can."

Gray spoke up and nearly choked on the spear at his throat. "You're wrong." Dalic twisted. Gray risked the wrath of the Algasi who held him to speak up. "We've a letter. With it we can get farther than you ever could," he answered defiantly. He hoped his words sounded more confident than angry, but the metal point scratching against his throat was planting a seed of wrath inside him to rival Zane's ire.

The two-banded Mundasi looked back to Ayva. "Does the Windspeaker speak truth?"

"He does," she said. "His grandfather is a very powerful threader of the spark. A good man and a leader much like you. He gave us a letter for the leaders of the city." Ayva neared and after a subtle gesture, her eyes speaking for her, the Mundasi stepped back. How did she...? Gray wondered but didn't ask, prying the slip of paper Ezrah had given him from his sleeve.

Ayva lifted the paper into the air. "This will get us to where we need to go."

"And if not?" Dalic queried sharply.

Her face was stone, matching Dalic's eyes and conviction. Blue eyes like icy daggers. Gray nearly swallowed, knowing that look. *Omni.* It was Omni's look, Ayva's predecessor and the previous Ronin of Sun. "It *will*," she said. "And if not, I will find a way to convince them."

"*Kara*," Dalic uttered. Gray knew *kara* meant *fire* in the Sand Tongue, for he'd heard Faye speak it before. The Algasi leader tilted his head, eyeing Ayva, judging her carefully. "But is it enough fire to see the duty done, or will you fail once more?"

Ayva stood her ground, straight-backed and defiant. Only a small movement in her throat showed Gray that she was the least bit nervous. Tension built as Dalic's eyes gauged her. His men behind him tightened their grip on their weapons, ready for the command, ready to kill.

Gray choked on the increasing pressure of the spear at his throat. He stared his captor in the eyes, but regretted it as the Mundasi looked into his soul with eyes like orbs of coal. Morrowil was close, lying upon the sand, but not close enough. Besides, even if he killed the guard holding him, what could he do to stop the rest?

At last Dalic spoke. "*Tas un varisu un salus.*"

The Algasi made sharp grunting sounds, ushering Gray and his friends to their feet. "What're they doing?" Hannah asked fearfully. "Are they… are they going to kill us?"

They were met only with silence and more prodding.

Together they were pushed out of the fog, weaving through the ruins, stepping over strange black fissures in the sand. With every step, Gray felt his power return. He inhaled deeper and easier with every footfall. Darius, Ayva, and Zane did the same, taking deep inhales and looking about in confusion as if emerging from a dark pit. Gray glanced back at the ruins only to see a pervasive mist. He couldn't explain it, but it felt as if being inside the Void, the black ruined plot of ground where no magic could be used, had been draining his life force. And perhaps it had.

He inhaled again, relishing the suddenly warm air of the Paragon Steppes.

Gray felt as though he was waking from a nightmare.

He turned, embracing the nexus, power flooding his limb and sensed the others do the same. As he did, the spear tips dropped.

Gray turned, facing Dalic and, for the first time, saw the man fully.

23

Dalic was far more intimidating than Gray had originally thought. What he gazed upon wasn't simply a warrior with a spear—he was a weapon of death. His broad shoulders rolled as if hungry for a fight, yet the rest of him was patience incarnate. He still wore tan cloth, but parts looked brushed with green grass to meld with their newfound surroundings. His arms were exposed except for the heavy cloth and leather bracers on his thick forearms. As opposed to his ebony-skinned brothers, Dalic's skin wasn't charcoal but deeply tanned, a dark brown, and heavily scarred. Strange black markings ran up his right arm. The markings were visible again on his thick chest—a portion of it was exposed by a loose shirt. Gray couldn't make sense of the glyphs. Even Kirin's memories didn't know what they meant. A thick crimson sash was woven around Dalic's waist. His starkest features were his sheer-blue eyes, the only visible feature gazing out from beneath his white-cloth shrouded face.

His men joined him at his side, a row of two-dozen fearsome, tan-clothed warriors with masks of darkest black. Where Dalic's eyes were a piercing blue, the others' eyes were glinting pieces of obsidian peering out shrewdly from a dark cave. Gray saw wisps of light hair curling beneath those black shrouds. Their hands—the only flesh visible—were charcoal-skinned, much darker than anything he'd seen before. He wondered why Dalic looked different, but Gray simply set the difference aside, remembering to note it for later.

Dalic pointed to the city with his spear. "It's two hours run or an hour upon your beasts. Once you reach the city, head to the Apex. That is where the prophecy will be. You have until the following dawn to retrieve the prophecy."

"The dawn isn't enough," Ayva interjected.

"It is all you get," the man said harshly, turning his head to face her. "If you try to run, we will find you and kill you. If you try to hide, we will find you and kill you. If you fail to find the prophecy—"

"—you will find us and kill us," Darius finished. "I think we get it."

Dalic's men stirred, lifting their weapons.

Gray wished that Darius could just hold his tongue sometimes, but despite his friend's rudeness, the warriors slowly lowered the spears.

"So be it," Gray answered.

"A final piece," Dalic said, and gestured to a nearby Algasi who also bore a red sash around his slender waist. The Algasi was as tall and broad-shouldered as Dalic, but where Dalic was compact muscle layered

24

upon muscle, this man was slighter of build. Gray noticed he had only one arm, but he stood close to Dalic in a position of honor. The one-armed Algasi unsheathed a ceremonial dagger from his back. Roughly shaped, with a wooden handle wrapped in turquoise wiring, and fitted with a red blade, it looked like a relic of insurmountable value. Dalic lifted the dagger. It gleamed in the sun like one of the mirrors of Vaster which were shimmering in the distance. Then he pressed the blade to his palm, flesh peeling, raising a thin line of blood.

He did it so fast Gray couldn't argue or oppose, but he knew what came next.

Dalic extended the dagger, hilt first.

Without thinking, Gray reached for it.

"No," Ayva said. She grabbed his arm, turning him to face her. "You've already committed to a bloodpact before with Faye and we're just lucky it ended as well as it did. This time it's my burden. After all, it's my..." she hesitated, then said at length, "*mission*." He knew she had wanted to say *sword*.

"Perhaps, but—"

"No, Gray. I struck the bargain. It's only fair that I see it through, or suffer the consequences." Then she smiled and spoke softer so only he could hear, giving his hand a quick hidden squeeze. "We're a team now. You don't always have to carry the whole load."

Gray knew she was right, but he didn't like it. He wanted to argue, to take the onus, and yet he knew that relinquishing control was something a leader had to do, no matter how much he hated it. Let others share the weight. Kirin's memories—those from his past life, when he'd just been Kirin, a young man with the simple life of a Devari warrior before his grandfather had stripped away his memories and set him on the path as Gray—echoed the statement. *A good leader knows when to lead, and when to let others lead as well.*

Even so, Gray touched his stomach—it twisted painfully as he witnessed Ayva slice her palm. It turned his insides. She sucked in a small breath, and slapped her much smaller hand flush with Dalic's large one.

"The bargain is struck," the Algasi leader announced.

The other Algasi raised their spears, giving a chorus of grunts, then turned silent.

Again, Gray's stomach churned hard, his gut wrenching as if he'd just eaten Mura's month-old mushroom pie. *No*, he realized as his gut twisted

25

again, and he clutched at it in pain. This was different. This pain was worse. Kirin, his old self, warned him as well. He ran through a thousand diseases in his head. *Miswall, Wartgal, Vistal Syndrome.* But he cast each aside. *No, no, no.* He groaned in pain, louder than he expected.

Everyone turned towards him.

Ayva still held Dalic's hand. "Gray? What is it?" Worry strained her voice.

"I'm not sure. It just started, as soon as he spoke those words and—" Suddenly, searing pain roared through his belly and he cried out, feeling as though a hot sword was piercing his flesh, and ripping out his entrails. Voices continued, muffled, as if Gray had been dunked in water and shouts rained above him.

"Heal him!" Zane said.

Through his agony, he saw Hannah's terrified face. Sweat broke out across her brow as she concentrated on Gray, then she opened her eyes in confusion. "I don't sense anything... there's nothing wrong with him..."

"What do you mean you don't sense anything?" Ayva said.

"That's just it—I tried to heal him, but I don't sense anything wrong with him. It's as if—"

The voices continued.

Then the pain abated for a small moment. Gray took a huge gasping breath and looked up at his friends through blurry eyes, trying to speak to tell them it was all right, to not worry. But as he did, the pain spiked again, as if a Darkwalker's black claws tore through him, only to tug roughly, ripping at his entrails. He gasped in agony, grasping at the ground, tearing up grass and soil as something continued to tear at his insides, pain reducing his surroundings to a dull blur. Images and words sparked inside his head like fire against a dark sky.

Si'tu'ah... Sword... Blood dripping from his hand... Clasping...

The words rattled in his skull, echoing down the chambers of his very soul.

He tried to speak, hearing shouts above him, hands upon his body, but no words came. The darkness, the agony, clawed higher in his body—from his belly to his chest. Something was inside him. Something foreign, like a creature trying to get out. Whatever it was, it was killing him. His hands followed the clawing thing, terror making sweat emerge from every pore. The clawing thing reached his neck, slithering higher. He felt his throat bulge, his eyes swell with terror, the grass beneath his hands becoming a smear of green and brown. He gagged, strangling as something thick and wet wriggled out of his throat. He was choking, dying. He couldn't breathe. He coughed and spat violently, blood splattering the ground around him, until at last the thing dislodged from his throat, falling to the earth.

He saw it distantly through his agony.

An inky darkness, like a poisonous black slug, oozing across the ground. Hissing eerily, it slithered on the grass turning black in its wake. The others backed away horror struck until a sunburst *destroyed* the living darkness. It disappeared into the air as a necrotic black smoke.

"What in the seven hells was that?" Darius asked, breaking the silence in a mortified voice.

"Death," Dalic answered from above.

And with that, Gray succumbed to darkness.

* * *

When Gray awoke the world was still a haze, and he felt as if stuck between dream and reality. He tried to open his eyes, but they only opened halfway. Even so, his sleep-crusted lids lifted to reveal fuzzy figures standing in a circle around him. He saw spears, and a bright sun high above. He thought he heard the cry of birds and the musky smell of wet wood, but everything seemed so faint he felt that it was surely his imagination.

"Where...?" he muttered, but the word came out, soft and garbled. Incoherent.

They were speaking, their voices clear.

"*Your friend is not well.*"

"*We can see that. What in the seven hells is wrong with him?*"

"*Magic.*"

"*Magic?*"

"*What do you mean magic? Who did this to him?*" The voice became angry, wild. Zane, Gray knew.

"*Do not threaten me, Firespeaker. It was not my doing. It was Farhaven.*"

"*Farhaven?*" Another softer voice asked. Hannah.

"*The magic he spat forth is a darkness that Vasterians and Algasi know well, the enemy of all elements. It is the balance of life, a pure darkness. Sungarsi. It is the blood of our enemy. Darkwalkers are born from this. It is the end of all life. As such, no human did this to your friend. This darkness is a thing of the land. It is Farhaven's doing."*

Gray continued to groan, wishing to speak, but he felt worlds away.

"*This blasted land can have its magic and all—*" Darius. Gray recognized the rogue's sharp, angry tone.

Another interrupted Darius. "*How can we help him?*" the voice pleaded. The voice was softer and it was a familiar comfort to his ears. Ayva, he knew. "*There must be some way. Please. Tell us.*"

"*Only he who broke the law of Farhaven, who twisted its rules, knows how he can amend his error. Your friend is the only one who knows.*"

"*What is that supposed to mean?*" Darius asked in frustration.

"*The malady he suffers from cannot be cured by anyone but the victim. He must fulfill his bloodpact. That is the law of magic.*"

"*Or what?*" Ayva asked, breathless with panic. "*What will happen to him if he fails?*"

"*He'll die. If not now, then soon.*"

Gray tried to speak, to tell them… something, anything. But all he could utter was a groan.

Someone turned to him. A slender figure… Through his narrowed eyes he saw her kneel beside him, taking his hand. He felt warmth radiating throughout his entire body. Yet his heart felt cold, as if there was a splinter of ice inside it. He tried to touch his chest, to feel for the splinter and pull it free, but the hand that held him was stronger.

Blue eyes.

Ayva.

She clutched his palm with both of hers, whispering something. But the pain screamed so loudly inside him that it was hard to hear anything else.

He strained to hear her whisper.

"*It's all right, Gray. We'll fix this. We'll find help…*" her words continued, soft assurances. He tried to rise, to speak again, but sleep dragged him down, pulling him into its dark depths. And the last thing he heard was Ayva's voice, issuing words of comfort, thick with empathy and terror as darkness washed over him like a wave.

PURE LIGHT

Rising above the gates was a city of pure light.

Ayva could hardly believe it.

She was here, at last. And yet…

A light touch on her arm made her twist in her saddle. Hannah's brown eyes were watching her. "Ayva… are you all right?"

Ayva hadn't realized she'd stopped. She looked down. Her hands were gripping the reins and trembling. Crowds swarmed about them, raising dust, noise and excitement. A steady trail of rolling carts headed towards the glossy golden gates that were wide open, revealing a city of brilliant light.

Zane pressed his dark brown stallion closer to her side, moving out of the way of a large, rumbling cart filled with shiny fruits—red and yellow, glinting in the sunlight. "You know, Ayva, we don't need you here."

Hannah sat behind Zane on their mount. They were sharing a steed. They'd left the other cormac and bay charger behind for Gray and Darius to catch up with, once Gray was feeling better.

"What I mean is," he amended, coughing into his gloved hand, "if you want to go back and be with Gray and Darius, I understand. We'd understand."

Hannah nodded. "It's not too late, Ayva. If you want to be with them, I wouldn't blame you. Besides," she said, and slapped Zane's shoulder again, this time affectionately, "we can do this on our own, can't we?"

Zane grunted. It could have been an affirmation.

"See?" Hannah grinned. In their journey, Hannah had called Ayva "pretty" and herself "plain" more than once. Ayva didn't know about that, and was inclined to think herself quite plain and Hannah far too critical of her own looks. But she did know that when Hannah smiled, the girl was absolutely radiant. "You can trust us," Hannah said, still smiling.

Ayva had trouble not smiling herself.

Zane she trusted, though she wasn't sure why. She'd known him for a month now, and in that short time, he already felt like a brother—an older, protective, quiet, brooding and fiery brother. Darius and Gray were different. Not brothers—of course. The comparison was strange to make in the first place as she'd never had a brother, but Zane was what she imagined it would feel like. No, Darius and Gray felt like... there wasn't really a word for it. Friends was accurate, but too soft. Soul mates was *way* too much in the wrong way. So was lov—

She shook her head, focusing back on Zane.

She trusted him. Perhaps because Gray trusted him, but not entirely. He had an air about him. He was powerful. His gaze alone unnerved others. Even now, as Zane surveyed the crowds, two Covian merchants felt his gaze and they flicked their mounts, encouraging them to move faster. Sweating in the sun, bearing the symbol of flesh—a stitched emblem of a heart—on their leather jerkins, the merchants quickened their pace.

On top of that, Zane was built like a brawler. Heavily muscled, with wild blond hair, a wide jaw, thick neck and faint scars that ran down his cheeks complemented his powerful appearance. Even his sharp nose was reminiscent of an axe blade. He might have been shorter, but he was sturdier than any of her father's bouncers. His control over fire, too, seemed every bit as strong as Gray's wind, and far stronger than her sun power or Darius' leaf power, and with more creative conjurations.

It bugged Ayva that she couldn't do more with her power thus far, but she wasn't in a terrible rush. Though she was eager to understand it, she was also afraid of it. For now, it felt like she was searching the boundaries of a great lake within her, testing its depths and seeing what lived beneath the surface, before diving into its mysterious waters.

Ayva returned to her previous train of thought, looking at Hannah.

Hannah was everything her brother was not: sweet, calm and without the dark shadow that seemed to follow Zane. Still, she had a tongue that could cut through a conversation with its bluntness and several times in their journey so far, her ire had roared to life, surprising Ayva. Hannah was the only one besides Gray who could temper Zane's fire, but Ayva feared for Hannah. It hurt her to say, but Hannah seemed way in over her head. Ayva knew Hannah would never leave her brother's side, but the girl still seemed more suited for a quiet life as a farmer's daughter than one filled with dangers. Back with the Algasi, Ayva had been truly terrified for Hannah's life.

"Did you know those are limfuns?" Ayva said, pointing to the fruit cart bearing the yellow and red fruits, rumbling away. "The yellow ones," she clarified.

Zane and Hannah looked to one another, confused.

She continued. "They only grow in Farhaven. They are apparently quite good for you. That is, if you can stand their terribly bitter *and* sour nature."

Zane scratched his head. "Uh… Ayva? Does this train of thought have a point?"

Ayva fixed them with a stare, confidence swelling in her breast, pushing down her fear for Gray. "My point *is*…limfuns only grow in Farhaven. My whole life I've read about them, along with a myriad of other things that only reside within Farhaven, and only now do I get to see them. I feel like a person who's always had the ability to see color, but up until now has been trapped in a world of shades of gray." She shook her head. "I don't know what lies ahead. It scares me. But what scares me more is shying away and turning my back on what lies before me. I never want to return to that world of gray." She realized there was a double meaning there and she winced, powering through it. "Besides, in a way Vaster isn't just my destiny, it's my home. It seems that I've waited all my life for this."

An amused smile tugged at the corner of Zane's mouth as he looked forward. "I guess that settles it. Shall we then?"

Really, there were a myriad of reasons why Ayva couldn't return to Gray and Darius. But foremost in her mind, they had only until dawn to return with the riddle or the Algasi would see their end of the deal fulfilled. At the tip of their spears. Trust for Zane or not, she wouldn't put their lives in anyone else's hands. Still, it didn't make the weight of guilt leave her chest, thinking about Gray vomiting darkness, his cries—

She shut her eyes to stop the awful images, nodded in reply to Zane then urged her cormac forward, blending back in with the crowds. Together they pushed their way through the gates that soared above them

31

like gold mountains and moved into the city.

Despite her anxiety, her breath was stolen as they entered.

The main road was breathtaking. It appeared to be shimmering glass, but beneath it glowed yellow, as if a sun were captured beneath its surface, straining to break free. It swirled and moved with motion. In pockets without light, it looked like a vast void. The effect was similar to walking on the sun, and the darkness simply empty space. The cormac's hooves touched on it lightly. They made no noise. Her hands tensed on the reins, fearful the glass-like road would break and send her to the swirling light-filled depths beneath. "Light and heavens," she murmured, stealing a curse she'd found in Gray's book. Others passed her with curious looks.

Hannah pulled her to the side, out of the flow of traffic. "We should have warned you. This is—"

"The Sunroad. One of the Grand Creations," Ayva finished. She dismounted and put her hand on the glassy surface. It was cool to the touch. What was she expecting? Warmth? Yet looking down she felt as if the sun were speaking to her, urging her to break it free. Something about it seemed so beautiful and yet cruel, containing such an energy. "It's doing something, isn't it?" she said, and looked up to see Hannah's surprised face. Zane was scratching his head in thought.

"How'd you know?"

"I've seen one before," she replied. "The water fountain at the entrance to Farbs. It was Gray's grandfather Ezrah's. He made it. Faye told me a little about them as well," she said, fingers still touching the glass. It reflected off her skin and off the buildings around them, turning white walls to living amber. It made the city look more like a grand painting than actual glass, metal and marble. But then she remembered. Gray's grandfather's creation was more than just a beautiful sphere of suspended water, two stories high. It gave water to all of Farbs and *never* ran out. In a desert, it was a gift of gods. "This is more than just beautiful. What's it doing?"

"It feeds the city with energy. Instead of watermills or coal or anything of the sort, the sun—"

"Gives life," Ayva finished in awe. She walked forward, following the golden threads. It moved like a golden river. It spoke to her, called to her, and she wanted nothing more than to break the glassy surface and dive into it and breathe it into her soul.

Zane cleared his throat. "Ayva—we shouldn't linger here."

"He's right, Ayva. Gray and Darius need us. Where do we find the Riddle of Sun?"

Zane continued to talk but Ayva paid no heed. "We should check in with the guards at the main gate. They will take us to whoever is in charge. We can't delay. Ayva?"

"...*Ayva*..."

The river began to hum in her ears, thrumming like a siren's song. Her hands grew warm on the glass and she rose, following the voice. The Sunroad's wide, main thoroughfare was a tempest of activity, but Ayva saw other smaller golden roads. They forked off left and right, into alleys and buildings, like little tributaries. The rays of sun seemed to be feeding something. She pulled her cormac behind her and followed where the voice led her. She tracked a thicker stream, taking a few turns. She wasn't sure how many. Suddenly, the stream led to the door of a two-story building of white marble. She glanced up and saw a sign made of glass. Etched into the glass were the words *Apothecary's Attic*. Beneath the words, stained glass depicted the portrait of a pot-bellied man guzzling potions inside a crawlspace.

As if in a dream, she tied her mount to a post outside and entered. Distantly she heard her name being called but she ignored it, drawn into the squat marble building.

Inside it was almost brighter than outside.

A woman stood on a tall ladder. She was squinting, eyeing the label of a glass bottle, before she placed it beside a hundred ones just like it. She was surrounded by hundreds of shelves that contained thousands of glass bottles with cork, wood or stoppers made of some black substance. The bottles were many different shades and Ayva immediately recognized it as a sorting system. The room itself was much bigger than all of *The Golden Horn*, her father's inn, but because every wall towered with bottles, the room seemed cramped and small. She saw a ladder in the back that led to an attic and presumed it was a sleeping loft. Otherwise, aside from the laden walls and few tables, the room contained only a long bar on the far side where cash was exchanged and several tables filled with odds and ends—instruments, flagons and decanters, white and black feathers and stacks of papers.

She heard Hannah clamber in behind her, with Zane close behind.

"Would you stop for one blazing moment?" Hannah asked breathless.

Ayva turned, looking to Hannah. Sweat dappled her brow. *Was I running?* She wondered. She touched her temple and felt a spot of sweat, and realized in confusion that this shop wasn't as near as she'd thought. "I…"

Memories flashed inside her.

A dark tunnel. Voices whispering in the shadows. Pulling Darius along—fear pumping in her veins, but she felt something drawing her step by step, pulling them to their destination.

It was just like back then, when she and Darius, without free will, had followed Gray in a daze—through the Sodden Tunnels and out of the Shining City. In a way, that had been the beginning of their journey together. And it hadn't even been of her volition. Not entirely.

The woman upon the ladder barely turned at their entrance. "Welcome," she said in a deep, strong voice. "You've come just in time."

"In time?" Hannah gasped, placing her hands upon her knees, nearly wheezing.

Zane stood at the entrance, his form filling the narrow doorway, only slightly winded. The crowds were thinner outside. It was clear they were no longer on the main road. *Where are we?* she wondered, but had no time to think as the woman spoke again, descending from her ladder.

"Yes, yes, just in time," she said, as if annoyed to repeat herself. In her hand she held a dark blue bottle with a yellow cork. Something seemed to move inside, but Ayva shook her head. It was just her imagination. It was terrifying to lose gaps in time, as if she were no longer in control of her own self. Even more terrifying was how completely peaceful she felt in that moment.

"Where are we?" Zane asked.

The woman took one last step and turned.

With a black bun mixed with wiry gray strands pulled tight and high on her head, she had a matronly look. She reminded Ayva of Mistress Hitomi—wisdom and secrets swirling in her eyes, but except for where Hitomi's eyes were a deep brown, this woman's were a spring grass-green with a hint of blue. Her face was smooth for her age—at least seventy summers, she guessed, knowing Farhaven's magic that slowed the process of aging. She wore a shrewd expression.

"The Apothecary's Attic, where else?" said the woman. "Can't you read the sign?"

Zane grumbled beneath his breath, but Ayva stepped in.

"I like the name," Ayva said.

The woman raised a thin brow. "See the play on words, did you?"

"Attic, addic*t*," Ayva said, emphasizing the 'T'.

"And a touch of alliteration, depending on your dialect—don't forget that."

"The painting of the man guzzling potions kind of gave it away."

The woman's eyes tapered in amusement. "My dear child, a joke is only as good as those who get it. Remember that not all the world is as shrewd as you."

Ayva blushed. "I didn't—"

The woman waved a hand. "It was a compliment. Don't be ashamed of your intelligence, child. It's a tool—a weapon to some, a shield to others. The real skill is learning when to use it."

Ayva nodded, not knowing what to say.

"Enough pontificating. Here, take this." The woman handed the bottle to Ayva. She held it in her hands. The glass felt oddly warm, like holding a mug of piping hot cider, but beyond the glass it was pure blackness. *A tad ominous for cider*, Ayva thought, and looked up at the woman, puzzled.

"It's what you came for, isn't it?" the woman asked, seeing her confusion.

Suddenly Ayva felt a tickle on the glass. She nearly dropped the thing, but instead held it lightly by the stopper and the top rim of the glass as to not uncork it. "What is it?"

The woman's eyes narrowed to tiny slits. "You playing dumb on me? If you're trying to pull the wool over my eyes, it won't work. No one fools Nell Perisphony Atwood. Not the Patriarch, not the Lightbringer, and definitely not you."

What in the seven hells was this woman talking about? "Is it alive?" Ayva asked, feeling the bottle shake once more.

"Course it's alive! You wouldn't pay that price for dead Brisbane. If you're trying to renege on your coin or change the price on me, it won't work. You paid. No refunds." Nell finally seemed to register the legitimate confusion on Ayva's face. She reached forward. "You are Helga and Moris, aren't you?"

She opened her mouth to say no, but Zane stepped forward. "That's us all right."

Ayva looked at him in confusion.

"Right, good," Nell said, looking relieved and heaving a breath. "Took you all long enough anyway. You said upon the new moon, and it's weeks past that."

"Right," Zane said with a sigh and jabbed a thumb toward his sister. "I thought I'd told you in our previous correspondence. This one ain't too fond of gryphons, or flying in general, for that matter. Had to travel by land and it cost us precious time."

Nell Atwood waved the matter off with a flick of her hand. Back turned, she shuffled through a stack of aged-yellow papers as if searching for something. "That's fine, fine. I don't care one lick so long as you're the ones." She lifted a paper, grabbed a quill, and brought it forward. "Sign here."

Ayva lifted her hand.

But Zane took over, signing.

In the corner of her eye, she saw the scrawled signature. MORIS — it read. Nell's hand darted out, snatching the pen and his hand before he finished. "Promise me one thing," Nell said, eyes like daggers. Something in them swirled knowingly. Did the woman smile? But when Nell Atwood looked to Ayva the woman's lips were one tight line, far from amused. "Use it wisely. Brisbane isn't meant for common consumption."

"I promise," said Zane sincerely.

Hannah opened her mouth, but Zane flashed her a look. She swallowed it down. Ayva's head felt full of cotton as she took the flask numbly. Zane guided them to the door, pushing them out and back into the street — into the light of day.

Light Versus Dark

Outside, Ayva whisked across the alley clutching the flask tightly. The others followed wordlessly. She felt their air of confusion as she set the bottle with its cork stopper down firmly in a crook of marble near a staircase. She then twisted to eye the stocky man behind her.

As usual, Zane wore a loose black shirt beneath his dark red leather vest, a gift from Ezrah. His face bore scruff from the days of travel, but with his blond hair lying flat for once, and dressed in his fine, if dusty, attire, he looked oddly distinguished — especially compared to when she'd first met him, a ragged-looking thief full of boiling anger. She hadn't seen his rage much lately, but she supposed it was a good thing. Last time he'd nearly brought down Shadow's Corner in an attempt to save his sister from Darkeye, a menacing thief-lord. The name alone inspired her stomach to turn circles, but if Gray were correct, Darkeye was dead. He had died at Faye's hands, no less, a woman she loathed more than... Well, *anyone*. Faye was her *Sunha* too. She still felt a bitter connection. Faye had trained her as they'd made their treacherous journey across the desert toward Farbs. She taught her about Farhaven and its many dangers, only to betray them to Darkeye when she and Darius had attempted to save Zane's sister from the thief-lord of the Underbelly. Could it be true? Could Darkeye be dead at Faye's hands? She shook her head, clearing the thought.

Zane wore a blank look now, only one brow mildly arched as if he were watching someone struggle and debating to help. "Might I ask what you're doing?"

She pointed. "Use fire and blow it up."

Zane's thick brows drew down to make an even ridge on his forehead—it was the look of mild annoyance. "I'm not angry," he said flatly. "Far from it, in fact. Besides, it doesn't work that way. Only our fearless leader can thread on command. You should know that."

"Can't you get angry?"

While Zane didn't roll his eyes, his look was what her father would give Ayva when she was being particularly obstinate.

"Shall I kick your shin?"

"Only if you want me to kick yours back," Zane replied, grunting.

Ayva sighed, and turned. She cast out her hands, trying to feel sun pouring through her from above. She felt her arms warm and golden light poured through her, as if the city were a conduit for her power. The flask rattled. She closed her eyes. The rattling grew, sun hot on her skin, until she opened her eyes with a gasp.

The flask sat, unperturbed.

Zane knelt and grabbed it.

He tossed it to Ayva and she gasped in pain. The glass seared her fingers and she tossed it from hand to hand like a miniature hot sun. "Well done," he remarked. "A nice piping hot cup of Brisbane and a few biscuits sounds delicious."

She growled and he smirked.

Hannah cleared her throat. They both looked to her. "Maybe we were meant to have it."

"Meant to have it?" Ayva asked. "I think the real Helga and Moris were *meant* to have it. We just stole it… or lied and took it, which I'm pretty sure is the same thing," she added.

Hannah didn't back down though. "You were the one that lead us here, Ayva. How do you explain that? Maybe it's fate after all."

"Fate to keep a bottle of poison?"

"You don't know if it's poison," Zane said.

"What else could it be? You heard what she said, 'not meant for common consumption.' I'm pretty certain that's shorthand for 'this is poison.'"

Hannah nodded as if that settled it. "That proves my point. We're keeping poison from the hands of two would-be murderers."

Ayva didn't know what to say to that. It seemed a reasonable assumption.

"Besides, what's the worst thing keeping it can do?" Hannah asked.

Zane looked up. The sun was in full bloom. Ayva saw his gaze settle on the crystal spires in the distance: where the prophecy would be and where they needed to be. "If you're truly worried, we can wait for the true Moris and Helga to show up and then question them in turn to find out their intentions."

Ayva sighed, reading his eyes. "Or we can actually fulfill what we came for, get out of this alley, find the prophecy and save Gray."

"You put a beautiful ring to my own thoughts," Zane said. "But it's your call."

"Well, fearless leader?" Hannah asked.

They both watched her expectantly. How had she become the leader? A part of it felt unnatural, as if she were stealing Gray's position, but another part of her felt right, as if it were in her nature. Second-in-command. *Fate.* And she spoke at last. "As much as I loathe the idea of keeping this thing—" she began, hefting the smooth glass container with its swirling black liquid. It looked like death in a bottle, and reminded her of Gray and where she had left him, sweating and groaning, blood forming about his mouth. Her gut twisted but she swallowed it down. "Gray is waiting for us and so are the Algasi. We'll safeguard it until we've found out what it is exactly and *why* the fates deemed we should have it."

Upon deciding, they entered the main road once more when the crowds began to ripple like heat waves in the sun. Riders appeared from around the bend with a young woman at their lead. Sunlight gleamed off armor. Men and women bowed, shuffling back.

Ayva instructed Zane and Hannah off the road as well, but the leader's eyes met hers and Ayva's heart skipped a beat, seeing recognition in the young woman's eyes.

"Quick, hide it," Ayva instructed, handing Hannah the flask.

Hannah tucked it in her bag as the group approached.

Ayva prepared herself, but all words slipped from her tongue as the crowds parted to reveal the young woman. Then Ayva saw the woman's mount and her mouth hung open. "An archwolf," she whispered.

Loping on all fours, the archwolf was half wolf, half creature of light. She swallowed, watching as great gold wings flared into existence as it parted the crowds. Then, abruptly, the wings vanished. She narrowed

39

her gaze, watching and remembering the tales. The wings formed again, solid one moment then insubstantial the next, floating in and out of existence, ethereal-like as if liquid gold loosed beneath water. Otherwise its body was fairly normal. *For a legendary beast*, she amended. Its head was that of a large wolf, but its tall pointed ears and bushy tail were made of light, with real golden fur along its graceful body. The last oddity was its eyes.

Yellow with gold flares fanning out in all directions—a sunburst.

As it approached, her heart clenched. Though one couldn't tell where it was staring—she knew it was staring at her. The archwolf was a mount of the Great Kingdom of Sun; it was bred when every phoenix had died, however, according to what Faye had explained, few archwolves still lived. It was a dying breed. The sun kingdom had little luck when it came to flying mounts. A part of her wondered why.

"Greetings," announced the woman on the strange and beautiful wolf-like creature. "My name is Evangeline, daughter to Lord Nolan, and High Lady of Vaster." *High Lady?* Ayva wondered, squinting—the woman had to be at least a year or two younger than her. And she was stunning. Evangeline had lustrous brown hair woven into a single thick braid that rested before her shoulder. Bright gold ribbons were threaded through her braid and dazzled in the sun. Evangeline wore a pure white dress and leather skirt. The center of the dress bore a hole that was fastened with a gold ring and accentuated subtle cleavage. It was far from Ayva's style and too brash for her liking, but Evangeline wore it well, she admitted. A blue cloth cape gave a dash of color and fell gracefully over her archwolf's form. The High Lady's ensemble was topped off with a rich brown, oiled leather belt looped around her slender waist, layered leather pauldrons that sat on her shoulders and sword in a simple brown sheath that rested at her hip with a few notes of gold decoration. Altogether, the outfit made Evangeline appear both princess and warrior.

Zane's gaze narrowed on the High Lady, almost imperceptibly. *Were his eyes drawn to her—?* Ayva's cheeks flushed. No, Zane seemed to only care for the welfare of his sister and that of his friends. His eyes weren't the wandering sort, and she didn't exactly peg him for a flirt or charmer like someone she knew. Zane and Darius were practically opposites, after all.

Evangeline nodded to the man on her right, a dark bearded man with a perpetual squint to his long face—like a typical snooty lord. "This is

Lord Magnis, of the Council of Twelve, and these are the Lightguards."

Ayva had heard of the Lightguards from Faye and a few books—famed warriors of light. They were highly trained men and women who wielded hook-like spears, swirling them about their bodies like whirling dervishes, and even dismounting charging combatants. They were nearly as famous in battle as the Algasi or Devari or... She smiled to herself. *Balance.* Each of the Great Kingdoms had it: first in mounts, then in magical facets, like the Grand Creations, and now in highly trained warriors. Balance and equilibrium to all things. And as soon as she thought she'd singled a kingdom out for being uniquely different, or creatures, like Darkwalkers, or even a type of plant, the world of Farhaven proved its balancing act.

Her mouth went dry, trying to respond, but she summoned her voice. "Greetings," she said, bowing on her snow white cormac. Her cormac dipped its long, graceful neck as if echoing her act. Ayva touched her chest tight with excitement and nerves. "I'm Ayva, and this is—"

Evangeline's eyes scanned them quickly. She took in their clothes, dirty and tattered from travel, their gazes, and finally her cormac — not impressed, like many, by the rare silken-haired elven steeds, simply calculating. No wonder, the woman practically rode a mythical creature. "—Zane and Hannah," she said, nodding to each respectively. "I know. We've been waiting for you. In fact, you're late."

"How do you know our names?" Ayva asked.

She sighed. "Unfortunately, there's no time to explain. You must come with us. He's waiting for you."

"*He?*"

"My father."

"Who's your father?"

"High Councilor Nolan, Steward of Vaster."

She turned to her companions.

Zane shrugged.

Hannah looked nervous and excited.

"Might as well," Zane said in a gravelly whisper. "That is why we came after all." "Your call," said Hannah, "but I agree with Zane."

She nodded, again confused how she had suddenly been put in charge, but glad that these two at least worked as one—unlike the bullheaded, indomitable Gray and the irascible Darius. She turned to Evangeline and gave another slight bow. *That's what nobles did, right?* "Lead the way, High Lady." High Lady—it sounded so awkward, but the woman seemed

41

accustomed to it and flicked the reins of her majestic beast, giving the command.

The Lightguards moved forward, reaching for Zane.

"What're they doing?" Zane asked, growling and reaching for his blade. He pulled his mount's reins back with his other fist, making the horse buck its head and whiny.

"Relax," Evangeline called, stilling the rising tension. "You don't need your blade within these walls, Zane. Vaster is a city absent of murder or crime. So you'll have no cause to draw such a vile tool."

Zane laughed as if she was joking, but Evangeline's face remained smooth and serious. "While I don't disagree that it *can* be a 'vile tool', depending on the holder... I don't see them giving up their weapons," he said, indicating the golden-plated Lightguards with their swords and wide bladed halberds.

"That's different," Evangeline said.

"Is it? How so?" His voice held an edge.

She looked confused that she had to explain this. "The Lightguards are holy symbols that have existed for a thousand years, and their blades are as much ceremonial as practical. Besides, their oaths are made as bloodpacts—each has made a solemn vow to draw their weapons only with just cause."

42

"Sorry, princess, but from where I come from '*just cause*' to draw a weapon is a rather morally ambiguous term, and, from one man to the next, it differs. I've seen men butcher innocent boys and little girls, but believe in their own dark hearts that it was for a 'just cause.' So you'll forgive me if I buck tradition and hold onto my blade." Then he added, lower and more menacing, "And if your men find 'just cause' to draw their blades now, then they'll find a less... polite reply. I'm not afraid of death." For any other, the final words might have sounded like an immature gibe, or at least the false bravado of youth. From Zane, however, it was the hard truth. His eyes blazed, and this was the first time Ayva saw him react this way. As angry as Zane seemed in that moment, and as much as his words seethed with venom, he also was oddly composed.

Evangeline seemed taken aback by this as well, as if expecting a very different answer. Her eyes gauged Zane as his muscles rippled. His hand still white-knuckled on his blade.

"Enough of this," Lord Magnis declared. "Take the petulant child's blade and let's be on with this. Lord Nolan is waiting."

The Lightguards marched forward.

Ayva opened her mouth to speak, but she was too slow.

"Halt!" Evangeline commanded, lifting a hand, speaking first. Everyone stopped, including the Lightguards. Evangeline's brown eyes went from serious and puzzled, staring at Zane, to... something else. There was a twinkle in her eyes and the young woman gave a small smile. "Leave him be. Zane and his friends are our guests and will be treated as such." She said no more, turning away.

Armor rattled softly as the Lightguards parted to form an empty space.

Ayva understood. She released a pent-up breath and guided her cormac along with the others to the front of the column beside Evangeline and Lord Magnis. Well, just shy of the front. Lord Magnis shot them petulant stares, his nose crinkling as if he wanted to speak, but he clamped his mouth shut and stared ahead.

Are you trying to get us killed before discovering the prophecy? Ayva asked through the bond.

Sorry, Zane said, but it sounded like lip service. He was busy staring at Evangeline's back, a small, unaware smile on *his* lips.

Ayva sighed and let it go.

Evangeline's archwolf moved with grace and agility. Ayva's cormac   43
and Zane's horse leapt to catch up. As she fell in line, she watched her cormac's short, powerful legs moving to keep pace. Naturally, there was an elegant flow to her cormac's gait as if inbred with the grace of the elves, though it was altogether different than the loping archwolf. Zane's horse, however, along with the Lightguards and Lord Magnis' steeds looked awkward, almost bumbling beside the two graceful creatures.

They rode for a short while. Ayva's mind was a whirl, thoughts of Gray all-consuming. All she could think of was Gray's face. That look of pain...and the blood. There was so much. She'd offered up herbs and advice to that strange Algasi woman, but she seemed to know every bit of it and more. Still, she wasn't daft. Whatever sickness lay inside Gray seemed more than it appeared.

Am I wrong to be here? she thought, and not for the first time... not even for the hundredth time. She pictured him again lying there, barely moving, face pale as death, chest rising shallowly. She shut her eyes. *No,* she told herself firmly, *Gray will be all right.* Besides, sitting at his side and wringing her hands would do him no good. That's why she came. There was something she *could* do here.

Zane dropped back a bit and gestured for her to do the same. Ayva slowed the pace of her cormac, coming in line with Hannah and Zane's mounts.

"What's our plan?" Hannah asked in a hushed voice. Her gaze flickered from the Lightguards to the gleaming streets and their crowds, then back to their straight-backed guide.

Ayva answered, "Find the prophecy and return to the Algasi before anything else bad happens." It sounded so simple in her head. But nothing was ever that simple. Not lately, at least.

"And Gray?" Hannah asked. "Perhaps Vaster has healers that can aid him."

"That will be my first question. Once we find the prophecy and appease the Algasi, we'll set about finding a remedy for Gray's sickness."

"You have the note, right?" Zane asked.

Ayva's hand reached for her pocket, feeling the neatly folded paper she'd read so many times and nodded.

"I hope it's enough," Hannah said nervously. "Do you think it will be? To convince this Lord Nolan to see the prophecy?"

She looked over and saw Hannah's face with its worried look—her brows were pinched and big brown eyes troubled—and realized she was scaring the girl. *Girl?* Hannah couldn't have been a year, maybe two younger than herself, but how much had Ayva aged in such a short time? Lakewood felt like a lifetime ago. She smiled for Hannah, putting her hand on her arm and spoke firmly. "It'll be enough, Hannah. I'm sure Lord Nolan will listen to reason."

Hannah's frown melted and she breathed easier.

Know anything about this Lord Nolan to back up that claim? Zane thought through their bond.

Ayva shook her head. *Just what Ezrah told us—that he's a good man.*

Zane grunted, mentally echoing her words. *A good man.* He was oddly proficient at it, speaking through their strange bond. Ayva, on the other hand, was still struggling to send full sentences that didn't get jumbled with the tangled web of her own constant thoughts.

He'll listen to reason, she sent again.

And if he doesn't?

Ayva only whispered beneath her breath, "Hope to light he does."

44

A Patient Man

Patience was perhaps Nolan's greatest asset. Some men were valiant—diving into a sea of swords bellowing battle cries—some men were wise, like Councilor Godfrey, with sagacity gained from many years of study and introspection. But Nolan, while he knew he had many of those qualities too, was above all patient. Yet now he was restless beyond measure.

He folded the note back up his cloth sleeve at a hard knock behind him and called loudly, "Enter!"

The beaten gold doors of the Light Hall swung wide and his manservant, Maldred, entered. The man might have been tall once but age, or perhaps the weight of running a whole kingdom's staff as head servant, had stooped him. Still, as always, Maldred's clothes were immaculate, his white robes slashed with black and gray were clean and perfectly pressed. His boots were oiled and gleamed like the floor beneath them. His skin, however, was barely wrinkled and surprisingly pale like most of the councilors—those men and women who were appointed by the citizens of Vaster to rule over the Great Kingdom of Sun. That pale skin was the result of staying inside the walls of the Apex and avoiding the ever-present sun. Otherwise, Maldred's features were unremarkable. If Nolan hadn't known the man for four decades, he'd have lost him in a crowd himself.

Nolan cared dearly for Maldred but knew the man was getting on in age. His hair was nearly all but gone—only a rim of gray hairs clung to his skull like the last remnants of stew clinging to the sides of a bowl. Looking at him now, he looked like Nolan felt. Twice he'd gifted Maldred a gilded cane. Each time Maldred thanked him stiffly, treating it with reverence, and yet never once had Nolan seen the man use the blasted thing. When Nolan would inquire about it Maldred would thank him again and say he would use one of them when the day came. He had a feeling that Maldred would never throw the canes away, but that he would also never use them. Each would be buried deep within his closet until the day the man died. *Pride, so much pride*—a trait all Vasterians shared and one he knew far too well. Maldred cleared his throat and Nolan shook himself, meeting the man's gaze. "They're *here*, my lord," Maldred announced slowly, waiting for recognition to spark in Nolan's eyes. *Ah, he must have already said it once*, Nolan realized.

"And my daughter?" Nolan inquired.

"She attended to them just as you instructed, High Councilor."

He smiled. He hadn't instructed that. Far from it; he had told her to stay away. The note said to trust these figures… But Nolan was not quick to trust. *Legends. Myths. Killers.* He would risk everything for them and soon, but not his only child—the dearest thing to his heart since the passing of his beloved wife. But it was just like Evangeline to twist his words. Likely she'd repeat what he'd told her, and he'd realized his words sounded like *aid* the newcomers, not *avoid* the newcomers. He knew she didn't do it out of spite. In fact, she only directly disobeyed him when she was concerned for his safety. In every way she seemed to prove herself a replica of her mother. He brushed the matter aside. "Where are they now exactly?"

"They are making for the Lightway and should be—" Maldred was cut short as Nolan strode forward.

The walls appeared to be white like clouds, but Nolan approached and put his hand to the nearest glass panel—the one that should overlook the Lightway. The panel turned clear, the white surface now transparent like fog banished by the sun. Sure enough, he spotted them. He narrowed his gaze. They rode on the grand walkway of yellow that crisscrossed back and forth, leading to the Apex's foot. The series of walkways, called the Lightway, hung over a moat that encircled the Apex, the central tower that housed all the nobility. The moat beneath was made not of water, but of white-hot gold. Unlike the Sunroad's friendly warmth, that yellow fire was not so friendly. It could sear the flesh from one's bones in a mat-

46

ter of seconds. Unwise critters, like redbirds and crows, occasionally fell into it, leaving only a sizzling hiss and the charred smell of flesh.

"Their mounts, is that a—?"

"—One cormac and two horses, my lord," said Maldred in his usual clipped tone.

"They're friends of the elves then." Perhaps that was a good sign.

"The lady Ayva rides it, and her friends are Zane and Hannah. Just as the note indicated, based on their appearance."

"Then you saw them clearly?"

"Yes, sire. From the battlements I did."

"And? Did they look like legends?"

Maldred hesitated, looking nervous or perhaps skeptical. Nolan had told his manservant of the note—he and his daughter were the only ones he'd trusted with the news. Not only because he didn't trust all the Council, but because the two of them were the only ones who'd believe him—or at least would be too loyal and kind to call him crazy. "I can't say I know what legends look like, my lord."

Nolan scrubbed a hand through his hair with a laugh. "I suppose not." He squinted into the sun. They were too far away to see facial features, but he could swear that the one upon the cormac twisted, her gaze falling upon him, and his heart skipped a beat despite himself. *Legends.* He couldn't help but smile. Nolan let his hand fall and the glass wall returned to its normal white fog. "Yet there's only three. Where are the others? I was told there would be at least four." *Four*—out of The Nine.

Maldred shrugged. "I know not, my lord."

There was a small silence as Maldred rubbed his balding head and Nolan knew that he wished to speak—he always rubbed his head or scrubbed that last fraying patch of gray hair when he wished to do so. Despite a thousand insistences that he speak freely, Maldred still acted as though he needed his lord's consent to speak. "Go ahead, Maldred."

"There's something else, sire. Your plans have been discovered."

"Discovered? By who?"

"Reaver Logan. He knows you seek a private audience but hasn't yet discovered with who or why. He's growing increasingly curious."

Nolan sighed. He had hoped to keep this whole thing a secret. But that man was far too perceptive for his own good, even for a four-stripe Reaver. "Fine then, put him to task. Let him wait for the others. There must be more coming, and not far behind. Allow him a dozen Light-

47

guards and have him meet the rest at the Light Walls; then bring them to my chambers at once. If you can, try to make the act seem inconsequential. Perhaps he will not spread the tale to the Council and make matters more complicated for me."

"And the rest of the Council, sire?"

Nolan hesitated and then waved his hand, dismissing his loyal friend. He was grateful for Maldred. He was nearly twice his age, almost eighty summers, yet still sharp as ever. Maldred had a stern hand with Nolan ever since he was boy; he had chastised him when he'd run too wild and when he acted as children often did. Nolan was always more rambunctious than most youths. Perhaps that's why he was so patient now. *Balance.*

But Maldred had never questioned Nolan in all their years together, nor did he now. The door closed on silent magical hinges.

A short while later another knock came on the door.

Three raps.

Just as he'd instructed.

Three heavily muscled men and one woman, who was equally as fearsome, entered the room. They stood at attention. Ungar and Azgal, were bears of men who were brothers by blood with bright red hair, trunk-like necks and piercing blue eyes; Dirk had scars riddling his misshapen face from another life as a bruiser and dockhand; and lastly, June—the woman. Though it was hard to call her beautiful, she held an air of dark grace—like a mantle of death and strength upon her shoulders, just like the others. With broad shoulders, she stood taller than Nolan. Her face and neck, the only part of her exposed, showed her fair share of training scars as well. Lightguards, each of them, and his personal guard.

Ungar took a knee as they approached and the other three fell in behind their commander. "My liege."

"You're late, they're nearly here," said Nolan.

Ungar's head dipped lower, nearly touching the polished gold marble beneath. "Apologies, my lord."

Nolan sighed, then realized he was doing that a lot of late. *Sighing is a sign of age, my love,* Vaselia used to chide him softly. *Smile and prove yourself young.* Though his wife was gone from this world, her words of wisdom always seemed to provide clarity in his moments of need. "Come Ungar, we both know it's my fault and not yours. And my frayed nerves are no excuse. Only a fool blames another for his own errors." Nolan

48

touched the man's muscled shoulder. He wore only black cloth now from head to toe. It was strange to see a Lightguard out of his or her normal golden garb—like a turtle who had shed its shell. Still, it didn't diminish his menace. Ungar's huge arms and barrel-chest bulged against the loose black cloth, and his brother Azgal, only slightly smaller, looked the same. Ungar had deep blue eyes and chiseled features, but a broken jaw that had never healed right sat askew like a damaged lantern. Aside from his face, only his hands showed. They were scarred, knuckles thick and calloused, and his palms were wide enough to engulf a child's head. He bore no weapon but a simple dagger at his side, just like the others.

Ungar rose at his touch.

"Come, let me show you." Nolan pressed his palm to the white-fogged glass and revealed the three travelers, ascending the yellow switchback road of light, nearly at their destination.

Ungar's eyes widened. "They're only children…"

"They best be more than children or this is all for naught."

Ungar hesitated, then inclined his thick neck. But his eyes said otherwise: *Are you certain?*

"Take your places," Nolan instructed, then pointed to either side of the door. Loyal to the bone, the big men and the woman moved to obey. "Remember what I told you. Don't go easy, but intend them no harm beyond what I previously instructed. You're to test, not to kill. And whatever you do, don't harm the High Lady Evangeline." Of course, it was completely unnecessary to instruct a Lightguard so—they could break every bone in your body, or just the exact twelve he specified and not a single other, all without breaking a sweat. But his chest was heavy and he wanted to be certain. No, he *had* to be certain.

What awaited him felt like a game of elements. He'd made his move; now it was time they made theirs and he dearly hoped the pieces fell where he wanted them to.

Nolan touched an orb of light that shone on a nearby pedestal. It was a dimmer switch that darkened the walls and let less light through the windows. His finger traced down, dimming the globe of light until it only shone a third full. The Light Hall darkened significantly until the room was nearly pitch black.

Silence. He heard only his rhythmic thumping of his heart as moments ticked by and time stretched. It could have been an hour, but it was likely only minutes when—

49

Four rhythmic raps.
His daughter's calling card.
"Come in," Nolan beckoned with a heavy breath.
And the door opened.

SUⴖGARSI

When Gray awoke, it was after midday.

He sat up, Dalic's words echoing in his mind.

"You have until the dawn."

Hours had been lost. Time was slipping by and he needed to find the others.

But when Gray looked around, he saw he was in a hut of wood and dirty thatch. A wet, cloying smell hung in the air, like the burning of sweet incense, clogging his nose. Nearby, a thick, low wooden table butted along the wall. On its rough-hewn surface sat dozens of drab light blue and gray clay bowls, a wood mortar and a pestle. Bushels of colorful herbs, flowers and bizarre shaped mushrooms were stacked high at one end of the table.

A woman sat over him, her face unreadable.

"Who are you? And where am I?"

"The others be gone," she said bluntly. Indara's eyes and skin were dark like the other Algasi. She wore a brown robe, and on top of that, an unusual red-fur wrap. *A Samigurian tiger from the Heaths of Samigur*, he and Kirin knew. She seemed old and yet young, and her words were the same choppy speech as the Algasi.

"Gone?" he repeated. "No... that can't be."

"They left you behind with me. To get better. They will return in the morning with the prophecy. My name is Indara. You are safe here."

Gray threw the covers off, leapt to his feet and then staggered. His world felt upside down and his head spun. He lost his balance and fell into a nearby chair and table. His hand swiped off blue and gray pottery, which shattered on the wood floor as he struggled to right himself. He groaned, grabbed his stomach as he fell back down, lying once more on his back like a helpless turtle. He gasped for breath, staring up at the thatched ceiling. At last, the pain died and he sat up, looking at his belly. There was nothing there. No cut, no wound, nothing. Even the wound he'd suffered upon the gates so long ago was healed, leaving unblemished tan skin.

"What's wrong with me?"

She handed him a mirror that had fallen to the ground, then spoke, "See for yourself, child," she whispered. In the mirror Gray saw his reflection. His gray-green eyes, jaw-length brown hair, stubbled cheeks, his bold nose and…dark red blood trickled from his nose. Panicked, he wiped it away but more flowed forth.

When he looked up, Indara was handing him a small cloth.

He saw it was already stained with blood. His fingers curled around it. "What's happening to me?"

"Farhaven be stripping you of your spark," she intoned.

"What do you mean?"

"You are going to die."

Dread rose inside him, his breaths coming faster. His head felt light, dizzy. His hands fell to the rough wood floor. His vision blurred and he gasped, his breath caught. "I… I can't breathe…" He had a sudden vision from long ago, of blood staining his hands, of screams of terror as he killed Ren and the others. Then of Ezrah standing over him as the horror of it all sunk in and his breath was lost.

Kirin's memories.

They were his memories now, too, but they still held the same horror. Just like then, he couldn't breathe. Gray gasped again, trying to pull in a morsel of air. His lungs burned, fingers clawing at the splintered floor.

"Breathe, child," the old woman crooned over him as the world spun. He tried to shove her away, angrily, but she held on.

"*Breathe.*" She repeated the word in a slow hum, over and over. Tears welled in his eyes, panic hummed through his body. Finally, after ages, Gray found his breath. He coughed and sputtered, his lungs filling slowly. The world returned to normal. He looked at her. She smiled, her thickly lined face creasing with warmth. "There you be. As long as we breathe we may find our way."

She reached out, handing him the cloth again.

He took it and put it to his nose, trying to come to his senses.

The bloodpact. Faye.

Dying.

A heaviness settled upon his heart, and yet it all felt too unreal.

He watched as Indara dipped a wooden cup into a clear pool of water and handed it to him. He grabbed at it. His hands were shaking, but he brought it to his lips and took a sip. It was cool and refreshing. He hadn't realized how thirsty he was. His throat hurt too, and he remembered that strange darkness he'd vomited.

Then he realized. "Indara…"

She looked up at him.

"Are you certain? What if you're wrong?"

"Not wrong, dear one. There be a darkness upon your heart. It will wring it dry if you do not find a way to stop it."

Still, he didn't believe her. He couldn't. In his mind, he felt the nexus stir. He even had his power, and felt small tendrils of wind creep along his hand and into the cup, stirring the water. "But I feel healthy. I don't feel like I'm going to die. How can you be sure?"

Her dark eyes took on a faraway glaze. "This disease is not new to me, I'm afraid. I have seen it before, in young strong men like you. Twice."

"And how long did they have?"

"The man who looked like you do? Two dalnas."

"Two weeks? So the man who looked like me, he didn't…"

She shook her head.

The knowledge overwhelmed Gray. He rose, gripping the doorframe for balance. Outside was a dark green scape of gnarled trees, watery puddles and muddy dirt. They were still in the Paragon Steppes, in one of those patches of woods he'd seen from the sandy dunes overlooking the plains. In the distance, over the trees, he saw the glimmering columns and towers of Vaster. *No more than a few miles away,* he judged. The others were there. They'd left him and he was dying. "What am I supposed to do?" he asked. "How do I stop it?"

"You must find the other."

He turned. "The 'other?'"

"The one you bonded with," she explained. She moved to his side and snatched his hand with fingers rougher than his. Her thumb pressed his white scar where he'd cut himself. Where he'd pressed his palm to Faye's. "The one who bears this mark."

"Faye..." he whispered.

"That be your answer. Find this Faye of yours and you can stop your death. Only then will you live."

"Why now? Why is this happening now?"

"If I was a guessing woman, I would say the bloodpact was patient like a panther in the reeds. And so it waited—giving you time to fulfill your bargain—but like a panther, its patience has limits, and now it waits no longer."

"Still, it doesn't make any sense," Gray said, gripping his churning stomach. "My bloodpact with Faye was to get us across the desert and hand her Darius' cormac—that's done, I don't understand. Why isn't it fulfilled?"

Indara squinted in thought. "Farhaven is not clever like humans, but wise, whole and pure. She will not twist half-truths, nor extract more than only what you said. But what words you uttered, she will hold you to them. Remember now," she said, and her voice grew ethereal and husky as she leaned in closer, putting her weathered fingers to his temple. The small room seemed to darken at the corners of Gray's vision as Indara leaned closer still. "*Remember.* Something you promised that you've yet to fulfill. Remember now." Gray watched, feeling entranced by Indara's eyes and with the last word, the woman blew a puff of white powder from her outstretched hand and Gray's vision clouded, his mind lost in memory.

"*One last condition,*" *Faye said, running a finger along the smooth steel of her blade. She stood before him, her wavy, deep red hair and charcoal-rimmed eyes were just like he remembered. She wore deep brown leather armor, worn leather straps with metal buckles that crisscrossed her body—the form-fitting leather accentuated her sleek, strong figure—hinting at curves of lean muscle. And though she had a fighter's body, she moved with a dancer's grace. Even the way the stood, one hand planted on her hip, was easy—apathetic. "I wish to teach you si'tu'ah. It is the sand tongue. In your language it means 'The Way of the Sword.'"*

"*Why?*" *he asked.*

"*I enjoy a challenge,*" *she said. "And a sparring partner is a rare thing for me. Back in Farbs, no one will play with me and I miss the practice.*"

Something in the way she said the word "play" gave Gray pause to wonder how many of her "playmates" were still alive. He saw her hidden motive, of course. I want to discover what you are, her eyes spoke. Devari? Reaver? No, what are you? He imagined her thinking. It was clever. Teaching him in order to learn something he would otherwise not disclose.

"Deal," he replied.

"Excellent." *Faye flipped her dagger, caught it by the handle then dragged its fine edge smoothly across her palm. Blood spilled forth. She wiped the flat of the blade clean across her sleeve and then handed it to him.* "Sorry, I trust my honor, but not yours. A bloodpact, however, is binding."

"How binding?"

"Farhaven will hold you to it," *she said simply, mysteriously.*

Without pause Gray grabbed the blade and cut his palm, sucking in a hard breath, water forming in his eyes. How had she not even flinched? He subdued the pain and gripped her hand firmly.

"It is done," *she said, still a breath away.*

The memory faded and Gray returned to the small hut and the muffled sound of pattering rain. Judging by her expression, Indara must have seen the recognition and the light in his eyes. "You see now what you must do?"

Si'tu'ah. The single word resounded in his skull. *I never learned.* They'd had a brief training session, but he'd spent the majority of that time getting his rear handed to him. As he heard the word again, something in his core resonated. He knew there must be something more she had to teach him—that *si'tu'ah* had to teach him something that it hadn't yet. Farhaven demanded it. Gray nodded. "I understand," he said softly.

"Good, good," Indara said and she patted him on his shoulder, a sad smile in her eyes as she bobbed her head and backed away. She shuffled back to the table where her mortar and pestle sat, then returned to grinding strange-looking herbs and multicolored flowers.

Gray watched her without words. His head felt full of cotton and his thoughts sluggish. *What do I do now?* First he had to figure out what in the Seven Hells happened to his friends. But he remembered her words and looked again towards the shining columns. "My friends—when did they leave?"

"They did not all leave," Indara said. He looked at her. She didn't stop from her work, but raised her arm coated by the red-furred Samigurian tiger, pointing out the door. "He's waited for you to wake all day."

"Who?"

"The one who speaks with the trees."

"Darius."

Gray left the hut, entering his strange new surroundings. It was Node-like. Nodes, magical sanctuaries, were created by Farhaven to safeguard its inhabitants—humans as well as creatures—from hot springs in the blizzards of the De'Gral mountains, or islands in the vast Kalvas Ocean, to oases in the endless Rehlias deserts. Nodes, however, only existed as long as necessary. Gray couldn't explain it, but the land around him now felt solid, like a permanent fixture of the land.

It was green swamp where moss covered every tree and insects buzzed in the distance. It smelled of rotting wood, rich earth and fresh rain. Standing outside, Gray listened to the soft patter on the thatch, watching as it ran down and mingled with a pool of fetid water at the hut's feet. He saw a rack where spears were held. He presumed the woman had something to do with Dalic and the other Algasi, but how exactly, he wasn't sure. Gray stood for several minutes, listening to the tranquil sound of dripping water, his mind adrift. Emotions churned inside him before he set his jaw and entered the mossy swamp.

He found Darius not far away, sitting on a stone before a pond, which was really an oversized puddle. About them, the swamp was quiet, save for a lisping trill of a cricket in the nearby reeds. Darius' back was to him as Gray approached. The rogue's brown hair was in its typical disheveled state—perhaps more so, as if he'd been running his hands through it in distress. His fancy green cloak, lined in a rim of brighter lime-green—a gift of the elven queen, Karil, after their near defeat on Death's Gates—was still in relatively good condition. Now though, its hem dangled in mud. Darius' head rested in his hand, looking heavy, his elbow planted on his knee while his other hand lazily made little circles in the air. Darius threaded the flow, like himself, the magic of the Ronin. But unlike Gray's power of wind, Darius was descended from Maris, the Ronin of leaf. As such, Darius threaded all things nature—manipulating plant, vine and root. In their two-week trek, Darius' knowledge of leaf and his abilities with it were nearly as strong as Gray's wind, and it was growing daily. Now, Gray saw a twig suspended by Darius' power. With twirls of his hand, he was mixing a leaf in a pool of mud. As per usual, Gray's presence alerted the rogue.

56

Darius turned. His face was a mask of emotions as he rose.
"Darius…" he began.

Darius embraced him. Gray felt distant. Before he could reciprocate, Darius pulled away, shrugging in his black shirt and green tunic, uncomfortable. His face was etched with worry and Gray delved into Darius' mind with the *ki*.

Terror. Uncertainty. Anger. His fingers flitted at his side—just like Maris', but it was more than nervousness. He itched in his skin, wanting to do something, wanting to help, but utterly helpless. He retreated from Darius' mind and opened his eyes.

"You know, don't you?"

Darius scratched his arm. "I don't know what to say…"

The oddly tranquil sounds of frogs croaking on nearby lily pads filled the silence. "I'm dying," he replied with a small laugh. "What else is there to say?"

They looked at one another. The rogue turned his gaze, letting it fall to the dripping water from a nearby bough into a large puddle. "I can't believe it. We've faced death so many times before, but now?" He shook his head. "Seeing you lying there on the ground like that… I felt helpless. For once it was an enemy I couldn't fight, couldn't swing a sword at. I just… watched." He shook his head, gaze distant.

Gray found Darius' disbelief somehow comforting, as if it made up for his own emptiness, and showed what he knew he should feel but couldn't. He grabbed his friend's shoulder and led him to sit back on the stone. "I'm dying, Darius. Not dead."

That made the rogue look up.

"As I see it, I'm still here, right?" He tried to make his words sound hopeful, true. "And I've never been one to give in before, so why now?"

"That much is true. You practically run yourself ragged. Sometimes I wonder how we've made it this far to begin with… Elves, dragons, Darkwalkers, madmen like Sithel, Reavers, Jian and his crazy Devari." Darius laughed darkly. "What's next, right? What's a little inborn darkness? Speaking of which, what is it, anyway?"

A voice spoke and they both turned. "It is called Sungarsi."

Indara stood between two trees on a dirt path Gray hadn't noticed leading to the small pond. With the dark-red fur of a beast from the dry plains wrapped around her arms, she seemed out of place in the wet greenery.

"Sungarsi?"

57

"It means 'the black void' in the Sand Tongue. All things be balanced in this world." She plucked a lone leaf from a scrawny branch and Darius snorted in objection. "Leaf's balance be metal, made by man. Soot, iron, acids and clouds of smoke erode the trees and take its life, its spark. But trees be the victors in time, like the Great City of Metal, where vine and leaf crawls and lays claim to those twisted, black walls like maggots eating away at a rotting skull. Water hisses at fire, the moon barks at the sun and flesh be nothing beneath stone."

"And wind?" Gray asked.

"Only wind be on its own. It be the overseer of all elements. Everywhere it is, in every breath, sitting upon all things. It be like the Great Father Wolf, its eye upon his cubs from above. But no man can thread wind. And like the great sword, our heart, our symbol of hope, it be a myth long forgotten. Not dead, but hiding."

Gray lifted a hand. A dozen twigs rose into the air on a gust of concentrated wind. Taking after Darius' stunt, he circled his hand. He felt threads of wind churn concentrically in the air. He made the twigs spin faster and faster, then higher and higher. His palm felt heavy, his heart tired. His nexus churned though, full of life, mocking him. Threading more bits of wind, he gathered debris to the small but growing tornado—more twigs, leaves, reeds, rocks and even a few insects got tossed into the mix. At last, satisfied at Indara's widening eyes, Gray clenched his fist. Dozens of twigs and leaves snapped, all of it splattering back into the wet muck. Lifeless. With a swipe of his hand wind rushed away, clearly visible, tousling their hair and cloaks until all was still once more.

Indara rushed forward, surprising him. She lifted his lids, staring into his eyeballs, examining him like an exotic beast. He didn't stop her. Her fingers dipped into one of a dozen leather pouches at her waist. She let flecks of green powder flitter in the air. The powder fizzled, turning white.

"Wind..." she said, breathless, backing away. Indara looked torn between falling to her knees or running from him as if he were a demon. She settled on putting her trembling hands to her lips, staring at him with wide brown eyes and muttered, "The blessed, cursed one at last..."

"You've no idea," he replied.

Darius snorted. "Cursed, blessed, who cares? What I want to know is how do we stop it?"

Gray felt a shred of a smile. Though he missed them all, he was glad it was Darius who'd decided to stay behind.

"As I told *him*," she pointed, looking uncertain if calling him a *him* was still proper, "he must find his bonder."

"By bonder, she means Faye," Gray said, filling in the blanks for Darius. "She's the one that bonded me to the bloodpact—the cause of my sickness, why I'm…" He didn't want to say it again. *Dying.* Then he corrected himself. *You're the cause, Gray. Your own ignorance—tying yourself to a woman you know absolutely nothing about.* But he knew why he did it. It'd been that look in her eyes. It was just like his. Haunted by a dark past and burdened by a terrible power within her. And so he'd tried to save her. *As if it would save me,* he thought with a snort. Like some gallantly dumb knight from the stories. Now he wasn't even sure if Faye was like him at all, or how much she'd been playing him or…

His thoughts were interrupted.

Darius abruptly leapt to his feet, excitedly, mud slopping. "Wait, that's all? Bugger me!" He cursed and gripped his heart, heaving a huge sigh. "Why didn't you say that earlier? You've no idea how bloody worried I've been. Holy hells, my heart's been stuck in my throat since that big oaf Dalic said you were a goner. But now? Faye—that's our answer! That's great news! We just have to find Faye and we'll set this all straight!"

Gray said nothing.

"Oh… right…" Darius said.

"Where is this Faye?" Indara questioned.

"That's a bit of a hard question," Darius muttered, stabbing a stick back into the mud. "We know where Faye is, right, Gray?"

"Farbs, I assume, but that's questionable," Gray replied.

"That's not the worst news. We'll scour Farbs, tear the Shadow Den to the ground if we have to! After all, we've got resources now, remember?" He lifted a finger. "First off, that damned Darkeye is dead, so the Darkeye clan shouldn't be a bother. Secondly, in case you've forgotten, you happen to have an *Arbiter* as a grandfather. He'll set the whole Citadel to the task. I can see it now, Reavers, *Devari*, even Jian running around like errand boys, combing the streets down to the last cellar." He laughed again, excitedly. "She won't be able to hide from us, Gray, I promise."

Gray continued his silence.

Oblivious, Darius snapped his fingers. "Wait, what about Faye? Will she feel what Gray's feeling?"

Indara nodded. "Aye. The bonder and the bonded will both feel the

59

pull of Farhaven tearing at their souls."

Darius swallowed. "You could have phrased that a little better… but still! That's even better news!" He thumped Gray's shoulder. "Don't you get it, Gray? She'll be searching for you too! We'll find her in no time!"

Finally Gray spoke, feeling empty. "Tell him how long I have."

"Two dalnas," said Indara blankly.

Darius scratched his unruly head of hair. "*Dalnas?*"

"Weeks. Two weeks."

Darius shook his head. Then the realization dawned on him.

Gray spoke his fear aloud. "It took us just under two weeks to travel here from Farbs, Darius. I've barely enough time to make it back to the kingdom of fire, and that's *if* she is there." Darius muttered a string of curses, kicking a tower of sticks he'd made, dashing them into the murky pond. Then his friend slumped, sitting back on his rock heavily, but his eyes flashed, deep in thought. Gray kneeled and gripped his friend's arm. "I'm not really a fan of lying down and giving up, so even if we have to run there, even if you have to carry me — we'll make it. I swear it." Darius nodded, but he didn't look entirely convinced. Gray raised his head at the crack of leaf-litter and a flash of movement. *What the…* He thought he saw a ghostly, slender figure dash from one hunched tree to another and a glimmer of scarlet hair. *Could it be?* No, he realized, seeing only a quiet swamp now. *My imagination.*

Silence settled over the odd trio. Despite the fact that it was still midday, the swamp was lit in a false twilight with rays of orange, red and purple. But as the silence deepened, Gray felt the world dim. His heart felt like a stone in his chest. His breaths felt short, his chest tight. It wasn't the poison — it was despair. Anger simmered somewhere beneath the surface, but mostly he felt disbelief. As if he were sitting in a dream, waiting to wake. He wasn't lying to Darius — he wouldn't give up, but he didn't see a way out. Not this time.

"You're right," Darius said suddenly, excited. The twig snapped in his hand. "You won't make it. Not by cormac at least."

Gray looked up. "What do you mean?"

Darius laughed. "Unless you've forgotten, Gray, I didn't find the Matriarch by running across the sands and searching every Node by foot. I mean, I'm a great runner and all, but that's just—" He wiped his hand through the air, grabbing Gray's shoulders, centering him. "My father always said, 'You can't make a sword if your hammer is making a horse-

60

shoe.'" Gray shook his head, confused. "*Gryphons*, Gray. We'll never make it to Farbs by land, but by air? How long will it take? A week? Maybe even less!"

Hope shot inside Gray, catching in his throat. He took a breath, feeling as if it were his first real breath since he woke. Life returned. The shadows all around him seemed to slink back, and the once-dark swamp brightened. He saw it all again, water upon the glistening leaves, Morrowil's smooth hilt in his hand. He hadn't even realized he'd been gripping his blade. Even the shadows in his mind retreated. How had he given into despair so easily? He felt annoyance and then anger at his weakness, but he pushed it down and gripped Darius' shoulders in reply, tears welling in his eyes. "Thank you, friend."

"I can't have you dying on me. After all, Ayva's tongue lashings are meant to be shared and conversations with Zane are a tad... one-sided." He smiled. "Besides, leader of legends, we've a long way to go yet."

Rays of light broke through the copse above, shining down as if echoing his words.

Suddenly, a phlegmy rasp drew their gaze. Indara's leather face was grimmer than death. "I be the bearer of bad news to tell you this, but there be no gryphons this side of the Aster Plains."

Darius' shoulders slumped.

This time, it was Gray's turn to laugh. "Gryphons, maybe not..." Then he pointed to the glimmering spires in the distance. He remembered in his book, still in his bag back in the small hut, the images of magical creatures. He still didn't know exactly the nature of the book—in some parts it seemed a history text, at other times a bestiary, at other times, a journal. In it, he'd discovered that each kingdom had a different magical creature. They stood as symbols, used as heraldry, each one an icon that embodied the persona of the city itself. For wind, it was translucent clawed, silver-eyed phoxes, for fire, majestic gryphons, but for sun, paradoxically, it was the bird of fire: a flaming bird, sunburst orange with red wings flying through the sky. "But phoenixes?"

Welcome to Vaster

Gray led the way, entering Vaster, steering his silver-haired cormac through the sea of people. He'd named the beast Cloud. Unlike Ayva's cormac, his had a grayish tint to its long, fine coat, reminding Gray of the dawning sun shining on clouds and casting a silver outline. He was tired. They'd ridden hard to get there in such short time, and Gray's side was in pain for it, but his guilt was louder. Cloud panted, silken hair slick with sweat. *I promise I'll let you rest soon,* he said inwardly, *just a little farther.* Cloud twisted his thick neck, his orblike silver eyes looked to him. He nickered, and as an Elvin mount, it had almost a musical quality.

Darius whistled through his teeth as they passed through the last marble gate. "By the gods, what is this place?"

Gray looked up and his breath was stolen as well. Neither Kirin's nor his past memories prepared him for the sight before him.

"There's enough gold to line every gambler's purse in Farhaven," Darius said, pointing to the gold that crusted fountains, pillars, staircases and even tiered balconies. "You sure this place was made by mortals?"

Darius was right. Soaring walls of beaten gold met them. Now inside, it was a sea of white marble, glass and gleaming mirrors. Most remarkable of all, however, a golden road sat before him. It reminded him of the golden walkway he created to save the villagers back in Daerval long ago. But this was different, not composed of wind, but sun. A burning gold light shone just beneath its clear surface as if the sun had been tricked, plucked from the sky and trapped here.

Even as dusk settled, life swarmed around them.

Carts carried bright yellow limfuns, boxes of citrus fruits and barrels of grapes imported from the Sevia countryside, pellets of iron ore from the shared Menalas and Esterian mines, wool bales from the Aster Plains, and even wheat bushels from the farmlands south of Cloudfell. Treading the gold road was an assortment of characters: travelers in dusty clothes, some refugees escaping the Aster Plain's bloodshed, some simple wanderers, and merchants in oiled leather or fine silks with caravans and single carts, each bearing the many different emblems of the Great Kingdoms. Gray noticed only the six surviving Great Kingdom's emblems, while stone, wind, and metal, the Forgotten Kingdoms, were noticeably absent from the heraldry.

63

With each wagon wheel, fall of a foot or hoof, the road pulsed. Golden filaments beneath the road seemed to light up, racing away toward a thousand different alleys and side roads, like veins in the city.

It reminded Gray of a beating heart.

Gray felt a sudden, sharp pinch on his arm. He growled, twisting to look at Darius. "What in the light did you do that for?"

"Just seeing if we croaked and went to heaven. Guess not—sorry."

"Pinch yourself next time," he said, in a tad testier voice than he intended for, but he blamed his surroundings. Clattering carts rumbled by, a loud-mouthed town crier in the distance shouted the news of the day, cloth masked vendors hawked their wares and more stimuli jarred his senses. Gray pulled his hood forward, feeling a darkness settle on his heart. It was all too loud and chaotic.

"You all right?" Darius asked. "I didn't think I pinched *that* hard."

Gray opened his mouth then closed it. His skin felt clammy, his eyes sensitive, his hand trembling on the reins. He clenched his fist tighter, silencing it. He reached for the small dagger at his belt, a gift Indara had given him, and it seemed to dampen the voices and the agony to a dull thud. Still, was this what dying feels like? *No, I still have two weeks. Then the bloodpact will kill me.* He squinted. "Just a little bright for my eyes," he said, twisting the truth. It was partly true though—with the sickness inside him, the sun felt too bright, and the world too loud. As if the darkness were hissing out at the gleaming world of Vaster from within.

Darius nodded. "Either way, we're in. What's next?"

Gray looked at his friend riding beside him and gave a sly smile. "Isn't this your area of expertise? Stealing flying mounts?"

Darius cleared his throat. "Right. *That.* Let's see." His eyes scanned the crowds, and then pointed to the spires in the distance, high above, still visible in the dusky skyline. The spires were breathtaking—a varying array, some white marble, some mirrored, and some even looked translucent, as if made of glass. The dusky skyline could be seen through them; only their faint outline even indicated they were real. "I'd say that's our best bet."

"How do you figure?"

"The nests back in Farbs sat high above as well. Easier to take off and all that, and easier to see conditions—wind, snow, sleet—"

"I don't believe those conditions exist in Vaster," Gray said exhausted, remembering Kirin's visions. A saying returned to his sluggish mind. *Expecting easy wealth is like expecting rain in Vaster.*

"It's as good a place to start as any. And I'd rather not dawdle here any longer," he declared, concern in his eyes. Gray wavered in the saddle and Darius' arm caught him, stabilizing him. "C'mon, Gray. It's time to find that damned Faye and get this sickness out of you."

Gray merely nodded. His head felt like a hundred pounds.

They moved into the crowds, climbing the city's rises to the spires in the distance.

He tried to take his mind off the pain in his gut and the thickness of his thoughts, studying the city and its people.

The citizens of Vaster wore curious attire. Most were dressed in robes in varying shades of white or gold. The robes themselves were unadorned, simply cinched with ordinary belts of leather and cloth, rarely tooled or jeweled. Each accentuated their slender forms as they walked, rode or worked.

No one is overweight?

It was an odd thought, but from Gray *and* Kirin's experience, towns were a crockpot or, in Kirin's mind—a *cesspit*—of diversity, filled with both old and young, obese and skinny, wealthy and poor. But everywhere Gray looked, Vasterians were slender and lithe. Few, if any, had facial hair, and their skin was either very pale or very dark, but not one was overweight.

Gray delved into a nearby citizen with the ki, unable to help himself. *Dedication. Vigor. Honor. Duty.* It pulsed from each one of them like the road they walked on, almost deafening. Were they all duty-bound to stay healthy? He shook his head, confused by the notion.

What caught his eye originally were their faces—or their obscured faces, to be more accurate.

Cloth masks everywhere. Men and women, even some children wore white, tan and a few colored cloth masks that covered all but their eyes, most of which were a startling light blue much like Ayva's. *No black cloth,* he noticed. No one wanted to emulate the dreaded Algasi. Not all wore masks, but many did—and those unmasked smiled and laughed, traded and conversed. Vaster, as far as Gray could tell, was a hub of life and joy. Nearby, a little girl without a mask clutched her mother's leg as the woman in a white cloth mask chatted with an older, gray-haired man. Gray smiled. The woman, and the masks as a whole, reminded him of Omni and her white cloth shroud. Gray lifted his head and froze, muscles tensing.

Amid the white clothed crowds—there she stood.

Faye.

Her ringlets of scarlet hair were in stark contrast to the white all around. Her skin was pale, and yet he thought he could make out dark veins spidering across her features, just like Vera's had, and something

65

strange upon her forehead. He touched Darius' arm, pointing. "Darius…" he said, breathless.

"Gray? What's wrong?"

Suddenly she was gone.

Gray twisted left and right, then spotted her again, huddled with a group of old men conversing a dozen feet away. Faye turned. She smiled at him, an indulgent, sorrowful smile and then he saw what had been strange upon her forehead—a ghastly wound as if her skull was cracked. Blood ran down her face in rivulets, but she seemed oblivious to it.

Her lips moved, but he couldn't read them or hear the words. Just then, the crowds shuffled once more and she was gone. Gray rubbed his heavy lids, searching frantically, but she was nowhere to be seen.

"A dream…" he whispered.

"What's a dream?" Darius asked.

He opened his mouth then closed it. "Nothing."

Darius grumbled. "Gray, you can tell me. You can't keep me in the dark. Not now. Not anymore." Gray felt his heart lurch at the desperate look in Darius' eyes. The ever-present mirth was absent. He was serious, hopeful and, buried beneath his green irises, fearful. "You have to let me help you."

"Faye," he said, knowing Darius was right. "I saw Faye."

"You saw…Faye?"

"She's in Farbs, I know." He shook his head. "I know it's a dream, Darius, but my mind tells me differently. I can't explain it." He ran a hand through his hair, grabbing a fistful in frustration, as if he could pull the sickness from his mind. "See? I didn't tell you because it's not important. I know it's just the sickness, and it's getting worse."

"On the contrary, it might be the piece we need to solve this puzzle. Was there anything strange or interesting about her?"

Gray nodded, remembering. "Yes. Her head. She had a wound on her head," he answered. "And what do you mean that it might be the piece we need?"

"I don't know yet," said Darius. "Just… tell me next time she appears. You promise?"

And Gray promised.

⁂ ⁂ ⁂

66

They reached a crossroads—the gold road split into four different directions.

"That was fast," Darius exclaimed, "I think we're lost already. Don't worry, I got this. Oy! You there!" he called, gesturing to a man who was leading a caravan of horses, ponies and a few mules while shouting orders. The man had a bushy, bright orange beard, sun-cracked lips and round belly. *Covian*, Kirin told him.

The orange-bearded trader looked around, confused.

"Yes, you," said Darius, approaching.

The trader was short—maybe three or four hands shorter than Gray. His balding head reflected the brilliant Vasterian sun. It was glossy with sweat in the mid-afternoon and the man periodically mopped it with a dirty kerchief. In contrast to his balding head, he had a furry face, as if all the hair upon his head had fled to his plump cheeks. As they approached, he scratched his stomach inside his ill-fitting jacket and straightened, regaining his composure. "What do you want? Can't you see I'm busy?" Contrary to his words, the man's hired help went on about their business, guiding the caravan with ease and looking thankful for their master's preoccupation.

"Only a moment of your time. Where are the mounts of this city?" Darius asked.

"Mounts?" asked the trader. Then his eyes glittered. "Come to the right man, you have! Mikkos Brasco is my name, and mounts are my game! What type are you looking for? Mules, horses, ponies? We've Sevian horses, fine racers, it's in their blood to run—nothing faster than them, other than the wind, of course. That's what the Sevians say, at least. And for you fine gentlemen? Only five gold marks."

Gray opened his mouth to object. *Five gold marks for a Sevian horse?* He didn't need Kirin's wisdom to know the man was swindling them. The price of his whole pack was perhaps only seven or eight marks at best. "You misunderstand us, we're not—"

Mikkos waved his hands adamantly. "No, no—stop right there. I've read your mind, young masters! Too rich, too rich for your blood. In that case, we've Covian stock, and even some hardy strays from the lands to the east—those white tufted ones over there," he said, pointing to a few small ponies with odd curling horns of white and gold. "Yes, yes, I see your eyes, good sir. You've got quite the eye for horseflesh! Strange bit those antlers, but the ponies are said to have bred with Landarian goats!

Mind you, I didn't believe it before, but on our way here I've seen the proof of it myself. Those little buggers clamber up a shale mountain quicker than an Esterian merchant for a gem! Really, quite the bargain too, for three gold marks. But, for you two, and only because I like you, I'll let you steal it off me for two Farbian golds." Farbian gold coins were thicker and fatter than standard marks, one was easily the equivalent of two in standard currency. Therefore, Mikkos' "steal" was more expensive than his normal fare. The man must think they were idiots.

More than that, Gray had had enough—the trader talked so fast it was hard to get a word in edgewise. He opened his mouth but then began to cough violently. His lungs burned and he covered his mouth. When he pulled it away, his threadbare gray cloak had a blotch of blood. No. Not just blood. Something dark seemed to swirl in that thick red membrane. Gray quickly scraped it off with his dagger, but the quick-talking merchant had already seen.

Mikkos backpedaled, putting his cloak to his mouth. "What sickness lies inside you? That looks like Darkwalker blood or—"

Darius snapped. "Enough! My friend is sick and your incessant rambling is only making him worse. Besides, we've mounts already, you bloody fool." Only now, the man's eyes panned down, as if the prospect of a sale had given him tunnel vision or perhaps the sheer oddity of Gray's mount hadn't registered.

"A cormac...." Mikkos breathed; then bleated, "I'll give you ten silver marks!"

"What?" Gray asked, feeling lightheaded. "No, Cloud isn't for sale." The silken-headed beast snorted, bucking its long, elegant head. Its tall, pointed ears flicked at the air, equally annoyed.

Darius snapped, "*Phoenixes!* Where are the phoenixes?"

"Phoenixes?" Mikkos' brows rose, trying to climb off his balding forehead. Then he began to laugh loudly, drawing eyes. "Dead. Or perhaps jotted down in the ol' storybooks for young ones like you to read."

"*Dead?*" Gray voiced, feeling hope drain from his body.

"Are you deaf? That's what I said! The last phoenix died a thousand years ago. Everyone knows that. Them and the dragons, back in the war of the Lieon. 'Course they say a few dragonkin still flutter about the caps of the Mountain of Soot, or dwell deep within the Drymaus Forest, but them's just wives' tales and folklore. Sad thing, too, that the City of Sun lost its majestic *official* animal." He chortled to himself, little round belly rumbling. "Makes you think all those fancy shields of the Lightguards should be scrubbed clean and painted with only the symbol of sun, don't it?"

Gray felt his heart drop to the pit of his stomach. "Are you saying Vaster has no flying mounts?"

"That's what I'm saying," he said, growing angry. "Now you two have kept me long enough—"

"Gryphons," said Darius. "Gryphons exist in Farbs. How is it there are none here?"

Mikkos squinted. "Where are you from? I can't pin you... Cloudfell folk? Your friend looks dark and swarthy—too pale for the surface and with that gleam of death in his eyes. Narim, I'd guess." He spat on the gold road and it sizzled in a tiny bout of smoke. "But *you*..." he crooned, peering forward, trying to see into Darius' hood. "Not good Covian stock," said the man with pride, "no, that's clear enough. Something weird itches inside me, those green eyes, that *noble* etch to your face, as if you've got the bastard of an elf within ya'. But if'n that was the case, even half-elves know the history as well as any."

Darius shook his head. *Did he just call me an elf?* he uttered to Gray in thoughts.

Half-elf, Gray corrected tiredly. *And I believe so.*

"Gryphons," Darius said tiredly, teeth grit. "Where are the gryphons?"

"You deaf as well as dumb? I told ya' already. The last gryphon Vaster saw was the day their precious sword was stolen."

"Why?" Gray asked.

"Why else? The world hates this light-cursed city almost as much as the Creator himself. That's why he cursed them. Forbidden to leave their precious city, they're locked inside their gleaming golden walls for all eternity. Sure they wear white and talk fancy, but if you squint just right, sometimes in the light, you can see the invisible chains about their necks. If you think about it, they're no better than common slaves."

"What are you talking about?"

"The curse you fools!"

"What curse?" Darius asked.

"Blood and flesh, the damn fools sparked the Lieon for the Creator's sake, the war that tore the world apart, made brothers kill brothers, and fathers slay sons." Mikkos Brasco shuddered, then took a breath and spoke again, lip curled. "It was then they were cursed. The Creator himself

69

did it."

"I don't see any curse," Gray said, looking at the joyful faces and listening to the buzz of life.

"Oh, it's there," Mikkos said, watching the cheerful Vasterians with a contemptuous look. "Peer closer and you'll see the darkness in their eyes and the weight in their steps. That's why the Great Kingdoms shut their doors—they don't want to catch the dreaded blight."

"That's not what I heard," Gray said. "I heard it was the betrayal from the lost sword of sun that made the Great Kingdoms turn on Vaster."

"Treachery, curse, what does it matter? The fact remains, when the sword was stolen, the Great Kingdoms shut their doors to Vaster so quickly you could hear the collective rush of wind across Farhaven." Mikkos made a *whooshing* sound, clapping his hands together loudly, and then smiled to himself contentedly because it made Darius jump slightly. "Henceforth no Great Kingdom, city or province was allowed to engage in official trade with this hellhole and flying mounts, being the property of each Great Kingdom, falls under that category. But us common folk make the trek on foot. Curse or no curse, coin is coin. And to a dying man in need of water, they'll pay a mighty fine price to stay alive. So no. No gryphons, no felbats, no nothing. Got it?" Mikkos' men were nearly out of sight, calling for their irritating taskmaster. The man griped, "See what you've done?! Gone and made me late, you have. The history lesson is over." Mikkos turned.

"Wait," said Gray, reaching out and grabbing the man's dirty sleeve.

He peered at Gray's hand like a venomous snake as it clutched him weakly. "There's nothing I can do for you, Narim filth," Mikkos Brasco said in a sneer. "Not unless you want to fix a few wings and feathers to one of my ponies, find the nearest cliff and—"

Gray reached out. His heart darkened and anger surged inside him. He was tired and in pain, and his vision was growing blurry. As the rage mounted so did the swirling nexus in his mind. His hand curled in the air and a thread of wind reached out, encircling the man's neck, tightening like a noose, when—

GRAY!

Darius had been shouting at him through their bond, but only now he heard.

Unholy hell, Gray, let him go!

Gray let his hand drop, the wind dissipating.

Mikkos' eyes bulged from the sockets of his head, wide with sheer ter-ror. "You're... you're a monster," the man spluttered, trying to back away.

Gray shook his head, opening his mouth. "No, I—"

Mikkos started bellowing, cursing at the top of his lungs, "Wind thread-er! *Demon! Devil!*"

Others turned to the commotion. The horse seller's shrill, panicky voice grew louder and Gray felt the hot glare of eyes fall upon him. Before the man could get any farther with his proclamations, Darius clicked his tongue and kneed Gray's cormac hard, pushing into the crowds, blending into the city. But still men and women watched them as they passed, curious and fearful. Gray's world spun. He gripped Cloud's silken hair as Darius took the reins, pulling them deeper in Vaster. He let himself be guided. When his senses returned, Darius had pulled him from Cloud's back and laid him against a cold marble wall, hiding in a narrow alleyway.

He felt sensation returning to his body.

He knew he couldn't use his power—it drained him too much and made darkness swim in his vision. Darius was wiping the blood from the corner of Gray's mouth with his sleeve, shaking his head in exasperation.

"Sorry," Gray said, looking up to his friend.

Darius looked up from what he was doing. He was still breathless from the flight. "*Sorry,*" he repeated with a laugh, shaking his head. He sounded less angry, however, and more fearful as he settled back down. "Just like you to be on death's door and try to bring down a mountain on someone's head—even if that loud-mouth idiot deserved it." He chuck-led despite himself. "You should have seen his face. What'd you do to him, anyway?"

71

Although both Gray and Darius could sense when the other used his power, they still couldn't always see *how* it was used. Darius' manipula-tion of vine, branch and root was a little more visible, but the others had trouble deciphering the power of wind for some reason. "I just..." he began. *I tried to choke the life out of him.* "It was just a trickle of wind."

"Whatever you did, I'm fairly confident that the great Mikkos Brasco will need clean underpants *and* britches."

Gray wanted to laugh with Darius but he hesitated, too lost in his own thoughts. Words he wanted to say sprouted to mind. *I tried to kill that man, and for what? Even if I survive this sickness festering inside me, am I destined to become the Betrayer of Men like my predecessor?* It seemed rash, but something had surfaced—as if the darkness of Kail that lingered inside him bubbled to the surface when his will grew weak.

When he looked up, he saw Darius was watching the white towers in the distance.

Gray knew what his friend was thinking.

No flying mounts. They'd never make it to Farbs. Gray's heart had darkened at that too, and now it came slamming back home. "You look awful," Gray said. "I thought I was the one dying."

Darius didn't look back. "That's not funny."

Gray sighed. "Listen, we have two dalnas, which is fourteen days, right?" Darius turned back and nodded, clearly wondering where Gray's train of thought was leading. Gray spoke, trying to push back the darkness, the fear that was swelling in his chest, sounding hopeful. "Then perhaps we're rushing to doom and gloom. After all, a flying mount will take only a week to get to Farbs. That means we have time still. Maybe we can head to Covai. It's only seven days hard ride from here to the kingdom of flesh. It's a mecca for trade—surely they'll have something."

Darius nodded, but they both knew that would be cutting it close. They still didn't know if Faye was in Farbs. It would leave them with no spare time to find out where she was, if not there. "What about your old memories? Do they tell you anything? Maybe a hidden transporter within Vaster? Or some sort of magical flying contraption? The stories used to talk about that kind of stuff."

But Gray shook his head, having thought of that already. Each Great Kingdom was supposed to have a mount—a symbol of their city. This had been a perfect plan, but now it was just another dead end.

Darius gave a heavy breath, looking away.

Gray put a hand on his friend's shoulder. "We'll figure something out," Gray said confidently. "I won't go easily." Darius smiled in reply. Of course, Gray's words felt like a lie—he felt his life leaking from him— it was terrifying to feel it slipping away like a bowl of water with a hole in it, dripping steadily, quickly even. But the least he could do was give hope to his friend, even when he didn't feel it.

"Agreed. In the meantime, no more wind for now, all right? I think people are a mite afraid of a legend coming to life before their eyes. Deal?"

Gray swallowed down the pain in his chest and simply nodded.

"Right, c'mon already. It's no longer safe here. That damned idiot horse merchant probably alerted half the guards in this cursed city."

They had mounted and ridden back into Vaster when a roar of hooves echoed from ahead. Crowds parted quickly, jumping out of the way as guards appeared, riding hard down the Sunroad. Their eyes fell upon Gray and Darius and the guards drew their swords. Gray and Darius were quickly encircled.

It all happened in a matter of seconds.

Gray looked up from his hood wearily. A figure pushed its way through the ring of gold-clad guards—*Lightguards*, his memories told him. Suddenly, every muscle in his body went rigid. She rode on a pure white mare, her beautiful face somewhere between bored and amused—just as he remembered her. Faye pulled a stray scarlet lock from her face and gave her usual dark smirk. "Welcome to Vaster, Gray."

✼ ✼ ✼

"Faye…" he whispered. "How?"

"Eloquent as ever. I'm pleased to see you too."

Gray shook his head, looking about. But as he turned, everything seemed frozen in time. There was a strange blur to the world, and moving his head too fast felt sickening. He looked back to Faye—the only clear figure in his clouded vision.

Her hazel eyes tapered in amusement. "You look confused."

"What is this? Am I dreaming?"

She had both legs draped over her mount's saddle, and as she neared, her leg brushed his. "Dreaming? Ah, but what is life if not a dream?" Her expression was cool as ever as she stared off into the distance. "Perhaps death is not an end, but merely a beginning—an awakening from this dream, this eternal torment we call life." He saw sorrow in her eyes, so deep and profound it tore at his heart—tearing away his breath.

"Faye—"

She interrupted him as she looked back. But the sorrow was gone, or perhaps covered once more in thick layers like her dark-plated armor. "Faye… *Faye*… Fa-ye…" She repeated, saying her name with different intonations, then at last shook her head. "Odd, all my life my name has been cursed, or whispered in fearful tones or even uttered by sad beings while they begged for their miserable lives. But not you. You've always said it differently. My name, it always sounds so… *soft* on your tongue."

Gray shook his head, coming to his senses. That face, scarlet hair, same curves, and even her smile—but like a statue's replica, he saw the

73

glaring flaw, the aberration from the original. Her eyes. There was a dimness to her normally sharp hazel eyes. There she fell woefully short from the real Faye. "Who are you?"

"Quite the question. What makes us, us? My skin, my flesh?" she neared, brushing him, and he felt *something*, but it was not flesh. Still, his cheeks heated as her finger played across his soft lips. "Who is Faye but an idea in your mind? And from your mind to another, I differ. I doubt they would see me the same," Faye said with a snort, gesturing to where the guards still stood, forming a ring around Gray and Darius. "They'd try to kill me perhaps, or lust over me, but never would they say my name like you say it."

"Then you're not real. Am I dreaming?" He could've sworn he was awake only moments ago.

Faye sighed. "You waste so much time on such boring questions. At least I know this version is truly you. To answer your question, what you see is the truest version you know. I am composed of the magic of Farhaven, made of the spark, as all living things are. All save the Ronin, of course."

The Ronin aren't even made of the spark? The flow... He knew, but kept his silence, choosing his questions more carefully. "Then the real Faye is still out there. Does that mean..."

"She will see a vision of you as well," she said and then began to fade. "Our time is up, for now."

"No, don't go," he said, reaching out.

Faye spoke, but it was just a whisper on the wind. *"I will return."*

"Wait!" He gripped the wisp of her cloak but it slipped through his fingers. *"Please, Faye! Where are you?!"*

Suddenly, noise began to thunder and the quiet sublime world faded.

His name echoed in his skull, louder and louder.

Gray? Darius' voice came back to him, sounding far away.

Horses rattled by on the Sunroad, crowds moved about, but kept a clear distance from the nearby riders who still held spears towards Gray and Darius. Darius was watching him, his dark brown eyes full of worry. He scratched his unruly hair fretfully. "Gray? Are you back?"

"I..."

Faye.

He looked around, searching the crowds.

But she was gone.

74

She was gone and he would die.

A Reaver was approaching with a group of golden armored men. *Lightguards*, Kirin, his memories, told him.

Darius was still watching him worriedly, and Gray replied at last, "I'm back."

But he wasn't, not yet.

THE DANGER WITHIN

Evangeline whisked to the double gold doors, her fist raised to knock.

"Wait," Ayva said, reaching out.

Evangeline hesitated, looking back, her pretty face confused.

"Do you sense that?" she asked turning to Zane.

"Danger?" he asked, reaching for his blade. He pushed Hannah behind him protectively but she pushed him off. She half expected a growl to emanate from the back of his throat.

"I..." Ayva closed her mouth. She didn't know how to explain it. All the way up she'd felt eyes upon her, from the sun walkway to the stables. Only now inside the halls she felt them fall. Something *else* unsettled her stomach now, standing before the doors. "I'm not sure, but something isn't right." She looked to the doors—seamless creations of gold with two phoenixes entwined upon the gilded surface. They were huge, as if all of Yronia's gold had been smelted down and forged into these giant double behemoths; but no light leaked from beneath the door's frame.

She realized she was still holding Evangeline's wrist and shook herself, releasing it.

Evangeline smiled serenely. "You've no need to worry, Ayva. We're in the safest part of Vaster—perhaps all of Farhaven. Lightguards guard every level of the Apex's hundred floors. An army, or the R—" she hesitated, swallowing her words. What was she about to say? Ronin? "Nothing can get to us here." And she knocked on the golden doors—four raps in rhythmic succession.

"You can't blame us for a little caution," said Hannah. "You see, we've traveled a long way for this moment, so you can understand why we're—" Hannah was saying, but Ayva wasn't listening as the doors opened and Hannah's words fell flat.

Darkness.

That was what Ayva felt. An absence of light. It made her heart clench and her palms sweat. The room was in almost complete shadow, save for a few shreds of light that seemed haphazard, as if reflected from outside the walls.

She narrowed her gaze.

At the far end of the room, a figure stood. He wore white robes, but his face was too hard to see from here. Ribbons of light fell on a glass casement in the center of the room. A glass case the same size as a sword.

Could it be?

"Father?" Evangeline's voice trembled, stepping forward. "Is that you? Father?"

"Evangeline, wait!"

Ayva, with the others close behind her, followed the panicked young woman into the room and into darkness. With growing dread, Ayva reached out to grab Evangeline's arm and abandon the dark room when the doors shut with a crash and the room plunged into a false night. Evangeline gave a cry of surprise. But Ayva was silent. She knelt to the ground and listened. "What's going on?" Evangeline called. "Father?" Ayva couldn't see Evangeline, but she felt her presence a few feet ahead, her voice sharp with panic. Just then, she heard a small scuffle of boot against marble.

Someone else.

Zane sent the same message through the bond. *They see us. They've had time to acclimate to the darkness.*

No, *it's too dark,* she said, knowing somehow, *they're sensing us through noise.* "Be quiet, High Lady," she said as softly as she could to Evangeline, who groped in the darkness beyond.

But the girl ignored her or didn't hear. "Father?" Evangeline called out loudly. "Where are you?"

Just then, there was a bellow. With her hand to the marble, Ayva felt the ground rattle, footsteps pounding. *Someone was charging.* Evange-

77

line cried out. Ayva was quicker. Judging where Evangeline stood, she dove, tackling the High Lady, bringing her to the ground. Steel flashed in the darkness. She sucked a breath in as the man's dagger missed. He rolled over them. Another figure was instantly on top of her. She felt thick, rough fingers grab her arm, prying them away from Evangeline with brutal strength. Ayva grit her teeth, and snatched her dagger from her side and cut. There was a sharp and angry cry. *Female?* Surprise shot through her and her attacker held on. Suddenly, Zane was there. He roared in fury, barreling into the figure on top of Ayva and the High Lady. There was a crash and they tumbled into the darkness.

Hannah cried out.

Ayva twisted, looking, but saw only a wall of pitch black.

She grabbed Evangeline. The High Lady's face caught a faint ray of light. "Are you hurt?" Evangeline's head trembled a *no*, big eyes even wider with fear. "Good. Then stay close to my side and stay quiet this time." She didn't wait for Evangeline to acknowledge. Ayva rose slowly, ignoring the bruises and pain from falling to the hard marble. "Hannah," she called.

Darkness… nothing.

78

She knew her voice gave away her position, but fear grew in her belly for Hannah's safety. She growled, hating the feeling, hating the darkness that cloaked her skin. Her heart was pounding in the bitter black and she wished she could see. "Hannah!" she called louder, searching the darkness. There was a moan, soft and muffled, straight ahead. Her anger spiked, but still, she saw nothing. She squinted. Suddenly, her eyes adapted to the shadows. Light seemed to bloom from nothing, as if she were pulling it from the faint rays in the room. The scene resolved itself. She took it in quickly, heart thundering.

The room was circular and huge.

In the very center of it, a glass casement sat empty. Above, the ceiling seemed to spiral into a dark abyss, but she caught glimpses of mirrors—thousands of them. They caught stray bits of light and reflected them to her eyes. Near the glass casement, grunts sounded. Thuds of fists against flesh—blows being exchanged. *Zane.*

Ten paces away a man pressed a dagger to Hannah's throat. Another stood at his side. Dark cloth made their outlines ambiguous in the dim light—but they were huge. Worse, she saw their eyes. Blue shards that gleamed icily, watching her. *Could they see her as well as she could see them?* Somehow, she doubted it. She moved forward, gripping her dagger, but hesitated.

Another.

She didn't turn her head, not wanting to reveal that she knew he was there.

She was surrounded.

"Let her go and I may let you live," Ayva said.

They looked to one another, clearly surprised that she could see them in the murky light.

"Who's out there? What do you see?" Evangeline asked, backing away fearfully.

"No!" Ayva turned, reaching out, but the big man was quick and he snatched Evangeline, enfolding his arms around her. She squirmed and cried out, but it was useless wrapped in his huge arms.

"It seems you are at a disadvantage." His voice was gruff and fearsome.

Ayva gripped her diamond-throated dagger tighter, facing him—the biggest of the three attackers. "Let them go. *Now.*"

The big man laughed. "Or else? I'm afraid idle threats will do you no good anymore, little girl. You may have the eyes of an owl, but you can't stop all three of us. Not with that little pig-sticker in your hand. Now who should I kill first? I'll let you choose." 79

Ayva's anger faltered. Everything inside her shouted at her that there was something off. It was his words. Dangerous surely, but the threat seemed tame, almost false. As angry and gravelly as he sounded, there was hesitancy in his tone. "You're not going to kill her," she declared in realization. "Who are you?"

He hesitated, blue eyes narrowing on her in surprise once more. "So sure, are you? Perhaps a dagger to this one's throat will—"

She ignored him and yelled into the darkness, "—This is a game, isn't it?"

Silence.

Her hand clenched tighter on her dagger, nervously, but she forced her voice to sound strong. *Who was out there?* "Come out now," she called, "before your pieces take this charade too far. Your men may be strong, but they're awful actors. Unfortunately, the light doesn't accommodate for that. They don't want to do this, so don't make them."

She felt eyes again—the same eyes as before, watching, judging.

But still only silence.

She breathed out as the tension built. "So be it."

"Talking to yourself?" said the leader of the assailants with a snort. "There's no one out there, little missy. You're alone." But she saw his eyes flick to the shadows, as if waiting for a command.

"Fine then," she growled. "Let's play this game of yours."

He pointed to Hannah and the dagger to her throat. "This isn't—"

"—I wasn't talking to you," Ayva interrupted, fixing him with a stare. Then she looked to Hannah. "It's going to be all right, Hannah. I promise. Do you believe me?"

And Hannah, her eyes wide, nodded.

"Well?" she said, looking to the big man. "What're you waiting for? Aren't you supposed to attack me?" In her left fist she felt something swirl, growing warmer and an image flickered in her mind.

Light.

A sun.

Her big attacker growled, looking obviously displeased in the dim light. "Prepare yourself, missy. I don't wish to kill you too quickly." With that he leapt at her and she ducked the blade. The attack seemed slow. Purposely. But still, he didn't stop. He brought his dagger down again and she reached up, parrying. He was far too strong. His one hand was enough to weigh down both of her arms. She winced, feeling her limbs shake.

"Is this it?" he asked, disappointed and… *fearful?* "Is this all you have?" Ayva stamped down on his foot but he barely flinched. "It will take more than that, little missy, if you—"

She didn't let him finish as she rammed her knee into his groin. *Hard.* The huge man let out a burst of air in a deep grunt, his body reflexively cringing but at the same time resisting, as if by instinct. He shook himself quickly, his crossed eyes focusing back on her, but she didn't waste the moment. She stabbed at his stomach. But he was too quick. He snatched her fist, engulfing it in his huge hand and squeezed. She cried out in pain, feeling her fingers crack, pressing painfully to the haft of her dagger. He squeezed tighter.

"Had enough?" he growled.

Ayva felt it before she saw it.

A searing bolt of fire, scorching at the air, hurling towards them.

The big man ducked but it was coming, and too quick.

She cried out.

It pulsed.
Light.
In her mind she saw it—a brilliant pinpoint of yellow, trying to push its way forward from the darkened recesses of her mind.
A golden sun.
Ayva grabbed it and raised a hand. Tendrils from all over the room gathered, flowing up her arm. She felt it draining her, sucking from her core, from her mind. Like dancing fireflies the light coalesced over her palm into a kernel of gold, and she flung out her hand. The kernel of light met the crackling ball of fire, and both erupted in a flare of luminescence, sending golden sparks into the air. But Ayva had no time to react. Zane was crying out, sending more. Bolts of fire flew forth at their attackers, one after another like flaming lances in the darkness. Her big attacker dodged the first few with surprising agility, but another exploded in a burst of flames at Hannah's feet.

"Zane, enough!" she yelled. "You're going to hit Hannah!"
But her voice was drowned out by the roar of flames and Zane's voice.
He was bellowing, anger consuming all.
Zane! she roared out through the bond, stepping forward as a bolt raced past her face, hot on her skin, causing a flush of sweat and scalding. But where normally she found his broiling thoughts, she found only a wall of fire—just as hot and impassable as her words. Another ball of fire seared out of the darkness, heading directly towards her. At the same time her big attacker leapt. He tumbled into her, throwing her to the ground. She fought, struggling to free her dagger but it was pressed to her stomach against his weight, twisting her wrist in pain. She reached up with her other hand, touching his neck. Again, something pulsed inside her.
Hope.
Light.
She prepared to explode her power into him when she saw the look in his dark blue eyes. He was smiling. "A mite close for comfort, wouldn't you say, missy?"
"You… saved me?"
Before she could say another word she looked over the man's shoulder.
Her eyes squinted, pulling at the fragments of light in the room. The darkness abated somewhat, and she saw Zane. He couldn't see, but must have been judging where the voices were coming from and directing the balls of fire. And he was threading again. Molten orange churned in his

81

hand, swelling with each of his breaths. His eyes were twin flames. The engorged globe grew until it was the size of a small cart, pressing back the darkness.

"*LET HER GO!*" Zane bellowed.

Ayva found her strength. She raised her hand to the big man's chest, feeling coarse cloth over his corded muscle. He raised a brow, confused. "Sorry," she said with a wince as a gust of light burst from her hand and the big man was blown back, harmlessly sliding across the floor.

Ayva slowly rose.

Zane's ire was like a sun, growing beyond its bonds. She knew what drove him to madness—his sister's protection consumed his mind, as when she'd been in Darkeye's clutches. But if he wasn't stopped, he'd burn them all to cinder. She took a deep breath and summoned her power. More light flooded her, filling her. At first, it took her breath away. She felt as if she'd crack at the seams, but still she grabbed more, light feeding her from all pockets of the room, crawling across the floor in gold snaking lines. The fire in Zane's hand grew, now a molten sphere the size of a house—his cry thundering through the room. The molten fire erupted forth. Ayva raised her hand. Her sphere, half the size, collided. Yet it was like a lance of light, piercing the molten bubble. Then, by instinct, she flared her fingers wide and her globe of light *exploded*. At first, the two spheres of magic fused as one—a terrible ball of blinding light and scarlet flames. Then suddenly, and abruptly, the ball stopped expanding. Instead, it pulled back in on itself. Air rushed forth, dragging at her clothes, hair flying in the air, but she rooted herself to the floor like a stubborn old oak. Her burst of light suddenly winked out of existence and they were left in silence. Ayva dug deep one last time and, like striking flint, a globe of light burst, rotating slowly in her upraised palm.

The room erupted in luminescence. She didn't squint against it. In fact, the white light that suffused the room, touching all—the walls, the mirrors, the man in the corner that hid behind a column—seemed *natural*. Their false attackers threw hands over their eyes as the sphere of light pulsed its radiance, matching her fitful anger. Her breath was ragged, watching the sphere churn in the air.

"Enough," she breathed.

Zane was frozen, but only for a moment.

He saw Hannah being restrained, and he charged.

Immediately the three brutes leapt on him, pinning him to the ground.

He growled and snarled, trying to claw his way to his feet, but it was useless beneath the mountain of muscle. Hannah leapt to his defense but Ayva turned from the two, knowing they wouldn't hurt Zane, and thrust the sphere forward. "You can come out now... Lord Nolan."

As expected, a figure in white robes walked out from the shadows.

"*Dad!*" said Evangeline, rushing to her father's side.

Lord Nolan drew near and Ayva saw him in the radiant light of her sphere: a proud, noble looking man with a sharp nose and intelligent eyes. She opened her mouth, preparing an angry tirade. But he gave a deep bow, gazing at the sphere, eyes wide, almost tearful. And Ayva's heated rant fell short as he spoke in reverent tones, "At long last, you're here..."

TRUTH VERSUS LIES

Lord Nolan pulled back his hood to show his features in full. His brown hair, with a touch of silver at the temples, was combed back and lightly oiled. His brows, also showing age, were silver eaves for his eyes—a deep, contemplative blue. His robes weren't just white, she realized, threads of silver were woven in seamlessly to the cloth making them shine in the light of her orb. A leather belt with a silver buckle and the symbol of sun etched into its center cinched his narrow waist.

Ayva couldn't hold onto her power anymore and the orb in her palm winked out. As it did, Lord Nolan touched a glass sphere sitting on a pillar near the center of the room. As he slid his finger, the sphere went from black to white and the room brightened. Ayva looked up in surprise as mirrors above them moved on silent hinges. At the same time, the windows in a circle around the room went from cloudy to clear. The mirrors caught the incoming light from outside and spread it about the chamber evenly, turning the room from night to brilliant day.

Lord Nolan stood straight, his hands clasped calmly before him. His face was smooth, but there was deep sorrow in his eyes. If not for the tears in his eyes from before, Lord Nolan could have been a statue—an artist's rendition of the perfect Vasterian. Ayva found herself having difficulty meeting his gaze for some reason. He didn't radiate power like some men, or even authority necessarily, but there was a sense of patience and perfect order about him. It were as if Lord Nolan were a pillar set into a deep foundation and nothing could unearth him. The rest of his ensemble was equally impressive. Large gold pauldrons sat on Lord Nolan's shoulders. Ayva reveled at the craftsmanship, as the pauldrons, a single mass of plate, had been shaped into the likeness of phoenixes bursting into flight. Silver vambraces adorned his forearms with a sunburst on each. Despite her distaste for him at that moment, he looked like a king. A *Steward*, she corrected herself.

She shook her head and found her anger again. "Lord Nolan, I presume? The puppeteer behind this little charade? I wonder, my lord. Do you always greet your guests by the tip of your Lightguard's swords? Or are we just lucky exceptions?"

Lord Nolan inclined his head humbly, genuinely. "I deserve that. I would hope that you're exceptions to the case. Though whether you're lucky or not, I'll leave that up to you." His mouth twisted as if he tasted something bitter. "As for my actions, I hope you'll forgive me. Integrity and honesty are what I hold dearest—not shadows and deception."

"Your actions don't match your words," Ayva said.

This time Nolan didn't bow his head, but gave a small, sad smile. "Sometimes necessity can break the codes of even honest men. And that necessity paid off. For here I am," he said. "Greeting the Ronin in person."

Ronin. Ayva's throat grew tight and her mouth went dry.

"Charade?" Evangeline asked. "What's going on?"

Lord Nolan turned to his daughter. "My apologies, Eva. What I did, I had to do, believe me. You're the last person I'd ever want to deceive. If I'd told you, however, they'd have seen through the ploy all the more swiftly and perhaps not used their powers as I hoped they would. They would not have revealed their true nature."

"True nature? You mean us being Ronin."

Lord Nolan nodded.

"You're not evil, I can sense that much. But that doesn't make you good. Not yet. So tell me—why?" Ayva asked. She still felt suspicious to her bones, but something in Lord Nolan, in his face and posture, made her want to trust him. She noticed he looked tired, as if Vaster itself sat upon his shoulders. "Why go through all the trouble? You could have hurt us or been hurt yourself. Not to mention if you're seeking something from us, attacking us is not the way to go about it. It often tends to make a person a tad more wary."

"All valid points."

"Then why?"

"It will be easier to show you. Come." With that he turned. Ayva was speechless. Lord Nolan's tone and urgency frightened her—almost more than all the chaos of the last few moments.

"Ayva..." Hannah said, looking to Zane. "Please."

"Wait! We're not going anywhere. Not until you let him go." She pointed to Zane who still struggled, groaning and wrestling like a trapped rabid badger beneath the huge muscled men. The men looked like they held him easily, but not without trepidation—the entirety of their focus was on Zane.

Lord Nolan watched Zane snarl and struggle. "'An unquenchable fire.'" He sounded like he was quoting something. Nolan looked to Hannah. "Your brother's in the grip of his own anger. Inflicting pain is the only thing on his mind. Calm him first, then I will give the command."

Hannah ran to Zane's side. She issued calm words until slowly, surely, the fire in his eyes died. As it did, the Steward of Vaster gave the command and the three men leapt away. Zane rose, but then he looked to Hannah once more. Sanity returned.

Nolan strode past Ayva, and past his daughter whose big brown eyes were wide, to the doors. Before either could speak, Nolan said, "Well, are you all coming? Time runs thin." And he was gone.

With questions bounding on her tongue, Ayva followed and they moved through the hallways.

Ayva glanced to Zane. He still looked different. A fog of anger and confusion—thick blond brows drawn, eyes glossed and narrowed. He shook his head from time to time, as if trying to shake off the anger. He hadn't returned to normal. Hannah held his arm, chaperoning him through the corridors. Hannah glanced to Ayva, worried.

Zane, are you back? Ayva asked through the link.

The response was delayed. Zane's gaze was glued to the Lightguards and Lord Nolan beyond. Evangeline walked at their side, drawn into herself. Ayva could tell she was still struck by her father's deception, if not more than they were. *Back enough to know that I don't trust this man,* he sent at last.

I don't either, but don't do anything stupid, she thought. But through the link, she only said, *We'll see. Just... let me do the talking.* White walls on one side, glass the other flanked their path. It was glorious outside. Vaster looked like heaven, and they were the angels peering down, but her attention was focused on Nolan.

"I still don't understand," Ayva said, tired of the silence, joining Nolan's side. "This was all some giant game? For what purpose?"

"To prove the truth," Lord Nolan said. His robes were of a strange, iridescent white cloth. And as he walked, they moved more like flowing water on his form than true fabric.

"What truth?" Zane asked, shrugging his shoulders as if still feeling the big men's hands upon him.

"The truth that you're the Ronin—and only the Ronin can stop what's coming and what's upon us."

Zane interjected. "You tried to kill us and now you want our help?"

Lord Nolan shook his head as they walked briskly. "Judge you, not kill you. A far different thing."

"How about we judge you? At the end of my blade." Zane unsheathed his sword.

The Lightguards slid between their lord and Zane, blocking Zane's path. Lord Nolan calmly touched the biggest Lightguard's arm. The sun lord wasn't weak. In fact, he had an air of experience. Ayva had a feeling he could hold his own with the blade at his side, and the armor on him looked more than merely ceremonial. But his slender hand looked almost dainty on the huge muscled man's shoulder.

"It's all right," Nolan said.

Grudgingly the Lightguards backed down, moving aside.

"You don't like me, do you, Zane?" Lord Nolan asked.

"No," Zane said. "I don't take well to men who hide in darkness with plots of deception." He put himself in a clearer path, blocking Lord Nolan's view of Hannah.

Lord Nolan gave a knowing, sad smile. "I know why you dislike me, and I don't begrudge you for it. But you should know I would never have hurt your sister, Zane."

"Because you want something from us."

"Because that's not who I am," Lord Nolan amended. He looked to his men. "Show them."

The biggest Lightguard stepped forward. Ayva touched the small blade he proffered in his scarred hands. The edge was duller than a spoon and had no point. He'd have more luck hurting her with insults than with that

87

sorry excuse for a weapon. "See, missy?" Ungar said. "Just toys."

"You were never in any danger," Lord Nolan declared.

"Why?" Ayva asked. "At least tell me *why*."

"Because of this."

Soon enough, they were at corridors with white-robed attendants whisking back and forth. Ayva noticed a peculiar gold insignia embroidered on the breast of their robes of a serpent wrapped around a sword. Her heart began to beat faster. They came to a door with another gold snake-and-sword insignia on it. Beside it, two guards stood at attention with cloth masks over their faces. Not Omni or Algasi cloth-like masks, but masks with two loops about their ears and of a different fabric. She recognized them from one of her books, '*Trades of Farhaven.*' *Sick-masks, for medicus' assistants.*

The guards saw Lord Nolan and bowed deeply.

They entered and Ayva was first struck by the acrid smell of herbs covering the faint, stomach-churning stench of decay. The foggy windows were more transparent here. The room was bathed in the ever-present but diffused light due to mirrors on the walls. Suspended from the ceiling were hundreds of green plants inside glass containers of varying shapes and sizes. Feeling a breeze, Ayva noticed a few of the windows were open. They apparently had tiny hinges to let in a cool, steady breeze of air.

But the most obvious were the people.

White stretchers from wall to wall. People filled them. Dozens, hundreds even. They were covered in bandages. Their coughs and groans filled the air. Everywhere men and women, even *children*. All dying.

"What is this?" Ayva asked, breathless, covering her mouth.

"My horrible secret," Lord Nolan replied.

"What's wrong with these people?" Hannah asked.

"They're dying," Nolan said simply. "Just like Vaster."

THE LOST BLADE

Robed attendants flitted among Ayva and the others like white doves administering aid. The robed men and women changed slightly bloody bandages, helped those who were too weak to hold cups sit up and drink water, exchanged bedpans and wiped sweat from the brows of the sick. More often than not, the robed helpers simply sat on stools, issuing soft words to the sick, creating a low hum in the otherwise quiet room. Ayva realized the loudest groaning patients were positioned in along the back walls with the most windows, as if they were given a chance at light before they departed this world.

A loud bloody cry sounded, punctuating the silence.

It came from a stick-thin woman with blonde hair and bright green eyes. She released her clutch on her blankets and reached up, toward the light, her fingers curling as if trying to grasp the sun. Her eyes were panicked, her breaths labored, short and quick. "Gods, no," she breathed. "I feel it coming. Please, not yet. I don't want to die. I—" Then her body convulsed and her eyes rolled to the back of her head, and she slumped back into the bed—dead.

Moments later, before Ayva could even register what had just happened, a man cried out, doing the same. This time, he merely clutched his heart and curled inward, sobbing until he was motionless and silent. White-robed men pulled his blankets over his head. A priest holding a worn tome rushed to his side, issuing rattled but practiced words over the man before the next cried out.

Another man, this one looking strong and healthy and built like an ox, with large muscles and hard-bitten features, died all the same.

Then a teenage girl.

Then an old man.

Then a little boy —

"No…" Ayva breathed.

The little boy's eyes were wide, scared. "Mommy, Mommy —" A woman who had been asleep, resting her head on his bed as she sat in a chair at his side, suddenly bolted upright, terror in her eyes. The boy reached out, also trying to grasp an invisible light. Fear grew on his features as he couldn't touch it and his bright blue eyes filled with confusion.

The woman cried for the healers over and over, and a balding older man rushed to her side. Just as he did, the boy's terror peaked, choking as if on blood. But there was no blood. He convulsed one final time and then fell over. A trickle of scarlet ran from his nose, but he remained unmoving. His mother gave a cry that made Ayva's blood turn to ice. Her body convulsed with heart-wrenching sobs. "No… please… Oh gods… Gerish… please, Gerish!" She pressed her face into his small, lifeless body, crying. "My boy, my little sun, please gods—don't do this to me."

90

Ayva felt sick. She needed air. She rushed to a window at the opposite end of the room, away from the cries, away from the horror and sorrow. Zane accompanied her; Hannah close behind. Then the others came. When she at last could breathe and the cool air of Vaster helped wake her from the nightmare she'd just witnessed, she tried to find words. "What is this madness?" she asked, looking to Lord Nolan, breathing steadily and slowly regaining her composure.

Lord Nolan glanced over his shoulder. The room was noticeably quieter. Ayva knew better, but couldn't help but attribute the newfound silence to how many lives were just extinguished. When she inquired about the sudden hush, Nolan answered. "The 'wave of dying' they call it. It comes and goes. No one knows for certain when or why, but my best healers and I believe it's because the Sunroad weakens in chunks, like a bridge with a hundred supporting beams. When one beam can bear the weight no more, it collapses. When it does, the wave of dying happens. And with it, another part of the Sunroad, and my city goes dim."

"How?" Ayva asked, her voice hoarse. "What's causing this monstrosity?"

"The sword."

Evangeline and the Lightguards all exhibited varying degrees of shame, bowing their heads and looking away like scolded children. Even Ayva felt a strange breathless guilt tugging at her heart. But Ayva shook herself, snapping out of it. *What was that?* It wasn't her fault. And yet she wondered if she had Vasterian blood in her. Was the guilt bred in the blood itself or was she simply sensing their guilt?

"A missing sword is doing *this?*" Hannah asked.

"All know the story of the missing Sword of Sun, but what you don't know is that the sword was more than just a symbol for Vaster. Housed in the Chamber of Sun, it was Vaster's lifeblood. It sustained us, kept the Sunroad alive, which, in turn, kept Vaster alive. Without the sword, Vasterians cannot survive. It's like surviving without the sun—at first we simply feel cold, but day by day its effects drain us, slowly killing us."

All of this was news to Ayva, but it made sense.

"How're you still alive then?" Zane asked.

"It's taken many years for the sickness to grow. Still, if not for the Macambriel, we'd be dead long ago."

"The Macambriel?" Ayva asked.

"A surrogate blade," Nolan explained. "Also known as the 'false blade.' It's lasted us this long, but it's breaking. After all, it was never meant to last this long. The Patriarch and Arbiter Ezrah helped forge the Macambriel from another relic, a very special dagger, but it was only ever meant to be a placeholder—a proxy until the Sword of Sun was found and returned to its rightful place. Yet still the Macambriel remains, enduring after all these years, like a lamp in the sky, trying vainly to replace the sun's light. But for how long? Our children grow weaker every year. Days begin to dim, nights are darker. Even now, I feel a weight upon my heart, suffocating slowly. And it's worse for some than others."

Ayva replied, "So you're saying if the sword isn't found, Vaster will die."

Nolan was stone-faced. "Put bluntly, yes."

Evangeline blanched, her pretty pale face growing even paler. "Surely Medicus Marlan will find a way. Didn't you say he was working on a cure?"

"To no effect so far," Lord Nolan said soberly. He took his daughter by her hands and spoke tenderly—the voice of a father replacing that of a Steward. His face appeared to age years in that moment. "I'm sorry to reveal it to you this way, my little sun."

91

Evangeline looked stricken; her eyes were for the sick around her. She looked like Avva felt—haunted.

"If only it were an enemy to hack at, or a spear to throw ourselves upon, but Lord Nolan is correct. The city weakens day by day and there's nothing we can do," Ungar, the Lightguard commander, said.

"How long will it take?" Ayva asked.

"A week… a month… a year? Maybe tomorrow? There's no telling exactly how long. The Macambriel cracks even as we speak and the residents feel its effects. When we retrieve the true sword the Vasterian people will be lifted from this plague. There's one last reason too… We cannot live outside the world of Vaster. We are prisoners within our own city. Vaster sustains us, but it's both our blessing and our curse. Yet if the sword is returned? Many believe we can once again travel the world." He flexed his hand, eyeing it like a ghostly apparition, then looked back at Ayva. Clasping his hands behind his back, making his silver vambraces click, he stood erect and asked with finality, "Will you help us? Will you return the sword and make Vaster whole once more?

Now that she fully understood Nolan's plight, Ayva couldn't help but feel his desperation. She looked to Hannah and Zane. Hannah's jaw hung and Zane scratched his head. "You're forgetting something," she said, pushing aside the weight the man had placed on her shoulders. "I can only find the sword if I know the prophecy."

"Then you'll help us? You'll retrieve the blade and save Vaster?"

Save… Vaster… Ayva swallowed. The man had a way of not mincing words. *Just save the Great Kingdom of Sun, Ayva. No big deal.* She felt all their eyes; Lord Nolan's, the Lightguards,' even Zane's and Hannah's. Ayva opened her mouth and then closed it, remembering. "You still haven't explained why you attacked us."

"Simple. I needed to prove you were you."

"Ronin," Zane said.

Lord Nolan inclined his head. "Ronin. Unfortunately, I couldn't simply ask if you were thousand-year-old heroes reborn as youths. Polite or not, the task at hand demanded that you proved yourselves Ronin."

"Why us?" Ayva demanded. "Why not send Devari, or Reavers or an army to find the Sword of Sun?"

"Forgetting the difficulties of ordering foreign nations to your bidding, or that this task is for Vasterians alone, or that thousands have already gone searching for the Sword of Sun, there's a simpler reason." He tapped his chest, upon his heart. "You feel it here, do you not?"

Ayva's chest was tight. She did feel it: a thrumming sensation that made her empty and anxious… Anxious to search—to find the Sword of Sun.

Nolan smiled, as if seeing the reaction on her face as confirmation. "It's calling for you. If the Sword of Sun was lost by Omni, the tales all agree, only her heir can find it. I believe it too. Of course, I'll provide you with anything I can to aid you in your journey. Horses, provisions, coin and anything else you'll need. Alas, I would go with you myself or offer my men to ride with you but…"

"The curse won't allow you to leave the walls of the city," Hannah finished.

"We can leave, but few live more than a day outside the Macambriel's influence. Supposing one could fare longer in the world beyond, even the strength of a Lightguard would be no more than a nuisance to you—their arms too weak to swing a blade or hold a shield." Then his eyes tightened. "That said, I was under the impression there were more of you. The stories say they were nine Ronin. One for each element. I can see now you are sun, dear Ayva, and you are fire, Zane. But where are the others?" His tone wasn't accusatory, simply curious, but Ayva felt slapped for some reason.

She took a deep breath. "It's a long story. Speaking of which, we need your aid. Our friend is sick and needs medical attention." She quickly described Gray and his whereabouts. She couldn't help her voice from sounding breathy and quick; her gold tunic felt increasingly constricting with each subsequent word. When she finished Lord Nolan simply nodded.

"I'll send a retinue to search the swamp and bring him back. Our healers, despite what you saw, are the very best in Farhaven." There was a long pause. "I've answered your questions. Will you help us?"

Ayva appreciated his directness, but she had one more request. "I wish to see the Macambriel first."

"As you command," Nolan said, his smile replaced by a dark look.

The Macambriel was held in a room beneath the Apex. As they grew close, Ayva's heart felt darker. There were no guards and no servants down here. It felt strange after such a bustling tower. They turned a corner and Ayva's heart began to pound. A large, arched doorframe sat in the center of the corridor, but with no door in sight. The white stone arch was in sharp contrast to the hallway's black stone. Cracks branched throughout the white marble as if the archway were crumbling beneath the weight of the Apex. Ayva noticed the symbol of sun etched on the archway's keystone. A dozen paces before it, a pedestal sat cradling a crystal orb.

"What is that?" Hannah asked. "It looks magical and *old*."

"Voidarches are very old, indeed," Lord Nolan agreed. "Some say they were created during the birth of the Great Kingdoms. They're one of many security measures to protect the Macambriel. As you can see, the archway looks open, but inside its frame is a magical barrier used to prevent intruders from crossing the threshold."

"Voidarches," Ayva said, noticing his pluralizing. "There's more than one?"

Lord Nolan said, "Nine to be exact."

Nine, Ayva recognized. "How do they work?"

"Simple. A Voidarch can sense the spark within a person, so I'm told. It's a bit gruesome to describe, but as one approaches the barrier, they feel warm, like the sun's smile on their skin. With the next step, heat envelops them—like the hottest day in the Farbian desert. Another step and your skin begins to crack and bleed. With the next step, its sears and melts the flesh from one's bones. How much you can endure depends on the person and his or her level of the spark, but nobody has ever made it within an arm's length of the archway itself."

Ayva saw sweat on Hannah's brow, though they were still a dozen paces away. Zane wasn't sweating but he wore a wary look. Evangeline had a faint bit of perspiration at her temple. Only the Lightguards were completely stone-faced. As Nolan's personal guard, she imagined they'd accompanied Nolan down here many times.

Ayva, oddly—or most obviously—didn't feel hot at all. Perhaps it was because she and Zane had the flow? Or perhaps it was because it was an archway of sun. Either way, it felt almost cool down here.

Nolan put his palm on the orb, but nothing happened. He lifted his hand, touching it again, eyes widening.

"What is it?" Ayva asked.

"I can't feel it," he said, panicked. As soon as the words left his mouth, there was a loud crash, sounding far away. "Oh gods… The Macambriel…" The crash was accompanied by a dreadful cackle, distant, echoing through the halls and making Ayva's blood run cold. Something about the terrible laughter was familiar, but it only grazed her awareness as she

94

and the others took off in a breakneck run—hoping against hope that they weren't too late.

* * *

They tore through the halls, following the horrifying sound of the cackle. The Lightguards led the way. Their powerful legs pumped in perfect rhythm. They looked torn between charging ahead and safeguarding their lord—but it was clear which duty took priority.

Just then, voices sounded from behind, echoing from the way they'd come.

"Behind!" Ungar said. "Turn and form ranks!" Like a dance, the Lightguards twisted and formed ranks between Ayva and the others, creating a barrier of muscle and dull-edged steel. *Now,* Ayva wished they had their real blades.

Lord Nolan gathered his daughter close, unsheathing his gold-encrusted sword.

The sound of footsteps grew.

Ayva's heart slapped against her ribcage. In the corner of her vision, she saw Hannah reach for her brother's hand.

95

Then they appeared from the dark tunnels.

Darius and Gray, beside a red-robed Reaver and several other Lightguards—men and women, all big but smaller than Nolan's personal guard, clad in resplendent golden platemail—approached at a breakneck run, a light bobbing ahead of them from the Reaver's outstretched hand.

Ayva released a pent-up breath.

"Thank the light," Hannah whispered, recognizing the faces a few seconds after Ayva did. Ayva's eyes seemed to adjust to the light better.

They slowed. Then she saw him. Gray, his face framed by the Reaver's light. He looked awful. Already dark circles rimmed his eyes, his breaths were labored, and sweat mingled with his dark brown hair, making him look ragged. But upon seeing them, a smile warmed his gaunt features. He opened his mouth to say something, but she didn't wait. Ayva rushed forward, embracing him. A gust of air was knocked from his lungs as she squeezed.

She hadn't realized how worried she'd been for him. Seeing that sickness pouring out of him... Now seeing him, relief flooded her. "I was so afraid," she said.

Gray simply squeezed back.

Darius coughed. The hug must have lasted a while. She wrapped her arms briefly around him too, knocking the air out of him with surprise. They exchanged a quick but heartfelt reunion until one of the smaller Lightguards asked, "What's going on here? We were coming to meet you in the Chamber of Sun, then we heard an explosion. Where is it?"

"This way," said Ungar. He was obviously second-in-command to Lord Nolan. Even a tall and leanly muscled Lightguard wearing a gold cloth band around his plated upper arm—*another captain,* she surmised—deferred easily to Ungar.

Ayva, what's going on? Darius asked through the link as they ran.

Someone's broken into the room where the Macambriel is held.

Gray and Darius exchanged looks. She read their eyes and their confusion, as if asking, '*Macambriel?*'

How bad is it? Gray asked.

Before she could say more, Gray found his answer as they reached an intersection covered in blood.

THE BLACK HiVE

O daren, the pudgy thief and right hand to the nefarious Shadow
King, moved with haste. His stout legs chafed as he hurried
with news certain to bring his own death. Turning, he entered
an intersection swarming with thieves, opening up to hundreds of
archways and canals—all of it coated in the famous turquoise glow of
Narim. It was a hub of sneers, dirty bodies and tangible threats—where
one cross look meant a swift dagger in the back. He tasted the tang of
sweat on his upper lip and covered his nose from the stench of death
that clung to the nefarious men and women who walked the pathways of
Narim, the Great Kingdom of Moon.

Death...

Odaren gulped a sweaty, fearful breath.

He stopped amid the watery halls. *What if I run?* He had a quick jolt
of hope and it made his pulse race. Dark thieves flowed around him like
murky waters. He looked up to see a dirt ceiling looming hundreds of
feet above—a barrier between the dark underworld and the land above.
A land of air, of light, of *life.* Yes... *I can head for the hills, then hide in
the crevasses of the Narim Foothills...* Smiling, Odaren grew emboldened
by the idea. *I can feed myself on the farms of the surface—those dim-witted
peasants would never be the wiser. But most importantly, I would live...*
Abruptly, his smile wilted.

All around him the people moved en masse, heading toward a coliseum-like structure that rose from Narim's grand turquoise lake like a shattered black blade.

The Black Hive.

No. There was no running, not from him.

The Shadow King's orders were always obeyed. Odaren was servile to his core. If he had a shred of pride, it was only in that. In a life full of depravity and sin—a life clinging *to* life, like the threadbare clothes upon his heavyset frame—Odaren was at least loyal.

With a heavy breath, he made his way up the long rise. Sweaty and tired, he maneuvered through the maze of arches and ramps, reaching the last barrier of guards—*thieves*, really—between him and the Shadow King. They lounged beneath a wide archway in their black rags. Festooned upon their breasts was a poorly stitched half-gold half-black crown, the symbol of their master. Odaren approached. They made no move to stop him, but beneath their breath he faintly heard the words, "King's Rat."

Odaren ignored them and entered the Shadow King's hall.

Perhaps at one time long, long ago, the hall was a place of grandeur, filled with rich rugs, tapestries, bloodstone murals and other symbols of the Moon Kingdom's wealth. Yet after the last rightful king of Narim was killed, everything was pilfered and wasted and those relics were now scattered across the lands. Now the hall was little more than a round hemisphere of worn stone. Broken chandeliers hung like giant paralyzed spiders far above his head. A fissure in the ceiling, not unlike a broken egg, showed the much nearer earthen roof of Narim.

Darkness was prevalent. It lingered in the air like cobwebs Odaren couldn't sweep aside. Luckily, on the far walls, turquoise light peeked through the slates of boarded-up grand windows. The light of Narim fought back against the dark aura of the Shadow King's throne room. It gave Odaren a strange sense of comfort to know that despite the corruption from a dozen years of defilement at the Shadow King's hands, the Great Kingdom still had a pulse.

Gaze fixed in deference to the stone, he made his way across the long, cold expanse of floor to stand before the Shadow King's throne. His heart thudding, the weight of hundreds of eyes bearing down upon him made Odaren twitch inside his skin. His peripheral vision glimpsed the crowded walls packed with an assortment of characters: sycophants mostly, and dirty little youths the oh-so-magnanimous king kept as errand boys to filch. But instead of keeping the little miscreants beneath the Black Hive, or in hovels like most cities, the grubby boys sat in the throne room of Narim, at his side. Odaren found it odd and often questioned the true reason for their presence.

His attention snapped back as Halvos the Shadow King spoke.

"*What news?*" the man asked from above, the words echoing through Odaren's skull.

"The news is..." he muttered, lip quivering, trying to conjure the right word. The silence stretched and he licked his lips, finally croaking out. "*Unsavory,* Master."

"My patience runs thin, Odaren," Halvos said. "Tell me of the rumors from the south of Farbs and Darkeye's Clan. Tell me or you will find your end equally *unsavory.*" Odaren glanced up finally, taking in the Shadow King. The man sat upon his throne, one leg draped over the arm of the twisted chair—a throne that made Odaren sick to his stomach. It was made of bleached white bones of all shapes and sizes: femurs, fibulas, tibias, ribs, with skulls as the armrests. Upon its crest, long, spindly bones of a creature Odaren didn't recognize sprung from the throne's back, re-sembling a massive white arachnid waiting to wrap the Shadow King in its terrifying embrace.

99

Halvos himself wore a black coat with a high flaring collar. A crown—one side black and the other gold—teetered upon his ghost-white hair. He stole it from the rightful monarch of Narim after murdering the man in his sleep some dozen years ago. He was thick with muscle, arms and chest like an Yronian blacksmith and his black coat was left open to flaunt them. But worst of all were his eyes... They were a cloudy white. The Shadow King was blind, but somehow his eyes pierced Odaren to the core.

At the man's side a woman knelt on the stone, her head bent. Odaren had never felt a woman's touch before, but this one was beautiful. She had been a present to the Shadow King. With long, curling red hair, a syl-van face—narrow chin, light eyes, and high, if a tad gaunt cheekbones—she was out of place in this dark hollow made only for the greedy and damned. Upon closer inspection, Odaren saw her hair barely hid a vivid white scar near her temple. Abruptly she glanced up and Odaren shiv-ered. Her gaze was vacant, dead. The woman may have been flesh and bone, but if her skin still held the warmth of the living, he'd be surprised.

"Well?" Halvos pressured in that eerily calm voice of his.

Where did he begin? "The Lair of the Beast has fallen," he stated bluntly.

"Fallen?" Halvos repeated.

"Crushed, Master," he answered. It was true; hundreds of accounts retold an epic battle and thousands of thieves dead upon the blowing sands.

"Then the rumors are true," said the Shadow King. "What of Darkeye? Does he still live?"

Odaren shook his head. "The rumors pile higher than a midden heap, Master. Some say he fled for his life, others that he was killed amid the fighting. I only know that there are whispers of a new ruler of the Darkeye Clan who's taken over The Lair of the Beast."

Halvos mused on this, tapping his lip in thought. He made a casual flip of his hand and a lanky, greasy-haired man shuffled forward out of the shadows of the raised throne. "Send word," the Shadow King ordered, "I wish to see this new ruler, tell him—"

"*Her*," Odaren corrected.

Halvos' head twisted.

Immediately he regretted the outburst, shrinking in his rags, trying to disappear into a ball of nothing. But Halvos' calm voice held a note of anger—that was when you didn't have to worry. It was only when it was absent of all emotion that men died at his whim—as he spoke again, "*Her?*"

Odaren bobbed his head, jowls quivering. "Indeed, Master. They are calling her Mistress of Shadows."

Halvos snorted and a smile creased his thin, black lips. "A woman... I was almost worried for a moment there. But yes... I see this is all working out for the greater good. *Strength is life... weakness death.*" His tongue licked at the familiar, comforting words well known to all thieves, especially of late. Halvos continued, looking up from his reverie. "After all, it only stands to reason that the Mistress of Shadows should meet the King of Shadows, should she not?"

"Yes, Master."

"Strength is life, weakness death," the man purred again beneath his breath. "Yes... Fortuitous indeed. With Darkeye gone, there is nothing stopping me from ruling all of the Clan of Shadow." He looked up, hand stroking the woman at his side once more. "This Mistress of Shadows... Do the rumors grace us with her human name?"

"Faye, Master."

His hand paused on his precious and beautiful possession.

The girl beneath his hand still looked like a doll, more dead than alive, but she stirred now. Her vacant eyes held a glimmering spark.

"That name..." the Shadow King began. "I know that name... But how? *Who is she?*" The girl beneath his hand trembled and Odaren saw Halvos' mighty grip was squeezing the girl's neck as if he were wringing a calvas vine for its juices, his anger flowing through him. The girl's neck would be crushed in a matter of seconds. Odaren didn't mind witnessing death, but watching her choke silently made something in his heart sting with pain. Maybe it was her beauty, maybe his lonesomeness, or perhaps he was simply warmer of heart in that moment than usual.

Either way he found his voice and spoke quickly. "She's no one, Master. No one compared to you. But if you wish it, I will find her for you directly and bring her to you ... under the pretense of reestablishing alliances." He was never silver-tongued, but somehow he found his words.

Slowly, the Shadow King's rage came back under control and that tempered voice, the one that sparked terror in Odaren's marrow, came in a bare whisper. "Perhaps you're right." He blindly waved the servant at his side away. "I shall give you the honor of this duty. Go now, and see it done, my fat little rat," he said, using the title all of Narim whispered behind his back. It rankled Odaren, but he kept his head bowed, hiding his anger.

Wordlessly, he flourished an ungainly bow.

When his eyes glanced up, he turned, leaving as quickly as he could— feeling sweat slowly dripping down his back as if he'd escaped the headman's axe once more. But as he reached the exit, he could almost swear the vacant shell of a girl at the Shadow King's side spoke, lips forming a silent word: "*Sister...*"

***

Odaren stepped out of the hall of the Shadow King and onto a balcony with no railing, one of hundreds that rimmed the Black Hive. The balcony watched over the dark halls of Narim. Beyond the lip was a steep fall—a sharp drop that ended in the churning walkways hundreds of feet below. Sharp black poles decorated the Hive, like barbs upon the back of a great nightmarish beast. Sweat dappled Odaren's forehead and he swiftly mopped at it with a dirty handkerchief, giving a shaky breath, eyeing the city that lay beneath it all. Narim sat hundreds of feet below the surface of Farhaven, the only Great Kingdom once called 'the subterranean gem' of the world.

The air was warm here. One might even call Narim serene, with its hundreds of slow-moving canals and the ever-present turquoise glow that clung where shadows should be, but beneath it all was a darkness.

Men and women moved among the canal's narrow pathways in droves, most with the sly gaits and shifty eyes of thieves. They were the Shadow King's legion. Really, they were just a ragtag group of lost mercenaries and once-bandits—those who sought shelter from the cruel world while adding to that cruelty in turn, their job to pilfer from the rich *and* the poor all in order to line the Shadow King's pockets. But now their numbers were growing, their training intensifying...

A chill breeze cut through the air. The breeze of change. Odaren knew what was coming. *Something grand...* Something that would shake the very pillars of Farhaven. His stubby fingers stuffed his kerchief away in his snug jacket as he looked up. Above, a dirt ceiling extended for miles, the odd murky half-light of the canals barely reaching the roof of the ancient Great Kingdom.

His thoughts turned inward.

The Shadow King had charged him with finding this woman, the Mistress of Shadows, but was it a death sentence? From the few rumors he'd heard, the woman was nearly as fearsome as the Shadow King himself. Well, no one was as frightening as the Shadow King, but the rumors of her *had* grown legendary practically overnight. Stories claimed she was taller than most men, with dragon scales for armor, who mowed down legions with fire-breath and brandished a sword of lightning and wind.

Wind! Odaren scoffed. That was preposterous enough, almost more so than the foolish notion of a woman breathing fire like a dragon of old. Those terrifying beings were now extinct from the world by all accounts. But the thought of the banished element of wind made him feel sick and coated in oil. Only one person had ever been able to thread that element—*Kail*, a Ronin, and worse still, the Ronin's leader. Odaren knew that stories always told a deeper truth. Just like this Faye, this Mistress of Shadows...

He wasn't daft enough to believe half the things he'd heard, but what he did believe and made him fear for his life were the *other* accounts—dozens of witnesses told of the woman killing men and women, both the enemy *and* her own. They said she slaughtered them while they called out her name, turning the tide of battle against the Darkeye Clan.

Perhaps she was simply out for power? What better way to supersede Darkeye? He shook his head. Something about all the tales didn't add up,

A deep fear told him this woman would be his death.

Again, Odaren thought about running and hiding in the hills.

"Yes... It can work..." he whispered, fumbling with the kerchief in his chubby fingers.

A rat squealed.

Odaren startled, nearly tumbling over the sharp abyss. A young man sat on the lip of the balcony, cast in shadows. The turquoise glow somehow didn't shed light upon his swarthy features. His feet dangled over the side as he stared out into nothing; something in his hands glinted brightly. A *dagger?* It moved methodically, as if cutting.

"You..." Odaren said, gaining control. "How long have you been there?"

The boy turned, looking up to him with eerie, alien blue eyes.

Silent and unmoving, Odaren suppressed a shiver when he recognized the boy. "You... You're the king's new pet, aren't you? The little rat that all the others fear." Odaren felt the irony at him calling another *a little rat*, but he still felt the wrath and sting from the Shadow King's *little* jab. Yet the boy before him didn't flinch. He just kept shaving something that Odaren couldn't see. Odaren decided to vent his anger. "Yes, that's right, his new favorite toy. The silent one... Modric, that's what they call you—yes, Modric, after the fabled stories."

The boy said nothing.

Odaren's curiosity spiked and he licked his lips. "They say you murdered your own parents. Is it true?"

Still the boy continued to shave, silent.

Odaren sniffed sharply, giving an uncomfortable shrug. "You're just a mute little rat. Scurry off and leave me in peace." He turned his shoulder but the boy rose. He was far taller than Odaren imagined outside the gloom of shadows. Odaren suppressed his unease, clutching the kerchief in his sweaty hands. With wide shoulders and a lithe build, the young murderer looked almost like an elf, but there was no threat to his stance. Still silent as the grave, the boy bit into the object in his hands, red juice spilling around his mouth. At last, with a faint smile, he let the object roll from his fist to the ground and moved off into the darkness.

103

Odaren released another shaky, pent-up breath, sagging in his skin.

Rumors of the silent boy had seeped into every corner of Narim—a boy who had slain his own parents, who had killed and raped his sister, who had done a hundred other untold things each more devious and dark than the last. The boy unnerved Odaren to the core. What the Shadow King wanted with the boy made him curious, and what the boy's role was in all of this was still beyond his sight...

Odaren hobbled forward and saw what the boy had eaten.

A skinned dead rat lay upon the cold stone, veiny and red, a chunk missing. For a flickering moment, Odaren imagined himself as the rat. Water dripped off the cavernous walls, matching his beating heart. He kicked the rat over the side of the cliff, watching it tumble to the masses below.

The world was changing, Odaren knew, watching the swarm of thieves like a pot ready to boil... and he would have to change with it or be cast to the wayside. Currying favor with the Shadow King was one option and the other was running. But what use was running when you were weak? Yet strength was not always in sharpness of wit or sword, he knew well, but also in the play of power and following those who rise and fall. And Odaren knew how to ride that rising tide—he could grovel and lick the Shadow King's boots, if only to live another day.

He looked up, deciding.

There is no running.

He had to go to Farbs, to The Lair of the Beast, and convince this Faye to see the Shadow King—to meet her death, and ultimately secure his life.

104

THE BROKEN BLADE

Silence held them all until they reached giant steel doors or whatever was left of them. The metal doors dangled on twisted hinges, exposing hints of a horrible sight within. Ayva slowed cautiously. The Lightguards and Nolan showed no such restraint, bursting into the chamber.

Torch stands before the door burned brightly, in contrast to the scrap metal doors behind them. Ayva brushed aside the oddity and moved to enter.

Gray glanced inside, then pulled his cloak over his nose as if to stop from being sick. "Don't, Ayva," he said, trying to hold her back, but she pushed him aside and entered.

Inside, the room was a circular chamber of stone. In the center of the room, Nolan was on his knees, cradling the broken fragments of what had obviously been the Macambriel. Nolan was weeping openly. The sight of so noble and proud a man crying openly tore at Ayva. But she felt numb. Distantly, she felt Lightguards brush past her, the golden warriors fanning out in all directions, searching for the culprit. But Ayva's eyes were locked on the horror before her.

Bodies were piled on the far wall. Their blood had been used to create a horror of art—words scrawled above them.

STRENGTH IS LIFE. WEAKNESS DEATH.

Ayva felt lightheaded, sick. She ignored the words and rushed across the room. *They can't all be dead*, she told herself. She touched a woman's ashen, lifeless skin. Her hand snapped back. The dead woman's skin was icy. Almost painfully so.

"They're all dead, girl. Don't bother yourself," Reaver Logan said. His eyes had a look of a perpetual glare and unsettling pale.

She knew he was right, but she ignored him. She had to be sure.

She turned over a body and found herself staring into the face of a young man. His eyes were peeled wide, his mouth slack. He'd seen his last moments, and whatever he'd seen was awful. Worse still, he was young; she realized he was not much older than her. A warm hand touched her shoulder. Gray was looking at her, his eyes full of compassion. "There's nothing you can do."

Before she could reply—

"—They fought well," said Azgal, Ungar's brother, stepping forward. He loomed over her, a tower of muscle. His big arms, the size of most men's thighs, were crossed, bulging. His face might have been handsome if not for a crooked nose. "See those two?" he pointed to two men with splotchy beards. They looked to be dressed in merchant's clothes, but it was obviously a guise. Their skin wasn't ashen or lifeless, though they were clearly dead. One had a huge axe-wound in his chest. "Those aren't Vasterians—that's for sure. The boy and the other guardians of the Macambriel must have felled them. And whatever took them out, if it did that to the doors, was surely no meek foe. So worry not, Lightbringer, their souls will find their way to the Shining Halls."

Ayva felt oddly heartened by Azgal's words. But not satisfied. Not until she found whoever did this. This looked like a scene of someone with power destroying at will those much weaker. Perhaps they'd been surprised. Perhaps not. In the end, despite what Azgal said, the scene looked like a massacre. No one here put up much of a fight—not one that had made a difference.

Ayva still knelt at the side of the corpse of the young man. His mouth was gaping, but no blood leaked from it, or his nose or anywhere else. In fact, only one person looked to have been cut and drained of their blood, and almost with a surgical precision—a woman with slit wrists and a long clean cut across her neck that had bled her dry. *What are you thinking, Ayva?* she asked herself and she answered, jaw grinding painfully.

106

That whoever did this was evil and deserves a slow, painful death. But she pushed her anger down with a breath, forcing herself to think rationally as she examined the skin of the young man more closely. Ashen, almost a dark grey... Not a pale white like the death-like faces she'd seen from most other corpses. Except *one* time, she remembered faintly.

Others bickered behind her, voices growing heated.

"*This must have been the work of Reavers.*"

"*Are you daft? What Reaver would risk open war with Vaster?*"

"*Who else would do it? More importantly, would is different than could. Who else but a Reaver could wreak this havoc?*"

"*Shall I explain it to you dullards in simple terms? A three-stripe might be able to. Might being the operative word. These walls are four hands thick of pure steel. And metal is a less favored element, as many think it's tainted, or distasteful due to the nature of the dark chasm that was once Yronia. Thus, very few Reavers have learned to thread more than a trickle of the element.*"

"*Perhaps a three-stripe wouldn't be powerful enough, but a four-stripe?*" It was Darius. He was antagonizing.

"*You think I—*"

Ayva tuned them out.

Images flashed before her eyes, running through them, as she was trying to remember.

Lakewood's destruction.

The battle on the sands—

She opened her eyes. *That was it.*

Gray gently touched her arm, breaking her from her thoughts. "Ayva?" he said, looking worried. "What is it?"

Zane and Hannah came with him. Darius noticed, and broke from his arguing with Reaver Logan, letting the others continue their heated debate.

"I know who did this," she said to them all. "It wasn't Reavers."

"Then who?" Gray asked.

"The Voidarches can't be destroyed by hand, right? And they weren't. They had cracks, but that's normal. Same for these people. Aside from only one of them, they've no axe wounds or sword cuts. Nothing on the surface."

"So?" Darius said.

"So how else can someone kill or destroy without even a scratch or without the spark?"

Darius shook his head. The others looked similarly perplexed. "They can't?"

"Of course they can. Look at the bodies, Darius."

He shrugged. "I thought it was a trick question."

"What're you trying to say?" Gray asked, steering the conversation back on track.

"The Voidarch and these people—what did they both have in common? What do we *all* have in common? Aside from us." The Ronin threaded the flow. She thought that would be hint enough.

"The spark," Zane answered.

She nodded. "Precisely. I never saw him kill, but I did see a few strange looking corpses during the battle on the sands. They looked just like this. Ashen faces, icy-cold skin, as if their warmth, their very soul had been sucked out of them. What other object could do that?" They must have known what she was going to say, but she said it anyway. "It was him. Sithel. And he must still have the voidstone."

Darius cursed, Zane took on a brooding dark gaze and Gray looked awful—it was hard to read his features through his tired, sickly expression.

"Who?" a voice asked. Lord Nolan had been listening.

She explained quickly, and Lord Nolan nodded thoughtfully. When she finished he replied, "Yes, that makes sense. I have heard of such objects of power but dismissed them as simply rumors until now."

"Rumors?" Gray asked.

"Whispers that Dryan, this new *king* of Eldas, holds a red stone. It sounds much like this voidstone you describe." Ayva shivered. Dryan was the elf who'd killed Karil's father and usurped the throne of Eldas, the Great Kingdom of Leaf. Even worse, Dryan deceived the world by making the great elf king's death look like suicide—that Karil's father, King Gias, had taken his life, too heartbroken to continue after his wife's sudden and tragic passing. Dryan's rule put a bitter, foul taste in Ayva's mouth that she wished to dispel by telling Lord Nolan that Dryan was a pretender and a liar and a murderer. But she knew it was a battle for another time. Moreover, she realized Lord Nolan had said "king" with a note of disdain, as if his rule was a sham.

Lord Nolan looked lost in thought after mentioning the voidstone.

"What is it?" she asked, noticing.

"First a dark blue and black stone, and now this red and tan one? It troubles me greatly, but those are just stories of old."

"Stories?" Ayva posed.

He waved the matter away. "Another time. This Sithel, what kind of man is he?" Lord Nolan asked.

"He nearly destroyed Farbs," Zane said bitterly, joining the conversation. "He's a bastard who hides behind others, weak on his own, but powerful in his ability to corrupt others to his side."

"Whoever he's corrupted this time is clearly no weakling, or this Sithel had found some strength of his own," Ungar said, not in admiration, simply observant. "Does this Sithel thread? Can he use the spark?"

"No," Ayva said.

"Then how did he do this?"

"I still haven't figured out the doors." She fingered the rent steel almost in admiration. The metal was thicker than she was. So much power and strength.

"A beast?" Gray asked. "They look like the work of claws."

She made a sound of agreement. "My thoughts exactly, but what kind of creature has this kind of strength? Nothing that I've ever read, or at least comes to mind. Nothing besides the myths of dragons in Drymaus forest." Ayva still remembered the "dragons" that had carted her to Death's Gates. That memory still left her skin feeling icy and throat dry, but from what she'd learned since then, those hadn't been full dragons, but drakes—the weaker brood of true dragons that had been manipulated to serve the Kage's dark army. Dragons would never serve another. But even those drakes couldn't do this either, and she hadn't seen them since that dark day.

Lord Nolan left them and moved to the center of the room—cradling the broken fragments of the Macambriel. Evangeline knelt next to him, arm about his shoulder, but Ayva saw the terror in the girl's own eyes. *Girl*, Ayva thought with a scoff. Just this morning she'd thought Evangeline a woman in a station a thousand feet above her.

Ayva stood before Lord Nolan, seeing the Macambriel, the false and now broken blade, at last.

It was beautiful but nothing remarkable. Fine steel, surely, with few impurities and a bit of a rippling pattern on the cutting edge—Faye had told her it was the process of old called a 'hamon' to make almost unbreakable blades, but otherwise? It was just a broken dagger. But she felt drawn toward it. And she knew why.

109

"It's her blade, isn't it? Omni's." Omni, the Ronin of Sun, and Ayva's predecessor. *This was her blade... Mine*, Ayva corrected, almost as an afterthought.

Lord Nolan looked up. The surprise in his eyes was confirmation enough.

"That's why it could be used to sustain the Sunroad. The Macambriel was her dagger—a blade forged by the same hand that created the Sword of Sun." Some believed all the Ronins' weapons were forged by He or *She* who'd birthed them, or brought them to this world—some called Him the Messiah, others the Creator, and a thousand other names, but whatever the case—a Ronin's weapon was not a mortal creation.

"Yes," he admitted. "A far cry from the sword itself, but it worked."

"How?"

"Long before my reign, the Sunroad's life force was transferred to the dagger. It was a miracle."

Ayva read his voice. "But?"

"There were drawbacks. A strange gnawing sensation like a hunger you can't satisfy or an itch you can't scratch. Awake or asleep—it's always there. Some call it a curse for starting a war that claimed the lives of thousands. Still, the Macambriel served its purpose. Until now. Now it's gone." He paused for a moment, jaw clenched. "Which only confirms what must be done." He looked up at them. "You, Ayva, with your friends, must go recover the blade of sun before it's too late."

"How long do I have?"

"I don't know," Lord Nolan admitted, shaking his head. "Before the dagger we'd count ourselves lucky at only a victim a day. Now? The death toll will rise. A dozen, two dozen each day? Maybe more." His face darkened. "I won't lie to you, Ayva. Even if you retrieve the blade before the sun sets tonight, hundreds will still perish. But too long and all of Vaster will crumble.

"Besides, if I claimed you had a week before the last child dies of sun sickness, what then? Would that make your job easier or harder? Would you search quicker, or would you break knowing that every moment you slept, every moment you ate, another of my people closed their eyes never to wake because of your delay?"

Ayva knew he was right. If she had a deadline it would haunt her, but the notion that every second wasted cost lives made her sick to her stomach and simultaneously anxious to move. "If I go—they join me,"

110

she said, indicating to Zane and Hannah and the others. But Gray wore
a mask she didn't understand. Darius, oddly enough, stepped closer to
Gray's side. Lines were being drawn in the sand that Ayva didn't understand.

But before she could question it, Lord Nolan nodded. "I wouldn't
have it any other way." He neared, holding the largest shard of the broken dagger. "I know what I ask of you is not easy, but it must be done.
What's more, I know it's you who must do it. After all, it's your blade." He
pressed the shard into her hand and she lit a small spark of sun to examine
it closer. As she did, the steel glinted, reflecting something on the wall.

"You said the Macambriel was a false blade, which means it only gave
off a false light. That means there was no light," she whispered. The terrible, beautiful understanding was slowly dawning on her. No windows
because of the depth, no air vents that could let in shafts of natural light.
Nothing. No light. "It makes sense—that's why no one has seen it until
now. He knew it as well. Sithel. Somehow he knew the secret."

Lord Nolan was staring at her, puzzled—as were the others.

Her heart was beating faster. "Close the doors," she ordered abruptly.

"What?" Lord Nolan asked.

"Do it," she said. Then, realizing she was ordering the monarch of a
Great Kingdom like he was a scullery boy, she said, softer, "Please, my
lord. Have your Lightguards close the doors best they can. Then snuff
the flames outside and any extra light."

Without hesitation Lord Nolan inclined his head. "Do as she says."
The Lightguards set about it. But despite a dozen muscled men heaving
with all their strength, the doors wouldn't budge—the hinges were too
ruined. Just then, wind rushed over all nearby, pressing into the doors,
making the metal grate along the stone. This time they *slowly* closed. But
she saw sweat break across Gray's sallow skin. His bloodshot eyes strained
as his teeth gnashed. She could tell it was draining him too much. Ayva
rushed forward, putting her shoulder to the door. Shortly Zane and Darius were at her side, even Hannah joining in.

"This better be worth it," Darius grumbled.

It worked, a little bit.

Then the doors began to hover and their pushing became useless.

"Move aside," Reaver Logan intoned, annoyed.

They slipped through the crack, and the doors slammed close with a
screech. There were still slits where the metal had been torn, but Ayva

111

hoped it would be enough.

She looked to Reaver Logan. He'd closed the two-ton metal doors without a flicker of effort. His flame still danced in his palm. As the last light in the room, it cast shadows, making everyone look like ghouls in the darkness. "That too," she said. Reaver Logan hesitated, then inclined his head, clearly amused at her giving orders. But she saw his eyes. Terribly curious. He curled his hand into a fist, smothering the flame.

The room winked into darkness.

Ayva reached deep inside. She felt blood pulsing in her ears. Everyone was waiting. For a moment her nexus fluttered. But she held on and it listened stubbornly. Sun blossomed in her upraised palm. She sheltered it with her other hand as it grew to a fist-sized orb, keeping the light at bay. Already though, through the cracks in her fingers, she could see glimmers on the walls, faint etchings that made her pulse race faster.

"There's a reason he ripped the doors to shreds," Ayva said, raising her hand. "He didn't want anyone to discover what he'd discovered."

Gold lines traced their way along the walls, snaking and arcing, twisting at points and crossing at others, like a line of yellow flames following black powder.

Words.

112

"THE RIDDLE OF SUN

The four will become five:
Five for the warrior of water,
Whose home he seeks - like war seeks slaughter,
But all will drown within the lakes,
If the Lady's word the Sun forsakes,
If word they heed, and cast no ear to song of *Dun*,
What's lost can still be won, that ancient treasure - a Sword of Sun.

"The prophecy…" Lord Nolan uttered.

"Just like the prophecy of fire," Darius said at her side.

Ayva nodded. The memory of them in the pit was a terrifying one, but she also felt a strange connection to Darius afterwards. Perhaps because he'd seen her at her darkest and most desperate. Or perhaps because they'd risen above and found a way out together. Thanks to Lucky, of course. Either way, she felt a special bond form after that moment.

Ayva watched Lord Nolan run his hands across the golden lettering in awe. The Lightguards too—all stared at the prophecy, looking torn between falling to their knees and shying their gaze, as if it were holy. Created by the Messiah a thousand years ago, Ayva supposed in a way, it was.

"How'd you know?" Gray asked at her side, sounding impressed.

"The torches. He kept them burning for a reason. No darkness means no reason to use sunlight. And if sunlight *was* used, it'd be hard to see the prophecy as it's obviously more clearly seen in sunlight only."

"Clever bastard," Darius said.

"Still, how'd you know it would respond to sunlight?" Hannah asked.

Ayva was a little surprised that Hannah asked the most important question. "This," Ayva said, looking to the globe of light in her hand. "It irked me that Sithel would allow two unharmed torches to stand in *front*, while those doors looked like the seven hells were unleashed upon them. But it wasn't until I was examining the shards in the sunlight did I see something flash on the wall. That's when it all clicked." But Ayva didn't voice the unsaid… First, the prophecy was invisible without sunlight, and down here, deep beneath Vaster, there was no sunlight. Therefore, Sithel had known this was here beforehand. That couldn't be his own doing. Someone was guiding him. And second, sunlight had to be threaded, which meant a Reaver worked as Sithel's accomplice. Knowing the location of the ancient prophecies or having Reavers at his side… She didn't know which worried her more.

Ayva approached Lord Nolan and the prophecy.

A line stood out to her.

"But all will drown within the lakes/if the Lady's word the Sun forsakes."

She knew prophecy couldn't be remembered, and so she took a mental note to repeat it all, but with different words, especially that one line. *All will die within the ponds, if I dismiss the woman's bonds.* She assumed that the sun was referred to 'her,' but tried not to take too many other liberties, knowing that could get her into trouble. Otherwise, she rhymed wherever possible for ease of memory, then said it over and over until it stuck. It took a few minutes, but soon she had the whole thing. Then she turned to Lord Nolan. Taking his hand, Ayva pressed the shard into his smooth palm. "I will find it, my lord," she vowed. "I swear upon my life, I will return with the blade in hand."

He looked at her as if seeing her differently. Then Lord Nolan smiled and it seemed to banish the darkness in his eyes. "You truly are her heir,

113

aren't you?"

The old Ayva would have blushed or dismissed the notion. Now Ayva simply smiled. "We shall see."

"That we shall," Lord Nolan answered. "There's one last thing—rest tonight. I'm certain you want to begin this very night, but you're obviously weary from travel and today's events. And your mission depends on your wits as much as on your will. So tonight find solace in slumber—my daughter will see you to your rooms. I will secure provisions for you for tomorrow. After all, tomorrow is a big day. You go to end a curse and save a kingdom."

Ayva nodded, joining Gray and the rest as Lord Nolan took his leave, his Lightguards trailing him like a whipping cloak.

Their task now clear in hand, the others looked purposeful.

Except for Darius. "Simple as that, is it?" he murmured beneath his breath. "Just save a Great Kingdom and end a thousand year old curse, but don't forget to be back in time for supper."

Gray elbowed him, causing a grunt and Zane smirked.

"Shall we?" Evangeline asked, joining them and they followed.

What Ayva hadn't said was that she wasn't just racing to find the sword: she was racing against a man who slayed a hundred men, women, and children just to distract them from his true cause—from a creature more monster than man. Sithel was searching for the blade, too, and she felt a cold sweat imagining what he'd do if he got it.

Once they left, they found Evangeline's archwolf waiting for them in the hallways above. An older gentlemen with fraying white hair held the archwolf's reins loosely. The old man had the air of a master servant—well-groomed and confident. His perfectly executed bow only added to the impression; not too low, not too high. She recognized him as the man who was watching them from Vaster's inner walls.

"Maldred will see to your rooms. I've something to see to," the High Lady said, seeming distracted. "Until tomorrow," she said. "Rest well." Leading her mount away, she paused at the edge of the corridor. "And thank you. Words aren't good enough for what you've done today. You've given us hope when we thought there was none left. You have my father's, Vaster's, and my undying gratitude."

Without waiting for an answer, she turned. The flying mount's majestic golden wings unfolded as it trotted away, following her. Immediately, Gray and Darius exchanged not-so-subtle looks, and Ayva felt something break.

Fearing, and deep down knowing, what those looks meant.

* * *

Later that night in the rooms Maldred had assigned them, Darius heard a rustle and watched Gray rise from the sleeping dark forms around him and move to a balcony that overlooked the city of Vaster. Darius followed him groggily, wiping at his sleep-crusted eyes.

He stumbled, nearly tripping on Zane, and careful not to squash Hannah's petite little form. But he was most wary to sidestep Ayva. As he looked to her though, he noticed her arms wrapped about her slender body as if she was terribly cold despite the warm room. He tiptoed near and pulled her blanket up slowly, and then joined Gray's side.

It was windless, but Darius hugged his cloak tighter to himself too.

Not cold, but a shiver of awe.

Gray said nothing as they stared out over the moonlit spectacle. Even in twilight, the city was a gem of unearthly white light. Leaning his arms upon the crystal railing, Darius took up a soft tune. He wasn't sure why. Perhaps it was the enchanting city that made him want to sing, or perhaps the desire for a tavern and a frothing pint of ale. Either way, the tune was a ditty he'd learned in Lakewood that had snagged his memory, repeated in his head and now burgeoned forth.

She danced about the Tining pole,
With ribbons in her hair,
The men came up and all about,
Singing how so fair,
Ol' Daisy was, ol' Daisy was,
A lass so pure without a care.

But soon they came a knockin',
Round about her door,
Ol' Daisy danced around the boys,
She'd treat them all like toys.
When each came time to ask her hand,
She'd tell them right and true —

115

Darius swallowed the next verse, silencing himself when he realized what he was singing. It was a song about a radiant maiden who feigned a horrible sickness over and over again to escape an onslaught of suitors. Until, one day, 'Ol' Daisy' actually became terribly sick and no suitor, or friend, or even loved one came to save her.

It must have come to his mind unbidden because of Gray's sickness. It was a Lakewood song though. So he doubted Gray would—

"'I'm sick, I'm sick! I can't be wed!
I'll infect you through and through!'

Gray finished the verse in a hoarse but even melody.

Darius gulped, looking to his friend, expecting the pale face to reflect anger or sorrow. But a simple smile crossed Gray's wan, gaunt cheeks. He was still eating, wasn't he? "Daisy's Lullaby?"

Darius nodded. "Sorry… I wasn't thinking."

"Don't be. It's got a catchy tune."

"How'd you even know it?"

"Old memories," he admitted. "I think the words are a little different in Farhaven, but the tune is pretty much the same. And the message."

Darius nodded, silent for a while, not knowing what to say.

"If you ask me," Gray said after a moment, "Daisy was an idiot."

Darius peeked up, lifting a brow.

Gray continued, looking out on the soft glow of the city. "She abandoned and pushed away anyone who cared about her."

"And she was left all alone."

Gray looked up. "I won't do that."

Darius grunted. "Good. You don't really have a choice in the matter, but good." And Gray smiled. Darius opened his mouth, seeing the darkness swirl in his friend's eyes, but then closed it, thinking to himself. *I hope I won't have to make you eat those words again later, my friend.*

Gray had tried to push him away before—to suffer his pain alone back in the Shining City. *When our cards are down, we become our true selves,* Darius knew. And Gray liked to suffer alone.

Gray seemed content in silence, so Darius left him that way for a while watching the dazzling nightlife of Vaster. The sun was gone now, thankfully. It seemed to sit in the sky forever this far north. But now it was just the bedazzling spectacle of mirrors, crystal spires, impossibly thin

116

bridges arching from one to the next and the huge golden wall. Darius saw reflections of the Apex off a nearby giant glass dome. At the center of it all, it looked like the golden sword of a titan — rising up to pierce the now dark heavens. Vaster looked like a city made of frozen water. And of course, the Sunroad. It snaked its way from the bottom of the city all the way up to the Apex where they stood, and even up that golden switchback landing.

Darius fiddled his fingers, a habit he seemed to do more of late, a comfortable feeling when he felt anxious, until Gray's silence stretched too long.

"I feel restless, Darius," Gray said. "Not because I'm terrified. I am that, too. But because I know now what I have to do."

Leave, Darius knew. He had to leave and find Faye. He knew it as well. "Should we tell the others?" Darius asked, watching Gray. He wasn't as worried as the others about Gray's condition, but rather focused on how to save his friend and take the necessary steps to do so. Gray seemed to feel the same way.

"I don't want to worry them," Gray said.

"But they deserve to know."

He nodded, looking almost sullen. "You're right."

117

Darius' fingers curled on the crystal railing of the balcony. His skin pricked, hairs raising nervously, not trusting it — the crystal looked like ice waiting to break and send them to their deaths thousands of feet below. He didn't like it. A railing without vines felt weird anyway. "I'm right... *but?*"

"But nothing."

"And yet you're still not going to tell them, are you?" Darius asked.

"Ayva will look after them until I get back. If we do it right, we'll be back before they have to worry long. And I think I know how." Gray's look was peculiar — light gray green eyes swirling, an eagerness like a coiled spring in his posture as he held the marble railing.

"What are you thinking?" Darius asked warily. "You've a look of mischief and no-good about you..." And Darius grinned as Gray looked to him with a sheepish smile, "and I like it."

His friend replied, "I intend to temporarily commandeer the High Lady Evangeline's mount."

"That's one fancy word for steal."

Gray held up a finger. "It's a fancy word for *borrow.*"

"Let me get this straight. You want to steal—sorry, *borrow*—one of the rarest mounts in the world from a woman who is, let's not forget, the daughter of the only man who seems to trust us, in the *very* center of a palace filled with deadly spear-wielding guards that are considered some of the most feared warriors in Farhaven?"

Gray nodded. It sounded about right.

Darius shrugged. "Fair enough. When do we start?"

Gray smiled. "Now."

Plots of Seduction

"Will it even listen to you?" Darius asked as they moved.

Gray led Darius down the halls, listening and following the faint threads of ancient air that would lead them to Evangeline's rooms to find the beast. Each thread was like another strand of rope, pulling him from his dark quagmire into the light. "I think *you* can make it listen," Gray answered Darius. "You seem to have an affinity towards animals. First the spooked horses way back when, then with the Matriarch and the gryphon."

Darius grunted. "Don't forget Mirkal who Faye stole."

Mirkal was Darius' cormac that Gray had promised the unpredictable woman in return for helping them to Farbs. It'd been part of their blood-pact. As he glanced over at Darius, the rogue's face contorted, his mouth forming silent curse words—*still* obviously a little bitter about the woman stealing his mount. Gray couldn't remember if he'd told Darius that he was responsible for brokering the deal that took his cormac. He felt a stab of guilt for that, but it had been a necessary price for Faye to help escort them through Farhaven's deadly deserts. Their lives in exchange for one beast? A worthy trade and one he would do again. Besides, if they saw Faye again, maybe he could bargain the mount back… if he lived long enough. "See? More things than I can remember. You and animals are meant to be."

"Maybe it's the elf in me," Darius joked. Then he blanched, his face turning pale as an underground dweller of Narim. It sounded closer to truth than jest. "Right then," he said, changing the subject. "I can help. What's your plan to steal this noble beast? You could just ask her, seeing as you are..." he left the rest unsaid, but Gray knew he wanted to say *dying*.

Gray rubbed his jaw. He'd considered that option, but then shook his head. "I doubt that she'd hand over a mount that's rarer than a golden sunpike. It's probably worth fifteen Ester Perfect Gems and a pile of armor and weapons from the Hall of Winds."

At his side, Darius groaned. "You're doing it again."

He looked up, caught in his thoughts. "Huh? Doing what?"

"That thing where you name mythical places that I know nothing about. It's kind of creepy, you know? Like talking to two different people."

Gray shrugged. "Sorry. But to answer your question, I don't think that asking is the smart choice. It's too risky. She could say yes, but she could say no, and then what? She'll suspect we want it, and then taking the mount will be all the more difficult. And that archwolf is our only chance."

"Right," Darius said, looking up, eyes lighting. "Seduce her?"

Gray rolled his eyes with a sigh. "No."

"What? I'm just throwing out ideas! You're being awfully unhelpful, being contrary to my suggestions. Granted, they're still a little rough around the edges—"

Gray shot him a withering look. "Seducing a princess of a Great Kingdom in my state is not one of your best ideas. I'd consider it more of a brain fart than a real suggestion."

"So you *are* considering it?"

"Darius," Gray growled, growing serious.

Darius nodded. "Sorry. She's not my type anyway. So just an old-fashioned smash and grab?"

"We'll have to be a little more clandestine than that. I believe I have an idea."

They crept through the mostly empty halls. He wondered about the strange absence of activity. He attributed it to the time of night, but the more they walked, the stranger the absence seemed. Perhaps being this high up in the Apex had weeded out the more common folk he'd seen upon entering? His guess seemed accurate as they passed royal looking quarters—rooms furnished with rich rugs, mirrored candle sconces of Es-

120

terian silver, golden lacquered tables and plush chairs, all well-lit despite the time of night. He wondered why a city this impressive would have so many empty rooms, but he hadn't thought on it too long when he came face-to-face with a wall of muscle.

Gray reached for Morrowil, then he saw who it was.

Zane stood in the center of the hall wearing a dour look. Even though Gray was taller than Zane, his friend struck an intimidating form. His arms were folded across his thick chest and were covered in red leather. His forearms bulged and his eyes blazed.

"Zane... I... We..."

He grunted. "How daft are you that you thought you could leave without saying goodbye?"

Gray realized he'd been half-crouched, skulking through the halls and rose, feeling sheepish. "We had to leave like this."

"Why?" he asked, looking unconvinced.

"It's... complicated."

"I do well with complicated. Try me."

Gray growled. He debated lying to his friend, but he settled on the truth — more for the sake of saving time than anything. The corridor felt painstakingly quiet, and he didn't know how long that would last. *That* and he knew that Zane had a strange knack for sensing fact from fiction. "Listen, what we're doing, Zane, it isn't the most... scrupulous."

Zane looked as unmoved as a boulder, his forearms still crossed. He grunted again. "The fact that you two are lurking about like rats in a cheese cellar didn't clue me off. What's your point?"

"*So* I didn't think you'd approve."

If Zane hadn't looked angry before, now he did. His jaw muscles flexed as he spoke, "What in the seven hells are you talking about? You know I've killed, right? Not to mention stolen, lied and kept secrets that would make your blood run cold. Hells, if there were an award for being *un-scrupulous*, I'd have stolen that too." He gritted his teeth, looking down. "I'm not proud of what I've done, but I am proud of why I've done it." He looked back up and grabbed Gray's collar — lightly. "Yet now I stand before you and you act like I'm some sort-of-dimple-cheeked youth?"

Any other time Gray would have trouble keeping a smile from his face imagining Zane looking like that, but now he felt only determined and sick. "That's not all."

"You mean, you didn't think Ayva would approve," Zane said, letting

121

him go.

"That," Gray replied, "but more accurately, I didn't want to get you all mixed up in it. If the guards or Nolan found out it could risk your task as well as ours. We all know what's at stake. You *have* to recover the sword. For Vaster and for its people."

This only seemed to pique Zane's curiosity. His eyes narrowed to slits. "What *exactly* are you planning?"

"Stealing," Darius said quickly, interjecting.

Gray shot him a glare.

"Sorry, *commandeering* the High Lady's fancy mount."

He smacked the rogue in the arm with a growl.

"*What?*" he asked innocently, rubbing his arm with a feigned look of pain. "You said yourself that time is of the essence, and this is taking entirely too long." His rubbing turned to a fearful scratch and he glanced down the corridor as if expecting the hordes that had descended upon Death's Gates to turn the corner any second.

"Right then, what are we waiting for?" Zane said.

Gray rolled his eyes. "This isn't a stroll in the Gardens of Eldas, Zane, it's—"

"Save your breath," Zane said flatly, "I'm coming."

Darius smiled, clasping Zane's arm. "We need more sordid folks in affairs like this," said the rascal. "Glad to have you aboard."

Gray grumbled, but thought he heard footsteps coming from the opposite direction down the well-lit hall. He realized that arguing was futile. "C'mon then," he snapped, stomach churning like the Abyss, "it's this way." *I think*, he thought.

* * *

As he hobbled, Gray distracted himself from the pain in his gut and the Apex's unnerving silence by taking in his surroundings.

The hallways were clean white marble—no dust seemed to settle there. Small alcoves, like scoops out of the stone, held artifacts from the other nine kingdoms. He noted a few: a priceless Sevian porcelain vase painted with tiny blue flower blossoms, a tapestry of the Median war fleet and a large tooth from some strange animal.

Despite his dour mood, that one made him gawk. It was easily the length of his forearm! He searched his memories, wondering what kind of creature it could have come from... A Drymaus inhabitant? Those misty woods were full of mysterious beasts. Or perhaps one of the famed Shadow Serpents? They were no more, but once upon a time they were long, scaled water beasts from the Frizzian Coast that, according to sailors' tales, swallowed whole ships in a single gulp. They'd been hunted to extinction, however, and if any still existed, tales said they swam in the depths of the crackling, terrifying Abyss—a maelstrom of death in the heart of the Kalvas Ocean. Gray could believe that. Man's greed and desire to conquer the unknown was a common thread throughout history and extinguishing an entire species was a part of that. Whatever the case, the fang from the Shadow Serpent before Gray seemed real enough. Kirin's memories told him that the land, The Dragon's Tooth, was named after the creature's notoriously long fangs. But Gray scoffed at that. He'd seen maps. More likely, the land was named "Tooth" because it looked like one.

Behind a thick glass case Gray spotted an uncut white gem—an Ester whitegem—a prized jewel from the famous mining city. It must have been worth the price of Lakewood and it sat here in some random corridor.

Lastly, Gray eyed a golden suit of armor. It was like the Lightguard's battlegear, but looked bulkier, with more straps, sharper angles and gold-leaf encrusting the horned helmet. *Perhaps an ancient version,* he speculated.

He ushered the others to stay behind him as they turned the corner, nearing a double wood-paneled door at the end of the hall, just as he'd expected. The scent of the archwolf was strongest here, a pungent and strange mix of musky, ancient and... he couldn't explain it, but *magical.*

"That's it?" Zane asked.

"Evangeline's rooms," Gray confirmed.

Darius cleared his throat. "Right, that was like a thousand turns. Are we going to just ignore how you mysteriously knew how to find this?"

Gray put a hand to the cold marble wall, steadying himself. *Was it getting worse?* he wondered, a flush of panic making a cold sweat form on his brow. *No—two weeks, she said,* and he clung to that thought as if drowning. "I thought you knew. Mounts have a smell, my friend. Even mythical ones," he answered. "My power feels limited. Like trying to breathe with a boulder sitting on my chest, but it's not hard to follow the creature's lingering scent. It hangs in the air almost as much as yours

123

does," he said with an eye to Darius.

"A joke?" Darius feigned a gasp. "My, you are in good spirits. Perhaps this whole bloodpact business was a ruse for my sympathy after all."

Zane grunted, looking back to where they'd come from—to the echoing footsteps. "Enough. We're running out of time. You two can flirt later," he said, cutting off Gray's retort. "What's the plan? Just walk in and grab it?"

"Not much of a plan," Darius replied, scratching his jaw. "What if there are some Lightguards in there?"

"They better not be lying in wait again," Zane said in a growl, touching his blade.

Before they'd went to bed, Ayva had informed both Zane and Darius of all that had happened. So much had transpired... They had procured a stopper bottle, originally meant for the alleged Helga and Boris, filled with a nefarious poison from a strange shop owned by an even stranger woman; they had met Evangeline and the mount of light; under direction from Nolan, they were attacked by the Steward's guards as a ruse to determine whether or not they were truly Ronin; and finally, they had looked upon a room filled with Vaster's sick and dying. Gray shivered, remembering Ayva's recanting and the look in her eyes.

Of course, Zane was still a little sore about Nolan's ruse. Gray didn't blame him.

"There's no one inside besides Evangeline and the mount," Gray said. He'd already sifted inside with his meager power and tested the room. Warmer air in certain spots clued him off that there were two bodies present—one exuded strange gusts of air. *The beast's breathing, or beating its wings,* he presumed. "That's not the problem," he declared.

"What *is* the problem?" Darius asked.

"Getting a five hundred pound mythical beast out of a guard-filled tower," Gray answered.

"Right... but didn't you say you had a plan?"

Gray nodded. He didn't say it was a very good one, but he had a plan. "I'm going to head to that room," he said, pointing to a closed door to the left of Evangeline's. Most likely it was a servant's quarters or guest room for nobility. "It's empty. I already checked. It has a balcony. I sensed air flowing in and out." He didn't say that it could be a window left open and not a balcony, but that'd be a problem once they started. "I'm guessing if it has a balcony, then so does Evangeline's. If the distance is right, I'll jump to hers. After I get inside, you two make some sort of distraction at the door and I'll—"

"Too complicated," Zane said and strode forward, cutting him off. He knocked on the door heavily. He looked over his shoulder at them, both scratching their heads. *You should hide,* Zane said through the bond.

And with Darius' help Gray shambled away, ducking around the corner of the hallway just as the door opened with a creak.

"Zane?" came Evangeline's soft voice heavy with surprise. "What is it? Is something wrong?"

"Oh no, nothing dire."

"Then what is it? This is most unusual—the hour is quite late." Her relief was replaced with confusion, even a tinge of anger and… embarrassment? That confused him, and Gray reached out with the ki and immediately squirmed as Evangeline's emotions flooded him.

Embarrassment. Confusion. All covered by a wave of practiced poise. Then another flush came over Gray's skin, cheeks heating. At last, dignity and composure like a heavy cloak, settled about the high lady.

Gray grimaced, shuddering. *That felt too invasive.* As always, he couldn't distinguish between female and male—all bodies felt the same, but their responses were what registered. Zane's muscled form making him, er, *her* sweat? He shivered again, not from his sickness. If he wasn't mistaken, Evangeline found Zane very good-looking, and staring at him hade made her nervous and excited. Feeling the emotions so intensely through his ki had made Gray flush with nervous excitement. Darius was looking at him strangely. Gray realized he still had a damp brow and he wiped it away. *Sickness?* Darius asked through the bond. Gray merely nodded, hoping he thought his flushed cheeks were just signs of the bloodpact too. Darius nodded to the door and their friend's voice. *Looks like he did it,* Darius sent.

Gray caught the ending of the conversation, "No, you did right," she said. "Take me to her, right away."

Zane grumbled something in reply that sounded like a thank you, and their footsteps sounded.

They are coming this way, Darius thought in warning.

Gray pointed and they dipped into an alcove, hiding behind the heavily polished display of golden armor.

They turned the corner.

Gray saw she was wearing a gown huddled around her frame—it was

125

layered, but light, hinting at her form beneath. She was slender, and he could even glimpse the hue of her porcelain skin beneath the pink fabric. *Perhaps that's also what she was embarrassed about*, he thought.

"Again," Zane was saying, "I could think of no one else to turn to, if there is someone else I could—"

"No, no," she waved off his apologies, "My offer holds true—you all are honored guests, but even if you weren't, it's all mankind's duty to aid those in need. Now I can't promise anything, but I will do my best. But you must tell me her symptoms, all of them," Evangeline pressed as they passed hurriedly.

Evangeline walked down the corridor with the confidence of a queen. Not a speck of the embarrassment he had felt before was displayed in her smooth face and regal posture. But he supposed that was the difference between what was inside and what was reflected outside. Ki truly was powerful. It almost didn't seem to have a downside. But he'd thought the same of many things before. Perhaps Kail had even thought that of Morrowil once upon a time.

"Surely," Zane said, casting Darius and Gray a quick look. And in their minds the words sounded, bold and compassionate. *Good luck*. And Gray nodded in reply. *You too*, he told his friend. And the simple blessing seemed to convey all it needed to. Zane looked back to the High Lady, his smile fading, returning to his furrowed brow of concern. "Where to start? She seemed a tad feverish."

"*Specifics*, Zane. I need specific symptoms."

"Irritability?"

"Good, good, what else?"

"She was muttering nonsense, as if in a fever-dream, but she was awake."

"Go on. What about shivering, did she complain of muscle aches? How about headaches?"

"Headaches? Oh yes, that's Ayva."

And their voices faded as they turned down another hallway.

Darius snickered at Gray's side. "Clever son of a… He was just describing Ayva without sickness, wasn't he?"

Gray nodded, seeing Zane's wit too, but felt tired, slumping against the back wall. He realized that using the ki and the flow to follow the threads of wind had taken a chunk of energy out of him.

"Oh no, you don't—it's time to borrow a mythical beast," Darius said, helping him to his feet. Gray wiped more sweat from his brow and nodded to the rogue that he was fine. He saw Darius' heavy concern and smiled in reply.

"I was just taking a quick nap," Gray said, "C'mon." He expected the door to be locked, but as his hand grabbed the silver handle, it gave.

"Something simple at last," Darius said. "It's about damn time, after all—" He entered first and his voice cut short with a strangled sound.

Gray pushed past him and saw what he was looking at.

The room was what he expected—ornate furniture along the walls, a plush red carpet, a grand, four-poster bed and lacy curtains that obscured another balcony.

But in the center of the richly furnished room, stood a boy. Well, boy was a tad strong of a word. He couldn't have been much younger than Gray or Darius, perhaps fifteen or sixteen, but with his red face and green eyes bulging in surprise, he seemed a boy caught with his hand in a sweets jar. At his side, he had a thin, ceremonial-looking blade. Otherwise, he wore white pants and a fancy white coat with silver-buckles. His fingers were frozen upon the final clasp, which he had apparently been doing up when the door opened.

"*This* is awkward," Darius said, scrubbing his neck.

127

"Intruders!" the boy yelped, overcoming his red-faced surprise, and lunged for his blade.

Darius snarled, reaching for the leaf-blade on his back, but Gray was quicker than both. He reached deep inside and touched his nexus, the familiar, comfortable swirling ball of air. As he did, his stomach lurched. It felt like he was scraping the bottom of a bowl, eating at the last contents of his power. He ignored it. Threads of air coalesced in his hand, forming a concentrated ball of wind, and he snapped his palm up. The ball of wind rushed forward, knocking the boy to the ground just as he'd unsheathed his ceremonial blade. Gray sagged in his skin, feeling like a brittle leaf, but locked his knees to keep himself standing.

Sprawled upon the ground, the boy looked stunned, but only for a moment as he shook himself and lunged for his sword. "Ah, ah," Darius said, wagging his finger as he stepped on the boy's wrist, leveling the shimmering leaf-blade between his wide, terrified eyes—making him go cross-eyed. "Move again and find yourself with another shiny adornment. *Right. Between. Your. Eyes,*" he said, emphasizing each word and squinting, while aiming the gleaming point.

"Wh-who are you?" the boy asked defiantly. "What do you want?"

Gray ignored him and looked to the corner of the room. His whole body felt lighter. He was right. It was here. A small smile, the first in ages, creased his lips. His journey felt long and arduous but, suddenly, not as impossible as it had seemed only moments ago.

The archwolf bucked at the commotion, but now sat on its haunches calmly watching him—two large, intelligent golden eyes gleaming out of the darkness. Gray reached out, expecting the archwolf to react, but it sat motionless. He touched its fur. *No, not fur*, he realized. Each one was a tiny white feather, thousands of them so small and close together that it appeared like fur. He ran his hand over its downy feathers, silken and smooth to the touch. He gazed into the creature's eyes—faint rays of moonlight streamed through the nearby balcony and lit the beast. He saw the eyes weren't simply gold, but sunbursts, bright yellow in the center, fanning darker bronze then a deep molten gold. As he continued to stare into the archwolf's eyes, he felt his heart beating faster, his pulse racing. Something tickled in the back of his mind, a faint brushing, like an awareness and, transfixed, he reached out to it when—

"—*Gray? GRAY!*" Darius shouted, shattering his trance.

Reluctantly, Gray pulled his gaze away from the creature's gaze and looked to Darius. "What?"

"*I said*, what do you suppose we do with him?" Darius was rubbing his jaw and eyeing the boy. "You know he's going to tell her we came here."

The boy's fire was back as he curled his lip in an ugly sneer. "I will—and there's nothing you can do to sto—"

Darius put the blade's edge to the boy's throat. "Shh. Not the time for bravery, kid. I wonder... What were you doing here anyway, huh? Isn't it past your bedtime?"

The boy's cheeks turned crimson.

"Oh really? I thought you were a little young for that sort of thing, but I'm impressed! With Lord Nolan's daughter, no less!"

"Shut up! Nothing happened!" the boy yapped. "I... Well, nothing yet. She just... *we*..." He grew more red-faced with each stuttered word and finally shut his mouth, settling on a glare somewhere between petulant and chagrined.

Gray groaned. "Nobles." He looked back to the creature, measuring its size as it heaved a huge breath, its wolf-like jaws opening in a yawn and stretching its huge legs, big paws retracting to show finger-length claws, as if bored and restless all at the same time. It was as restless as Gray was. His heart was beating faster. And he considered his options... then decided. "Bring him."

"What?" Darius squawked.

"*What?*" echoed the boy.

What are you thinking? Darius sent through the bond. *You know the little whelp will turn on us as soon as he can. I don't know his deal, but he's clearly one of those entitled snotty buggers.* Gray wasn't sure when Darius had developed a chip on his shoulder for the rich and youthful, especially considering the boy was nearly their age, but it wasn't the time to ask.

Then what do you propose? If we leave him here, he's going to bolt to the nearest guard as soon as we go. He'll tell them what happened and ruin everything.

If we —

Kill him? Gray asked.

Darius held his gaze in the darkness, blade still hovering over the boy's form. The boy gulped, gaze flickering between him and Darius. They must have looked quite the pair — just silently glaring at one another, different emotions flashing across their faces. *I hope that's just your dark, moody version of bad humor. No. Not kill the dopey noble, but we could hit him over the head, tie him up, and leave him in the closet. When he comes to...*

Gray wavered on his feet. He hated that Darius had, even for a flickering moment, thought he might have been serious about killing the boy. How bad did he look? How much of Kail did Darius see in him to question that? *We aren't hurting him, Darius, there's no need. Besides, Evangeline will come back tonight. You think she won't wonder about a strange muffled thumping in her closet?*

What then? He joins us? He's going to get us caught, if not killed, Gray. I've a bad feeling about him.

Gray sagged. *Just trust me,* he said. *We'll take him to the outskirts of the Paragon Steppes and dump him there. That way he'll have to run a dozen miles back to tell anyone what happened. By that time, Zane and Ayva and Hannah will be long gone, and we'll be halfway to Farbs.*

Well... Darius wavered. *Why didn't you say that before?*

I was hoping I wouldn't have to — we don't exactly have the luxury of time and therefore, words. Suddenly Gray felt his chest clamp, a sharp pain splintering inside his heart. It was the second time it had happened — as if little tendrils of some of the mysterious, deadly poison were seeping into his heart and slowly shutting his beating breast to a standstill. At last, the pain eased. The darkness receded and he found the archwolf's sunburst gaze staring, gauging him, reading him. Bumps of unease traced up his arm, and Gray looked back to his friend.

Darius looked apologetic and worried, but wasted no more time on words. He sheathed his blade and turned to the boy. "Up you go, Lord Snooty Pants," he said, snagging the boy's fancy white coat and hauling him to his feet.

"It's Cidolfas," the boy snapped. "Or *Lord* Cidolfas to you. And I'm not going anywhere with—"

Darius wiggled a throwing dagger before the boy's eyes. "That's way too long of a name. I'm calling you Cid. And the next word out of your mouth, Cid, you'll be absent a tongue. I'm sure that'll make you and the High Lady's little pillow talks a little less…"

He cut short as Cid began to quiver in indignation. Still, Cid swallowed any further objection and approached the animal. The archwolf emitted a low, terrifying rumble as the boy neared, lips peeling back to show huge incisors the length of Gray's hand. It was a terrifying sight, even to Gray in his dour state. "How do I even ride this cursed thing?" Cid asked.

"You don't know?" Darius asked. "Haven't you seen your girlfriend doing it?"

Cid flushed again. "I don't watch her every move! And don't call her that!"

Gray growled. He turned, scouring cabinets when the presence touched his mind again. *Urgent. Powerful. Heavy.* It felt like a gust washing over him. When he opened his eyes, the archwolf rose and approached an oversized white dresser on the far wall. The archwolf nudged the dresser with its huge wolf-like head, making the thing rattle and nearly fall. Gray opened it. Inside were leather straps and two huge well-oiled saddles. One that could easily fit two, the other made for one rider. He grabbed the larger of the two, and with Darius' help, fitted the saddle to the archwolf who made it easier by lying flat, then rising when they needed to loop the straps beneath. Gray felt the creature was almost indulging them. *Bloody hell. This thing can practically put the saddle on itself,* Darius thought, echoing Gray's sentiments through the bond. When they tightened the last buckle, the beast flicked its head to where the door stood open.

A strident voice sounded in Gray's head, not in words or sounds but feelings and images.

Danger! It sent. Then... *The glint of steel. The smell of human flesh and sweat. The clank of well-made armor.*

The images were powerful and confident, seeming well-practiced, but it was an unfamiliar language to Gray. Luckily, it wasn't complicated. "Lightguards," he said, pointing to the open door. "The guards must have heard us. Get on, quick!" he ordered, and Darius threw the boy over the saddle, then leapt on himself. The archwolf was the size of a large Covian draft horse, and luckily Cid was as scrawny as a scarecrow—the beast easily accommodated the two, leaving a snug spot for Gray. Gray grabbed the feathery mane of the beast, but the strength in his arms waned and his legs trembled. Darius snatched his arm and hauled him onto the beast just as the footsteps burst through the door.

"Go!" he commanded the archwolf, but the beast was already moving. It pushed open the windowed doors and trotted out onto the balcony. Then, with one press of its powerful legs, it leapt from the wall to the sickening drop below. Gray clung for his life as wind rushed in his ears and his eyes watered. Distantly, he was aware that Cid was screaming. Suddenly, huge arcs of golden light appeared in the air—taking shape. He watched through watery eyes as the light formed into golden wings that caught the rushing wind. As if yanked by a rope, Gray's insides slammed against his ribcage. He fought down the desire to be sick as the archwolf beat its golden wings, once, then twice, and they lifted into the air, riding the winds.

"Do you think they saw us?" Darius shouted over the roar of wind.

The archwolf's feathers tickling his face, Gray peered over his shoulder. Standing on the balcony were tiny golden figures like pieces on a cyn board peering at them as they flew away. Gray felt their angry gazes even from here. He prayed they were too far to recognize—but deep down, he realized it was just semantics at this point. When the guards checked his and Darius' rooms, they would see that they were gone. "I think so," Gray replied. "But it doesn't matter."

"*Why not?*" Darius yelled.

"Something tells me Lord Nolan needs the Ronin more than the Ronin need him," he answered. Cid seemed oblivious to their conversation, still crying out as they wove between glassy pillars and over crystalline

131

white homes. It was too late in the night for crowds, but a few tired-looking citizens cast them jaw-dropping looks. *Just a white blur in the night to some,* Gray thought, *and tavern tales for others that their friends won't believe.* Surely many knew of the archwolf and Evangeline as Lord Nolan's only daughter, but he doubted the beast's appearance was commonplace to any onlooker. Besides, three males on a legendary beast's back riding the wind in the dawning light? He knew that it must be a sight to behold. Below, the Sunroad could easily be seen—a bright golden snake, winding through the glassy city. But Gray's heart was elsewhere. Ignoring the rush of wind, his eyes panned above the glimmering spectacle, looking to the distance towards the dark stone of the Citadel and Faye.

As if reading his thoughts, a hand clasped his shoulder warmly—the first real warmth Gray let touch him since their moment in the swamp with Indara. "She's waiting, Gray. We'll find her and end this bloody sickness, then return to Ayva and Zane with time to spare. I swear it. Then we can deliver High Lady Evangeline her stolen mount with a bow and a ribbon attached to it—brand new and shiny, and never the wiser."

Gray cracked a smile through his dark mood, lifting a finger, "Right on all accounts. But remember, not stealing, *commandeering.*"

And Darius laughed over the rush of wind while Cid gave a whimpering cry, clutching to Gray's back for dear life.

* * *

Zane led the High Lady to their rooms, hoping Ayva was there. *That would be awkward if she wasn't, wouldn't it?* he thought. He didn't like lying. He was good at it—but just because you were good at something didn't mean you liked it. Zane felt the same about killing and his jaw clenched at that thought. It'd been so long since he'd had to take a life. He never wanted to do it again. Those memories of his time as Shade, thieving from Darkeye and doing what was necessary to keep the Lost Ones hidden and safe felt like a lifetime ago. Now it gave him nightmares. It was a plague on his consciousness he hoped to one day dispel—a plague that felt as real as Gray's sickness. And while less life threatening, it was far more threatening to his sanity.

Had he been a murderer? Never a saint, clearly. His hands were too bloody for that, he thought, eyeing his scarred, heavily callused palms. The calluses *were* shedding, skin peeling day-by-day, just like his shell and like his past life. *No, not a saint,* he thought again. That's what Hannah was to him—the ray of light amid the darkness. But the tenuous line between morality and what was necessary for survival had always been a blur—one he had always tread with a heavy heart. Yet now he was different. Now—with Darius, Gray and Ayva—he'd rarely had to even draw his sword, and long gone were the days when it was stained in blood.

He saw the door at the long end of the hall as they walked. Evangeline seemed content with silence, casting him occasional sidelong glances he couldn't decipher. Twice she tucked her shiny brown hair behind her ear, seeming uneasy. Again, she looked at him, her almond-shaped eyes flicking to his, then away. *Is she trying to read me?* he wondered. It's not often anyone walked side-by-side with a man who threads the flow, he knew.

Suddenly, a red-robed Reaver appeared out of the side corridor.

It was the man from before: Reaver Logan. Zane had been so preoccupied at the time, he had noticed the man, but had been focused on the blade above all else.

Seeing him again, he was immediately intimidating, even to Zane.

Long brown, wavy hair that fell to his shoulders, framed the Reaver's strong jaw. His lips seemed almost stuck together in a hard-flat line. The man approached with a look somewhere between condescension and indifference. But the actual *air* around the man... Zane felt his jaw tighten. It felt hot. *Power,* he knew with a sickening feeling in his chest. Zane might have been a Ronin, but he was a child playing with a soldier's blade. This man was a battle-hardened veteran. And his dark eyes shone with a ferocity that nearly made him feel soft. Zane knew the look of a man with plenty of blood on his hands, and Reaver Logan was practically drenched in it. He was certain the Reaver could obliterate the whole corridor with a casual swipe of his hand and then use the hand to stifle a yawn.

As the Reaver approached, his robes whisked just a hairsbreadth above the faultless snowy marble floors. He seemed distracted, too, but when his gaze caught sight of both him and the High Lady, his eyes focused like an arrow notched then loosed. Reaver Logan stopped, letting them approach. Zane had half a mind to take a different course to avoid the man altogether, but the High Lady seemed intent on speaking with him.

"Reaver Logan," she said in greeting, giving him the barest of nods that his title would demand.

"High Lady." He added a sneer, not even a nod. Zane was as far from

133

a noble as you could get, but he was keen enough to see the Reaver's greeting as a breach of etiquette tantamount to a slap, or in the Shadow's Corner, a dagger to your side. He felt his ire grow, his fist wanting to smash the sneer off the man's haughty face, but he refrained. Barely.

If Evangeline cared, she didn't show it. "We're in a hurry—I can see you have some pressing matter on your mind as usual, but it will have to wait, whatever it is."

"It's your father," he said tersely.

"Is he all right?"

"He's... not unwell, if that's what you're asking. But—"

Evangeline hesitated, as if to inquire further but decided against it, clamping her mouth shut. "Then he can wait," she said, cutting him short.

They continued on, heading toward the door, leaving the man standing there with his hands inside his blood-red robes, watching them in the bright hall—the four-stripes on his cuffs like the dark side of the moon on a sunny day.

"Well done," Zane whispered.

She cast him an eye and smiled. "I don't like that man."

"Then you're a better judge of character than I thought."

Her smile deepened again and a faint red came to her cheeks. Zane noted it, but didn't quite understand it. "You're not alone in your dislike of him. My father finds him equally distasteful, as does most of the Council... at least the more favorable ones on the Council do." Zane had yet to see this Council. He wondered if they held themselves up in the highest parts of the Apex like figureheads or if they were commoners who held rank, and came and went as they pleased. He wasn't curious enough to ask.

"Who is he?"

"He arrived several weeks ago, two weeks after the Patriarch assembled the heads of the Great Kingdoms to decide the fate of Farhaven." *The Patriarch.* The name sent a shiver through Zane. He wasn't one for grand titles or legends, but the Patriarch was the most powerful threader of the spark in the entire world. It was hard not to wonder at such a man. Evangeline continued, "He is meant to be an 'ambassador of good will' or some such nonsense, but I sense *spy* would be a better term. He lurks in the corner of my vision like a spider that's made his nest in every dark spot of the Apex." She shivered. " Still, for the first time in who knows how long... centuries... we may actually bring the Great Kingdoms together again, thanks to the Patriarch and my father's ties. And Light be praised, I fear if we waited any longer…"

She must have seen his confused, raised brow.

"You haven't heard?"

He shook his head.

Evangeline's pretty face pinched in worry. "Let's just say Farhaven needs the Great Kingdoms now more than ever. Their union couldn't have come at a better time."

Better time? he wanted to ask, but they were approaching the doors. Besides, he had a feeling he knew what she would say. In their journey to Vaster, they'd heard any number of rumors, but although Zane had heard them for years now, they grew more real and more numerous each day.

Rumor had it that pirates inhabited the Frizzian Coast, amassing a horde that could rival the Median warships. Their purpose was unknown. The great pirate city of Hagvas was always a cesspit, but now, the city was in pure chaos and death was more common than a sneeze. In the ensuing chaos, a new ruler had arisen and claimed to be a descendent of the legendary Maglock.

But there were more rumors: Nodes dying; more Voids appearing; Cloudfell fisherman pulling up whole hauls of dead fish; the Abyss growing; the Algasi's movements.

And a thousand other rumors of madness that besieged the lands. Zane didn't worry about it though. As long as he could protect those close to him, that was all that mattered. He wasn't like Gray—worrying about some distant unknown, or trying to protect the whole world. Not anymore.

They approached the doors.

Was Ayva there?

He wished he could sense his friends like Gray could sense them. His ability to speak through the link, or what Gray had begun to call the 'bond'—Ayva had apparently read about it in the strange book that Gray kept, a gift from long ago—was strong. But it had its limits. Nobody could communicate through even simple barriers like doors or stone. He wondered why. It wasn't like normal speech; why would it be hindered by normal objects? Each had taken to deciphering their own facets of what it meant to be a Ronin—his task had been the bond and uncovering its secrets. He'd had little success thus far.

He shook his head, realizing he had been gawking at the wood door to

135

their rooms for a good few seconds as if he'd just lost his wits. Evangeline arched an elegant brow to him, waiting. "Well? Didn't you say this was urgent?"

"Uh... yes, sorry."

With a breath, he knocked on the door and entered.

The room was empty.

Bloody hell, he thought to himself. *Time to conduct some elaborate lies.*

A Remarkable Theory

Ayva trailed Gray and Darius through the halls of the Apex. At an intersection they stopped, debating which hallway to take. Ayva's instinct was to duck behind a corner. Instead, she stood frozen for a long moment, wanting to call out, but words wouldn't come—her throat was dry. Moments passed like hours. Finally Gray nodded, with his nose in the air, and Darius followed. And just like that, the two turned a corner, and were gone. The last image she had was of Gray's crossed-swords emblazoned on his threadbare cloak, whipping behind him. "I can't say goodbye and I can't follow them," she whispered to herself, now alone. *It's their journey now.*

Feeling drained, Ayva returned to her room to find Zane standing side-by-side with High Lady Evangeline. Ayva's hand lingered on the door's handle, confused. They were both staring at her oddly. The look on Zane's face was bluff as always—perhaps a little more pinched of brow indicating annoyance. But that was it. The High Lady however, was another matter entirely.

Ayva nearly blushed eyeing the girl—er, *young woman's* attire. *She's your age, Ayva,* she reminded herself.

Evangeline wore an almost scandalous nightgown—layered so as to hide her curves, but still each sheet was gossamer thin and faint shades of pink. The combination allowed the High Lady's flawless porcelain skin to be clearly seen beneath—save for the most indecent areas. Her arms were crossed, her mouth drawn to a tight line and one brow arched in puzzled study.

"High Lady?"

"She doesn't appear to be affected by too dire of a malady," Evangeline said, her words clipped and dubious but not *entirely* certain.

"Sorry?" Ayva asked. "Am I missing something?"

And Zane spoke in her mind. *I told an elaborate lie that you weren't well to aid Darius and Gray. It'd probably be best to go along with it or it'll likely ruin our good will with Lord Nolan.*

Ah, she thought, all the pieces fitting together like a puzzle she'd rather not have fit together in the first place. She gave him a tight-lipped smile that rivaled the High Lady's. *Fantastic. Thanks for telling me.*

He shrugged. *What? I'm telling you now.*

She grumbled inwardly and turned back to Evangeline, putting a hand to her head, adding a warble to her voice she hoped didn't sound *too* affected. She was a terrible liar—an inherited trait from her father that she normally took pride in. Now it only made her sweat nervously. "No, you're so right," she said, "I am feeling much better. I think I just needed a little fresh air and a walk. I was just feeling anxious, what with everything that happened yesterday. Of course, I told Zane all this and insisted he not wake you. But telling Zane what *not* to do is like yelling at a brick: lots of frustration and very little reward. I promise I wouldn't have summoned you if it was my choice."

"No," said Evangeline, a strange look coming over her face, as if suddenly convinced. "Zane was right to call me. I'm happy to help. I can see now that you are suffering from something. You're just good at hiding it. Concealing your emotions won't help me, or you."

Ayva gawked. "Hiding... my... emotions?"

The High Lady didn't reply though as she whisked her to a nearby couch and sat her down—swiftly, firmly, but kindly. "Enough talk. I can see you're going to be a difficult patient to work with. Zane told me of your symptoms and I can see a few of them already."

"Symptoms?" she couldn't help but ask.

"See?" Zane said. "I told you she suffered. We all do when she's like this," he added.

She cast him a heated glare over the High Lady's shoulder that satisfyingly made him wilt, if only a little.

"You must understand," the High Lady was saying as she worked—lifting back her head and pressing her fingers to her throat, leaning in close as she did so—which made her chest a hairsbreadth from Ayva's face, and in that sheer nightgown… Ayva felt a flush of sweat. The High Lady looked down, noticing her heated cheeks, then pulled away and nodded at this, as if it was the expected reaction, or at least *very* telling. "…it matters little what you say. In fact, what you say can be very informative, for how much you try to hide, or how you confess, but I've seen many healers working in my time and the conclusion is always the same. Some patients are just downright *difficult*. I can tell right away you're one of those."

"I am not!" she said, then immediately winced—seeing the irony.

The High Lady lifted her pretty face, giving her a questioning look. "No?"

"No," she said, a little more composed. "I'm not difficult, I'm just not—" Zane sent a message, *Not what? Do you wish to expose my lie? For what benefit? Your own self-image?* He narrowed his eyes, looking disappointed. Was he being serious? She could never tell with him.

For my own… she retorted then bit the words off. She groaned, slumping back into the seat. Evangeline apparently took this as an admittance of her difficult nature and gave a sharp nod, continuing with her examination and her explanation, poking and prodding at will as if Ayva was meat for the tenderizer. She pressed two fingers to the side of her neck. "Racing pulse…"

Ayva was still glaring at Zane. *Indeed*, she thought.

"Cough," she ordered.

Ayva coughed.

"Anyway," said Evangeline, with perfect dignity as she tilted Ayva's head back to peer down her nostrils, "as I was saying. Oftentimes patients can make the work of a healer much more difficult than necessary. It's not always their intention—some people are just a little more closed about their emotions. It can be a fear of looking or feeling weak that makes them downplay their symptoms, as I believe is the case with you. Like I said, you hide your emotions well, but you needn't do so."

"No? And why is that?" she asked, hoping her voice didn't sound too sarcastic.

Apparently if it did the High Lady didn't notice. Ayva's armpits were far too interesting. She'd lifted Ayva's arms and pressed her fingers to her armpits. This of course created another flush of sweat, and a snarky reply which Ayva bit back.

139

"Because it all comes down to energies," Evangeline explained. "You see, the aura Zane exudes is very different than the aura that I exude, or you exude, or Gray's and so forth." When she said Gray's name, Ayva noticed her eyes tighten, and Zane's name seemed to give a different response entirely.

"What's an aura?" she asked, baffled.

"Auras are emotions that people exude. At least, that's the layman's way of putting it, but it's much more. Have you ever been able to deter someone with a look—" Ayva cast a look toward Zane, but he was leaning against the nearby wall with legs crossed, pretending to rifle through a worn green tome, "or invite someone closer without saying a single word?"

"That's because of the look on my face, not my energy," Ayva retorted.

"Ah, that's what many people think, and you're partially right. But there's also a heat behind your gaze that pushes someone away, or a lust that pulls them in. This is your energy. A simple furrowed brow or simpering smile is just the mask you wear. It's nothing without the emotion, or aura, behind it."

"I'm afraid I don't understand," Ayva confessed. It seemed the tactful way of saying, *I think you're full of Cerabul manure.* Unfortunately, she knew saying that would be taken as a challenge by Evangeline.

Evangeline sighed, an eternally patient sound. "Of course, let me try another explanation." She parted Avya's lips, examining her mouth. *What am I, a draft horse?* Ayva wondered, clamping her mouth shut. The High Lady ignored this and pressed her pretty brown eyes close to Ayva's gaze—scanning—and continued. "Think about it. Have you ever won someone over in speech? Perhaps a person who was so stubborn, or close-minded you were certain that there was nothing you could say or do to convince them, but you poured your heart and your will into the words you spoke and you found them nodding their head in agreement?" Ayva mulled over this, slowly nodding herself, then realized the irony and stilled her head. "How about the opposite? Knowing you had the words, the right emotions, but were unable to summon them forth—whether through fear, or the like—and you weren't able to convince someone. Perhaps the words were right, the very same ones you would have spoken before, but the emotion, the sentiment just wasn't there, and thus they fell short."

Ayva had a memory of her father. A flashback to a time when she'd

140

convinced him to let her study later than normal, into the wee hours of the night when all other children would be fast asleep, out of sheer force of will. She'd thought it was the clever words she'd used, but perhaps it was more. If only she could have used the same words on him that day in Lakewood, found him before the chaos, and convinced him to leave with her before the Kage—those nine terrible facsimiles who had posed as the legendary Ronin and who were the *true* evil—had destroyed the town with their nightmarish army and ultimately taken his life. She found herself thinking of him more and more of late. She wondered why. And even stranger, wondered why she had buried it so deep down for so long. Something about what the High lady had said before felt like a knife now. '*You hide your emotions well.*' Again, she stubbornly swallowed down thoughts of her father and looked back at Evangeline.

The High Lady gave a small smile, seeing the recognition in Ayva's eyes. "You understand, don't you? *That* is a person's energy, or aura. The ability to affect another person, or yourself, with the energy you exude is something far more potent than a silly smile or a plaintive whine. Animals can do that, humans can do more."

"Do these energies have any relation to ki?" she asked. Ki was the ability to sense another's emotions—what Gray and other Devari wielded. *Ka* was the elven equivalent. They didn't let those of their rank join the order of Devari; she wasn't sure why. She wondered now if there was some cultural or historical significance. Gray had told her that the Devari were once tied to the Ronin, and the more she read, the more she realized the truth in those words. How close they'd been or in what capacity, she still wasn't certain.

"Quite astute," Evangeline replied. The praise made Ayva warm, and lessened some of her engrained defensiveness against the High Lady. "Yes, I believe ki is just a manifestation of one's innate aura, however, instead of being contained in your own body, the wielder—like the Devari, for example—can extend outward. They can sense another's energies with their own. In order to do that, they must have an extreme understanding of their own body in relation to others. Some believe that all humans could do this at one time, but now we've become selfish and too concerned with our own affairs—the mind has blocked the heart. Of course, it's all the mind, most likely." Then she shrugged. "Or perhaps it's both. Even the wisest Vasterian scholars aren't sure where auras or even the ki originates."

141

"How does that relate to the spark?" Ayva asked.

Evangeline now sat back, hands folded across her lap, as if forgetting her purpose and examination entirely. The desire for intelligent conversation had consumed the two of them. "A fascinating question with few answers," the High Lady admitted. "The spark is energy too—it is our very life-force. One cannot live without the spark, yet one *can* live without the ki or an aura—though it'd be very difficult, if not impossible, to never exude an aura. Even a terribly boring man will live a life with moments of great conviction or sorrow, emotions which almost always exude an aura. Anyway, that's how they differ, at least. One you can live without, one you cannot. I believe that's the key or the answer to solving the riddle between the two, but beyond that?" She shrugged, as if mystified, and looked excited by her own befuddlement.

Ayva completely understood the sentiment. It made her heart race faster just thinking about the complexities of the world, of Farhaven, and all its mysteries. And she ventured, feeling her brain straining to pull at the answers. "I can only assume then, if the spark requires life and the ki doesn't, then the ki might not have always been present since the beginning of human life."

142

Evangeline tilted her head. "What do you mean?"

"I mean, the notion that we've all lost our empathy with time. It's a nice notion, but it might not be true."

Everything in Evangeline's face implored her to elaborate. "Are you going to make me keep goading you to explain? I'm the High Lady of Vaster after all—don't make me pull rank."

Ayva smiled. She didn't voice the fact that a Ronin was neither above nor below the hierarchy of rank or that even kings and queens could not command a Ronin. To be a Ronin was to almost be detached from humanity itself. She wondered if that was necessary in order to safeguard them, in the same way a criminal needed an unbiased tribunal or an artist a free-tongued critic. But that had been a long time ago, during an age when the Ronin were considered virtuous heroes and protectors of peace.

Back then, as a Ronin, Ayva would be greeted with awe and perhaps respectful fear. Now, her gut told her Farhaven had changed. Outing herself as Ronin, if not met with disbelief or laughter, she would be condemned as a demon. As a bringer of war and death. Ayva found it reassuring that Evangeline hadn't treated her, or the rest of them, as evil. But Ayva didn't quite feel a Ronin... Not yet. And she wondered if that's why Evangeline didn't fear them—because, despite her father's claims, deep down the High Lady didn't believe they were. Ayva wouldn't blame her—how could seventeen-year-olds possibly resemble what the stories claimed? Instead of thousand-year-old legendary warriors with unfathomable powers and confidence to match, Evangeline must have seen a girl who had the power of a low-ranking Reaver at best, and still blushed at gossamer-thin nightgowns. But Ayva didn't belittle herself for the obvious gulf between herself and Omni, her legendary counterpart. She knew even Omni had to start somewhere.

Shoving aside thoughts of the Ronin, Ayva continued her explanation of the ki's origin, "Well, obviously the spark had to exist since the beginning of life—without it there wouldn't be life, and without life there wouldn't be the spark. Correct? But the ki is different. Humans can exist without the ki. In fact, there's plenty of them. From what I've seen, to be a Devari is rare. Being born with the ki is practically like finding an Ester gem too big to swallow." Only after she used it, did Ayva realize she had used a Farhaven metaphor without trying. "That means if we can live without it, maybe humans lived thousands of years without the ki even being a part of this world."

"Then how did it come about?"

"That's the curious part. If not borne innately, it could have been created."

"Created?" Evangeline asked, her eyes wide.

"*Imparted*," Ayva said, finding a more accurate word. "I mean, if it's so tightly connected to Devari it makes me wonder... From what I've read, stories say the Devari were beholden to the Ronin long ago—a strange and intimate tie. And the Ronin were said to come with the Messiah."

"—Or the Diviner," Evangeline added, gesturing with her hand, indicating that she also knew the stories and His many different names, depending on the Great Kingdom and its people.

"—Or the Creator, and so forth," Ayva agreed. "So—"

"If the Diviner created the Ronin, than perhaps he created the Devari too?"

"And thus, the ki was borne."

"And spread," Evangeline continued, now suddenly breathless, "Devari can mate—though they often live celibate lives. There were said to be thousands more Devari long ago, a whole army. Perhaps that's the basis for people thinking that *all* humans once had the ki. It was more

143

common, but still…"

"Still just limited to Devari. Thus the origin was not innate to humans but magically divined."

"If this is true, it only stands to reason that many more things could have been created by the Diviner then. We know *The Three Rules*—engraved by His hand alone—and the Ronin, of course, but now the Devari? What else could He have had a part in? Things we wrongfully believe innate, or things we've yet to discover?"

Ayva shrugged. "I mean, it's still only a theory."

Evangeline's eyes were wide. "A remarkable theory." She let loose a heavy breath, sitting back as if she was lightheaded after running a great distance. "You realize Ayva, that you just created an entirely new twist on the origin of life in a single moment, a new theory that scholars will scratch their heads about for centuries to come, and all in the time it takes to have a cup of tea." She shook her head. "You truly are a marvel."

Ayva blushed so deep she thought the blood would pop from her pores. "It's just a theory, High Lady, nothing more. But you flatter me, and far more than I deserve."

"And *you* do no justice to yourself by assuming so humble an attitude," Evangeline said with a small smile, trying to take the bite out of her words. "Own your intelligence."

And Ayva looked up, matching Evangeline's gaze and nodded with a confident smile. "Thank you."

Zane coughed, and the moment shattered. "What about the flow?"

"The flow?" Evangeline asked. "Contained only to the Ronin, it's the essence of all magic. The rest is just theory. The flow is the source of all life, and it can either create that life or destroy it. To the most interesting… it's the divine source. The spark is the source of magic for us mortal beings, but the flow is derived from the Diviner, and thus is more pure."

"I've heard that last one," Zane said with a snort. "Long ago, the Messiah created man, but He messed up or something. Turns out we're a greedy, selfish lot that nearly destroyed the world. Something about twelve kingdoms vying for dominion and power. The Messiah saw this from up in His pearly white clouds and instead of casting us all to the bottom of the Seven Hells where we belonged, He took pity on us and gave us another chance."

"Exactly!" Evangeline said, growing excited. "That's when He created the Ronin, crafting each one out of His deepest emotions—fire for wrath, water for patience, light for reason, stone for will, and so forth."

"God's wrath," Zane snorted, eyeing his hand.

"Us," Ayva added, knowing the story well.

Zane continued, "But that wasn't enough. His guard dogs needed teeth, right? So the Messiah gave His creations magic swords. But He knew even these wouldn't be enough—the world had descended into a state of madness. So He gave us the *flow*, the very essence of His being, pulling the threads from His own body to do so. With the power of the flow, the Ronin could break down the world and reform it in order to overpower His flawed but loved creatures known as humans." Zane held up a finger. "But then, and this is my favorite part and most idiotic of all, the Messiah hesitated. After seeing the flow, He worried He'd deprived mankind of a *precious* gift and so, while not trusting them with the same divine power, He gave humans the watered down version. The spark."

"I'm surprised you know that story," Ayva said.

Zane's mouth made an ugly sneer. "I hope that's all it is. If not, God's a bloody damned idiot."

Ayva swallowed. "What?"

"Think about it. He gave humans, creatures already proven to be mad, hateful beasts willing and capable of destroying one another, an immense power. That's like giving a murderer, *and a young one too*, a sword and telling him to have fun." Ayva saw his fist ground into a ball at his side, tome going forgotten in his hand.

"Zane… The spark isn't evil, it's a gift—"

"—A *gift*," he bit back derisively. "I've seen children burnt alive by men with the madness of the spark dancing in their eyes. You call that a gift?"

"And how many have you seen healed by it too?" Ayva snapped back, rising to stand. "How many lives saved by those without darkness in their heart? Would you damn your sister because she's human and she has the spark?"

Zane ground his teeth, growing quiet. He took a breath, reining in his anger, but didn't give any sign he agreed. "Anyway, that's just a story. A child's tale."

"Often stories have threads of truth," Ayva said. "After all, did you ever believe the Ronin were real until you found out you were one?"

Zane grunted.

"Anyway," Evangeline said, looking glad that the tension cleared,

145

"some believe, if this theory is true about the flow, that if the Ronin were killed and banished forever, then the spark would vanish as well—like a river drying up at the source—and thus all life, which is dependent on the spark, would come to an end. But these are only theories."

Ayva nodded, mulling over the different notions—having a few of her own. The last seemed closest to the truth, but something was still missing. She wondered if Gray's book would help flesh the truth out more and it made her wonder at the power in her own veins.

Abruptly the door opened, and Hannah entered. She looked confused, taking in the book-strewn room and the three inhabitants with curiosity. "What's…. going… on?" she asked hesitantly.

Evangeline was lightly holding Ayva's hands and she let them drop.

"Ayva's sick," Zane grunted, snapping his book shut.

Ayva looked up at the High Lady with a smile, "Yes. What's the prognosis?"

"You're fine, I suppose. Just a bit of a cold, perhaps, and a heavy case of stubbornness."

This time Ayva didn't blush, but smirked and inclined her head. "Back at you."

Evangeline smiled warmly. "I sense, if anything, a great deal of stress on you—on you all—which is something I can do nothing for, I know. If I could, I would. I should leave you now. Rest will be your best ally, second to companionship." She paused on this, her gaze flickering between Ayva, Zane and Hannah, "Which you all seem to possess in abundance. Speaking of which, where are your friends, Gray and Darius? I wished to speak to Gray in particular before you all left."

Zane looked ready to speak, but Ayva spoke first. *You've done enough lying tonight for the three of us. Allow me.* "He's resting," she said, coolly dipping her head to where the beds were hidden by a set of dark gold curtains. "I can wake him if you wish," she gambled.

As expected, Evangeline made a dismissive gesture. "No, no, I couldn't do such a thing. It can wait. Tell him it isn't urgent either, but I would love to… ask him something."

With that the High Lady rose, gathering her sheer gown about her trim, petite form and made for the door with her chin held high. Hannah left the door open and Evangeline bowed her head in thanks. She turned back, "I've been thinking about the prophecy… The words are falling from my mind, but I couldn't help but wonder… Do you know where you're going to start looking for the Sword of Sun?"

The question was so direct that Ayva was stunned for a moment.

Evangeline mistook her pause. "Forgive me if overstep my bounds, I—"

"—no," Ayva said quickly. "It's not that. I just… I don't know how, but with all that's going on, I haven't even thought of it." She smirked, adding, "But I'm open to suggestions."

The prophecy echoed in her head. If she was right, she was the only one who could remember the prophecy of light. Only the Ronin whose element mirrored that prophecy could retain its words. "But all will drown within the lakes/If the Lady's word the Sun forsakes," Ayva said the words aloud—they had a musical quality to them—and they lingered in the air for all to hear. "Have any idea which lake it's referring to?"

"There are many bodies of water in this world," Evangeline said. She hesitated, looking deep in thought. "It's difficult to say for certain."

Ayva knew that was true. Cloudfell Lake. Taerian Bogs. The Nimue Everglades. Agreas Pools. Even the Kalvas Ocean, with its hundreds of small lakes that dappled the Frizzian Coast and fed the great sea.

Evangeline smiled, but there was a mischievous light in her eyes. "Sorry I couldn't be of more help." Ayva dismissed her concern with a smile of her own. "One last thing, know that what my father wishes of you, and what you do is far more important than you could ever know. The fate of your people and even the destiny of Farhaven—toward darkness or light—rests in your hands."

Ayva was acutely aware of her choice of words and her gaze. *Your people.*

"And read deeply of that book, Zane. I fear you will need it." She let those words linger, and with that, she gave one last smile in Ayva's direction, a slight bow, and left, closing the door.

"What in the Seven Hells of Remwar was that all about?" Hannah asked. "I stepped out to grab a bit of fresh air and see I was missing out on all the adventure. Sickness? Gray sleeping? Fate of Farhaven? What were you all talking about?"

But both were silent as Zane hefted the green tome again, eyeing its tattered cover with faded gold lettering.

Read deeply of that book, Zane.

And Ayva noticed the title: *Mysteries of the Nimue Everglades.*

147

Fanfare or Something

The next day Zane stood in the courtyards of Vaster, surrounded by shiny white buildings and glass edifices, like translucent toothpicks, and looked over their mounts. The sun was glaring above, and there was a farewell parade crashing about him, but mostly he just noticed the sun. Zane squinted at it. He preferred the sun of Farbs—it was hot and angry. This far north the sun felt glaring and ever-present, like a light that wouldn't turn off. But really, Zane was distracting himself from what surrounded him. Moodiness. And excitement. But mostly moodiness.

Ayva had discovered what had happened—everyone had connected the dots when both Gray and Darius didn't arrive that morning to pack up the mounts. Zane had picked up on the small whispers and looks.

They were given a royal farewell, despite the strange moods lingering in the air like a fishmonger's day-old catch. As he tightened the strap on his mount, looping one end over to secure the favored black cloak Father had given him, he glanced up.

The courtyard was alive with hundreds of spectators, long lines of gleaming soldiers in silver plate, and even a row of golden-plated Lightguards on the steps beside the Lord of Vaster. Nolan watched them with an unsettling gaze. He recognized what swirled behind that man's eyes, those very familiar emotions. *Need. Hope.* Just like a Lost One. And just like a Lost One, the city of Vaster was an outcast, a refugee to the rest of the world. And their acceptance would only come in the form of a missing sword. It was ironic that for all the city's opulence and grandeur, they had so much in common with the dirty street urchins and lost waifs with tattered rags and sunken eyes. But as Zane looked around, he thought he could see another similarity.

Vasterians had dark-rimmed circles about their bright eyes, and several glanced behind them as if a shadow nipped at their heels, while others still clutched their children tighter than normal, glancing about fearfully. *The sickness,* Zane knew. *Rumors must be spreading already.* Nearly ten years ago, Zane had seen Farbs torn apart by plague rumors. He hoped Vasterians were wiser and calmer than most in the face of death, but doubted it.

Smells assaulted him — clean as usual for Vaster, but horse and manure mingled among the fresher scents. There was the smell of baked goods and of roasted vegetables on wooden skewers, some dipped in fragrant, colorful spices — though oddly, no meats. The sweet scent of cooked fruit drizzled in honey wafted from nearby lean-to stands of enterprising sellers who wished to profit off the impromptu event. Judging by their attire and looks, Zane figured not many of the sellers were actually Vasterian — instead they had the look of traveling merchants hailing from Great Kingdoms like Covai, Farbs or Median. Layered over the smells of food and horses, was the pungent smell of sweat from the crowds standing in the hot sun.

149

Zane finally saw the Council. They were stuffy old men, as he'd expected, standing beside Lord Nolan, but there was something strange about them. He couldn't put his finger on it but he didn't care.

The mood was oddly heavy, despite the cheer. Laughter from children sounded as they weaved in and out of the watching crowds. Flower petals fell from the air. Zane grabbed one as it twirled and danced its way down from the spires and glassy terraces overhead. His rough hands pressed it between his thumb and forefinger, feeling its silkiness. *Pink.* It crushed, turning a deeper shade where he pressed too hard.

Hannah's familiar sigh sounded at his side. "Must you destroy *every* pretty thing?"

He grinned. At least one person hadn't been such a melancholy mess. "I've kept you around, haven't I?"

"Was that... a compliment?" Hannah sounded genuinely surprised.

He shrugged. "Was it?"

Zane looked to Ayva standing a stone's throw away. She stood beside her cormac, eyes distant—brushing the same patch of silken hair for the thousandth time. He could tell those blue eyes were staring beyond, and from time to time, she'd glance up to the sky and south—toward Farbs and toward Gray, and then return to her absent-minded brushing. He knew what she felt, for his gaze flowed south as well, thinking of Gray.

Hannah waved her hand before his eyes, drawing him back to the moment. His sister smiled. Gray's disappearance didn't seem to bother Hannah. He was certain she didn't know how bad Gray's sickness was... If she did, he doubted she would be smiling. Of course, he'd grown closer to Gray than her. Zane had forged a bond with him during Hannah's absence, when Darkeye had kidnapped Hannah. And Zane knew—the bloodpact was killing Gray and quickly.

Hannah's dark brown eyes drew him away from those dreadful thoughts though. They looked bright in the light of the sun. Like russet fields. He'd never seen russet fields—only heard about the endless rows of golden wheat and the lush vineyards of Sevia to the east. He supposed the journey of a Ronin would bring him many new sights. He was... all right with that. The rest of Hannah spoke of excitement. Her brown hair, normally flowing about her shoulders, had been neatly plaited into four braids, two woven into a braid down the back of her neck like a Devari's Komai tail, and two thinner ones that wrapped around her head like a circlet of hair. She'd even managed to weave in a few yellow and flame-colored flowers. It was pretty, he admitted. She almost looked elven today. "Who helped you do that?" he asked, pointing to her hair.

She blushed for some reason. Women seemed to be doing that a lot around him recently, and for different reasons he suspected. "No one taught me it," she said in a huff, brows drawn down, "I've always known it. But I felt today seemed... appropriate." She gently caught a falling petal with a smile, watching the jubilant crowds. Somewhere music was playing—a horn and a stringed instrument, mixing with the noise of the crowds. "Grand, isn't it?" Hannah's voice was airy.

"A bit much," he grumbled, wiping the petal from his hand.

She ribbed him with a sharp elbow.

"Why'd he order this anyway?"

"Really? You don't know?" She planted her hands on her hips, giving him a level stare. "We're going to recover the most important artifact this city has ever known. That's not enough?"

"And if we fail?"

"I imagine he's hoping that we don't."

"I..." He shook his head. That was a strange path of conversation. "You're right."

Ayva moved closer, guiding her cormac to them. The elven mount with its long silken hair was still strange to Zane. Stories from other thieves and miscreants in Farbs did the creature no justice. Its round eyes were too intelligent and were large, easily the size of his fist—taking in everything at once. But with no pupil to focus on any single thing, the cormac's silver eyes could have been staring at Zane or at the sun, or both. The slope of the creature's back was more than a normal horse, its ears long and sharp, like something between a rabbit and a fox. Everything about them seemed elf-like in appearance. Having grown up on the streets and more than once escaped death by way of narrow alleys or vaulting from three-story rooftops, Zane preferred his own two feet to the hassle of mounts. "I heard your conversation," she said. "Hannah's right."

"Of course I am!" Hannah said triumphantly.

"Look at their faces," Ayva said to him.

"I can't, they're in masks," Zane said.

She rolled her eyes. "Their *gazes* then, or those who aren't in masks. What do you see?"

Zane took in the crowds. Many were unmasked. Those faces wore smiles. The ones with masks had light-colored eyes that shone with hope. No, not only hope. *Redemption.*

"Don't you see? The sword is more than a symbol. It's reclaiming their pride and alleviating their guilt. A thousand years of guilt is a heavy thing to bear."

Zane looked at her. Ayva sounded as if she was speaking from personal experience. But then she looked up and crossed her arms beneath her breasts, fixing him with a glare that would make milk curdle. "What?" he asked, swallowing.

"Well? Are you going to tell me?"

"Tell you what?"

Her gaze didn't flinch. "Gray and Darius."

"What about them?"

"Don't play dumb, Zane. You saw them leave. I've a good feeling you practically packed their bags and patted their bottoms goodbye. And don't try to deny that you had something to do with them stealing Evan-

151

geline's mount."

"Patted their… bottoms…" Zane repeated, practically stuttering. Hannah let a burst of laughter escape, and Zane shot her a glare as she clasped her hands over her mouth, containing her laugh, but mirth still danced in her eyes. "What're you laughing at?"

"You. She's calling you out. I like it. And you deserve it. You let Gray and Darius escape and you haven't even told us a thing about it."

"I didn't *let them* go. First off, I couldn't have stopped them if I'd wanted to, and I didn't want to. They had to go, Ayva."

"I know," Ayva said, putting a hand on his arm, as if letting him know she wasn't upset. "I just want to know what happened. Tell me, Zane. I deserve to know. We both do," she said, looking to Hannah.

Zane looked south where Gray and Darius had flown. In his chest, he felt a tinge. His heart hurt thinking of Gray and the sickness in his eyes. At last he spoke, telling her everything: of finding Gray in the hallway, of forcing them to tell him why they were leaving, of how they'd gone to Evangeline's rooms, and how he'd lied and told Evangeline Ayva was sick so that Gray and Darius could steal into her chambers and thieve the archwolf. All so Gray could make it to Farbs to find Faye before the bloodpact's disease consumed him. When Zane finished, Ayva slowly nodded as if digesting it all. "But you knew all of that, didn't you?"

Ayva's gaze fell to the Sunroad as her thumb grazed the cut on her palm—the bloodpact she'd made with Dalic. Zane eyed the cut. It was sore and red still, but healing quickly—almost unnaturally quickly. Perhaps a sign they were on the right path with the sword? Or perhaps it was Ayva's preternatural, innate ability as the Ronin of sun in her home of sun to heal quicker. But what Zane *really* noticed was the air about Ayva. It shimmered. Only now did it fade as her eyes resumed their normal cast.

Zane shook his head, feeling drugged. *What was that?* His tongue had nearly wagged on its own—the truth ripped from him.

"I didn't really believe it. That they could be gone," Ayva said.

"They left because they had to," Zane replied, still confused by what had just happened. "Gray's death—"

"I know, Zane," she said, stopping him. "I know. Gray would have died if he hadn't have left. The bloodpact demands that he find Faye and fulfill his bargain. *Whatever that was*," she added with a shake of her head, and then looked up—strong once more. "But it doesn't make it any easier. We'd finally found a modicum of peace, a measure of unity, and now he's forced to leave. It doesn't feel fair, that's all."

Zane slowly nodded. He knew that feeling well.

Hannah spoke, "I know you're worried, Ayva, but you know better than both of us that Gray is something special. With his eye on a goal, he's like a gale force wind—unstoppable. And with Darius looking out for him? They'll make it to Faye. I know they will."

"It's just this time I fear it's different," Ayva said. "I fear Gray's always pushed for another's life, self-sacrificing. I worry when it comes to his own life he won't…" She fell silent, then looked up with an uneasy smile. "In truth, I'm afraid."

"We all are," Hannah said, placing a hand on Ayva's arm, then one on his.

Zane glanced at his sister's touch, debating whether he should say something, but held it back as he felt both their eyes on him and only gave a gruff nod. Luckily, Zane was spared from a moving, teary-eyed speech as Ayva spoke for them all. "Whatever the case, we're on our own now. They'll return to us. But until then we have to find the Sword of Sun or there will be nothing to return to. Vaster, not to mention Farhaven itself, needs the Sword of Sun once more."

There was commotion in the masses.

153

Zane looked ahead. He knew who it must be as the jubilant crowds grew quieter than a dead thief. Algasi. They didn't need to push their way through. Vasterians parted willingly—the white cloth-masked citizens looked like pretenders next to the lean, black-clothed warriors. Dalic, their tall, imposing leader who seemed crafted from tempered steel, parted the milling masses. His mask was also white—though not nearly as pearly clean as those that watched him with wide, fearful eyes. Stained by sweat, sand, dirt and blood, it only made his icy gaze all the more fearsome. His gaze sought over them—which wasn't hard as he was a good several hands taller than most—until he saw Zane. He approached like an arrow.

Dalic nodding in greeting, saying nothing. His Algasi fanned out behind him.

Zane did the same, a small nod of respect.

Hannah rolled her eyes. "You know it's okay to exchange speech." She turned to Dalic. "Greetings, Dalic."

Dalic's face didn't soften, but he narrowed his eyes and Zane was certain he was smiling. "Greetings, Firespeaker." It was a title he normally reserved for Zane. "You have the prophecy?" Dalic asked Ayva.

"Yes. Though you know prophecy can't be contained to memory, I have it."

"Give it to us and our bloodpact is complete. We will leave this... city and its people alone," Dalic replied.

Ayva's brows knit together. She seemed to steel herself. Her back was straight and her head high, her gaze narrowed on Dalic. Only her hands seemed restless—fidgeting slightly. Zane had seen that look many a time, always the moment before blood was drawn. "I'm afraid I can't quite do that," Ayva said in a measured tone.

Several Algasi shifted subtly. None reached for their spears but they appeared more wary, looking to their leader for direction.

"You side with them and do their bidding?" Dalic asked, looking hurt. "These pathetic creatures who deem themselves better than us? For what reason? Because they hide in stone edifices instead of tents? Or because they eat their food with metal tools and not hands? Or is it for the way they hold their noses high and look at us with contempt, even now?"

Sure enough the crowd was watching them, but not as much contemptuously as warily and fearfully.

Ayva's fist clenched at her side, taking a step forward, looking *up* into Dalic's face. "You speak of contempt, but listen to you—can't you see? You're just as spiteful as they are." Dalic glanced away as if guilty. "And no, I don't *side* with them. I side with the path of light. Thousands of lives are at stake. Vaster crumbles without the blade. I go to find the Sword of Sun before any more die needlessly. That's my path."

"Then you won't give us the prophecy?"

Zane spoke to Ayva through the bond. *He doesn't seem to be listening.*

I can see that, she replied, then she spoke again in her thoughts, but it seemed more to herself. *I need to speak to his reason, not mine.*

What?

She didn't answer Zane but spoke aloud, "I have a better option if you'll hear me out."

Dalic looked to his hand, eyeing the unhealed wound of their bloodpact. The cut on Ayva's hand from the bloodpact looked painful to Zane, but Dalic's was a deeper, nastier cut than hers. "No. If you won't give us the prophecy then you're an oath breaker as well. As bad as them." He spat at the ground near an old woman wearing a white cloth mask, making her startle, and a few men drew forward as if preparing to fight. They had the slight, lithe build of scholars and two wore strange metal and glass instruments on their noses—*glasses*, she remembered. They were fodder to Algasi but they didn't back down. Their fists trembled at their sides. Dalic ignored them. "You will make us draw blood right here before all these people, Lightspeaker? We may fall, but not before these many men of light fall first."

"To what purpose?" Ayva asked. "You kill me, you lose the prophecy and thus any chance of finding the Sword of Sun. *Or* there's another option."

Dalic grunted. He waited a long time, spears gripped tighter in his men's hands, until at last he asked in a grudging low rumble, "What do you propose?"

"First, these are your people. I won't have you condemning an entire populace because of something your ancestors' ancestors' *ancestors* did." As if seeing Dalic's raised brows—a look of incredulity for the hardened warrior of sand, Ayva added, "At least not in front of me. Not anymore."

Dalic seemed to suppress a sneer. "And second?" he asked cautiously.

"We go together." Ayva looked to him and Hannah. "All of us."

Dalic stared into Ayva's eyes for a long moment as if trying to read her soul. A moment so long Zane thought he wouldn't answer. At last he extended his thick, tanned and clothed forearm to Ayva. She gripped it, her fingers barely wrapping around a portion of it. "So be it," the Algasi leader said. "Together."

That settled easily, Zane said through the bond.

Ayva nodded, looking more than a tad surprised. *Reason,* she replied through the bond. *Not mine, but his. Death and torture hold no sway to a man like Dalic. But honor and duty? He knows the only way to reclaim the Sword of Sun, and thus his honor, is through us now.*

So he'll play along.

For now, she agreed. *As long as we know the prophecy, he needs us.*

Is it worth it? Zane asked. *Forcing him to join us could put us in danger. He'll be looking for a moment to slip the chains.* To Zane it felt too much like trying to control a lion by putting a string around its neck.

I had no other choice. I won't see bloodshed here, especially not between these two people. It could start a war. Besides, we can use their help. We'll just have to be careful. As long as I'm the only means he has to find the Sword of Sun, Dalic is on our side.

Zane didn't like it, but he didn't see any other option.

155

Ayva at the lead, Zane at her side and Hannah at his, they turned collectively to Lord Nolan who rode forth on a white charger, leaving the Council on the steps. Zane noticed the lord's large charger had a golden blaze as if bred by Vaster for that peculiar mark alone. The lord dismounted. Despite the presence of the twelve Algasi and the menacing Dalic at their lead, Nolan held himself with confidence. He wore simple white robes today, like the other Councilors—yet his were absent of gold trim. Over the robes, however, he wore a golden breastplate that started with a plated gorget, protecting his neck. Gold medallions swung from the breastplate—the whole of the plate itself was etched extravagantly with sun patterns. His golden pauldrons, crafted to look like phoenixes in flight, were polished enough to make Zane squint, shining in the dazzling sun. It was obviously royal attire. Nolan himself had a little unshaven scruff about the edges of his mouth and his face seemed more lined today. There was a haunted shadow to his blue eyes as if he hadn't slept. Otherwise, the lord struck a gallant figure like something Zane imagined painted on walls or tapestries—the type of gaudy decorations hung in castles for lords and ladies with riches to waste. Zane looked to Nolan's feet. Leather boots peeked from beneath the lord's white robes: well-oiled, with a few straps and thick soles. *You can judge the make of a man by his boots,* Father always told him. Good, solid boots, nothing ostentatious—Nolan knew a need for flair and presentation for others, but for himself, he preferred the practical and the reliable. Despite himself, Zane found a strange, growing affinity for the man. As Nolan neared he noticed the Steward of Vaster discreetly tucking a dirty piece of cloth into his plated vambraces.

"Together, is it?" Lord Nolan asked, looking only a little surprised.

Dalic nodded. "The Lightspeaker is… *compelling*."

"That she is," Lord Nolan said earnestly.

This time Ayva couldn't hide a slight coloring.

Compelling… Zane scoffed inwardly, using the bond. *Perhaps if she were a little less compelling we wouldn't have a Samigurian tiger riding in our midst.*

Ayva kicked him in the shin, low and hard.

"Enough talk. It is time," Dalic said.

This seemed to suffice for the lord, and he looked to Zane. "Be safe and travel well," he intoned grandly. His words carried over the heads of the nearest milling masses. They had created a natural barrier, allowing

156

the courtyard to be open. No guards or roped lines to hold them back from the procession. Zane found it peculiar, as if they instilled order within *themselves*. He shook his head. Nolan continued, and as he did, Zane heard an echo in the distance. He realized city criers were spreading the word through the packed streets for those who couldn't hear. The speech must have been written down and well-rehearsed. "So begins your journey to reclaim what has long been lost to us, but never forgotten. The road you travel I do not envy, for it will not be easy. Many a hero have sought the sword and died for its cause, but the time for its return is now. And there is no greater honor than what you do. You go to reclaim the pride of a nation. I speak for all Vasterians when I say you hold our honor in your hands. Go in light, and return with it in kind."

A great cheer went up, and then talking continued.

"By the way," said Lord Nolan, speaking over the cheers. "You three haven't seen a young man, have you?"

"Young man?" Ayva asked, pulled from her thoughts.

Nolan nodded, palm playing at the gray stubble on his chin. Zane saw a breadcrumb in his beard from where he'd likely fallen asleep in his meal. A sleepless night, Zane noted. "Yes, it seems a young man in my daughter's care went missing last night after Eva saw to your... malady." He said the word oddly, Zane thought. Did he realize it'd all been a ploy? He shrugged inwardly. Did it matter? They were leaving. Besides, Lord Nolan wasn't above ruses of his own. It served him right. "When she returned to her rooms he was missing, as was her mount."

"Her mount is gone?" Ayva asked, aghast.

Zane hid a groan. *What an awful lie.* If she'd slapped her hands to the side of her face it wouldn't have been any more obvious.

"...Yes," said Lord Nolan, almost polite at her awkwardness. "Missing along with the boy. You don't happen to know what happened to either, do you? The mount's recovery is important. Its worth is more than coin. Obviously, as one of the last archwolves in Farhaven, priceless would not begin to describe it. Yet the boy's disappearance worries me more. I believe the creature can fend for itself, and will not be gone long." Zane coughed into his gloved hand. The others cast him looks. *Were they idiots?* The man practically admitted that Gray had stolen it. How much did he trust them? What lengths would he go through to let them find the Sword of Sun? If Zane was more like Darius he would have abused the privilege... Darius, better known as twigs-for-brains, would've gone gallivanting in taverns and inns, stolen a few priceless Sevian vases and Alakai oil paintings, then waved Nolan's seal of approval. Luckily, he wasn't like Darius. Well, Darius wasn't *so* bad, he admitted grudgingly.

"The boy, however," Nolan continued, "he's the youngest son of one of the Council members. A prominent member *and* more importantly, a good friend. Lord Godfrey is most worried about his boy, and I can understand his sentiments. I would love to allay his worries if I could."

Zane scanned the eight other stuffy old men. They all looked the same. Varying amounts of black in their white hair and beards. Stiff postures. White and black robes lined with gold stitching. Their clothes alone were probably enough to feed a family for a month with some to spare. One man, however, had a glint to his eye. Sorrow and a keenness. His head hung a little as if stooping beneath a low archway.

Lord Godfrey.

Then Zane grimaced, seeing Reaver Logan at the man's side.

"No," Ayva said, sounding honest. *This time.* "We don't know anything about a missing boy. I'm sorry we couldn't be of more help."

"Maybe he's drunk in some tavern?" Zane posed. "Young lords do that sort of thing, don't they?"

Lord Nolan shook his head. "My guess as well at first. But Evangeline assured me he's not that type. Still, I've had Vaster scoured from the Apex to the lowest cellar, but to no avail."

Did Gray and Darius really kidnap a young lordling? Ayva asked through their bond.

Zane shrugged inwardly. *I didn't see anyone else in Evangeline's rooms. I'm sure there's no connection.*

Ayva nodded but looked uncertain.

The Vasterian lord grew suddenly serious and he took two steps forward, his voice turning to a dark hush—barely loud enough so all four could hear, but not a breath farther. "I'll be forthright," said Nolan. "I know Gray is gone. I saw the sickness in his eyes. If he stole the mount I can only assume it was to save his own life or another's." He sighed. "I can hardly begrudge a man who wishes to live, nor can I harbor any hatred for you three in trying to protect him. However..." He grew deadly serious. "You leave me in an awkward position. The other lords are... *skeptical.*"

"Skeptical?" Zane repeated.

"They want to keep us here to prevent our journey, don't they?" Ayva asked.

Nolan gave a dark laugh, lowering his voice even more. "They want to throw you in a dark and moldy jail cell until you prove you're not thieves and miscreants or until you rot and Vaster falls down about our heads."

Zane opened his mouth, anger rising.

Nolan raised his hand. "I convinced them otherwise. Barely, but I did it."

"Then why are you telling us all this?" Ayva asked.

"Because it's the truth. You leave Vaster in two very different states. One with hope," he gripped the air as if holding hope, "and the other with mistrust." His gauntleted fist grabbed another fistful of air, wringing it and then let his fist drop. "There are much larger things at work here than politics, but the others don't see it. And for now, mundane human affairs rule their minds." He sniffed at this. "An attempt for some modicum of control, I suppose. Nevertheless, if you prove me a fool for trusting you, then my fragile rule might end at the edge of the headsman's axe."

"The Council would kill you?" Zane asked, incredulous.

"If you return empty-handed? Even the wisest of people still fear their end, Vasterians included. And when the rising tide of bodies come—and they will come—my people will look to their leaders, to us, for answers. And what do you think will happen when the other lords have none? When there's no one else to blame for the endless death?"

"They'll blame you," Ayva said in grim realization.

Nolan took one more step forward, a hand length away from being chest-to-chest with Zane. He was a good hand or two taller than Zane, and while his frame was smaller, his grand suit of armor and hard eyes were intimidating. "I'm willing to do whatever it takes for this kingdom. If that means playing the martyr and giving my very life, so be it. But if you don't retrieve the Sword of Sun, it's all for nothing."

"I—*we* will retrieve the blade. I swear it," Ayva declared, and Zane and Hannah nodded in turn. But the heavy weight of Nolan's words sat on Zane's chest like an anvil.

Nolan nodded. "Don't let me down." Then he spoke much louder and Zane understood. *There must be an eye or ear of one of the lords planted nearby that would relay all of their conversation.* All of it beside the hushed bits Nolan had specifically chosen. Nolan's voice carried smoothly, absent of the sharp tenor, "Anyway, I didn't figure you would know. I simply thought to ask. I'm sure he'll turn up soon." Evangeline

159

kept her distance, Zane saw. Apparently, the good will they'd garnered last night hadn't been enough to soften the blow of her mount… or her missing boyfriend? She sent them frosty glares now, arms crossed below her breasts as she sat on her mount—a horse—beside the other Council members.

They moved to the entrance of Vaster, crowds and cheers following them as they tread the gleaming Sunroad and then halted before the vast gold gates.

Here they bid the Council, Nolan and the others one last goodbye.

Zane felt a gaze and he turned, catching Evangeline's eyes. She gave him a peculiar look. Then her eyes darted away. It was so fast he'd almost missed it, but that look… Lingering. *Longing?* No. He was imagining things. He shivered despite the warm sun, shaking it off.

"Did I just see what I thought I saw?" Ayva asked.

"Huh?" he replied.

"Her gaze softened on you," Ayva asked. "*Considerably.* And soften would be the polite word."

"What? No, it didn't."

Hannah lifted a dubious brow. "I think it did… If I were High Lady Evangeline, I'd say that was practically a simpering smile."

He shifted uncomfortably in his clothes. For the first time in ages he felt hot. Why was his red leather so chafing? It was this damned sun. He grumbled. "She didn't glare at me, so what?"

"You clearly don't understand women," Ayva answered.

"It means she likes you," Hannah explained slowly, as if he were daft.

"No, she doesn't. She's a High Lady. I'm… *not.*"

"For one so savvy, you're quite the idiot sometimes, brother."

He gave a heavy breath. "Isn't it time to go?" He marched to the Algasi, ignoring the two women's amused smiles. A wall of the sand-clothed warriors met him—their eyes looked like black coals of anger and duty. He could see why the crowds behind shifted nervously on their feet. He moved toward Dalic but the Algasi held spears out, stopping him.

Zane's fire rose, but another Algasi stepped forward. He was tall, with sharp blue eyes and had one arm. A sleeve was tied off right below the man's shoulder. The one-armed Algasi snapped a few harsh words and the other Algasi lowered their weapons, their dark eyes looking almost chagrined as they stepped back.

Zane grunted. "Thanks—"

"—Yunwa," the one-armed Algasi answered. "And you don't need to thank me, Firespeaker. I simply see a friend where they see enemies. After all, this world is too big to make all of it our foe, and life is too short to live it in anger."

Yunwa extended his arm. Zane clasped it as Yunwa led him to Dalic. "Will you be able to keep up with us on mounts?" Zane asked as he approached. He squirmed, *still* feeling the girls' gazes and whispers on his back. "I'd rather not linger."

Dalic gave a snort, turning to face him. "Here I thought your leafbinder was the one who made the jests." And then he rammed his spear into a leather holster on his back, the double-ribbed blue lines showing above his broad, imposing shoulders. "You shall see. Let us go now. The Sword of Sun awaits no man."

Ayva and Hannah joined them, and he felt Ayva churn at his words on her mount. *No man*, she thought in amusement.

Zane wasn't certain what she meant, but he could still sense Ayva's unrest as they ventured forward. *Gray will be all right*, Zane reassured her again through their bond as they pushed through the last crowds, moving beneath the gate—toward the green Steppes with the Algasi flanking their sides. But secretly he hadn't said it for her. It had been for him. The darkness in Gray's eyes, the words Ayva had spoken before… They seemed too true. Gray sacrificed for others, but for himself? Would he push as hard, search as frantically to find Faye and end his sickness?

161

On the other side of the gates, standing on the sloping hillside of the Steppes, he saw the familiar faces of Ungar and his brother, as well as Dirk and the Lightguard June. This time they wore their formidable, gleaming Lightguard armor, helms tucked beneath their arms. The armor made their already huge frames seem practically gargantuan, especially the two brothers. And he knew they could move in them with ease too.

They gave sharp salutes of respect. "We're to lead you to the edge of the Steppes. From there, you're on your own." Zane remembered what Nolan had said… With the sickness eating at them, venturing too far away from the City of Sun was impossible for a Vasterian. They were bound to their city. Then he thought again and realized *trapped* might be a better word.

"It would be an honor," Ayva replied, sounding commanding.

Ungar dipped his head. "It's all ours, missy. It's all ours."

And with silvery bells chiming behind them and pink petals raining down, they embarked. Toward the Nimue Everglades. Where death awaited.

Zane had flipped open the book last night, reading through it when all the others had gone to sleep. One passage echoed in his head now. *"Leave your darkness behind, for upon the steps of the Everglades all your fears will come to play. It's not tests of blade that lays a man down, but strength of heart. For what nibbles at your conscience in the light of day, in the dark of Nimue will eat you alive."*

Chasing Darkness

Odaren slipped off his stout Cloudfellian pony and landed in a puddle of mud outside the grimy stables. He grimaced, wiping muck from his already dirty clothes—caked with sweat, dirt and dust from days of travel.

He'd traveled hard to get here—one week with no shuteye, save for the few winks he'd snatched beneath a farmhouse's eaves during a storm that had pushed him from the road.

Some men were lucky, but Odaren didn't count himself among them. Nevertheless, only once did he run into trouble, harassed by bandits on the Aster Plains. Despite his plump, ungainly appearance, he was quick with a knife, and the two men, barely more than boys, had run off crying. If he wasn't a servant of the Shadow King that would have unnerved him—the Aster Plains were always rife with bandits and bloodshed, but the world was changing. Thieves were getting younger, good men turning bad and thriving towns where neighbors were once family were shutting their doors, turning inward… a shadow was slowly descending upon the world of Farhaven and it spoke the words *"Strength is life, weakness, death."*

A stableman came forward from the shadows into the ruddy orange glow of a swinging lamp. "Here for a stay?"

"Just the night," Odaren said, grabbing his heavy saddlebags.

"You pack heavy for one night," the stableman replied. "Heading somewhere?"

Odaren twisted, narrowing his gaze warily. The man was old, teeth likely rotting from his head. His ratty clothes were damp from the rain outside. But age aside, his eyes were keen, taking in his surroundings like a moonorb, a spark-infused object that sucked the light from a room. Odaren knew there were spies in all corners of the world, some with and some without allegiances, simply looking to sell information to the highest bidder. And where Odaren stood now, in a sinister part of Farbs, in a dark back alley called Shadow's Corner, a man would sell his mother for a loaf of bread. The city of fire was dangerous for one with a loose tongue. "My business is my own," he answered, pulling the saddlebags off the rest of the way, throwing them over his narrow shoulder with a grunt.

"Just asking," said the man coolly.

Odaren handed the reins of his mount, Unta over.

"Two silvers," the stableman grumbled.

Odaren laughed in reply. "You're kidding, aren't you?"

"Two silvers," the man repeated, humorless.

"You'd rob a blind man, wouldn't you? This stable is barely fit for a pig."

The man opened up his palm, letting the reins slide out.

Grudgingly, Odaren slapped a small silver into the man's waiting palm. "That's all you get. Treat Unta well or I'll know," he threatened emptily. Though the stablehand was twice his age, he still stood head and shoulders over Odaren.

"Ya?" The man's leathery skin peeled into a sneer and he spat on Odaren's boots. "And if I don't?"

The nearby lamp creaked, swinging from a breeze.

Odaren felt his anger for all the hard days of travel, all the disrespect he'd suffered slowly rise like bile in his throat. "You don't understand, do you? Who I work for doesn't treat those who disrespect his followers kindly. You might have heard of him…" he trailed off with a wicked grin. "The Shadow King." And he spat upon the man's dirty, hay-covered coat. "Understand?"

The old man's sneer melted. With a string of apologies, more mumbles than real words, he backpedaled, disappearing into the stables with Unta in hand. Odaren didn't feel too smug about putting a stablehand in his place, but some men had to learn their rank in life. He swallowed a lump in his throat, but his mouth was too dry. It was time he did the same... And he reached for the inn's brass handle.

"Around the front," said a voice from the shadows.

Odaren swiveled, nearly slipping on the mud and falling to his rear as he did. He caught his breath and peered into the murky darkness of the stables, glimpsing only a swinging boot and the faint smile of a tall figure perched upon a horse's stall. *"Excuse me?"*

"I said I'd use the front door," the man repeated. His words, though undeniably confident, were smooth and held a strange lingering accent to them as if he was used to singing more than talking—the lyrical note caught Odaren by surprise. It was somehow familiar, but he waved it off.

He peered harder, wincing into the dark. "Who are you? Come forward into the light," he demanded. "A man doesn't need to hide if he's nothing to fear." Odaren himself did not believe the words, but the man was unnerving him—at least in the light he could see what he was up against. He checked his weapons in his mind—a dagger nestled close to his thigh, and another on the inside of his forearm, ready if the man made a move.

The dark figure laughed, remaining where he was. "Unfortunately, we do not live in a world where that is true anymore. A man who works for the *Shadow King* surely knows that."

Odaren gritted his teeth.

"As for who I am?" he paused, musing on the question, and then answered in amusement, "A helper, it seems." A thick forearm pointed out of the darkness. "The door beyond leads to the common room, but before that is a room that is being occupied. A woman, someone you should fear far more than me, is using it... seeking questions. I doubt you would want to interfere."

Odaren's squat muscles coiled, tensing in fear and excitement. *A powerful woman? Could it be?*

Yet he heard the unsaid message in the man's word of caution.

This woman was fearsomely powerful. If so, it might be her indeed. His quarry. His Mistress of Shadows. He wanted to ask, but already felt a fool for revealing his connection to the Shadow King. Information had its weight in more than gold—it had its weight in blood. Besides, greater men than he had died for revealing less, Odaren knew.

Keeping an eye to the shadowy man, Odaren hobbled forward. "Stay there," he ordered. He felt silly saying it, but somehow he felt the man would listen. Cast in darkness, a faint ray of light lit the man's mouth

165

and jaw. His sly grin widened but the man didn't move from his perch. Muffled voices sounded from beyond the thick oak door. Kneeling in the muck, Odaren put his eye to the small, glowing keyhole.

Inside, he saw a large room: tables, chairs and walls lined with dusty books and a ceiling with a black blanket—both well-known tactics for dampening voices. It was bright in the room, especially compared to the dusky stables. A wall obscured some of his view, but on the far end he saw a woman sitting in a cushioned chair. Her face was too hard to make out, but she was garbed in silks and a purple shofa hid her face. *Is she alone?* Suddenly, a figure strode forward. Odaren nearly leapt back, scampering away from the door as he dropped his saddlebags, but froze just as the man paused, two dozen paces away—his back now faced the stout thief, mostly blocking his view of the woman. Odaren's heart missed a beat, recognizing the man's dark red robes.

A Reaver.

He couldn't be certain, but the Reaver seemed to have four stripes upon the cuff of his scarlet robes. *Four? The man is nearly an Arbiter!* Reavers were denizens of the Citadel who threaded the spark. He'd heard of three-stripe Reavers, but never four—tales of them reached even the City of Moon, of three-stripes leveling hilltops with fire, or summoning torrents of water to drown a city... His dry throat scraped as he swallowed a ball of mucus. *What in the seven hells could a four-stripe mean?*

Odaren broke from the door, looking back to the shadows—the figure still sat on the stall door watching. Odaren hesitated, then realized in the wet muck of the stables he'd hear the man's approach, and he put his eye back to the glowing keyhole.

The Reaver was speaking animatedly, but through the door it was too low and garbled. Odaren's curiosity spiked. He hated his inquisitive nature, which he tried to squelch at every turn of his miserable life, knowing that it could mean his death one day, but he couldn't help himself now as he pressed his ear to the door and listened.

The words were still muffled by the thick oak, but he heard snippets:

"*What you search for isn't here... It isn't... likely even in this world anymore... If it was ever in this world... The voidstone was a fluke, an anomaly. For the rest, all you have is books, scraps from ancient texts and... Forgive me, Mistress, but how do you know you're not merely following myth and legends?*"

Mistress? Odaren questioned. *Who could possibly outrank a Reaver of four-stripes? Who in the blood and dice was the man speaking to?*

A softer voice, full of quiet confidence like the one in the shadows of the stable replied. The words carried despite their low tone, slithering into his ear like a serpent's tongue. *"Myth and legends, Izul? Like the Ronin?"*

The man stammered something in reply.

"Precisely... Now after the battle upon the sands, you seem to be a believer. The Ronin have returned," she said bluntly, *"and so have the Nine Stones. Now, you will do as I say and head to Narim... or you won't. In which case I will turn you into a pile of ash like the others. Four-stripe or not, I will not suffer disobedience. Now which is it, Izul? Will you question me again? Or shall I have your brother kill you after he succeeds with his mission in Vaster? You have two brothers, and I only need one of you."*

The man slowly knelt. *"I will do as you say, Mistress. Rath and Logan will not outdo me. I will recover the stone of Narim and find the boys."* Silence followed and his blood beat like a drum in his ears. At last, Izul rose and the woman was gone.

Limbs quaking, Odaren pulled away from the door.

He stood slowly. "I suppose... I'll take the front." His voice trembled like his body, frail and quiet for fear of being caught. But as he looked to the shadows where the man had sat, he saw only darkness. He didn't dawdle or wait for him to return. Quickly shouldering his saddlebags he retreated from the stables, leaving the ruddy orange light, muck and the dreadful conversation behind.

Still filled with fear, Odaren moved through a dark side alley, glancing over his shoulder repeatedly, but only the yellow moon above watched him as questions bounced inside his skull. *Who was that woman? The man in the shadows—if he was a man—why had he saved him? For he clearly had saved his life. What were the Nine Stones?* And lastly and most terrifying were her final words that chilled Odaren's bones and set his teeth on edge.

The Ronin have returned.

And for the first time in Odaren's life, he prayed. He prayed that the woman was wrong.

167

THE LORDLING

"Here you are, your *magnificence*," Darius intoned, throwing the lordling a spare woolen blanket, then adding in an absurdly grand bow for good measure. Over the top surely, but as smooth as a court bard, if Darius didn't mind saying so himself.

Cid gawked at him. Again, Darius realized Cid wasn't particularly bright. "Huh? What am I supposed to do with this?" he asked, clutching the rolled bundle to his chest. The lordling looked ridiculous. His hair was a frizzy, unruly mess of brown waves standing on end and a hand's length in height as a result of the rushing wind. His eyes were still wide and bloodshot and his lips were cracked. At least he'd stopped crying several hours back, favoring a muted stupor and soft whimpering instead. Now he swayed on his feet as if unfamiliar with solid ground and took in the glade. It was a quaint little green enclave they'd spotted from high above. Cid, however, didn't seem to think so. His fingers dug into the blanket, eyes flashing to each rustling leaf.

Darius gave him a level gaze. "You really don't know what that's for? Haven't you ever…" He shook his head, realizing the lordling had probably only ever slept on cushioned beds of down and silk. He sighed and left the boy standing in his own puddle of confusion to go about making camp.

"It's for sleeping," Gray said, throwing his own bundle on the ground and lying down with a groan.

"Or *flying*," Darius said as he brushed down the archwolf's feathery fur with a spare shirt, cleaning it of any debris it had accumulated during the flight. The beast unnerved Darius enough already, so it was comforting to know that even legendary creatures got dirty.

Gray sighed. "Ignore him. Sorry, my lord, it's no goose feathered bed, but it'll keep the twigs out of your back and the burrs out of your hair."

"*Or* you can use it for sustenance," Darius added. Then he turned to the young lord and wrapped his cloak about his head, hiding the lordling from view and spoke, words muffled. "Or perhaps make a new fashion statement." He pulled the cloak down then pointed to Cid's disheveled head. "You're already on the cusp of one with that hair of yours."

You're one to talk, Gray said tiredly through the bond.

Bah, Darius replied.

Cid's face was priceless. Darius could practically *see* the young lord's brain struggling, realization dawning that he was being mocked. His almost feminine features twisted into a snarl, and he made some rude gesture with his hand Darius wasn't familiar with. Darius only snickered as he tied the archwolf's reins to a nearby bough, which felt silly. The beast was smart. He half-expected it to shake its head and tell him not to bother, but its huge sunburst eyes only watched him patiently; then it yawned, showing rows of gleaming white teeth that made Darius shudder. If it wanted to, its wolf-like muzzle could engulf his whole head.

"You…" Cid gulped, eyeing the forest floor. "You don't actually expect me to sleep here do you?"

Darius rolled his eyes.

Gray was more patient, unsurprisingly. "We do."

Cid looked at the ground as if it were crawling with snakes. "*How?*"

You can't be serious… "Watch," said Darius, as he pantomimed pressing his hands together, resting his head on his hands and making exaggerated snoring sounds. "See? Now you try."

Cid snorted. "Ha ha. Very funny. You're a riot."

Darius bowed again. "I know. Thanks."

"You can sleep here or you can run back home," Gray said, silencing them like a father with two bickering children. He pointed back the way they came. *North*. There were many thickets, rolling hills and empty farmland, but it was fairly easy terrain. "It's a two, maybe three day walk, but there are plenty of towns along the way where you can get food and shelter. It's your choice either way. You're no one's prisoner. Not any-

169

more. You're on your own now."

For some reason Gray's words etched *more* fear onto the lordling's face. "My own?"

"But be careful of bandits," Darius said, lifting a cautionary finger.

"Bandits?" Cid choked.

Darius waved the matter away, like shooing a fly. "Oh, just a few. I wouldn't worry about it. Besides, they want coin, not blood." He paused for perfect emphasis—waiting until Cid's face went slack, easing a sigh. "*However*... It's the Saeroks and Nameless that you should watch out for." Cid piqued up. "With claws like daggers, they'll tear the skin from your bones and wash it down with a nice, tasty pint of your blood. In fact," he said, looking around the glade as if noticing it for the first time, rubbing his chin, "they like glades like this." With each subsequent word the blood in Cid's already pale freckled face drained a little more. "Of course, that's if the Darkwalkers don't get you first—"

Gray growled. *Enough*, he snapped through their bond. Darius almost yelped at a sudden sting. *Had he sent pain through their bond?* Darius shook his head. No, he had to be imagining it. But Gray was growing more irritable, not that he didn't sympathize. Still, it was lame that Gray didn't allow him to have even a *little* fun at the lordling's expense.

Cid looked to Gray. "Is it true? Are there really Darkwalkers out there?"

"Yes," Gray said. "But you won't run into any."

"How are you so certain?" Cid asked.

Darius understood his fear. Darkwalkers were intensely nightmarish creations. Their bodies seemed to be hewn by a dark god. They differed: sometimes with five, ten, or even twenty limbs, but they were always made of obsidian evil—all hewn at sharp, odd angles. Almost as if the dark god had attempted to craft spiders, ants, beetles, locusts and millipedes from black glass and failed miserably. Bigger than an oxcart in size, they moved with frightening speed, each limb coming to a gleaming razor-point. If that wasn't enough, their touch alone meant death. And if *that* wasn't enough, fire, stone, metal, flesh, sun, ice, moon and even leaf were all useless against them. Of course, the worst were the ones that walked on two legs. Those gave Darius the creeps.

"That's a long story," Darius interjected. It was true. They'd fought a blood-soaked battle on the sands against Darkeye, Sithel and a horde of Darkwalkers and bandits. It'd been a terrifying army. But with Ezrah,

Gray's grandfather, and an army of Reavers, they had fended off the creatures. He fondly hefted his leaf-blade, pulling it out of its sheath half an inch. It shimmered like green glass. *A good turn of luck that the blade could slice Darkwalkers in two*, he thought. Not for the first time, it made him wonder about the powers of the blade. *Masamune*, he remembered. That's what the stories called Maris, the Ronin of leaf's blade.

Casually Darius saw his hair reflected in a silvery buckle of the archwolf and realized Gray was right. Granted, he didn't look nearly as bad as Cid, but he looked quite a sight. Wincing, he licked his hand and smoothed down a few stray strands.

"I'm coming with you," Cid said suddenly, rising.

Darius laughed, still smoothing his hair.

"No, you're not," Gray said.

Cid hugged himself, watching the bright green woods. "You don't understand. I've never been outside the walls of Vaster. Not in my whole life."

"You've never seen the outside world?" Darius asked, pausing in his work.

Cid shook his head.

"Not even once?"

Shrinking in his clothes, Cid shook his head again even more timidly. The lordling stood out like a white lantern in the deepening night; his skin was unnaturally pale.

"And how old are you?" Darius asked, bemused.

"Eighteen summers," Cid admitted.

Suddenly Darius felt bad. The lordling might not have been the sharpest chisel in the shed, but he realized much of his daftness was simply inexperience... Everything was a stimulus overload to someone who'd never experienced *anything*.

Gray cleared his throat. "Then this is a great experience for you. You'll be fine."

"No, I won't—I'll be eaten alive! If not by bears or dragons or—"

Gray interrupted him. "There are no bears this far north, and dragons dwell deep in the Drymaus forest."

"Balrots? Drakils? Falchions? What about them? They could be out there right now."

"Uh, I think you're confused. That last one is a type of sword," Darius said. Then he had trouble not laughing at the image of a broad, slightly

171

curved sword lying in the bushes, inanimate and unmoving, while the lordingly chewed his nails in rising dread.

"And the rest are child's tales and myth," Gray continued smoothly. "You're a Vasterian. You've scholar's blood in you, for light's sake. Your people pride themselves on intelligence, dedicating their lives sorting fact from fiction. Stop being so superstitious. You're worse than a Cloudfellian barmaid."

"Fine. Dragons aside, I won't survive a day," Cid said again. "Trust me. What if someone sees me, and my clothes, and wants to use me as ransom? My coat alone is worth more than most people's homes."

"He does have the look of a free meal," Darius said reluctantly, hating where this was going. "I don't like to admit it, but perhaps leaving him out here isn't the safest thing. Food for the lion's den, if you catch my drift," he said, eyeing the boy, imagining the perspective of a thief, scrubbing his chin. *Gold. Silver. Fine coat, nice belt, fancy playsword that could have been a butter knife for all it was worth in battle.* Yup, he looked like a haunch of lamb left out for... a cerabul... or something like that. He still hadn't gotten a handle on the creatures of this world like Ayva and Gray.

Gray's back was turned.

172

"Gray?" Darius ventured.

Gray was silent, muttering to himself.

Darius shivered, skin crawling. He hated when Gray got like this. He knew he was talking to Faye again. Or Faye was talking to him. Gray suddenly cackled and swiped at the air, turning his back on his imaginary conversation. He always grew angrier or more distant after conversations with Faye. It made Darius hate Faye all the more.

"Gray..." he said softly, "The lordling..."

Gray was silent, hunched in on himself, shaking.

"Gray?"

"I DON'T CARE!" Gray bellowed, twisting—there was a mad look in his eyes and his mouth twisted in an ugly snarl. "Come, leave, it doesn't matter a damn. He's going to die on his own or he's going to die with us." And then he let out a huge breath, throwing a stick into the darkness, his angry tirade giving way to forlorn, muttered musings. "Who cares how it ends? Who cares in general? After all, it always ends. We all die. Why the hell should I care so much how? There's no control. It's an illusion. A sad little dream we tell ourselves that we can control our fates. But children die and thousands starve every day, and none of it's in our control."

A dark, depressing silence settled over the glade.

Cid opened his mouth, but Darius shook his head. Darius dropped his voice to a whisper. "You can come." Cid's eyes grew wide and Darius raised a single finger, stopping whatever praise or thanks the lordling was about to spout. "*But* only until we get to our next town. Then we drop you off there, make sure you're in good hands with the local magistrate, and they can cart you back to the City of Sun."

"Why don't you leave?" Gray snapped, staring into the fire.

Darius ignored him, gesturing Cid to his bed.

But Gray continued, "Not him. You. I don't get why you're here, Darius. It's not your life."

"Because we're friends, Gray," he said softly, not biting on his friend's antagonism.

"Are we? You just feel sorry for me. My death is like the long, drawn-out look you give a beggar. You feel bad, sure, but really you're glad you're not one." He spat angrily, and Darius saw a little bit of black in the spittle that bubbled on the ground. It burned a hole in the green grass, sizzling.

Darius looked up. "You really believe that?"

Gray was staring at him, eyes like hateful black marbles. "I do. Admit it. That's who you are and who you've always been. You can play the role of the white knight, pretend to be my savior, but that's me. Not you. You're the rogue who only cares about himself. We both know in the end—as long as it's not your own hide, you really don't give a damn."

Darius felt his ire rise despite himself. His blood grew hot and he opened his mouth, angry thoughts streaming, *What're you bloody talking about? I've been here—every damn moment! Waiting, trying to help.* Uselessly, mind you, *but I'm bloody trying at least!* He grit his teeth, molars grinding as if wanting to crack. *You want to push me away? Fine! But I don't want you to die! I don't know what to do! What do you want from me? I... I...* He felt tears in his eyes as all the words bottled up inside him, wanting to be freed, to be bellowed with spittle flying from his mouth. But as he stared at his friend, he did the hardest thing he could. He swallowed his rage, his pain, the feeling that he truly was worthless and settled back down in his bed, feeling the soft cushion of his bundled clothes cradling his head. "Go to sleep, Gray. We've a long day tomorrow."

And in the darkness Darius saw the evil in Gray's eyes, the burning hatred suddenly vanish. *Was it the disease?* Darius wondered. Part of him wondered how much Gray was speaking, and how much the bloodpact

173

spit out those hateful words—hateful, but true. Darius consoled himself, telling himself that Gray wanted him there but he was simply afraid. And Darius was afraid too. Terrified, even. But he wouldn't let Gray see it. And as Gray grumbled and settled down in his bedroll angrily, Darius let out a breath he'd been holding in, feeling tears flow. "I'm sorry," he whispered. Too soft for Gray to hear and then he found his way into a dark, restless sleep.

The next morning the great plan to get rid of Cid went quickly awry. They found a city to drop the lordling off in, a cozy little town with sharp wood-poled walls and a center green that reminded him of Lakewood. Darius pulled on the reins, veering closer. As they neared the archwolf beat its wings, swerving away.

"Where are you going?" Gray asked.

"Not going anywhere, I'm trying to lead him down!" Darius yelled. But the archwolf stayed his course as Darius yanked, tugged, and yelled to no avail. After the third town, Darius caught a trend. "He's definitely avoiding towns. Looks like he likes the little bugger. Whatta' we do now?"

"Eventually we have to land. Then we can track back a few miles on foot to the nearest town and..."

"... And waste precious time?" Darius finished, completing what he knew Gray was thinking.

"He could go by himself," his friend ventured into the wind.

Darius shook his head. "Not around here. You know that he can't."

Later that night when they stopped, dozens of miles from civilization, Gray brought the conversation up again while eating a roasted hare that Darius had caught with his throwing dagger. Thankfully, the shadow in Gray's gaze was less tonight. "Cid... I've gathered a pack for you—spare tinder and flint, enough clothing to replace that fancy coat of yours and—"

Darius interrupted, feeling a heat enter his voice. "No, Gray. The time for dropping him off was many miles ago. These are the Aster Plains. You heard what Ayva said, and Faye, *and* Ezrah. We spent days avoiding these plains."

Gray held his gaze. "So?"

Darius didn't let his gaze drop—and matched his friend's fire. "So? It's death. Bandits are more rampant here than hiccups in a drunkard's speech. If you drop him here you might as well slit his throat yourself," he said sharply.

"He can make it."

Darius felt his anger reach a peak. He was usually not an angry soul, but Gray's irrationality hit a nerve. He stripped a throwing dagger free that was strapped to the inside of his arm, throwing it down—raising a puff of dry dirt. "Then do it. End him here and save him the trouble and the fear."

Cid looked between the two, dread in his eyes, clutching his meal and edging away.

Gray hesitated.

"Look at him, Gray," he said, losing some of his fire, pointing to the boy. "He's just a boy... No offense," he added to Cid, who shrugged. "I don't even think we would be able to survive without skipping the bloodiest patches." It was true; dozens of times they'd flown over small or even larger skirmishes of a hundred men and women fighting tooth and nail with makeshift weapons and armor. The Aster Plains were a deathtrap—embroiled in a civil war that never ended. And if the endless fighting between nations didn't land you on the end of a pike, Asterian bandits would—hordes of depraved thieves who picked at the edges of the fighting like vultures. "Think of us crossing the Rehlias Desert without a mount, without Faye, and this is twice as bad. Now picture him." Every point he knew was like a dagger, sliding deeper into Gray's gut.

175

At last, Gray sighed.

Darius nodded.

"Then I come..." said Cid, sounding cautious and hopeful.

Gray eyed him hard. Darius swallowed. Cid flinched too. Had his friend always had such a sharp glare? "Where we're going, it's not what you think," Gray said.

Cid looked up. "I don't care where we're going."

"You joined us awfully fast," Darius said, catching Gray's implication. "What're you so afraid of back in Vaster? I thought it was all light and sunshine, where people farted rainbows that smelled like cinnamon buns."

Cid gave a slightly puzzled, slightly baffled look in response to Darius' attempt at humor, then the lordling shook his head--as if clearing the imagery and started scrubbing his arm nervously. "It's... complicated."

Now that Darius thought about it, Cid hadn't even protested *that* hard to being whisked away from his home.

"Who are you running from?" Gray asked. "Who are you really?"

Darius leaned in closer.

Cid's gaze flashed between them, unsure what to say.

"Now that I think about it, shouldn't you be all pale and sick, being so far from Vaster?" Darius pressed.

Cid's eyes gained a bit of fire. "None of your business," he snapped. "I... I don't want to go back. Not yet." Then he turned pleading. "Please."

"Answer the question," Darius said. "Why aren't you sickly?"

"I'm... I don't know."

"You're not Vasterian, are you?" Gray interjected.

Cid shook his head. "As far as I can remember... I remember white walls. It's my first memory. I have to be... But I've felt different all my life. My eyes, my hair, everything—but I don't know any life outside of Vaster."

Is he lying? Darius asked Gray through the bond.

He believes what he's saying is true. Whether it is or not, that's another question.

His past sounds as bad as yours, Darius replied. But despite his best efforts, Darius found himself feeling for the boy who watched them, now uncomfortable at unearthing his confused past.

Gray's dark glare softened. Slightly. "Where we're going might be less safe than bandits, Saeroks or Darkwalkers, Cid. It's not safe with us. We're..."

Are you really going to tell him what we are? Darius asked through the bond.

One day the world will have to know, Gray replied. But he didn't say it. "We're not who you think we are. Danger follows us. You could be hurt. Killed. It would be much safer for you to risk the plains, find a town magistrate and then tell him your story. Surely they'll understand and—"

Cid was shaking his head the whole while. "No. I'm coming. As long as you're willing to take me."

"So be it," Gray said.

And the matter was settled.

Later that night, as twilight was settling down and the skyline was a velvety-orange spread like burnt wax running down a wall, Darius approached Gray who stood away from their camp gazing into the distance.

Gray was watching the horizon. "If Faye's not there..."

"She'll be there," Darius said with every shred of confidence he could muster. But inside he was terrified. Gray looked to him. Darius had felt fear before, but the look in Gray's eyes was different. It was a look of complete uncertainty. He'd never seen it before in his friend. He held his gaze as long as he could until his confidence broke and he looked to Cid to hide his uneasiness. "Get some sleep. I'll take first watch. We'll get a few hours of shuteye and then head out before first light. Who knows, we might even shave off a few days. That way if she isn't there, we'll have plenty of time," he said.

Gray's eyes said what he was thinking too. *And if she's farther than a few days? If she's a week away? What then?* But he didn't ask Darius. Instead. he gave a smile — more for Darius' benefit than truly heartfelt — and moved to his bedroll.

Darius spent a few more minutes staring into the sunset.

It was truly beautiful, but the feeling was fleeting.

Twelve more days.

There was a howl from a wolf in the distance and Cid shivered in his bed. Darius took a heavy breath, setting up first watch.

Puppets on a String

S ithel kept his arms clasped behind his back, standing upon the
precipice of the windy cliffs of Ren Nar, looking out over the world
of Farhaven. He grinned wickedly, seeing the Great Kingdoms
spread out beneath him like pieces on a cyn board that were waiting to
be played like the last scraps of food pushed around on a plate before
being consumed.

Standing on an outcropping of rock, wind raging about his massive
form, he felt like a god dealing out death and judgment.

He gazed to the west.

"*Median*," he gurgled in delight.

It was called the Great Kingdom of Water, but it was a half-lie. Median was a fragment of its former self—Seria, the true Great Kingdom
of Water that was lost to the ravages of war and time. Still, Median was
impressive. It was like a white hand stamped upon the Frizzian Coast.
He sniffed the air, smelling the tang of salt from here. Hourly, Median's
high white walls were pounded by the fierce, salty waves, as if the Great
Kingdom of Water had tamed even the great and powerful Kalvas Ocean.
*Isolated and smaller than the rest. Like a sickly beast separated from the
herd, you'll be culled. That will be your end, water folk.*

He twisted towards the north and east.

"*Vaster*," he hissed as if he could feel the brilliant sun on him.

The bastion of light was only a pinpoint of gold from here, but Sithel knew its thousands of mirrored columns, resplendent and breathtaking in the rising sun. *Pride will be your downfall, Jewel of the North,* he thought, tongue playing across his razor-sharp teeth, savoring his meal further.

He peered deeper east, but the rocks of the great Thousand Spines obscured all sight of Lander, city of stone. *A dead, lost city,* he knew, *no meat on the bone to pick there.*

Eldas — *consumed even as we speak by Dryan and his machinations.*

Yronia — *devoured.*

Narim — *eating itself from the inside out.*

Morrow — *lost.*

That left the best for last.

Wind raged about him as he gazed south.

He reached out slowly, almost tenderly, but instead of a normal human hand, thick, glossy black claws curled at the air, engulfing the dusty city of Covai in the distance. He pictured planting his dark talon in the center of the Great Kingdom of Flesh and raking it across — spilling it open like the belly of a hog for the Harvest Festival. This tickled Sithel and he continued, dancing his clawed fingers in the air in amusement as if pulling strings and causing havoc, and grinned wickedly.

"Master," said a sniveling voice behind him.

Sithel, caught in his moment of joy, felt a spike of annoyance. His mirth fell along with his dark clawed arm. He didn't turn. "What is it?" His voice was dark and sinister now, like thick sheets of metal being ripped.

"Master," it whimpered, "Master, I've brought one."

Sithel slowly turned.

Kneeling upon the windy cliff was a small man like a shriveled shrub, clinging to life just like the tiny trees that gripped the cliff's face beneath him. He was nothing and nobody. Just some small thing that Sithel picked up in his retreat from Farbs — a cobbler or something else equally worthless. He called himself *Hammand* and he was part of the *kin* — pathetic humans groveling for a false promise from Sithel's master. Sithel was the only *true* servant. The rest were just puppets on strings.

Two hulking Vergs trundled behind Hammand, stamping at the grounds and snorting huge gusts of billowing air as if attempting to compete with the windy heights.

The beasts were nightmarish, hellish even. They had a lumbering presence, with leathery skin and no necks, they were twice as tall as the

179

average man, but surprisingly and annoyingly exhibited sharp wits. Their arms were huge and long enough to scrape the ground and their legs were thick and stocky. Each hand engulfed their prisoner's arms and thick veins ran beneath their gray skin.

For the most part they looked like what childhood stories called trolls, but twisted, *darker*. He'd heard of Vergs and Saeroks from tales of the Lieon, but these were more. Like him, he supposed. Parts of their flesh were armored. From their backs, flesh became dark metal spikes like black briarthorn, if briarthorn was made of Yronia steel. It looked like wicked black pauldrons upon their monstrously broad shoulders. The chitinous black metal was elsewhere too—down their huge curved spines and affixed to their muscled arms. The black plate was fused to their gray flesh like a second skin. *No*, he realized more accurately—not fused, but *growing*, a seamless blend of flesh and metal. What had his mistress done to these creatures?

The presence of the Vergs, however, was odd.

Normally she'd just use Nameless to do her bidding because their sudden dematerialization made for perfect scouts and assassins. But a Verg? If an errant farmer or traveler saw the beast, they'd think the Seven Hells had opened up before their eyes. That made him smile. Oh, how he wished to unleash the creatures upon Covai to watch those pitiful beings tremble in fear, to feel true helplessness as he once knew, but his mistress had forbid it.

He remembered it now, *standing in that strange room of living darkness, the walls crawling, alive, like writhing black snakes.*

"The war is brewing, Sithel. A war to tear the world asunder." The voice echoed from everywhere at once—not feminine nor masculine, but a rumble from a god, echoing inside his head and inside his blackened heart,

Sithel grew excited and he stepped forward, his clawed hoof stamping down. The writhing snakes moved as if parting to make way before his fierceness. "Why wait?" he growled. "We can rip the pathetic creatures from this mortal coil. I can be your harbinger! Let me show the world our true strength."

"No." The reply was simple but sharp.

Sithel grew annoyed; he stepped forward again. This time the dark writhing snakes didn't part. Where his hoof touched, he felt pain lance through him. He pulled away, confused, but it didn't quell his annoyance, "Why?" he asked, voice not nearly as menacing, but still a guttural rumble.

Inhuman. "*I grow tired of waiting. How long has it been? We sit idle in our dark crevices, like beasts afraid of the light while they sit eating off the land, filling their bellies behind their high walls thinking they're safe. They must die! Yet I sit here like a—*"

Sithel was cut short as the writhing feelers lifted into the air, dancing about his form menacingly. He remembered what they could do—remembered clearly the agony they'd caused him, and he felt a shiver of true fear again. He quelled his frustration, changing tactics. His voice became soft, pliant, almost pleading, "*I've seen the armies, Mistress. I've seen what you have coming.*" His voice grew frenzied and breathless, almost human as he remembered what he'd glimpsed, if only for a mere moment. "*It's... beautiful,*" he crooned, eyes watering in memory of the endless sea of Vergs and Saeroks filling the vast halls of Yronia. "*It will kill them all. A clean slate, just as you promised, for us to create our new vision.*"

"*Our new vision?*" the voice asked, amused.

He'd inclined his dark head, confused. "*Certainly,*" he said with less conviction. "*A new world where no one is weak.*" He sensed amusement in the air. "*That is your vision as well, is it not? That is why you spread the seed, 'Strength is life, weakness, death', isn't it?*"

The voice laughed. It echoed off the walls, deep and rumbling.

Sithel grew confused and afraid. This whole time... his mistress had different plans? Different motives? "*Why else spread the mantra?*" he asked, too curious. "*Why else convince and sway the world to the belief if—*"

"*—So many questions.*" The words smoothly cut him off, sounding condescending and short.

He could tell he was treading too far, the ice thin out here. He licked his lips—an old nervous habit of his, but his forked tongue only felt rows of barbed teeth and no lips. The living tendrils loomed around him. He remembered his old life, his Sunha pierced by giant tendrils of living darkness, blood spewing from his wretched mouth. The living feelers danced in the air, circling about Sithel, toying, threatening to do the same. "*I live only to serve,*" he answered at last.

The reply came, sharp and clear, "*You learn, my pet. Slowly, but you do learn. For now follow my orders and find the boy. All else unfolds as planned. Soon you will find your vengeance.*"

Sithel returned to the moment. He understood. She wished to keep her secrets for as long as possible until the perfect moment—and then spring her evil upon this world with such force that the titans themselves couldn't hold them back.

It wouldn't be long, he told himself.

He focused on the creature the Vergs held.

A short man with curly, black hair and dark, caramel-colored skin—white tattoos—the pigment of which was drawn from marlberries—were scrawled across his skin in some language Sithel couldn't read. And he wore sand-colored rags that were bloodied and torn. Blood ran from the corner of his mouth. Only his eyes, a light shade of copper that fluttered in and out of consciousness, showed any sign of life.

An Algasi. At last.

He hung like a limp sheet in the wind between the Vergs' massive arms. "What is this?" he asked.

"An Algasi, ju-just as y-you instructed, M-master" Hammand stammered.

Was I ever that pathetic? Sithel wondered. He had a flashing vision. A huge bellied man with blood upon his blacksmith's apron—eyes flaring like coals in the night, wielding a hot branding iron and a creature kneeling before him, simpering and begging forgiveness. *I suppose I was,* he thought, amused, the memory fading. There was a shred of annoyance at the memory, but none could deny that he had changed. He flexed his claw at that and looked down on Hammand who watched him with dull brown eyes. "I told you to return with an Algasi, not a corpse," he said, gesturing to the Algasi and grabbing a fistful of curling black hair to expose a huge gash that ran from his temple to his jaw. Sithel growled. "He looks like the Seven Hells of Remwar chewed him up and then spat him back out. What happened?"

Hammand wilted, mouth working soundlessly until Sithel stepped forward. "It was just as you said! Th-they were leaving Vaster, heading west! We captured him on the Green Hills when we found him scouting away from the rest. He put up a fight, he did. Strong and deadly, like a Devari mated with some sort of—"

Sithel stepped forward again, cutting him off, keeping him on track.

"—H-he even killed Entrius and Hessia!" Hammand said quickly, looking shaken and eyed the man angrily, fingering a bloody cut on his arm. *A wound suffered from the Algasi,* Sithel presumed. "I'm the only one of the kin that survived, Master." Sithel sighed. Two other members of the kin. They would be annoying to replace, but beyond that, they mattered nothing. But there was no use telling the fodder it was fodder.

"He still breathes—I suppose that's all that matters. Did the others notice?" he asked.

Hammand shook his head adamantly. "No, I swear it, Master. They were too preoccupied."

"Good, they have to believe us gone. That's the Great Lord's wish." He hadn't told any of the kin yet their master was a *woman*. He wasn't entirely sure she was a *she* anyway. Gods of death didn't exactly have genders. "Has he spoken yet?"

Hammand mopped at the sweat upon his face, pushing back the black hair that fell into his eyes from the raging wind. "Not yet, Master. I figured if anyone could pry out where they are going, it would be you," he said, licking his lips nervously.

Sithel stepped forward, lifting his hand

Hammand cowed, worming in his skin—knowing his touch meant death.

"You did well," he said, petting the man with his human hand. Hammand, like a servile hound looked up with brown eyes, smiling through his terror. He ignored the man and turned to their captive.

* * *

183

"Welcome."

The Algasi said nothing; his copper eyes only burned with hatred.

"Do you know what they say about this place? What used to exist here, Algasi?" He walked the grounds, dust pulsing with each step of his huge, armored feet. "Hmm?"

The Algasi remained quiet, watching him.

Sithel knelt, patiently. His real hand—the only piece of living flesh on him touched the ground beneath, feeling the hard-packed earth. It felt warm, and not just from the sun, but as if ancient power still rested beneath the sands. "Of course you do. Morrow," he answered in a sneer. "The Great Kingdom of Wind, home of the banished element. All know the tales. Even uncultured filth such as you."

Still the Algasi's eyes burned with silent wrath.

He laughed menacingly. "Right here!" He stamped his heavy boot down. He sniffed as if he could smell the foul stench of the elemental power of wind and its fallen people, but there was nothing—just the smell of actual wind and dust clogging his nostrils. "Can you believe it? Right now we very well might be standing in the Hall of Winds, gazing upon the famous weapons forged by the gods themselves!" His laughter and smile wilted as he continued, almost sadly. "But where is it now? *Gone.* A whole kingdom engulfed by the tragedy of the Lieon, leaving behind only this sad patch of dust and this incessant wind. But I wonder…" He pinched a bit of sand between his human fingers. He brought the sand to the Algasi's nose, rubbing it, letting him smell. "Where did it go, hmm?"

The Algasi pulled away and spat. The dribble fell upon Sithel's claw, sizzling and hissing like butter upon a hot pan.

He only smiled, amused, and continued unfazed. "Think about it. Even great beasts leave behind bones to remember them, but there's nothing here, is there?" He made an amused, thoughtful sound to himself and twisted back. "If the greatest city in the entire world can be turned to dust so easily, what tales will be told a hundred years from now? A thousand? Ten thousand? When all the Great Kingdoms turn to rubble, what legacy will remain?"

The Algasi's eyes pinched, curious.

"Care to venture a guess, warrior of sand?"

But the Algasi only snarled in reply.

"Incorrect," he replied and turned, cloak fluttering. "How about you, my pet?"

"I—I," Hammand stammered, shaking his greasy black hair, "I don't know, my lord."

"I shall tell you. *Men,*" he answered to all those in attendance, speaking grandly. "My hope is not in wood or stone, or other artifices that crumble, but in hearts. Don't you see? If we can change the world with the minds of men, then all else can fall to ruin, but as long as humans exist—so too will those ideals."

Hammand clapped uproariously but it was taken by the wind. "Yes, my lord! Beautifully said!"

Sithel cast him a glare and the man froze, shrinking back into his dirty rags. Sithel turned to the Algasi. "*Weakness is death, strength is life.*" He licked at the words, savoring them. They were the only truth he knew now. "You know this, don't you? You are the very testament to it. If you were only stronger, you would have killed my friend here and escaped."

He ran a finger along the Algasi's brow, dragging sweat with it.

"But you failed. Now Gray and his little friends are attempting to rebuild something and inspire hope in this world, but it's too late. This world is a broken thing. Why save a beast, breathe false life into it, only to watch it linger and decay once more? This world needs a rebirth. This world needs *me*. Now that you see what I'm trying to accomplish, you will help me, won't you?"

The Algasi looked away.

"Where are they going?" he asked. "Your brethren and my little lost ones—Gray, Ayva, and the others. Tell me."

The Algasi spat again.

This time it hit Sithel on the cheek and he felt his ire rise. He wiped it away with a dark grimace and neared, raising a dark claw. "You don't like to speak, do you?"

The Algasi only shivered in rage, trying to attack Sithel, arms straining against the huge Vergs. But it was useless. Better to try and uproot a Great Kingdom from the ground.

Sithel took a single claw and traced it down the Algasi's cheek, slicing a long line of blood from his temple to his chin. As he did, the man screamed an inhuman cry. It was bloody, loud—a death shriek. But when the Algasi finished, panting from the effort, sweat dappling his brow, he looked around, confused and breathless. "You'll die now," Sithel declared, "but unfortunately, it will be slow and painful. Yet I can save you from that. I can make it quick, *painless*. A breeze, if you will… if only you share with me *where* they are headed and what the prophecy said."

The wind raged around them, tugging at the Algasi's clothes, but his words were crisp, cutting through it all. The dawning of his words seemed to settle in on the Algasi like a stone sinking to the bottom of the river, but then, to Sithel's complete bafflement, the Algasi *smiled*. His smile became a grin.

"I don't understand. I just gave him a death sentence and he smiles?" Sithel said.

Hammand wrung his spindly hands. "I believe that's the way Algasi are, my lord. They're said to be fearless in all things. They don't fear death. Not like you and I, at least. Some say they even embrace it."

"Idiots," Sithel sputtered in his gravelly voice, booming over the windy heights. "Fools and idiots. They wish for nothingness? That's madness."

Hammand shrunk farther, as if wishing to disappear.

"Only one way to find out, I suppose," Sithel said, a smile creasing his black skin. He slowly stabbed his dark claw into the Algasi's stomach. The man gasped. Sheer agony filled his eyes. "Does it hurt? You can

185

scream, you know." He pushed harder. A scream erupted from the man's lips, bellowing forth and cutting the sound of the tempestuous heights. Sithel felt warm entrails and gripped, playing with them, just like he had played with the Great Kingdoms below. He danced his clawed fingers around, tugging and scraping at the man's innards, watching each shift tear new agony across the man's features, and sprout fresh tears of anguish in the Algasi's eyes. At last he pulled his hand free, still smiling, then gripped the man's curling hair with his human hand, pulling him in close, whispering fiercely. "Now you feel it, don't you? The terror? The darkness creeping at the corners of your vision? It approaches—your death. An end to all things. The great void. *Nothingness*," he hissed, tongue forking out, licking at the air. Head held up, the Algasi gasped like a fish torn from water. He seemed to be searching, eyes looking for something. Perhaps he was simply seeing his life slipping away. "But I–*I* can save you. You don't need to die, little fish." His flicked his hand out dismissively. "Or I can end you, whichever you wish. If only you tell me what the prophecy is..."

Slowly the Algasi twisted against Sithel's hand to stare him in the eyes. With the last of his strength, he lunged and bit—hard. His teeth gnashed, clamping onto Sithel's black ear and he tore at the lobe. Sithel screamed in pain, feeling flesh rip. He gripped his head, feeling blood—dark, with still a hint of red.

"You filthy son of a—"

"Ah, ah! A *gift*," the Algasi said, speaking at last, staying Sithel's hand.

"A gift?" he growled, still feeling blood pouring out around his human hand. "Tell me, how is *this* a gift, you filthy piece of refuse?"

"You see, the prophecy speaks only to the righteous. It's not for the ears of the undeserving, for cursed things such as you." The Algasi's eyes glinted. "But then I realized if I removed your cursed ears, then I could tell you. So you see—a gift." He smiled, and blood covered his teeth and gums—Sithel's blood.

Sithel raised his fist, but then the Algasi coughed and hacked—dark stringy strands of blood flew from the man's mouth onto the parched earth. He tried to catch his breath, but nothing came—only sharp, dry inhales. "Ah, it seems our conversation is nearing its natural end. You have but moments to tell me where your friends are headed and what the prophecy says before you die. Perhaps if you do, I will spare some of your kind—or at least give them the quick and gracious death that you were too foolish to accept."

The Algasi hacked more, struggling and trying to get a breath. His eyes bulged from his head, his muscles coiled and strained against the Vergs' grip. Sithel watched the poison work its way—seeing his veins slither and crawl like worms beneath his skin. The man opened his mouth to speak.

Sithel leaned in. "Yes?" he asked. "Any more clever retorts with your last breaths?"

"I will tell you this, *unrighteous*. The prophecy of sun…it names you."

Sithel hesitated, a grin peeling back his lipless mouth. "Does it now? Tell me then, what does it say? What fate does your oh-so-glorious prophecy spell for me?" He leaned in closer, knowing the man's dying words would be but a hoarse whisper now.

A single word, clear and sharp breathed forth: "*Death.*"

With that the Algasi's lids fluttered.

Sithel sneered, raising his clawed fist into the air to finish the deed. But as he did, the man exhaled a long, peaceful breath and slumped. His head fell forward, the last of his life fleeing his body—Sithel glimpsed an orange essence fading into the air. *His spark…* or what the naïve called *souls.* He remained motionless for a long moment, thoughts churning, darkness and anger brewing inside his heart until he cast his hand sideways at last.

The Vergs understood. They flung the Algasi over the cliff. A powerful zephyr blew, alive. It tore at Hammand, sending the small man sprawling and clutching for a root to keep himself from being knocked off the cliff. The Algasi's body tumbled off. But instead of smacking against the cliff's face and causing a bloody smear as Sithel had hoped—the wind seemed to catch the Algasi, and carry him away from the jagged rock's face. The Algasi continued to fall until he was only a tiny dot, and then was gone from sight, depriving Sithel of witnessing the gruesome scene and what he'd thought would be a fitting finale for the cursed man. Another disappointment that left a sour taste in his mouth.

"Leave me," he said to the hulking Vergs, pointing away. The beasts grunted and left, heading to the dark tunnels—a nearby set of avenues beneath the surface, a hidden passage back to the breeding grounds of the grotesque creatures.

As they left Sithel's mind was a dark cauldron. *Was he lying?* Yet he'd seen the look in the Algasi's eyes speaking the truth. He pondered the words of the Algasi savage, denying their reality. "It can't be," he mut-

187

tered. He felt Hammand shift nearby, nervous and confused. "He has to be wrong. He's must be. He used his dying breath to place one more pitiful jab – the bastard. The prophecy can't name me. Pathetic." He laughed callously. Sithel's eyes rose as Hammand made a fearful sound. He returned to the mount, his black clawed grip hovering over his pet's head, a mere breath away. "Hammand."

"Y-yes, m-my l-lord?"

Sithel saw a pool of urine forming beneath Hammand. *Pitiful.* "West. That's what you said, correct? Where Gray and the others were headed when you saw them last?"

Hammand nodded, terrified.

"And they were all accounted for?"

"All of them?" Hammand repeated.

"Gray and his friends."

Hammand swallowed. "How many?"

Sithel's rage stirred. "Three boys and two girls. How many did you see?"

"I saw children. I'm sure it was all of them—"

"How many, my pet?"

"Traveling with the Algasi? Two girls and one boy, but perhaps I counted wrong, Master. That must be it."

Sithel tried to restrain his anger, but he knew his disappointment was only a fraction of what hers would be. "You don't know where the others went then?"

"I... I don't know. I had my people watching the gates at all times. A mouse couldn't have snuck out of Vaster without me knowing!"

Sithel took a long, even breath, looking away. *They've split.* Another thorn in his side.

"Master, you believe me, don't you?" Hammand asked behind him plaintively.

"I believe you."

Hammand smiled.

Sithel finished. "I believe you've lost track of them. *Half* of them at least. You've proven to me you're as useless as I expected all along. I could have trained a dung-eating dog to follow my orders with more success and less... cringing." At this, Hammand cringed. Sithel stretched his palm over the man's skull, his black claws hovering right above touching. "Stop cowering." Hammand continued to shake. "Stop it." Sithel's

voice grew louder, but still Hammand's quivering continued, now accent-
ed with snivels. "*Enough.*" But it didn't stop him. Hammand was now
openly crying—his sobs grating agonizingly on Sithel's ears.

He played it out, crushing Hammand's skull in one quick squeeze, feeling the satisfying crunch of bone, ending the horrible sobs. They sounded so familiar—so painfully familiar and so pathetically weak. They hurt
him, scratching like a claw on his brain, and Sithel bellowed. The sound
was demonic and thundering. When his bellow ended, he looked down.

Hammand had stopped crying.

But he wasn't dead.

Slowly, Sithel pulled back his dark claws. The man watched, confused. Then Sithel waved his human hand and Hammand scampered
away. The cowardly man didn't object, didn't ask questions—though his
eyes repeatedly glanced back as if Sithel would change his mind—he just
ran. Sithel didn't know if Hammand would return, but he didn't care.
He wasn't opposed to killing in cold blood, but Hammand hadn't done
anything terribly wrong. Sithel just never wanted to hear that pathetic
sound again.

Sithel turned, looking to where Gray and the others should be. "West,
is it? Where are you headed, little rabbits? And why?" Heading westerly,
fractured and separated from one another. It made no sense. He snarled
in annoyance, knowing he'd have to follow one group and not the other.
Why did they part? Which miscreants had gone after the sword and who
hadn't? It didn't matter. He knew where they were headed.

The missing sword would be the perfect bait for their death.

His vision was different now, too, more powerful. He squinted and felt
miles disappear, thousands of feet racing before him as he glimpsed the
Covian dust, almost feeling as if he could see the long train of caravans.

His homeland.

I will return to you soon, he thought, claws reaching out like a lover's
embrace towards his land. He couldn't wait to savor his peoples' fear and
to watch their wide eyes as he peeled the flesh from their bones.

189

Pride of Median

Helix found himself in darkness.

He didn't hate darkness. He didn't love it. It was what it was. The rats that nibbled at his toes, however, the constant creak of planks above him and the droplets of water that fell into his eyes, waking him from his intermittent moments of shuteye—it was all beginning to grate on him. The only thing that truly comforted him in the pitch black was the soft splash of the ship's hull crashing against the waves beneath it. That was the one saving grace to this leg of his journey.

A journey to find his homeland and reclaim his ancestry.

It was his seventh day on the *Pride of Median*—a dumb name for a boat if ever there was one. He'd chosen it not for the name, however, but for his ability to sneak on without the crew or captain noticing. He didn't like the term *stowaway*, for Helix planned on paying the captain and his crew back eventually when he found his homeland and its lost wealth, but for now he was out of money.

He'd run out a week ago and had been scrounging ever since, but he knew himself well. He had integrity, and, one day not far from now, he planned to pay everyone back that the things he'd 'borrowed' from along the way: the farmer's apples in the orchard of Tovai, the pie on the windowsill of that little village, the copper in the beggar's cup, of which he still felt especially guilty about. *But he'd needed it,* he thought again, adamant. To continue his quest and to survive. The world was a harsh

place for a seventeen year-old orphan from Median without coin or con-
nections.

But for now, there was nothing to do but find peace in the soft lapping
of waves just outside the ship. Always they lulled him back to sleep, back
to the darkness within darkness. And so they did again. Helix shut his
eyes and found himself in the world of dreams.

They came fitfully.

He saw a vision.

*A city of wind and salt, sitting mightily upon the northern banks of the
Frizzian coast. He watched it from the cliffs of Ren Nar, standing far away.
Barges, fleets of warships, dinghies, trading crafts, and all manner of sea-
faring vessels lined the silver docks that extended for miles into the Kalvas
Ocean — the water a tranquil blue.*

Median, he knew — The Great Kingdom of Water.

"The false kingdom," he whispered.

*Suddenly, as if his words had sparked it, the sea roiled, turning tumul-
tuous. It churned and frothed like a diseased animal. A storm was coming.
It surged, becoming a sheet of water a thousand feet high, looming and
creating a shadow over the land, darkening Farhaven, promising to flood
the world with change, with chaos... with death.*

The vision dissipated, evaporating like water in a dry land.

*It was replaced by a vision of a man with a dark beard and bright eyes
like a shallow lake, just like his... Anger spiked inside Helix and —*

He awoke with a start.

Helix wasn't sure how long he was out, but diffused bits of light tried
vainly to peek through the outer hull. The faint call of gulls echoed in
the background and his limbs were stiff with disuse. He looked around in
the pitch blackness, confused. *What woke me?* Helix wondered, slightly
unnerved, yet the ever-present creak of the ship and crashing of water
threatened to soothe him back into sleep when a voice called, sharp and
loud, "Oi! How many of thems does ya want, Captain?"

A dull echo answered.

He peeked over the barrels before him, just barely, and made out a man
peering down into the darkness of the hold. Light shone from outside,
shouts of men and more, before the man dropped inside with a thump
and the hatch snapped shut, plunging the hold into darkness. There was
a scratch and a hiss, and a lantern roared to life. The sailor stumbled,
squinting, and Helix ducked as his gaze glossed over him. His footsteps

191

thundered, mirroring Helix's beating heart as he pressed his back to the barrels, quieting his breaths.

He knew the price of being caught.

For many boats, especially those run by Median captains, a captured stowaway meant a lost finger or even a hand, depending on the captain. But that wasn't what he feared. Thrown to land and cast in shackles, he'd never reach his destination. His quest would end, and the thought of finding his homeland and the lost city would be all but hopeless.

With steadying breaths, he calmed his racing heart and reminded himself that he wouldn't be caught. Growing up in Median and taught by his father, he knew all about ships. Helix was pressed against the bilge, hidden behind a dozen barrels of limfuns—tart fruits used to abolish a sickness that only occurred when sailors were adrift too many days on the sea without proper nutrition.

Luckily, this was only a quick jaunt—a two, maybe three-week excursion along the Ker stream. No one would develop the malady during a silly river trip. He was safe.

Yet the man's footsteps creaked, getting closer.

"Dicing captain… Dark as death in here, it is," the man groaned.

Closer still.

His even breaths quickened, and as he always did to calm himself he imagined the water moving on all sides of them, blending and rushing through him, becoming one. He felt a warm glow on his face and his eyes snapped open.

"Wot's this we 'ave 'ere?" Heart pounding against his ribcage, Helix twisted, looking up and staring into a sailor's amber-lit face. The man's dark beard rustled into a smile. "A stowa'ay, is it?"

"*How?*" Helix whispered to himself, confused.

The man snatched his ear. "Come 'ere, then." He pulled him from behind the barrels, making Helix scramble. "Roight, the captain won't be all too happy 'bout this… Yer makin' me job not-so-easy, y'know?"

"Please," he pleaded. "You can just leave me here, can't you? What harm am I doing to anyone?"

The sailor raised a brow. He pushed his lantern back over the barrels, lighting up Helix's not-so-safe cubbyhole, revealing fruit rinds, several fish bones that'd he scrounged from the trash, and a half-eaten loaf of bread. "Roight, that's not goin' to get me strung up from the riggin', noot at all," said the man sarcastically. "Come on, then," he groaned with a sigh, prodding Helix forward. "Let's get this over with."

Helix pleaded with the man as he was dragged out of the hold but the sailor was silent, face grave as death. The man kicked open a pair of double doors and light assaulted Helix as he was thrown to the wet planks of the deck.

"What's this?" growled a deep baritone, rumbling inside Helix's head.

He twisted, looking up to see a massive man hovering over him while holding the edges of his dark blue coat. Helix squinted, eyes still adjusting to the light and sounds of the surface world. It was all too much after seven days below deck.

"Found us a mite small bilge rat," his captor said, nudging Helix with his boot. "Wos locked up thar for quite a while, he was—since the port of Eldas would be me guess, judging by the scraps he'd found and fed 'imself on. Quite the little den he 'ad."

Helix scrambled to his feet, brushing himself off, taking a deep breath, and standing as poised as he could.

He stood face to face with the captain, a short, stocky man with a typical, lengthy white beard and hair. His face was well-darkened from the sun, and he had bright eyes just like… Helix shook his head, stopping his rambling thoughts as the captain spoke in a low gravel, jabbing him softly with a pipe. "Is it true then, boy? You a stowaway and a thief on my fine ship?"

"I'm no thief," he said sharply.

"No?" asked the man, raising a silver brow.

A small crowd began to form, sailors dropping from the rigging and gathering around the captain, forming a circle. Helix watched them and answered stubbornly, "No—well, not precisely… I plan on paying it all back in good time."

Several men laughed or snorted.

"Do you now?" the captain asked.

"I do," he snapped back.

"And as for the stowaway bit? Do you deny that claim as well?" asked the gruff-faced captain.

Helix answered with a small smile, "You say stowaway, I say—" He searched his mind quickly, feeling the weight of eyes. "Borrower of space? Temporary guest?"

A roar of laughter erupted from the sailors.

Helix felt a bit of pride and surprise—he never thought himself a man

193

of humor—but he stood tall as the captain's face judged him, too hard to read. His white brows drew together, he lifted his hand, and the second mate bellowed at the men to settle down. "What's your name, *borrower of space?*" he questioned, and a wave of chuckles rippled through the crowd.

"Helix," he replied firmly.

"Helix, is it? What am I to do with you, Helix?"

Helix shrugged. "Let me stay?"

This elicited no laughter from the men, simply blank stares. Helix felt his skin grow hot. "Blond hair… bright eyes… light skin… slender as a sail… You're Median, aren't you?"

Helix's gut twisted at the name, feeling a stab of betrayal and anger, but he tried to hide it from his face as memories resurfaced like boiling water. At last, his fist uncurled and he shook his head. "Covai," he lied, distancing himself from that wretched city.

"Well then, *Covian*—though you do not have the look of it—do you know the price of a stowaway?" This time Helix nodded, slowly, swallowing the hard lump in his throat. "Then what do you suppose I do with you, Helix?"

"There's no law that says you have to…" He couldn't say it and he grabbed his fingers, wringing his wrist nervously. He could already feel the blade upon his skin. Words suddenly poured out of him like a faucet. "I'm not bad or evil. I wouldn't be a nuisance on your ship—I promise you. I…" His gaze panned around the ship, past the mainmast, over the shrouds, eyeing the swinging boon as if drowning and looked for something to help him escape when it dawned on him. "I know my way around a vessel too. I wouldn't get in the way at all."

His captor stepped forward. "Well, 'e was in the least likely place to be found on the 'ole ship, Captain Xavvan. Smart lad, he is, hiding behind the rations we don't use for the river runs. He was confused and angry as a devil's hornet when I found 'im there—he must 'ave known it was a damned good hiding spot too." He laughed. "If it weren't fer yer love of da limfuns, Cap'n, he'd 'ave been wid us to the gates of the Seven 'ells."

The captain snorted. "Clever lad, indeed." Helix felt a note of pride for the man's compliment, then anger eyeing his captor—he was still the one that found him—and finally a slow, dawning realization, seeing the oblong bulge in the captain's coat pocket. A limfun fruit. *Who in the light eats limfuns for taste?* he wondered, baffled as the captain spoke in a loud, commanding voice, "Yet the question remains—what do I do with you?

I'm not one for bloodshed—seen enough of that to last me a lifetime, and the next few to boot. But this shipment of Menalas coal must be delivered in the week, and we're already behind as is—"

"I can help," he said quickly.

"You're from the city of flesh, a town of dirt and dust as far as the eye can see, and you say you've worked a ship before? Manned the lines of a vessel this size?" he asked dubiously.

"No," he replied honestly, "but I learn quickly, and I'll do whatever it takes for me to stay aboard this ship."

"And tell me, my temporary guest, what makes you want to stay on my ship so bad?"

Helix opened his mouth then snapped it shut. In a quest like his, he knew it was foolish to say too much. Besides, the captain was clearly born and raised in Median, and to men of Median, what Helix sought was no more than a fairy tale… a dream that they'd shoved deep down, subdued until it had turned their once warm hearts to ice. No, despite the kind look in the captain's eye he couldn't risk ruining it all. "I can't say," he admitted. "My journey is my own, but I promise to do as you say no matter what if it means staying on this boat. Even if it means losing a finger."

"Keep 'im, Cap," a sailor called.

"Oi, let the little runt stay," said another.

Helix felt his heart buoyed, smiling.

Even his captor shrugged. "He really didn't do much harm, Cap. Just a few fish bones and sum soggy bread. Besides, he's skinnier than a codler fish." He jabbed a thumb back over his shoulder at the milling sailors. "He'll eat half what these louts do."

The captain harrumphed. "You've gone and become savior, have you, Gambol? It seems there's a soft, mushy side to my first mate after all."

Gambol scrubbed his messy, white-splotched hair with a chuckle.

"And whose rations will he take, hmm?" asked the captain, looking around.

The men behind him turned suddenly silent.

"Mine," said Gambol, "I can share a bite or two." Then he fixed a hot glare on the others that made them rustle guiltily.

"Ah damnation, I suppose I can make do with a scrap less bread," said another.

The man was ribbed by a taller man. "You can and you should—yer getting rounder about the waist than your sister, Morgan." There was

195

sharp laughter and jostling followed by a serious silence as all eyes fell to the captain. Helix's heart pounded.

"Keep him, you say," the captain grumbled to himself, echoing the sailor's sentiments. He rubbed his beard, salt and spray falling from his crusted whiskers. Gulls cried out overhead and the grassy banks passed by in a steady blur. Helix swallowed nervously. He wasn't a nervous person, but the man's silence stretched. Above the sun burned angrily, like a brilliant flare of yellow after the darkness of the hold, making him squint in annoyance and raise a hand to his eyes as a shield. "Don't like the sun, do you?"

Helix realized his mistake, shaking his head, pulling his arm away.

But Captain Xavvan was surprisingly spry. He leaned forward and snatched Helix's wrist, lifting it up to the light of the sun. A flush of fear filled him, panic nearly taking over, and he tugged hard on his arm. "Let go," he pleaded. But the captain was too strong. He yanked down on his white sleeve, exposing branded flesh in the mark of an "X" on the inside of his forearm that reached all the way to the bottom of his wrist.

The captain sighed, splayed lines at the corner of his eyes tightening. "The last thing I need is a boy getting in the way. Especially one who has the banished mark on his arm…"

There was a collective rumbling of murmurs among the sailors.

Helix felt their eyes, hot on his neck, and their unjust glares of judgment. He knew what their thoughts were: crass words he'd heard time and again, cursed at by mothers, hissed and spat at by old men, or thought by once-trusted friends. *Thief. Liar.* But worst of all… *Murderer.*

He forced himself to turn, standing tall and facing their gazes.

The white sails snapped at the rigging as the captain spoke. "I don't know what you did to deserve the banished mark, and…" He held up his heavy palm as Helix opened his mouth. "I don't *want* to know. You've lied to me already and I can't trust you. And a man I can't trust has no place on the *Pride of Median.*" The vessel creaked, accentuating his words. Helix's heart dropped like an anchor into the pit of his stomach and deeper, carving a hollow in his chest. The captain gave him a last long, disappointed look, blue eyes heavy and lined face unreadable, and he waved his hand, turning. "Tie him to the mizzenmast."

Helix cried out. "No! You can't, please! I can explain—"

But his words were drowned by the captain's booming decree, "We'll drop him off at the port of Hagerton and hand him over to the authorities

196

there—" Each word rolled over the deck, hitting Helix like a dull hammer in his chest, robbing his voice. Hands grabbed at him and he wanted to fight, but he felt his hope and his journey collapsing beneath the weight of the captain's voice, "—make sure he's fed and well taken care of, but if he speaks again, gag him until we've made our stop."

Immediately Helix felt sick, stomach churning like the sea in his dream as he was dragged to the quarterdeck. He vomited abruptly but the men, accustomed to such sights, sidestepped it and continued. The world spun beneath Helix, the heaving ship lurched, making him sway, and he knew he was going to faint. The last thing Helix took in before he fainted was the captain's dark blue coat and the gentle sound of the river lapping against the vessel's keel—dull, distant and hollow.

For he knew his dream had just died.

An Unexpected Visitor

O daren opened the door to the inn, letting rain and wind crash through like opening a storm drain. Men and women—all thieves—turned to his entrance, grousing at the rain and cold and he quickly shut it and hobbled in.

Light and noise assaulted Odaren's ears as he stood at the threshold of the inn's doors.

The Hand of Fate, its sign read in cracked gold paint.

After visiting a dozen inns and bending enough fingers, he was told she'd be here. Oddly, though tangible fear laced every voice he'd met, they all seemed to know where she was. His *Mistress of Shadows*. He wondered why that was… but feared he knew the answer. *When walking a ledge you make sure you know where your feet are relative to the abyss, so you don't find your feet scraping too close and foolishly fall to your untimely death. Faye was that abyss.* He swallowed, not letting his thoughts get ahead of himself, and focused on the common room at hand.

The room was bright for a thieves' hideout—candles lined the walls, the bar, the tables and the large fogged windowsills, casting a hoary orange glow. Cobwebbed chandeliers swung from the rafters where hot wax fell to the dirty hay-strewn floor. Were it not so wet, Odaren feared the whole of it would alight in flames, but then eyeing the subdued patrons like heaps of flesh huddled over dark brews, he wondered if anyone would notice.

Quickly he took in the dangers. A big man stood in the back. Neck thicker than a bull, his one eye grazed lazily over the patrons as he leaned against the wall with his trunk-like arms crossed. Otherwise, it was the customary scene—groups of gambling thieves with daggers just beneath the tables, ready at the bad roll of a die or greedy fingers reaching too quickly for the copper glittering dully upon the table.

Yet the only person that mattered was not there. She was not among them.

Odaren's thundering heart slowed, both relieved and worried. He reminded himself that all fingers had pointed here and he knew the night was far from over. The clock was ticking, his life seeping out of it like an hourglass with each breath wasted if he didn't find his prey soon.

Hiking up his saddlebags Odaren slunk up to the bar, dragging his right leg—he always limped, but twice as bad during a good rain. The joints in his knee seemed to lock up like steel hinges with too little oil.

The innkeeper stood behind the bar polishing a pewter mug. He was a corpulent man whose bulk strained against his too-small, dirty apron. It might have been white at one time, but now it was a brown smear of dirt, sweat and other unknowns. As he approached, the man's beady eyes shot him a glance, then returned to his work. "No rooms," the man groused then continued, talking almost to himself. "Not since the Patriarch, in his infinite wisdom, opened the gates of Farbs to the riffraff of the world have we had any rooms or any respectable guests for that matter." He glanced up, squinting one eye. "Speaking of, what are you? You've a dark, swarthy look to you… Covian? Vasterian?" His lips curled in an unsavory, disgusted manner. "Pray tell me you aren't from Menalas, are you? They're almost as greedy and miserly as their Esterian brothers."

Odaren ignored the man and his prejudices. He pulled out two silvers and slapped them on the rough bar, pulling his hand away half-expecting splinters, then spoke beneath his breath. "I'm looking for a woman."

The innkeeper's sour face twisted into a wry smile, his rosy cheeks looking like two balls of dough. "Aren't we all, friend?"

"A particular woman," he corrected, not wanting to play the man's tongue-in-cheek game. He felt death on his shoulder and humor was the last thing on his mind. "Her name is Faye."

"Can't say I know the name…" the man said, scraping the silver into a large cloth pocket in his apron. "This woman of yours go by any other names? We've mostly Darkeye ilk in here…" He pointed across the

199

way to a dour woman in a brown jerkin. "Nine Lives Kara." Then he shrugged an elbow to his near left where a slender woman with a gaunt face was tapping her fingers rhythmically to the tune of a minstrel and his lute playing on the center stage. "Freya Fast Fingers." He nodded to a nearby table where four men were playing a modified, simpler game of elements. Instead of glass pieces the figurines were lumps of wood and the board was half the size. "The one in green, though I know she don't look it, is a woman —"

Odaren interrupted him, eyeing him deliberately. "*Another* name."

The man looked befuddled.

Sighing, he gestured him closer and the innkeeper leaned in, bulk pressing against the bar. The noise of the tavern turning to a quiet dull thud in the background of his mind, Odaren whispered, "*Mistress of Shadows.*"

The innkeeper backpedaled as if he'd been slapped across the face, stumbling, his pewter cup clattering to the ground. He scrambled for the coin in his pocket but Odaren was quicker. Half-expecting this reaction, he grabbed the man's stained apron and yanked him closer, pulling his dagger under the folds of his many chins. "Take your thieving hands off me," the man sputtered, fear still bright in his eyes. The innkeeper's eyes flashed and Odaren knew he'd gestured to the big brute in the corner he'd seen as he entered — the muscle used to subdue unruly patrons. Odaren knew he only had a few moments before the man was on him.

"Now you're going to listen closely," he breathed, frustration and anger welling up inside him. He tried to imagine he was the Shadow King and what that tyrant would say. He let the darkness of despair, the apathy enter his voice. "As we speak I'm a dead man standing. My life is forfeit if I don't speak to this *Mistress of Shadows*," he snarled the name, truly angry at his predicament. "So do you think for one moment I would hesitate to spill your blood across your own bar? I've one foot in the grave already." He laughed, feeling a crazed note enter his voice. "I'd laugh, I would, as I watched you gag on your final breaths, watch the life bleed out of you…" He swallowed, feeling sanity return just a bit as the man's eyes widened — the room still a dull thumping in the background, the sound of heavy steps nearly upon him. "*Unless* — unless you tell me where she is…" As he spoke the final words and the world seemed to return to its normal pace, the light returning.

Huge hands dug into his shoulders.

Odaren cursed. It was too late; the innkeeper hadn't bought his ploy, or perhaps the insanity in his own eyes had stilled the man's tongue, making it thick in his own mouth. Desperate, he pulled his last gesture. He dug the dagger beneath his glove, ripping the fabric and exposing a black mark on the back of his hand that resembled a sickle moon with nine black dots in its center, standing for the nine Great Kingdoms.

It was the Shadow's Mark—the emblem of a man from Narim, and a servant of the Shadow King. In truth, it was once the mark that all thieves wore—when the Mistress and Master of Shadows ruled the world. Or so the ancient stories went. But the Shadow King had adopted it again, and all who knew of him knew of the Shadow's Mark.

Upon seeing it, the innkeeper's pale lips went slack, fear riddling his face.

The brute's huge hands loosened on Odaren's shoulders but didn't let go.

Odaren spoke quickly, "If you kill me the Shadow King will hear of it… But for a favor?" He licked his lips. "He always repays those who serve him wisely."

Something churned in the man's dark gaze—a light—and for a moment, a seemingly greedy glimmer flickered and then was gone. The fat man looked up, waving away his hired muscle. "Be gone, Goram, you thick-headed oaf," he cursed, rubbing his neck, "And next time be quicker or I'll throw you back where I found you, into that miserable pit you called a life." The big man's shoulders slumped and he slunk back into the shadows. "My apologies…" the innkeeper crooned, dipping his head in deference. "Had I known who you were—"

"Enough," Odaren snapped. He'd wasted too much time already. "These events are far over your head." *Over mine as well,* he thought distantly, almost wanting to laugh or cry in dark humor, but instead he simply said, "I've told you too much already. Now tell me where she is."

"Right," said the innkeeper, nervously watching those nearby. No one

201

had seemed to notice their little skirmish, or, if they had, the world needed to fissure beneath their feet, cracking and opening up to the Seven Hells for them to care. "She's… she's upstairs… second room to the right…"

Odaren twisted.

Chubby fingers gripped his arm. "If you die up there," the innkeeper said anxiously, eyes flickering to the ceiling and rooms above as if he could see the angel of death. "The Shadow King will not blame me, will he?"

"For his right hand man?" Odaren posed, feeling a greasy smile cross his face. "The Shadow King would burn this rat-infested heap to the ground and you along with it." With that he ripped his arm from the man's sweaty grip and turned to ascend the staircase, leaving the common room behind. *If I die*, he thought darkly, knowing the truth, *the Shadow King would never care.*

∗ ∗ ∗

The innkeeper's words sent a tremor beneath his skin that Odaren couldn't settle. 'If you die up there…' How many men had died before him? Yet Odaren feared the Shadow King more. He might even be watching now. The Shadow King often sent men to watch, waiting to end his life if he tripped up in any way. Maybe Odaren already had messed up. He'd given the Shadow King's name *twice* now and Halvos didn't like unnecessary attention. The fear of eyes made Odaren eager to leave the common room and he scurried up the stairs.

Resting at the top of the landing, he gripped the handrail, trying to stop his body from trembling. He couldn't stop the tremors, however, so he continued. As he reached the second room, the walls and the very air seemed to darken. He almost expected the door to come crashing open or daggers to pierce the thick oak and enter his body.

He shook his head, banishing these dark thoughts and reminded himself, *I work for the Shadow King.* Yet somehow he knew those words wouldn't be the protection they'd been from the innkeeper. If anything, he feared mentioning his master would only ensure that his blood would spill even quicker. He remembered his hand, ripped a shred of cloth from his sleeve and wound it around his palm, hiding the Shadow's Mark once more. With a heavy breath, he turned the door's grimy handle. As he did, it swung open with a slow

202

creak.

"*Enter*," a strong voice called from within.

Swallowing, feeling the raw scrape of his throat, Odaren obeyed.

The door slammed shut behind him as if shut by an imaginary gust of wind. The room was big—far bigger than he imagined possible for such a dung heap of an inn. But as he glanced around, he saw paintings on the wall of ordinary men and women, including the likeness of his portly friend, the innkeeper. On the bedside table he even glimpsed a framed picture of the innkeeper himself beside a plain-looking woman. *She'd filched the man's own room*, he surmised, amused. It didn't surprise him. The rest of the furnishings were meager, but he quickly eyed the whole room to distract himself and get his bearings. A small, round table was placed near the center of the room. Upon it sat a wooden board with a dozen meticulously carved figurines on checkered black and white poplar—cyn. A battered chest with a limp, broken lock was near it, as if dragged out, inspected, then forgotten. Draped over a coat hanger, and making the wire bend from the weight of it, was an ornate, dark armor piece of overlapping plates, lacquered a black so deep that it seemed to suck the light out from the room. A tremor of recognition shot through him. He'd seen the like of it before: Dragonborne armor. Made of metal from the depths of Yronia and wrought in the smithies of the Deep Forge, legend claimed that each piece was destroyed in the great war of the Lieon. He could hardly believe it possible, but it had to be—for the Shadow King had a few pieces as well. After taking this all in, finally Odaren's eyes lay upon the worst of all: a pile of dusky clothes and leather straps from garments before a bed.

203

Upon the rumpled bed, almost completely in the nude save for a tightly fitted pair of midnight black breeches was his quarry…

The Mistress of Shadows. Odaren gulped.

She lounged in flickering shadow. The candles of the room lay on the table and near the door—casting *him* in the orange spotlight as the center of attention. While darkness obscured her slender body, what he could glimpse made his cheeks flush, seeing a sleek, muscled figure—her silver buckle and her light-brown eyes were all that glinted from the darkness. His gaze lingered until he pulled it away, focusing on a red stain on the floor.

"Welcome," she rasped in a dark husk of a voice. There was no emotion to it—no anger, no hope, nothing. If there was anything to her tone,

Odaren noted a deep, buried note of sorrow. "Care to join me?"

If he'd flushed before, now he flushed all over, sweat soaking his skin. "I…"

There was a flare of light in the darkness of her bed as she lit a pipe and tamped down its contents. In the orange glow, he glimpsed her top and… She spoke, drawing his attention. "At a game of cyn," she said, motioning coolly to the board on the table as if it were obvious. "I saw your eyes catch on it. You can play, can't you?"

He turned his head, answering in a voice as smooth as he could muster, "I can play."

In the corner of his vision and in the faint glow of the pipe he saw her smile wistfully as smoke curled around her features. "It's been a long time since I've had anyone to play with—anyone who was my equal, at least." Her toe caught a stray piece of clothing on the floor. She brought it up, slipped it on and quietly rose. Odaren turned back and saw her in full. She'd donned a white shirt stained with sand and blood that he very much doubted was her own. It was loose and thin, hinting at her form beneath, even *more* alluring somehow, knowing what he'd glimpsed before. He swallowed the thought down, focusing again on the task at hand, imagining the Shadow King's dagger slipping into his gut and the light fading from his own eyes like that little rat he'd kicked over the edge of Narim.

"Sit," Faye commanded, pulling his attention back.

He wiped the sweat from his brow with a dirty handkerchief and meekly obliged.

She sat at the table less than an arm's length away, propping her feet up and eyeing him coolly. He took in her features—strong nose, flaring almond-shaped eyes and dark scarlet, almost chestnut colored rings of hair that fell around her tan skin. She was truly stunning. Yet where other women would have a certain air, knowing their beauty and its effect, Faye seemed to be aware and yet completely apathetic to it. "Well?" she asked. "Are you going to tell me your name? I've a feeling you know mine already. You're not Darkeye brood either, so I hope it's not Fingers, or Seven Toes, or some nonsense like that."

"*Odaren*," he managed with a gulp.

She smiled. "You know what that means in Yorin, the old tongue, do you not?"

He did. "The rat," he answered, more confidently. "Not many know the old tongue, luckily for me. My mother had a cruel sense of humor

and my father had a cruel way of not giving a damn." He wiped his damp
hands on his pants as she stared deep into his eyes—he couldn't tell if he
was simply a plaything to her or if she was genuinely intrigued by him.
He cursed his own foolishness, knowing it was the former.

"It seems we have something in common," she said at last, amused, but
her eyes had flared with a note of wrath as Odaren had said the word 'father.' *She loathes her father*, he noted, setting the morsel aside. It was another reason so many called him the King's Rat, for the scraps of valuable
information that others unknowingly cast aside, he gathered and saved for
later consumption.

"I believe we do," he answered, "Mistress of Shadows."

Faye laughed humorlessly. "Such a silly name."

"Fitting, though," he retorted, trying to gain some ground.

Again her lips curved, but it chilled him more than if she hadn't, for it
brought no warmth to her eyes. Calmly, she grabbed a short, pawn-like
figurine, the carving of a man wielding a two-handed sword, and placed it
one checkered space forward on the wood board, fitting its small peg into
a hole that kept the figurine secure. "Flattery didn't save the five men I
killed before you when they entered my room hoping for something. And
don't tell me you're not hoping for something, *Odaren*… We're always
hoping for something." Her eyes glazed dark as if seeing something painful and far away, then settled back on him like daggers.

Odaren swallowed. He decided to pull the conversation back, keeping
it more practical and less of the witty sort, which he was never good at.
"I'm here for a reason," he said bluntly.

Calmly, Faye pulled out a dagger, letting it play along her fingers nim-
bly as if it were dancing. He waited for it to cut her but it didn't. "Go on,"
she supplied.

He leaned forward. "I'm here—"

She jabbed the dagger into the table. He gazed down. It sat a hairsbreadth between the first two fingers of his right hand. *"The game,"* she
advised coldly. "Make your move first."

Odaren shook slightly. He tried to hide the tremors but it was no use.
Quickly he surveyed the board. He saw his side was already being played.
A person could play cyn alone and clearly Faye had been playing both
sides. Unfortunately, his side was losing. He was never great at cyn, nor
was he clever under pressure, but he did learn quickly and knew how to
stay alive. He moved a small man who was clutching his round, naked

belly—a piece called The Uncle—one space back, away from the line of sight of the thin figure with the two-handed sword—The Brother. He'd saved the figurine from a killing blow.

She pulled her dagger free from the wood and took a long, slow drag from her thin-stemmed pipe, letting smoke curl around her beautiful features. "I knew you had the look of an intelligent man," she commented. "I wasn't lying when I said it'd been a long time since I'd played an equal. Granted, you're a damned idiot for entering my room, and I've made no promises that I'm not going to kill you if you utter a single word I don't particularly like... I'm not known as a patient woman or one with a sunny disposition. But oddly, I think I like you, so your death would be... *unnecessary, perhaps.*" Through all of it her face was as blank as a stone.

Odaren tried to swallow, but again his throat chafed like two rocks grinding. His eyes darted, eyeing the cup at her side, feeling his throat grate again. "Mind if I...?"

She raised a brow as if daring him.

He snarled. *To hell with her and her mind games.* He snatched it up and gulped down the contents like a man dying of thirst. Long burning gulps, the liquid spilled around his mouth until he slammed it down upon the table. He opened his mouth to breathe a sigh but choked. His throat burned! "What in the seven hells did I just drink? It burns like a Devari's blade!"

"Never seen someone drink Bilch Brew so fast," she remarked. "I'm impressed and now you have my attention. Speak your peace and find my answer. But know if you lose, or if your answer displeases me in the slightest, I will wet this blade with your blood and roll your fat little body out the window and into the alley for the rats to feast upon."

Odaren was running out of time. Her voice was bored—she was growing tired of him and this was his only chance.

She made another move on the board. The second brother, a smaller man with a long flail, shuffled two spaces forward. Odaren knew his face was wet with perspiration. He saw it all like a maze before him. Her first move had been a diversionary tactic—a plan to lure the uncle, who had been protecting the father, away. If killed, the father was the only piece on the board that ended the game immediately. Fortunately, the father had to be hit twice in order to fall. His father, a bearded man wielding a wood axe, sat exposed—surrounded on both sides by the two brothers—their long weapons meant an attack from three spaces or more... The father had only two spaces on all sides.

He was trapped.

Odaren licked his lips, trying to find a way out. He looked up, deciding that if he couldn't win the game, at least he could win the conversation. Luckily, he had the trump card. "I know why you won't kill me. Your sis—"

She raised a brow and her dagger flashed, pressing against his neck. "Ah, ah, ah," she said, wagging a finger, "that's cheating. Your move first."

He swallowed, trying to speak. "But—"

The dagger pressed tighter and he winced, feeling skin peel and blood trickle. *Blood and flesh!* he cursed. His eyes scanned the board quickly, fear rising. The dagger continued to press slowly tighter until he worried his throat would be cut before he could make his move. Fear made his thoughts churn like muddy water as he tried to think of a way out… panic rising… He couldn't do it—there wasn't a way to win! He tried speaking again. "Your sis—" he choked, feeling the blade bite so deep—too deep, he feared in terror.

Suddenly the door crashed open behind him.

Faye's eyes flickered up. "Yes? Can I help you?"

"Let him go," said a voice tremulously. *The innkeeper?*

A heavy grunt echoed behind the man—the brute, Goram.

"Why would I do that?" Faye asked, head tilting.

Odaren's vision clouded. Choking out, he tried to call for help.

"If you kill him you'll bring the Shadow King's wrath upon our head."

"Will he?"

"I've heard it before, in Cloudfell," the fat man stammered. "A man bearing the was killed by a tavern's patrons. The Shadow King burned the whole tavern down, murdered every man. Then he slit their families' throats in their sleep. Kill him, and the Shadow King will kill us all." The innkeeper must have pointed to Odaren. "See for yourself. He bears the Mark."

Faye raised a single eyebrow. "Amusing. That's why you're here?" she asked Odaren and he groaned weakly.

"Well…" the innkeeper stuttered, answering in his place. "That, and he's worth more alive. Think about it… We can ransom him back to the Shadow King for a mound of gold more than he weighs!"

Faye *tsked*, disappointedly. "I'm afraid I can't do that… you see, he's lost and I'm afraid my word is my bond. I take it very seriously. He has to

207

die." Meanwhile Odaren's eyes fell to the board, tears clouding his vision. *The Child…!* Where had it been? His hand reached out for the tiny figurine, feeling its rough-hewn edges barely out of reach, attempting to pull it free from its pegged hole.

Suddenly Faye's eyes glazed, distant. "*Gray?*" she whispered, breathless.

The blade lifted Odaren higher as Faye rose, standing. Suddenly she eased the tension on her blade, letting it clatter to the table and Odaren collapsed to the floor in a gasping heap.

She spoke again, looking past Odaren, through the door and beyond. "How am I seeing you? Is it… is it truly you?"

He clutched his neck, keeping pressure to his wound as he glanced behind, but the men looked equally as baffled. *What in the Seven…* he wondered, dumbstruck. *Who was Gray?* Faye seemed to be having a conversation with someone who wasn't even there. *Was she mad?*

"It's the bloodpact, isn't it?" She laughed darkly. "I told you Farhaven would hold us to it."

Odaren scrambled backward as she stepped forward, almost on top of him, oblivious.

Faye's face darkened like a storm, recognition settling into her features. "We'll both die, won't we?" she whispered, then shook her head of scarlet hair. "But I don't even know where you are… How am I to find you?" She laughed. "No, I don't care anymore. Believe me or not, it doesn't matter. If I die, if the whole world burns… None of it matters," she seethed. Then her voice dropped to a whisper. "*Why?* Because she's dead…." Tears began to stream down her face. "You deserve more… you both do."

The innkeeper suddenly began to cackle. "Priceless. You can't be serious." He laughed again, fear fading from his face. "Don't you two see? She's mad. The Mistress of Shadows is a raving loon." Goram, the hulking mound of muscle, still looked terrified but he began to chortle alongside his master. "Quick," the fat man said, "end her life now, Goram!"

"Why?" the big man asked, stepping back.

"Think about it," the innkeeper raved. "She's the next leader of the Darkeye Clan. Whoever kills their leader, you dumb lump, inherits the crown. We'll kill her, take her head to the clan, and prove ourselves the rightful leaders…" He began to laugh maddeningly, tears forming in his eyes. "Can you imagine the wealth Darkeye's amassed stealing from the

Citadel and the people all these years? The gods have pissed on me my whole life, but finally a stroke of luck—and in the form of a madwoman."

Faye was reaching out, not speaking, but listening.

Goram asked, "Why's she like that?"

"How would I know?" the innkeeper replied. "Probably from the battle and death upon the sands, but who knows and who cares?" The innkeeper prodded him with a dagger. "Just kill her!"

Goram shook his head. "It don't seem right," the man grumbled.

"Do it, you useless mountain of flesh. Kill her quickly before she snaps out of it," the innkeeper ordered. Goram heaved a tempest of a breath and lumbered forward, wringing the grip of his iron-studded cudgel nervously. He lifted the huge bludgeon.

Odaren still clutched his throat, trying to find his voice. "No..." he pleaded in a dull croak. "Don't do it."

Goram hesitated.

"She tried to end your wretched life," the innkeeper said. "What are you complaining about, you worthless worm?"

He growled through the blood pouring over his hand. "I don't care... If you kill her, I'm as good as dead."

The innkeeper growled louder, "Ignore the fool and end her life now!"   209

"Don't go, Gray," Faye whispered, reaching out a hand, as close to a pleading voice as Odaren thought was possible from her. Despite his pain and anger, he felt a pang of sympathy.

Goram hesitated, but only for a split second as he cried out, smashing his cudgel into the oblivious woman's skull.

There was a loud crack and Odaren shielded his eyes.

Suddenly the room was still.

He looked up, opening his eyes. Faye's right arm was bent at a weird angle, dangling at her side, but then he saw Goram's chin. It had sprouted a dagger. Faye's dagger. Somehow in the time it had taken his cudgel to connect with her skull, she'd grabbed her blade from the table and stabbed it through his chin. *Quick*, Odaren thought in disbelief. How can anyone be that quick? Now, blood fountained from Goram's jaw as he worked it uselessly, trying to speak. Goram fell to his knees, rattling the floor. Slowly the big man reached for his cudgel but Faye growled and kicked it from his reach. With brutal efficiency she pulled her blade from his jaw and stabbed it into his temple. Goram fell over dead.

The innkeeper gawked. His gaze flickered up, backpedaling, raising his hands and forming slurred, panicked words. "I... I told him not to, your Mistress... I said to protect you and the fool went and—"

Faye sighed. Instead of reaching for the blade embedded in Goram's skull or bothering a reply, Faye pulled a long curved dagger from her boot. The action was slow, calm and almost lethargic. No, Odaren thought. As a child he'd plucked the legs from an ant, one by one, slowly, taking his time with torturing the tiny insect and amusing himself with its helplessness. This was the same. The innkeeper backpedaled, breathless and blubbering. "Please, no! Oh gods show mercy. I didn't... I never..." When Faye didn't slow, the fat man stopped his pleas and turned only to stumble and fall. Crying out, he shambled to his feet and sprinted for the door. Odaren heard a soft whistle, watching as the blade flipped end over end and embedded itself into the back of his skull. The innkeeper flopped onto his belly, rumbling the floorboards, lifeless.

Cradling her shattered arm, Faye now grabbed the dagger in Goram's skull, freeing it with a sharp tug and a spurt of blood, then turned. She neared Odaren and knelt, nearly a breath away, fingering her dagger. Odaren was speechless, feeling something warm running down his pants, knowing he'd just wet himself.

He couldn't speak, but knew even if he could, it was worthless.

This woman was death.

He was right from the very start.

Faye's eyes fell to the board beneath her, eyeing the pieces.

He knew what she looked at. In the moment before his collapse, he'd placed the child into the peg-hole in front of the two brothers. The move was called 'Mother's Safety.' It wasn't a perfect move, but it meant she'd lose her second most important piece and buy his Father a stay of execution. 'Mother's Safety' was the only glimmer of goodness in a game of utter brutality and familial bloodshed.

"You know that doesn't mean I lose..." she said, almost disappointed. "If I kill the child, I lose my mother, but I can still win without her."

He shook his head, still unable to speak.

"You were hoping I won't kill the child, because why...? You believe I have a conscience?" She sighed, sounding weary. "You're several days too late for that, my little rat." Her words turned dark and hollow. "If I had a conscience, it died... along with my sister."

She lifted her dagger.

Wordlessly he fumbled, grabbing the wooden figurine and placing it

210

in her limp hand. She uncurled her fist with a grimace, seeing that the child was a small girl. Faye eyed him, confused, but looked searchingly into his eyes, trying to grasp his meaning.

And Odaren spoke, a raw rasp, "Your sister… still lives."

A thousand emotions flashed across her eyes: sorrow, pain, confusion, but above all, hate and rage. She raised her blade, thick syrupy blood still dripping from its point. "If… you're lying to me…" Her voice cracked, the threat of danger all but cutting into Odaren.

He fell into a fit of coughs, clutching his neck.

She rose, leaving him. Suddenly she returned, throwing him a cloth. He snatched it. "Apply pressure. You'll live," she said offhandedly, and then beneath her breath, menacingly, "*You better live.* At least until I find out if you're telling the truth or not. And if not? I'd say may the gods help you, but even they won't stop my blade."

He rattled his head, feeling his cheeks shake. "I…" he coughed. "I swear it—upon my life."

Faye laughed. "Let's hope that means more than mine," she answered, lugging him to his feet. With alacrity, using her foot as a wedge, she ripped the bed sheets and wound a makeshift sling around her shoulder, cradling her arm. "Tie," she ordered. He did and she nodded in satisfaction, and then grabbed her armor from the metal stand, throwing it into his arms. He grunted but it was surprisingly light. She flung her brown pack over her good shoulder, then pulled a wet-looking black sack from beneath the bed and turned to him. "Shall we?"

He nodded dumbly.

And together they left the room, stepping over the bodies, as dark blood pooled around his boots on the rough timber. Following her back, Odaren shut his eyes and swallowed his fear, throat still dry as bone. Juggling his saddlebags and the Dragonborne armor, he followed her, knowing where he took her would be her end… And yet it would be his beginning.

If he could get her there…

Still he followed her, blood sprouting from his neck as they entered the murky stables. And he realized whom he followed, and it wasn't the Mistress of Shadows.

It was the Mistress of Death.

And she was going to meet the one man who was practically death himself.

Light save the world when that happened. Odaren gulped. *Light save me.*

211

Reborn

B alder walked along the white, outer stone wall examining Queenstown's burgeoning defenses.

He was doing his rounds as he always did each morning, but today it was merely a distraction. As usual, a flock of people trailed him as he moved—advisors, masons-in-training, woodworkers, a blacksmith and a few messengers to relay important information to Karil if need be. He always had a thousand things to say, but today, Balder was silent as he marched with his hands clasped behind his back, eyes scanning. He admired the smooth seamless joints and was impressed by the plane of the long horizontal course. It would be a strong wall—perhaps the best he'd ever made. He felt pride swelling in his chest, but his fear was sharp-er, louder. Time was running thin… Balder glanced up. The Forest of Aenor was dark today and looked like sinister storm clouds with its canopy shrouded in mist that poured from its maw.

Balder was shook from his reverie as a servant brought forth a sample of mortar on a wooden plate. As customary, Balder rubbed the mortar between his thumb and forefinger, feeling its grittiness, then sniffed it. At last he put his tongue to it, tasting. "Too much lime," he said aloud at last. "This city will last for ages. We can't have water and wind stripping it down before its time." And he gave instructions to add more white clay to the mortar. But his words were absent, his mind troubled—when, over the shoulders of his entourage, he saw a peculiar figure sitting on a stone bench.

"That'll do for now," Balder announced, spirits lifting. "Same time same place tomorrow and don't dawdle." Each glanced at one another, looking slightly confused at the sudden dismissal. But upon hearing his kind, curt tone, they left silently to see to their duties.

Balder's attention was no longer on his attendants. He neared and sat at Finn's side.

Reaver Finn was silent as usual; his dour mood was an ever-present raincloud floating over his head. As soon as Balder sat at Finn's side, he felt stares. Men and women passed furtive glances towards him as he sat next to the brooding Reaver. The people of Queenstown feared Reaver Finn and Balder couldn't blame them. The darkness in Finn's eyes and the way he moved about the camp like a shadow didn't make the Reaver seem the friendly sort. He half-expected Reaver Finn to comment on the stares but he didn't. Instead the man sat with his hands folded neatly upon his scarlet robes, which were still dirty as if they hadn't been washed since the day he arrived in that wagon from Farbs—a wagon filled with a chest of gold that gave them the means to build their city and wage war on the foul Dryan.

Finn's blue eyes gazed into the unknown. Balder coughed and settled back, pretending to watch the nothingness as well.

"You aren't as clever as you look," Finn said suddenly, feigning interest in a group of elves who were stoking a large kiln and feeding in white-stone bricks that made a marblesque finish. That clay was a rare find with both beauty and strength—a mason's dream.

"Hmm? Not clever? How so?"

"Sitting next to me marks you both fool and outcast."

"Ah," he nodded, as if thoughtful and unaware of this.

"Master Architect and fallen Reaver, sitting side-by-side," Finn explained more slowly. "Surely you see their gazes, unless you're merely a blind fool."

Balder shrugged, throwing his hands behind his head and leaning back against a vine-covered wall. Already life began to crawl over those newly finished constructs—lichen along the benches, vines along the nearby fountain, moss between the stones and grotto. Verdant moss crawled up an unfinished square-faced building that would soon become town hall— each flora in vivid hues of blue, red and green. Whether it was the elves' work or the close proximity to the Forest of Aenor, Balder wasn't certain,

213

but nature followed the budding city like a lover, giving it a sense of vitality and animation. He enjoyed it and it seemed to mimic the life of those who inhabited the camp.

Nearby men stripped to their dark breeches tossed jokes as they worked the roaring kiln—the kiln of his design. It was built on a slope to allow for a better draft, with a series of chambers to allow for more efficient firing times. The men were stacking wood for the front firebox while sweat glistened upon their bare chests. Balder watched several women pass, casting flirtatious smiles at the shirtless men then giggling as the men noticed. As per Karil's orders, many of these women did the same jobs as men and vice versa—men cleaned laundry by the river while women helped haul stones from the northern quarries—all needed to be strong if they were to succeed in retaking Eldas from the tyrannical Dryan.

Balder pulled away from the sights, watching as more elves and humans cast sidelong glances at the strange pair. "Let them talk. I care not for foolish rumors. I care more about the true character of a man—a character defined by his actions."

"Actions..." Finn whispered, then fell silent.

"If you remember, or unless you were still in that dark void of yours, it wasn't two weeks ago I was the camp rapscallion—a beggar and a drunk."

Finn took in the bright pin on Balder's chest. "And that pin changes you?"

His tone was neutral, but Balder knew what he was getting at. "This? Simply a trinket, but in here is what matters." He tapped his skull meaningfully. "When others believe in you, we tend to believe in ourselves."

"And what or who believed in you?"

"Karil. A queen's word can change a lot of things," Balder said offhandedly. "Today a drunk, tomorrow a Master Architect... Today a fallen Reaver, tomorrow the town healer. Or head sorcerer of war or some such, if that's your kind of thing."

Finn turned silent again.

Balder cursed inwardly. He'd pressed too sharply, too quickly. The man was pricklier than a maggleberry pear.

A woman with a tight black bun on her head and pretty eyes that reminded him of Hitomi, without the keen dark glint, came over to hand him a bundle of reports from the north end of camp. He heard her wish him "good morning" and he replied back offhandedly. From the corner of his gaze, he saw the woman hide a shiver as she gave Reaver Finn a

214

tight-lipped, fearful greeting.

Finn said nothing.

Scanning the reports, Balder sighed.

The northern wall's well had run dry, which meant no more bricks... The stone quarry in the northeast was nearly used up—they'd have to search other avenues but he'd known that was coming—and there were several questions for the Master Architect to answer.

Ashfall, oak or marlberry trees for the buildings?

A combination of gypsum or zanic for more mortar?

Ashlar masonry versus rustication for the outer bailey walls?

The last one was preposterous. Rustication? Who on earth would propose that? It was a fine looking pattern, but as structurally sound as a paper fort compared to ashlar. Not much good against Dryan and an army of dark elves. He took a ledger from the woman and ticked off a few notes on each report, then handed them back.

She inclined her head respectfully. "Master Architect." And her eyes glinted for a mere moment—a flash of... attraction? Balder shook his head as she wove back into the camp's bustle, heading north. Perhaps it was the title? Men with power were a magnet for women... but it had been a long time since he'd gotten looks like that. His mustache and grizzled cheeks, though a distinguished gray, were beginning to seem more like an old man's and less like a dashing gentleman on the cusp of aging. He knew his eyes still held a sharpness, but the lines about them had grown just as sharp throughout the years. And the last time he gazed at himself in a water reflection there was a droop, a slight one, but a droop nonetheless, beneath his dark blue gaze. The look from the younger woman, only thirty or so years in age—young especially for Farhaven—made him sniff in amusement.

"You've an admirer," Finn spoke.

Balder turned to the man but the Reaver's face was grave, as if he was a statue that had come to life to speak, then returned to stone once more. "I believe she reads my immaturity, and not my wrinkles, as an identifier of my age."

"How old are you?" asked Finn.

Balder grumbled, raising a brow. "How old are *you?*"

"Seventy-seven summers," the Reaver said unemotionally.

Balder grumbled louder and watched a group of women pass with flowers in their hair carrying more wood for the kiln. "Now I'm surely not telling you," he said and blew a heavy gust of air out his nose and mouth. "That's downright preposterous. You look as if you could be my son, or grandson for that matter, and you're—" he stopped himself. "*Older* than me."

Finn twisted to him and the man's dark brown eyes took on that strange glimmer—that unreadable, faraway look many threaders got when summoning the spark—as if looking through Balder to Eldas a hundred miles away and then beyond. Balder squirmed beneath his gaze. Then his skin pricked, giving him goosebumps. "Seventy-one," said Finn. "You're seventy-one."

Balder's teeth gnashed. "That… you…." he began then laughed, frustration seeping out of him. "That's cheating, you know, using the spark. Not all of us can thread, after all. Though I am curious how you can tell such a thing."

"Flesh," said the man. "I can read it, not in your wrinkles but in the skin itself. The very tissue of humans holds a record of their age. It's an ancient threading that not many know anymore—I might be the last." He hesitated. "I learned it from a woman more talented than any I've ever known." The Reaver's eyes turned glassy, then he changed the subject. "Regardless, I believe true age is gauged in the eyes—hoary and fogged or clear and sharp."

"And mine?"

"A man of much younger years," he said frankly.

Balder scrubbed his stubble. "A compliment from a Reaver. I'll remember that. This woman, she must have received your silver tongue as well. Where's she now?"

Finn's eyes roiled in pain, sorrow and anger, but then settled again in the distance. He rose, folding his arms in the sleeves of his dusty scarlet robes. "Best of luck with your kingdom, stonemason. I'm afraid you'll need it." With that he stalked off, leaving Balder alone.

Balder sighed. "You're an old fool, indeed, Balder." His comment had clearly opened the gaping, raw wound in Finn he'd been hoping to avoid. Instead, he'd jabbed his finger in the man's pain with lighthearted ignorance. Balder couldn't explain it, but there was something in Finn that drew him in and made him curious and determined to help the man. He only hoped he hadn't blown his chance.

* * *

A few days later, Balder found Finn again, sitting beneath the shade of a Silveroot tree. Finn's eyes were closed in meditation, his face placid. Careful not to disturb him, Balder wordlessly plopped himself down at the Reaver's side. Moments passed and Balder distracted himself, watching the buildings—*his* buildings—the elves and the camp's usual flurry of activity. He grew bored and began to hum. It was a catchy little ditty. While he didn't expect the Reaver to sing along, part of him hoped Finn would shake his head or even berate Balder for disrupting his peaceful trance, but instead Finn's eyes remained shut, seeming unaffected. His arsenal far from depleted, Balder got out a bundle of fruit and offered a piece to Finn. He waved the ripe combersul before the man's nose, knowing Finn could sense his gesture, even with eyes closed, but still he said nothing.

Balder shrugged and bit into the fruit just as there was a spark of commotion. He knew who it was before he saw him: Lucky, the boy otherwise known as the beloved 'Hero of Aenor.' The eight-year-old had arrived only a month ago alongside the Gray's shipment of gold to aid Karil's army in the battle against the nefarious Dryan—the dark elf who murdered Karil's father and now ruled Eldas, the Great Kingdom of Leaf, home of the elves. Within that short span of time, Lucky wormed his way into the townspeople's hearts *and* Balder's with his antics and jovial nature. When their task seemed impossible—other Great Kingdoms turning a deaf ear to their cause or Dryan's dark reach seemed too vast—Lucky's boyish charm was a ray of light. The boy now barreled down the dirt street, weaving through humans and elves. Balder felt a smile tug at his lips. Despite a handsome golden cloak that wavered behind Lucky—a gift from Queen Karil to the Hero of Aenor —Lucky's blond hair was messier than a tuft bird's and his white ruffled shirt was still smeared in dirt and grime. Balder could sense he'd been a street urchin or cutpurse before he was given purpose and life. All people needed a purpose. Someone had done that for Lucky, Karil had done it for him and someone needed to do it for Finn… But he had a feeling the Reaver would be tougher to crack than a Landerian seal.

Breathless, Lucky landed at his feet.

"Whoa there, lad, slow down. You look as if the Ronin are nipping at your heels," he said, then realized how that phrase didn't have the same meaning anymore—the Ronin were no longer the evil all the land feared. The Ronin, legends of a different age, thought to have fallen and believed

217

to have nearly destroyed the world, had turned out to be heroes. It was the Kage, nine imposters posing as the Ronin who had done the real destruction.

Of course, much of the world still didn't know that. And Balder glimpsed what lay ahead for Gray... Finding the rest of the Ronin and proving to the world that they weren't the true evil was a grand task indeed. He swallowed the lump in his throat, now suddenly glad for the task of building a Great Kingdom from nothing. By comparison, *his* job didn't seem so daunting. Still... Whatever spawned the Kage—that's what kept Balder awake and sweating at night.

Thoughts of Gray made Balder miss the young lad. Perhaps that's why he'd apprenticed Lucky? He wasn't sure.

Balder shook himself, casting aside his heavy thoughts, seeing Lucky anxiously prancing on his toes as if he were about to wet his trousers. "What's got you in such a ruckus now?"

"I'm late! You said an apprentice is never late for his master."

"Did I?"

Lucky nodded, still trying to catch his breath. He looked to Finn. "Hi, Finn."

Finn said nothing but he nodded amidst his trance.

Balder growled to himself. *All my tactics and charm and Lucky gets the only acknowledgment. Should've figured.*

Lucky turned back to Balder. "Well?" he asked excitedly.

Balder scratched his chin. "Right. First lesson," he said, raising a weathered finger emphatically, "a good leader knows how to follow and a good teacher knows how to be a student."

The boy scratched his head, confused. "Leaders following and teachers... studenting? Why would a leader want to follow? I don't get it."

"You will," said Balder. "For now, why don't you gather Entrius's reports on the southern wall?"

Lucky looked disappointed. "But today you promised to teach me bonds and seals and—"

"—in time, my good boy, in time."

With a sigh the boy turned, then paused. "What's inside Drymaus Forest, Balder?"

"Why do you ask?"

Then, as if a dam had been broken, Lucky purged his thoughts in a long, breathless deluge. "I heard there's this grove where dryads sing to trees, making them stronger, and they turn into heartwoods. *And heart-woods'* wood is harder than steel. Harder than *anything*. Is that true? If so, you could make the city's walls out of it. That's what the Gates of Eldas are, aren't they? If we made Queenstown out of it, then nobody could ever knock our walls down!"

Balder narrowed his gaze. "Who told you all this?"

"Entrius," Lucky said sheepishly. "And Mistress Hitomi has a piece of it too for her bar, but she won't let me touch it. She says that I'll 'make it all dirty with my grubby paws'—but I think it's magical, like Dared. I don't think anything can hurt it. I see it glowing purple at night. And then I thought about you and the city and our defenses. We can use it, can't we?"

Balder couldn't hide his smile. He liked the way the boy thought. Of course, he wouldn't enter Drymaus Forest if he had a sword pointed to his back, and perhaps not even then. But he didn't want to dash Lucky's dreams or enthusiasm. "You're getting ahead of yourself. I'll answer that and your typical thousand questions when you return with my reports."

Lucky sighed but ran off, giving a quick goodbye to Finn.

"Quite the army you have," said a sudden voice at his side.

Balder didn't turn—as if looking would spook Finn like a reclusive and mythical phox peeking its head from a burrow. Instead he just kept watching the swarm of builders, movers and messengers move about, creating a city from nothing. "It's not Rydel's," he confessed, "but it'll do."

They sat in silence for a while longer. Balder was content. He loved talking, but he knew better than any that a crowbar wouldn't pry a man's heart—but silence and compassion would... And where those failed, alcohol. He opened up a canvas pack and extracted a ceramic jar, offering Finn the container of *hame*—fermented bark from a dola tree.

Finn cracked an eyelid, gazing at the *hame* sidelong. "You're not one for giving up easily, are you?"

"Not my nature. Nor, I believe, yours."

The Reaver's features were smooth, but he accepted it and took a long draught, then handed it back. "Good *hame*."

Balder grunted his thanks.

"What's your grand plan?" Finn asked, watching the flurry. "To build a new Great Kingdom from scratch?"

Balder laughed. "Something like that. At least, the Master Architect was charged with that task..." *How to bring up the death of the man's love*… He'd already done it once and Finn had shut down and left him further behind than where he started.

"Impressive," said Finn. It sounded hollow, like a man closing down before even opening.

"It's a beginning," said Balder. "We all need a new beginning…"

Finn turned to him as if reading Balder's mind, but his tan face was as emotionless as always.

Balder set the ceramic vase down. He scrubbed his hands together, feeling the soft clay of dried mortar rub and fall onto the new shoots of grass beneath his feet. "A new beginning… Think about it." He stood up, but Finn grabbed his arm. Balder hesitated. He looked down at the Reaver's hand. *Calloused? A swordsman? Odd…*

"Wait…" said Finn, a tenor of something that wasn't hopelessness in his voice. "What do you want from me?"

"Live. You've grieved, now it's time to stand back up," Balder said.

Finn sighed. "I understand. If I'm some sort a nuisance or a blight on your little camp, I'll leave."

"This isn't about us. Though we could use you—light knows what a Reaver of your ability could do around this place. It's about you. Moping and acting as if you're already dead."

"You don't know what I've lost," he said, a hard edge to his voice.

Smart Balder. Taunt a Reaver. But Balder couldn't help it. "Look up from your own grief, Finn," he said and then eyed the villagers who moved carrying a long line of bricks, elves wheeling barrows of clay and wood. Many carried an extra, unseen weight on their shoulders of loved ones lost in Daerval, or of lives left behind, but they all moved with purpose. And there was laughter too. "We've all lost something. Every one of us. What we do next is what matters." He sighed, his vision fogged for a moment, lost in memories. "I see that gleam in your eyes. To destroy everything in your path or to slip, sinking into the darkest hole you can find. But what you don't know is that it doesn't last. You don't want to hear this now, but you will heal. The wound upon your heart won't fade, not completely, perhaps not ever… I can't promise you it will. What I can promise you is that it *will* heal, then scar. But most importantly, you'll live. How it heals is up to you… Some heal with an anger like a splinter beneath their skin, some heal disillusioned by the world, and rarest yet, some heal and live more fully than ever before. Perhaps for those they lost or perhaps because they realize—why live any other way? What does sitting in darkness serve you or anyone else? Truly, the greatest loss can be the greatest gift, but it's up to you."

Finn played with something in his hand, touching it tenderly. It looked like a strip of a Reaver's scarlet cloth. *Was it hers?* Balder wondered. At last Finn looked up. Though his eyes still held sorrow, a thin, faint smile traced his lips. "And here I thought you were just some drunkard with a shiny pin and a god complex."

"You got the first part right."

"And the second?"

"I'm not sure about playing at god. We've got enough legends in this world now for that kind of thing—I'll leave that to Reavers, Arbiters and Ronin. But Karil charged me with a task and I'll see it through. We all have our duties. This will become a Great Kingdom."

Just then a young elf messenger came running up. The youth spoke frantically, voice quavering with terror, "Master Architect, they've come! They're here! Dear spirits, I saw it for myself in the form of demons possessing trees come to life. I—"

"Who's come?" Finn asked, rising, cutting him off. "Speak cleanly!"

"The gates," he breathed in terror. "Dryan! We're under attack!"

"Which gate?" Balder asked, gripping the elf firmly.

As he spoke there was an echoing crack, like two tons of wood splintering upon stone, and the man didn't need to finish his sentence. Balder, Finn, even the heavens themselves heard the direction of that terrible sound.

The Southern Gate.

Of course.

And Balder ran, hearing faint cries in the distance, with only one thought on his mind.

Lucky.

221

An Apprentice Stonemason

Lucky donned his clothes quickly—a faded white shirt and brown britches. Both were clean and pressed, despite his best efforts. He bolted down the staircase, bubbling with excitement for today was his first day as Balder's apprentice. He took the stairs two at a time and had a flashing memory.

"Tomorrow begins your training!" Balder announced. "You are hereby anointed to Master Architect's apprentice."

Lucky beamed, then hesitated, confused. "Um, what's an architect do anyway?"

"An architect, or at least a good one," he said, holding up a weathered finger, "is someone who can grasp the big picture and sweats the details."

Lucky scratched his head. "Both? Sounds hard."

Balder grunted. "Tell me about it. But what other job compares? We give shape and structure to the world around us... We build buildings that comprise cities, and cities that comprise kingdoms, and kingdoms that comprise the world. The world, Lucky. And every edifice you create, if you do it right, will last a thousand years. So, many years after you're gone, men and women will look to your work with awe, and wonder who the man behind the stone was and what life they lived. You are ready for that kind of responsibility, aren't you?"

Lucky gulped then nodded, more faintly.

As Lucky took the last few stairs, he glanced around the inn.

The inn was alive as it usually was, even for this early in the day. Lucky liked it that way. It felt like home, like the bustling streets of Farbs. Plus, he liked all the people that worked for Mistress Hitomi. Elves, humans, villagers, everyone seemed to drift toward the innkeeper like bees to honey. The only person with more pull in the camp was Karil herself, the elf queen. A queen! Lucky shivered. He still couldn't believe it.

But today Hitomi was nowhere to be seen.

He crossed the nearly built common room, weaving through elves carrying large beams and villagers hammering in a bannister that would wrap around a large center platform where singers, musicians and all sorts of performers would play. The rest of the inn was equally impressive with over a dozen stained glass windows and a huge bar, made of beautiful purple wood called Heartwood by the elves, wrapped around the whole back of the inn. A vaulted ceiling with heavy beams held up the *five*-story inn. "If I'm going to build this, it's going to be an inn to make other inns blush," Hitomi had told him once.

"Stop right there."

Lucky skidded to a halt, freezing.

He knew whose voice that was.

Lucky turned red, still facing the door. He didn't want to show his face. He could feel her stern eyes on his back, a glare that pierced flesh and bone. All work in the inn seemed to slow as ears began to eavesdrop—the clank of hammers and the chatter of pleasant work subsiding. *Does she know I've been stealing sweetcakes from the pantry?* he wondered fearfully. "Morning, my lady," he said, "I can't talk. I—"

"Don't 'morning, my lady' me," she said sternly. He twisted to look at her. She was surrounded by her standard army of workers. "You've been skirting me for two days now, flitting in and out of here at all hours. It's not becoming of a boy your age. You're too old to act like a puppy without a leash. A boy your age needs boundaries, rules."

Lucky scowled, reddening in anger, his hands balling into fists. But before he could retort, Hitomi held up a hand.

She seemed to read him and her stern face softened. She approached and *tsked*. He looked up to her. Her frown slipped, replaced by a smile, and with that smile, Lucky's ire faded. Hitomi smoothed his blond hair. "I was worried about you, that's all. You've heard the reports. I know you've a keen ear—the scouts of Dryan are getting too close. I fear..." She shook her head but her eyes still looked troubled.

223

"I'm sorry," Lucky said, and he did feel it. He knew she was just worried for him.

"Tell me then, where've you been sneaking off to?"

"Balder," he confessed.

A flash of emotion passed Hitomi's face. Her lips became an angry flat line, but something in her looked... did her cheeks color? "You know how I feel about that man, Lucky."

"He's not bad," Lucky said, his anger returning. "You're wrong about him. He's good. You're just... you just are..." *Did he dare?*

"I am what?" she asked, arching a thin brow while big brown eyes bored into him.

"Too stubborn," he said at last. "Just like him."

Most surprisingly, Hitomi didn't look angry as he expected. Instead, she looked amused. She laughed and cupped his cheek. "You're too bloody astute for your own good." She sighed. "I suppose I've been a tad... *strong-handed* with you and Piper of late. But know I only do it for your own good." Her workers waited behind her patiently like a shadow. "Go on then, Hero of Aenor. But be careful," she added. "The woods, they don't feel safe today."

Lucky nodded excitedly, turning to leave.

"And Lucky?"

He paused at the door.

"Tell Balder... Tell him... Tell him hello from me."

Lucky shrugged, but then leapt to action. *Adults are strange,* he thought.

He reached Balder. He was sitting beside Finn. Unfortunately, Balder told him off—redirecting him to go see Entrius, one of the chief builders under Balder's command. *Ugh... that elf was the worst.* Then Lucky winced, feeling bad. Entrius wasn't *that* terrible. The elf was always nice to him, but Entrius always made him do boring tasks like stacking bricks. Lucky wanted to do more; he wanted to learn what made a kingdom a kingdom. He wanted to do big things like heroes did in stories. Real heroes. Not just pretend ones like he felt he was sometimes. And real heroes didn't stack bricks. But he obeyed Balder and moved off.

As Lucky ran, men and women tossed him friendly smiles and waved in greeting. A lot of people knew him. Word had gotten out that he was the one who had brought all the gold. He'd helped *a little* in spreading that. And he liked talking to people, too.

Lucky found Entrius surrounded by humans and elves at the edge of the camp. *Belegrun Fields*, it'd been called. Now it was all the City of Aenor, called 'Queenstown' by most, after Karil of course. She was the heart of this space, so it only made sense. He approached.

The elf was tall and with hair that was white for his age, Entrius looked older than he was, Lucky wasn't sure what made an elf old, though. Twenty, maybe thirty years? That was pretty old. Entrius spotted him over the heads of others and parted the crowds. "There's my little thief! Come with orders from Balder, have we?"

Lucky colored, but nodded.

Entrius was the only one who knew about Lucky's habit of filching things. Lucky tried to wean himself off, but he still occasionally pocketed things. A chisel with a bright gleam to it or an abandoned pocket watch—nothing *pricey*—but somehow Entrius always caught him. Still, it surprised him that Entrius hadn't ratted him out to Balder yet. Maybe he was waiting. But that'd be odd. Entrius was always nice to him, especially for an elf. The elf clasped his shoulder. "Come, I've something to show you today, Lucky."

Most went back about their business, but a small group followed as Entrius led him to the edge of the wall. It was a long white stone barricade several feet high. Not much taller than Lucky was. But it was growing by the day. Soon Balder said Aenor would rival Eldas or even *Farbs*.

Entrius knelt beside the wall then pointed to something. Lucky saw a small bug with a hard green back, blue spots and six legs. Lucky didn't see anything special about the silly bug and he grew annoyed. He was still disappointed by Balder's dismissal so he grumbled, crossing his arms. "A bug, Entri?" he said, using his nickname for the elf. He didn't like calling the elf by his full name. It was hard. "I'm not five, you know? I'm *eight*. Bugs are for little kids."

Entrius nodded dutifully. It was that kind of tight-lipped nod that adults gave him when they were trying to hold back a smile. It only made him more angry. "My apologies, my liege. I did not mean to make you feel inferior. But do you see anything special about this bug?"

Lucky squinted, watching the creature walk over smooth seamless stone. The stone was more interesting than the bug. Balder had showed him how hard it was to create such seamless masonry—a Landerian seal, he called it. He shook his head at last, frustrated. "No. It's just a dumb ol' bug."

225

Entrius folded his arms, looking disappointed, and arched a thin brow. Yet, his face still held a certain composure, smooth and unruffled, like all elves. "You aren't looking very hard. A good stonemason can see the tiny cracks in even Balder's near-faultless masonry."

He reddened, angry. "Balder doesn't—"

"—It was an expression," said Entrius. "Look closer," he advised.

And as he prodded the bug, it suddenly turned red, green, blue and yellow. Lucky gasped as the creature unfolded wings the size of his face and landed upon his outstretched hand. It flapped its wings that looked like big leaves, its tiny feelers tickling Lucky's skin then suddenly... it disappeared. Lucky squinted, and then he saw it. No, it hadn't disappeared, but it was the same color as his skin! Exactly the same color! Only the outline of its wings and its tiny black eyes made it obvious it hadn't moved. That, and the tickling feelers. "How did it do that?"

"There are frostbugs, metalbugs, even windbugs but this is a leafbug. It can blend with anything it touches. And it bonds with whomever touches the leafbug first. It's yours now, until you release it."

Lucky smiled up at the elf, opening his mouth when—

There was a crack from the woods, and Lucky and Entrius twisted.

"What was that?" Lucky asked.

The tall elf shook his head, eyes squinting, as if trying to see within the darkened forest several hundred feet away. "I'm not sure..." He turned to one of his followers, a stick-thin human woman with curly hair and pouty lips. "Find Rydel. At once," he commanded. The woman nodded and was turning to leave when the ground rumbled. Lucky rose, stepping forward. The leafbug flitted onto his shoulder, as if also watching, when the woods rattled once more.

A roar sounded. It shook the trees and birds took to air as huge creatures stomped forth out of the woods. Lucky gulped in terror.

An Old Friend

Odaren kicked his feet up, watching Faye in the corner like a rabid lion waiting to bite. Her arm was still cradled in her makeshift bandage, but she hadn't made a single moan or wince of pain since it happened. He could hardly believe it. He'd seen *bone* sticking out, and yet she treated it like a sprain or a bad bruise. Even now, the Mistress of Shadows limply gripped a hunk of wood with her bad hand, cutting with the other.

She made smooth strokes, whittling something he couldn't see. It reminded him of that strange boy in the shadows of Narim who'd eaten the rat. He watched her the same way—like a creature he didn't understand, and one without a leash. He liked to think he *was* that leash. He imagined that she wouldn't kill him because he was guiding her to her sister, but he knew that was a foolish notion and it was the reason he slept with his eyes open.

He remembered her ruthlessly killing the innkeeper and his hired muscle, dispatching them with the ease of a practiced butcher chopping up a fresh carcass. The image of Goram fountaining blood from his chin and the innkeeper's terror before he died kept replaying in Odaren's mind. No, Odaren didn't feel so safe. Worst yet, he'd seen true evil, but Faye was different. Her moods flickered, changing constantly. It was like she was a hundred different people, impossible to predict from one moment to the next. In one breath, Faye seemed absolutely apathetic, then in another she was dark and violent, and then every mood in between. In their brief journey thus far, occasionally, he thought he spotted something more lurking behind her eyes—a rare glimmer. Something like humanity or kindness. *No.* He snorted to himself. Not kindness. He was being hopeful again. This was a woman who would quirk a brow at that word and question its meaning. Still, she hadn't killed him yet. That was something, wasn't it?

Odaren took an uneven breath, feeling his damp palms. He consoled himself with the notion that if Faye wanted him dead, she would have done it by now. But instead of sounding truthful, Odaren knew he was being profoundly optimistic. He growled, but she didn't look up from her whittling. He wanted to ask her, to shout at her, '*Are you going to kill me? Do it already if so, because this waiting grates on me.*' But Odaren was too much a coward to say those things. After all, he liked living. Well, not so much that he *liked* living, but that death scared him. Terrified him even. And so he licked his lips and continued to watch her—a black cat in the corner of the room, haughtily ignoring a cornered, plump rat.

"Where is my sister being held?" she asked abruptly from the shadows.

It was the question he'd been waiting for. He clutched his pant legs, fingers gripping his thigh in fear, but forced himself to look out the window as if apathetic—as if the answer didn't matter and as though his usefulness extended beyond his next words. He watched the slow rattle of carts on the well-paved streets, the orange glow of street lanterns and the steady stream of well-dressed people, a surprising majority of them wearing the black garb of the guard with the orange flame upon their leather chest.

It was the second day of their journey. They were in a town just north of Farbs called Abernathy's Crossing, but all called the middling port town simply Aberton, or in fearful whispers, *Deathville*—its title bestowed by thieves.

Because it was the only outlying town and fief of Farbs, Aberton received a small but steady stream of revenue from the Great Kingdom of Fire. And it put its coin to use. The town was well known for its strict laws and stricter folk. Unlike Farbs, a caught thief didn't lose his hand in Aberton—he lost his life. Worse yet, the small size of the town made it easy for the horde of guards to patrol all the shadowy corners. It was a thief's nightmare and it made Odaren's skin crawl, imagining over and over the door to their small room bursting open and guards carting him off to a dark cellar or a short rope. He rubbed his bandaged throat, feeling the coarse twinge already.

A husky voice cleared her throat and he startled in his chair, nearly tipping over.

"Daydreaming?" she asked—again her voice flitted between amusement and anger, a baffling mixture. Yet since he'd told her of her sister and how she still lived, Faye didn't hold much amusement. In fact, she'd barely talked, her eyes instead speaking for her, roiling with wrath and questions.

"I..." he swallowed. "I was just wondering what we're doing in Aberton," he said, changing the topic, hoping she'd forgotten her original line of questioning. "It's not the safest place for persons such as us." *Safer still to hide us in the Citadel or in a pit of Devari,* he added wryly in his own head.

"Aberton is a wretched place, but it suits my needs," she countered.

"But—"

"—you aren't very good at this," Faye interjected.

He shook his head. "At what?"

"At manipulating the conversation," she said dryly, making a long stroke on her carving. "Where are we headed and what's your plan?"

He fumbled, realizing he was a fool. Perhaps if he'd conducted a long convoluted answer, a lie about how he was going to aid her. He could have said he knew secret passages to the Shadow King's lair and special passwords, then she would see his usefulness and—

Faye sighed. "—I know we're headed to the Shadow King, to Narim, Odaren—to the heart of his lair. I knew it almost as soon as I saw you." She gestured offhandedly to his boots with her dagger. "In your laces is Mireweed. It's a deadly poison, second only to Brisbane, that I hear the Shadow King has a fondness for, of which he grows in his personal garden in the hub of Narim, in the Black Hive."

"If you know so much, then what are you asking me for?" he snapped.

"Because," Faye replied darkly, "As we both know, I'm looking for a reason not to slit your throat and leave you behind," she said, then kinder, "I'm trying to find your usefulness, Odaren."

He swallowed, softening his tone. "What... what do you want to know?"

"He plans to kill me, doesn't he?" she asked.

The candles flickered in the room. Odaren's throat went dry once

229

more and he watched her light brown eyes.

"I figured," she replied. "It seems a common thread. If he kills me, he will take over the Darkeye clan and become their leader, just like our fat friend back in Farbs had planned to do when I—" she paused, trailing off, then shook herself and turned to him, "—but what I haven't figured out, my little rat, is what do you get out of all this? What is your grand prize for delivering my head to the Shadow King? Gold? Fame?" Her eyes smiled but held no warmth. "Women?"

Odaren licked his lips, watching the steady stream outside the window. "My life," he answered at last, simply, honestly.

Out of the corner of his eye, he felt her watching him. She settled back into her chair with a small smile, and he wondered if his honesty had just saved his life for once. But her answer came from the darkness, lethargic. "Amusing. The life of a rat... I wonder... how much is it really worth saving?"

Her answer cut him to his core. He felt dizzy.

Suddenly she rose, dropping her wood object. He saw it now. A *pipe?* Faye snatched her heavy black cloak from the wall with her good arm, throwing it around her shoulders and heading to the door.

"Where are you going?" he asked.

"I need some air," she muttered and the door slammed shut.

✻ ✻ ✻

Faye stalked the streets, sticking to the darker parts—but it all seemed to be light. The orange glow of the lanterns flanking the street of seamless gray stone seemed to watch her as she moved, as she searched, eyes roving and thoughts brewing like black pitch.

A man approached from amidst the crowd in a Devari gray cloak with crossed swords. His bright green eyes held her, moving with graceful purpose. She slowed, mouth forming the word lingering on her tongue, "Gray..." At her side, her small, concealed blade that flitted through her fingers slowed as well, watching as Gray neared. Something cut, snapping her from her trance. When she looked up the man brushed her shoulder, and she saw his face in the amber streetlamps—grizzled, tired lines around his too-round eyes, and he was short—at least two-hands shorter than her, and far shorter than Gray. In fact, up close and in the ruddy light the two looked almost nothing alike save for the bright green in their eyes. The green-eyed man passed, disappearing into the fog, and she shook herself. *What in the Seven Hells is happening to me?* she wondered.

She glanced down to her fingers as townsfolk flowed around her in a blur. She'd cut herself. A gash on her thumb oozed a steady red stream. Cursing, she tore a piece from her makeshift sling and wound it around her thumb. But the foreboding reminder was thick as fog upon the Ker Stream.

The bloodpact.

Gray… It had seemed so real, she thought, remembering the vision in *The Hand of Fate*—an inn she chose for its irony, planning to waste away in drink and sorrow until Odaren had arrived and she'd seen Gray. She'd heard her father talk about bloodpacts, making her swear to never enact one. He'd told her they took varying forms, but the magic of Farhaven always found a way. *Was that all it was, truly? Her own memories ran together to form—*

She shut the thoughts out, shaking her head—there were too many things swirling in her mind now, too many forces at work pushing her in different directions, but only one thing made sense, and that was Leah. She'd had enough fresh air for tonight, and Faye turned down another alley, planning to head back to the room when she had the distinct feeling that she was being watched, hairs rising on the back of her neck. She continued, her pace even, making sure she gave no sign that she'd caught on. As she moved, she scanned her surroundings peripherally, catching it all.

On her left was a stone turret, one of dozens of guardhouses where dull-faced guards watched the steady stream of people. *Not them.* Men and women moved at her side, most richly dressed merchants from up north or south, or refugees from the Aster Plains in rags that hung from their frames. *Not them, either.* The feeling of eyes grew, a tingling that began to crawl across her skin and make her good hand itch to touch the blade at her side, but it wasn't there. She'd left it in the room.

Aberton had a ban upon outsiders with swords. It left her with only a dozen daggers positioned around her body, concealed against her skin, though not as easy to grab with her new injury. She growled, growing annoyed, waiting as a set of guards walked down in a two-by-two file, their torches hissing at the damp air, then she ducked into a darker alley between two squat stone buildings. She stalked the alley, waiting, acting oblivious. But it took another twenty steps until she heard a scuff of boot

231

upon the rooftops and she slowed.

The streets were empty here, devoid of guards or life, but she knew it wouldn't be like that for long. Patrols roved every scrap of this god-for-saken city. Faye's heart thudded rhythmically in her chest, fingers flitting lightly, gripping her blade, readying herself…

From the darkness of a side alley a pebble flew, bouncing off her shoulder.

She growled and followed it, stalking into the dark warren.

As she entered another gray-squared courtyard another pebble flew, whizzing from her left and she squinted, a memory tickling the back of her mind. Again she followed it, a little more hastily. And again it led her down a dark alley and into a square like the others, this time ringed by golden lamps. The air whistled and Faye twisted, snatching the pebble from the air. Her heart thudded in her chest now, loud in her ears… memories pushing their way to the front, but nothing tangible came. "Your game is cute, but I'm bored with it now. You can come out."

She heard a soft, familiar laugh and footsteps sounded from a patch of nearby fog, a black form slowly resolving itself as it spoke in a deep, strong voice. "You used to play the game at least for a smidge longer. You forget you're supposed to find me."

Her heart thundered now. *That voice…* "I've lost my patience with games," she answered, then ordered, "Show yourself."

The figure in the fog replied, sounding sad. "Is that all you've lost?" He stepped out of the mist and Faye felt her heart drop, seeing that devious smile.

"Davian…"

Davian's smile grew. "I'm glad you haven't forgotten me." He made a quick, subtle gesture and two-dozen thieves dropped from the rooftop in near perfect silence. In dark cloth wound around their frames and faces like black shrouds of death, they looked like shadows come to life, *Nameless* almost—all but the white of their eyes covered. Long blades protruded over their shoulders, and their black cloaks wavered as they settled behind Davian like black statues.

Davian was a striking figure. He was tall, nearly as tall as Gray, but with broader shoulders. His face was strikingly handsome—a rugged jaw, hooded eyes rimmed in black kohl, and a dense, dark beard broken by a white scar that ran down the side of his face, near his lip that made his smile almost a dark smirk.

Faye couldn't believe her eyes. And she rubbed them, wondering if this was merely another vision when a memory took her.

"*My father can beat your father,*" *Faye said.* "*That's why you'll never beat me.*"

"*Take it back!*" *Davian yelled and lunged at her, throwing her backward. She clung to him as they rolled, tumbling through the sand. Her training kicked in and at the end of her roll, she pressed her feet off of him and leapt to a stand.*

She snagged the nearby wooden sword from the ground and stood over him, a haughty grin crossing her face. "*Say it,*" *she demanded.* "*Your stubbornness isn't cute anymore. I'm going to win. I always do.*"

The boy lay on his back. His long, black hair was a tangled mess but it didn't hide his charming features. Worst of all, he knew it. But right now, Davian's face was angry. The boy wore a loose-fitting white shirt and a gray tunic that looked like an adult's clothes on his small frame. But unlike the other youths they played with sometimes, Davian's clothes, just like Faye's, weren't caked in Farb's grime and dirt. The others were street urchins, while Faye and Davian were something more. Davian's father worked for her father; and when Davian's father or her father spoke, all listened. They listened and obeyed.

233

However, while other eight-year-olds were just part-time troublemakers, Davian was the 'troublemaker king,' a titled he'd smugly took upon himself. "*Never,*" *Davian growled and kicked at her feet. She fell but held onto the sword, knowing that was always his next move. He dove upon her but she extended the blade in the nick of time. It sat an inch from his throat.*

"*Defeat?*" *she questioned.*

He glowered at her, annoyed and angry, but grumbled, "*Defeat.*" "*Now help me up.*" *Faye grabbed his hand and they joined Leah who sat on the well, braiding strands of silveroot bark. She'd been at it for hours. Her sister looked up again from her work as they joined her.*

"*You have to let him win eventually,*" *said her sister.* "*There's only so much a man's pride can take.*"

"*He'll win when he deserves to win,*" *Faye replied, then leaned over her sister's shoulder.* "*What are you making?*"

She handed it over. "*For you. It's a necklace.*"

Faye accepted the braided root carefully. "*It's beautiful,*" *she said and hugged her sister tightly.*

"*Aww, where's mine?*" *complained the boy.*

Leah elbowed him playfully. "Nothing for you, Davian. Unless you like necklaces or maybe a pretty bracelet?"

"Hey, I might," said Davian. He grabbed his chin and made a silly pose that Faye realized resembled the famous statue of the Ronin, Seth and the Patriarch. Davian was a scoundrel at times, but his anger always died quickly. He was good at forgiving—a trait Faye didn't quite share or understand. "I may look like a scary legend," Davian said, fixing a stern glare ahead—imitating the statue, "but don't judge a man by his rough and fierce cover."

And they laughed, but Leah's laughter cut short. Faye followed her sister's gaze, seeing their father approach from the distance like a storm cloud—fear returning like a familiar nightmare. And with it, the moment evaporated like water upon the hot sands.

Faye returned to the present, seeing Davian stand before her.

He stood at the fog's edge, watching her as if she were a legend or a Ronin. "I can hardly believe my eyes... It's really you..."

Dark as her heart felt, Faye could hardly believe it herself. She'd thought Davian dead or lost to the darkness of a thief's life. None of her other so-called friends had ever made it out and now here he was like an apparition from another life. *"How?"* It was all she could bring herself to ask.

He smiled, making his scar curl. "If you're asking how I've lived all these years? With difficulty," he answered. "As for how I found you? The answer is the same. You're a hard woman to track down, Faye. I've been following you like a whisper, barely out of earshot. We've hardly slept, hardly ate, but now we've found you." His eyes glimmered with hope, almost desperate. "At last."

At last? she wondered.

"What happened to you?" he asked worriedly, looking to her arm, coming forward. She half-expected him to reach out and she pulled back.

The bone had been broken clean in two but it would fuse with time, especially with the merdwart she'd applied, aided by Farhaven's natural affinity to quicken healing and lessen rest.

Up until now her single-minded drive had shut out all else, but the pain was there, waiting like a gnat in her ear if she turned her attention to it. The pain was nothing, however, compared to her thoughts of Leah and the agony of not knowing whether she was being tortured or not, living or not—*that* wondering burned like a thousand cuts upon her mind.

Faye shook herself, coming to, and found the edge to her voice. "Why are you here, Davian?"

He laughed as if that were obvious. "I'm here for you."

One of his men spoke, urgently and cautiously as footsteps echoed in the distance from a nearby patrol. "Tell her, Sunha, she doesn't know..."

Sunha? She wondered. Sunha meant 'the learned' in the sand tongue, a term used from apprentice to master. Davian was the master of these men? She eyed them again, seeing their intimidating forms — tall, wide of shoulder like Davian, and blade slender. But Davian... The Davian she knew was a scoundrel. A fool bent on getting in as much trouble as he possibly could and hoping to get away with it. Now? The man before her was... Taking him in again, she realized he was more than a pretty face. Her eyes caught his posture, the thick swordsman's callouses on his right *and* left hands, the stiff blades hidden on all parts of his muscled form and most menacing of all, his gaze. The gaze of a hunter taking in the roof-tops, the alleys and all else, muscles coiled, yet relaxed. She wasn't sure why she cared, but somehow the change made her want to sigh. *Why?* All things were destined to change. Even her childhood friend.

Davian stepped forward, breaking from his men. He neared, but not too close, luckily. He was a memory, not a friend. Not any longer. "You're a legend now, you know that?" Davian asked.

"Don't remind me."

Davian's face turned grave. "Unfortunately, that's why I'm here. You have to come back, Faye. I'm not sure if you know this but..." He hesitated, and reached out as if to comfort her, but simply spoke, "Your father's dead."

Faye remained stone-faced, hiding a dark smile.

Davian looked confused. "Did... did you hear me?"

"I heard you," she sighed. She looked to the silvered moon. The hour was getting late. Her thoughts were still for getting out of this cursed town, for Leah, for her next move.

"Faye..." he said, grabbing her arm, turning her.

Anger and fighting instincts spiked inside Faye and she grabbed the man's fingers with her good arm, twisting them. Davian collapsed to his knees. She eyed him, dark heart swarming with emotions. Davian's face contorted in pain but he didn't cry out or beg her to stop. She felt his tendons and bones creaking, wanting to pop. His face was a mask of fury and pain, but he said nothing.

235

At last she pushed him away and he fell back to the stones.

Before he fell, his men rushed forward like black phantoms, swords ringing in the alley, and Faye readied herself for blood. But paces away, Davian lifted a hand. His men froze. Davian slowly rose, curling his fingers to see if they still worked. And though they'd bruise like month-old fruit, they weren't broken. She made sure they would bruise badly. The man had a surprisingly high pain tolerance.

"What do you want, Davian?" she asked, weary. "Time is short, and if you came to reminisce or swap childhood stories, you came to the wrong place. Make your case for why you've really come or leave me be."

His gazed panned up darkly, but the question in his eyes was clear. *Who are you?* Instead, his answer was the softer sort. "What's happened to you, Faye?"

And she answered, "You came seeking a legend, did you not?" She raised her hand, offering a mock curtsey. "Here she is, your Mistress of Shadows. For I can see the look in your eyes, *old friend*. You're not here for Faye." The gray courtyard seemed to darken, the fog moving about the two as if alive.

Davian's jaw tightened. "I'm here for both. The rumor and what stands before me."

"For both? Or for neither?"

He hesitated, raising a brow, dubious.

"You're not here for Faye or for the Mistress of Shadows, are you? No," she said in realization, sounding the word out slowly, feeling its dark implications. Despite seeing him again for the first time in a decade, Faye felt a stab of disappointment at what was unfolding before her. *Even you, Davian.* "You're here for my claim to a throne. A throne full of liars and thieves, a throne of death and destruction." She'd thought him better than that, but perhaps her fondness was just childhood nostalgia. Still, Davian's treachery was only a small dark pebble in an avalanche of pain.

Davian's eyes widened in surprise, then narrowed in anger. *Ah, seems I struck a nerve.* "You pretend to cut to the heart of the truth, but it's the furthest thing from it. I'm not here for your bloodline, Faye. I'm here for you."

"Doubtful, but I'll allow you the chance to prove me right," she said, waving her dagger. "Speak, by all means."

"Your father stood for darkness, for deception and all the worst things a man can hold dear... But you are different. We can be different." He pointed behind him to his row of loyal shadows, and the men stood straighter. "These are my men. We've traveled through the underbellies of Covai, Narim, Median, Vaster and more, nearly all the Great Kingdoms, wading through the muck and the filth, seeing the depravity of man that you believe I possess. But…" His injured hand curled into a fist and hope tempered his deep voice, "…even in the darkest pits, Faye, we found rays of light. And we've gathered them, those who not only value strength, but truth and honor, those who see strength as not only an endowment, but a responsibility. Those hoping to see a clan of shadows reformed into something more, into what once was."

She listened quietly, his last words making her waver, a chill coursing down her spine. *Once was…* The words sounded like the prophecy of old. The legend all thieves told one another from a young age of a perfect time in history when all were ruled by the Master and Mistress of Shadows. But she hoped it was simply unintentional phrasing, giving him the benefit of the doubt and replied, "More, Davian? What *more* are you talking about? It's always been a clan of dark vermin, of diseased rats spreading their false ideals."

"But your father was the harbinger. He's dead now, with your father—"

"—My *father* was simply the rat king," she interrupted. "He was not original and he was not alone. Even as I left, another rose to his place, a thief calling himself 'Salamander.'" She laughed but it held no mirth. "Don't you see? There'll always be men who value *death* over *life*, who will protect their own miserable hides over those less fortunate, and who will rise up to put others down. You wish to save the world, to save the clan, to save *me*, Davian? But there's nothing worth saving."

Davian's words came, a slow burn. "There's still good in this world, Faye."

She sighed, "Ever the knight, my old friend." She paused and her vision flashed into memory. She saw the dark, damp passageways leading to the heart of the lair of the beast, seeing the thousands of thieves dead, their copper and silver-capped teeth pilfered, fingers cut off in a haste to free too-snug rings… Death and mayhem and the rise of a new ruler. She had been told her sister was dead and left it all in her wake, her claim to a shadowy throne, and even the shred of hope that she'd found in the presence of those bright-eyed fools. Gray, Ayva and Darius. She'd thought the last good thing in this world had been taken from her, the one thing she'd promised to protect, and the one thing that she felt could spell her

237

salvation—that is, until Odaren told her differently. "At our hearts we all crave power. Yet you want me to believe you and your men are somehow different?"

"No," he answered. "I want you to believe you're different."

Faye rocked back in surprise, but only for a moment until she breathed in the wet air and sighed, turning to leave. "I'm not, Davian."

"You are, Faye. The Faye I knew wouldn't run. The Faye I knew protected those who were weaker than she was. Like Leah. Like me." He pulled back his sleeve to expose a scar that ran down his right arm, gnarled and knotted, just like hers.

And she remembered, gut twisting in memory, in searing pain.

Faye pushed it aside and looked up. Davian's eyes burned with passion and she could not see the darkness that roiled in most men's eyes—that lust for power, for a more that has no end, for dominion over other men thinly disguised as 'protection' or leadership. No, something in her wanted to believe Davian, to see him as something more. But her heart felt too dark and the night was too cold for inspirational speeches of peace. She knew where she had to go and it wasn't with Davian. It was to her death and to Leah's life. Her answer was a cold rasp, carrying across the gray stones. "Your trust is misplaced, old friend, and your memories of me are simply that. Memories." She turned.

"Faye—" he called, reaching out and grabbing her shoulder.

Suddenly there was a familiar, sharp cry from the rooftops above.

Odaren fell in a heap to the stone, landing between her and Davian. "Stay back!" he snarled. "I may not look like much, but I'll cut you ear to ear if you touch her again."

Davian didn't move. He looked baffled.

Faye was equally surprised. "Odaren... what in the Seven Hells—"

But the stout thief was transfixed, eyeing Davian like an adder and ignoring her as if she were just another stone in the wall behind her. She opened her mouth to speak, but before she could, Davian, without turning, made a flashing hand signal to his men, and they prowled like black Suntha panthers at his command, encircling the fat thief with deadly grace.

"Get away from her," Davian seethed.

With surprising nimbleness, Odaren juggled two long arrow-bladed daggers between his hands, readying himself. "Too afraid to fight me yourself? Need your pets to do it for you?"

Davian unsheathed a long silver blade from his back with a crystalline ring and stalked forward.

Faye shook her head, baffled. The two proud fools were about to kill each other and she didn't care about either of them. And yet... A growl grew in her throat and she snapped, both freezing in their steps. "Are you two mad or just idiots? Or is it both? You both want to protect me and you both plan on killing each other?" Still a part of her was disappointed that she spoke, stopping them.

"Whatever he wants is not what you want," Odaren replied quietly. "I saw it from the rooftops."

Suddenly boots thundered, but this time from all sides. The guards had clearly heard the commotion.

The men behind Davian spoke animatedly, "Sunha—we must leave *now!*"

Davian didn't move. "Last chance, Mistress of Shadows... Come with us."

Faye remained silent as stone.

Davian sighed at last. He looked up, setting his jaw as the pearl-white clouds shuttled, parting to reveal a slivered moon like a splinter in the sky. "If you change your mind, find me at the courtyard of Wayfayer's Hall upon the next full moon. I'll be waiting..." He turned, but hesitated. "There *is* still good out there, Faye, and it's more than just a dream." She hesitated, his eyes once again burning with a light... *Could he really be telling the truth? Could he really want to change the world for good?*

He pulled away as his men called for him urgently, disappearing into the fog once more, and she was left standing alone.

She glanced behind her and down. *Well, not alone.*

The clatter of footsteps grew.

Faye grabbed Odaren. "C'mon, it's time to go. We've outstayed our welcome." They left the gray square, turning a corner and entering the stream of life once more—a sharp contrast to the quiet of the alley. Faye's mind swirled, emotions churning. She felt as if she were a string, its threads frayed and coming apart, suddenly pulled in a dozen different directions.

Odaren moved at her side, saying nothing, his face an equally confusing mask.

"Thank you," she said at last, softly. He turned to her, looking confused by the compliment. "There is a scrap of bravery in that coward's heart,

239

isn't there?"

His smile twisted sourly and he shook his head as if surprised he'd expected any different. "But did I do it to save your life and save mine in turn? *Or* am I the hero you're afraid to admit I am?"

She laughed. "That's yet to be seen," she replied. "But one thing is certain. I was wrong. You're not as concerned with your own death as I previously thought if you leapt at that man and thought you'd live."

Odaren shrugged, stout legs making a small leap over a storm drain to keep up at her side. "So... who was he?"

Faye thought she detected a note of jealousy but kept the smile from her face. She extracted a twisted strand from her pocket, eyeing the silve-root's metallic glint in the streetlamp's soft glow. It was the treasured relic she never let leave her side. She stuffed it back and looked ahead. "A memory from a different life—nothing more," she answered as they took an alley heading a different way from their rooms. She smelled the musk of wet wood, knowing she was getting closer.

Odaren noticed. "Where are we headed?" he questioned, confused. "Aren't you going to join those men and—"

She grabbed his shoulder, stopping him. "Listen closely. Head back to the rooms and gather our supplies," Faye instructed. "After that, find a sta-ble for my cormac and your little pony." She lifted a finger threateningly before his eyes, making Odaren go cross-eyed. "A *good one*, mind you, or I'll ignore your acts of bravery earlier and finish what I started," she said, eyeing the bloody bandage around his neck. "I won't have my cormac eaten for some curious noble's bizarre fetish." She extracted two fat, gold Farbian coins from her purse—the last of her money and placed one in his chubby palm. "That should cover their cost."

He raised a brow, puzzled. "Won't we need our mounts?"

"Not where we're going."

Slowly Odaren followed her gaze. In the distance, through the thin-ning crowds she eyed the dark blue rush of the river.

And she announced, "We leave tonight."

Death Then Life

Every muscle pushed Balder onward and he heaved himself over stone walls, through disoriented crowds, dashing with his tired old limbs toward the Southern Gate. Toward Lucky. Toward the cries.

Reaver Finn was at his side, barreling through the chaos of the camp.

Many people didn't even seem to notice they were under attack, while others fled with blood upon their faces and arms. Elves came to arms, running at Balder's side, but not enough for his mind.

"Where's Rydel?" he cried, grabbing a Lando who was running at his side. But the elf shook his head, uncertain. When Balder turned back, Finn was before him on a mount, reaching out a hand. Balder took it and Finn sprung the mount to action. They arrived at the Southern Gate in a flash.

It was pure chaos.

Hundreds of villagers, elves and humans, were running away, but still more were packed on the stretch of grass. They had focused nearly all their efforts here—builders, water-carriers, masons and brick builders. Here, their defense was weakest. And here, they were closest to Dryan's dark forest, where the sword of that mad elf could pierce deepest. And the bastard knew it.

Then he saw, over the hundreds of heads, the origin of the terror.

Monsters.

A dozen creatures—tall, with long, spindly, bough-like arms and trunk-like legs. Each was easily two or three men tall. He saw no outward weapons, but they plowed into the defenseless villagers with abandon. They looked like trees come to life, swinging their branches and cutting down swaths of humans and elves. "You find the boy, I'll stop those things!"

"*I'll* stop those things, you find the boy," Finn amended fiercely. "You're no use against Dryan's forces. And Lucky needs your help. Besides, if I don't stop those now…." He left the rest unsaid.

Balder growled but then nodded.

He dismounted to search the crowds, pressed down his terror as he'd been trained to do when he was in the guard of the Shining City and scanned the faces. Luckily, no children were allowed this close to the border, except the one a foolish old man had sent. "Where is he?" he voiced, afraid.

Something grabbed his arm and he twisted to see a woman's face. It was the same pretty, too-young brown-haired girl who was flirting with him what felt like only moments earlier. "Lucky," Balder panted, grabbing her shoulders, "where is he?"

"I-I'm not sure," the girl answered, panicked.

She was no use and Balder turned away, but the crush of people was overwhelming—he felt swarmed over, his anger and frustration reaching higher as he searched faces and screams clawed at his ear. He moved to leave when the girl suddenly cried out—

"There!"

Balder saw she'd gained purchase on the half-built white wall for vision, and pointed out over the crowds. Balder followed her gaze and his heart sank. Lucky. The boy was stuck between the wall of fleeing people and the monstrosities come to life. Finn was nearly to the towering creatures, but he was to the eastern line of them and Lucky was being flanked from the west.

"He doesn't see him," Balder breathed.

He cried out, trying to get Finn's attention, but it was much too far.

There was no other choice. Balder ran. He felt a presence following him as he tore through the fearful masses, racing to Lucky. Fire ignited the air over the heads of the running masses and Balder knew. *Finn.* Unearthly shrieks followed. Two tones—the dying of a beast layered with the dying of a man. The oddity struck a nerve in Balder, but he didn't slow.

He pressed his way through the last line of thinning, fleeing villagers and saw Lucky. Everything in Balder tensed and cringed in terror.

The boy was surrounded.

Three of the tree-like creatures trundled forward, taking lethargic, earth-rumbling steps. Lucky whimpered, cowering, pressing himself to the low-lying wall as if for protection, but it was useless. The boy's gaze searched for help but there was no one near. A dozen other elves fought the main contingency of monsters—but these had recently stumbled free of the Forest of Aenor, happening upon their first prey.

The biggest of the three attacked.

It raised its black-coated limb like a club, preparing to smash the boy to rind, and Balder could do nothing but watch. He was still a dozen paces away and completely weaponless. Everything in him cried out, but it was futile. Still, his training kicked in and he ran. The huge beast's trunk-like arm crashed down. Lucky leapt in the nick of time. Soil and stone littered the air, but the others were next. Another smash and Lucky rolled beneath it. As if keen to Lucky's agility, they attacked together. They took turns, hammering down on the boy and Balder bellowed, watching, running, helpless.

Lucky's cries were cut short as they continued to rain blows. Stone, dust and earth became a pulverized mound. Rage overwhelmed Balder's sorrow and, as he neared, he screamed a battle cry that would make the Da'Grael Mountains tremble. Every instinct shouted at him that he was an old fool, that he was running to his death, weaponless and bleary-eyed with rage, but he ran anyway.

The beasts turned on him, slow, confused, and he saw something—inside their torsos, something not covered by twisted branch and vine—*a face?* Balder saw eyes coated in eerie, churning black oil—but the terrified face was obscured again as the beasts attacked.

Running full force, he ducked beneath the first huge swing. The second came closer and he skidded across the dirt. Pebbles and fractured stone scraped at his legs and body, and the skid became an awkward roll. Dazed, he looked back as the beasts circled in on him. Suddenly, his brave attack had come to a complete standstill. Balder stumbled back and fell, scuttling back on his rear as the terrifying beasts closed in.

He saw them in full now.

Trees-come-to-life was accurate—if trees grew in the fetid Seven Hells of Remwar. They were three times the height of a man. Their bodies and limbs were not one solid piece of wood, but thick boughs woven together

243

to form two lumbering arms and thick legs. The woven legs fanned out like a tree trunk's roots, crawling and moving, still alive.

A root crawled over the ground, wrapping around Balder's leg and stopping his retreat. The root encircled his leg and he tugged, but it was like Yronia steel. The root pulled him closer, slowly, painfully toward the reach of the hellish living trees. They cried as he neared, as if hungry and preparing to feast. The cry was human yet inhuman as before—like a bear bred with a man. And he scrambled, looking for something—any-thing—as he was drawn closer. The biggest one again reached his huge limb into the air, preparing to end Balder, but Balder saw a dead elf's sword at his side and grabbed it. He yelled as the limb crashed down, cutting the thick tuber holding his leg and rolling to the side. Still, the creature's trunkish arm clipped his side and Balder's left arm exploded in searing agony, knowing it had broken. The world swam in darkness, but he regained his vision.

Looming over him, the creature sluggishly realized it'd missed a killing blow as the dust cleared. This time it didn't make the same mistake. All three beasts attacked as one.

Balder roared and rolled, diving beneath the attacks. He leapt to his feet, half-stumbling on roots and his own clumsy feet. But he regained his balance and twisted as a huge arm came roaring forth. He barely ducked aside, then jammed his blade into the center of the biggest crea-ture, aiming for the face he'd seen inside. He heard a sickening sluice of flesh. The creature stumbled back and shrieked—not from its mouth, but from its chest. It fumbled around looking confused, even terrified. Huge black eyes suddenly turned moss green. As they did, the two nearby beasts turned. With terrible efficiency, they clawed into the biggest of their kind. The big one fought, but it was no use. They tore it limb from limb and it shrieked—a single cry and it fell, rattling the earth—dead.

Balder was dumbstruck.

"What in the Seven…" he muttered.

But the beasts turned back on him. He had no time to question as they attacked. They snatched him, lifting him up into the air, and he felt wood coil around his body, constricting his air and blood. He couldn't breathe, and he felt his tendons and muscles stretched agonizingly.

Just then, there was a cry.

Rydel.

The big elf launched himself through the air and cut—an impossible jump, twenty or thirty feet—and, with a single stroke, sheared the head off the nearest creature. The beast toppled and Balder fell with it. The pain abated, but as he looked up the other beast was reaching out, grabbing for him. Balder rose with a cry, his limbs working like lead weights. He realized he still gripped the elf's sword and he clumsily struck out at the creature's root-like fingers. The beast cried out, clearly in pain. Balder took advantage of it. With his next exhausted swing, he hacked at its chest. Vines, roots, and branches broke beneath his strike. More seemed to fill in where he cut, but he didn't stop. He screamed, and he realized he was screaming Lucky's name as the beast toppled over.

He saw another sword in its chest.

He turned to see Karil.

She pulled her blade free, heaving a breath. Her silver eyes glinted at him but he had no words.

"Aim for the center, not their heads!" came a shout, cascading over the chaos.

Finn.

Rydel, Karil and the other Lando obeyed.

They ducked and dodged the lumbering attacks, cutting and slashing at the hearts of the beasts. Karil took out one. Rydel another three. *Four*—Balder amended as he launched his blade end-over-end and it pierced a mammoth living tree's center. The rest of the Lando swarmed over the remaining creatures and suddenly the action and chaos stilled.

Blood pounded in Balder's ears and he gripped his heart—fearful it would pound its way through his chest. But elation filled him, realizing he somehow still lived, and even better, as he looked around the causalities were—

He twisted, remembering.

Beyond, Lucky was lying on the ground.

Balder ran towards him, horrified. As he neared, the boy, lying in a fetal position, groaned and opened his eyes. "By the gods, you're alive!" And Balder scooped the boy up.

"What happened?" Lucky asked, dazed.

"What happened is that namesake of yours is truly paying off," he said with a thin, fearful breath he hadn't realized he'd been holding onto. In Lucky's hand, Balder spotted a strange little statue the boy often kept and called Dared. He had a sinking suspicion something else was at work, and that something was the spark.

Lucky looked too afraid and glad to speak. Tears leaked down the little boy's dirty face and he gripped Balder's arm tightly, as if holding onto him for dear life. Balder gripped back, then turned to see the depth of the chaos and destruction.

Bodies littered the ground, but not as many as he'd anticipated.

Perhaps a dozen, maybe fewer — a few were Balder's masons, including Entrius — his heart clenched at that, he'd been a good elf and friend — but mostly the dead were Lando who'd rushed to the aid of the defenseless. Otherwise, the ground was torn up. Balder noticed spots of shriveled grass. *Where the creatures had stepped?* he wondered.

Balder wrapped his arm around the boy, holding him close, as Karil and Rydel met them with several dozen Lando at their sides and a good chunk of their army behind them. Balder realized Rydel had brought them to force. That must have been why the casualties were so low. Still, one life was one life too many. Especially when they fought a war against Terma and a true Great Kingdom and… whatever in the cursing hells they had just fought.

Karil cast him a thankful eye and nodded to Lucky, wearing a sad smile.

Balder finally noticed the queen's outfit. It was remarkable — the battle garb of a true warrior queen. She wore gleaming plate armor at her shoulders and chest and elven mail and leather elsewhere — a bright lacquered green of the Lando. It all gleamed in the sun and if not for the sorrow tearing at his heart for the deaths before him, it would have seemed majestic. Still, he'd yet to see her in battle attire, and the sight *was* stirring, and as he gazed around, he saw he wasn't alone. Others watched the queen, a light in their eyes as if her presence was a boon greater than a thousand trumpets and a hundred banner men. And he realized: it wasn't stone or metal that made a Great Kingdom. It was her. A great leader and *heart*. For all the stories of the other Great Kingdoms, Balder knew, they were only pretty, hollowed shells without a leader like Karil.

Karil saw Finn nearby, too, and gave a mysterious look before turning away.

Rydel stepped forward and unsheathed his blade from the huge beast he'd felled with a sickening slurp — something between hacking wood and flesh — then flicked the blood away. Balder's eyes pinched, noticing it was a mix of green black *and* red.

"What were they?" asked a Lando, echoing his thoughts.

"Baalrots," said Karil softly.

All turned to her. She knelt over a fallen Lando, her silver gaze full of sorrow, eyeing the dead elf's lifeless stare. She closed the elf's eyes gently, whispering a prayer.

Karil wore her heart on her sleeve each time one of her elves died and all knew it. The chaos with Hadrian had caused her to grieve for nearly four weeks. But Balder saw it as strength, not a weakness. Compassion, or as Karil said it, *heart*, would be their greatest ally in this war. She continued, "My father told me of them in the old storybooks. But ancient elven scrolls have accounts of them too. From everything I remember they are kind-hearted. Gentle, even. Peaceful beasts who tend to the trees and the land of Drymaus Forest."

Balder blew a breath through his mustache. "Peaceful," he guffawed. "Then what turned them to such a frenzy?"

And Finn stepped forward.

"I fear I know the answer to that." He moved to the biggest creature and lifted a hand. Thick, gnarled branches upon its torso peeled back swiftly. Some snapped and cracked, others bent to create a hollow cavity in the creature's chest. Balder leaned forward, Lucky at his side doing the same, as Finn's eyes gleamed brighter. Balder could see the spark roaring to life in him, showing what it meant to be a three-stripe Reaver. At last, Finn lifted his other hand and a body floated through the air then came to rest gently on the ground in the center of the gathering.

Soft sounds, mostly gasps, emanated from all nearby.

Balder felt his throat clench—yet somehow he'd known.

Lying on the trampled green grass was the body of a Terma. His chest was pierced by Rydel's sword, and blood coated his mouth, but otherwise the elf looked unharmed. Roots still twined around the dead elf's arms and legs, and Balder knew that was what he'd seen inside the beast.

A once-living Terma.

"How? I don't understand."

Finn shook his head. "I don't either. Not entirely. On a basic level, it seems the Terma controlled these creatures. By killing them it freed the Baalrots... Or so I thought at first."

Balder agreed. "The beast I killed seemed to prove that. Its eyes turned from black to green as soon as I ran it through the heart, but then its foul brethren started smashing it to bits." Somehow the memory of the creature being torn apart alive and by its own kind was truly horrifying—even

247

if they were just trees come to life. All life was sacred, and he'd seen the Baalrot's eyes as it had been laid into... Afraid and confused. Balder shivered.

Finn nodded sadly. "I'd hoped to save them, but I believe the darkness from the Terma was a poison that has spread too deeply. Thus, as soon as the beasts had been pierced through the heart they seemed to come back to themselves, then instantly die.

"My guess is the Terma are the only things that can maintain the darkness. Since they could still *live* with the poison in their veins, they were used as a dark, hatred-filled fuel for the beasts." As he spoke the words, a black poison dripped from the biggest of the creatures, falling upon the crushed grass. Where it touched, a hiss sounded and earth burned. Balder sneered and even a few hardened Lando stepped back.

Finn cast out a hand. The air seemed to go drier for a quick second, and then the huge Baalrot was turned to cinder and smoke, leaving only a patch of withered grass.

A Lando stepped forward. He had long blond hair, sky blue eyes and a smooth expressionless face, looking almost too typical of his race. He bore a larger fragment of Karil's father's crown. *Temian*, Balder remembered his name. The man was the highest-ranking member of Karil's army, aside from Rydel. *And me*, he supposed. But Balder's was a purely non-militant title. Temian seemed to be a good elf from the little Balder knew of him. He'd spoken to Balder on a few separate occasions before his rise in rank. Mostly about the 'eminas,' Gray. The elf had taken a fondness for the boy, like many. But as Temian spoke, he now bore a hard edge to his voice. "I believe I speak for all when I say no life lost is a good fight, my queen, but at least these creatures were not difficult to defeat. Dryan has expended his element of surprise and at our weakest point. We will not be so weak again and he cannot strike us twice thusly. If this was Dryan's great attack, then we should count this day a victory."

Other elves began to nod, seeing the wisdom in Temian's words.

Until Rydel spoke. "These were not the strongest of his creatures," said the big elf suddenly, quietly. His words were like a dark wind over all in attendance. Rydel was still wiping his blade on the cloak of the nearby Terma, cleaning black blood from its brilliant surface.

Balder scratched his jaw. "Then what is?"

"I fear if he has learned how to manipulate the hearts of even the most peaceful beasts of Drymaus, then he must have learned to do it with others, and those darker or more neutral of heart."

"What else lives in the Drymaus Forest?" asked Finn. "And how exactly would you know? Reavers dare not even venture into those enchanted woods. I thought elves also had enough wisdom to avoid those dark woods."

"I am a Hidden—it's my job to know."

"An evasive answer if ever I heard one," Finn snorted.

"Says the child who only now has decided to become a man, the one who hides among us, cowering from his past and his future."

Balder leapt to Finn's defense. "Everyone knows he's been… *troubled*." He coughed into his hand, clearing his throat, and continued, "But Finn came here, did he not? How can you fault a man who puts his life on the line and—"

Finn raised a hand, stopping Balder. The three-stripe Reaver's eyes blazed in anger *and* power, but Balder noticed the rest of him was remarkably under control—his posture relaxed, arms resting at his side. His one hand still loosely held a ratty strip of red cloth. All in all, he looked… changed. *It was a start*, Balder thought with a small note of pride. Finn held Rydel's gaze—staring up into the powerful elf in his gleaming green plate. "I know little of your race, and even less of your rank, but I can tell when a man or elf is trying to hide something, when he is redirecting a conversation with insults to avoid a darker truth. What you don't know is I have certain talents with the element of flesh. Talents that allow me to wag a tongue that doesn't wish to speak." Finn raised his hand and little orange sparks danced in the air above his fingertips, glowing brown and red. Balder's throat tightened and Rydel's eyes narrowed, the grip on his blade tightening.

"Finn—" Balder started.

Finn's eyes weren't mad or filled with anger. They were stern, serious—determined. Balder's pulse pounded. The Reaver continued to talk as if Balder hadn't spoken, as if no one else existed aside from him and Rydel. "All your muscle and speed will be useless against such talents." Then his smile vanished as he clenched his fist. The sparks vanished. "Luckily for you, I will never pry truths from an innocent again. A stubborn, blockheaded innocent, but an innocent nonetheless. So hide your Hidden secrets, but know that you put us all at risk if we don't understand and prepare for the dangers that we may face in the days to come. And when others die, the blood of innocents will be on your hands."

Rydel looked torn. His handsome elven features, normally smooth like glass, were now hooded and wary. He looked to Karil, but she still knelt, closing the eyes of another fallen elf and whispering a prayer. Rydel looked to the other Lando, then sheathed his blade with a sharp snick. "To be raised a Hidden is to be raised in Drymaus. We are taught to learn its ways, but forbidden to speak of the woods and what lives within. The spark is deeper there, more powerful, and thus more dangerous. But it's there we learn to harness the spark fully in order to become what we are."

"You... thread the spark?" Lucky piped up, asking hesitantly beneath Balder's arm like a bird beneath its mother's wing.

"We cannot thread it, not like a Reaver, but we can breathe it into our bones, our skin and muscle—to our very souls. This makes us faster and stronger, the same way Farhaven allows one to live longer, sleep less and move quicker than those who live in Daerval.

"Yet other creatures have harnessed this spark, too. Powerful creatures. Creatures who have had an eternity to imbibe the powerful spark of Drymaus forest. That is what I fear from Dryan. Compared to them, Baalrots are rodents, small and insignificant."

Balder's heart hammered. *Eternity.* That word struck a chord, stories springing to mind and he opened his mouth, but another ventured his question first. It was the woman who had spotted Lucky. He hadn't realized she'd followed him all this way. She stood at his side like a sentinel, with Lucky on the other, but her voice trembled as she asked, "What... what sort of creatures?"

Karil answered for him. She rose from the dead, her fist clenched tightly. She unfurled her fingers showing a golden fragment of her father's crown that had made spots of blood on her hand. Balder noticed the broken fragment was in the shape of a winged serpent—and Karil's voice was hollow and quiet, but it carried over all in attendance like a gust of wind. "Dragons."

* * *

When the chaos had settled and Karil's ominous words had sunk in, they began to see to their necessary duties to set the camp straight. The pretty woman turned to him. "Is there anything I can do?" she asked, touching his arm.

He eyed the touch and grunted. "In fact, there is. Take Lucky to Mis-

250

tress Hitomi, will you? Tell her what happened. Perhaps she can lend some aid in cleaning up this mess. At the very least, our ears and eyes should know of what transpired today."

Lucky tugged on his jacket. "I..." He looked embarrassed, but not much, "I don't want to leave your side."

Balder's heart was warmed by the boy's words and he gave a kindly smile. "Nor I yours, lad. But I've some matters to attend to—words that little ones ears shouldn't be privy to. You've seen and heard enough for one day, I think."

Lucky grudgingly nodded. And Balder left the two to join Karil who sat on the low stone wall. They watched elves clear away the dead and haul the Baalrots into a pile of wood and vine, like the makings of a camp-fire for titans. Balder sought to fill the silence and ease the pain in Karil's eyes. "They died in defense of what they believed..."

"They died all the same."

"Many more would have fallen if not for you."

She gave a sad smile. "It does not change the simplest fact, my dear Valkyrie. I—we," she amended, looking to Rydel who was ordering about a group of elves, "were late, and far too slow. Too many died today. Had only I arrived earlier, then—"

251

"Then we'd still have lost men. You can't save them all, Karil. Be-sides," he added, scrubbing his jaw—it felt loose from his skirmish with the Baalrots, "if we could make wishes spring to life, I'd wish for the head of that bastard elf Dryan on a plate and a cup of mead beside it that never went dry."

He glanced over his shoulder, seeing if it got the appropriate response, and sure enough found Karil's faint smile and then an almost pretty gri-mace. "That sounds... unappetizing."

Balder smiled, but he still saw the sorrow in her features as she looked out over her citizens. Rydel was managing the gathering of corpses while another clutch of elves wrapped rope around a Baalrot who'd collapsed upon the half-built wall and dragged it free of the rubble. "Find pleasure in what you have and give grace for what you've lost. They're the wisest words I know and the ones I almost always forget."

Karil gave him another one of those looks. The look that said she was impressed—raising a single brow. It made him want to give a wry grimace and place his hands on his hips, and yet the other half of him felt that look was a sincere compliment. Karil answered, "I give it equally—but am not foolish or misguided enough to be ignorant to the facts. The truth remains that every Lando is worth a hundred of Dryan's dark elves. He outnumbers us a thousand to one. So for every attack like this where he loses few and we lose many, we grow vastly weaker. I feel as if I lose a limb with each new reprisal of his… First Hadrian and now this…"

Balder knew Hadrian was still a soft spot for her. He'd heard accounts of the elf's capture and release around camp, and knew from everything he'd heard, many mistakes were made that night. "You couldn't have known what Hadrian was, and this? We knew this was coming—that's why you had me focus my efforts here."

"But we were too slow."

Balder growled, rubbing his graying beard. He wanted to throw up his hands in angst, but he needed to be composed. And he replied, looking out over the quiet field of corpses and dead Baalrots, "We will succeed, my queen. By the gods, I promised you a Great Kingdom and I will deliver." He looked to her, staring into her silver gaze. It was difficult, even for him. He made his voice hard as iron. "I swear it."

At last, Karil gave a flicker of a smile. She laughed, and it was light. "You are something, dear Balder. I saw what you did with Finn."

Balder rubbed the back of his neck. "What'd I do?"

"Don't try to deny it," she replied. "I've eyes and ears, you know."

Balder grumbled. *Hitomi.* It must have been that pretty brown-haired woman who'd 'flirted' with him. He knew he shouldn't have trusted a pretty woman. She must have been under Hitomi's thumb this whole time, feeding the woman knowledge of his exploits.

"Grumble all you want—no one saw life in him but you. And no one could have gotten that man to do what he did today. No one but you." As she spoke, Reaver Finn raised his hands and the huge pyre of Baalrots suddenly burst into flames. The fire licked the bright air—tongues of red, orange and even black. "Now he's back."

"It's a start," he admitted, not quite as confident. Balder knew that some demons didn't die so easily. "He's a good man, he was just a tad dour. And his wounds are deep, but I believe he will heal now. Or hope. He just needed a reason to live, not a reason to die."

"He needed someone to believe in him," she said. "And here I am, giving you only a downpour of complaints and misgivings, and you choose to inspire rather than enflame. You really are a master builder."

He scrubbed a hand through his hair, trying to hide a reddening of his cheeks. *Am I truly blushing? What a foolish old man I am,* he thought, but then grew more serious. "Then you haven't given up hope?"

"Far from it, my friend. I only think of plans beyond this."

"Plans beyond?"

"Mura is out there still and Jiryn too. He seeks the prophecy of leaf, the relic hidden within Eldas that I hope will spell the end to my people's suffering and Dryan's rule."

"But?"

"I fear for him… in the heart of Dryan's dark den and surrounded from all sides. I believe he will need help."

Balder saw the look in those eyes as she gripped her sword, watching elves pass. "This sounds like a task for Mistress Hitomi," Balder said. "A missive to that boy, is that what you're thinking?"

"If the Great Kingdoms will not join us as we stand, perhaps they will reconsider when we have a Ronin—or several of them—on our side. I believe it's time to make a grander move. One that will wake the sleeping giants of this world and rally the true Great Kingdoms, or turn them against us. I believe it's time Gray joins our fight."

A New Friend

The splash of waves woke Helix. That and something sharp in his side. He groaned, feeling splinters and wetness against his cheek, and cracked open his tired eyes to see damp timber. His tongue felt around his mouth, tasting something sour and awful. *Bile?* And memories returned, landing on him like a crashing wave...

A lantern in the dark, finding him.

His mark, revealed to all.

Vomiting on the deck.

Chains.

He gasped, jolting upward, yet came up short, steel rattling. He looked behind him. His wrists were pink, his skin chafed from the metal manacles latching him to the mizzenmast. "It wasn't a dream," he whispered, starting to feel sick once more. Then he remembered his sore ribs, but didn't see anything nearby that could have been digging into him.

Strange...

The cry of gulls came back as his world became clear like a spyglass coming into focus.

He looked up, squinting. The sun was bright above—too bright—as if the sky were on fire. He tried to rub his sleep-encrusted eyes but the shackles shook again, mocking him. Slowly, a figure resolved itself.

A woman.

Sitting on the boom, perched precariously, her steel-tipped boot swung a hairsbreadth above him. Helix glanced about. Normally the quarterdeck was reserved for officers—but he noticed only a swarthy-faced helmsman manning the ship's wheel, and the man was out of earshot and his gaze fixed ahead. It left Helix and the woman essentially alone. Helix scampered backward, pushing himself upright to get a better view of her and he felt his mouth go dry.

She had scarlet hair and wore tight, faded black leather pants and a loose shirt that might have been white at one time but was marred with dirt and blood. Her slender arm rested on her bent knee, leather and metal-strapped vambraces on her forearm and bicep, and he watched a dagger dance amid her fingers. Her other arm was crooked in a makeshift cloth brace.

She looked down.

"Morning," she said with a faint smile. Her voice was husky yet light, and her piercing brown eyes—a faint band of black charcoal circling them—narrowed on him. It reminded him of the Algasi he'd read about in the stories, fierce tribal warriors who fought for honor, yet while she had neither the wildness nor the darkened skin of an Algasi, there was a certain feral quality to her. She watched him, curious yet disinterested. Helix wasn't sure how she seemed both, but she managed it. In the same way that she was pretty *and* fearsome.

Helix rolled his shoulders, trying to get feeling back into his muscles as he sat up straighter, pressing his back against the mast. His ribs still smarted as if riddled with tiny splinters, and he looked down, trying to find what had pained him so. He groaned. *Had I slept on a steel bar?*

"You were out solid," the woman voiced. "I was bored. I woke you up." She lifted her boot.

"*You*—why would you—" he growled, confused and angry. "Wait, who are you?"

"Who are *you*?" she replied.

He groaned again as his side throbbed, and his back and… In fact, *everything* seemed to ache, but none of that mattered in the wake of his memories. *My dream is dead.* "It doesn't matter," he said forlornly and hunkered back down, huddling into a ball, feeling sorrow settle over him like foam upon the sea, his heart heavy. Gulls cried, as if cackling at him.

"My, my, aren't we young for such thoughts of melancholy."

The waves sloshed the *Pride*, making his empty belly churn as well. He hadn't eaten and he felt irritable and tired, but still not hungry, oddly

255

enough. Her words played in his mind, buzzing like a gnat. He sat up finally, unable to find the reprieve of sleep. "You wouldn't understand, all right?"

"Try me."

He rejoined hollowly, "I'm never going home."

"See? Already off to a good start," she said. "I'm never returning home either." He watched her, uncertain if she was just mocking him or if she was serious. She seemed serious.

"Well," he corrected, "it never was my home."

"No?" she asked. "Where is home then?"

"I…" He hesitated, then admitted, shoulders slumping, "I'm not sure."

She raised a brow. "Curious for a home… did it up and run off? Made of magical bricks, perhaps?"

Now she was mocking him. A thread of defiance rose up inside Helix. The voice of his father taunting him: *Don't be a fool. Stop looking for what isn't there, lad.* "I'm going to find it. I don't care what anyone says. I'll show everyone. I'll show them and—" He stopped and looked up, realizing that he was ranting.

The woman wore a curious smile but her eyes spoke of intelligence, watching him, and he shivered under that intense brown glare. "I see..." she murmured. "I think I know what you're looking for, but which of the Forgotten Kingdoms is it?" she mused, tapping her rosy lips in thought. She slipped from her perch and knelt. Helix tried to scoot away, but he was held by his shackles and she was too quick. Her fingertips pinched his dirty clothes, taking him in. "Strange clothes… bright blue eyes like Ester sapphires… blonde hair brighter than the Vasterian sun… You're Median. So Seria, is it? The lost Great Kingdom of Water? That's what you're looking for?"

Helix swallowed a lump in his throat. "*Who are you?*"

She sighed. "I get that a lot. Better that I don't answer that," she said, waving it off. "But the Forgotten Kingdoms aren't so easy to find."

Helix's heart pounded in his chest, he leaned forward, shackles scraping tender flesh, but he didn't care. "Do you… do you know where she is?"

"Seria? Did you try to the south and west? That's the rumor I've heard. Tucked behind Yronia, hidden in the shadow of the Mountains of Soot, deep in the forest. But I've never put much stock in rumors."

"I tried there," he muttered. He still remembered the prick of spines from magluck brush, the fear of large predators' eyes watching him in the thickets of the woods and seeing those strange, multicolored worms that could kill with a single bite. "I spent two weeks roving those woods. *Nothing*. The rumors lied. It was emptier than the Rehlias Desert. That's when I boarded this hunk of junk. Everything was going fine until…"

"Until they found their little stowaway, their little bilge rat," she finished.

Helix cursed, kicking a bucket over and spilling dirty water over the already soaked deck. He breathed a shaky breath, trying to control his anger. He never was very good at controlling it—not like his father, the epitome of calm, a sea without a storm. But the man had no backbone, no guts, as if he'd been filleted and left out to dry.

"Where are you going to look next?"

He had his ideas… And the note in his pocket was the biggest piece of advice. He felt it crinkle in his pocket as he shifted. He'd discovered it a day after his failed venture into the woods, trapped beneath a rock when he'd woken from his slumber under that farmer's eaves. The letter was what had advised him to take the ship. "It doesn't matter," he replied at last and began picking at a splinter in his palm, digging at it with his thumbnail, distracting himself. But his nail only pushed the shard of wood deeper, embedding it in his skin. He dropped his hands in frustration.

257

"Why not? You've a grand quest ahead of you, you can't stop now." Her tone sounded dark, almost hollow. She wasn't being fake, but something in her voice sounded hopeless… Like a boat headed to The Abyss, knowingly.

Helix laughed and rattled his chains. "Unless you haven't noticed…"

"So?"

"What do you mean? I'm stuck."

"You're stuck," she replied flatly, "not dead."

Helix was struck dumb by her words, unsure how to respond.

The woman picked up a piece of mooring rope that was oddly blackened at the tips, twisting it in her hand. He finally realized she was cradling one of her arms, holding it limply as if it were broken.

How had she broken it? he wondered. But he was too afraid to ask.

She saw his gaze, however, and lifted her limp arm. "Wondering how I got this?"

He nodded.

"Woke up from a bad dream and it was like this," she said.

"Fine, don't tell me," he replied in annoyance.

She smiled as if amused. "Why'd the captain string you up anyway?" she asked, curious. "He seems too soft a type to shackle a ten-year-old boy against his will."

"I'm fifteen-and-a-half, *first off*," he said sharply, and the woman arched her brows in surprise."

"And-a-half? Excuse me."

"You're excused, and *secondly*, because he's a fool and a brute. He's planning to throw me overboard the first chance he gets." And yet he knew it wasn't really the captain's fault. After what the man had seen, it only made sense. In fact, he was surprised Xavvan hadn't done worse. He gazed across the deck, seeing sailors swinging from the rigging as gulls cried and the ship swayed, but there was no sign of the captain.

"Is that so?" she asked. "If he plans to throw you from the ship why didn't he do it already? We were docked at Aberton."

He shrugged. "I don't know…" he said, uncertainly. He turned to her, still feeling his blood boil. "Why do you care so much anyway?"

She said nothing. Calmly she leaned forward, dagger flitting amid her fingers like a sprite on the surf. A wave of fear flushed through him. She was pretty, but she had the look of a killer. He didn't know whether she was going to kiss him or kill him.

"I'm not evil, I don't know—" he said, flustered.

Her face brushed his.

Helix's heart thundered. Suddenly he heard a click and felt his hands drop to the planking. Rubbing his raw wrist, he looked at her, confused. "Why?"

"No one should be in shackles," she answered. A flash of pain crossed her visage, then was gone. Her eyes flickered, glimpsing his wrist and the tip of his white scar—his mark of banishment. Panic flushed through him. He scrambled back, pushing down his dirty white sleeves. The woman didn't flinch. Instead, she loosened the ties and removed her leather bracers on her injured arm to expose a long, sinuous white scar that ran nearly to her elbow. It was hideous. Twice as thick and unruly as Helix's. Transfixed, he wanted to ask why or how, but she slid the bracer back on and he snapped his attention back to her eyes. "We all have our demons, boy. I don't begrudge you yours."

Helix nodded, softly, wanting to change the subject. "The captain won't like you for this," he answered, rubbing his tender wrists.

"I've a tendency to not be liked."

"I don't think you're all that bad," Helix said after a moment. "Maybe you're just misunderstood."

She laughed. "You are a curious one… Just like him."

Like who? Helix wondered.

"Do me a favor, will you?"

He nodded, rising.

She pointed across the deck to a figure in scarlet robes staring out over the railing. "If that man comes to talk to you, say nothing. And if you do, say nothing about me, and more importantly, say nothing about you or your quest."

Helix opened his mouth to ask why. But he was clever enough to know when to ask questions and more importantly, when not to. Suddenly footsteps sounded on the quarterdeck's stairway and a squat, seedy-looking man with a patchy beard appeared. He stuck his thumbs behind a belt that was trying vainly to hold in his belly, like water over a dam. "Did I… interrupt something?" he questioned.

"Yes," the woman replied tersely.

He didn't seem to be upset, though. Instead, his face grew serious. "We need to talk, Faye."

259

"Faye, is it?" Helix asked. She looked like a Faye.

"One of a few titles," she answered. "The softest of the bunch."

"I'm Helix."

"A strong name," she remarked. "'*Maker of waves*' in Yorin, correct?"

"That's what my mom always thought, but she's…" He swallowed the lump in his throat. "My dad never had the same opinion, at least not in a good kind of sense." He smiled wistfully. "My mom always thought I'd do something great with my life. '*Shake the world from its slumber, my little maker of waves, and it change it for the better,*' she'd say." He affected her tone, then his smile faded. "She knew my habit for causing… disruption."

"A troublemaker," Faye said.

"Something like that."

"You loved her very much, didn't you?"

Helix managed a small nod. "Somehow she always saw the best in me."

"And your father?"

"He thought the opposite. We were very different, he and I. In every way. My dad thought my 'restlessness' as he called it, would only lead to a shallow, early grave." He realized he was in chains and his dad's opinion seemed to be the more valid one. But she made no comment on it.

Instead her eyes held pain.

"Faye…" the pudgy man insisted.

The woman shook her head, returning to the present. "Right." She waved him on.

Helix continued to rub his wrist, watching her go, her dark form moving with sinuous grace, but then she paused at the stairs. "Helix," she said and he met her eyes, "If you like those wrists of yours I'd change your thoughts on the captain. He's dropping you off at Hagerton, a town where you'll get no more than a slap on the wrist. If he'd dumped you at Aberton you'd be massaging stumps right now."

∗ ∗ ∗

"Why are you talking with that boy?"

Faye took the steps, feeling the boy's gaze on her back. She shook her head. She couldn't say why exactly, save for one reason. "He reminds me of someone… but younger. I think he's more than he seems."

Odaren raised a brow, keeping his voice low as they found themselves on the main deck. "Does he have the spark?"

She waited as two bearded, leathery skinned sailors passed and she flashed them a small, wanting smile. The men fumbled with the thick, long coil of rope they were holding, nearly tripping, and she continued on. On the opposite end of the ship, she watched a carpenter toiling away, placing a gooey substance between the seams of two planks, but she used it as an excuse to eye the back of the red-robed Reaver in her peripheral vision.

"Our Reaver friend hasn't made a move for him, so I doubt he's an Untamed, but he's cast a curious look in the boy's direction more than once. He's tried to be subtle about it, but I've seen his dark glare."

The Reaver had appeared on the ship at the same time they had.

Worse still, her gaze panned down to his cuffs, eyeing the number of stripes.

Four.

She could care less if the ship was occupied by fanged, black-limbed Darkwalkers or the Ronin themselves. It made no difference to her mission, but still…

"This is a side I haven't seen of you before," Odaren remarked, pulling her from her thoughts. She looked at him. His thin lips were ruffled in bemusement.

"What side?" she asked, annoyed.

"Protective."

She sighed. "Cautious," she corrected. "We're trapped on a piece of driftwood for the next day or two whether we like it or not. In the meantime, we've the delightful company of a Reaver that could blow us all out of the water, and a captain who is starting to catch on that I'm not a seamstress of Aster, nor you a gem merchant from Ester," she said, once again regretting their choice of alibis. "We can use the boy and anything else." She didn't believe her words, not entirely at least, and Odaren probably didn't either, but wisely he didn't question it.

"I thought Ester was a fine choice," said the stout thief, thumbs looping around his leather belt smugly. "I always figured in another life I'd make a fine swindler of precious commodities."

She admitted his was the more likely backstory. She was the one falling down on her role, very much unlike her. She should have chosen something grittier, like a butcher's wife, or even a Farbian guard. As it stood, if she had to pretend to be a simpering seamstress for another day she'd either sink the bloody ship or throw herself overboard to end the whole charade. "Why did you call me aside? Your timing on ruining a good conversation is impeccable, by the way."

Odaren scratched his layered chin, then used it to indicate the red-robed Reaver. "Him."

"What about him?"

"He's more than he seems," Odaren replied.

"In case you haven't noticed, he doesn't need to be more than he seems. A four-stripe Reaver can rip the flesh from the bones of everyone on this ship before we could reach for our daggers and barely break a sweat. The man is a near god of the spark, surpassed only by Arbiters." That thought reminded her of Ezrah the Arbiter, Gray's grandfather. Even now she shivered in memory, for the man's gaze had always been unnerving, looking at her as if seeing inside her, like a Devari's ki.

"His name is Izul."

She raised a brow. Another deckhand with a few missing teeth passed, casting her a wary glance. She smiled again, her best doll-eyed smile, but

261

he eyed her as if she were a doll with fangs. She hadn't fooled *all* of them. She pulled Odaren to an empty pocket between the front mast and the side railing. "How do you know his name?"

"Before I ran into you I heard two people talking in the back room of *The Hand of Fate*. One of them was this Reaver Izul. The other, I'm still not even sure to this day… a woman, but she was twice as fearsome."

"More frightening than a four-stripe?"

"Much."

"More than me?" she asked, glancing to his neck.

He swallowed and gingerly felt at his blood-soaked bandage, but then responded, gravely, "*More.*"

She sighed. "I'm losing my edge. So what about this Izul is more than he seems?"

"He's headed to Narim like us, but he's after something."

"The boy," she guessed, already feeling a strange inkling.

"My thoughts, exactly," he answered, and licked his lips—his nervous habit, "And something more. I overheard their words. The woman told him to look for… uh… um… " Odaren squinted, rapping his noggin through his oily black hair in frustration as if the memory were stuck and he was trying to dislodge it. Suddenly his beady eyes lit up. " That's right! The Nine Stones!"

She clasped a hand over his mouth, covering it as a big sailor with thick arms and a hairy pelt of a chest covered with a dirty red sash passed by. "The stones, are you certain?"

Odaren's eyes crinkled, not realizing what he'd just stumbled upon. "I am. What are they?"

She had a vision of a dark stone, crackling, sucking at life. She remembered seeing it upon the battle of the sands amidst the chaos wielded by the madman Sithel.

The ship became a dark room as memories took Faye.

"I don't understand," she said, lying in her hard cot, a sword gripped in her little hand. It was his custom that she always hold a blade as she fell asleep to become accustomed to her blade's handle. Another sword hung above her bed, a pace away, suspended by a thin, fraying string ready to fall at any moment. She was forced to stare at it before she fell asleep, reminding her that death could come at any moment. "Why though?"

"Why are they evil?" her father, Darkeye asked, standing above her, immersed in the shadows of her small clay room.

262

She nodded. *"If they protected the Great Kingdoms I don't see why they went bad. It doesn't make sense, Sunha."*

"Because they are, disvala." It meant 'little blade' in Sand Tongue. *"Don't you see? They couldn't handle their strength. They couldn't handle what true power meant. As a result, Kail and his minions turned their back on Farhaven, and on us all. Their reliance on their swords and the hubris of their magic was their downfall as well. For there is always someone stronger, always something more that can be our undoing, just like the Nine Stones. That's why we must always be ready."*

The Nine Stones… Faye heard distantly.

"But…" she began, trying to have it make sense. *"The Ronin aren't good at all?"*

"No," he answered, *"even the weak or the broken serve their purpose, my daughter. Thanks to them, the Great Kingdoms began to break and fissure and the clans of shadow rose to fill those cracks, to save the people from their own weakness, their own misery. You and I—the clan—are here to rebuild the land and—*

She broke from the memory, knowing her father's awful rants too well and his twisted truths. Her stomach was sick, not wanting to travel down that road again. The wet black sack in their rooms below deck didn't even give her any satisfaction. It simply was what it was, and soon it would be over. Still… the Nine Stones. Only a rumor, she'd thought.

Until she'd seen the voidstone.

Faye shook her head, answering Odaren at last. "It doesn't matter."

The stout thief was watching her expectantly. She realized how helpful he'd become. What had started as a thief planning to offer her up like raw meat to his beastlike master was now becoming… well, she still wasn't sure. But Odaren wasn't what he seemed, that much was certain. Still, she knew conflict was bound to happen when they arrived at Narim. A time would come soon when he would have to hand her over like a lamb to slaughter, and at that time she couldn't hold ties to anyone. If the time came, she would slit his throat faster than he could blink. But the sentiment didn't stop her from gripping his shoulder awkwardly. "Thank you. It was good that you told me." The pudgy thief seemed to warm at the compliment. She eyed the Reaver. "Keep an eye on him and the boy as well. Do your best to keep him from Helix. All that matters is that we reach Narim without dying."

"Always looking at the bright side of things," he replied.

"The honest side of things," she amended.

Odaren tipped his head in obedience. Nearby a rat scuttled into a pile of ropes, searching for food. The big-armed sailor with the red sash and hairy chest stepped forward, squashing it with his boot, guts splaying across the deck. Odaren swallowed, gaze riveted and answered, a tad breathless, "I'll... I'll do my best."

Across the way the Reaver turned, taking the quarterdeck's steps.

"Go," she ordered.

"I'm not your lackey," he snapped and then winced, looking self-conscious, as if he'd overstepped his bounds in turn.

"Fine," she sighed. "Pretty please go."

Despite her tone that dripped with sarcasm, Odaren smiled, looking satisfied. "You do soften with time... slightly."

She rolled her eyes and the pudgy thief left to intercept the Reaver.

Faye looked out into the river, the keel splitting the water with ease. The *Pride of Median* seemed to glide, almost soaring above the Ker Stream. She watched the river churn at the ship's flanks, not pressing, but *pushing* her bulky hull forward—toward their destination. She was not daft and recognized the spark, knowing the Reaver's appearance had quickened the ship threefold.

Faye whispered, playing the name over in her mind. "Izul..."

Odaren was right on another thing as well. Whoever this woman was who commanded a four-stripe Reaver, and whatever she wanted, was far more terrifying than a Reaver, the Shadow King, and all else. The world was becoming a dark place indeed, she knew.

Davian's words slunk back into her memory.

A shadow is rising...

A Blade Coated in Blood

Dogs loped across Gray's path. The smell of horses and fish filled his nose. To put it mildly, it was a pungent, unappealing scent that stuck in Gray's nostrils ever since they'd entered the city of Aberton. All about Gray, guards in black tabards with orange flames cast wary glances, making him want to sneer in reply. The streets were unusually packed and only upon entering them did he remember why. Today was the Day of Trade. From his memories he knew it well. A day once every year when *all* could sell their wares and gave supposed discounts. It brought a flood of people, sightseers, deal seekers, and a plethora of makeshift merchants to even this middling town. Aberton was normally a strict, medium-sized city on the outskirts of Farbs, but today it could have been mistaken for Covai. Markets and small stands were set up in every spare scrap of space, reducing traffic to a crawl but creating a strange blend of sights, smells and sounds.

Again, most notably to Gray, the pungent smell of fish.

Sidestepping a hound on a leash that peed onto the cobblestones, Gray pointed ahead. "There." The sign read *Gunthar's Tack and Feed*, just as the guard at the entrance had indicated. Beneath was a painted red horse, poorly rendered, munching contentedly out of a trough. A larger sign swung beneath it. "NO CALLERS."

"You really think it's going to be there?" Darius asked, pulling him back to the moment.

Gray swallowed down his surge of emotions—disgust, hesitancy, even anger toward the archwolf and its food of choice—and simply shrugged. "No idea. But it's our best bet. If not, the owner may know where we can find one."

Darius scrubbed a hand through his hair, looking uncomfortable. "I can't believe we're going through with this."

"What other choice do we have?"

"Are you certain that's what it told you?"

Gray nodded with a shiver. The image flashed again. *White. Meat.* And he wondered why. It seemed strange... something didn't add up, but without knowing what, Gray had no choice but to obey.

"Then it's what we have to do. We just have to figure out a way to pay for it, seeing as it's worth a kingdom," Darius said.

"Or *commandeer* once more," Gray said.

This time Darius didn't smile or laugh. He made an awkward grimace, hiding a shudder himself, and they strode forward. Gray tugged his threadbare Devari cloak closer, hobbling toward the splintered sign.

Time's wasting away, my death looms, and we're getting food for a mount, of all things.

It'd been ten days hard riding, stopping only to catch a quick night's rest. There was little to no conversation as they focused grimly on their destination. What they had to do was obvious, there was no room for debate, and even talking seemed a waste of time. Every morsel of Gray's attention was focused forward. That, and because Gray was stuck in his own morose thoughts.

Darius seemed content to let him be. Not always, of course. From time to time, he'd feel his friend's lingering gaze. Gray would remain huddled in his cloak before their campfire, silent, feeling Darius' empathy like a tangible thing hanging in the air. This exchange was obvious. Darius wanted to help but he couldn't. And Gray wanted to tell him something, to help dispel his friend's fear, or even tell him off, but he couldn't. And so Darius' eyes would drop and he'd return to whittling or stoking their pitiful fire or the like.

Darius sometimes told quick stories as they fell asleep. Little tales he'd heard from the inns of Lakewood. Mostly to keep Gray distracted. But it never worked. Gray's mind was plagued like his body. He found sleep difficult, tossing, turning, and sweating each night. Like a fire's afterimage, visions of Faye flashed in his head. And every waking moment was spent staring into the distance, waiting to catch a glimmer of the Citadel on the horizon, urging the archwolf's great, golden wings to press even swifter than it already did.

They'd passed several large, teeming towns, avoiding them each time—always waking in the painfully early hours of the day. Sleep was scarcer and scarcer. Barely enough to get by—to keep moving. Food was equally scarce, nibbled bites of dried provisions while they flew or right before they went to bed, scrounged from Vaster's kitchens. Gray's body craved to sleep for days, but the only upside of his sickness was that his stomach felt a dried knot. He was rarely hungry. Except for more haste. Hungry to keep moving.

On the tenth day, however, the archwolf suddenly stopped.

The conversation had been simple and brusque.

Wind rustled in Gray's hair as they suddenly descended.

"What's happening?" Darius shouted.

"I don't know!"

The fabled creature landed next to a stand of bark-stripped dola trees with green fronds in the center of a Node.

The creature tossed them from the saddle with a sudden, violent shake. Darius shook the dust from himself, cursing, and Gray rose slowly, realizing the archwolf was emitting a strange growling sound. He neared despite Darius' protests and put a hand to its wolfish head by instinct. He got an image and his hand darted back as the creature snapped. Not at him, but at the air. "It... he—" Gray still didn't know what to call the fabled creature, then settled on 'he.' "He's hungry."

"Well? What does 'he' eat?" Darius asked.

"How am I supposed to know?"

"He ignores grass and turned his nose at the hare you caught."

Then an image was placed in Gray's mind. Meat. White. Silken. "I think I know what he eats..." he voiced.

Darius had crested the rise and saw the town a half-a-day's walk away. As if the creature had known all along. They'd left the archwolf back in the Node, tying it to a tree, leaving Cid to watch over the beast. Cid had griped about it and looked a little nervous being left alone, but eventually Gray had made the task seem gravely important. The boy's eyes had widened to the size of Farbian coins, as if he was some sort of hero in an adventure. Fool boy, he'd thought. Young and good-hearted, but so naïve, exactly like Gray had been.

267

Now they were here.

Gray returned to the moment.

They passed a few strange mounts that clattered along the cobblestone road of Aberton led by a pink-faced caravan leader that looked a little like the obnoxious horse merchant from Vaster. But Gray's eyes were drawn to the creatures. All different shades. One even had a shade of light red to his coat. Almost pink! The lead mount was most curious, tall and hairy with curling ash-colored horns, looking like a blend between goat and horse.

It made him wonder about what existed to the east. They heard a few rumors. Even wisps of words that mentioned "Lander," the lost Great Kingdom of Stone.

They entered the shop and found it was next to useless. The jowly, pinched-faced owner of the shop who smelled of manure and horse — that was a distinctly unique smell — had nearly called the guards on them for asking about purchasing such a *thing*. He'd blustered and grown red-faced, waving Gray away as if trying to blow away a storm, and Darius had barely calmed the man down.

Now they were back onto the streets, no closer to getting the archwolf's food and no closer to finding Faye and curing Gray's sickness. Men and women passed by in a steady blur, ignoring the two wayward travelers. Gray shivered, an icy chill seeping beneath his skin. He felt suddenly very cold and his teeth chattered. Darius noticed and immediately un-pinned his green cloak, putting it around his shoulders and ushering him onward, "Come on, let's get you out of here," Darius said. "We'll think of something else. I'm sure we will."

Gray merely bobbed his head. He hated being taken care of, but saw no use arguing. He was running out of ideas, and a part of him was growing tired... Not merely sick, but tired of trying. Tired of fighting. His bones ached and his mind was a foggy stew. Murky corners of the ill-kept city grew more enticing. He started to see why the beggars had lay down. Once he lay down though, he feared he wouldn't get back up.

Four more days, his mind echoed.

A beggar bumped into him and there was a crash of coins as they flew into the air. Suddenly the crowds froze — the dull bronze coins hung in the air, suspended. Gray drew an even breath. This was the fourth time she'd come. Each time she imparted a bit of wisdom but each time it wasn't enough — never telling him exactly where she was for certain.

He twisted, looking through the frozen faces, searching for her. "I know you're here," he called tiredly. "You can leave me in peace if you've just come to taunt me again. I'm in no mood today." It was true. He felt angry today and teetered on the fine line between despair and rage.

"No mood? How very *Sons of the Flesh* of you," came the echoing voice, sounding from everywhere and yet nowhere. *In his head.* "You know they can't... " she coughed suggestively, "*you* know."

He gripped his skull, fingers digging into his hair, tearing at his brown locks as if he could pry her from his brain. "Just go away..."

The beggar before him lifted her head, turning into Faye. She gave an impish twist of her rosebud lips. Her light brown eyes peered out of a dirt-smeared, sun-darkened face, shining in the light of the sun. Yet her teeth were a blazing white—unlike the missing, yellowed ones of the beggar. Her scarlet hair fell like fire about her. "Go away?" Faye asked, leaning nearer. "In case you forgot, that's not so easy. You and I are one. I'm a fig-ment of your imagination given life by Farhaven's magic. So really you're just talking to yourself." She sucked in a breath, wincing as she crossed her arms beneath her breasts. "Talking to yourself, Gray. That's a little embarrassing, wouldn't you say?"

Gray felt a confusing mix of emotions. He could smell the filth, the rankness of unwashed skin, of urine on her soiled clothes, but she was also so close he could smell her breath. It was sweet and musky. Again he wondered if that was truly how Faye smelled or if it was just his idea of how she *should* smell. It was a weird mix of emotions. He read her with the ki and sensed amusement, surprise, and tried to cover his thoughts by looking away. "Are you serious?" she asked. "This is your type?" She lift-ed the rags, as if finally realizing what she was wearing. "You *are* an odd one. Is that why we never had anything?" Her finger traced his arm, her lips parted invitingly, tongue playing across her teeth as if hungry.

"Sometimes you're a poor substitute for the real Faye. She would nev-er mention us, not like that at least."

Faye's imposter shrugged. "Perhaps she's—I'm—not what you think."

True enough. The woman was more mystery than person, but Gray still found himself giving a dismissive snort.

"You don't believe me. You don't think I care about anyone, do you?"

It was strange how the imposter slipped between 'I' and Faye, as if sometimes certain of her identity and sometimes not. When she spoke in first person she sounded more like the Faye he knew. In those times

269

he *almost* wondered if she were Faye, and if his mind were doing more than playing tricks on him. *Almost.* Gray gave her a level stare. "Am I wrong? Do you care about anyone else? You've almost admitted as much before. That me, Darius, Ayva, none of us, nothing matters to you. Even your own life."

Faye's eyes lost some of their ferocity, that burning golden-yellow turning to plainer copper as she slipped back into the imposter—the shadow of Faye. She flicked her hand as if it were a stupid conversation and she regretted bringing it up. "Again, perhaps you're wrong, and perhaps she was too. Perhaps Faye was lying to hide a deeper truth. But maybe you're right. And if so, I'd say you should take a lesson from her. After all, that's your greatest weakness."

"What're you talking about?"

"Self-sacrifice. How noble, and how utterly pointless and weak when a martyr isn't needed."

The words cut deep, but a wound didn't bleed the same when someone was bled dry. "Enough. What do you want this time?" he asked, looking away. "Speak your piece then leave me alone."

"Four more days," Faye said.

"I know."

"You're afraid."

"I'm not afraid," he lied.

She didn't laugh or smile. When he looked back, her face was smooth, unreadable. "Everyone's afraid of death," she answered.

"Even you, then."

She shrugged. "The real me would probably stab you for that. But yes, the fake me knows the truth. Yes, even me."

Gray wiped away the illusion, turning, searching for Darius. "I'm not afraid. I'm just tired."

"That's the first sign," said the figure behind him. She stepped nearer and he felt warmth. *That couldn't be true, could it?* He swiped a hand through her, again turning her to smoke, twisting again. But Faye appeared, rising like steam from a vent before him. "See? You push away the truth, but it can't be pushed away."

"What truth?" He knew he couldn't avoid her forever. Each time she came to tell him something. Something to taunt or something to help, but always something. It was quicker simply to ask, but his stubbornness always rebelled.

"A depressed man grows tired; a man afraid does nothing. It's the first sign of true fear. You pretend not to care, but really it's just your own terror bubbling up inside of you. And so instead of confronting your fear, breaking free of its shell, you let it suffocate you. The suffocation is the tiredness, like a cloak that whispers for you to sleep, the same way a man freezing to death feels warm in the moment before his last breath." She put a finger beneath his chin. "And you will die if you stop moving."

"What am I supposed to do?" he asked, growing angry. "I'm trying, but time is wearing thin."

"Then you know what you have to do." Faye's voice grew serious, losing its humorous edge. Gray's heart beat slower, time slowing. "Use it."

"It?"

"Si'tu'ah," she said.

Si'tu'ah... The single word seemed to crash in Gray's head, a bell tolling with perfect resonance—as if there was a song in his head, and that was the note that was missing. That word. He remembered once more. *That* was the answer. *Si'tu'ah.* "And if I do?"

"It will lead you to me."

He didn't understand. Her sun-tanned face smiled deeply as she rose to her full height and he noticed a bit of crystal white sand fall from her sleeve.

With that, she was gone.

As she vanished, a vision replaced it.

An elf on a cormac trotted through the crowd.

And he knew the archwolf's meal awaited.

271

⁂ ⁂ ⁂

"Gray?"

Gray turned, realizing Darius was talking to him. "Sorry, I..."

"Her again?"

He nodded, gaze fixed. Unfortunately as the throng of unwashed masses milled, Gray took a closer look at the elf that moved a dozen paces ahead, and his chest grew constricted. He didn't need the ki. The elf was truly dangerous.

"Luck," Darius breathed, following his gaze—seeing the cormac and its rider.

"Not quite," Gray said, taking in the elf. With a blade on his back—

wrapped much like theirs—the elf wore the guise of a simple wanderer. He was concealed in a traveler's cloak of rough-spun wool, but Gray caught glimpses of his clothes beneath. They fit him strangely, bulging at specific places, and his shoulders seemed to flare too wide. He voiced his concern. "His clothes sit on him awkwardly, bulky-like."

"He might be fat."

"He's wearing armor."

"So?"

"So why would someone hide their armor?"

"Because it's tarnished? Maybe he's fashion conscious?" Darius scratched his head, "All right, you got me. I'm not sure. Why? And when did you become cleverer than me?"

"I've always been cleverer than you. I just don't relish rubbing it in."

Darius smiled at the riposte, clearly glad Gray was making jokes. Most often after a Faye visit Gray would prefer to sit or ride in somber silence—stuck in his own brewing thoughts. Something in what Faye said nagged at him, however. *Si'tu'ah.* The word pounded in his head.

"I concede," Darius said, drawing him back. "So why the armor?"

He was doing what he did with Faye. Using subtle clues to understand the true nature of the elf on the cormac, but he had another way to decipher the elf's hidden motives.

Gray delved into the elf with the ki, sifting the divide. Yet as he touched the elf's mind, the ki rebounded like a sword clattering against a shield. He retreated back into his own body, annoyed, but as he did the elf glanced over his shoulder, looking directly at Gray. No smile. A flush of sweat broke across Gray's skin. *He knows.* Then the elf shifted, looking back ahead. "He can detect my ki," Gray voiced.

"Is that a bad thing?"

He shook his head. "It's not a good thing." Then Gray saw several men shadowing the elf, trailing through the crowd like stalking Suntha panthers trailing a giant Marluke. Images popped into Gray's sluggish mind. *Great midnight black cats loping, leaping from tree to tree with perfect stealth. Ahead, a huge albino beast broke root and boughs as it lumbered with as much gracelessness as the cats exhibited grace.* The image of the Marluke was in fragments. *Huge curling tusks. Hoary clumps of matted hair clinging to its leathery hide. A giant, flat snout that rooted and sniffed at the ground, aware of the danger, but confident in its raw power.*

That was strange. It was an image from Kirin. But had Kirin actually seen that? He had a feeling that it was a story told to Kirin. That was the first time a memory of Kirin's hadn't been firsthand experience and had come in the form of imagery. Most of the time if Gray *saw* it, Kirin had actually *seen* it. If Kirin hadn't seen it, he only knew a rough description.

Either way, it was obvious the trailing thieves saw fat gold coins at the sight of a cormac. It was a rare treasure. Thus why Faye had bargained Darius' away. But despite the elf's rigid gaze, something told him the elf was well aware.

He pointed, and Darius saw the trailing thieves too.

"What do we do?" Darius asked. "They're sure to try to corner him in an alley, or the like. Should we try to save him?"

"I'm not sure if he's the one that needs saving," Gray said, then pulled his friend along, "C'mon." Something in Gray's gut churned nauseatingly at something that wasn't the bloodpact. He felt eyes on him. Not the elf rider, or thieves, but something else… Something powerful. Something dangerous. Something told him the smell of fish would soon be replaced with the smell of blood.

But in a way, it didn't matter. Gray remembered had his answer to the bloodpact—the answer that would save his life.

Si'tu'ah.

That was the part of the bloodpact that hadn't been fulfilled. *That* was what was killing him. Faye had promised to teach him *si'tu'ah* but their training had been cut short. But knowing that *si'tu'ah* was the missing piece wasn't enough. He had to learn it. Then the obvious, dumb question hit him like a hammer blow to the gut that nearly stopped him in his tracks.

What was *si'tu'ah?*

273

A Losing Game

Faye eyed the pieces on her board, but her vision seemed to glaze, looking past. She was playing a game with Odaren. They'd finished their game of cyn. He'd lost. Now they were playing ele-

ments. The board was interchangeable—a slat of checkered wood could be slid out and flipped over, exchanged for the many-squared board of elements. Inside the hollowed wood she'd found the colored glass pieces of elements. They weren't flawless like some she'd seen—they still had the bubbles, an imperfection she rather liked, but it made her think of the fat innkeeper she'd killed. He must have filched the board from some rich patron, and then she'd *borrowed* it in turn. She was glad to be playing elements over cyn. Both were tactical games, but cyn was a short, rough game of betrayal and death. Elements, on the other hand, was a game of long-term planning.

Elements was a game that took after *si'tu'ah*, which in sand tongue translated to 'the way of the sword,' but most considered it a manual to life and living. Just like *si'tu'ah*, elements had strategy and planning, and required reading the clues in your surroundings, and more specifically in your opponent, to gain an edge. And there were always clues.

In truth, she felt both games stirring inside her. The rage inside her wanted nothing more than blood and death, but she'd need to think long ahead of the Shadow King's plans if she hoped to save Leah. "So... What's the Shadow King have planned for me when we arrive in Narim?"

she asked her partner and opponent in a brusque tone.

Odaren looked up from the board. "Planned?"

"Surely he doesn't expect me to come bound and gagged like some stuffed pig ready for the Harvest Festival."

Odaren scratched his chins. "Why not?"

"Isn't it obvious? He sent you, my little pudgy friend."

The thief grimaced, turning his attention to the board. "So?"

"So you're no great assassin—"

"But I—"

"—or handsome prince—"

Odaren growled.

"—or handsome *anything* for that matter."

He grew silent at last, pouting, eyeing the glass pieces with sullen anger. "Your tongue is crueler than your blade. I'm not sure if I should be impressed or sorry for you."

She sighed, leaning back and kicking up her feet. "That's just because you've only tasted my blade, but you had the fortunate and rare chance to feel the full breadth of my tongue." She didn't mean the words to be interpreted erotically, but Odaren turned red, somewhere between lust and anger. She rolled her eyes. Always sex first with men, even in the face of impending danger. "Why you?" she questioned again, "and what's the Shadow King planning?"

"You've already proved I'm an ignorant fool to his plans—why keep harassing me?"

"Because you're shrewd, and because you know him, and because…" she hesitated, glancing around the deck, seeing only deckhands moving to and fro, gulls cawing and passing by in the thick briny air. "Who else am I to ask?"

"By the gods you have a way with compliments."

She sighed again, leaning forward and grabbing his grubby hand. She felt the dirt, but it was surprisingly warm in her cold, slender fingers. And a little sweaty. "I'm not one for compliments, and I'm not…" She didn't know how to phrase her next words. Her heart was never warm, but now? It felt like ice in her chest. Still, Odaren didn't deserve her lashings. "Forgive me." Then she sought the truest words she could. "I need your help, Odaren. You know the Shadow King and his ways. I need to prepare for what's to come if I'm going to save Leah."

Odaren seemed to judge her eyes for a long moment. He turned back

275

to the board—he made a move, pushing an orange shard of fire closer to her water—it balanced the two, and both were shoved from the board. "I can't help you."

"You can't or you won't?"

"Both, either, pick your favorite."

Faye's jaw clenched. "You still side with him then?" She felt her heart darken further.

Odaren laughed, which made the barrel he sat on quiver beneath his weight. "You truly don't know me, do you? I can't and won't, but not because I don't want to, but because it's simply not possible."

"Explain."

He sighed. "The Shadow King isn't a man. He bleeds like you and I, but his thoughts? I can't predict them." Faye remained silent. Odaren shook his head, gripping his dead orange shard tightly in his stubby fingers. "He can see without seeing, he moves faster than any man but cannot thread, and—he's *not* human, Faye. I once saw him kill his head servant in cold blood for no reason. It wasn't natural. He ripped the man's throat from his neck, then let—"

Faye sighed heavily, raising a hand to stop Odaren. "You aren't help-

ing."

Odaren scrubbed at his neck sheepishly. "Sorry."

"Let's try this again. I don't expect you to erase all your years of hatred and fear of the man, but let's think about this logically, shall we?" Odaren nodded. "If he wanted my head on a platter he'd send another, correct?"

"If he thought he could get your head," Odaren professed. "I did tell him of your rising legend—that you killed Darkeye and a horde of thieves with ease. Perhaps that was never an option in his mind."

"Perhaps," Faye admitted, a little happier that she was including Odaren in her thought process. "Then why send you?"

"I can be… convincing."

"No, you can be perceptive."

Odaren sighed. "Then you think he wanted me dead?"

"No," she said. "Still, I think you're too valuable for that. At least, if I were him." Odaren's too-wide mouth split into a smile he couldn't seem to help. She scowled. "Don't make me throw you overboard and cool that swelling head of yours. I didn't say you were invaluable, just too valuable to throw away without use."

"So if I'm too valuable to send to death, too worthless to be used as an assassin… Then… why me?"

Faye moved a green shard of leaf forward, thinking. It crowded closer to the golden shard of sun—the two worked powerfully together. She was now only several paces away from Odaren's white-shard, and though that piece could move nearly at will she intended to trap it. "An assassin might push me away or die trying to kill me, a charmer might make me see the snake waiting in the brush, but a pudgy thief? My curiosity is too much."

"So I'm used as an innocent lure. But still, why not kill you? Why not send a dozen assassins? A hundred?" Odaren asked, pushing his white shard away, running.

Faye had planned for that and put her white shard in the path of his retreat. "For something greater." She realized it as she pushed her lesser clear piece to the edge of the board, raising it to an element as well. "To turn me."

Izul approached, casting a shadow upon the table.

Faye's stomach soured, mood darkening.

"Elements, is it?" the Reaver intoned. "You're playing it wrong."

Odaren's bulk twisted on the barrel and he grimaced, taking in the Reaver looming over him. He flashed a look to Faye that read, *Why didn't you tell me he was coming?*

277

She shrugged, looking back with a *Would it matter?* sort of gaze.

"Wrong?" Odaren sniffed. "How so?"

"Elements is a game meant for Reavers, for threaders of the spark, and not for those sparkless souls such as yourselves."

Faye remained silent, unfazed.

"Thank you for that enlightening morsel."

Izul snatched a bauble of blue glass, eyeing it in the light of the sun. Only two of the tear-shaped glass baubles remained on Odaren's side—*shards*, they were called. The blue, or *water* shard, in Izul's hand, and the clear bauble on the back squares—*wind*—the most pivotal shard. "This game is over," he declared.

"Not yet it isn't," Odaren said in a near growl. "And we were playing, in case you didn't notice."

Izul ignored Odaren, staring at Faye. He put the piece back in its place using the power of stone. It floated down smoothly. "Play aggressively and you could win in the next move," he told Faye, pointing to the shard of wind. "You're aware of this, aren't you?"

Faye slid the golden shard—sun—a square forward, still ignoring Izul.

Honestly, she'd wanted to move the wind shard — it could leap over the others and attack Odaren's final pieces with ease now that she'd trapped it. But Faye listened to no man, and immediately she could feel it rankle the Reaver. A muscle in Izul's face twitched, eyeing the safer move.

"How droll," said Izul. "And weak."

She had trouble not laughing, and traded the mirth for a small sigh. "Can I help you with something, Reaver Izul?" she asked, at last looking up to the man, sun glinting in her eyes. Izul had refined features — a clean jaw with a thin patch of fashionable beard adorning his chin — a recent style of Farbs — and thin, dark brown hair that fell almost to his eyes. His red robes were pristine, almost glowing, like fresh blood in the morning light. In another life he could have passed as a noble man of some province of Seria known for its vineyards — but his expression seemed perpetually strained, and a burning lust lingered in his gaze. Beyond that, seeing him up close for the first time she noted he was attractive — something she looked for in all men, but didn't really care to hold onto after the notice of it. Unfortunately, his narrow jaw and angular nose made his face too sharp to be truly handsome. In another life, if she felt anything but darkness in her heart she might have toyed with him, but instead she just felt tired and annoyed.

278

"You know my true name," Izul said, eyes snapping wide, impressed. "How might I ask?"

She looked back to the board and answered dully, "I'm good at guessing."

Faye *felt* him darken above her as if storm clouds were forming around his head. "Do you truly know what game you're playing at?"

"Elements?" she asked, growing bored.

"So clever, *Mistress of Shadows.*"

Faye tensed.

"How could you be surprised? By the gods, you're famous! Even deaf beggars in the hills beyond the gates of Farbs know of you and what you did at the battle upon the sands." He snorted. "You'd be lucky to find some backwaters farmer in the Narim Foothills who hasn't heard of the Mistress of Shadows!" His voice took on a grand air. "The one and only... The woman who killed the thief-lord Darkeye." Faye tensed. Her knuckles grew painfully tight on her concealed dagger, but she kept her face smooth. "*Not to mention,*" he added, "the same Mistress of Shadows who threaded the nine elements upon the sands. Even the power of *wind*—a fearsome rumor, indeed."

Faye snorted, but her blood was still cold in her veins. "I figured you too old to believe in child's tales."

"Oh, I'm not so daft to believe that you are a threader." He wagged his four-stripe cuff in her face. "After all, I can sense the spark. But you know that, don't you? And you don't have a whiff of it in you. Nor does the pudgy thief… Sorry, *gem merchant*."

Faye felt her fingers curl even tighter around the dagger at her right hip. The man was revealing all his cards and she feared his next words. She kept her eyes on the board, shaking her head slightly at Odaren's look, sensing his hand inching towards his blade.

"No, no… Menacing and mysterious, perhaps." He scratched his jaw as if she were a puzzle missing several pieces. "But you are no dreaded threader of wind. If you were, sorry to say, I would have wiped the deck with your blood. However…" he said, then leaned in closer next to her ear and whispered, "if your pet interferes with me and the boy again, I will give you the pleasure of mopping his ashes from the quarterdeck. And you…" His fingernail scratched its way along her cheek, carving a path down her salt-slicked skin, down her neck, over her scars, farther down toward her chest. "I can find uses for you as well. I'm not always considered creative compared to the others, but the element of *flesh* has remarkable uses if used aptly." His breath was hot across her skin as he leaned in closer.

Faye sighed. The man was clearly used to controlling conversations by flashing those four-stripes and it was time she played her cards. "I see you're not one for mincing words or feigning charm. Not like your brothers."

"My brothers?" he asked, reeling for once.

"You are the youngest, are you not? Is that why you were charged with this sad mission? That of watching over a small boy and two harmless, sparkless souls like me and my brother, the gem merchant here?" she asked, motioning to Odaren. "While your brothers, much more powerful and much more charming, I assume, were given missions of actual consequence. What irony to be four-stripes and yet still so weak." She gave a toothy grin. "Wouldn't you agree?"

"How did you…" His face turned red.

She continued, pressing her advantage, "You said you know the game of elements. You're correct, by the way—it wasn't meant to be played by such base creatures as my portly traveling companion and I. But I don't think you truly know its origins." She plucked the white shard of wind, bouncing it in her hand. It had a nice heft to it. *Who had you stolen this from, innkeeper?* "You see this piece? It's the shard of wind. But you know that already, don't you? And so you should know that no Reaver, no Arbiter even, threads wind. Not even the Patriarch himself. This game wasn't meant to be played by Reavers, it was meant to be played by the Ronin."

Izul was shaking now. *"That name…"* His limbs trembled and Faye felt the air grow hot; the planks seemed to rattle on the deck, men glancing to their feet fearfully. Rigging snapped and the waves thundered against the ship's hull. Faye held onto the game, digging her feet to the ground but felt the boards curl beneath her toes as the ship creaked and groaned angrily beneath the Reaver's boiling wrath.

Izul stepped forward and suddenly his eyes widened, tensing.

The rocking ship stopped in a rush.

She tapped the inside of his leg, right beside his groin with her dagger. "Do you enjoy your manhood, Reaver Izul? If not, I'll gladly remove it for you, free of charge."

Faye's hand grew hot and her dagger began to glow. It fell to the deck, steel melting like wax into a puddle on the wet planks. She grimaced— she'd liked that blade. Yronia steel was hard to come by. But at least Izul's wrath was drained from his features. "Interfere with me and the boy again and find your end quick and far from painless." With that Izul turned on his heel and stalked away.

"That was foolish beyond measure," Odaren breathed after Izul was out of earshot. Sailors still gripped the rigging fearfully, watching the Reaver pass—even the captain cast a curious eye to Faye and Odaren, as if having watched the whole ordeal from his place on the quarterdeck. "He could have burnt us to the ground!"

"Life is a confidence game, my friend. If you didn't already notice, he *already* has the capacity to bring me into those cabins and have his way with me as his eyes and words suggested, or to peel the flesh from your bones with little to no consequence. But now?"

"He's afraid of what you, what the Mistress of Shadows, is capable of…"

"Hardly. Now he's just not so sure. Ideally my charade has gained us a leave of absence, at least until we reach Narim," she replied. Then shrugged. "Or not, and he will kill us tonight." A tight breath left her chest. Whether from the mere glimpse of the Reaver's vast power or from the idea of death as a reprieve, she wasn't sure.

Odaren cursed loudly. "I'm not sure if you're the most…" Her gaze flickered up, stopping his next words. "… Or the *smartest*. But at the very least it's clear you're the maddest woman I've ever met. But one thing doesn't make sense." He frowned, scratching his fat lower lip and settling his bulk back into the small, wood barrel. "How did you know he had brothers and he was the youngest?"

"*Si'tu'ah,*" she said.

"Excuse me?"

Faye sighed. "Four-stripe Reaver or not, that man had runt ridden all over him. Besides, he compared himself to '*others.*' He could have meant Reavers or Citadel ilk, but a three-stripe Reaver, let alone a four-stripe, believes themselves in a league of their own. So it could only have been family. Old or young, rich or poor, powerful or powerless, it doesn't matter… Family is the one thing that can get under anyone's skin."

Odaren made a thoughtful sound, nodding.

However, if Izul is that powerful and clever and he is the runt of the litter, I dread meeting his brothers…

Several hours later as darkness settled upon the ship, Faye found herself alone on the deck for a brief respite. She gripped the railing, staring into the night, a sea of stars hanging above. The land below passed by in a gray blur—small cottages, farms, and the grasses of the Sevian plains. Tomorrow it would make way for the shadowy, fertile lands of Narim. Gray was out there somewhere wrestling with the darkness and death that awaited him, just like it awaited her.

"Evening," a voice in the night said.

She turned, expecting Odaren, but instead found herself looking up into the wild, white tangled beard of Captain Xavvan. He tugged on his blue coat—his customary habit—joining her side at the rail. Faye didn't keep up the pretense of the simpering seamstress, and somehow she sensed Xavvan didn't believe it anymore anyway, especially after the conversation with Reaver Izul. Instead she simply leaned on the smooth railing, feeling the light spray upon her skin and listening to the splash of the river beneath them. Moments seemed to slip by until Xavvan spoke at last. "Get some sleep, Mistress Sophi. You'll need it. Tomorrow we should arrive in Narim."

Gaze fixed on the distance, Faye kept silent.

As Xavvan turned he paused. "I've seen that look before. Whatever you're searching for, I hope you find it."

Faye said nothing, clutching Leah's silveroot necklace in her hand. "Captain…" she began as he turned. She heard the planks stop creaking, waiting for her to speak. "There's one more thing."

He returned and she handed him a letter. He unfurled it and read.

"Are you certain?" he asked.

She nodded. "Where I go, I go alone. Only promise me no harm will fall upon him. He's no saint or scholar, but he's not a bad man either, and I've a feeling that before this song has sung its last verse he might still play a role for good in this world."

"You talk in riddles, but…" He hesitated, then blew a great gale of an exhale out his nose, making his wiry white mustache ruffle. "So be it. As long as you're the one doing the deed—I can be the one to finish it."

"You're a good man," she said, listening to the lap of waves against the hull.

Xavvan grunted. "I once met a traveling minstrel upon the Frizzian coast. He told me that none of us are good or evil by nature—that there's no such thing. If that's the case I'm no good man, simply a man trying to do good."

"No such thing…" she repeated with a sad smile, the face of her father, of the Shadow King, of a thousand other evils ghosting before her eyes. "If only that were true… Luckily for your bard friend, his wise words only testify to one thing—that he never met true darkness. Be glad for those who don't." She said it softly, but the words were like a knife to the conversation, cutting it still. The captain cleared his throat as if knowing he was out of his league in this debate.

"If… there's nothing else?"

"That's all," she replied.

And he retreated, the planks creaking beneath his weight, and headed toward his cabin.

She looked down, feeling a sudden wetness at her hip. She reached her fingers under her shirt and brought them before her eyes, into the bobbing white light of a nearby lantern. Blood. It coated her fingertips. The wound she'd sustained from a Devari years before?

The bloodpact.

It was coming to fruition faster than she'd ever expected.

She gave an even breath, looking out into the crashing dark waves.

At least let me reach Leah she prayed. *Then it can end. Once she is safe... Then it can all end...*

283

Narim

They arrived at Narim in the morning, but Faye watched as the ship lurched, taking a sharp left from the main river. An hour later they were in the infamous shadows of the Narim Foothills, home of the Great Kingdom of Moon. Simple shadows seemed to draw longer now that they were closer to the city of moon. A once glorious surface was now toppled ruins. At one time it was the outskirts of Narim, a thriving city, or so it was said. Now it was no more than a forgotten city of tumbled-down, scattered stone, like an abandoned quarry, ominous seeming. The ruins' shadows stretched despite the morning sun, as if trying to reach out and grasp the passing ship like black claws. *My imagination…* she knew.

The true danger was ahead.

"We're here," Odaren announced.

Faye squinted but saw nothing.

Suddenly shouts echoed across the deck, men adjusting the sails and battening hatches. Eventually she saw it… wood structures, dozens of them, rising from the flat land flanking the river. As the ship neared, Faye squinted into the rising sun, eyeing the rickety wood structures. Upon their heights, dark-clothed men wielding bows stalked and watched them with wary gazes. Faye's hand itched to touch her blades.

"Sentry towers," she whispered. *But what are they guarding?*

As if in answer to her question, the river grew louder. Too loud. She heard it before she saw it, the rush of water deafening.

A dozen wooden towers stood in a semi-circle. In the center was a waterfall pouring into the earth. The river didn't continue, she noticed. Instead, it fell into the wide, pitch-black abyss, as if Farhaven was swallowing the Ker Stream whole, like a hungry beast.

"The stone beast of Narim," a sailor remarked.

She'd heard of it before, of course, but to see it now... She wasn't sure how the river could still be so full and yet be emptying so much of its...

Then she noticed.

Water didn't *only* fall into the black pit, it came out as well, flowing both in *and* out of the vast hole. One thick channel of water on the right fell into the dark hole never to be seen. The second channel on its left vomited up the dark river, creating a sort of reverse waterfall.

"How?" she whispered, more to herself than anything.

Somehow, over the din Odaren had heard or seen her quizzical look. "Magic," he replied. "Built into the kingdom."

Faye had seen magic, or the spark, in action—from the Grand Creation of Arbiter Ezrah's, a globe of suspended water four men tall that nourished the city of Farbs, to a thousand and one magical acts done by Reavers with the power of the spark, some fantastical... others less so. But this? "Built by who? A Grand Creation?"

Odaren shook his head. "No," he said. "That's to come. No one knows who built it. The Harbinger who brought the Ronin? The Ronin themselves? Most say it was the Patriarch—seeing as he is the only Arbiter to have constructed multiple Grand Creations."

She'd heard as much. Arbiters had to construct a Grand Creation as a requirement to rise to their legendary rank. There were only two stipulations for a Grand Creation as far as Faye knew. One, it had to last for all time. A simple feat, she mused. And two, it had to impact the world for good—a truly remarkable good. Or at least that was the rosy notion of it. The only one she'd ever witnessed in person was Ezrah's Grand Creation. Unending water for a parched city stuck in the endless sun was a remarkable thing indeed. This? Remarkable surely, but not with the elegance she expected. Most Grand Creations had a flair from their creator, not to mention they were often intertwined with the nature of the Kingdom. The Endless Sphere of water for the Great Kingdom of Fire, the Gold Road paved with endless energy for the Great Kingdom of Sun... The rest of the Grand Creations she'd never paid much mind to. "And the

285

Patriarch? Pray tell. What does he say?"

"He's your king. How would I know?" said Odaren grouchily, wiping the sweat from his face with his small cloth, watching the towers near.

She raised a brow. Her little thief seemed moodier as they got closer to Narim. He hadn't looked her in the eye all day. It fit her just fine—she had death on her mind, not friendship. "He's no one's king, especially not mine," she replied. Rumored to have lived since the Lieon, since the Ronin themselves, the Patriarch was more god than man. *If he even existed...*

She felt the ship gain speed, but not due to the Reaver's aid. The beast was drawing them in, waves crashing. Shouts went across the deck. The spray of water became a gush, the chasm spitting its fury upon the *Pride of Median.*

Faye rocked, while others were thrown from their feet.

Odaren clambered to a nearby rope—one of the first. "You better grab hold."

Faye growled. Reluctantly she grabbed a loose rope, wrapping it around her wrist as the *Pride* took a sudden plunge into the darkness, falling into the depths of hell. Light was extinguished in a rush, but before it was, she glimpsed a passing shadow. *Is that...?*

It passed by a rock that gleamed blue, lighting the dark silhouette.

Not a shadow, she realized. *A huge black pirate ship.*

The pirate ship ghosted by them on the second channel, heading to the surface. Her eyes widened, but then the world plunged to darkness and her heart and stomach slammed against her ribcage, choking on whatever words she was about to say. She fell like a rock in free-fall until... The hull hit water—hard. The rope snapped tight and she clenched her teeth as her weight sunk to the ship's deck, knees nearly collapsing beneath her, but she managed to hold her feet.

Then it hit her—her stomach flipping over and bile rising sickeningly. She clasped a hand to her mouth, stifling a gag.

"You all right?" Odaren's snarky voice came in the dark.

"I'm..." she gulped down bitter bile, answering tightly, "... fine." Faye listened as even a few hardened sailors vomited across the deck and laughs resounded in the darkness.

Odaren sniffed. "I'm surprised, almost disappointed you didn't vomit—it's practically tradition."

She wiped a hand across her mouth, biting back an answer.

Calls were made for light, but as flint struck, light bloomed from all around. A turquoise glow bathed the walls, revealing a black cavern of stone. As if by the hand of an invisible wind, the ship pushed forward, gliding along the water. As always, the thought of wind made her think of Gray and her hand touched her wounded hip, but she shoved the thoughts down, urging the vessel to quicken its pace.

The Shadow King's death awaited.

The *Pride* skimmed beneath low and tall archways and through a maze of bubbling canals. The ship's tall masts grazed the tops of the archways but always, as if by magic, they would slip beneath and deeper into the shadowed kingdom. Faye spied the mark of Moon on a nearby wall.

A clumsy hand had attempted to chisel the mark of the thief into it.

She noticed other hints of the past in the strange turquoise light.

Empty sockets, cracked clay braziers, rusting steel brackets.

Gems. Gold. Silver—long filched.

"Shadows of the past," she whispered.

"Pity, isn't it?" said Odaren. "Now they only serve to show what this kingdom has become, what we've lost."

While she agreed, words came to mind. Davian's. Words he'd told her long ago when they were children—the last thing he'd ever told her before he disappeared. And she'd held onto those words, thinking he was dead until he'd risen from her past, attempting to sway her to a future she'd never see. The words returned. *Holding onto the past will only haunt you, Faye,* he told her as they had stood in a moonlit courtyard, moments from parting those dozen years ago.

"And the future? How much brighter is that?" Odaren asked.

Faye hadn't realized she'd spoken aloud and turned silent, focusing ahead.

Around them on the walkways and in the shadows, she saw sinister figures. Eyes watched them, gauging their wealth and weighing it against the level of threat. She kept her blades close but the eyes always retreated back into the darkness—and she had a feeling it wasn't her doing when she saw flames dancing upon Izul's fingertips. Eventually they turned a corner, unveiling canals full of thieves—hundreds crowding the narrow walkways or trundling upon the overpasses.

The smell of sweat, blood and fear hung on the air.

Faye squinted as the ship rolled past a strange edifice of moss and stone with metal bars that glistened a curious red, tucked into the corner.

287

"What's that?" It appeared to be an ancient jail.

"No one knows. The lock to the door is held by some ancient spark and the bars are infused with bloodstone. Yet it holds no wealth. And whatever doesn't glint with gold the Shadow King pays no mind."

And the *Pride* glided onward, leaving it behind.

"You never answered. What's the Grand Creation of Moon?"

Odaren licked his lips and smiled. "Wait for it."

Suddenly the vessel lurched, turning a corner.

Faye's eyes widened. The crowded canals ended, opening up to a huge vaulted black cavern. It looked like a hollowed out sphere, the dome of which was so high and fragile Faye imagined an errant foot from a surface dweller could fall through. Most magnificent of all, however, was the light. It was everywhere. A sea of strange turquoise light, hanging like fog in the air.

They were here... At last.

Narim—the Great Kingdom of Moon.

"This," he said, cupping a wisp of blue turquoise, and it ghosted through his fingers like fog. She arched a brow. "You're looking at it," he explained. "The light *is* the Grand Creation, feeding the city."

"How can light feed a city?"

"Thanks to the light, nothing in Narim ever rots."

Faye scoffed. "Impossible. Decay is a part of life, just like death."

"Not in Narim. A can of beans left out for two moons? Not a speck of mold. As such, food goes a long way in the city of Moon." He eyed the crowds with disdain. "Sometimes it's a problem too. A dead carcass in the streets will stay fresh as the day it was killed. The Shadow King likes it that way—serves as a reminder of his favorite phrase. Strength is life—"

"—*weakness, death*," she finished, feeling a bitter taste on her tongue. Odaren spat over the side of the boat into the dark roiling waters. "I know the phrase well. It's a favorite of men with diseased minds and even more corrupt hearts. Is that all the light does?" *All*, she scoffed. Preventing rot—if all the stores of food in the world never rotted, hunger wouldn't exist... But Faye knew a type of hunger always existed, whether the hunger of greed or the hunger of the body.

"No, not all. The light also acts as a sort of... nutrient. Like a second sun." The fat thief scratched his oily head. "Never quite understood it myself."

Faye's hand ran through a thick patch of light blue. "I've seen it," she whispered. "My father liked to test the limits of a human. Once he kept a small boy in darkness, hoping he'd grow accustomed to the lightless world and become a secret weapon. Instead his bones turned brittle and his legs bowed before he could stand, as if he'd ridden in a saddle all his life." She still felt pity for the boy who'd been condemned to darkness. He'd been no older than she. Although, when he had failed that little project, Faye had become her father's secret weapon.

How'd that turn out, father? she thought with a sneer.

Odaren bobbed his head in agreement. "Teeth, eyes, skin... Too much darkness makes you sick, makes you weak. Not in Narim." He chuckled, gripping the ship's railing. "'Course, you still get old and wrinkled here just like the rest of the world. It stops rot, not aging."

Faye took a deep breath.

She breathed the unusual air in—something between mist and blue light, a vapor. She tasted the blue vapor. It felt cool, tingly even, like silken essence. Xavvan shouted. Mooring lines were grabbed and calls were made to drop anchor.

The *Pride of Median* glided into a large dock.

Calling it a dock was generous, Faye thought. It was no more than a square patch of water with several rickety piers on the verge of collapse. No servants, no dockhands, no guards. Just ships and wood. It did house two or three dozen vessels—some smaller, a few bigger than the *Pride*. But instead of crisp white cotton sails like the *Pride*, each was fitted with ragged, mouse-eaten black canvases and blacker wood, giving the appearance of ghost ships.

More narrow canals flowed outward from the dock, deeper into the warrens of Narim, but none the *Pride* could fit in. Men and a sprinkling of women—or what might have been women, for their shapeless black rags and dark swarthy faces made it difficult to tell—moved about onshore. Thieves slowed, eyeing the unusual ship with a dark gleam in their eyes, but then shuffled onward.

"It's time," Faye announced, turning to the thief at her side.

He gulped heavily. "For what?"

"What else? To kill a king," she said with a toothy smile, moving away. Odaren followed on her heels. As she walked she undid her sling, casting it aside. She felt at the bone of her arm, giving it a full rotation. It felt sore and a little tender, but it didn't smart.

"That mended quickly," Odaren said.

"Surprisingly so."

"Seems Farhaven is on your side," he remarked.

Faye only grunted. It was said if one healed quickly, the 'spark of Farhaven was watching over you,' and that the land had decided to feed its energy into you. She wasn't sure if that was true, but if so, she figured it was about time Farhaven dealt her a good hand of cards. She paused before the captain's quarters, hefting her Dragonborne armor. She noticed Captain Xavvan was on deck, busy shouting orders to men who rushed in a whirlwind—lowering the gangplank, while others tossed mooring lines; and still more pushed over several large, cylindrical rope-woven objects that cushioned the *Pride* against the rickety landing. Xavvan must have felt her eyes because the big man glanced over. He gave her a knowing look and an almost imperceptible nod before returning to his red-faced bellowing. Faye's abrupt stop caused Odaren to tumble into her. "Do you care to join me?" she asked with a small smile. "I need to change and I know you have a penchant for catching me without clothes."

Odaren turned crimson. "I'll… wait out here."

"Gather your things then join me inside. I have something to show you." Odaren nodded, rushing off. "And be quick, will you? Death waits for no man."

All the blood that had rushed to his head seemed to vanish just as quickly as the portly man turned pale as a sheet. Faye chuckled darkly, disappearing into the captain's quarters.

✳ ✳ ✳

When Faye walked out onto the deck she was alone. And though her heart was heavy, her mind was steeled. Her Dragonborne armor was affixed—it fit her frame snugly, tight enough that no spear could pierce the overlapping black plates, yet loose and light enough that she could still scale walls or run a mile without winding.

As she walked out of the cabin she was met by Xavvan and Helix.

"He's making me stay on the ship," Helix griped loudly. "He says I have to stay on this rickety heap until we get to Phern's Valley. Phern's Valley," he repeated, incredulous. Faye shrugged, confused, not knowing the name. "It's a coastal fishing town! It's no bigger than a flea on a dog's back." Then the boy stopped, thinking. "You know, you could drop me off at Hagvas."

Hagvas was a pirate's den—a great lawless city tucked inside the Dragon's Tooth.

"Nice try, boy. Phern's Valley sits at the crown of the Frizzian Coast, away from all that nasty pirate business that's taking place down south. It's a quaint town, a tad on the small side, but with real nice, hearty folk. Lucky for you, too, I know a few of the folk there. Agrea and her husband Mobus—real sweetheart she is. Mobus is a good, solid bloke, and the town mayor to boot. Agrea's got three girls of her own but always wanted a boy. She'll take you in, I'm certain. If you won't go back to Median, then I'll leave you there until I'm done with this trip. Once finished, I'll come back up the coast and take you back to the City of Water, back to Median. I know a few folk in high places… If you're real nice to me, they might lend an ear to what I have to say and perhaps help with that mark you bear."

Helix seemed aghast and angry, covering up his forearm with his hand—though his shirt already hid the mark. Xavvan simply continued, "In the meantime, Agrea will set you straight. I'll admit, you remind me of myself a little, and if that's the case, a firm hand is what you need. I won't have you becoming a dullard, short of temper and short of wit like these louts." He hooked a thumb over his shoulder, at the men behind him. "The world knows we have enough of those." Then he shook a pointer thick finger as Helix tried to protest. "Nor will I have my conscience bloodied by leaving a boy to fend for himself. I happen to like my sleep and nasty thoughts like that at night just won't do me much good."

"See?" Helix said. "You have to change his mind!"

Faye glanced around for Izul but he was nowhere to be seen. She grit her teeth. She wished it were a good sign—he'd left the boy alone after all, but she knew it wasn't. Faye shook herself, realizing Helix was still gripping her arm. She pried it free with a grimace. "I wouldn't complain were I you. Free of shackles and a far cry from Aberton? You should be thanking the man, and me," she replied absently, eyes still fixed on the Black Hive.

Time was growing short.

"See? Mistress Sophi, wise as always. You should listen to your elders, boy. You've a good heart, I see that. As I said, I see a lot of myself in you. But you listen about as well as a gnatfish in a storm and are about as reckless as one too." Xavvan looked up from the boy to notice Faye in her intimidating armor—the other sailors had noticed, too, and were giv-

291

ing her a wide berth. She half-expected them to jump ship into the dark waters if she made any sudden moves. Then the captain's eyes drifted to his quarters…

He raised a questioning brow and she nodded.

It's done, she thought.

Helix was oblivious to the whole exchange.

"That's it! Leave me here," Helix pleaded suddenly. "Leave me with Faye."

"And your quest to find Seria, the Great Kingdom of Water? You'll so easily abandon it for a pretty face?" she mused.

Helix blushed but didn't fall for the bait. "That's easy," said the boy, "you'll help me find it."

Captain Xavvan guffawed, mustache quivering like a flag. "Nonsense! No offense to you, Mistress Sophi," he said with a wave of his hand and she shrugged, then twisted his wrath back to the boy, "but I swear upon my brined heart that I won't be dropping you off in a pirate's cave, a lawless den of hoodlums and—"

Faye held up a hand, ending the captain's tirade. She looked down at the boy, though he nearly met her eye level. With tousled blond hair and bright blue eyes, he was handsome, youthful and full of hope… and naïve. She hadn't the heart to tell him Seria was destroyed, lost in the war. Or that the banished mark upon his wrist meant he wouldn't survive more than a day in any Great Kingdom that favored Median as an ally. Or even more simply, that Farhaven was a land riddled with danger for even the wise and experienced. Worst of all, he was clinging to her as if she were a mother hen and not a killer by trade. Finally, she settled for a truth, or a version of it. "As touched as I am, staying with me is as bad an idea as I've ever heard. Where I go, I've no interest in lost kingdoms nor wayward boys." *Or my own life.*

Helix tried to hide his disappointment but it read on his face clearly.

Faye added with a reluctant sigh, "*But*—what I do recommend is that you go and find your treasure. Don't give up, not if the Seven Hells up and swallow you—let nothing stop you, not even me. And when you do find it," she said sharply, looking to his still red-chafed wrists, "I expect you to return my favor and share your fortune. If not I will find you, and I always keep a promise." *Except for you, Gray*, she thought, thinking of the blood-soaked wound upon her hip.

Helix nodded, though sullenly, still looking like a wounded pup, then fell back in at the captain's side.

Xavvan spoke, placing a hand on Helix's shoulder. "Now that that's settled, I suppose this is farewell." He reached out a meaty forearm and Faye grasped it. "Until next we meet," he said heartily, as if trying to usher a promise out of her.

Faye returned a dark smirk. *In this life or the next.*

With that, Xavvan pulled the boy with him, moving away and rattling orders in his deep baritone—sailors fell to task, dashing like wind sprites. They prepared to unload large boxes of cargo hoisted by rickety pulleys that sat on the dock's landing. *Their shipment was made,* she thought and looked to her own. Hefting the black cloth sack, Faye set off.

* * *

Somehow the route up the winding black canals seemed simple. It required ducking under arches, dipping up slanted paths—eyes watching her from the shadows all the while—but her sights were set like a black arrow, and Faye didn't slow.

As she moved, words echoed in her ears.

"Please, Faye. You're smarter than this. Not bound in chains and with that fire in your eyes, he'll kill you before you can even lay eyes on your sister. This... this is a death sentence."

Odaren.

She'd left him bound inside the *Pride* with specific instructions for Xavvan to untie him only once they'd left Narim. Only then did she know he'd be safe and he wouldn't try another harebrained scheme like trying to save her. She wouldn't risk his life. Not for a cause that wasn't his own, and not when he'd proven himself to be a thief with a conscience. But his words kept echoing in her skull and the memory resurfaced like the sour taste of limfuns.

"Faye—wait!"

Faye lingered, gripping the doorframe of the captain's quarters, letting the false light of Narim scatter across her face. It felt cold, like her heart. Light should not feel cold, and yet Narim was a city borne in darkness, mired in greed. Even the dull thump of hearts in the crowds lingering on the dock beyond seemed cold in her eyes. Only the Black Hive, standing on a rise above the vast subterranean city, seemed to hold life... Her sister's, and the Shadow King's, soon to end.

293

She turned the key in the door, unlocking it and moved to close it behind her.

"Don't! Don't throw away your life like this..." Odaren's voice was hoarse.

Faye didn't turn, didn't look back. "Why not?"

"Because..." *he fumbled, nervous,* "because you don't deserve to die."

Faye merely smiled. "You're sweet, my pudgy thief, but very wrong." *Her eyes fell to her calloused palms.* "No, death is perhaps the one thing I do deserve. In the end, you can't change your fate."

Odaren had paused then. She thought her answer had cut him short, but when his response came, slicing deeper than a hot blade, it resonated in her head again.

"You changed mine. The world needs you, Faye."

With that, she shut the door and left.

Now frozen light suffused the Kingdom of Moon, cold against her hot skin—flushed as it always was before battle—as she strode to see the Shadow King's demise and to feel his blood upon her hands.

Odaren's words were a gnat in her ear, but it changed nothing. *Leah...* that was all that mattered. Her sister could be the beacon of light the world needed, a symbol Faye could never be. Abruptly pain lanced Faye's side and she groaned, falling to her knees at a shadowy fork in the road. Blue lamps around her seemed to waver, darkness pressing in. Tenderly, she reached beneath a fold in her dark plates and... She winced, sucking a breath through her teeth. She pulled back a red-stained hand. Pain made her knees weak but she staggered back to her feet. "Cursed body. Don't you give out on me. Not yet..."

At last she stopped before a columned walkway. She knew it was the main entrance because her heart thudded in her throat. She could sense evil emanating from behind the large double doors at the end of the hall flanked by large, ratty-looking guards, just as she could sense the presence of her sister—the warmth and serenity—everything she was not.

She approached the guards that flanked the door.

The first sneered. "Where's the little rat?"

So they had known she was coming. Odaren had been right.

The second guard lifted his pike to block the doors. "Halt. Whoever seeks to enter the domain of the Shadow King must relinquish their weapons."

Faye reached out as if to grab a letter from her sleeve, but in its place were two small silver daggers. They flipped end over end, embedding themselves into the guards, pinning their throats to the wall behind them. "Gladly," she said as they gurgled blood. Without slowing, Faye used her momentum, bashing the wood doors open with her foot and entering the grand hall of the Shadow King.

Fetid Plans

"This doesn't feel like the *smartest* idea," Darius said, wisely beneath his breath.

Gray couldn't help but agree. But what other choice did they have? Without it, the archwolf wouldn't budge. And without flying, Gray was as sure as dead.

They were in a fetid alley, the sun blocked out by shrouded buildings. Gray kept his distance, following what the wind told him—the lingering foul smell of the thieves—which was *difficult*. The alley smelled rank like piss, feces and food left to rot in the moldy wet nooks of stone. But they took the narrow corridors, winding deeper, away from the crowds and noise.

"They're herding him," said Darius. "Away from the crowds and away from witnesses. Bloody clever bastards."

If only, Gray thought, growing more wary of the prey they tracked, knowing the truth.

Again visions flashed to mind.

Seven sleek-coated Suntha panthers with fur darker than the shadows of Narim. They moved warily, stalking their prey into a steep-faced basin, only to find the Mukla with his back turned to the cliffs, facing them. Bones littered the earth about the flat-packed ground. Suntha panther bones. Some bloodied with the flesh still clinging to the white ribcages. Huge flies buzzed, nibbling at the carcasses, and the Suntha panthers understood.

The beast had led them into the deep bowl on purpose. A killing ground.

The prey had become the predator. Death and chaos exploded as huge tusks gorged, trampling and roaring with primal anger. The Sunthas leapt and struck with perfect grace. But it didn't matter. Not here. Suntha claws scored along the Marluke back, tearing huge groves. But still it fought heedlessly; if anything, it was enraged by the pools of blood its attackers spilled. It ended, and there were only limp black corpses and silence. The beautiful, prized hunters were now simple food as the Marluke tore the fur in huge ripping bites and gobbled on the lifeless creatures—claiming his prize. Gray shook his head as if waking.

The story was vivid—he could smell the carcasses. He could almost taste the hunger in the Marluke. Marlukes were great white albino beasts resembling giant boars that lived in the enchanted Drymaus Forest. They had huge curling tusks, a leathery hide with tufts of patchy fur and a snout with three-pronged holes—nostrils that gusted air like a forge's bellows. Gray had felt the Marluke's raw power and the sharp, visceral fear in the Sunthas. *How?* He pushed the oddity aside, returning to the moment.

Voices sounded around the bend.

Gray leaned against the wet wall, feeling his clothes soak through and pulled back as he listened.

297

"*An elf! A bloody elf!*"

"*Are ya as daft as yer ugly?*" griped another. "'*Course he's a bloody elf! Look at his cursed mount—you don't get scum like us ridin' fancy beasts like that, do ya?*"

"*Doesn't matter, does it?*" asked one.

"*King, queen. Unless you're an Arbiter in disguise, you're as good as meat for the grinder,*" another said with a cocky swagger. The leader, his fighting senses told him. The voice *sounded* like a big man. "*So do what's keen, elf, and lay down your sword. You ain't got a chance against a dozen men.*"

"*Hear that, elf scum? Talon Snakeeye gave you a command! Do as he says and we promise we won't hurt you... too bad!*"

A round of sharp laughter echoed at this.

Another squawked, "*Don't lie to the fool—he knows he's a dead elf. But we're the softhearted type. We'll make it quick and painless.*"

"*Aye,*" another added, "*we'll end it real nice for you. Won't hurt a bit. Promise.*"

What do we do? Darius thought through the bond. *Maybe we should wait until they've bloodied each other up enough and then —*

Taking a page out of Zane's book, Gray interrupted the rogue by striding forward.

"Oi, look, cap!" a thief said, pointing.

The leader twisted, along with a dozen others. "What in the bloody hells?" the leader, this *Talon Snakeeye*, snarled upon seeing him. "Lost your way, boy, have you?"

Gray unstrapped Morrowil from his back, pulling the string that held the wrapped bundle with a trickle of wind. The cloth fell, revealing the brilliant white blade — glowing silver in the dusky alley. It was just for effect.

Most looked up, eyes wide at the blade

A few of the thieves were gaping.

But Talon wasn't.

Talon was a giant of a man, maybe two hands taller than Gray and three times as thick. He wore black and red cloth — the only colors amid the ragged, mottled bunch — that hung loosely despite his obviously thickly muscled frame. Talon gave a sneer and lust entered his eerie eyes at seeing Morrowil. It was almost tangible. The ki practically reeked of the man's greed.

Darius grumbled behind him and stepped out into the alley, unsheathing Masamune — giving the alley a pulsing green and silver glow.

The thieves began to chatter amongst themselves — half facing the white mounted elf and the other half twisting to face the new threat, fearful whispers sifting among them.

"Who in the bloody hells are they?" one mumbled.

"Ain't sure, but that's elven-work, ain't it?" a tall, skinny one said, crooking a bent finger at their swords.

"No, Menalas worked — Menalas men make the best steel."

"Not true. Maybe it's Yronia steel," ventured a portly thief.

They each guessed at Gray's and Darius' blades until their leader cut their bickering short with a wave of the hand. "Shut it, you groveling maggots!" Talon growled. "It don't matter none what the blade is or who they are, got it? They're just more dinner on the plate and it's high time we ate well." He unsheathed twin blades that rested on his hips, each grating loudly, and then pointed. "Whores and beers until he drowns in both for the first man who takes that silver pig sticker from the boy with death in his eyes."

"Death in his eyes," Gray repeated with a cold laugh, surprised at how dark his voice sounded. "Fitting words."

Talon's eyes flared. "Kill them."

Several thieves moved forward.

"No," said a huge thief, stepping forward from the others. "He's mine." He was even taller, if less muscled than the leader. He wore a leather vest, its thongs untied to show a thick, tanned chest, heavily scarred. His face was even more frightening, and grotesque. A hideous pink scar ran down his cheek—still puffy and inflamed. *Infected*, his warrior side knew, seeing the hints of pus at the corners and a trickle of blood. The hulking thief gave an insidious smile and hefted a huge blade with spots of rust along its edge.

"Beer and whores enough to quench Goliath's hunger? I'd like to see that!" said a thief.

Goliath roared, charging forward.

And Gray closed his eyes and let him come.

❊ ❊ ❊

"Gray?" Darius' voice was soft.

The charge brought the big thief closer and closer. He didn't see it. He felt it. The wind distorted as he moved the last few paces.

"GRAY?" Darius shouted.

But Gray waited—one more instant.

One more breath.

In the next inhale he felt the wind part.

He stepped to the side, exhaling, and opened his eyes to see the rutted thief's blade. It cleaved the air where Gray's skull had just been a breath before. The rusty blade clipped his shoulder, cutting Gray's vest. His old memories shouted, seeing the opening. *Monk Presses Back the Tide.* His whole body was like a coiled spring, striking. But this time he added something.

The wind whispered, need filling him.

Threads ran across his arm like tiny snakes—something he'd done before—but instead of powering a jump, it powered his strike. Gray thrust his palm out, smacking it into the huge thief's chest, sinking into the move. His hand burst against the behemoth's brawny chest and he felt ribs crack beneath his strike. Spittle and air burst from Goliath's mouth

299

and he flew a dozen or so paces back, skidding across the dirt to fall at the leader's feet.

Vomit and spittle dribbled onto the ground but otherwise the hulking thief remained motionless, not even twitching a muscle.

Silence hung in the air.

Behind him, Gray felt Darius' fear. *Did you...* Darius thought through the bond.

No. He'll live.

The now eleven thieves now clutched their blades nervously, eyes flickering from their fallen companion, then back to Gray.

"Dicing hell, he dropped Goliath with a single blow! That boy's got the strength of a Cerabul!" a thief gasped.

"He didn't even look at 'im!" said another.

"What are you blithering idiots doing?" Talon fumed, "Get him! He's just a boy!"

"No, he ain't no boy. He... he ain't even human," another muttered, stepping back, a few joining him. Fear was rank in the air—the ki felt it. Like the smell of a beggar's despair or Gray's desperation. It made him feel sick. Gray looked up slowly, knowing his eyes blazed white. They all stepped back.

"Those eyes..."

But then Talon pointed. "Look!" he cried exultantly.

Gray followed his gaze as pain lanced through him. He looked to his left arm. The gargantuan thief's blade had clipped closer than he thought. His vest was torn, and a shredded bloody gash marred his shoulder from the blade's dull edge. He saw spots of flaking rust buried into the wound, left over from the tarnished blade. And it hit him. Agony tore through Gray, shuddering his body, making tears sprout. He wanted to cry out, but he contained himself to a sharp breath through his teeth, keeping his gaze locked ahead.

"See? He bleeds, you cowards. Same as any man. Now kill 'im!"

They hesitated still.

"KILL 'IM!" Talon bellowed louder.

And they attacked, spurred on by the sight of Gray's blood.

A lithely built thief was the first to Gray. He moved with a fighter's grace, his fingers curling repeatedly around the haft of a dark blade. His eyes boiled with anger. Gray sensed the thief with the ki. *Anger. Pain. Tears brimming in his eyes, his breaths hot, a fire growing in his muscles as a tightness spread across his chest.* Gray read all the signs, growing familiar with distilling emotions from physiological reactions. *Sorrow, wrath, pain.*

"*Bastard*," said the lithe thief. "You bastard. I'll make you pay for what you've done."

Gray understood.

Goliath was the thief's friend, and he thought him dead.

Before Gray could attest otherwise the man attacked. Gray dipped beneath the lithe man's strike to his head but a shock ran through him, seeing a second blade flashing toward his face. With no time to evade, Gray lifted Morrowil with his waning strength, hoping he could fend the blow. He parried and steel rang then *pinged*, giving a sharp crack. Luckily, his arm didn't jar with the weight, as the thief's shoddy blade simply shattered beneath the parry. Gray lunged forward. But two more thieves replaced the first. He lifted his hand, clapping them together.

Anger and stillness.

The nexus pulsed.

Threads pulled to his will, and a gust of wind lifted the thieves, smashing them together. They crumpled as a pair. Two more charged and Darius leapt toward them. Gray released a shaky breath, staggering beneath the weight of using his power in his weakened state. But he had no time to pull in a breath as the lithe thief had regained his feet and stabbed toward Gray.

Pulling on his training with Zane, Gray sucked in a breath—letting the blade miss his abdomen. He pulled Morrowil around, his arms straining this time and hacked at the man. If he'd had his normal strength, it would have hit. Not a killing blow, but one intended to clip the man's wrist and disarm. As he stood, the man easily dodged it, leaping back. The lithe man grinned at this, a greasy smile. "I knew it," he said, looking mollified, "A lucky blow that took him. Goliath would never fall to the likes of you."

"Your friend isn't..." Gray began, but the words were almost as draining as the sword, and so he shut his mouth as the man charged again—saving his energy. *Enough of this*, he thought.

He lifted his hand to use the nexus.

Anger and...

His legs trembled and he locked them with gritted teeth, feeling his ire rise. Tiny threads tickled along his arm, wanting to form—

Anger and...

301

But stillness wouldn't come. Gray was a storm of rage and despair and the nexus flickered, remaining a half-formed ball in his mind. He cursed, lifting his blade. The next strike from the lithe thief nearly took Gray at the wrist, lopping off his hand. But Gray yanked Morrowil back—sluggishly—and the pitted blade rang again. It sounded on the verge of breaking, but Gray couldn't count on it. He needed to finish this. Now. The bloodpact was draining him. A longer fight would mean his end.

His whole body slumped—Gray didn't need to exaggerate the motion—and he watched the thief's grin widen, looking confident as he lifted Morrowil in a grand gesture overhead, charging forward. The thief raised his blade in an easy parry, focusing on the two blades, but Gray smashed his foot into the man's chest, launching him back. The lithe thief staggered backward and Darius, finished with his two thieves, flowed forward. He took the opening, flipping his blade and hitting the flat of it against the man's face, drawing only a line of blood. The lithe man looked confused as he smacked against the alley's wall, as if wondering why he wasn't dead. Darius lifted his palm, his brown eyes swirling with a deeper shade of green. Green tubers that had taken up residence on the damp wall, soaking up the fetid water suddenly sprang to life, wrapping around the thief—pinning him to the wall.

Just as five more thieves charged forward.

Gray lifted Morrowil.

As he did, his legs shook and he staggered, falling to his knees. He knew it was the agony in his arm and the sickness of the bloodpact eating away at him. *I... I can't...* he sent through the bond. Darius understood and met them, leaping before Gray. He ducked and dodged with more grace than Gray had ever seen in his friend. With each pommel strike to the head or smack of the flat of the blade, Gray knew Darius was doing his best to merely incapacitate the thieves. But several were skilled fighters and Darius hadn't the skill with a blade yet. Two blades cut closer to Darius and he barely dodged them. Gray stepped forward but his legs trembled again. And he knew as he stood that he was next to useless in a brawl like this.

Beyond he saw the elf on the cormac was fending off blows with ease. His silver blade hacked off a thief's arm. It sent a hate-fueled cry, splitting the clash of swords. The elf wasted no time running the man through the stomach and turning to the other five.

Gray flinched at the sight of so casual a killing.

The death sparked something inside of him.

He sighed.

This had gone on long enough.

Each breath of his, each attack felt more sluggish than the last... Faye was waiting. Ayva was waiting.

He raised his hand. *Anger and stillness.* He repeated the words he'd learned to summon the floating ball of air and this time he found his stillness. The nexus flared in his mind.

Gray lifted his hand. Threads coursed along his body just as two thieves ran past Darius toward Gray, obviously wishing to face the weaker, easier prey. Gray clapped his hands, smashing the two against one another. They collapsed like limp dolls. Three more leapt at Darius, going for killing blows. He flung his hands to the right and left. A gust picked them up and threw them to the wall. Just then, the lithe man broke free of his root-based shackles and threw a glinting piece of steel at Gray.

The dagger flew through the air. Gray saw it in the nick of time. *Pulse.* The nexus throbbed in his head and he slowed the air—no, that wasn't right. He didn't slow the air. He *thickened* it. The dagger hit the cushion of air, slowing just before it reached Gray. Gray caught it, snatching it like an apple from a tree, pulled it around—keeping its momentum going—and flung it back with all the strength in his arm, adding a bit of wind. It flew.

He hadn't seen the others though.

A second dagger sailed, grazing his cheek.

Then a third.

This he couldn't stop. It spun toward him and he watched its edge catching in the ruddy light of the alley. He lifted Morrowil but his tired arms were too slow, strength sapped like a bucket with a hole in it. He cried out, trying to summon more wind—but that faltered too. He'd extended his power too much. A flash of green. Metal clanged and when he looked up, he saw Darius was standing before him, fancy green cloak wavering behind him. He cast a smirk over his shoulder. "Got to be more careful," he said and Gray joined him at his side.

The clash was over, as simple as that.

Thieves lay on the ground, several unconscious, two dead from the elf on the cormac, and the rest groaned—clutching their battered selves. Above all of that were cries of agony and foul curses.

Darius turned to Gray, worming a finger through a dagger hole in his

303

green cloak. "That was close," he breathed. Gray smiled, then Darius'
face contorted in pain.

"What is it? What's wrong?"

Darius reached beneath his cloak, clutching his side. When he pulled
them away, his palms were slick with blood. With a paling face, Darius
gave a sickly smile. "I guess I spoke too soon." His knees buckled and
Gray caught him, nearly crumbling beneath his friend's sudden weight.

The elf on the cormac laughed. "Foolish humans. You saved me only
to get killed in the process." He unsheathed his blade, cruel blue eyes
focusing on Gray. "The Great Elf will be pleased by your demise, he—"

Rage, anger, and sadness collided through Gray and he lifted his hand.
A blast of air moved from his core, along his arm and shuddered the air,
slamming into the elf on the cormac. The elf flew and smashed against
the wall. Gray knew the blast would have killed any normal person, but
the elf wasn't human. Dazed, the elf stabbed his blade into the ground
and moved to rise, blood frothing from his mouth, hand quivering on his
handle. "You... blasted..."

This time there was no hatred, no anger in Gray's heart as he lifted his
hand. Stillness. The nexus swirled powerfully, and he knew it ate at him
deeply. Threading felt as if he were carving a chunk of flesh from his body.
"No," Gray said softly, shaking his head, and the elf froze midway to standing, "I don't have time for you." Tiny threads coalesced, but each powerful, like a thousand blacksmiths' hammers. Wind pressed from all sides.
The Terma's armor suddenly crumbled, turning inward, sharp shards of
the well-crafted elven plate stabbing at the elf from all directions. He
shrieked in agony. Gray quietly and quickly picked up Darius with the
last of his waning strength. He ignored the terrifying feeling of Darius's
limp body and the slick warmth of blood running down Gray's arms as he
staggered to the cormac. The beast was motionless. It could have been
sitting on a field of green chewing grass for all the expression its silver eyes
showed. Gray's legs trembled with each step, his breaths short, and the
darkness in his heart burned like fire. He knew all the flow he'd just used
had nearly killed him. He didn't care. None of it mattered.

Darius breathed wetly, softly, as if trying to speak. "Don't speak. Stay
with me," Gray ordered, teeth grit, moving relentlessly. He reached the
cormac, and carefully with threads of air, lifted his friend onto the cormac's silken back. His mind was rage and stillness. Empty. Like the land
after a storm had blown through. The memory of the destruction and

violence were still a breath away, but only stillness remained.

In the corner of his vision, Gray saw a figure he'd missed. The leader of the thieves. Talon Snakeeye. The man was visibly shaking, listening to the elf's terrible cries. His gaze flickered up to Gray. Greed was in his eyes, but his terror was much more obvious. Gray eyed the dagger in his hand, threads of golden wind swirling up his arm and his eyes filling with power. Talon staggered back, dropping his dagger, and pressed himself against the wall as if he could blend in with the wet stone. Talon's lips flapped, muttering an incomprehensible string of words. Upon nearing, Gray realized it was the same word repeated. "Wind... Wind... Wind..."

Gray ignored the man, letting the flow drop, his body sagging as he did and then he vaulted himself onto the animal with strength he didn't have. "Ride," he commanded, gripping the cormac's silken mane and it obeyed, leaping forward into a full gallop. Gray left the alleyway with the groans of thieves, the shaking thief leader, and the terrible cries of the Terma in his wake.

A Good Death

"Welcome, Mistress of Shadows."

A dozen thieves ringed the far wall of the round room; a marble-cracked ceiling let in dust and blue light. Aside from that, the

hall was empty. Were Faye not filled with rage she'd find that odd.

Instead, Faye's heart hammered, seeing but ignoring it all.

Her wrathful gaze was for only one man.

The Shadow King.

He lounged in a throne made of bones that towered over him like a wave. Strange, glossy black plate covered every inch of his body, save for his thick arms and head. His face was smooth and deathly pale. He had long ghost-white hair that fell to his broad shoulders. A crown rested on his head, one side black metal, the other a tarnished gold. That face watched her emotionlessly, save for a bare flicker of a smile as hands stroked his armrests made of skulls. Worst of all were his eyes—white orbs with no black iris, like a blind man's. She'd heard he was blind, yet she watched his gaze center on her. "You're late," he declared, his eyes tightening. "And alone. Where is my little rat?"

The only sound in the room was a slow drip, drip, drip, from an unknown source. It echoed off the domed walls, matching her heartbeats.

Faye repressed a snarl, replacing it with a venomous smirk. "Dead."

"Dead?" The Shadow King's eyes flared, anger consuming his face; then it fled just as quickly. "That's unfortunate. I rather liked my little pet, though he always was one foot in the grave. How'd he meet his end?"

"I killed him," Faye answered, stalking forward.

"You... killed him." His cheek muscle twitched in fury. "*Why*, might I ask?"

Without slowing, Faye unslung the black sack on her back. It had been black for a reason—to hide the blood. She gripped the matted red hair and threw it—with a sickening *thunk* the severed head landed and rolled toward the Shadow King, a trail of blood staining the white marble beneath. Pain and agony rattled her whole body. She wanted to scream and cry for what she'd done, both in relief and revulsion, but instead she merely smiled. "He died for his sins. Just like Darkeye..." Her eyes fell to the head, the eyes still caught in shock. "My father... And just like you are about to be."

The Shadow King's eyes widened.

Before he could respond, Faye bellowed, charging the throne.

Suddenly, pain erupted in her stomach, blindingly sharp. She cried out as it wracked her limbs. Faye staggered and fell to the floor. Her eyes split wide, tears blurring her vision, but she fought to maintain consciousness. *Please, gods, not yet. Not now...* But the pain continued to wrack her limbs like glass shards piercing flesh, cutting bone. With effort, Faye pushed down the pain. Gripping her stomach with one hand, she slowly rose to her feet.

The Shadow King's face no longer held the glimmer of horror. The skin at the edges of his mouth pulled, showing a spreading grin. Something about his face unnerved her, aside from those pure white orbs for eyes. He had pronounced cheekbones, a strong and wide jaw, a bold nose and deep-set eyes. All of it was perfectly symmetrical. She realized why it unnerved her—with his bone-white flesh, the Shadow King's face reminded her of a skull.

The rest of him was heavily muscled, with round, boulder-like shoulders, a broad muscled chest—which flexed occasionally, showing the strain of muscles wanting to be used—and a tall frame. In many ways, it was a flawless, masculine physique and yet something seemed horribly off, as if he were too perfect.

Her father had a lieutenant once that liked to stuff dead animals. She remembered staring at their lifeless eyes, their postures frozen—a stalking cougar, a deer caught in mid leap. They imitated life. Just like the Shadow King. The Shadow King's body seemed too perfect, like a

307

large skeleton wrapped in pale human flesh. Adding to this effect was his ghostly white skin, so absent of color it almost glowed. The Shadow King laughed, a dark haunting echo that reverberated through the empty chamber. "My, my, how amusing… What death flows through those veins of yours?"

Wavering on her feet, Faye spat blood defiantly.

"What fire…" the Shadow King said. His huge white palm pawed at the skull armrest as if stroking a head, then he glanced to his hand and the skull with a smile, before looking back to Faye. "Just like her."

Faye unsheathed her long blade from her back, letting its weight take it to the ground. Forged of Yronia steel, like her armor—it was light, but it felt like a hundred pounds now. "Shut up and die."

The Shadow King's amusement fled his face. "So be it. Come then, let's see the skills that killed your father. I only pray you didn't stab him in the back or this will be over all too quickly." He inclined his skull-like head, a bare dip. At this, the dark thieves that ringed the walls that had been watching Faye like an adder in the brush, stalked forward.

It must have been her lucky day though. Not all of them left the safety of the wall. Only the bigger, most brutish-looking thieves decided to join her little party. The biggest of these said something to his compatriot and they laughed condescendingly, then turned and licked their tongues out at Faye and drew blades.

"You men must get all the ladies," Faye said seriously.

"Ladies?" The big, crude one who'd uttered the joke questioned. "There 'aint no such thing. Just whores, like you, that need to be taught a proper lesson."

Faye sighed. With lustful sneers, ugly scars that marred their uglier faces, topped off with arrogant swaggering, these men had the look of 'I beat women and like it'. While they could be storybook gentlemen, Faye somehow doubted it.

Faye laughed. It hurt the wound on her stomach. She nodded her head to the big stalking thieves. "This is pathetic. You're the worst kind of coward. A spineless, heartless, gutless bastard that doesn't have the nerve to face his fears. Even your pet, Odaren, had that strength. You on the other hand sit back, watching, feigning smug, but we all know the truth. You're less than nothing. If you think different, fight me and prove me wrong."

Halvos didn't rise to the taunt. "Don't disappoint me and you might just get your wish." His eerie smile widened and his eyes swirled like a snowstorm. "Come now. Your sister is waiting."

Faye's anger sparked and she turned her attention to the stalking thieves. She stumbled forward, not trying to hide her weakness, but showcase it. Lucky for her, it wasn't hard. Her sword dragged, scraping on the stone beneath her. Her arms felt terribly heavy, as if she gripped an anvil in both hands. It wasn't an act. Now that she had let her muscles relax, she feared they wouldn't respond when needed. The stalking, dark-clothed thieves watched her stagger and catch herself. Again, not an act, but Faye saw a hungry, eager look flash across their dirt-smeared faces seeing her weakness. They drew closer. But instead of slow, stalking movement, they walked boldly, straight-backed, almost sauntering like fools. They neared, and in the moment before they approached Faye straightened.

Surprise flashed across their faces at her swift movement. They leapt back, but too slow. One took her blade across the throat, leaving a clean, red gash. He died with wide eyes. The other was quicker. He stabbed. She sidestepped, but her leg gave out. His stab sliced her ribs. She growled and threw her weight forward. The thief raised his blade, but she was too fast; her knee slammed into his chest and she tackled him to the ground. He grunted as air fled his lungs. Eyes flaring in rage, lying on his back, the thief snatched her throat with big, strong hands—fingers tightening like metal cords around her small neck. But it was useless. Her killing blow had already come. He just didn't know he was dead yet.

Holding her blade with both hands, she slammed it down, the Yronia steel plunging into his chest, piercing leather and dirty rags with ease—ending his life. His hands fell limply from her neck. Looking up, two more thieves approached quickly from either side. Still kneeling, Faye left her big sword swaying in the thief's chest and unhooked the crossbow on her hip. She fired two bolts to the left thief. One bolt found his chest. He grunted but didn't slow. The next pierced his neck and the big man gurgled blood but before he fell, he cried out, hurling his sword. It flew end over end. At the same time, the last thief was nearly upon her, bearing down on her with a rusted scimitar—bellowing so loud and hatefully she could feel the flecks of spittle hit her face. His rusted scimitar swung toward her head. Faye ducked, barely, feeling wind and the hairs of her neck sliced by the blade.

Glancing up, the flying blade was almost to her. It made its last rotation. It was still flipping end-over-end, waiting to revolve the last bit and

309

dive into her throat. But time slowed for Faye. It hadn't completed its rotation. She heard the slow drip. Drip. Drip. Water echoing through the chamber. Her heartbeats followed, one slow pulse at a time, pounding. And she reached out, timing the moment between heartbeats, almost unaware of what she was doing. Her hand grabbed the handle before it could turn to its blade's edge. Snatching the flying blade from mid-air, she twisted, not wasting its momentum. With a full spin, she found herself facing the spittle thief once more—and like letting a spear fly, she merely held its grip, guiding its flight. The blade soared forward, punching into the spittle thief's chest. It slid in easily, sinking nearly to its hilt. The spittle thief gasped. Faye let the blade go, as if freeing it now that it had completed its journey, and the thief staggered back. He stared at the metal protruding from his chest, confused. Bright blood spilled from his mouth. He looked to the Shadow King, eyes wide—then to Faye as if she were a demon—then toppled, rattling the marble.

Slowly Faye rose, taking in the deathly quiet hall.

Even the drip of water was now silent.

A slow clap resounded, echoing off the halls, and she looked up to see the Shadow King standing, appraising her. "Impressive."

He stood, watching her, not reaching for his sword which lay casually against the wall a dozen paces away. Now was Faye's chance. Faye cried out. Grabbing her swaying blade from the thief's chest, she charged the throne.

Suddenly she was pressed to the ground by an invisible force, nerves twitching. She moaned and tried to rise, but was slammed back down to the marble. What was happening? It wasn't the bloodpact. It felt different. Not internal but external. As if someone was doing it to her. She'd felt it before… a familiar memory she couldn't place in her anger-addled brain.

The Shadow King's voice thundered, a powerful, resonating baritone. "You're just like him, you know? You even have a flair for the dramatic." He stood over her. So close. Faye's fingers crawled, trying to grab the sword that was inches away. But it could have been in the bottom of a pit. Her fingers spasmed, shards of pain making her eyes water and limbs twitch.

She craned her neck, feeling muscles in her neck pull and strain with the effort.

The Shadow King's eyes were on her father's decapitated head. He didn't seem to be aware that she was watching him. Strands of red hair, like hers, still stuck to her father's face. The Shadow King wore an almost sad look—no, not sad. Disappointed, and curious. As if he were wondering why the man's head lay there, staring up at him vacantly, dripping blood onto his floor. What was he thinking? Faye wondered. Then the thief king's look vanished and his cloudy eyes flashed to her. Because his vacant eyes lacked pupils, it was difficult to tell that he was looking directly at her, but she felt his gaze and a terrible violence and hatred that burned within it. His words were slow, amused. "Like father, like daughter."

Faye thrashed against her invisible bounds, gazing up and snarling through gritted teeth at the man. "You bastard," she snarled. "Where is my sister? GIVE HER TO ME!"

The Shadow King loomed over her, filling her vision. He knelt at her side, and softly stroked her head. Like a pet. Like a wild horse he was eager to geld. His pale hand was huge as he touched her, making her seem like a child by comparison. She flinched, trying to pull away from his touch but it was no use. So she did the next best thing. Using *si'tu'ah*, Faye took in what information she could. His hand was warm. So he *wasn't* an animated corpse. She wasn't sure if that was a point in her favor, or not. At least he was human. He pulled a strand of her red hair, feeling it between his fingers. "So soft, yet so hard."

She ignored his words, again forcing herself to notice his details. *Use* si'tu'ah *to find his weak points*, her mind shouted. Despite his hands girth, they curiously looked soft and milky. Swordsman's hands were calloused at certain points. So were a bowman's. Even a brawler had thickened knuckles and scars across the back of their hands. Not the Shadow King. His hands could have been a courtesans for all their lack of blemishes. They were smooth as if he lotioned them, with large, round manicured fingernails, and not a single scar or raised callous. She felt a spike of confidence, realizing what that meant. He wasn't a fighter. And yet, why possess such a big sword if he couldn't wield it? Compensating? No. Something was missing. Something nagged at her; so close to understanding and yet still out of reach like the blade at her side.

"Fight me," she growled, still unable to move.

"In time," he said, almost sweetly. "Be patient, my Mistress of Shadows. It won't be long now." He sounded eager. Faye's mind raced. *What is he talking about? What won't be long?* The Shadow King rose, turning

311

his back on her and moving back to his dais.

Faye pushed herself up, trying to rise, trying to fight her restraints, but agony wracked her limbs. She looked up and saw a red-robed Reaver appear from behind the Shadow King's throne. Through her blurred vision she squinted, trying to make out the figure, but knew who it was even before the man's features resolved.

"Izul…"

Izul only smirked. His fetid brown hair fell into his eyes while his fingers danced as if he were playing a puppet. With each movement of his fingers, fire and pain erupted beneath her skin. She tried to suppress her cries, to not reveal the pain, but each new flare felt like a glowing hot ember placed beneath her skin.

The Shadow King returned to his thrown and sat calmly, his thick arms resting on the skulled armrests, soft hands cradling the skulls.

"Enough," she heard at last.

It was the Shadow King. She reviled him, but had tears in her eyes, thankful for his intervention in her agony. It made her hate him all the more. "Coward," she spat. "The great and powerful *Shadow King*, too scared to fight a woman upon her knees. You have to resort to others to do your dirty work."

"Is that what you think? That I'm afraid?"

She smiled and felt blood upon her teeth. "We always fear what we don't understand."

The Shadow King rose once more. He extended an arm, and several servants moved forth from behind the throne. Apparently there was a corridor hidden from sight behind the hideous throne. The servants grabbed the blade that rested against the wall, hefting it reverently—she was acutely aware it took two of them—before placing it in the Shadow King's outstretched hand. Faye took in his armor and blade.

His heavy plated armor had two massive spikes on either shoulder. It must have weighed an immense amount, but he moved smoothly as if it were light linen. He casually hefted the giant blade. It was the size of an ordinary man. Along the surface of the dark steel blade were tiny white stones that glowed faintly—the blade itself looked like curling fire, rising to a wicked, gleaming point. That and the glint of the black carapace seemed familiar… *could it be?*

"Do you know who gifted this armor and blade to me?" the Shadow King asked, turning over the blade, admiring its craftsmanship. His eyes

312

flashed. "*Your father.* Dragonborne, just like yours, found in the ruins of Yronia. But unlike you, Darkeye was smart enough to know I was the destined ruler of this world. That you betrayed him is no great mystery—the strong eat the weak, as is the natural way of things. I believe he always knew you would kill him. But sometimes... I wonder... if he always intended for me to kill you."

Faye gulped. His words sunk through her skin, hitting bone, jarring her. *Always knew?* Questions raced through her agile mind. Had her father really bent a knee to this cretin or was there more to the story? Had her father given his youngest daughter to this monster? If so, was the Shadow King more than he seemed to be or was her father's offering just a ruse for greater power? She shook her head. No. None of it mattered. When she looked up, her death mask had returned. "You'd be better suited to a cocktail dress than that fancy armor, *my liege,*" she said mockingly, spitting blood upon the white marble.

Izul let his fingers drop, but his face looked disappointed. "Really, you should let me kill her, my lord—she will only cause you trouble, Great One." *Lord? Great One?* Faye questioned. Had she hit her head and lost all sense? What in the Seven Hells kind of game was Izul playing at? Four-stripe Reavers did not play servant to false thief kings. Perhaps the bloodpact was starting to drive her mad, but she didn't think she could be imagining all this. Besides, Gray always arrived in her imaginings and he was nowhere to be seen now. She wished he were here, even as just a figment of her imagination, even for a fleeting moment, if only just to see his face. She laughed inwardly. *I sound like a girl with a crush. What's happening to me? How much blood have I lost?*

The Shadow King sighed. "No, I'm afraid not," he said, after weighing the idea. He settled back into his throne. "I have need of her, as she has need of me. Do you not, *my* Mistress of Shadows?"

Faye shivered to her bones. The way he said it...

The Reaver's bonds slackened, disappearing.

Despite the agony of her wound, Faye rose, but a dozen thieves were there, blades upon her neck. "*Where... is.... she...where is Leah?*" Faye asked.

The Shadow King ignored her.

"Before the ceremony starts might I take my leave?" Izul asked.

The Shadow King waved his hand dismissively.

Izul started, then stopped at the Shadow King's booming voice. "Re-

313

member, Reaver. This is not your Farbs. Tread lightly in my city and do not be late." Despite his even tone, the Shadow King's threat was unmistakable.

Izul swallowed nervously. "I'll need a servant. I'll take him." He pointed to the boy with raven hair.

The Shadow King weighed Izul, tilting his head with an eerie madness in his white eyes. Then, slowly, he nodded.

"By your command, I go to see our promised deed done." Izul's final words shook, his voice practically breaking.

Promised deed? Faye wondered woozily. The world swam. She was losing too much... Her thoughts were beginning to get muddled and the floor heaved like the *Pride's* deck. She fought to rise but several thieves leapt forward, pinning her down.

Gathering his robes as if they could protect him, Izul walked briskly down the marble dais. He reached her with a cocky smile. "In the end we all get our deserved fates, it seems."

Faye felt a shiver to her core. "What're you planning?"

"Wouldn't you care to know?"

She laughed, looking to the thief king in his throne. "Him? Really?"

"You don't know the half of it."

"Whatever bargains you struck he will break them, and then end you like the fool you are."

He lowered his voice, the Shadow King watching them with a narrowed gaze. "Oh, and I hope he tries. Nothing would give me greater satisfaction. Then my orders will be clear—I can kill the lot of them. Until then he follows my plans and my orders unwittingly." Izul grabbed her hair, and planted his lips upon hers in a rough, sadistic kiss. Unfazed, Faye bit his lip. Hard. Then she ripped it away, spitting a chunk of pink flesh to the ground. Izul roared in agony and she smiled up at him sweetly. Eyes like pools of fire, he stared intently at her and another jolt of pain spasmed through Faye's body. Like the bastard he was, he focused the shards of pain right upon her bloody wound. Faye forced herself not to cry out. Tears sprouted from her eyes, but she grinned through them until the scraping, cutting agony slowly dimmed.

Izul rose, wiping thick blood from his wounded lip.

Faye licked the salty blood from hers—tasting it, watching his anger still pulsing from his body. "Well? Off you go, little pet," she said jauntily, as if she weren't the one bound in shackles.

Izul touched his bloody mouth and threads of flesh wove his lip together—pink and new, but whole once more. His sneer deepened, eyes glistening with hatred. "Enjoy your final moments, Mistress of Shadows. Not long now and you'll join that whore of a sister of yours in the afterlife."

Faye's whole body stiffened, but she remained silent. She didn't want to give him the satisfaction that his words affected her, but Izul must have known. *She's not dead*, Faye thought. *She can't be dead.*

Izul knelt, but this time the Reaver used threads of flesh to keep her in place. Her face was locked, staring forward as he whispered hotly in her ear. "So you know, I never approved of the way the Shadow King treated her. Like a pet. Nothing more than a willing hound at his beck and call. He didn't see her beauty like I did... just like you. So lovely on the surface, yet so empty and so cold beneath." Izul gripped her chin and leaned in even closer. She felt his tongue licking her ear as he spoke, making her body shiver and her skin crawl. "Behind closed doors, however, she was surprisingly eager to please."

Faye didn't move, her rage mounting. Her lips were clamped together by threads. She fumed hot breaths through her nostrils, but Izul's oily leer only widened in the corner of her vision. "I wonder if you're the same. All fire and fury on the surface, but a willing treat when no one is looking. A shame, really, that I'll never get to find out." He sighed as if truly sad, and rose. "I suppose I'll take solace at least in knowing that your death will be slow and painful. Goodbye, Faye. This will be the last we ever meet. " Izul didn't strike her again, didn't lash out with the spark. The four-stripe Reaver's thick robes swished as he turned and left. Only when he was out of earshot did she feel the bonds on her lips and body break and Faye gasped a breath, feeling hot tears leak down her cheeks. Was he right? Was Leah really dead? No, he'd just been goading her.

A servant appeared. "My liege. The others are here. It's time."

"Perfect," crooned the Shadow King upon his throne, settling back. "Put her in her chosen place—make sure to hide the blood—then send the others in." Two thieves nodded, moving to obey.

Time? Others? Chosen place? Faye wondered, watching her blood leak down her armor and onto the marble beneath her. Izul's prod must have opened it even wider. She could almost feel it flowing freely from her. She felt lightheaded, almost loopy, but she kept her face a mask. She'd seen the same before in her victims when they lost too much blood—they rambled, laughed, then were caught with panic-stricken moments of fear

315

and begging. But not Faye. She would not die a floundering fool.

She grabbed her sword with one hand and stood.

The two approaching thieves slowed. They eyed her hand that gripped her flowing wound, blood gushing around it, then more pointedly at her blade made from Yronia steel. They wavered visibly, and Faye grinned a bloody smile.

"She's half-dead," the Shadow King declared. "What are you two waiting for?"

"My lord…" sniveled the bigger thief, "It's the Mistress of Shadows, not some petty thief."

"She's half-dead. Does she need to be flayed and staked for you as well?"

"Come now, don't be shy, boys," Faye goaded, stepping forward past the dead thieves before her when pain lanced through her abdomen once again. Crying out, she fell to her knees once again. *Seven Hells*, she cursed to herself as she hacked up thick, stringy strands of blood. She wiped them from her mouth, more in annoyance than actual pain. *It's made its way to my lungs.*

That was bad.

Heaving breaths of relief, the two thieves ran forward. They snatched her limp arms, binding them roughly and then hauled her to her trembling feet.

It didn't matter.

None of it mattered. She would live, she vowed—at least long enough to see Leah survive and the Shadow King die, and then it would end…

At last. But Izul's words tremored through her.

Promised deed…

And deep down she feared her life was not the only one in jeopardy. Her sluggish mind tried to think. Helix. The way Izul had looked at Helix. Izul wanted the boy. Why, she didn't know, but she was certain he wouldn't have stopped until the Reaver had the boy. That's why she'd been surprised when Izul had left the *Pride of Median* and its company alone. Now she realized he wasn't leaving it. Izul just needed to fulfill an errand first and ensure Faye was out of the way.

It was only speculation but she feared its truth.

Izul wasn't finished.

With that thought, she hoped the captain had been wise enough to leave her behind and set sail already. Light willing they were long gone by now and on their way to the Frizzian coast and Izul would find an empty dock. But Faye knew the light was never that gracious.

※ ※ ※

Faye let herself be lugged by the two thieves, her feet dragging on the marble. Perhaps *let herself* was an overstatement. She found consciousness difficult. Standing wasn't quite in the cards. Still, as they hauled her to the large dais where the Shadow King sat on his throne looking like a regal jester, she told herself that the weaker she seemed, the more she could leverage that. It was a twisted half-truth.

The two men gruffly set her in a red-velvet cushioned chair.

Woozily, she glanced to her left and right. *Eight*, she counted the chairs. Four on one side of the vainglorious thief king, and four on the other. Each had gold stained wood, now flaking. More remnants of Narim's fading glory.

"Be gentle," she said softly, mockingly, as they bound her hands and feet to the chair's arms and set about staunching the flow of blood that was making her thoughts wander.

Her head dipped, feeling heavy, but she turned it into a nod, gaze falling to the man in the throne, hatred raging through her.   317

The Shadow King's white gaze was set ahead, as if seeing a coming storm.

"Where is she?" she growled.

He was silent.

"Show me Leah, you coward, or… or do you not really have her? That's it isn't it—you've never had her?" She laughed, feeling a tad mad. "Then you've no leverage on me. Kill me then and be done with it."

"Gag her," he ordered, flipping a hand.

A thick cloth was shoved into her mouth, and a strip wrapped over it to silence her. She had to breathe through her nose, which made it difficult to get enough air. She distracted herself from her rising fear by taking in the men around her.

One was big and bulky. He'd moved her like a ragdoll, easily setting her in a chair… the other? He was slighter than most women, but his face was covered in a black mask as if he were some sort of Algasi. Oddly enough, it only covered his mouth. Just above the mask, she glimpsed a light birthmark. It resembled a sword. She hesitated. Was she just delirious?

The man looked like…

No, it couldn't be.

Still… Sun-tanned. Odd for a thief whose home was the endless dark of Narim. The most notable contrast to the others, however, was his eyes. They watched her with bitter hate and she knew it couldn't be him. Besides, Melx was dead. She knew first-hand because she had killed him.

The men tried to strip down her armor to find the wound, but without the proper knowledge, they would never take it off. There were no clasps, no hooks or easy-to-cut straps. The releases were known only to the wearer of the armor. Finally, they settled on lifting up the skintight plates to place a thick cotton pad upon the wound. But when blood seeped quickly through the pad, then the next, and the next, their eyes grew wide.

"What's taking so long?" the thief king demanded.

"There's a problem, my lord," said the blue-eyed thief. Something shone in his eyes for a flickering moment. A hint of… *sorrow?* No, just her imagination.

"What problem?"

"We cannot staunch the flow… Only slow it."

It will not heal, she knew. *You cannot use me as a puppet.*

The Shadow King sighed. "How long does she have?"

"Several hours, maybe less, maybe more."

The Shadow King turned to her. "I would be most disappointed if you died on me so soon, Mistress of Shadows. I have…" His pale lips twisted, but not in a smile. And despite his gaze of pure white nothingness, she felt the hot glare of something akin to lust in them. "Plans for you and I."

Faye snarled, but knew her words would only sound muffled and ineffectual.

"If I cannot stop it?" asked the thief with the black mask who was trying to heal her.

"Keep her breathing long enough to sign the treaty. If she dies, you die. And your death won't be as pretty as hers. If she lives beyond that? Then I will see her to Reaver Izul's talented hands."

A guard came with sweat straining down his face, making his black livery wet. "They're here, my lord."

To Witness The Moment Before

Helix watched the men prepare to set sail while he played with a small woodcrafting knife he'd found, digging at a small hole in the ship's grab rail. He chipped away at the varnish—tung oil most likely—that kept the salt and water from seeping into the wood, carving absentmindedly. Whittling at Xavvan's ship was pointless and it was unlike Helix to mindlessly vandalize, but he was frustrated to the point of screaming. He had no idea what else to do. His thoughts were on his homeland. And so he dug, glancing over his shoulder, knowing he'd get an earful if Captain Xavvan spotted him.

But the big bellied man was preoccupied arguing with his first mate, Gambol. Their heated exchange wafted in the air like the sting of salt, biting at Helix's senses, distracting him. Even the other sailors were half-heartedly going about their duties, leaning one ear to listen to their leaders' squabble.

"—and oi' say, that ye be'in a blubberin' fool, Cap. Waitin' here be a damned fool's errand and y'know it!"

Xavvan's hands gripped the railing, looking to the Black Hive that rose from the turquoise and black city like a shattered blade, saying nothing. He turned to Gambol, calmly. "Is that all ye' have to say?"

Gambol growled and grit his jaw. As he did his hollowed cheeks looked to Helix like two sails with the wind sucked from them. "No, it ain't all! I don't get it. Not one bit. She ain't worth piss and shill, and ye' be waitin' on 'er 'and an' foot all this way. Now we be charged t'er, sittin' on our damned 'ands in this blasted city and wait for 'er royal princess to return? Wha' next? Let her man the 'elm and take the *Pride* 'erself and all us with it into the Seven Hells of Remwar?"

Helix had never seen Gambol angry. Usually he was all snorts and sly smiles. But now he was worked up into a full lather. Unfortunately, the captain was three Gambols in one, and his size gave him a significant sort of presence. That and the fancy blue coat he wore smugly, always tugging on the edges. Xavvan rose from the railing, gripping his blue lapels once again—his pockets still bulged with limfuns, the man's curiously annoying habit. "We stay, Gambol."

"But ye' told 'er we'd leave! Why wait?"

Xavvan's jaw clenched. "My gut. It tells me there's something coming."

Gambol licked his lips and drew nearer. He grew nervous, then realized all of the *Pride* was watching. He turned on the sailors. "Oi! Get back to it, ye' filthy land lovin' freeloaders or I'll 'ave you swabbin' the planks until yer flabby arms fall off!"

The deckhands jumped too, but only for show, still trying to listen in.

Gambol lowered his voice so only the captain could hear beneath the sound of licking waves upon the hull. Luckily, Helix was close, and the water became a distant murmur as he leaned in, listening. "Oi Cap, my gut speaks it too. Something be coming. But I don't like it none. None at all."

That tone… Helix felt his pulse stutter.

Xavvan hesitated too, casting Gambol a dubious eye.

"How long 'ave we known each other, Cap? Too long, right?"

"Too long," Xavvan agreed.

"Right," said Gambol. "And how long in all that time has me gut been wrong? I'm tellin' you, Cap, somethin' ain't right here," he said, watching the milling thieves onshore. Helix hesitated. The thieves and dock didn't look any different to him. Just a bunch of greasy-haired figures with stubbled faces in soiled rags. Sure, they watched the ship as they passed with greedy, beady eyes like rats from a dark hole, but the dozen sailors with swords on the gangplank deterred them as surely as the scent of a cat. "Trust me now."

Gambol pleaded one last time, gripping Xavvan's coat. Xavvan opened his mouth as if to object, but read Gambol's plaintive eyes. At last, the captain sighed. "So be it," he said, as if casting a death sentence. "Give the order. We cast off."

Gambol bobbed his head gratefully. "Right, Cap." He turned, and then paused. "For wha' it's worth. Yous' doin' the rat' thing. Thank you," he said in his gravely voice. The last two words sounded awkward coming from the hard First Mate, but sincere.

But Xavvan didn't reply. He turned his gaze back to the Black Hive sitting like a shattered black blade above the turquoise mists, looking even more troubled as shouts rattled across the gangplank and orders to hoist off were given—the sounds of the lapping dark waters returning again to Helix's ears. As Gambol dipped away, he shot Helix a glance.

Gambol had said all of two words to Helix, but he seemed to be watching over him. Since he'd been captured he'd felt Gambol's gaze from the crow's nest, or peering over the tiller. When that man, the Reaver in the red robes had approached, Gambol had saved him once already—telling him off at nearly the cost of his own flesh being flayed. And the first mate didn't have much to spare.

Gambol had been giving Helix a big helping of his own food too—almost more than he could eat. Why was the man so generous? He hadn't asked for his help. It almost annoyed him. If it was pity… Helix's jaw grit, gripping his dagger tighter. But it didn't seem like it. Nor sympathy. Medians weren't one to look kindly on Banished folk. Perhaps he felt guilty for capturing him in the first place? He grew too curious. "Gambol!" he called.

The man was yelling at a deckhand, and he approached. "Oi, what's it, boy?" His words were crass and direct to all, but when speaking to Helix he seemed to soften them and his squinting eye.

"We're leaving, I see," he said, leaving the statement a sort of question.

The man hooked his thumbs in his leather belt and nodded. Despite being many years older than Helix, the man wasn't much taller. He had an almost child-like frame, but it was hard-bitten like the rest of him and deeply tanned, almost as dark as an Algasi. He had a strange gait, and Helix noticed that as he rested his thumbs on his tooled belt his right arm seemed awkward, bent at a weird angle, as if it had been broken and never healed right. "That's right. Cap's orders," said the man. "No need to be sloggin' 'round this dark pit any longer. No place for civilized folk

321

or young ones." He spat toward the milling thieves on the docks beyond; his spittle fell to the dark waters. An awkward silence settled between the two until Gambol's eyes lit up suddenly, digging into his pocket. "Ey, you wants any more food? I got a bit of nuts and larba fruits I hadn't eaten this morning."

He handed over a handful of slivered nuts and dried red berries despite Helix's protests. "No, I'm fine, really..." But Gambol didn't listen, pushing the food into his hands. Helix stopped trying and looked up, smiling in thanks. "Why are you so nice to me?" he asked bluntly.

He had a sudden memory, standing before a fruit seller's stand and a heavyset man who blushed a crimson deeper than a Reaver's scarlet robes.

His father grabbed his arm, pulling him away. One hand on his arm, the other yanking his ear and drawing sharp pain. Helix winced, rubbing his ear as his father let go. "What'd I do this time?"

"You asked him why he was fat."

"So?

"You don't see what's wrong with that?"

He shook his head. "It's a fact, isn't it?"

His father sighed, his white brows drawing together. As always, he blocked out the majority of the man's features, blurring them. He didn't *want to remember. He wanted to forget. But the memory continued despite his blurry face.*

His father pointed out to the sea, a glassy surface that extended for miles, now placid as usual in the Median dawn. "Look there. Water is smooth, boy. It wears away slowly, carefully, knowing just the right path to take, like carving away sand from the banks of the Ker Stream. You? You're blunt like a hammer. Smashing and banging away to get what you want. People don't like blunt. Be honest, but be tactful. Be like the sea." Helix gave a sharp snort at the memory of his father's words. His father was wrong. Water could be a tempest, wrathful and sudden, destroying whole cities with a single tidal wave, or mysterious and terrible like the Abyss that sucked thousands of ships into its nether-like black hole. Perhaps the man had been simplifying it for a child's mind back then, but Helix didn't agree in general. Smooth was boring. Water, when soothing, was boring. A hammer made more sound. Besides, blunt was all he'd ever been.

He looked back, remembering that he'd asked the hard-bitten first mate a question. "I... uh..." Gambol was still squirming like a worm left in the baking sun. At last, the old seaman relinquished. "You remind me of someone," he confessed. "That's all."

Helix peered up at the man. "Who was it?"

"Jus' someone who 'ad dreams behind 'ere," he said, pointing a scrawny finger to his squinty eye, "like you—it's nice to see after this cursed lot. More dreary than a mortuary they are."

Helix ventured a guess. "Did this person... have this?" He pulled back his sleeve and exposed the banished mark. A sinuous white scar that took up nearly his entire forearm. Luckily no other deckhand was near enough to see the hated mark.

"No, 'fraid not," admitted Gambol, and Helix shrunk in his clothes, feeling exposed—he knew the man was curious how he'd gotten the brand, but he didn't ask. He had a feeling Gambol would never ask unless offered. Gambol added, "'owever, she was sharp like you."

Was... "I'm sorry," said Helix. "How'd she die?"

Gambol looked away and laughed. "*Direct* like you too."

Helix realized he'd touched on too tender a nerve. Perhaps this time his father was right and he was too blunt. He opened his mouth to apologize again and tell the man it was all right.

But Gambol answered first. "When I was a lad I found myself on a fishing schooner in a storm. Was my first voyage to sea, it was—I was giddier than a gull digging into a bucket of day-old chum. But no one was happier than me sis. You see, the sea is in me—I breathe it in, taste it, but to her? It was her *life*, her very blood. She would've found a way onto that rust bucket of a ship even 'ad I chained her to the docks with Yronia steel. And that's that same sheen you have in your eyes. I see it. A dream that stirs in yer blood."

The man was right. It was his search for the true Kingdom of Water, but Helix was transfixed by Gambol's story. "What happened?"

Gambol's eyes glazed in memory. "Not one day into the voyage a storm sucked us right up, it did. We fought, putting oars to water, raging against the winds with our all might, but it was no use. Swells came about us, rising about our heads. Bigger and bigger they grew—bigger than a mountain, taller than the cliffs of Ren Nar crashing upon us. Still we clung for dear life. I held Ala's hand below deck, but the storm dragged us ever deeper... to the edge of the Abyss itself." *The Abyss?* Helix had never heard of anyone reaching the Abyss and surviving. It was supposed to be a whirlpool of black, leagues wide, plagued with lightning and thunder and torrential rains. Tales only said men who caught glimmers of the giant,

323

angry, dark vortex were pulled into it and never seen again.

"Did... you see it?"

"And wished I never had. Still do, too. In my dreams, in my night-mares, every night," answered Gambol with a haunted look.

"What," Helix said, and licked his lips, "what happened then?"

Gambol took a shaky breath. "I still remember the sound of it... The ship flexed, its long planks twisting and buckling beneath the pressure of the heavy waves, beneath the beast of the Abyss—as if the titans them-selves had their grip upon us. I looked around at the huddled men be-neath that rickety deck as the storm besieged us, pulling us into the angry eye of the devil itself. I felt it then, in my gut. The truth. We were all to die." His eyes went glassy, looking faraway, something dark and terrifying passing over them; then it was gone. At last, Gambol looked up with a heavy breath. Though the turquoise light of Narim still pressed in on them, Helix felt his breath return, breathing in a huge lungful as if he'd narrowly escaped the black Abyss himself.

His mouth was as parched as the Rehlias Desert. He worked some saliva into it and asked, hesitantly, "How'd you survive?"

"Can't say," said Gambol with an honest shrug, back to his roughhewn self. "A miracle some said, or perhaps a curse. All I can recollect is dark-ness and the crash of lightning, then water everywhere, taking me... And then waking up in one of them white infirmary cots in Media, 'earing the faint cry of gulls and the truth that my sis and all hands had been lost to the dark waters, and I was all that remained."

"I'm sorry," said Helix again, not knowing what to say.

The first mate scratched his gaunt jaw. "Eh', nothing to be done fer it. In the end it was no one's fault but the Almighty's 'imself, and he can't be blamed." Then he fixed Helix with another squinty glare and a smile. "Oi think Ala woulda fancied you, tho'. She 'ad a sense for the good folk. That was never my strongest hand. Now I try to look for 'em. I guess that's why I've been keepin' one of me eyes to you."

Helix felt uncomfortable under the praise.

Thankfully, Gambol didn't let it linger. "As for Ala, she's gone to a better place. She found her home in the Crystal Seas. And one day I'll see 'er again."

Crystal Seas.

It was where all sailors, and most Medians, believed they went when they died—a pure crystal-blue ocean with white sand beaches as far as the eye can see. According to legends, the water was so pure you could drink from it and so clear one could see to the deepest ocean depths, and the swells were always calm. It sounded beautiful, but it was just a fool's dream, Helix knew bitterly. A story, every bit as fabricated as the Ronin themselves. Nothing came after death, and if there was anything—it wasn't happy.

He shut his eyes to hold back tears, remembering.

Gasping… Blood-soaked hands clutching at Helix's clothes.

He shut the memory out, gritting his teeth against it. No, death wasn't pretty. The dying didn't smile nor did their eyes warm to the future. His father had looked afraid, terrified even. Worst yet—helpless. Just as Helix had been.

But he didn't tell Gambol that. Helix was only supposed to be a fifteen-year-old boy who believed in fairy tales and the Ronin, like all other boys his age. Helix had never been a big believer in fairy tales or delusions, and that included the Crystal Seas. Helix offered up another lame condolence and Gambol took it.

"I ought to put this sorry lot back to work, for the sooner we set sail and fly this dark pit the better, as far as I'm concerned," said Gambol. With that he turned, shouting orders for sails to be raised, anchor to be drawn and the mooring ropes to be cast off.

Helix popped a handful of nuts and dried berries in his mouth, chewing, mulling over Gambol's story as the crew moved about him like a famous Sevian carnival under Gambol's lashing tongue. He rose and leaned on the railing, watching the crowds when he heard a bit of commotion again. In the streets beyond, he saw an entourage of hooded thieves, a figure at their head. Their leader drew nearer and Helix saw who it was…

Izul?

The Reaver was weaving through the crisscrossing, creaking docks, pushing aside any who got in his way, moving with impetus and a dangerous looking air.

Something flittered inside Helix, palms growing sweaty on the rail.

What was the man doing back here? He figured wherever Faye was, that man wouldn't be far away, but as he scanned the faces he saw only two-dozen or so cloaked figures moving at his side—all bulky. Men. No Faye. Izul reached the gangplank. Suddenly he raised a hand. What was he doing? Gambol abruptly grabbed Helix's arm and yanked him

325

sideways.

"*GET DOWN!*" he bellowed.

A huge fiery explosion erupted, sending shards of wood and chunks of fire into the air and all across the deck. Cries echoed in the air. The world turned inside out. Helix tried to breathe but sucked in only sharp, acrid smoke. He coughed and gagged. It stung his lungs and eyes. He couldn't see. Terror filled his veins as he clawed across the deck, feeling rough wood. He stumbled over something wet and flesh and brought his hands to his eyes, seeing red. Blood. The face resolved itself.

Gambol?

No—a dark, hollow-cheeked sailor who looked a little like Gambol. He remembered the man now. The sailor had given Helix a few nods and easy greetings, but not much more. Now the sailor's eyes stared into a world beyond, glazed in death. *Just like him. The same eyes*—the thought came like a lance. Helix felt a flush of sweat. He backpedaled until his back smacked the ship's railing, his breaths coming hard and fast.

As his head began to clear, ears still ringing, he saw figures through the shroud of dust and smoke. Dark cloaked men. Helix's hearing returned as he grabbed onto a barrel, peering over it. He heard groans and plaintive cries of men and the crackle of fire amid the smoke.

Suddenly a sailor spoke, a voice in a sea of gray. "*Please no—let me live, I don't want to—*"

The words were cut short by a gurgled cry and the sickening cutting of flesh, like a butcher's knife into a carcass of meat.

And Helix understood.

The cloaked men were killing any who showed signs of life. Though still woozy, Helix's instincts told him to run, to flee as fast as he could. And he moved to rise when he saw a flash of scarlet push through the cloud of debris. Anger and hatred spiked inside of Helix. Reaver Izul stood at the top of the gangplank peering about. He saw the man's eyes— twin molten orbs scanning the fog. They settled on Helix and he felt his heart skip a beat. Just then something flickered and there was a groan.

A sailor.

He reached out for his cutlass.

Izul sighed, extending a hand.

The man burst into flames. Blood splayed the air, but the Reaver swiped a hand and a thin layer of black sprung to life. *Moon.* Like a black shield, it caught the spray of blood then winked away. A stray droplet of blood had fallen on Izul's cheek though and he wiped it free, flicking it aside with a sigh. "Where is he? The Shadow King has only given us a sliver of time. I have to return to help deal with that insufferable woman." He sounded impatient, anxious even, and the Reaver licked his lips as if hungry.

He? Who is he searching for? But Helix had a sinking suspicion.

"We're searching, Reaver Izul. But if you could make this cursed dust go away, it would make our jobs at lot easier," a thief growled.

Izul snorted, turning to the thief—a stocky man with stubby limbs. "And how exactly would I do that? Shall I burn the hanging debris and set you all on fire?"

"I..."

"Or perhaps you think I should use the banished element, hmm? Unfortunately, none but the dreaded Wanderer himself can thread wind. Perhaps you can? Are you Kailith, my fat little friend?" Helix couldn't see the man's face, but the thief's head rattled in protest, looking petrified at the fire dancing in the Reaver's eyes. "No? You can't? Then shut your mouth, stop wasting my time and look for the boy. He can't have gone far."

"And if he's dead?" asked another.

Izul laughed. "There's a reason I used fire. His power is based off need. It would have saved him. If not, then he's not the one we are searching for after all."

Power? Helix wondered. He figured they were talking about him until that...

Helix peered over the railing, looking into the dark waters. *I could jump,* he thought. *What then, genius? They'll hear you and then Izul will light up the waters.* He looked to the gangplank, but a dozen dark thieves blocked his path. There was no way off the ship. He began to back away when he felt a rough hand clasp his mouth. He let out a stifled scream and looked over his shoulder.

Gambol.

The rough-faced man pulled him away into the fog, away from the voices. They crawled over bodies and shattered wood. Abruptly Gambol grabbed his arm, pulling him back. A thief passed in front of them, head twisting and growling his annoyance. Gambol waved a hand, ushering him on. Smoke stung Helix's eyes, making it difficult to see, but he watched Gambol extract a key from his tunic pocket and unlock a door.

327

He pushed it open and they slipped inside.

"I thought you were dead," Helix whispered in a bare breath as soon as the door closed and Gambol silently locked it once more and slid the huge metal bolts into place.

The first mate wiped the blood from his mouth. "Not yet. But no time for talk of life or death," he whispered. "They will be here in moments or less, and that lock is more like tinsel on a tree than steel to that lily-livered, red-skirted coward Izul."

Helix still couldn't believe what was happening. Why was Izul slaughtering them? But Helix knew why. Izul was searching for him. But why? He felt a wave of guilt but even more so, though he was ashamed to admit it, he felt fear. He didn't want to die. "What do we do?"

Suddenly another voice sounded. "We fight."

Helix twisted to see the big-bellied captain. He stood in front of his desk—and Helix realized they were in the captain's quarters. Compared to the rest of the ship it was enormous, almost kingly. It even had paintings on the walls of ships on raging seas and a painting of the white-walled fortress of Median gazing out on the grand Kalvas Ocean; in the corner, Helix spotted a bolted-down table with a game of elements on it, midgame. Helix looked back to the captain. Xavvan's blue coat was singed in a few different places looking like burnt parchment, and blood ran from the corner of his ear and smeared across his cheek—ash and soot stained his once-white beard, but he still gave a grizzly smile. "Xavvan," Helix whispered, elated. "Praise Median, I'm glad to see you!" He rushed forward, hugging the man.

"Aye, I'm glad to see you too, boy," said Xavvan, patting him on the back.

Helix saw the big captain held wicked weapons in his meaty fists. In his left hand Xavvan gripped a cutlass of fine, dark steel with a golden crossguard, and in his right he hefted a thick truncheon with metal studs that looked almost as heavy as Helix.

"The blithering rat Izul and his cronies will be here any sec, Cap," Gambol said, nodding to the door. "We 'ave but a moment."

Xavvan grunted, then his blue eyes grew steely. "How many?" Helix understood. *How many dead?*

"Just us left," Gambol said.

"And them?"

"Two dozen, maybe more."

He exchanged a mysterious look with Gambol and the man nodded. *What was that about?* Helix wondered, confused.

Xavvan handed the cutlass toward Helix.

Helix swallowed. "I don't know how to fight—" he began.

"Luckily it's not for you," said Xavvan, reaching beyond.

Gambol took the blade in one hand. Helix saw now, one of the first mate's arms was bent at an odd angle, blood pouring down his arm and dripping to the deck, but still he wore his customary half-grimace, half-smirk. Xavvan trundled quickly and moved behind the captain's white silveroot desk to snatch what looked like a letter opener from a drawer. He handed it to Helix.

"Take this, boy."

Helix wanted to argue, but the greater part of him didn't even know what to do with the small blade. And he admitted as much. "I've never fought a day in my life."

"You'll learn quickly enough," said Xavvan. "But with luck, not today." *Not today?* He nodded to Gambol and the man seemed to understand. He set his blade down, then grabbed a chair with his one good arm, propping it beneath the door's handle. At the same time, Xavvan shambled to the mosaic glass windows in the rear of the cabin. He lifted a small lever that locked the window in place and pushed it open, letting in a trickle of turquoise light, and the cool air of Narim.

329

"I don't understand," Helix whispered nervously, palms already sweaty on his little dagger.

Xavvan gave a heavy breath, speaking urgently. "It's time we parted company, boy. Unfortunately, this is a fight for those with a few more years under their belt," said Xavvan in a low breath. "A few years you don't have. Go on now." They slid a chair over and ushered him up onto it. He peered out the window and saw a rope dangling, falling all the way to the darkened waters below.

"I…" he paused.

Helix felt the pressure of the moment—seconds ticking by.

He glanced to the door, waiting for it to burst open any moment.

"You could join me," he said suddenly, hope rising.

Xavvan snorted. "Even if I could fit through that window, and it's been many years since I could do that, they'll never think I just up and left the ship. They'll know we ran and that bastard Izul will light up the waters before we're two strokes from the *Pride's* stern. This way at least we can stall that bilge rat and buy you time to get away. Besides. it's you he's after, not us. He might leave us be." Helix knew that last part to be a lie—adults always tried to lie to him as if he didn't know the difference.

He turned to Gambol, desperate, hopeful.

The first mate's grimace deepened as he lifted his lame arm. "'Fraid the Cap's right this time, boy. Arm's busted seven ways to hell. Damned thing wasn't much use before, but now it's even less. I can still lift a blade though, and while there's breath in these here lungs I won't go down without a fight."

"But... I..." Then he felt something strange and wet. Tears. Leaking down his face. He suddenly felt very young and very afraid. And he didn't care. "I don't want to be alone," he confessed. But more than that, he was afraid for them. "Don't leave me. Please."

Suddenly the door rattled, and then there was a shout.

"Climb, lad!" ordered Xavvan in a dark rush. "Now!"

Helix clambered up and out the window. His hands were slick on the rope as he prepared to descend.

As he did, the door burst.

Gambol gave a rallying cry, charging with his black cutlass.

Dark clothed thieves met him.

Helix watched as Gambol stabbed the first thief, taking the man through the belly. Another thief made it through but as the first mate slashed, the thief raised his sword—the blades clashed, ringing steel. But Gambol became an angry dervish. He pulled the blade back and twisted, cutting the man's legs from beneath him, turning his legs to stumps. The thief gave a bloody cry, toppling as Gambol swung mightily and buried his heavy black cutlass into the man's chest in a spurt of blood. More thieves stalked forward, surrounding the man, and the first mate heaved heavy breaths.

"Well? What are you waiting for?" spat Gambol with his customary grimace-grin. "Come at me you, brine-crusted dogs of men, if you dare." The thieves wavered and Helix's heart rose. *They're afraid.*

"Let me," said a voice.

And a figure Helix hadn't expected walked forth out of the dust. He wore similar black rags to the thieves but his had a note of dark blue to them at the cuffs and a similar blue shirt peeked from beneath his black coat. The boy's eyes were hooded in shadows, like sunken pits as if from too little sleep. He also bore the thieves' half-gold, half-black pin on his breast. His face was pale and sharp-featured. He might have been attractive to girls, Helix guessed, with his dark fall of black hair across ice blue eyes. But the look in those eyes made Helix afraid. But not like Izul made him afraid. Izul, standing beside the boy, was mean, cruel, and powerful. This boy... And he couldn't be a year older than Helix... He was evil. There was a mystery and an anger in his eyes too. And while Helix felt a burning anger for his past, for his banishment, for the death of those he loved—the dark-haired youth looked as if he'd been born with tragedy in his heart like a black splinter.

The boy stepped up, holding only a small black dagger in his hand. The threat was clear.

"Modric... I can handle this—you were told to merely watch," Izul commanded.

But Modric said nothing. He also didn't step back. His blue gaze held Helix's and Helix felt fear, swallowing nervously. But he forced himself not to look away.

"I won't kill a boy," said Xavvan.

"I will," said Gambol with a snarl. "'Specially ones with devil spawn lurking in their eyes. This ain't no boy, Cap. Is you, demon spawn? You's a killer. Come on then, killer. I sees what you are and what you want—and you ain't gettin' the boy."

Modric said nothing. Not even a flicker of a smile. He only palmed his black dagger, waiting.

And Gambol cried out, charging. His sword was fast but Modric was quicker, if only by a hair. He sidestepped the blade. Gambol's blade flashed again, quicker and quicker, but with each slice Modric ducked, dodged, and slipped. "Fight me, you demon spawn!"

Sweat formed on Gambol's brow. Helix spotted Modric's breaths—harder. The two were of the same lithe build and stamina, but Modric was several hands taller. Helix felt a growing terror. There was something strange to the boy's movements. And why wasn't he attacking? Gambol struck again but despite the first mate's skill and speed, he seemed to strike always a second too late. As if he was striking at Modric's shadow.

Suddenly Gambol caught him, pinning him with his sword. The black cutlass hovered before Modric's throat. "Die, you—"

And Modric struck. Helix didn't know how he did it. He'd only blinked but the boy was *inside* Gambol's range, past his sword. And he stabbed his black dagger in the first mate's neck. Gambol fell and Modric leapt upon the first mate, attacking with abandon. He cried out, stabbing over and over again. Blood fountained from Gambol's neck.

"*Stop! Stop it!*" Helix bellowed. He clambered back into the room, running to Gambol's side but Xavvan grabbed him first.

Gambol reached out with his one limp arm, as if to fend off the flurry of blows or perhaps beg an end to the stabbing, but Modric didn't stop. He continued to stab, relentless, silent, an evil burning in his eyes. Gambol's arm fell back, flopping lifelessly. Still Modric stabbed. Blood no longer fountained, only the sickening thud of flesh and wet splashing followed.

"He's already dead!" Helix cried out, sniffling, reaching out. "Stop!" And as if hearing, Modric stopped and slowly rose, blood coating his body all the way up to his elbows like red paint. Gambol's blood. Helix felt sick to the pit of his stomach. He vomited and when he looked up, Modric's eyes fell on him. Colder than ice. Colder than death.

"You're a monster! You killed Gambol!" Helix bellowed, tears streaming.

"He wanted to die so I gave it to him," said the nightmarish boy in a soft, almost delicate whisper—a complete contrast to the demon that had only moments ago torn into Gambol. His words sounded strange too, as if it were the first time he'd ever spoken.

Helix's throat closed in pain and anger. It boiled up inside him until he thought he was going to explode. He felt something flicker and suddenly the whole boat rocked. Thieves and Izul reached to grab onto walls, hanging rope, or else fell to their knees. But then the *Pride* settled, as if it was only a sudden huge swell. Helix fell to his knees, suddenly exhausted.

"Don't kill yourself, child, by taking on too much. At least not before we do. My mistress has great plans for you. And you..." Izul turned to the gore-covered Modric. He cackled, "What a delight you are, boy! Even better than I'd ever hoped for. The Mistress will truly be pleased by you. Yes, I can see it now."

Helix tuned out the madman and tried to claw his way forward to rip Modric's blue eyes from his head, but Xavvan pulled Helix back. It was easy for the big man, but Helix ripped into him too. "Let me go, dammit, let me go!" he cried, teary-eyed.

There were tears in the captain's eyes as he spoke. "He's gone, boy. Nothing to be done now. It's time you ran." He pushed him back. But Helix stayed. Xavvan rounded, fury replacing his sorrowful eyes. "Go, I said. Now! Do not let Gambol's death be in vain."

And the fury in the man's eyes made Helix hesitate. He looked to the bloody corpse on the ground; Gambol's dead, vacant eyes stared into nothing, his blood running in rivulets and the wood planks soaking it up—but then Xavvan's words sunk in. *Do not let his death be in vain.* And he knew there was nothing he could do here. He had to run. He couldn't fight these demons. Not yet at least.

But Izul spoke. "Oh, the boy is mine too. He's not going anywhere. Orders are orders."

Modric stepped forward.

"Not this time, boy. You're much too vital to risk." Modric suddenly cried out as his legs collapsed beneath him. He fell to the wood deck as if rooted there, his muscles twitching, trying to resist. He turned to Izul lifting his dark blade, but then it glowed like an ember in a blacksmith's bellows and he released it, blood and flesh bubbling upon his hand. "Ah, ah," said Izul. "You forget who you're dealing with. Now sit back. I can handle this one." He turned to the captain.

The captain fixed Helix with a stare before turning.

And Helix wanted to help—every muscle begged him to help, his will shouted that it was the right thing, but his terror was like a wave washing over him. At last he did as Xavvan commanded, telling himself he had to, and not because of his fear.

It was a lie.

And hating himself, Helix ran.

As he did he felt his legs fold beneath him with a mind-numbing pain that felt like small daggers spreading across his legs, piercing flesh. But the result was flexed muscles that wouldn't move. *Move!* he screamed at his body.

Xavvan growled. "You won't get the boy, you bastard. Not upon my—"

Izul curled his five fingers to a single point and Helix watched with wide-eyes as tiny particles of light pulled from around the room, darkening the space. Izul flicked a single finger and a concentrated beam of sun shot forth. It pierced the captain's neck, burning a charred hole into the wall behind him. Xavvan gurgled blood, falling to his knees. Izul sighed again, "Such noble protectors, but that was destined to be a terribly boring speech," he said, then glanced over his shoulder. "Grab the boy and bring him to me—and be quick about it. Patience is not the Shadow King's finest trait, nor mine." A clutch of black-clothed thieves moved to obey.

333

But to Helix's and Izul's surprise, Xavvan suddenly bellowed. From his knees he swung, taking the legs from beneath the first charging thief, then bringing the truncheon up and smashing it into the man's skull, exploding it like an overripe melon. The captain spat his own blood to the deck and lumbered back to his feet.

The other thieves froze in their tracks.

The distraction was enough. Helix dove for the window. He jumped, ignoring the rope. As he did he heard another loud bellow from above. He hit water. He waited for the hard smack—like hitting brick that gave, but instead the water seemed to soften beneath him as he pierced its surface. Helix swam. He swam harder than he ever had. He looked up and saw fire blossoming all around him. He felt a bolt of fire sear past his leg, scorching, and he swam harder, diving deeper into the murky blackness. As he did, the water seemed to resolve itself—on the surface it was turquoise, but beneath it was a black void. It scared him, whatever lurked down there. But as fire rained down, getting closer, he knew what he had to do. He pushed deeper. His breath began to grow short and panic rose. But the fire still rained down. He found a small alcove in the darkness, hands grasping a watery wood-like purchase. A *sunken ship*. He relied on his single lungful of precious air. Growing up, Helix could always hold his breath for minutes longer than his friends, more than even most adults.

I can do this.

He held the wood, looking up. More fire. But it couldn't penetrate the water's depths. *I'm too deep*, he thought in success. But his lungs were beginning to burn. Then the fire stopped. His lungs wanted to burst, crying out for air. *He's given up! I can surface!*

Wait, shouted another voice. And something in him trusted it. Helix held onto the shattered sunken vessel, waiting, his brain and thoughts growing woozy from a lack of air. Then the water seemed to crystallize. Izul was turning the water to ice.

Helix would be trapped—he'd die. The icy water reached out to him and he swam back. Terrified, he knew he had to swim, but ice was coming towards him from all sides. And he was already out of air to the point of drowning and swimming would drain him of any remaining air and energy he had left. He swam anyway, diving beneath the crystallizing water, but he was too slow. The ice gripped his arm. He yanked on it, but it coated his arm like a casing of stone, moving higher. The icy flakes

spread across his chest and he gasped from the sheer surprise and frigid-
ness.

As he did, water filled his lungs.

The world froze around him.

His lungs filled with ice.

And Helix knew he'd failed.

Failed his father, failed his quest to find the true Kingdom of Water,
failed Xavvan and Gambol. He'd failed them all. And pure terror came,
knowing what was next. The end he'd seen in his father's eyes—the endless darkness. The last of the ice crawled over his face, coating his eyes,
locking his gaze in place for all eternity.

* * *

Thump.

The feeling pulsed through Helix, not a word, but a feeling amid the
eternal darkness.

Thump.

Was he dead? He had to be dead.

Then why did his lungs still burn? Why could he still think? His
thoughts were sluggish. Trying to grasp one felt like reaching through a
murky brown puddle with his hand coming back empty. His brain hurt,
and he knew his mind was slowly breaking down. He'd heard of it before—sailors drowning, lasting for several minutes without air. But each
minute shut down a different part of the brain, until they either came back
a vegetable in a human body, or dead. But something was saving him.

Thump—it came again.

His heart. It beat slowly, one slow thump every few seconds. Somehow he knew that was saving him, but not for long.

Think! He pleaded to himself. *If only I could see!*

A swirling ball of water pulsed in his mind.

See! he begged.

He felt ice turn warm and wet on his lids and he opened his eyes. Panic filled him again. Ice—blue and endless. He was still encased in a solid
block of ice as far as he could see, but he wasn't dead. His heart started to
speed and he felt his brain shutting down even faster. *Slow!* he urged his
heart, but it wouldn't. Time was running out like sand from an hourglass.
He tried to rattle his limbs but nothing moved. *It's no use!* Again the pan-

335

ic surged inside him, tears running down his lids and blurring his vision. The ice in his lungs was cold and terrifying—a solid block...

A solid block.

The phrase seemed to call to him, to shout at him—something about it was wrong, but his mind was so slow, he felt so sluggish and so scared. He could feel his brain dying, parts of his mind blackening with no air, no more than—

A *solid block!*

The word screamed in his dying brain.

And Helix saw it. Little bubbles suspended in the blue ice, floating before him. Hundreds of them. Thousands. *Millions.* The ice had frozen from the outside in, Helix at the center, and so the air had nowhere to go. He felt his limbs shudder—a part of his brain that was too important was shutting down, he knew. He was about to black out. But the icy orb in his mind churned, pulsing. *Use me!* Helix grabbed with the last shreds of his consciousness. He watched dizzy and delirious as the water melted around him. Thousands of bubbles coalesced to a single orb of air. Suddenly he felt the ice in his lungs turn warm. He hacked the water back out, coughing and sputtering—in its place he sucked in the waiting bubble of air in a desperate gasp. It filled his lungs—one piercing, painful and beautiful gasp. His eyes snapped, much needed air rushing to his dying brain and Helix felt the swirling ball of water pulse louder. The endless mass of water above him began to melt, and he swam.

Helix pierced the water, gasping, expecting the turquoise light of Narim.

Instead he was on grassy banks. *Where am I?* he wondered. One moment he had been asphyxiating in those dark waters and now? He squinted beneath a burst of sunlight. The sun. His mind throbbed, confused, exhausted, painful. Dumbfounded, Helix groped at his body.

I'm alive... It doesn't make any sense.

He felt joy and hope, and a surprising small laugh escaped his throat. "I'm alive," he repeated, almost as if to reaffirm it. There was a tickle in his lungs and he coughed, making more water jettison from his mouth, and splashing upon the wet dirt. It trickled from his lips, and he pointlessly wiped his mouth with the back of his even wetter sleeve. "But how?" he whispered, eyeing his hand, remembering ice coating every limb, filling his lungs, burning him up from the inside. That had been real. *Then how did I—*

But Helix knew. *I used magic.* The spark? It had to be. He'd heard of Untameds before—threaders of the spark that the Citadel hadn't caught, whose latent abilities sometimes surfaced much later in life. "Maybe that's what I am…" It was a terrifying thought. He didn't know much about Reavers, but what he did know, he didn't like.

Izul…

Scenes of blood and fire and smoke flashed before his eyes, hammering into Helix. Pressing the heels of his hands into his eyes, he tried to shut out the awful visions.

Gambol.

Xavvan.

Dead, and for what? For trying to protect him. He felt a sickening wave of guilt and nausea wash over him.

"It's not my fault," he said aloud. That blue-eyed bastard and Izul were the cause of their deaths. He curled his fist tighter, pounding the grassy ground and decided to embrace this newfound power. He didn't know anything about it but he would learn to use it, and then he would seek revenge. Modric and Izul would die with the same merciless cruelty they had exacted. Xavvan and Gambol would be avenged.

337

He put thoughts of the spark and vengeance to the back of his mind as he took in his newfound surroundings. It was a grassy tree-filled glade. Water lapped at the verdant banks. The river was mild behind him, lazily flowing by. To the far west, he saw a shadowed mountain range. *The Foothills of Narim.* They were far in the distance compared to when he'd seen it earlier that day, but even so, they still loomed.

He judged the sun in the sky and the position of the faded moon—a thing his father had taught him and speculated that he was about three or four leagues north of Narim, or about twenty miles from the city.

The Ker Stream must have dropped him off somewhere north. The river was too small for it to be the Ker Stream itself, so perhaps an off-shoot? Maybe the River Rel or another tributary, but something about the land didn't feel correct. Narim was bleak and lifeless, only soil and low foothills dotted with occasional farms and homesteads, but on this part of the river, life abounded.

Deep-rooted trees with shaggy green moss and slate-colored bark, looking as if covered in soot, surrounded him on the eastern side of the river.

Butterflies flitted beyond, birds trilled and small reptiles slithered up the metallic trunks. A forested wetland? He scratched his head. Odd in such a desolate land. Then he realized, feeling the latent spark in the air.

It was a Node.

He needed to find somewhere to sit and think, to piece out his tangled thoughts.

Helix found a small pond of deep blue and began to take off his clothes and wring them dry as the sounds of magic and life sifted all around him. Something squawked in the distance and he swiped at a red butterfly that mistook his nose for a flower.

Nodes were sanctuaries spawned by the magic of Farhaven. Life flourished in a node like a chalice overflowing with water. They were filled with birds, beasts and reptiles, and the spark saturated the air, providing rest and relaxation. But Helix couldn't feel all the beauty around him. He felt empty and confused. He couldn't help but notice that the Node was oddly quiet. Aside from the occasional warbling bird, flitting butterfly or skittering lizard, he seemed to be alone.

It made him shiver, reminding him of stories.

Nodes were almost commonplace these days. Before he'd stowed away on the Pride, he heard tales in his journey of thousands of Nodes appearing all over Farhaven. The land had never done it before, why now? Some said it was a sign of the next "Return," of another Lieon that would destroy the world. They said the Ronin were coming. Helix wasn't sure about that, but he did see signs of evil. Cities and people becoming darker, whole towns closing up before sundown, whole flocks of birds dying, livestock slaughtered without a mark, and a hundred other tales of a growing evil. Helix believed it. Something was coming.

Clearing his head, he set his mind back to drying his clothes.

He squeezed the last few drops from his dark blue pants and hung them on a nearby branch with his shirt, socks and boots. There was a little bit of a breeze, but it was still warm—warmer than most of Narim had been and rays of light broke through the canopy to dry his sodden clothes a little quicker.

What do I do now? he wondered. He'd always had such singular purpose. *Find Seria. Find the Great Kingdom of Water*—the true home of his people. Without an idea where Seria was, Helix felt lost and aimless. With a sigh, he settled down on a patch of moss, overwhelmed, sad and confused. He curled into a ball as exhaustion took him.

His dreams were fitful nightmares.

A *huge tidal wave washing across the land of Farhaven before being stopped, barely, by the impossibly tall cliffs of Ren Nar.*

A *man with blue eyes.*

His *father.*

That one over and over again.

Helix awoke. Sweat covered him from head to toe.

Looking about, he saw a bright morning sky. Had he been asleep for a whole day? Nodes were confusing. They didn't reflect the world outside, not always at least. Sometimes they did, but more often they were different. Some said they were a portal to a different part of the world or their own place in time—as if separated from the realm of Farhaven entirely. Rumors abounded, but one thing was fairly certain.

Nodes only came out of need.

Had he needed it? If so, why?

Stories told of travelers who, on the brink of overheating and dehydration, found a sudden oasis of water and shade in the middle of the Rehlias Desert. A sudden hearth of fire and light appeared through a snowstorm amid the ice-capped mountains of the De'Grael when others were on the verge of shutting down from the frigid cold. Fire would appear in a land of ice; ice or water would appear in a land of fire. So Nodes weren't tied to any one place. They were just symbols of their land, occurring all over Farhaven. But never at random.

"Never at random," Helix repeated to himself. He didn't believe in coincidence either. So why had it appeared all of a sudden? Why now, when he had no idea where to go? When he was lost just like a wanderer in a storm?

It was *then* the Node had appeared... When he needed something. And it dawned on him.

The Node... It *was* the clue. It wanted to help him find his way and discover the lost Great Kingdom of Water.

Helix did a full turn and realized.

Water.

It was everywhere. A waterfall fed the huge green pond. To his right were shelves of rocks with crystalline blue pools like a thousand tiny birdbaths. Water even hung in the air, dampening his breath.

And he understood. *Seria.* "Of course... that's it."

Sand and dunes for the fire and flesh kingdoms. Forests for the Great

339

Kingdom of Leaf. A Node filled with shadows and darkness for the moon kingdom. And water for the water kingdom. Nodes were based off of their kingdom of origin.

A Node could spawn randomly in the center of Median—at least it could in theory. This Node was from the Great Kingdom of Water, and it was pointing him to it, toward the lost kingdom. And he whispered in realization, "Whatever elements are in this Node are clues to where the lost Kingdom of Water is hidden!"

Breathless, Helix pieced together the clues, hints like dots on a map. *Warm desert air.* Only two deserts were this dry and warm, Covai and Rehlias. That limited his options. A salty breeze. Not far from an ocean then. He touched a nearby tree, feeling its craggy skin and long curling fronds with thick husked nuts. *Mablebark.* As far as he knew it only grew in one place.

The Nimue Everglades.

Everything fit together. The Nimue Everglades were forested wetlands slightly southwest of the Kalvas Ocean—near enough for the tang of salt, and close enough to Covai to explain that dry heat. His pulse raced, pride swelling in his chest. *I've done it. I've discovered the origin of the lost Great Kingdom of Water!*

340

But… he thought, rubbing his jaw, *how do I get there?*

He had no mount, no town nearby to buy one in, and the tributaries were too small to carry him any farther by a makeshift raft. *I suppose there's only one other option.* And tugging on his soggy clothes, he picked up a nearby stick. He stripped its outer twigs and tested its weight as a walking staff. Exhilarated, and not wanting to waste another second, Helix set off.

A burning, painful anger still stirred in his heart, but it was mixed with purpose.

He would find Seria, and in the process find the strength to seek vengeance for his fallen friends. *I swear it,* he thought, *upon my life.*

A Tide of Darkness

The Shadow King lounged in his throne of bones, surveying his flock. The grand chamber filled with all manner of disreputable scum: murderers, thieves, pickpockets, brigands, pirates, arsonists and even your average forest highwayman. It seemed every scrap and piece of refuge of Farhaven had assembled here. Faye was surprised that with this much trash in one place, it didn't smell something foul. Well, maybe a little. But mostly of sweat, grime, fear, impatience and greed.

They were the growing armies of Narim and of the thief lords. The Shadow King's gaze turned to the thief lords upon the platform sitting in their chairs of honor. They'd recently arrived, each with small entourages in tow. Faye was baffled to see them. *They actually arrived*, she thought again to herself. *What fools.* Somehow, the man had convinced shadows to step out of their dark hovels. Thief-lords each, they wore masks and clothing that covered all but their eyes. Their masks matched the kingdom they called home—blue for water, gold for sun, and so forth. Faye caught rare hints of flesh, but for the most part, they hid anything that could hint at their true identity. A distinctive scar, a bit of jewelry, and a tattoo or marking all had to be hidden. All knew the names of the great thief lords, but none knew their faces—just like her father. They were the kings and queens of the worlds beneath the surface.

"Welcome—all of you. At long last we are gathered beneath one common roof: Gared of Covai, the Great Kingdom of Flesh; Salizar of Eldas, home of leaf; Mathelstan of Median for the water folk; Six-Fingers Sendra of Vaster, bastion of sun; and even those once broken and fractured from us, thought to be lost to forever." He pointed at a stocky man with a graying beard that showed beneath his brown mask. "Ufantis of Lander, dominion of stone," he said, then looked to a hard-bitten creature with sunken eyes. His face was hidden, but what she could see was dark, but not by sun. "—and Thalis of Yronia, fortress of metal." *Soot*, she realized, his features were darkened by the Mountains of Soot. *Yronia and Lander, metal and stone... the Lost Kingdoms, that meant they still existed...*

"Each of the Shadow Clans assembled in one place, save for the Great Kingdom of Wind, of course—the most loathsome of elements. And last, but not least, the Mistress of Shadows of Farbs, the Great Kingdom of Fire." His gaze fell to her in her shackles. Oddly enough, the powerful men and women at her side glanced to her with wolfish hunger in their eyes. And she realized... They were legends each, but she barely knew them. For all they knew she was just another pet sent by Darkeye, like her sister, to be ruled over. They would be of no use. The Shadow King continued, "Here we stand, masters of the underworld, thief kings and queens alike—"

She turned her mind off, ignoring the ramblings of a mad king and turned her attention to her escape. She cursed her weakness but did not blame anyone but herself. If only she hadn't made the bloodpact with Gray, then she would have the strength she needed. But she was not one for lamenting about the past.

'Cry about the past and be dead in the present'—her father's favorite words. As always, they held a bare hint of truth dipped into the mire of insanity. But they reminded her to think. *Think.* She shrugged off her wound and took in her surroundings, looking for anything of use, going through a mental checklist as she had been trained—in order of most useful to least.

First, *herself.*

The bonds.

The rope on her wrists and ankles was thick—too thick to break with strength. She had a dagger tucked up her sleeve but her forearms were pressed too tightly to the wooden arms. She tried rattling her arm to shake the dagger loose, but they were positioned so that would not work—simply falling free while she was walking. The crossbow had been a nuisance when they were trying to bandage her, so they'd left it on the ground

342

beneath the next chair. She judged the distance, but her foot was too far to clip it and bring it close—even so, it would make a laughable and awkward scene: scraping a crossbow slowly across the marble with her leg stretched like a Farbian whore before the thousands of watching thieves. No, that option was out. She grimaced, hating her choices. She was scraping at the bottom of the barrel and still coming up empty.

Her personal space was of no use.

Fine. Next, the developing situation.

There were thousands in attendance. Perhaps one of them could be helpful. But as her eyes scanned the swarthy-looking faces of the crowd, she felt hundreds of eyes already upon her. Why so many? Most were familiar looks: lust, rage and fear. Then, over the heads she saw a redhead even taller than the rest, brandishing a dagger, eyes gleaming. He seemed familiar. But how? Her blood-drained mind struggled to connect the dots until... She grimaced. Curly red hair, freckled face, cliff-like nose and taller than the Apex of Vaster. *You killed his brother, Faye,* she told herself. Or... was it his sister? Of course the sibling had been deserving of death—a child-killer, if she remembered. It was the case with all thieves of Farbs who didn't fit in, who were too dark for even Darkeye's standards. If not killed, they were punished and then banished. Usually they'd seek sanctuary in the dark folds of Narim or the neighboring pits of Menalas, Ester or the pirate coast called The Dragon's Tooth. But of course who dealt Darkeye's punishment? None other than his beloved daughter. *Great,* she thought, *how many are eager to see the blood of the punisher on their hands?*

As much as she couldn't blame them, she sighed, shaking her head.

No, they would be of no use.

She had trouble not coughing—blood was starting to fill her lungs. It felt like drowning in reverse. She swallowed, but it did no good. Faye's heart began to pound, slapping her ribcage. Her breaths became short, little panicked half-sips as she watched the Shadow King upon the platform spew his nonsense. She needed to keep her senses keen if she would save Leah, but the world blurred.

Think!

She coughed wetly.

I... I can't...

Something seeped into her mind like cracks in her armor.

Fear.

I'm afraid. The realization was almost scarier than the fear itself. As her fear rose, an old memory resurfaced.

Faye was inside a giant vat made of bronze. It was the source of the grand sphere above—hundreds of pipes ran to the surface to feed the Grand Creation. But none knew the Arbiter's gift originated here. She felt something warm and glowing beneath her as her small arms tread the dark water. She looked down and saw a strange blue light in the water's depths. The source, her father told her. It created water from nothing, then heated that water to make it safe to drink for all of Farbs. Even now her toes felt warmer than her chest. The closer one got to it, the hotter the water.

"It's time," her father announced and then instructed in a cold tone, "Grab the sword from the bottom near the source and then return to the surface. Do this and the water will stop. If you do not, you and your sister will die."

She glanced over, seeing her sister in another bronze vat. Leah sobbed loudly, blonde hair plastered to her innocent face. Leah was six, only a year younger than Faye, but she might as well have been a toddler by comparison. Faye's sobbing had ended long ago. Still, her heart clenched as Leah's chains rattled. Her sister was shackled with her head scarcely above the water, but not for long... When Darkeye pulled that lever, water would fill Faye's huge vat, and then it would drain into her sister's through a series of pipes, filling it in turn—sanitizing the water, her father told her. Of course, once that vat was filled it was pulled to the surface for all of Farbs, but not before her sister drowned.

"Wait..." she said, trembling in the dark water. "I promise I... I won't be weak again... Just let Leah go."

His dark eyes watched her, lifeless and full of hate, which made her feel helpless, small and angry, as always.

"Please..." she begged. "Father..."

Darkeye sighed. "You never learn, do you? The strong don't beg—they take," he declared. "You are weak, my daughter, but you will be strong. Even if it kills her, even if it kills me, you will be strong... or you will die."

He pulled the lever.

It clanked and a torrent of water fell from above, falling upon her head. Faye's neck bent beneath the weight of what felt like an avalanche. Immediately she was slammed beneath the water. She cried out, but the water stole her words.

She kicked hard, gulping for air. She saw her father's face through the

344

water, vision blurry and panicked. He watched her. So close, he could help, could grab her flailing limbs, but he did nothing.

"Father!" *she called, coughing almost as much as speaking.* "I can't!"

"You must, or you will die," *he voiced softly.*

Faye reached out for him, tried to grip the wall but only clawed smooth bronze. The tip of the wall was too high. Worst of all, the deluge was too heavy. She was shoved down again, beneath the surface, into darkness. She drank in a breath in surprise.

Water filled her lungs, taking over her thoughts as she sank.

She was turned around, couldn't tell up from down, and sheer terror gripped her. This is it... Suddenly all her flailing stopped. She felt a strange calm. Her panic-stricken mind slowed. Above, water pounded. But she twisted, looking down. The blue light pulsed, beckoning her. Yet everything in her body wanted to reach for the surface, to make one last attempt at life. Instead, she turned and dove—down—deeper into the water. Bubbles of water rose from the glowing orb, making it difficult to see. Still she swam. Heat enveloped her. Thoughts blurred into one lump, one word.

Swim.

Her skin felt hot enough to crack and burn, searing her insides.

She couldn't do it.

345

But when she turned, through the hazy water, she saw her father's gaze. Anger stronger than she'd ever felt overtook her mind. Her body may give out, but she would never give in to those dark eyes.

The last bit of air mixed with water in her lungs burned like a fire. She let it go and sucked in another full gulp of water, reaching out. Her hand burned as if passing through a ring of flames, but then... Something metallic. She screamed inwardly at her fingers to curl, to grip the object. They did and she bounded off the burning bottom, shooting toward the surface. Her vision turned black and her limbs gave out just as she reached the surface.

Suddenly, the pounding water stopped.

She hacked watery coughs, spewing it all forth—emptying her lungs.

Then breathed.

Her lungs sprang back to life, filling with air—burning and sharp as daggers but sweet too—sweeter than anything she'd ever tasted. Arms grasped her, pulling her from the water. She opened her eyes and saw those dark hateful eyes staring down at her in cold approval.

"Well done, my daughter. Remember this lesson well. Conquer your *fear or it will conquer you. Do this and you will become stronger than you can ever imagine."*

Faye returned to the moment.

Again, she coughed wetly into the gag, tasting copper. Hatred filled her from the horrible memory, but her mind was clearer than ever. She looked around at the crowd of thieves. And despite the blood filling her lungs and her clipped breaths… she felt calm, fear falling away like leaves on an autumn branch.

She shifted and then felt it.

The chair—it was weak.

The back legs wobbled beneath her.

And she grinned beneath her cloth.

The Shadow King was coming to the end of his dark tirade. He paused on a high-note, letting the crowd roar and cackle like animals, and he closed his eyes. Faye watched him take a long, deep breath, as if inhaling their adulation, drinking it in. As if he were their god. Worse yet, he almost looked the part. The grand chamber was filled to its cracking walls and he stood over his flock, staring down from his platform. To top it off, adorned in his great black coat of armor over his pure white skin, he looked darkly divine. Save for his yellowed teeth that flashed as he gave a wide, repulsive grin. Rotting teeth really ruined the effect for Faye. And with the rest of his face so pale and colorless, his yellow mouth looked like he'd swallowed a lantern. But those hands… they were the worst. They curled, huge and soft, gripping at his skulled armrests.

"Too long have we settled—eating and accepting their pathetic scraps like obedient hounds before their lavish tables. *Yet no longer,*" he seethed. Another cry went up and he rose at last. The crowd nearly took a step back from his presence, while others jostled forward as if wishing to touch their dark god. The Shadow King tightened his huge fist, raising it into the air, seizing on their fervor. "Join me, brothers. Join me, and together we will make the almighty Great Kingdoms shudder and piss themselves before the face of true strength—together we will watch as Farhaven bends her knee before the will of the Clan of Shadows!" Another even louder round of cheers went up from all the thieves. The Shadow King let this continue on for a while until at last he dropped his hand. His cloudy eyes surveyed them as he spoke in a deathly cold tone that rippled over the crowds, "Then all will know the greatest and only truth, as we know. Strength is life, and weakness—*death.*" His words sent a shiver down Faye's spine. Because he didn't seem mad, not like Sithel or like a thousand other evils she had known, but his smile and those eyes, seemed intelligent, calculated.

A master at his craft.

The thieves noticed his ending note and practically erupted. They jostled one another in a frenzy—shouts, snarls and cheers resounded through their ranks. They took up his words, echoing them like the mindless drones they were and it thundered through the domed hall,

"STRENGTH IS LIFE, WEAKNESS, DEATH."
"STRENGTH IS LIFE, WEAKNESS, DEATH."

How fitting, Faye thought and seized upon the moment. Grinning, she pounded her feet to the ground, pressing off. The chair rose into the air—a foot or two, no more, then came down hard. The weakened back legs crumpled beneath her weight and the chair splintered beneath her. She shrugged off the pieces and rose. Beneath the torrent of noise, only the nearest Shadow Lords noticed. Several drew daggers, but her dark rage wasn't for them. She ignored them. To her annoyance, her hands were still bound, but her chafing had coated her wrists with blood. A superficial wound, but it lubricated her wrists. With her arms unbound behind the chair, she had room to maneuver. She shimmied her wrists, feeling the rope cut deeper into her skin before slipping one wrist free, and then coolly dropped her shackles.

By now, others in the crowd had noticed, but still absorbed in the adulation of a thousand fools—he hadn't. Not yet. Her gaze settled on the man in his throne of skulls watching as the Shadow King grabbed a ruby-throated chalice from a servant and raised it in a toast.

Faye rolled, snatching her crossbow from beneath the nearest man's chair. Mid-roll she notched the bolt to sight, came to her feet, aimed—seeing the glaring white temple of the demon thief—and shot. It had all happened in a matter of moments. As the Shadow King put the chalice to his lips, she shot and the bolt flew through the air. All the crowd saw, and the world seemed to freeze as Faye watched the bolt fly, its fletching fluttering.

A silver flash.

A dagger flew, nicking her dark black bolt.

The bolt struck. Pushed off course, it sliced through the web between

347

the Shadow King's forefinger and thumb—the chalice flying into the air. He twisted, his white glare falling on her.

She didn't waste a second; her hand tied, she fumbled to notch another bolt and—

Another silver flash.

She felt its direction and she ducked, but it zipped past her and thudded into her crossbow, snapping the taut string. She looked at the crossbow, now worthless in her hands, and let it fall. Then she twisted, wrath filling her, to the object of her rage and desolation.

He was short. He had a deep blue mask that matched his blue eyes and blond spiky hair that peeked out from his cloth mask. The thief-lord of Median. She hadn't bothered to remember his name.

"*Why...*" she found herself asking in a pained breath. Faye swallowed down the blood that wanted to spill forth, clutching her bandaged stomach. She staggered on her feet but caught herself, barely, keeping herself upright.

The bastard only scrubbed his blond head. "Why? Simple, really. Amusement. Isn't that why we all came?" He looked to the other thief-lords but they remained silent, judging, calculating. "I merely want to see this little bout play out. If you kill him now, it's all over. Instead, this prolongs my enjoyment and gives even ground to both parties. A fair match, you could say."

"A... fair... match?" She had trouble catching her breath. "I'm nearly dead and you call that a fair match?" Faye regretted sparing the words, feeling blood dribble over her mouth and she wiped it away.

"Sorry, should I hinder you more?" the water thief-lord mocked, but he looked genuinely curious.

"That's quite enough," said a man, rising from his chair. He was tall. His mask was flesh-colored. Covian? His eyes were dark and unsympathetic, but they watched Faye with curiosity. "You prod a dying beast that bakes in the cruel sun, Mathelstan, and you find mirth in this?"

"Don't be such a bleeding heart, Gared, really," the blond mocked.

"That joke wasn't funny the first time, Mathelstan. You're a cruel man for one of water. Even among thieves there is honor and you, as always, have none."

Mathelstan, the thief-lord of water *tsked*. "You really mistake my position. I thought Covians were supposed to have a keen eye for flesh, and yet you're as blind as an Athi bat. A dying purebred steed is still a purebred. Have faith in my decision, my dust-eating friend."

And Faye turned with a growl, ignoring the idiots. One blabbered about honor while she was dying and the other seemed to only want to watch her for sport. She turned her attention to the real problem. The Shadow King had risen from his throne of bones and now faced her. All in attendance had grown silent, watching the half-dead Mistress of Shadows face off against their nightmarish lord and master.

"Give me a sword," she demanded.

But the crowd didn't stir. Her voice echoed hollowly.

She twisted to the thief-lords. While their names were well known, their faces were a secret, and each wore masks that hid all but their eyes to disguise their true identity. She reached out a bloody hand, feeling the Shadow King's gaze upon her—his white eyes like oil on her skin.

None moved.

Mathelstan lounged back in his cushioned chair. Faye gripped her stomach and staggered forward, sending shards of pain shooting through her abdomen. "You *bastard*. You started this. You want to watch me dance on strings? Then give me something, *anything!*"

Mathelstan lifted his hands apologetically, as if there was nothing he could do.

349

And Faye rounded on the thief-lord of flesh, Gared. Her hands still bound, she grabbed his tan rags that were still coated in dust from travel. "*You!* You want to spout on about honor? Then prove it now. Give me your blade."

Gared hesitated, reaching for the long curved blade at his hip, but then his hand froze. She read his dark eyes. *Greed, lust, power,* but above all, *fear.* Just as his eyes had flickered to the Shadow King, Gared brushed her aside and backed away.

Faye stumbled forward, realizing she'd been using him as a crutch.

"It seems you are alone," the Shadow King called from behind her and his deep, terrible voice echoed off the hall's domed walls. She could feel his mirth roiling across the distance between them.

The laughter echoed in her head and Faye staggered and felt a hand catch her.

She looked up into a smooth face—unblemished, with thin arcing brows over light blue eyes. Her skin was pale, not the ghostly Narim pale indicative of an under dweller, but fair-skinned and with high, noble cheekbones. Though there did seem to be a flush to her cheeks, and the woman had dark circles about her eyes. *A sickness.* Still, it was clear who the woman was—Sendra Six-Fingers of Vaster, Great Kingdom of Sun. Sendra had taken off her mask to expose her face and she looked about at those watching in defiance. All knew what that meant. To see a face was to know the true ruler of a thiefdom—and to know the true ruler was like seeing a pot of gold unveiled. For to kill a true thief-lord was to claim their title. Sendra's exposure was as outright a challenge as Faye had ever seen.

"Here," Sendra said in her silken tongue and clipped Faye's bonds, then slapped a handle into her palm. Faye examined the blade quickly— wire-handle with the symbol of sun, balanced, four-hands in length, and remarkably of Yronia steel that held a faint yellow glow. It was infused with… something. But what? she wondered.

Sendra gave a wicked smile, betraying her true nature, and answered Faye's unasked question. "I'd hoped to poison him, but my dealer and the Brisbane were never delivered. I came here to see his demise myself for the trouble he has brought me, but this seems a fitting conclusion if I've ever seen one. So save me the trouble, will you? End the man's ranting drivel once and for all."

Faye didn't thank her. She simply nodded and turned.

350

Strength was still leeching from her body, but she locked her knees and pointed her blade to the demon-king. "Fight me, you coward," she breathed venomously.

The Shadow King had watched the whole exchange, unmoved. Now he merely smiled. "A tempting offer, but why would I do that when I have others to do it for me?" He sat back in his throne and with a motion of his hand, dozens of black-clothed figures stalked up the stairs. Faye gripped her stomach, swallowing blood. She could take a few, but more than that? Besides, she needed to save her strength if she was to defeat the Shadow King, especially as she 'stood' now. Then she saw him in her periphery. The tall redhead with the gleam of vengeance in his eyes was the first up the stairs.

He bellowed, charging forward and swinging.

Faye had judged the distance. She didn't turn. Instead, she simply cut. Her blade carved through the air, then hit something solid. Flesh. The *thunk* still made her sick inside. Faye turned to look at the towering behemoth, seeing her blade cracking his skull in two. The big redhead looked confused at the blade in his head and Faye pulled the blade free, whipping blood from its edge with a flick. "This is where you die…"

To her bafflement the huge thief took another step, anger in his eyes. "My brother—" he seethed, blood pouring from his mouth.

"—murdered an innocent little girl and paid the price. Now he's dead, just like you."

The seven-foot redhead took another lumbering step, raising his blade. Faye sighed and cut, severing the man's head from his huge body. He collapsed, head bouncing as his body flopped lifelessly forward, shaking the floor. Because the giant, the leader of their charge, fell so easily, the other men hesitated.

Faye ignored them and turned back to the Shadow King. "My offer is simple—which should fit your simple mind. I challenge you to a duel to the death. The winner claims the throne of both Narim *and* the Darkeye Clan. The loser, well…" She rolled her shoulders, but it sent spasms of pain she tried to hide coursing through her broken body. "That should be obvious enough. His or her warm blood will run freely, and we shall celebrate that single great truth. The strong survive and the weak die."

Silence lingered.

"What say you?"

All eyes were focused now—not on her, but on the Shadow King.

Faye's cold heart pulsed. She kept her face impassive but every part of her thundered. *Please. Accept. Take the damn bait, you stubborn fool.* She stepped forward, raising her sword, her arm trembling with the weight of it. "*What… say… you?*"

And slowly the Shadow King rose. His armor was soundless, plates seamless. He gripped a handle upon his back and unsheathed his blade in a dark rasp that shuddered through the hall and into her soul.

The blade was nearly as tall as she was. Its edge was wicked, curling like black waves. Runes were etched into its surface—Yronia steel, just like her blade, but almost a hundred times the weight. And as he lifted it, she could tell it wasn't solely for show. He *could* wield it. Then why were his hands so soft? And the dark thief-lord smiled, looking as if he'd hoped for this all along. "I accept your offer."

And darkness fell upon Faye's heart, realizing—*he had*. This had been his intention, his move the whole time. To weaken her, cut her down within an inch of her life, and then goad her, forcing her to make the offer then claim her throne in front of all the kingdoms to establish his legitimacy. Of course, if he hoped to steal one kingdom, he could have killed her outright, but to slowly consume all eight thiefdoms? The

351

white madness in his eyes was all the more terrifying, for she recognized it now—it was not simply madness, but the cunning of a man who planned to conquer the world. The blade in his hand was not death.

The Shadow King was death.

Missing Hearts

Ayva's thoughts churned while her hand gently felt the book's worn cover and its symbol of wind. The others slept, but she couldn't. It was the first day of their journey and everything felt wrong. As she stared out over the hills, she felt cold and wrapped her arms around herself, clutching her blanket tighter. She wished it wasn't a blanket warming her but Gray's arms, and she wondered if he was thinking about her.

"Can't sleep?" a voice asked.

Consumed in her own thoughts, Ayva nearly leapt out of her own skin. She turned to see Dalic. Broad-shouldered, tall and crafted of lean, hard muscle, Dalic was the epitome of a warrior. Ayva admired him again as he stood over her.

His tan clothes were tied to his muscled frame by strips, keeping them tight to his form. But here and there, cloth strips were loose and wavering in the evening breeze. A thick leather belt girded his thin waist. She noticed it had a strange red fur lining, as did his leather shoulder pads and the leather bracers on his sinewy forearms. Recognition struck: a plains beast called a Samigurian tiger. Ayva remembered Faye's stories about them. Algasi, if they wished to test their mettle and earn the blue-stripe of a Mundasi on their spears, had to fight a Samigurian tiger. But to attempt the task was tantamount to suicide. Samigurian tigers were apex predators. During the War of the Lieon, they helped the Ronins and overnight, nearly decimated a thousand warriors that had tread too close to the Heaths of Samigur, a grasslands east of the Aster Plains.

Their pelts were worth an absolute fortune that few, but the wealthiest and most powerful, could afford. Faye said that every year, some adventurous idiots would rally a caravan with stories of untold riches. They'd gather hungry mercenaries or recently reformed bandits from the Aster Plains and would brave their way into the Heaths of Samigur to try to skin the fur from Samigurian tigers that had died of old age or other natural causes. When Ayva had inquired what happened to those men, Faye had laughed, saying only dead fools ventured into the long grasses where the Samigurian was king. Few ever returned—and fewer still could even tell the horror of what they'd witnessed. A dozen trained warriors were no match for one of the cunning beasts. The fact that Dalic was outfitted in it and probably didn't know its monetary worth, or more likely didn't care, only added to his status in her eyes. He sat down at her side upon the rolling knoll to look out at the shadowed Paragon Steppes and Vaster. The City of Sun now sat behind them. Even in the night, its columns of glass and mirrors soaked up the moon's pale white glow, gleaming like an Ester diamond. "No," she admitted. "It feels wrong."

He grunted. "Leaving your friends?"

She gave him a glance out of the corner of her eye.

"Algasi does not mean stupid," he muttered without returning the look. He plucked a blade of grass, squinting at it. "I saw the way you looked at the boy who speaks with the winds and that other one who talks to the leaves."

Then he glanced at her and Ayva felt her cheeks heat. She cursed herself, feeling like a little girl with a crush—*but for which one?*—but if Dalic noticed it, he didn't make mention. "Yes," she said with a breath. "But it's not what you think. It feels wrong *because* it feels right."

He grunted again. "This I understand too." His white cloth mask moved lightly as he spoke. She wished she could have seen his face—not that it mattered, but all she could make out were glimpses of deeply tanned skin. *Why were Algasi and Vasterians so different of skin?* she wondered. "But you will see them again. Even with those I have lost, brave warriors, men and women, I will see again. We do not lose the souls who bind us, who make us who we are."

Ayva nodded, *feeling* the wisdom of his words. "I still wish they were here."

"That book," he asked, pointing. "The boy of wind?"

She pressed her palm to the smooth leather cover, fingers feeling the embossed symbol and nodded, then shook her head, clearing her thoughts of Darius and Gray and focusing on their path. *Only fools and historians linger in the past for too long*, her father would say. "So…" she said, looking to the shadowed hill in the distance—toward the Nimue Everglades. "What's our plan?"

"Sleep. We talk soon—long journey ahead."

With that he rose, leaving her alone.

Ayva lie down, thinking sleep was far from coming, eyeing the other slumbering figures and Vaster, which seemed like a pale light that wouldn't extinguish. But it came. Her dreams were deep. She dreamt of a glowing sword, of Gray, and the strange last look he'd given her. When she awoke it was to the sound of laughter—Darius', but then she remembered he was gone. She rubbed the sleep from her eyes and saw the others were not only already up, but that she was the last one still in bed. Guilt coursed through her and she threw off her covers.

The others sat in a large semi-circle. There was a low mist over the ground and a fire crackled in the center, heating a small black kettle.

Dalic waved her to sit at his side. As she sat, the one-eyed Algasi spooned out a bowl of steaming porridge for her. Zane gave her a nod and Hannah gave a warm smile while sidling closer to her and touching her arm affectionately. Ayva returned the warmth and listened as a tall man with curly straw blond hair was speaking. "Then it's settled," he said in a deep voice. "One of us will return to our people who wait for us upon the Steppes to let them know that they should make camp and wait for our return, but make no move toward Vaster or any other town. The rest of us, those two dozen who sit here, now, shall journey forth with the lightspeaker and her companions to find the sword. Agreed?"

A rumbling of grunts echoed through the Algasi; even Dalic added a grunt, as if casting his vote. There was a sudden silence, and Ayva felt expectant eyes looking at them. Zane grunted. The eyes shifted to Hannah. Hannah grunted too, a small one. Ayva felt their gazes next, and she gave a grunt. Then, as if the matter were settled, the Algasi turned to their bowls and the next topic.

Ayva's annoyance at being late washed away. She smiled at the whole exchange. *They make decisions together as one*, she thought, and Zane heard at her side.

Just like the Ronin, he answered in thoughts.

She nodded.

Just like the stories of the Ronin—they all seemed equals. Ayva glanced at Dalic. All but one, she supposed. He sat on the same level as the others but his white-cloth mask, sharp blue eyes, and two-banded spear made him a sharp contrast to their black masks... they all made him seem *different.* Just like the Ronin too. 'First among equals' was what the stories called Kail. It must be the same with Dalic.

"Next," said a wiry Algasi with a scar that ran over his right eye. "Which pass shall we take?"

"No one makes it through the western pass," said another Algasi. "We go east."

"What's the east pass like?" Zane asked.

"To the east, it differs. Sometimes a burning savannah. Sometimes not."

"Sometimes not?" Hannah asked with a gulp.

Ayva merely sat, content with listening. She took a bit of porridge—nutty and not too sweet. A little bland, but if she knew anything about the Algasi, it was surely nourishing.

Dalic answered smoothly, "It is different each time. Sometimes fire and flame, sometimes cold, sometimes torrential rains. Beasts too, stories say, guard the Lake. It will be no easy task."

"Then why not west?" Zane questioned.

"The west incline is a bitter blizzard more harsh and angry than all the Da'Grael storms combined. You would not survive. None of us would. It is an impossible thing. Only those who wish for a quick death travel the west pass."

Zane shrugged. "Sounds like a good enough reason to me." But Ayva saw him shiver too.

"You just don't like the cold," Hannah said.

"Death-like cold," he corrected. "Can you blame me?"

"But why?" Hannah asked, turning back to the circle of Algasi. "I thought the Everglades were merely a marshy green land. Why's it so horrible?"

But Ayva knew that answer. She swallowed her mouthful of porridge and spoke. "The Lake is a Node, isn't it?"

Dalic grunted. It could have been a negative, but she'd started to grow accustomed to the subtle distinction between his affirmations and his denials. Was that strange? She supposed it was a little.

"If it's a Node, a Node's first purpose is to protect itself—that's all it's doing," she said. The other Algasi gave nods and small affirmative grunts. But something in Ayva made her question her own words. A constant Node? She'd seen a small one in Vaster, but this one was huge. Why was it there? Solely to safeguard her sword? She looked to Dalic, but his eyes were unreadable, his face hidden behind his mask.

"Then it's settled," the Algasi leader declared, setting his bowl down. "We make for the Eastern Pass."

Dalic appeared at her side again as she was readying her cormac. He was wrapping his hands with white cloth, staring out over the green hills, to the rising Everglades. *White cloth*, she noticed again. He looked down on her, his blue eyes shining. "*Salna.*"

"Salna?"

"It means 'hungry.' Your eyes, they are hungry."

She laughed. "I've questions, if that's what you mean. More than a few."

"Ask," he said. "I will answer what I can."

Her heart and voice leapt at the opportunity. "Your mask, it's white. Why?"

357

"Why not?"

"I mean, why do you have a white cloth mask when the others have black?"

"The leader of the Algasi has always worn white cloth for his mask. It is the way of things. As it has always been."

It's not the answer she was hoping for but Ayva stowed it away, something tickling in the back of her mind. "You avoided saying something before in front of the others, didn't you?" she asked.

Dalic hesitated. "Ah, that. Only stories."

"What stories?"

"Algasi have stories for the Enchantress. They say she is a demon, a witch and a trickster. No one knows exactly. I fear she will be our greatest threat." He paused, as if waiting for her to agree or deny or be surprised, but she was distracted watching Zane sheath his sword and strap it to his mount.

"If we do get the sword," Ayva said, risking her next words. "What do you plan to do with it?"

She couldn't be certain, but she could have sworn Dalic was smiling behind his mask. "You ask a question to a problem that is too far from sight—such types of questions my people are not fond of. But you are the lightspeaker, and you are not familiar with our ways, so I will answer." He finished wrapping his hands and grabbed her palm suddenly, putting it to his chest. "The Great Sword is my heart. It beats as fiercely as what you feel inside yours." He pressed her hand to her own chest, and gently let go. "To part with it would be to carve out what beats inside my chest and hand it over to you."

Ayva swallowed but held his gaze, not backing down.

His voice gained force, like a rock rolling down a hill, "The sword is our honor and our birthright. As such, the sword belongs to my people. We have risked everything for it." He paused and gave a deep breath. "And yet… I am not foolish enough to ignore your claim to it as well. If you are truly the lightspeaker, then the blade is yours as well. It belongs in your hands, and you have every right to the great blade." He glanced out over the hills to Vaster, and then south where Gray and Darius should be. "Those who you care for deeply, your friends, they also hold great blades, do they not?"

Her throat clenched, pained, but she merely nodded, remaining silent.

Dalic grunted. "Then I believe I understand your pain more clearly. You do not only feel the blade's absence, as I do, but you see others with their rightful hearts in their proper places and this pains you, does it not? For you feel your absence all the more clearly, like a man who sees his friends holding loved ones when he is without."

"I couldn't have said it better. But why do I feel this way?" she asked and couldn't help but give a small, frustrated laugh, shaking her head. "It's nothing more than a sword… I've never in all my life cared for material things, and yet I feel for a blade the way I'd feel for a person."

Dalic placed a hand upon her shoulder. "Others do not understand. The great blade is a soul." He unsheathed the dagger he kept at his belt—it was fine steel with a handle made from strange black rock. "This is metal and rock. It has no value but what I see in it. The great blade is more than metal, more than…" He shook his head. "Words fall short," he said at last gruffly. "We have a saying, one of many. 'The heart knows the truth.' I believe it is such with the Great Blade."

Ayva nodded. "There's one last thing," she said, looking to Vaster. "The people of Vaster will want the sword as well. Nolan and the people need it." She felt bitter and envious, voicing the words. It felt as if the sword was a meal and she was starving, only to hand it over to another hungry mouth. But she could not ignore the Vasterians' plight. Her people's plight. The little boy's dying face and the sickness ate at her slowly, driving her forward.

"A difficult decision if ever there were one," Dalic confessed at last. "The river though, has not taken that turn. When we retrieve the sword we will visit your question again."

Ayva only hoped that conversation wouldn't end with the point of a sword.

An Algasi came forward and spoke. "Tu sa, unarsa alatha."

Ayva didn't understand Sand Tongue well, but she understood urgency. The Algasi was breathless, panicked—especially for one of his kind. "What is it?" she asked worriedly.

And Dalic answered like the cold rasp of steel, slamming his blade back into its sheath. "My men, two of them are missing." He looked over the rolling, shadowed hills, his blue eyes blazing. "We are not alone."

"What are we going to do? Should we form a search party?" Ayva asked but Dalic said nothing. "We have to do *something*."

"They are dead."

Ayva was aghast, and defiance rose up inside of her. "How do you know that?" She shook her head. "You can't give up on them so easily. What if…" But she couldn't think of anything else.

"You are kind of heart and full of hope, but Algasi do not simply 'go missing,' lightspeaker," he said sharply. "And I have felt eyes this night."

She shivered, rubbing her arms as if from a sudden chill. "Me too," she admitted. "I'm not sure what it is, but something is out there. What do we do?"

Dalic turned and gave a few quick Sand Tongue words to the Algasi messenger. The man bowed his head solemnly and hurried off. "We will bury our men's possessions and give them the honor they deserve."

"That's all?"

"Beyond that, there is nothing we can do. We will simply have to be vigilant. And I should have known." *Known?* she wondered. "The sword is a treasure beyond worth. It only makes sense. We will not be the only ones searching for it. Something else is out there, hunting as well."

Sithel, Ayva thought in dread. "What if they aren't hunting the sword, but hunting us?"

Dalic seemed to ponder this for a moment, grabbing his clothed chin, then nodded. "Yes. This makes sense. If they kill their foes, the sword can be theirs alone without competition."

Ayva shook her head. "No, not for the sake of the sword. What if they are simply out to kill us?"

Though she couldn't see his face, she felt his puzzlement. "The Algasi have many enemies, this is true. But who would do such a thing? And to what end? Besides, who knows of our task?"

And Ayva told him. Of Sithel. Of the Macambriel and the room filled with bodies. Of everything. She wasn't sure why she hadn't told him until now. Perhaps there had been too much else on her mind, or perhaps she thought to use it as ammunition against him if it came to that. A shrapnel of guilt hit her, realizing that perhaps her silence had cost two Algasi their lives. She said as much, but Dalic assuaged her. "No. You did well. My men know the risks they take. Expecting an easy foe is not the Algasi way. This Sithel is no different."

An End to All Things

Faye staggered down the dais, pushing through the horde of thieves, her blade leading the way. They parted reluctantly. None attacked. She almost wished they had. Then the pain would end. She shook her head. No, she didn't care about pain or suffering, just Leah.

A space was made as the crowd of thieves reluctantly stepped back to watch the coming spectacle of death.

Faye turned, gripping the woman's sword in her hand. It felt slick in her grip—her wounded arm wasn't fully healed and it had ripped open. She was bleeding from everywhere. But she locked her legs, forcing herself to stand upright.

The Shadow King stepped through the crowd, parting it like a dark sea. He was easily head and shoulders taller than the nearest thieves. As always, his skin was a chalky white, at odds with the swarthy faces around her and the dark armor that fit his huge frame. *Dragonborne*, she cursed again. Every sliver of advantage she'd hoped for was slipping away like water through her fingers. "Well, well…" said the man in a rumbling bass, standing amid the center of thieves. He lifted his muscled arms to the domed ceiling above them—a huge crack ran down its center, fissured like a broken egg. From that fissure, turquoise light peaked through as if she were in hell and she could see the heavens above. "Standing here at last. The Mistress of Shadows to face the Master of Shadows. I almost feel this moment was fated from the start, don't you?"

You planned this, you cursed demon… she thought. But she spared the words. Words took effort. Effort which she needed to kill him.

Still, one thing grated on her and she needed to know. "You're no king, no master of shadows. You're a lie. I see through you. Your hands are soft. You've no idea how to wield that blade of yours, do you? You're an imposter." She hadn't pieced out this part and she needed to understand why. Why? It taunted her, right at the edge of understanding.

"You don't have to call me that. The Shadow King is too formal for you and I. Call me Halvos." Then Halvos glanced to his huge soft hand, flexing it, then placed it back to his hilt. "And you've a keen eye, but you don't see as deeply as you think you do. Consider this a riddle then. Tell me, if you truly learned *si'tu'ah*, show me that wit of yours. How can a man wield a blade and not show its signs?"

Faye's weary mind struggled to work. She was too tired for games, too tired to use *si'tu'ah*. "You can't," she snapped, angrily.

"Come, you're smarter than that," he chided. "Think."

Faye hated him. Hated how he was trying to teach her before killing her, how he sounded like her father, but her curiosity, her *si'tu'ah* took over. He had the muscles of a fighter. They coiled and rippled as he moved smoothly—not deterred by his girth or muscle-bound as some men were. Then why not the hands? His posture too. Halvos stood straight, loose, shoulders down, knees lightly bent, and turned to only expose one side of his body—all signs of a blademaster's posture. Then why? And it struck her. Those were things that didn't fade quickly. Muscles, posture, attitude, training—those things were engrained, or at least faded very slowly. Callouses, on the other hand, *they* faded quickly.

Halvos, The Shadow King, had no need to lift his blade because no one had ever presented enough of a challenge for a long enough time. He'd killed, and likely often, but then had been deprived of a worthy opponent, leaving his hands to go soft. In the end, callouses faded. Training didn't.

"Ah," Halvos said, smiling his yellowed grin. "You see, don't you? I've had no reason to pick up a blade. When even the greatest blademaster of Covai and scores of Sword-Forged Devari fall with little effort, there's not much reason wield a sword. As much reason for a master to cut wheat in the field beside his slaves. They get the job done just the same, and I don't have to—"

362

"—Dirty your soft hands?" she cut in.

"Be disappointed," he corrected.

Despite her snarky reply, the realization sent a cold shiver down Faye's back. When she thought the man couldn't get more terrifying, he found a way. The greatest blademaster of Covai? She heard a story of a great swordsman, some said it was Jian, the Devari Leader's brother, who lost in a duel while heading to Narim. No one said how or why. But it made sense. And a score of Devari? Faye had faced off against a single Sword-Forged Devari, the highest of their ilk aside from their leader, once—she felt lucky she was still alive to tell the tale.

Halvos continued, unperturbed

"I always knew we were to be one or the other, lovers or bitter enemies. But that legend was always merely a myth told to young thieves with the gleam of greed in their heart." He spoke almost familiarly, bitterly. *Was this the true Halvos?* she wondered. But when he looked back up his features were smooth, his ever-present grin returned. "*Master and Mistress of Shadows.* There can only be one true Master of Shadows."

The only thing that mattered pierced her thoughts like an arrow and she let it through, slipping past her still bloody mouth, "Where... where is she?"

363

"She?"

"My sister. Where... is my sister?" The words were like a sword—so cold and so angry. Even the Shadow King's smile wavered at them.

"Safe," he replied, looking down the length of his menacing blade as if examining its black gleam and keen edge. "For now." His white eyes flickered up to her. "But that answer doesn't suit you, does it? Really, think about it. Why would I harm her? She's quite... talented."

Faye's anger spiked, but she kept it concealed. *Si'tu'ah.* Show emotion and the enemy could use it against you. In some battles Faye showed her rage, pain or even fake emotions to lull the enemy toward the direction she wanted—overconfidence, insecurity, fear... But she knew that wouldn't work against Halvos. She'd debated it, surely. If she showed fear, maybe he'd grow cocky and expose himself. All she needed was one overconfident strike, but she had a feeling a battle of wits, *si'tu'ah* at its heart, was not her greatest asset as she stood. Something grated her still. "My father," she breathed, refusing to look at the bloody, wet sack that sat beside Halvos's skull-made throne. "He gave her to you, didn't he?"

"An excellent deduction."

"Why?"

"To unite the clan of shadows, why else?"

"You can't honestly believe that, can you?" She swallowed down blood, pointing her shaking blade to the thief-lords on the dais beyond. "You can't truly believe that they buy your lies? A unified kingdom? Under your benevolent rule?" She laughed, but it caused a spasm of pain in her stomach. "Spare me. It's nauseating even saying it aloud. You're a disease. Power hungry, a mongrel. Just like my father."

"Your father," said the man, amusement in his eyes. "He wasn't what you think he was. Nor are you. Yet I suppose that's something you'll never discover now."

"What do you mean?" Faye said through gritted teeth. She knew she was wasting time. Time she didn't have, but curiosity was always her greatest weakness.

The Shadow King circled her, wearing his typical thin-lipped, cruel smile. "What's the truest human condition, Mistress of Shadows? I'll tell you. Laziness, indolence. *Weakness.*" He pointed his blade to the earthen roof above, past the dangling broken chandeliers. To the surface world. "You see, I don't pity them. Not fully, at least. I *sympathize.* They could be more and yet they fall to their baser desires. As we all wish to do. But it's the mark of the strong to resist such temptations. Don't you see? You're one of those, Faye. You're like me. Something burns inside you to break the human condition, to be stronger, to be more. We're not so different."

"You really are a delusional idiot, aren't you?" she spat her blood toward him, but he caught it in the air with his blade. "The difference between us is simple. I was bred to be this monster. You chose to be one."

His hairless brow crinkled in amusement. "Is that what you still think? You were forced?"

Faye hesitated, but she shook her head. *Si'tu'ah.* He was simply using it against her—making her question her most basic tenets, trying to shake her foundation. But she was nearly dead... did he really need to break her will as well? She shut the thoughts out and raised her blade.

The Shadow King lifted a black-gauntleted hand, curling his fingers toward her in invitation. "Well? Come on then. I'll save the secrets of your true nature for another time. Show me what you've got, won't you? Show me what killed Darkeye."

And Faye's bloody grin grew. "With pleasure."

Faye calculated her odds quickly. She knew immediately she wouldn't win in a prolonged fight. Perhaps not even in a short fight. But every creature had a weakness. What was his? She cursed, eyes frantically scouring her opponent. His giant sword rested on the cracked marble floor, content with watching her, not attacking.

That was it.

His sword.

The five-foot monstrosity dwarfed her little three-foot blade. It was practically the height of her. But its sheer size was also a hindrance. Perhaps she could use that against him. If she could get inside his range, he couldn't swing that black behemoth.

"What are you waiting for? Come and—"

And she cut his ranting short, dashing in.

Halvos swung his blade. Fear shot through Faye, watching the blade slice through the air with inhuman speed. All plans washed from her mind. She had only a fraction of a second. She ducked barely in time as the black blade nearly lopped her head clean off, a gust of wind brushing over her.

She scrambled back across the floor.

Thieves laughed, but Halvos didn't. He didn't even smile. His white eyes merely fixed on her. *Scratch that,* she thought, gritting her teeth. *What's next?* she thought woozily. *His armor?*

It was impenetrable, but there were clean gaps.

Shoulders. Neck. Face.

She shook her head. *No use, she couldn't even get close enough.* Frustration welled over her. Every question met a brick wall. Where was his damned weakness? *Si'tu'ah* had trained her. Every *creature* had weakness. Every single one. Even a Shadow King.

His white eyes.

They swirled like clouds—red veins forking across their surface, unnervingly seeing into her. She tested him, shifting her stance, but the white eyes followed her. He could see her? No. She'd seen blind before. He *was* blind. Then how did he sense her? Something didn't add up. It yelled at her, but she was so tired, so sluggish. Even her warm blood seemed to be growing cold upon her arm. She had mere minutes. Even if she killed Halvos she knew she wouldn't survive this day. *Search!* she cried out. *Find his weakness!* Leah was depending on her.

Halvos stalked forward. "Those eyes. I've seen them before. Your fa-

365

ther told me such a thing. *Si'tu'ah*, am I correct? Searching for the cracks in my armor? But I wonder, what happens when you find none? What happens when your fears come true, your questions fall short, and you're left with only one truth? I will win, and you will die."

Faye snorted. "Arrogance."

"Confidence," he countered. "You have but two paths, Mistress of Shadows. Join me, be my right hand and take your sister's place… or die."

"You… you would let her go?"

"Ah, the very same crux you faced before. If I did let her go, would you accept my offer?"

Faye didn't hesitate. "I would. My life, my body, anything. Let Leah go and it will be yours. I'll… be yours." The words nearly made her sick up, but she held the bile down, swallowing.

Halvos mused, tilting his head. "So very tempting. But I decline. I believe you two are a pair and come as such. I'll take both of you as my pets or nothing."

"Then you'll get nothing."

"So be it. Either way I win. You die and I get Farbs. You choose to live and I'll get an apprentice and slave to do my bidding until the day you die. You see, Faye, I can't lose."

Faye didn't have any more time to waste.

She'd have to kill him in one, maybe two strikes at most, or she'd die. *Si'tu'ah* had failed her. *Attack now or die*, her instincts told her. And she did. Faye screamed, charging forward. The Shadow King swung his blade but she slid beneath it, between his legs, aiming for his shins. He didn't bother blocking the attacks, knowing his Dragonborne greaves would save him. But she switched the angle of her blade at the last moment. She slashed, but this time at his groin. The blade scraped along his black-plated loins, harmless, but then the blade roared with a sudden light as if cutting through the folds of dark armor, slicing as she skidded across the marble. She came up.

The Shadow King grabbed his manhood then raised his white hand to his face, seeing blood. "You… you filthy whore!" he roared in agony and anger.

"That worked, did it?" she mused, surprised with herself. "I debated that—attacking your manhood—figuring you had none, but I guess I was wrong." Still, her attack had been next to useless. She'd expended almost all of her energy, sagging in her frame, blood almost raining from her, and she'd only scored a superficial hit and a crass insult. She'd die for those two minor pains and he'd win. Part of her relished the move, realizing he might never reproduce, but it was a small, pointless victory.

The Shadow King was still howling, anger coursing through his body, his huge white muscles flexing in pain and wrath, looking around like an enraged beast. It was the first time she'd seen him as he truly was—without his façade. A nightmare. He was terrifying. She felt that flicker of fear and his eyes snapped to her. And that's when it struck her…

Fear.

Her emotions.

He couldn't see after all.

She could win.

Suddenly, Faye's chest felt constricted, feeling tight, as if someone had rested ten stones upon her breast—and she struggled to breathe, falling to one knee. *What is this?* But her training shouted at her as sweat broke across her skin. *Rapid pulse, profuse sweat, heavy chest.* She knew what was coming.

Shock.

She'd lost too much blood. Shock would hit her soon and she'd lose control.

Now was the time.

Fight or die.

Faye charged.

❊ ❊ ❊

She understood what she had to do now.

The man could sense her emotions.

She had to use that against him.

But she had no chance to think *how* as Halvos charged forward like a cerabul, bellowing in fury. He swung. She dove to the side, barely. Marble cracked beneath his sword, chips flying into the air. She rose sluggishly, but again the monstrous blade came. Again she leapt. *Too slow.* It clipped her, hacking into her black pauldron and her whole body rattled from the force of it, as if nicked by a two-ton hammer. She skidded across the ground, landing at the feet of a thief.

She felt the floor shudder beneath her hands.

Faye twisted as Halvos lumbered forward with earth-rattling steps.

"You had your chance, Mistress of Shadows. You could have sat at my side, been my queen and ruled the world of Farhaven, savoring my benevolence and enjoying life's sweet pleasures. But you chose your pathetic sister. You chose death."

"I would choose death a thousand times before I knelt at your feet and served another demented soul exactly like my father."

Halvos hesitated. "Served?" His head tilted, amusement rippling across his smooth too-pale features. His thin pink lips twisted into a cruel smile as he panted from anger. "All that time you really think you were sacrificing your body and soul for her?" Faye felt confusion to her core. Halvos must have seen it or *felt* it as he snorted derisively. "Oh my, before you die, this will be fun. Let me let you in on a secret, then—the secret of who you *truly* are. Two daughters. Odd that you were the one that became the killer, isn't it?"

"I killed because I had to. I saved her from a fate worse than death," she said. "I saved her from becoming me."

"Is that who you did it for? A fate worse than death, you say. Then it seems to me you would have killed yourself once your duty was done. Yet here you stand, living a fate 'worse than death.' Who did you say you fought for again?"

Faye's pulse began to flutter, her palms growing sweaty. She shook her head. "My sister…"

"*My sister, my sister!* I was trying to save my sister!'" Halvos cackled loudly. "If that was your ultimate goal why did you never try to flee with her, run from your mad father, hmm?"

"He would have found us! His rage had no boundaries."

He sniffed. "And yet you never even tried. If you are the martyr you think you are, you could have died in the process, killed yourself. Your father wasn't vindictive, simply efficient. He'd have ignored your sister like a toy that had lost its use. She'd have been freed."

You lie! You don't know him. You're wrong! Words thundered inside her head but she remained silent. She was a coiled spring of rage and confusion, his words hammering into her like a metal splinter into her brain.

"Instead? You chose to use your sister as an excuse, to follow your heart's desire and become what you are today, a being much like me. Adaptable, strong—one who would do whatever was necessary to achieve her goals." He pointed to her broken body with his giant sword as if it were proof enough. "All you ever wanted was to see your true limits, your true potential. Just like me."

She shook her head, shutting her eyes. "No…"

"You see now, don't you? Your eyes are opened to the truth. You chose your fate from the very start. You never wanted your sister to live." Halvos's upper white lip curled, twitching in rage. "The greatest truth you've blocked out, your father told me… You both were given the blade that fateful day. But only one of you picked it up."

Faye's vision was taken in memory…

Faye turned at the gates of the courtyard and knelt. Gremwa leapt into her arms and she laughed. He panted, tongue out and he wagged his butt, hoping for Faye to scratch his favorite place.

"Good boy, Gremwa!"

Leah caught up with her, catching her breath. "I told you to wait!"

"Sorry, I couldn't hear you," she lied, continuing to pet Gremwa. Faye loved Gremwa, but the only thing she wanted more was her father's love. And today he'd promised to train her. She couldn't be more excited. She turned but ran into what felt like a solid wall. She rubbed her head, glancing up. A big man blocked out the sun, looming over her. He lifted her up gently. She was only tall enough to touch the blade at his hip if she stood on her tippy toes, but he ruffled her hair and gestured her onward. "Go on, little ones, your father is waiting for you."

369

Guards made a ring around the open courtyard. It was one of the few courtyards in her father's estate outside the city of Farbs.

"I will be blunt," said her father, standing in the center of the yard. "I can only have one heir and that means I can only train one of you—the other will have another purpose. I will not lie to you. The result will be simple and profound. One of you will be strong and one of you will be weak. And what happens to the weak, my little ones?"

"The weak die," Leah recited before Faye could.

"Good, Leah. You know your tenets well."

Faye felt a stab of jealousy despite her fear. Leah was always quicker than she.

"And do either of you want to die?" her father asked almost gently, rubbing his hands together, still staring at the dirt before his feet.

Both girls shook their heads fearfully.

Faye didn't want to die. She wasn't sure what happened, but she'd only ever seen one person die. Her mother. And the memory of it scared her more than anything. More than even her father.

"How... how will you choose?" Leah asked, a tremor in her voice.

Faye felt her whole body shaking too and her tongue was thick in her mouth—she was surprised her sister could even speak. And their father reached out a hand and his guard put a small dagger in it. He took the dagger and threw it in the sand, a foot between both Faye and Leah. Then he looked up and pointed to Gremwa. Faye's heart dropped to the pit of her stomach. "Kill the dog and I will train you. Kill the dog and become strong."

Faye's body went limp with fear. At her side, Leah clasped her hand over her mouth. But Faye felt her father's eyes—his love and judgment weighing on her heart.

Kill the dog and become strong.

Something inside her clicked.

And before she knew what she was doing, she knelt and curled her small hands around the blade.

Gremwa was wrestling with a stick in the sun. She called him to her side, feeling distant, and he obeyed like a good dog. He brushed his soft curly fur against her leg, waiting for her to scratch his favorite place as she always did, but instead she raised the blade.

"Faye, no!" her sister cried out, rushing forward.

But Faye ignored her. Her heart broke and she stabbed down. Gremwa yelped in pain and surprise. But Faye didn't stop. Chopping and hacking. Blood coated her arms, but still she stabbed. At last, Gremwa's cries stopped, and she looked up. Her father nodded approvingly, and suddenly guards stepped forward, pulling Leah away. Faye's sister wailed, but Faye was lost in a world of her own horror.

When Faye returned to the moment, she felt hot tears streaming down her face.

The Shadow King had raised his blade with a thunderous cry, fury in his red-white eyes. He slammed it down and every instinct in Faye made her want to lift her sword, to parry it. But she knew what would happen, seeing events unfold before they did. It would shatter her mending arm, her bones turning to dust. Or it would simply cleave through. She had to move then, but she couldn't. Every muscle had been spent. She felt the blood thickening in her throat, rising.

Her vision blurred. Halvos stood before her like the demon that he was, blocking out the light above.

It was too late… she had nothing left.

Use it against him! Si'tu'ah, her instincts, screamed.

His emotions.

He read emotions.

The gigantic blade crashed toward her head and Faye took one last long deep breath. She imagined herself in that tank of water, drowning from all sides, feeling it clog her throat, and she did as she did back then. She stuffed it all down — her fear, her anger, every single scrap of emotion.

Halvos suddenly paused — his sword came to a standstill, a breath away from her face. His eyes roved as if searching for her, confusion in those chilling white orbs. Faye wanted to feel surprise, elation, anything, but she stuffed that down too and rose slowly, scraping past his hovering blade. She limped to her feet, muscles quaking with the effort — but even the pain she ignored, shutting it away in that black lockbox she'd formed so many years ago. She staggered back, sure to be as silent as possible as Halvos twisted this way and that, snorting in fury like a bull, now truly blind.

When she was far enough away she spoke, "All creatures have emotions," she said flatly. "Thus you can see every being in here, can't you? Unless they have no emotions. But that's not very human, is it? Not unless they've learned to suppress them. Unless they've been trained to push them so far down, they don't exist. No fear, no anger, no pain. Nothing." She watched him twist and turn, fury in his body. The thieves around watched in befuddlement too. And slowly, breathing evenly, Faye approached. A huge gusting strike swiped through the air, the black blade an inch from her face. But she remained still, letting it pass, then walked forward again. Nothing. Her heart was a dull thud, so soft it practically didn't beat. Another pace.

Halvos bellowed, "Show yourself, you whore! Show yourself now or your sister will taste —"

She shut him out, refusing to hear his taunts.

Another step.

Halvos twisted in a giant circle with his blade, cutting. She smoothly ducked beneath it, stepping in the last pace. The thief-lord gave ragged, rage-filled huffs, and his hideous white eyes stared directly into hers — but he saw nothing. Her breath was almost hot on his skin now, but she kept that withheld too as she lifted her borrowed blade and aimed it at his neck. Everything in her wanted to kill the man, to slice his arteries wide

371

and let him suffer as her sister had suffered, but she refrained, remaining impassive. Cold metal touched flesh. As it touched his throat, his eyes widened. "*Where... is she...*" Faye breathed, ready to stab.

"You would kill me?"

"*Strength is life, weakness death,*" she quoted bitterly.

He sneered. "Then you'll never find your sister."

"If I kill you this city is mine."

"And if she isn't here?"

"*Where then?*" She pressed the sword tighter, skin peeling. "You will tell me or you will die."

He turned to her with a grin that made her skin want to crawl, *leaning* into the blade, causing more blood. It poured over her blade. "You believe I fear death?" he asked, amused.

Faye smiled. "No, but I believe you fear me."

"And what if your sister is already dead? If I've already broken everything you thought to save in her? What if you traveled all this way only to find what you've always feared—a creature precisely like you?"

"Then..." Faye's rage welled upside her, "I'll return. And I'll finish what I started. I'll flay that soft, milky white skin of yours and burn this depraved cesspit of a city to the ground."

"And if I do it first?"

Faye hesitated, puzzled.

But Halvos made a strange gesture, raising his hand.

Just then, the ground beneath her began to shudder. The whole of the moon city seemed to quake and rattle, and—

BOOM!

The earthshaking explosion nearly tossed her from her feet, but she held her ground as something crashed between her and the Shadow King, sending shards of marble and dust into the air and throwing her back. She rushed forward, anger exploding. But fleeing thieves smashed into her, bolting in fear as stone fell from above and she was carried like a leaf amid the current.

"*No!*" she bellowed, struggling against the tide of thieves.

The Shadow King stepped back into the crowds wearing a faint smile.

Faye cut those in her way, crying out, but more thieves replaced them like water to fill a hole. She screamed out in rage and agony, clawing her way forward, helpless as the man she hated more than life itself slowly slipped into the folds of the crowds. Something groaned and she looked

372

up. Wrist-thick chains snapped as crystal chandeliers fell from the roof, but it didn't matter, something was happening in her body. Every muscle was shaking like a leaf in the wind, uncontrollable. *Shock? Had it finally come? She'd…* No, it wasn't that.

Sharp pain spiked in her arm.

She looked down. Blood coated it, but beneath that her vein *bulged*. Something was inside her body, trying to get out. Something black against her pale skin. The bloodpact. It was winning. She gasped, feeling it snake through her veins, scuttling higher, toward her heart. If it reached her beating heart, all was lost. How she knew wasn't clear, but she was certain.

She reached for her sword and cut, dragging the sharp blade across her arm.

The darkness poured from her vein like black ooze. It coated her limb, hot and sticky, burning, and tears sprouted from the pain of it. Quickly as she could she ripped a scrap of cloth from her shirt beneath her black armor, then wiped the black liquid from her arm, tossing the shred of cloth to the ground. It ate at the cloth, consuming it as if hungry. But the darkness had already taken its toll. She knew that wasn't all of it. The bloodpact and the blood loss were too much. She couldn't continue. Faye staggered forward, her rage and will pushing her onward, like a husk of a human being lashed to continue. But each step was lumbering, slow, hopeless. Her knees buckled like dry wood. *Cold marble* — she felt it on her cheek. Before darkness took her, she saw a fissure in the domed roof, cracking wide.

A block the size of a house broke free, plummeting toward her.

373

* * *

Through her bared slits, she watched the block descend. Its course seemed to shift, or perhaps she'd misjudged its trajectory, and it smashed into a group of running thieves with a sickening thud, rattling the domed hall. The sound made Faye's head ring. Cries of the damned echoed about her, muffled. At the same time, feet scuffed and trampled her broken body. Still, she didn't care, could barely feel it. *So dizzy, so tired.* She didn't want to get up. All she wanted was an eternity of sleep — it beckoned as dirt and chaos reigned from all sides.

Get up, a voice shouted.

But she couldn't move a muscle. She'd spent herself too far. She'd attempted everything to kill the Shadow King, and it had failed.

Get up! It bellowed.

And she looked up, to see a face she recognized.

Gray.

She blinked in surprise and dismay. He looked awful—as she must have looked. Face bloodied, some of it dark red, cracking and days old, but most of it fresh and new. It ran in streams, soaked his clothes. His gray tunic was little more than tatters and his once-white shirt now a dirty brown. Splotches of blood and char were on his collar and sleeves as if he'd wrestled with a dragon and lost. But his eyes. They were the worst and best of him—hollowed black pits, as if he hadn't slept in weeks, but inside that gaze she saw... bright and gray-green. They held her. "Get up," he said again, not pleading or angry, not even hopeful. Desperate. Afraid. But determined. It was a face she'd never seen before from him, and she realized he'd finally understood. There was a power nearly as great as sacrifice. The will to live. It shone in his eyes. But still he would die without her, she knew.

He stood over her, reaching out a hand.

Faye reached for it.

She grasped it and rose. Every muscle in her groaned in protest, her wounds like a thousand needles, but she did it anyway. As she looked up, Gray wore a smile. He said nothing but his eyes seemed to speak for him.

Suddenly Gray burst, as a massive thief with a face full of scars barreled his way through the apparition, turning Gray's image to smoke. The giant of a man was pushing swaths of thieves out of his way in an attempt to flee, and where others moved too slowly, he laid into them savagely with a huge battle-axe, shearing thieves in half. He neared Faye. She slipped his axe, dodging to one side, brought her foot on top of it, running up its length, and lopped his head free. He tumbled, but she didn't look back as she jumped and rolled to her feet and ran.

Stone rained down about her and still she ran. Pieces smashed over her armor but she kept an eye to the roof above, ducking and dodging pieces that came too close. She cut down thieves that tried to barrel or shove her as they fled, several stabbing at her. She twisted beneath their dark shivs, staggering as a small man's blade pinged off her Dragonborne armor. He dashed in again, but she lifted her blade just in time to catch him in the stomach. Abruptly, Faye found herself through the double doors and looked behind.

A figure stood on the platform beside his throne of bones.

The Shadow King.

The hall trembled as if on the verge of collapse.

Every muscle in her body wanted to stop and to fall to a bloody heap, but those muscles that didn't wanted to wade back into that hall and kill Halvos, however, she knew it was a miracle that she still stood. Despite the distance, she could feel his slick smile. Suddenly a huge stone smashed into the exit, sending blood and bones flying, sealing off the hall. She stood, frozen for a moment as thieves ran about her, others standing in shock or nursing wounds in the long corridor. She prayed he'd be killed amid the wreckage, but knew that was wishful thinking. Bastards like Halvos didn't die that easily. Besides, she had somewhere to go. Faye limped onward, coughing blood, making it to a series of black archways— to a shadowy cliff of stone that overlooked the city. As she suspected, the rest of Narim was unharmed. The Shadow King had clearly set up a trap to only self-detonate the Black Hive and no surrounding area. It was an extreme back-up plan, but it worked.

But none of that mattered.

Words washed over her.

"*I go to see our promised deed done…*"

Words that Izul had said, grating on her all this while, and the Shadow King's taunt had confirmed it. West, she looked, peering intently out over the dark city to the watery tunnels and saw what she'd dreaded.

A spot of orange.

Fire.

Something burned, a bright flame amid the vast dark city.

The docks.

Odaren and the boy.

And Faye thanked Gray in her mind and began to run.

375

THE GATES OF ELDAS

Mura slowed to a stop as the thick stand of trees broke, revealing what he'd seen in the distance and what he'd feared. A gate. If it could even be *called* a gate—the Gates of Eldas looked as if a titan—the size of the Mountains of Soot—had plopped a titan-sized dam of wood smack in the middle of a forest that belonged to much smaller beings. All that mattered, however, was that it stood between them and Eldas, between Mura and his hope of reclaiming the elven kingdom from the king killer known as Dryan.

"Closed," he uttered in disbelief, and a tad in awe.

Jiro, the tall High Elf healer fell in at his side. "I told you it would be closed."

"I hadn't disagreed," he replied, "I merely didn't want to agree." His hand stroked his now lengthening beard.

Standing at the tree line, Mura scanned north and south, but saw no elves. He scoffed inwardly. Of course he wouldn't see them—that was the point. Dryan was a king killer, bearing a bloody crown that rightfully belonged to Mura's own niece, but he wasn't a fool. Nor were his elves. Perched in trees with bows a Terma—elite guardians to the kings and queens of Eldas—wouldn't be seen unless they wanted to be.

"It's safe," Jiro said.

Mura cocked a brow at him. "Is it now? Has your memory gone foggy or don't you remember that elf trying to slit your throat in your sleep not two days ago? Dryan's elves are crawling all over Relnas Forest and you're somehow certain that the very *Gates of Eldas* are not watched?" Mura didn't rub in the fact that he'd come to Jiro's rescue in the nick of time preventing the near fatality—probably because Jiro had saved his hide from roaming squads of Dryan's elves several times prior… *and* after. Luckily none of their encounters had been Terma.

"It is safe," Jiro repeated simply, ever the elf.

Mura sighed. "For my human side, mind elaborating?"

"I know Dryan."

"*And?*"

"He is efficient," said Jiro, almost bored. "If the Gates of Eldas are closed there is no cause for guards here. It is impenetrable."

"Nothing's *impenetrable*," said Mura, striding forward.

The Gates of Eldas rose to the soaring canopy above. It reminded Mura of Death's Gates, rising heavenward, which reminded him of the boy… *Gray*… He shook his head, keeping his thoughts to the task at hand.

His hand grazed the purple wood, feeling its smoothness—almost metallic and yet clearly a rich, burnished wood. It felt warm as if it were alive and he half expected it to beat with a pulse. Mura hacked at it and rope-like cords of wood came to the wall's rescue, reinforcing where he had made only the tiniest of nicks. "It is alive," he breathed.

"All wood lives, my friend, and heartwood lives just as much, but the gates are reinforced with magic." Jiro raised his staff, gazing up with as close to a look of awe as he'd ever seen on the elf's face. "It is a seamless barrier covered in stone, roots and moss, and beneath that is woven heartwood thicker than the metal doors of Yronia, rivaling even the stone gates of Lander. Unless you have a sword the size of the Spire, you will never breach this wall. Not with a hundred armies."

"But how is it possible? Since I was a boy these gates have remained open and lifeless."

The elf looked troubled. "I know not. Not since the war of the Lieon have the Gates of Eldas been closed, or been able to close… The magic used to close the gates is similar to that of Death's Gates. It requires the Great Sword."

"Morrowil?" asked Mura. "The boy has the blade—"

Jiro interrupted. "The Great Sword of Eldas—the leaf-blade Masamune. Each of the nine swords opens their respective gates, or they are

377

some greater key to their own kingdom. Because Morrowil is Kail's blade, however, it might work." The elf seemed to turn inward as his brows turned down, pondering.

"It opened Death's Gates," Mura answered. "You believe since both are made by the elves, it may open the Gate of Eldas?"

Jiro stroked his green beard—an elf with a beard was still a strange thing, especially since it had a fern green tint, but apparently High Elves, a dying breed, were quite different. Mura took in his traveling companion.

Jiro wasn't his real name, of course. High Elf's names weren't so plain as a human's or an elf's name. Instead, Jiro was actually Jiryn Ial Rimwalerian Ondasarial. But it seemed a whole lot easier to just call him Jiro, taking the first letter from each of his names. Jiro didn't seem to mind. The High Elf's emotions ranged between composed and *totally* composed, so Jiro never seemed to mind.

Mura had known the High Elf ever since he'd been a boy growing up in Eldas. Even back then Jiro had seemed ancient. When Mura had left the magical world of Farhaven to find Gray in the world of Daerval, he'd returned to discover that while he had aged decades in Daerval—a land without the spark—Jiro and others like him had remained the same, faces unmarked by the passing of time. In all the time Mura had known him, the High Elf rarely talked. He'd been the royal healer to Karil and her family, and a sort of behind-the-scenes advisor for countless years. But he and Mura had never said more than a dozen words to one another. Not until this trip.

The High Elf's physical appearance was fascinating. Jiro had angled eyes, hooded by faintly green brows like drooping moss, long pointed ears and a sage silver gaze that was almost shiver inducing. His gaze was even more striking than Karil's, and always seemed to brew with hidden thoughts. Jiro was one of the last High Elves left in Farhaven, perhaps the very last. Even his arrival all those years ago as the new healer to the royal family had been a mystery. When questioned about the last of his race and his origin, Jiro made non-committal answers to mysteries within the Drymaus Forest. Each time, Mura sensed his pain and let the question drop.

But his companion's green beard reminded Mura of his own grizzled cheeks and how long it'd been since they'd seen Karil and the others. He felt as if he were a hermit all over again, back in the Lost Woods. *Simpler*

378

times, he thought nostalgically.

"I know not," the elf replied at last. "The leader of the Ronin's blade is said to be different, but the blade isn't our creation. Still, it might work."

"You think it might be a master key, don't you?"

"Or it might not."

Mura sighed. He supposed it wouldn't have mattered anyway—the boy was off fighting his own battle in Farbs. He would see him soon; until then, reclaiming Eldas was all that mattered. "What now?" he asked.

Jiro raised a brow. "Elves are not all prophets, you know. Your sister and Karil are—"

Mura stopped him with a raised hand. "Right, right. No need to lecture me on the history of prophets and elves again, I understand. Let's just look for a way around." He shouldered his pack. "I'll head south, you north—meet me back here once you've reached the end of the gates, or if you find something."

"And if I find the Terma?" the elf asked.

Mura smirked. "Let's hope you don't."

Jiro, far from defenseless, raised a mossy brow, then nodded.

Mura left the wizened elf, heading south, brown leaves crunching beneath his feet reminding him that winter was around the corner. Farhaven was prone to vast changes in temperature, but as a boy he'd learned that the elves, threading a vast amount of the spark, had cast a spell upon the Relnas Forest, shielding it with ancient magic. As such, the sharp cold and burning heat rarely pierced the canopy above. Seasons, for elves, were consistent.

After a while his feet began to ache, and all he'd seen was more of the gate. He ran a hand along the hard purple wood, feeling it change and shift subtly beneath his fingers like running his hand across a snake's belly. He stopped, leaves rustling, eyeing the looming wall, knowing Eldas was on the other side. But there was nothing he could do.

"Looking for a way around?"

Mura twisted, gripping his sword's hilt, ready to whip the blade from its sheath. But as he turned, he saw nothing. The wind whistled slightly, his breath and heartbeat the loudest thing in the quiet glade. "Come out," Mura called. "I know you're there."

Silence, save for a mocking bird that trilled in the distance. Then a voice spoke again from within the trees beyond. *"Ah, but what if I'm not a friend, but a foe? Do you still want me to show myself?"*

379

Mura grinned. "I'd rather you were a friend, but a foe seems all the more likely. I present you the offer of showing yourself and proving me wrong."

"*And how are you to know which one I am? Noble or wicked? Are you good at guessing the heart of a man?*"

His grip tightened harder on his sword's obsidian hilt. Though he itched to unsheathe it, Mura had learned long ago that often the difference between living and dying was in that first ring of steel, and in the draw lay Mura's skill and his element of surprise. "From your voice, I'd say you were a man conflicted."

"*Astute,*" called the voice with a laugh. "*But are you any less?*"

"Why don't you show yourself and let me be the judge?"

A figure dropped from the trees at the forest's edge, a dozen paces away, alighting softly on the ground. He raised his head and a ray of sun broke through the copse above to show a handsome elf in near rags. His shoulders were wider than most doors, and his arms, where the faded green cloth was shredded, showed coiled muscles like wound ropes with many scars. His eyes were green daggers that held Mura. For once in his life, Mura had trouble meeting another's gaze. The elf smiled lightly and strode forward. Mura noticed the elf was weaponless, but still he gripped his own sword's handle. The elf stopped before Mura an arm's length away. The elf, a good two hands taller reached out, extending his arm. "Friend."

"That's your name?"

"That's who I am," replied the elf. "A friend, not foe."

It was strange for an elf to introduce himself, and even stranger to reach out and clasp forearms, a traditional Devari greeting. Mura reached out, gripping the big elf's arm in turn and replied slowly, "Mura…"

"A pleasure, Mura."

"I hope I can say the same…"

"Have you judged my heart yet?" he asked, amused.

Mura still gripped his forearm — it was like holding onto a log, his calloused fingers barely wrapping around half. "Not yet. I cannot see the good through the fearsome," he said. "And I've yet to see a man with great power wield it with great restraint."

"You speak openly," the big elf replied. "I like you already. I feel we will be fast friends." He scratched his jaw with his free hand and his expression darkened. "However, to speak openly in turn, I must warn you. We have only moments until we are surrounded from all sides and attacked." Mura attempted to rip his grip from the big elf, reaching for his sword, but the elf's face turned to stone and his grip did as well.

At that moment, Jiro came racing from the north. "The Terma are coming!"

Fear shot through Mura like an arrow. "You…"

The big elf held his arm—it was Mura's sword arm, and he had a distinct feeling the elf knew that as Jiro joined their side. "Who is this?" he asked sharply, his staff thumping the ground threateningly.

"A foe."

"A friend," the big elf amended.

"Yet to be seen," Mura replied. "Let go of my arm."

The big elf sighed. "Not until you listen."

Mura's anger rose but a voice of reason subdued it. "Speak quickly."

"I left my sword in the woods to prove to you my intentions. You are too clever to miss a hidden blade, and too fearful to trust anything but a man or elf who is defenseless."

"You left your sword when you knew we're about to be attacked?" he asked, incredulous. *Was the man mad or simply a fool?*

The big elf shrugged. "Call it a game of trust—or, if I fail, as I seem to be doing now, I figured I could simply take your sword."

"To what purpose?" Jiro asked darkly.

"To save you, of course," the big elf replied, emotionless. "Now… May I?" He extended his left hand, waiting for his blade.

Mura was speechless.

"How many?" Jiro asked.

"A dozen, maybe more," the big elf said bluntly.

"Can you take them?" the High Elf healer replied.

The big elf said nothing but his eyes spoke for him.

Mura's mind raced, trying to catch up to the two emotionless elves. He was always a man who felt calm in the midst of chaos, but in that moment he felt like a child bickering in the middle of two adults. "My sword… that's what you want?" Mura tried to read the big elf's stoic features but found nothing. Would he even mind if Mura said no? There seemed to be an apathy there… Not a death wish, but a spark waiting to be lit behind his eyes like a fire that had gone cold.

At the tree line figures emerged from the shadows. They stalked into the light. Their movements were graceful and precise, moving like the

381

wind through the trees. Light fell upon their emerald plated armor. Terma. Mura felt fear reach his bones. He'd seen a single Terma rip into four normal elven warriors before they'd even gripped their blades.

"We can't take that many," he voiced, stepping back. "We have to run."

The big elf turned, looking over his shoulder. "Give me your blade."

Mura hesitated. Something shouted at him to do it—*instinct*, he was certain. But his senses, his good judgment told him it was madness. At last he sighed, offering his sword. "Tell me truly, can you kill them all?"

The big elf grabbed his sword's smooth obsidian handle. "I've only ever made a promise to one woman, and to her I will keep it." Mura caught his gaze, noticing that it flashed for the briefest moments to a fragment of a golden crown pinned to his vest that had been Karil's father's, a mark of the Lando.

With that, the big elf turned as the Terma unsheathed their blades, stalking forward, surrounding them, death in their eyes.

* * *

Mura's fingers itched, wishing he had his blade as the Terma glided forward.

The big elf lifted his sword into the air and slammed it into the ground, burying it halfway to the hilt, then spoke. The elf's words carried across the glade as the elite elven warriors fanned out in a wide circle. "I know what clouds your vision, what haunts your thoughts and whispers in your ear…"

Jiro spoke, his heartwood staff stamping into the ground. "You can't reason with them, they aren't elves anymore."

The big elf continued stubbornly. "… A darkness. But you don't have to listen to it."

Still the Terma continued their death march.

Darkness? Mura wondered.

The Terma either seemed oblivious to the big elf's words or willfully ignorant as they glided forward, relentless, step-by-step. Mura's vision blurred as the Terma's spark-fused elven armor blended with the ground and the air, as if they were a part of the woods, but their eyes stood out—orbs of black, soulless pits in the bright glade.

The big elf didn't even raise his blade. "One last chance …" he called, but he sounded resigned, distant. His back was a muscled wall, dark despite the bright sun glaring down from above, watching the encroaching circle of death.

Suddenly all things seem to pause, and Mura could only hear the soft thump of blood in his ears, of a halengal's titter in the distance, of a soft breeze rustling the multi-hued leaves.

The Terma lifted their blades, steel glinting in the sun.

The big elf's words came, a soft utterance. "So be it..."

And the Terma attacked.

Ducking the two blades aimed for his neck, he snatched Mura's blade, diving back. But two more swords met him from behind, cutting at his legs. His—Mura's—blade tip dove into the ground, steel clanging and rebounding. He continued, parrying and evading with liquid ease. Quickly Mura realized the big elf was doing everything in his power not to kill. But the elves were too fast and too strong. He slipped a tall Terma's blade, but its point clipped his shoulder and blood flayed out, dashing the ground.

Silence.

The big elf was a statue, now facing Mura. When he looked up, darkness like fetid oil shuttled across his green gaze. Then, like ice shattering the Terma launched at him, six blades crashing down from all sides. He bellowed. It shook the woods and rattled his bones, and he exploded into action.

Like a wisp of wind, the big elf glided between the elves, cutting and slicing. He found the miniscule weak points in their armor, bashed in knees, carved heads from their shoulders like trimming brown leaves from a trembling branch. The elves made no sounds except for the gurgle of blood as they fell. Still they fought as if possessed, leaping at him from every angle. He ducked two keen blades, steel sparking in the air and brought his sword in a semi-circle beneath, cutting their legs at the knee. They fell and he ended their lives...

It was over in a matter of moments.

Blood stained the brown carpet of the woods, running in rivulets.

Mura was speechless. He'd never seen killing like that. It seemed more like pulling weeds from an unruly garden than the taking of life. He felt detached, cold, even a tad woozy—and he'd killed before, many a time. Something about the whole incident seemed dreamlike.

But it was the little things that proved it to be real... The metallic scent of blood that filled the damp air, the now eerie call of a halengal in the distance once more, and the big elf's even breaths. Mura felt sudden

383

warmth creep beneath the sole of his boot and looked down to see hot blood spilling across the ground, soaked up by the hungry earth, but not quick enough to stop the puddle around his foot from forming.

The big elf knelt, shutting an elf's eyes and whispering a prayer.

"You did what you had to do," Jiro said at last.

Mura pulled his boot away. "Did what you had to do?" he repeated. "This is not killing... this is slaughter..." He looked up, eyeing the big elf who wasn't breathing hard, his green gaze now returned as he surveyed the scene, as if searching.

Suddenly the big elf found another large elf nearly the same size as him and began stripping his armor from his body.

"What are you doing?" Mura asked.

"Changing," said the big elf coldly.

He watched him tug on the armor, the limp, dead elf like a ragdoll in his hands. "Can't you wait?"

"For what?" the big elf asked as he threw the tattered rags he'd worn to the ground, exposing his body to the chill air. He slid the thin breastplate over his frame. Despite the huge Terma he'd found, the armor still bulged, plate groaning in the shoulders and chest, barely fitting him. "He's not even cold yet."

384

Slapping the translucent forest green bracers over his wrists the big elf replied, "The elf won't get more dead, friend. I'm afraid death is death. Besides, I've been in these rags for far too long."

Mura gritted his teeth, looking away.

Suddenly he heard a wet, sputtered breath.

One's still alive, he realized, hope rising, and he swiftly knelt at the elf's side. The elf had a youthful face; blue eyes without wisdom blinked away tears. He still had the traditional *elai* blond braids over his sharp ears. The age of passage for elves was twenty, which was when an elven boy cut his braids and ascended to adulthood. *Not yet twenty.* For elves, the Terma was only a boy. Mura was astounded he'd had been raised to the rank of Terma so young. The boy had no visible wound, but it was clear he was bleeding from the inside; likely his armor had spared him from being severed in half from the big elf's monstrous blows, but had left his insides shattered.

Mura's heart panged, looking to Jiro. "Heal him," he demanded.

But the High Elf healer remained stationary, his staff planted into the ground like a root. "We both know the malady this elf suffers from cannot

be healed… even if I heal his wounds I can do nothing for his darkness…
He will rise and try to kill us again."

The young elf began to choke.

For a flash of a moment, Mura saw another lying on the ground.

Gray-green eyes. Dark brown hair.

Gray…

It reminded him of Death's Gates and the boy's near death upon the
stone altar. Frustration welled up inside him, watching. He couldn't do
anything just like back then… He'd had to watch helplessly as Gray's life
slipped away before his eyes. Mura lifted the elf to keep him from choking on his own blood. "Can't you try at least?" he insisted. "By the gods,
he's just a youth."

"And what then? Even if I'm wrong, and I'm not, we know nothing of
this disease," Jiro countered. He watched the boy, struggling to breathe.
"There's a high chance if I do heal this boy the darkness may infect me.
If I am turned, what then?

"My knowledge, my power, my aid may all be turned to the very cause
we're attempting to subvert. Not to mention, my life and the young Terma's will both be forfeit."

A sharp gasp drew Mura's eyes. The young elf's eyes were beginning to
glaze as he stared up at the blue sky, blood forming around his pale lips,
leaking down his pure, fair skin. The elf began to shake in his arms and
fear roiled in his eyes, subduing the inky darkness if only for a moment.
Mura began to whisper a long prayer, issuing words of comfort when—

Efficiently, quietly the big elf neared, a shadow over Mura's shoulder.
He knelt and moved Mura's blade slowly across the elf's throat. Blood
issued forth, spilling to the ground, the Rehlias floor eating it up like a
hungry animal until the young Terma's head lolled lifelessly to one side,
heavy in his arms.

Mura rose, feeling angry and tired. He heard his voice, hoarse in the
back of his throat. "He didn't have to die…"

"Yes, he did," Jiro answered. "You know that as well as I, as well as any
of us."

Mura looked to the big elf, emotions roiling inside him. He was still
hunched over the green-plated Terma as if the Spire itself weighed upon
his back, and his words came, a dark roll like thunder on the horizon.
"I've seen these elves. Trained many of them myself since they were
small. I've watched their smiles as they scored their first strike on their

385

friends. Friends that now lay lifeless next to them…" His voice was desolate, forlorn. "I've killed so many. Each I've tried to reason with, tried to…" His gravelly voice broke as he pinched his eyes, then looked up at Mura and Jiro, green eyes like pools of anger. "I held one down once. Pushed the young elf against a tree, tied him until he couldn't move. I made certain the rope was good and tight, and as I tried to question him, to pull the darkness from him, his eyes rolled into the corner of his head and he slumped lifeless. I swore I didn't tie the bonds upon his neck too tight, but the darkness in his eyes fled with his final breath, as it does with all."

Jiro joined his side, staff making leaves rustle as he neared. "You cannot reason with them," said the High Elf healer. "Whatever possesses them has turned them more creature than elf."

The big elf shook his head. "You don't understand. It tugs at your soul, whispers to you… "

The man sounded too familiar with the malady that infected the Terma. Mura wished he could grab his blade. "How do you know that?"

"Because…" the big elf answered and his lids shuttered as the darkness floated across his eyes like a film of night. "… I have it as well. Dryan has infected me with the same darkness."

Mura eyed his sword still in the elf's huge hands. "And why aren't you turned by the darkness?" he asked, a touch more condescendingly than he knew he should. The elf had saved their lives, and yet… He shook his head, not knowing what to make of it all. He knew the vision of Gray had turned his thoughts toward irrationality—they were all doing the best they could with what they'd been given. But it didn't make Mura trust him any more—there was a power and a darkness, and more importantly, he sensed a confusion to the big elf… as if he had yet to choose a side. Mura pressed more sharply, "Why should we trust you if this evil can convert even the strongest of us?"

"Because I'm not like them. Terma are trained since they are youths to be blades, to be weapons. I was trained from birth. I can control the darkness. For now, at least."

"What are you?"

The big elf looked up. "I believe you already know the answer to that, friend of Karil."

Immediately Mura knew where he'd seen eyes like that, where he'd seen an elf move like that, all of it slamming home. Rydel. The big elf resembled him in so many ways, and yet he was different. "Hidden," Mura replied.

"More than a Terma, but less than Dryan," he answered.

Less than Dryan? Mura wondered, but Jiro spoke first. "You kill Terma. But the question remains—where does your allegiance lie?"

"To myself," replied the big elf without looking up. He was admiring Mura's blade, turning it over in his hands. His huge palm nearly consumed the black handle, pressing against the rare metal guard, or tsuba, that flared like a dragon's talons. "Fine elf-work indeed. A weightless *stoneworked* handle, Dragonborne *tsuba,* a blade folded with bloodstone to cut through the spark, and..." He turned the blade over, eyeing an etched white symbol on the pommel in the shape of a leaf and an *E.* "Esmeralda's hand, if I'm not mistaken?"

Mura nodded, eyes squinting, hiding his surprise. Few knew of the High Elf armorer aside from royalty. Tucked away in the depths of Eldas, she was almost as old as the Spire itself and had crafted only two blades in all her years of existence, trying her hardest to replicate the Ronin's blades—an attempt she knew was all but folly, but still the swords were near indestructible. "She's made only two blades, yet you handle that one as if you held it before."

387

"Again, another answer you already know," the big elf replied with a smile. "My blade as well and two more, aside from this one."

"She created four blades?" Mura replied, incredulous.

"One for each hidden, and this," said the big elf. "Though I'm surprised she made a blade for you... Whoever you are is a mystery indeed."

Jiro interjected, "You've yet to answer the most important question, Hidden."

"Always the High Elves that get to the root of the problem."

Mura had the same burning question. "How did they find us?"

"They didn't find you, they found me," the big elf said, "and they'll be coming again. More this time. Two dozen, maybe three. Even with your powers, High Elf, and with yours, my mysterious new friend, we can't take them."

"Then we run."

He laughed. "We cannot run. I'm faster than you both, and they've nearly caught me a dozen times already. Now I realize they've been corralling me like a loose fox."

"To what end?" Jiro asked.

"To here," he answered, pointing to the massive Gates of Eldas looming over them, a purple, white and green spectacle. "Pinned against the gates that cannot be opened and surrounded from all sides, I'll finally find my end and you, yours."

"Then we leave you," he said decidedly.

"And be hunted down in turn. They are coming from all sides."

"Then what?" Mura asked, growing angry. "Die with you? You led them to us! You better have a way out of this."

The big elf smiled as if amused. "You can save your threats, my mysterious friend. My plan stands before us." And Mura followed the elf's gaze, seeing as it panned to the immense wall, crawling up the tangled bulwark of heartwood, moss, and vines.

The Gates of Eldas.

"It's time to climb," the big elf declared.

***

"Are you mad? We can't climb that," Mura said.

"You can't climb that without *me*," corrected the elf.

388   Jiro neared, putting his staff to the gate. Vines and wood unfurled, grabbing it and trying to tug it forward, as if attempting to absorb the High Elf's walking staff. Jiro uttered a few elven words and the vines shrieked, letting go of the staff as if seared and becoming still as stone on the wall once more. "Mura is right. What you suggest is folly. The gate has precautions against those who wish to scale it. It can sense an individual's motives, sensing an attacker or an intruder and respond appropriately. It will break us like driftwood if we attempt to climb it."

The big elf laughed. "That's the least of your worries."

"The least?" Mura posed, almost afraid to ask.

"The gate has hundreds of defense mechanisms," he explained. "Elves created Death's Gates, but the Gates of Eldas are a work of deadly beauty that far surpass that monolith of stone. Don't forget, Eldas weathered the chaos of the Lieon more unscathed than most—the Gates of Eldas are much to thank for that. It's called the Wall of Death by some for a reason."

Mura scratched his head, trying to contain his exasperation. "Then how in the Seven Hells do you propose we climb it?"

"With empathy."

"Empathy?"

"If the gates believe you wish it harm it will attack you, kill you, throw you from its face to a bloody death, but if it believes you mean it something else? Then you can climb unscathed."

"You mean to redirect our intention," replied Jiro, his white eyes narrowing like an archer's slit in a keep.

The big elf nodded. "That and more. You cannot simply think on daffodils and summer days. The gate and the ancient elves who created it are too intelligent for such a simple loophole. Instead, you must climb the gate as if you *are* the gate."

Be the gate? Mura wondered. "And... how do we do that?"

"You are the one with one of Esmeralda's blade. I'm sure you can work it out," the big elf replied then shrugged, stabbing Mura's blood-soaked blade into the earth at last. "Or... you won't, and you shall die here."

Mura's jaw ground in infuriation when, suddenly, the woods shook. Flocks of birds took to the air from the green canopy and made the blue sky appear a sea of white. More Terma had arrived.

"They're here," Jiro declared.

"Then it's time." The big elf composed himself, a deep hum emanating from the back of his throat, and then began to climb. His hands gripped a vine and it shifted slightly but held. He reached out again, finding a foothold of rough lichen. Then his pace quickened, scaling the wall as if he were running, graceful and purposeful with every movement. "I suggest you begin now," he called, already a dozen paces up.

Mura looked to Jiro. "Well?"

Jiro gave a shrug and turned to the wall.

Mura joined him.

With a breath he reached out, grabbing a wrist-thick tuber. The tuber twisted, as if doing a wrist release and grabbed his arm in turn. It coiled around him, slowly but surely. Fear spiked inside Mura. More roots came to the tuber's aid and moss slid over his skin, cold and wet, coating him. *Empathy!* his mind shouted, reminding him of the big elf's words. *Let me help you,* he thought forcefully. *I'm here to help.* Instead of tugging or pulling away he gripped the tuber back, issuing thoughts as if they were a sheer force, exuding into the wall. He felt the rough grip upon his arm lessen, and he opened his eyes in amazement to see the tuber and vines retreat back into the living wall once more.

He turned to Jiro in astonishment. "It works."

389

But Jiro wasn't there.

He looked up. The High Elf was already two dozen paces up, moving, if not with the same alacrity as the fearsome Hidden, at least with ease. Mura sighed. "Good, Mura, now hasten your pace, you're—" Jiro fell silent as he looked down, eyes widening.

He followed the healer's gaze.

Over his shoulder the tree line rustled. Elves stepped out. A dozen, then two, then three… Each with green-plated armor. A hundred Terma with madness in their eyes stood at the tree line.

And his words were stolen from him.

"Climb, Mura!" Jiro cried out.

And the Terma charged.

Mura needed no incentive. He grasped for the wall. But fear made his thoughts slick and the roots, instead of reaching out to grab him, slid beneath his hands like water. He grabbed a vine but it sucked itself into the wall like a timid creature. *No,* he cursed inwardly, knowing the elves were getting closer by the moment. He gained several feet on the wall until his fingers clutched a patch of moss. It ripped free and he cried out, falling to the ground. Again he leapt, digging into the gates, but the wall held no more purchase than a waterfall.

He looked over his shoulder. The Terma were nearly on him. He had to fight. He reached for his sword, turning.

A voice crashed above. "Think!" the big elf bellowed. "Don't give up!"

Mura growled, thoughts like a storm, slamming his sword in its sheath. This time he let it all go. He closed his eyes and leapt, reaching for a thick, green root. He gripped it. "I am you," he whispered, trying desperately to believe that he and the root were one, that he *was* the wall.

Something clicked and it made sense.

The root began to slip through his fingers and he began to tumble backwards into a sea of swords, but then it twitched. The root looped his wrist like a shackle and he gripped back. This time the root didn't solely hold him, it pulled him. Mura felt his body heaved into the air, arm nearly wrenched from its socket. He looked over his shoulder as the Terma leapt from the ground, reaching out. He wasn't gaining enough ground, not fast enough. A sword lashed at him and he unsheathed his blade in a ring, parrying. Another Terma leapt with elven strength, grabbing his ankle. He staggered, the root halting. The Terma unsheathed his blade and rammed it into Mura's calf, hitting bone. Pain erupted and he cried out, letting go, but the vine held on.

Suddenly, Jiro was at his side.

"*Suthas un varisus!*" the elf's voice was like a crystalline boom, echoing through Mura, thudding in his chest and in his ears. A chunk of the wall erupted, shards of wood flying into the Terma who leapt for Mura. But still the Terma gripped his ankle, clawing higher. More leapt, grabbing for the wall, but slid free. Several others clutched vine or root, only to be wrapped by leg-thick shoots or a thousand sprouts and pulled into the wall, crushed in a pile of blood and armor. Still they leapt, possessed.

All the while Mura clung to simple words, repeating them through his agony.

I am you.

I am you.

Tears sprouted in his vision in pain, watching in terror as the root that held his wrist began to stretch and break. *No*, he growled, but instead of anger, Mura pleaded to the wall, beseeching its help. *His* help. A dozen more sprouts wrapped around his wrist, baby-like tendrils trying to keep him out of reach from the prickling steel a breath away.

But as they did the Terma holding him cried out, reaching out a hand.

"No..." Jiro whispered.

391

A dozen more green-plated warriors leapt, grabbed the Terma who held him, the influx of weight tugging at his leg, popping his knee and causing another explosion of pain roaring through him. Worse still, their weight was too much. The roots and nubile sprouts holding Mura snapped. His weight was lost and Mura fell, tumbling toward the ground and toward the briar patch of swords.

There was a cry and Mura looked up to see the huge Hidden plummeting from the sky like a rock. The big elf's boot slammed into the Terma holding him, fountaining blood from the elf's nose. The vine wrapped around the big elf's thick forearm snapped short, halting his descent. At the same time, he snatched Mura, stopping his fall. Mura wasted no time. He grabbed his dagger, slashing the Terma's hands holding him. The Terma cried out, falling.

Yet as he did, the root the big elf held began to twist and break.

"Climb," he ordered. "It cannot be done for you."

Mura understood. He reached out, grabbing a chunk of moss. It fell away as his thoughts began to slip. *I am you.* He pleaded and reached up, holding a knotted tuber. It shook, then held. His teeth grit and he repeated, louder, "I am you." Above him, a dozen round nubs formed like rungs on a ladder and Mura grinned, if only to distract him from the numbing pain in his leg. He grabbed root after root, gaining space between he and the death below. Fingers felt, fumbling over moss, root and vine. The living footholds came to his aid quicker now, like gentle hands pulling him up the purple wall, but occasionally his mind would slip and he would question his thoughts. At those points the roots would shudder, pulling back into the wall, but he would forge his belief stronger, his thoughts harder—willfully imagining that he was made of the wall before him, his skin *moss*, his sinew roots, and his blood sap, and the wall would listen once again.

At last, when his heart began to slow, his near death experience slowly fading, he slowed. The big elf was nearby, two fingers casually holding a palm-sized rock, his feet balanced on an outcropping of rough lichen. Mura closed his eyes and kept his thoughts strong. Two tubers that stretched from the wall to form shackles on his hands and a vine that curled around his waist allowed him to look down.

The Terma were only small figurines on a board of cyn now, their steel blades like tiny glimmering shards in a sea of green and brown.

How long had he been climbing? His muscles ached.

Jiro was nearby, his staff on his back, held by a vine, and his feet held by a small landing of roots. Mura was surprised by the High Elf's adroitness. Clever, surely, he knew all too well by now, but graceful too. He was a High Elf after all, but his age, like Mura's, was a false indicator of his true grace. "You are your mother's child," Jiro claimed. "Tenacious to the end."

"If you expected me to fall before we're finished with this, my elven friend, you're less wise than I give you credit for."

"A mystery, indeed," the big elf declared, eyeing Mura's holdings. "You're beginning to catch on. But we've a long way to go yet," he said, and Mura twisted, looking up into a sea of clouds, and more wall stretching endlessly, much like Death's Gates. But ahead was different. Vines and tubers moved, waving in the air menacingly, like an Algasi *Dance of Spears*, and he saw huge hand-length thorns protrude like daggers from the living wall.

"Great. What's happening now?" he asked. "Why is it doing that?"

Jiro put his palm to the wall, a small, green glow blossoming and he spoke, eyes closed. "The wall senses us... it's unsure of what we are... I sense... *confusion.*"

The big elf pointed to Mura's hand where tiny, green sprigs reached out to hold him, then curled back like a shy maiden then reached out again, as if warring with itself. "I told you the wall is alive. Like any living thing there are parts that feel and are more aware... If the bottom of the Gates of Eldas are its feet, then we are about to climb its face." The warrior-elf glanced to Mura's blade. "Keep your thoughts strong and be ready, for you will have to use that soon."

As he spoke the wall rumbled, and twigs and branches broke from Mura's grip and reformed again, barely catching him before he fell. "I am you," he breathed, eyes closed, hard and powerful, picturing himself and the wall as one entity. "I am you!" Still the wall shook, rumbling beneath his hand as if a rockslide was happening.

The big elf's voice cut through the rumble. "It's not your thoughts."

Mura opened his eyes. Upon the wall the thorns broke, and something began to bulge from the wall's surface, rock and lichen taking form into some sort of creature.

And he heard the thread of fear in the elf's voice, "He's come..."

✳ ✳ ✳

"Who's come?" Mura voiced.

"Moglai," Jiro whispered. "It's him, isn't it?"

Moglai? Mura had heard the name before, long ago as a child, and distant memories resurfaced. Moglai was a name for the ancient protector of Eldas, taking form in all manner of creations—birds, and beasts, all formed from the woods themselves. But it had always been a friendly story, told in reverent tones, as if Moglai was a benevolent god, not some evil creature.

"The Gate's guardian has come," the big elf uttered.

At his words, there was a pop and snap of branch and root from above and to the west, a hundred paces away. The wall seemed to be coming alive. "We cannot fight this creature," Jiro declared. "We must run..."

Mura heard the words but his gaze was riveted. His hands shook, watching as legs sprouted, made of sinewy dark wood. Its bulbous carapace was comprised of mossy limestone, and from its stone face a hundred black marbled eyes sprouted. His grip faltered as he stared into the forming creature. The rumbling and scratching of rock sounded in his ears and above, a voice shouting once more, "Climb!" the immense elf bellowed. "If you value your life, climb *now!*"

And Mura climbed, but when he looked back to the wall where Moglai had been it was nowhere to be seen. The creature had disappeared. But rather than comfort him, his stomach dropped, eyes roving to his left and right but seeing only more tangled branch, vine, rock and moss.

"*Where is he?*" he cursed.

Jiro froze at his side, equally perplexed.

"Don't wait for him! Climb, you fools!" the big elf shouted. "If we reach the summit we'll be safe!"

"*Safe,*" he scoffed, but he didn't question or slow and grabbed a huge rock when he saw Jiro's face—it was pale as snow.

He glanced up and the big elf was equally frozen in time.

Mura looked down as the rock beneath him began to rumble, breaking free from the wall. Moss shed itself, blinking, and two black-marble eyes formed. Then three and four, and the eight black eyes of a spider appeared on a mossy face. They stared at him, a breath away. Pincers formed as well, sliding free from its stone mouth, a dark snarl rasping from its earthen maw.

Mura tried to find his breath.

"Climb…" Jiro whispered.

"*Climb!*" bellowed the big elf.

And Mura leapt, but Moglai was quick.

It snapped down on top of his leg, digging into the wound from the Terma. He gasped a cry but couldn't find the breath. Shutting down the pain, Mura slammed his foot into the creature's face. Still the pincers held. Again and again he rammed his heel into those black eyes but it felt as if he were kicking granite. His grip on the wall began to slip, his thoughts breaking and roots shredding as fear began to conquer his thoughts of empathy.

"Use the wall!" the big elf called.

Drowning in pain and fear, the words were too distant, too confusing.

The beast let go of his leg. Now numb with pain, Mura crawled higher. He tried to pull away, reaching for the next root, but saw the rest of the wall had gone slick like the bottom of a boat. A clicking emanated from the creature's maw. It pounded in Mura's skull.

Em— He tried to hold onto the word. *Empa*— The spider's legs made from thick boughs smashed into the wall, moss sprouting where it touched. It crawled over him, shrouding him like a second night. He found himself staring into its many eyes. The clicking now throbbed in his head, deafeningly loud, as if tearing his mind in two.

Moglai's mandibles lowered.

Mura reached for his blade. He gripped the obsidian handle at his side when the spider's weight pressed into him, jaws nearing. His arm was tight, stuck against its heavy stone carapace. He couldn't retreat, couldn't fight...

It was over.

He felt stone pincers slide around his neck, his death certain.

And he had one final thought through his terror.

Gray...

Stout Surprises

It was hot on Faye's skin, even from a dozen paces away.

Sweat broke out across her face as she watched roaring flames consume the ship and smoke lift into the air to mingle with the turquoise ambiance. But she didn't slow. She hobbled onward, pushing her way through the crowded docks as a resounding *boom* sounded from the Black Hive. It shook the city and she fell to her knees, feeling splintered wood beneath her hands. Thieves stumbled and others turned, more interested in the desolation of their capitol building than some dying woman. She used that to her advantage, but she didn't think it would last long.

If Halvos lived, they would come for her.

She rose to her feet and limped up the gangplank, choking on a wave of putrid smoke and the scent of charred flesh and viscera. Ripping her right sleeve free, she wound it around her mouth. The hot sting of smoke was dampened, but not gone. She kept low, ducking beneath it as much as possible. Bodies littered the ship's deck. Each time Faye quickly flipped them over, checking for a pulse and desperately scanning their faces. Her pulse itself was rapid as she flipped over a fat man. She breathed a sigh, seeing the man's swarthy black skin and missing teeth. A sailor. Not Odaren.

Faye kept moving, crawling across the deck toward the captain's quarters. Her hands were wet with blood, some of it her own, some of it from the blood-soaked deck. She had no idea if Izul and his men were still onboard. In her present state, she couldn't fight a small child let alone a four-stripe Reaver. But it didn't change her resolve. Whatever happened now would happen. Faye slipped into the captain's quarters and saw what she'd dreaded.

Blood—everywhere.

It lathered the ground, making the once-brown deck a gruesome red.

Two corpses.

She let her black cloth fall from her mouth to the ground.

The first corpse was a small, spindly man with a surly scar. His face was plastered with horror, as if he'd looked upon a demon before he'd died. *Izul*, she cursed. They'd been no match for the Reaver. But as she stepped over him, she saw his neck was gashed wide open as if he'd been stabbed a thousand times. "What kind of madman…" she whispered and closed his eyes, then looked to the other.

She knelt beside the bigger of the two.

Captain Xavvan.

Her gut twisted. All emotion had seemed to be bled from her, like a pig for slaughter, but it raced back now. Xavvan's soft blue gaze stared into the beyond. She examined his wounds quickly as she'd been taught. He had a small, charred hole through his neck but looked otherwise un- harmed. Half a dozen thieves lay scattered around the man with bashed-in heads or shattered limbs. She smiled to herself. *Si'tu'ah* read her battle, and told her he'd fought bravely. Fighting insurmountable odds of evil and nearly prevailing, there's no better way to go than to not go at all. But still he'd helped her, said kind words to her. She even thought the Captain had taken a small liking to her, like a father she never really had. She put her hands over his eyes, closed them and whispered soft words—not a prayer; she didn't believe in such things, but kind words for whatever lay beyond this life and rose.

As she did, there was a *thump*.

She twisted to the closet and opened it.

Odaren came tumbling out like a barrel. He looked just as she'd left him—stubby arms bound behind his back, his wrists and ankles tied by thick coarse rope she'd acquired. Odaren hit the timbers of the deck and grunted. *Still alive*, she thought thankfully. Faye let go a breath she hadn't known she'd been holding. Accustomed to darkness the thief blinked and squinted up at her with a thousand different emotions—anger, sorrow, but above all, elation.

397

"You're alive," he whispered.

"Something akin to that," she muttered. She saw a gold-hilted sword lying in a puddle of blood nearby and reached for it, cutting the thick ropes at Odaren's wrists and ankles.

As soon as she did, Odaren leapt up and embraced her, careful of her many wounds. But this time she didn't retreat. If anything, she gripped back. "So much death," she uttered. "So many."

He seemed to understand and didn't reply.

At last she pulled away. "What happened here?"

"I…" He fumbled for words, gruffly wiping away his tears. "I couldn't tell you. Not exactly. I only heard it all, muffled as it was. There was an explosion and I… I hid. I didn't know what else to do. The cabin doors were locked so I figured the closet was the next best thing. It wasn't easy. I rolled mostly. But I managed to close the door then kept my mouth shut as the chaos began." He looked haunted. "Those two…" He looked at Xavvan and Gambol and sorrow entered his bulbous eyes. "They fought bravely. Heroes, if I believed in that sort of thing. They died for the boy."

"Helix?" she asked.

Odaren nodded.

"Did he die?" She was surprised how easy the words were to say. That was what she feared most—Odaren and Helix's death. Somehow, Odaren's would wound her hardened heart, but the boy's death… She feared it would be something awful for the world. But she wasn't sure why or how.

Luckily, the thief shook his head. "I don't think so. I heard Izul yelling, cursing, but as much as I can tell the boy escaped."

Faye eased a pent-up breath, nodding, glad for it. "We have to go," she declared, looking at the bodies.

"Why?" said Odaren. "Did you not kill that bastard?"

She shook her head.

"And Leah?" he asked.

She choked, not having words. *Dead. Alive. Did it matter?* The Shadow King's point was all too vivid. If Leah lived, how much of her truly did live? How much of her was what Faye remembered, and how much of her would be what Halvos had done to her? She would be exactly like Faye then. Tainted. Broken. And worst of all, no longer human.

She put it all down, saving her wrathful questions for another time.

"Come," she said, "we have to get you out of here. There will be time for questions later." Smoked seeped through the cracks in the timbers near the cabin door—it wouldn't be long before the whole thing was consumed in flames. And yet, the *Pride* should be a bonfire already. Why wasn't it?

As they left the ship, Faye noticed the flames hadn't changed. Something about the turquoise air seemed to be both feeding the flames and yet keeping them at a minimal roar. It reminded her of what Odaren had said—the air *sustained* life.

"Which way is out?" she demanded upon the docks.

Odaren pointed. "Two ways out. That's the quickest."

And they moved, but as they maneuvered down alleys, sticking to the shadows she felt eyes. A group of men bearing the Shadow King's half-gold half-black pin upon their breast barreled down a wide walkway. She grabbed Odaren, stuffing him behind a nook in the vaulted black archway, hiding behind him in a crouch.

"They're gone," said her chubby friend.

She nodded and they continued.

Suddenly, Odaren grabbed her arm and she winced in pain. "Wrong arm."

He apologized but then pointed.

Faye saw.

399

A dozen black-coated thieves blocked the exit, standing beneath a large archway. Faye glimpsed the light of the surface-world beyond.

"Those are the Shadow King's men," Odaren said nervously. "I recognize them. If they see us, they'll stop us. If they don't kill us they'll take us back to him. I'm sure of it. Can you take them?"

"Not as I stand."

"Then what?"

She sighed. "The other way?"

"Will you make it?"

"I have to—what other choice do we have?"

"None," he answered.

And they moved.

More thieves swarmed the walkways though, and this time Faye saw their eyes—searching ravenously. She pulled her hood forward, hiding deep in her cowl and hunching in her skin. It didn't take much; she wanted to shrink into a ball of nothing, to crawl into a corner and never move again. But she followed Odaren silently. He led the way now. Her mind dozed in and out of reality. She felt her lungs burning, heat and sweat breaking out across her skin. Shock was returning. She wasn't sure how she'd staved it off this long. Perhaps the bloodpact? Either way, it would come again soon and she would die or become an unconscious hindrance. Then Odaren would have to carry her out of the city, and that would be a death sentence as sure as sticking a blade in her heart. But she kept her mouth shut and followed.

At last, Odaren stopped at a narrow archway. "This is it," he declared. She nodded.

He peered around the archway and swore. "Cursing damnations."

"That doesn't sound promising," she said, swallowing more blood. It was gurgling up now, threatening to become more blood than air.

He shook his head. "That bastard must have planned this. There's two-dozen of his dark ilk there, and more seem to be coming like rats from of the storm drain. He must've gotten word to them that you're trying to flee—the whole city is going to be locked down at this rate, and soon."

She gripped the wall, falling back against it, taking the weight off her weary limbs. "I deduced most of that from your cursing." She gulped. "A-another... way?"

He looked back to her and worry sprouted across his features. "Not unless you want to break open the ceiling above us and crawl to the sur—" He turned, and worry and panic spread across his features. "Cursing hells, Faye! You look..."

"Gorgeous? *Radiant?*" She swallowed more blood.

"Awful."

She smiled instead of laughing. It took less effort, but blood felt sharp and bitter across her gums. "You know... how to... compliment a girl."

"I learned from the best," he replied and she smiled, but the thief shook himself. "Don't worry, Faye, I'll get us out of here," he said worried-ly, looking around, licking his lips as was his tendency when he was lying.

"You're a horrible liar," Faye grumbled and slid down the wall, falling to the ground. More thieves swarmed past them, but none seemed to be agents of the Shadow King's. "Besides, there's no use," she voiced. "I couldn't move another dozen paces if I tried. It's over, my pudgy friend."

"You can't...." Odaren voiced.

"It's all right," she lied. "I'm all right. We all die, and the spirits know death is a deserved end for me." She took a desperate gulp of air. "Besides, I've lived a longer, better life than I've a right too." But in her heart, Faye *wasn't* content with dying. Not yet. Not even for Leah anymore.

For she knew her death meant Gray's demise as well. And just as Helix's death would eat at her, Gray's end felt a passing all too painful for Farhaven. She whispered, watching the tranquil aquamarine stream continue by, paces away, softly to herself, "I'm sorry, Gray. I truly am. I tried." Bloody hells had she tried.

She looked up.

At a crossroads, beyond the canals, she saw a figure. He stood motionless.

She narrowed her eyes but her vision was blurry, her mind fogged.

Odaren followed her gaze. He'd been speaking but she hadn't heard a word.

The figure moved through the thieves.

He parted them, standing over her. He was hooded, face obscured.

"W-who are you?" she asked.

He was silent, saying nothing.

Odaren put himself between Faye and the youth.

"Move."

"Why should I?"

"I can save her," he rasped.

Odaren stumbled back, unsheathing his dagger. "That voice…" he blubbered, eyes splitting wide. "It's you… Modric… you killed them. You killed that sailor Gambol!"

The youth pulled back his hood to expose attractive dark features. Tilting his head, he examined Odaren, but didn't reach for a blade—nor did he have one as far as Faye could see. "Your friend will die, but I know a way out. Do you want to leave or do you want to fight me?"

Trembling, Faye watched Odaren sheathe his blade. "Save her," he whispered, desperate. "Please."

Modric nodded. "Then help me."

He reached down, grabbing Faye and throwing her over his shoulder, and Odaren grabbed her other arm. Every pain in Faye's body roared anew, her wounds stabbing her with agony until tears sprouted in her eyes. But still they ran. She clutched onto the little strand of silveroot in her hand, as if it were a life raft in the Abyss, while they wove through pathways past thieves. Her world turned to mush. Cries sounded. She saw Odaren watching her but still they ran. They turned a corner and entered a strange empty room. It felt familiar.

Black metal bars covered in moss.

401

Modric extended a hand. Something black and jagged slid from his sleeve, into his fingers, and the huge ancient-looking lock vibrated, then clicked open.

They set her down on the ruined stone steps.

Words came to Faye, distant.

"This is it," Modric declared.

"This is what? What is it?"

"Salvation."

"Where will it take us?"

"I don't know," he admitted. "But it won't be here. Isn't that enough?"

Odaren nodded in the corner of her vision.

She watched as the youth backed away.

"Who are you?" she whispered again hoarsely.

His eyes were shadows, churning with anger, hate and sorrow. "An even exchange. A life for a life." And he hit a stone on the wall. It slid out on hinges, rattling the room, moss and lichen cracking as it moved. And as it did, a purple sphere formed in the air. Faye felt it slide over her skin, encasing her and then…

She was gone.

Narim was gone.

A Confused Ancient

Moglai's pincers slid across Mura's neck.

Jiro cried out and the big elf was moving in the corner of his vision, but they were all too slow. The hermit whispered a silent prayer. He wasn't afraid, but he was sorrowful, knowing he'd failed. The prayer was for Gray, for Karil, for the war he couldn't help stop—for all those whom he'd tried so hard to aid, and yet had gotten only this far.

He had failed.

He waited for it to come, but the stone scraping along his neck hesitated. He stared deep into the creature's many eyes. Hundreds of beady black gems blinked in confusion. The stone pincers slowly slid free of his skin. The beast shook its lichen-crusted head as if railing against something. Mura blinked in confusion as he watched Moglai, but he didn't waste time. He climbed. Scraping against the rock belly of the creature, he slithered higher. Behind him Moglai screeched suddenly, a multitoned cacophony—both reedy and guttural. Whatever the creature was warring with seemed to be winning, but Mura didn't know for how long.

He climbed, desperately, not looking down.

The wall listened and he grabbed root after root, one stone outcropping after another. Higher and higher, Jiro and the big elf were ahead of him, nearly to the top when the sound of the beast's screech reached a crescendo.

All turned.

Whatever had been wrestling with the creature had clearly lost.

Moglai turned his many eyes to the three climbers and gave an angry cry, seeing that his prey had escaped. A dozen more limbs sprouted from its huge body and it began to climb. Fast. Too fast. Mura's heart leapt into his throat watching the dozens of limbs crash and pound against the huge wall, the creature a blur as it sped toward them.

"We cannot outrun it," the big elf declared. "Not this time."

Mura knew the sound of those words. The sound of sacrifice. He opened his mouth to argue with the strange elf, but he was too slow.

The big elf turned on the wall then lifted his arms wide, and the roots pulled themselves back and he fell. Mura reached out, trying to grab the plummeting elf, but he dropped like a rock—too fast. As he passed, the big elf swiped the sword from Mura's back and bellowed, sword out-raised. He landed on the beast, but it did nothing to stop Moglai's ascent. He slashed and hacked as the beast climbed, chopping away stone and lichen, freeing limbs from its body, but still Moglai roared and climbed, slower now, but relentless. Mura understood—it was enraged, and its sights were for only one person.

Him.

Moglai reached them and lunged for Mura. Mura dove, letting his hands fall free. *I am you!* he cried to the wall, pleading for it to listen. A stone outcropping rumbled from the wall and he gripped it with the tips of his fingers, clinging on. The beast twisted, lunging for Mura. The big elf still rode the creature, hacking like a whirlwind of death, limbs falling free—but where he cut, more rock-and-root-and-vine replaced it, forming new appendages. Still, sensing the true threat, Moglai planted itself and bucked suddenly to throw the big elf. He stabbed Mura's obsidian blade into the wall, dangling. Free of the true threat, Moglai turned its full attention to Mura again. Its pincers rattled, stone clanging, a terrifying and loud hiss that made Mura want to cover his ears emanated from its slathering maw as it scuttled forward.

And Mura understood—they were words. Strung together in a long, slow hiss, all bleeding as one, but words nonetheless. *Has, handaria.* El-vish. And he knew their meaning.

Die, intruder.

But Mura wasn't ready to die. He closed his eyes, holding onto the wall, and with every ounce of his being he poured himself into his thoughts. He bled into the intention with his very being. *I am you.* The world disappeared—light, sound, color. He felt cold. Quiet. He felt ancient. He breathed, but it was not a normal breath. It was of the sun and the spark of Farhaven. What he was did not need to breathe. He was not dead, nor living, not in the traditional sense, but still very much alive—he felt… One. He was a part of the great wall. Distantly he was aware he'd let go of the wall and it had encased him, pulling him into it, creating a living barrier of vine, stone and root. Moglai reached him and gave an awful cry. The beast pounded against his barricade, reaching for Mura, but Mura was not Mura. He was the wall. Every facet of him bled this thought, and the wall absorbed it. He felt roots circling his limbs, trying to enter his mouth, but he quietly closed it. The wall hesitated but continued to absorb him as its own. Moglai pounded fiercely against Mura's enclosure, the creature's huge stone pincers cutting chunks of vine while his massive limbs ripped away the wall as quickly as it was built. Quicker even—Mura's distant human-side realized. He was going to get to him.

There was a cry and a blast of light assaulted the beast.

Jiro—the Mura-who-was-not-the-wall knew.

Another cry echoed through Mura's cold barricade. Elvish, deep, powerful. *The Hidden.* Through slits of vine and stone, he saw the huge elf laying into the beast once more. Moglai roared against the onslaught. But still it pounded toward Mura, relentless, almost to him. Its stone pincers reached forward, nearly at Mura's neck. And Mura's concentration wavered. Suddenly, thousands of tiny black spiders poured out of its maw. They crawled over Mura, coating his body, entering his ears and mouth, trying to claw into his eyes. He grit his teeth—thinking of stone and leaf and—

His concentration shattered.

He coughed and gagged, crying out. The roots fell from him and Moglai's pincers lunged. Mura dived away from the first lunge, then the second he skimmed by breathing in, but the third latched onto his leg and clamped. Pain erupted as he felt bone crack and blood rupture. Moglai crunched down upon his leg, eating his way higher. Mura felt agony like never before. Just then, there was a bellowing cry and through Mura's haze of pain, he saw the big elf suddenly cut the last of Moglai's limbs. The huge spider fell. It reached out for the wall to latch on, but Jiro sent a blast of summoned stone into its carapace and it flew—far from the wall—too far to grasp.

And he continued to fall, plummeting to the forest below.

405

Mura gasped, black spots swimming before his eyes.

He let go of the wall but strong hands clasped him. Words sounding from far away, encouraging, hopeful, but distant... so distant. Blood poured from Mura's leg; he felt its sticky warmth coating everything. He felt fear for that—knowing he was losing too much. But even the fear was distant, simply pain as the hands grabbed him and pulled him higher, the forest a spiraling dot of green beneath.

Mura tried to speak, tried to tell them to leave him, but his words were garbled and the pain made everything sluggish and his thoughts mush. A light, cool hand touched his head and words issued forth again in Elvish, "*Sethara siltha.*"

Sleep and be still.

And Mura fell away to emptiness.

His last image was of Jiro's face, an impossible drop, and blood. So much blood.

* * *

A howl and the sound of ripping flesh awoke Mura.

Mura blinked his thickly crusted eyes open. He knew by that alone that he'd been out for at least a day. Memories slammed back into him. *Hundreds of beady eyes glaring into his soul. Stone appendages chewing. Agony.* Chest tight, he bolted upright, eyes flying to his leg.

A dark green cloak was wrapped around his right leg. The cloak was bloody, more red than green now. He unwrapped it quickly and swallowed down a wave of emotions.

His right leg ended a little before the knee. Beyond that it was a smooth, round stump—skin unbroken. "So it was more than a dream," he whispered, voice still hoarse from his howls of pain.

"I believe they call that a nightmare," said a deep voice.

Mura looked up to see the big elf.

A fire parted the two, crackling and pushing back the evening. Trees encircled them. But Jiro was nowhere to be seen.

The big elf was eating. His face was cast in shadows from the fire—but it wore a brooding, mysterious look. Not pity, but something akin. Sympathy? It couldn't be. Not from the hardened elf. But there was a touch of compassion in his green eyes. "Can't say that's the way I'd want to wake up," said the elf and looked back down, gnawing on a leg bone.

Gristle crusted his mouth, glistening in the fire's light. He spoke between bites. "You're one tough man, Mura Andrasa. One tough man, indeed. Ever consider becoming a Hidden? I believe you have to be a full elf and trained from birth, but they might make an exception for a man like you."

Surprise washed over him, overriding thoughts of his missing limb. "How do you know my last name?" Mura asked sharply.

"Been out of Farhaven that long, have you? You're the rightful queen's uncle, my friend," he said, amused. "That makes you elven royalty. That's sort of how bloodlines work. Shouldn't a subject know those who rule over them?"

Rule. The word put a sour taste in Mura's mouth. Whatever Dryan was, King Gias— Karil's father and the previous monarch—had been the opposite. Loyal. True. Honest. Kind-hearted. The perfect elf. And now he was dead, assassinated by Dryan for the throne. But he saved his energy. Arguing with the big elf was low on his list. He lay back down, resting his head on the hardwood of a log, gazing up to the sky, but it was oddly shadowed—no stars could be seen. "Speaking of names, you've never told me yours," Mura voiced.

"You never asked."

"I'm asking now. What's your name?" Mura had a sinking feeling he already knew. The talk of Karil. It was the way the big elf looked and the fragment of crown from Karil's father. Even the way the big elf moved and killed with brutal efficiency gave it away.

"You already know who I am—do you wish for me to say it, or for you to admit it?"

Mura sat up. "Hadrian," he said, speaking the name Karil had told him.

"The one and only, I hope," Hadrian replied.

"You…" Mura felt rage and confusion. "Why did you save us?"

"I listen to Farhaven. She told me you're…" Hadrian hesitated. "Necessary. I fear a world without those like you or Karil. And so I'm here."

Mura grit his teeth against sudden pain. "Why does it still hurt?"

"Jiro mentioned something about that. Can't remember what though."

Mura felt an absence and a brief sorrow looking at his leg. How would he fight now? How would he even walk normally? He felt an anger too. If only he were stronger, or if he'd moved a little bit quicker or—

"Will you be alright?" Hadrian questioned—his voice dark, stern.

Mura caught the elf's squinting eyes in the firelight, as if he were

407

deeming Mura's worth. He remembered those same eyes judging that Terma and then quickly ending his life. It had been the right thing to do, of course, but it hadn't made it any easier. Something in Hadrian's eyes was simply that: cold and calculating. But Mura didn't care about his gaze, or even about his mistakes. He would make do with what he had, and with time, rise above it. "I'll live—that's enough."

Hadrian smiled. "Glad to hear."

Mura grabbed the cloak and tossed it to the elf. "Thanks for the cloak."

The elf gave a dip of his head through the flickering flames.

"Jiro?" he asked, looking about the darkening glade.

"Gone—somewhere," said Hadrian casually. "He's not one for conversation, is he?"

"No," agreed Mura. They'd traveled for two weeks together and he barely knew more about the High Elf than the stories.

"It's true what they say about High Elf healers... He had the look of a High Elf about him. Those pronounced cheekbones, green beard and that quiet, lofty air. But I thought they'd all died in the Lieon—killed off by the Ronin, so they say."

"And you believe that?" Mura questioned.

408

Hadrian merely smiled in the fire's light. Mura had the distinct feeling that every time he tried to put a prying eye to the elf, Hadrian would immediately turn it back upon him. Hadrian ignored the question, twisting it. "Does he do this often? Wander about?"

"It's not unusual. He has a tendency to roam the woods and search for..." Mura hesitated. Did he dare tell Hadrian why they were here yet? He redirected the conversation but knew the Hidden had sensed his awkward pause. "I believe it's his way of being alone. Being the last of your kind bears a weight upon one's shoulders neither of us can comprehend."

Hadrian nodded but it seemed non-committal, as if he *did* understand. *What else was the man hiding?* "I suppose." Hadrian dug back into the rabbit with abandon. The rest of the creature still spun on a skewer over the fire. Fat dripped from the carcass, falling into the flames, making a sizzling hiss and pop. Mura was uncomfortable, starving from his wounds, and queasy by the sight of the charred rabbit.

It'd been weeks since Mura had eaten meat. Being around Jiro and seeing his cool, quietly arbitrating looks had made Mura return to eating typical elf fare—roots, tubers, fruit and the like. Not that it was all that bad. Mura liked all food. Meat included. And the soil of Relnas Forest made even plain old roots taste like a Farbian delicacy.

Hadrian continued to munch and gnaw away; Mura's stomach continued to curdle. The elf's eating made him uncomfortable. It wasn't exclusively his atrocious manners, but then he realized why. "I thought elves didn't eat meat."

Hadrian glanced up from his meal with a toothy, meaty grin. "I thought you'd have deduced by now that I'm not your typical elf."

Mura huffed at that and rolled onto his side, throwing an annoying stick that was poking at his back. "I'm honestly not sure what I've deduced from you. You're strange, certainly—but I wonder if *you* even know what you're after."

Hadrian looked thoughtful, as if picking at Mura's words the way he picked at the bone of the hare. But then he smiled and dug back into his meal. He tossed the bone into the fire pit and Mura listened to the fat and marrow inside the bone crackle from the flames. Mura lost himself to that crackle, gaze lingering in the orange-hued flames, the warmth of the forest coating him. His leg only throbbed dully—he figured Jiro had given him mendwort or perhaps found a rare silveroot tree to nullify the pain and speed the healing. Of course, Jiro was a powerful healer too. He'd brought Gray back from the brink of death long ago during the battle at Death's Gates, and while flesh and bone could be knit back—a whole leg? Mura knew such a thing wasn't possible. Worse, it wasn't the wound itself that hurt. That had been healed. The pain of his *missing* leg hurt. Why did it hurt so?

409

"It changed," Hadrian said suddenly. "One day. I don't remember how or why, but I changed."

Mura perked up. He sidled up higher on the fallen tree branch that his back rested on and listened intently. "When?" he asked.

Hadrian's eyes glazed as he spoke. "I'm not sure. The last of my memories before I changed are indistinct… like looking through broken, hoary glass. I remember it wasn't long after King Gias' death. I'd been training in Drymaus Forest when I got wind of the tragic news. I knew nothing of the treachery behind it, but something felt afoul. I returned home and discovered Eldas was in shambles, Karil had fled and the Terma were no better than Asterian scoundrels. But it was still early. Dryan hadn't corrupted everyone—only those he needed. Mostly the Terma and the Council. Then it gets hazy. I remember…" He reached out with his huge hand, as if trying to touch someone or something in the firelight.

"Soft velvet… then an orb of red… then…"

He shook his head as if the vision shattered.

"That's the only clear memory I have before I became… *this*. Since then, I've craved only meat, felt a strange anger brewing in my veins at all times and other strange things."

"Like what?"

"A hunger," said Hadrian.

"What kind of hunger?"

"It's more than just the appetite for flesh. It's for the sun, for dust, for battle." Hadrian looked up. "Make anything of my madness?"

"Not really," Mura admitted.

Hadrian looked disappointed, as if he'd been hoping for an answer.

And Mura ventured, hesitantly "This isn't anything more than an educated guess but… You sound like a caricature of Covai. Craving the sun, hungering for flesh and dust? Those are attributes I'd ascribe to a Covaian."

Hadrian nodded at this, agreeing. "I don't see why though."

"You said Dryan infected you. With what, or how?"

"I'm not entirely sure."

410

"Others are infected by it too?"

Hadrian nodded.

Mura scrubbed his stubble in thought. Then he suddenly realized where he was. He looked behind him and caught through the flickering firelight a shroud of black rising over them—blocking out the stars. That's what was obscuring the night.

The wall.

Hadrian saw his eyes. "We didn't want to travel far while you were injured."

Mura saw the greater ramification. "That means…"

"We're inside Eldas," Hadrian finished with a smile. "Of course, that was the easy part. Next will be harder, much harder. But I will see it done." Hadrian's eyes glowed in the fire's light. The rabbit's bone in his hand cracked as he squeezed it in a fist. "I will kill Dryan and heal this plague that festers inside me. And you will…" He hesitated, waiting for Mura to fill in the gap, but Mura was silent. "Why are you here again?"

And despite the pain, the sorrow, the sudden emptiness at losing a part of himself, hope rushed back inside Mura like a sputtering flame fed with a rush of wind. He hadn't failed. Not yet at least. He would find the Prophecy of Leaf and he would end the war for Eldas before it even began.

A Demon Speaks

When they had reached the Eastern Pass they found two more dead Algasi. They had stumbled on them as a group and Ayva was the first to them. Ayva stopped her cormac short and dismounted.

Dalic was at her side.

Ayva put her hand to her mouth. Hannah and Zane neared. Hannah gasped, falling into Zane's chest and turned from the horrific image. He held her but didn't look away, his eyes tight with anger. Ayva was glad it wasn't just her. She felt her stomach churn in horror, anger and a thousand other emotions, eyeing the bodies. Dalic and his Algasi, on the other hand, wore stony expressions, eyeing the gruesome scene with dead eyes, but Ayva felt their fury and sorrow.

The two dead Algasi lay in the middle of the small dirt road that led upward, deeper into the forest of the Nimue Everglades.

It was two days since news of the disappearance of the first two Algasi. Since then, their journey had been smooth and effortless. Green rolling hills and hours were spent chatting with Zane and Hannah about life in Farbs and their upbringing. Ayva spent the rest of her time trying to extract what information she could out of Dalic, but any mention of the sword had been deflected with 'that road is out of sight still' or answered with mere silence. She was growing almost more afraid of finding the sword than not finding it. Now with the Eastern Pass nearly in their sights,

Dalic had sent ahead two scouts.

Their deaths had clearly not been painless.

Guts sprawled across the dusty road, entrails in strange patterns. Their torsos were ripped apart, claw marks down their chest, their arms and legs severed, and other signs of terrible violence. The only part of their bodies that hadn't been mutilated seemed to be their faces. Though their faces were twisted in agony their dark skin was unblemished, and their eyes, though bulging from the pain, left intact. If one didn't look below the neck they would have looked otherwise unharmed—as if the killer had made sure they would be recognizable to those who cared for them.

"Who could do such a thing?" Hannah whispered.

"A monster," Zane replied.

"Sithel," Ayva said clearly. She narrowed her eyes, squinting at the snaking red guts, realizing. "Those are words aren't they?"

Dalic answered with a grunt. "Our tongue."

"What's it say?" Hannah asked timidly.

"A threat," said another.

Unta Suris, Ayva read, and her mind clicked—memories, Omni's or hers speaking for her *"Death comes."*

The wind switched directions and the putrid smell of entrails made Ayva gag. She brought her cloak to her mouth to keep the smell from making her vomit. Tears formed in her eyes, anger rising. *We have to find him. We have to make Sithel pay.* She was surprised by the fury in her tone, even through the bond.

We will, Zane said firmly.

She knew nothing would bring back these men's lives, but Sithel's slow and painful death would be a good start.

Dalic closed the eyes of his men and looked up. "We've no time to waste here on funeral pyres or burying. We must continue. The winds and sands will see to their bodies."

Zane looked to her and she understood.

She cleared her throat. "Allow us."

The light of the sun from above filled her—it felt full of hope. An odd contrast to the grisly scene before her. She felt as if she were doing a dis-service to the Algasi's memories, but it *had* to feel hopeful, otherwise her power fizzled, and so she let it spiral through her. Fire and light seared the corpses, burning their torn-out entrails and bodies to piles of ash, then the ash was lifted on a gust of wind—until only stains of red remained on

413

the dusty road. The Algasi gave them nods of respect. A sincere compliment from the somber warriors, and even Dalic grunted in what could have been thanks, and they continued.

Soon they reached the mouth of a wide trail. The Algasi fanned out as if before a horde of enemies, but Ayva saw nothing intimidating beyond. Ahead was a bright forest of sapling trees. Light streamed from above through the airy canopy and a bed of bright green needles covered the forest floor. "This is the Everglades?" she asked. "Why is everything so new?"

"Not the Everglades," Dalic countered. "This is the Eastern Pass—a land of constant change. It is the path to the Everglades, to our destination and to the sword." He looked to each of them in turn. "Are you certain you want to continue?" Dalic looked troubled. "Beyond this trail much danger lies. I cannot promise your safety."

They looked to each other. "I'm coming," Ayva said.

"And we're joining you," Hannah said firmly.

Ayva's heart warmed.

Zane made a sound of agreement. "What she said." He dipped his head back, indicating his sister. "Besides, it's been getting a little boring recently."

Hannah smacked his arm.

"We started this together, we'll end it together," he said more seriously.

"Then come now—we should make haste while it remains so, before it changes its mind and turns to anger," Dalic said.

"You make it sound alive," Hannah asked, raising a brow.

"It is alive."

"How does a land get angry?" Zane asked, dubious.

"Wait here and see with your own eyes," Dalic said, then motioned to his men. "But we will not waste this blessing." He said no more as he continued on with his Algasi folding around him. Ayva looked to Zane who shrugged and followed.

A light rain began to fall as they rode. Ayva continued to notice signs of new growth everywhere, from tiny colorful flowers trickling onto their path to sprigs of new trees peeking forth from the bed of green needles and leaves.

Many sounds seemed to follow them, a light breeze, the trickle of a distant brook, the rustle of leaves, but altogether they seemed harmonious—musical even. She shook her head, holding her reins. She remembered

414

the prophecy. *The song of Dun… is this it?* No—it was just the sounds of the woods. Her imagination was running wild. Oddly, she noticed no other signs of life—no birds, or bees or beasts of any kind. Not even any crawling insects. It was as if the land had suffered a wildfire or a terrible flood, then new trees were planted in its wake. She began to ruminate on Dalic's words.

Dalic and his men walked, but it was no normal walk—their long legs and tireless pace made Ayva feel breathless and she kept her cormac at a near canter. How the Algasi never tired amazed Ayva, and she wondered if it wasn't partly due to what she'd read and what Gray and Faye had told her about *si'tu'ah*. *Si'tu'ah* trained you to draw the most out of the land and out of your opponents. Faye said that people who could use it fully could better embrace the spark; like breathing deeper, and running faster, jumping farther, fighting longer and even healing quicker.

Dalic walked at her side, leading the way.

Ayva asked, "You said the Everglades are alive. You made them sound like a creature."

Zane veered his steed closer to listen.

Dalic spoke, watching the woods with wary eyes. "All Farhaven breathes the great breath of the spark—some parts more than others, and in those parts the mind of the land exerts itself and shows its true form. Some places the land shows anger, some places, peace and stillness. You often call these places Great Kingdoms. We call them *Altaras*, pieces that comprise the great body of Farhaven."

Ayva squinted. She *almost* understood what the Algasi leader was saying, but Zane made no such pretense.

"That made no sense," Zane said.

She shot him a glare but he ignored it.

Dalic seemed unaffected. He rubbed his clothed jaw as if looking for the right words. "How to explain… All creatures, humans too, have moods—yes?"

Zane nodded at this. "Sure."

"Farhaven is the same. It is a creature of many moods. The blustering sorrowful cliffs of Ren Nar, the mysterious and unstable Drymaus Forest, the angry hot sands of the Rehlias Desert… Do you not feel these things when you enter those domains?"

"Yes," said Ayva, "but they're not angry or moody, they're just… *lands*…." She settled on at last. "They merely happen to have different weather."

Dalic grunted. "Like a man who gets angry and throws a stone—you see only the stone being thrown, only the reaction of the land, but never the origin of its feelings." Ayva wasn't entirely convinced. But she wanted to believe. She had mixed feelings. Thinking of the land as alive was both breathtakingly inspiring—like discovering the grandest creature in existence—and terrifying—like finding out the bed you slept on, the air you breathed, the very water you drank could have sentience. She shivered.

Perhaps it was no more than the notion of a tribe's people, beings who 'connected' and anthropomorphized the land, but something in Dalic's words rang true. The bloodpact sapped Gray's life, and this place seemed to fit into that strange puzzle. She had a feeling Farhaven was alive.

"So the city of fire is angry, city of water is calm, city of stone is stoic, and so forth?" Zane asked.

"Yes," Dalic said, "something like that."

"Sounds simple enough," Zane said.

"There is more. The magic, the feelings of these cities, are felt more deeply by some than others." Dalic paused, thought for a moment, then his gaze tightened as if pleased. Again Ayva found it odd that she was now reading his eyes like a book. "It is like faint music, some can hear it, others not, yes? It is the same with Farhaven. Those who do listen and embrace the land's song become like it, while others choose not to. Like a child who listens to calm words, he grows up calm, yet when a parent speaks angry or hateful words, the child grows up angry. But not all children listen to their parents," Dalic said, then grunted as if amused by his own words—a private joke apparently as he glanced behind to his men.

Ayva understood. "That's why not all water-folk are calm or Farbians are angry." She glanced to Zane. He was from Farbs, and the rest was fairly implicit, due to Zane's often and easily stoked temper.

Zane scratched his jaw, shrugging. "Only the best ones I suppose."

Meanwhile, Dalic answered her rhetorical question, "That is correct."

"What about the Everglades?" Hannah asked.

"The Everglades is a land with many different moods. It is angry like fire, calm like water, enduring like stone, passionate like flesh, nurturing like leaf, fierce like wind, sharp like metal and mysterious like moon. Not many enter the Everglades and live. Only stories exist. Stories told by my people of sun for over a millennia, from the days before the Ronin, before

416

the Great War."

"What stories?" Ayva asked.

Dalic grunted. This was the most she'd ever heard him speak, but he didn't seem reluctant or excited, but dutifully recounting the stories, as if he were fulfilling a necessary tradition. "Most believe the Everglades were formed from leftover elements that could not find a home within their proper bodies—their *altaras*, or 'kingdoms' as you call them. With no place to go, these emotions wandered the land until they found one. The Everglades."

"And how does the Enchantress come into play in all this?" Zane asked.

"They say long ago—no one knows how long—that the Enchantress was a powerful threader of the spark, much like your Reavers. She ruled the city of Menelas and Ester, but at that time it was just one kingdom, a place called Esterlas. Then a great war happened. All Farhaven vied for dominion over the land. From this, the nine kingdoms were born, along with the Ronin. Esterlas was not among these nine kingdoms. It claimed no single element but all of the elements, save for wind. Such a thing was blasphemous. Esterlas was fractured into two, cities that you know now as Menelas and Ester. As the ruler of Esterlas, some say, the Enchantress could not live with her fractured power, while most say she was driven from her home by the Ronin. Fleeing Esterlas, she found the Everglades—a land that was unclaimed and where all the elements existed. There she made home, growing her powers and biding her time until she could return to finish what she started—to conquer the world at last and make all the Great Kingdoms bow to her."

417

There was a collective silence after his words. Dalic didn't have a storytelling air, but his cool, collected delivery was almost more powerful. He continued, "She has only grown more powerful with time. The Enchantress touches all within her domain—and none of it is..." he searched for the word, "...normal." He settled on. "Trees that are not trees. Stone that can change to water, and water to stone. And each can change faster than one can grunt."

"Sounds awful," Hannah said with a shiver.

"It is neither awful nor good," said Dalic. "As with all things of the spark, it simply is."

Ayva understood. "It's a balancing act. Where the Everglades is a constant state of flux, changing every moment, there exists stability elsewhere in the lands."

Zane grunted, sounding like an Algasi himself. "And here? This Eastern Path is a breeze. For being so close to the Everglades lands, I expected something scarier."

Dalic rounded on him with a fierce frown on his brow. "You are a fool then. For what appears soft rarely is. The magic of the Everglades is not contained—it seeps out and overflows into the Eastern Path. It is not as potent here, but neither is it as it seems. If you value your breath to flow, stay vigilant, for change is the only constant within these lands. All the elements will—"

Dalic stopped midsentence, turning an ear up. "Listen."

Everyone paused. Ayva opened her mouth to ask when thunder rumbled, sounding like crashes in the distance. Hannah's horse nickered and Ayva's cormac dipped its head. She patted its neck, soothing the beast. "It's just a bit of rain and thunder, nothing to fear."

But the silence of the Algasi was unsettling.

Worse still, there was no rain or lightning. Moments passed, and only a breeze disturbed the deathly quiet.

The thunder sounded again, shaking the woods.

"Run," Dalic commanded—the single word grave, hard and menacing. And suddenly they broke into a run. Ayva, flustered, kneed her cormac and Zane followed suit. Soon enough they were blazing through the forest, passing it in a whirling blur. Her heart thundered and she cried out as Dalic and the other Algasi sprinted ahead, but it was lost beneath another cascade of rolling thunder.

What's going on? Zane sent.

I'm not sure, I—

As she sent the thought, something collided with her shoulder. It hit hard, nearly unseating her from her mount, but she gripped the cormac's fine mane, holding on. She glanced behind her, wind whipping and saw a huge chunk of ice. *Hail.* But it was the size of her fist. Her shoulder throbbed painfully, but she lay low on her cormac's back and rode swiftly.

Don't stop, she sent and Zane nodded.

Another ball of ice flew toward her and she veered her cormac left, but too slowly. It skimmed off her beast's flank, taking a chunk of flesh. The cormac made a sound of pain, bucking its graceful head. Several more chunks of ice whizzed toward her. She ducked the first, which was aimed for her skull, but two more were right behind it. She cringed, tensing and

418

preparing to take the blows when small bursts of flame erupted in the air, melting them. Hot water splashed upon her face.

She thanked Zane and he nodded in return when—

Something whistled through the air. More by instinct than anything else, Ayva leapt from her cormac just as something huge and clear descended from the heavens. She rolled on the ground, water splashing as the object collided with the ground. The earth shook beneath her from the force of it, dirt mixing with the rain, and when she looked up she saw it. A spear of ice the size of a man impaled her cormac through the saddle, exactly where she'd been sitting, pinning it to the earth. Her heart broke, words caught in her mouth. The beast thrashed for a moment as if trying to free itself, giving those strange tragic cries as it flailed uselessly, and then the light in its silver eyes vanished.

Dead.

Sorrow rent Ayva's chest. Her heart still pound fiercely, but just like that... there was silence.

"It's over," Hannah whispered.

Ayva glanced to the hair on her arms. They rose slowly, standing on all ends as if pointing upwards. She looked up to where they pointed. It was quiet. No, not quiet. Eerily silent. But the sky roiled, clouds forming and growing, darkening ominously. Just then, the sky cracked and deep thunder rattled in Ayva's chest, stealing her breath with how loud and close it sounded. Zane horse nearby whinnied and bucked, and everyone else—even a few Algasi—jumped.

Silence.

Her eyes were still glued to the dark sky.

Against the black clouds, something glistened. It looked like white gemstones against the curtain of black. And she knew why. Her mouth hung in terror. Huge, crystal clear spears of ice, dozens of them, hundreds even, were falling from the clouds like translucent spears of death.

Zane cursed. "*Gods, no.*"

Murmurs of fear echoed from all the nearby Algasi.

They were falling—heading directly towards them, spears the size of the one that had skewered her cormac.

"There's no running from this," Dalic voiced, looking to the sky, his blue eyes resolute. And he turned to her. "Save yourself, lightspeaker. You and the firespeaker might be able to get away. There's still time." But Ayva was tired of running, tired of being weak, tired of listening to advice

419

from others. She wanted to save the others: Hannah, who she would never leave, but the Algasi as well. They had fed her, talked to her and even watched over her while she slept. In this moment, not even they could protect her; they could do nothing but watch the sky and know their impending death. Ayva couldn't run any longer. She'd run all her life. Run from Lakewood, where she'd been helpless to watch the only home she'd ever known burn. That fire, and the Kage, had taken her father from her and she'd been helpless to stop either. Then in Farbs, she'd felt mostly helpless—following Darius and Gray, but rarely helping. She'd felt a victim again. Not anymore. She wouldn't run or be a victim to her events. She would stand her ground.

Hope surged inside Ayva, seeing the looks of her friends—afraid but determined, and Ayva smiled. "We're not going anywhere," she declared into the terrible silence. Zane and Hannah smiled, fearful but resolute, echoing her sentiment. Then, staring up into the sun, Ayva prepared herself for the end as the shards of destruction came raining down.

✶ ✶ ✶

420 The icy shards fell and the heavy silence was shattered.

The land rattled with the first round—most hitting at the edge of their cloistered group.

But the rest followed quickly, aimed straight for them.

Two shards were quicker than the rest. They fell into the crouched Algasi who held spears aloft—but they could have been toothpicks against a giant's sword. The shards slammed down and—

Hope. A small sun bloomed in Ayva's mind, growing as she fed it her hope—and she smiled, feeling a wild, almost crazy, grin come over her, light filling her limbs. Ayva flung her hands as the two shards fell. Small points of light formed inside the icy spears before they made contact, then they erupted. The act both invigorated her and drained her. Those two bursts of light made a small part in her mind grow a little cold, and she felt her arm grow heavier. Still, it worked. The shards melted and water splashed down. Washed in the now icy water, the Algasi spun to her—eyes wide, but Ayva wasn't done.

She ran. The ground rattled beneath her feet as a spear crashed to the earth on her left, dirt flying. She kept her eyes to the sky, watching as the spears fell like volleys of huge, frozen arrows.

Ayva rolled beneath another, then came to her feet. Feeling her heart warm, she cast her hands and two huge spears whistling toward her face turned to slush. She gasped, feeling icy water pour over her, but she continued to run. To her left several Algasi were pinned in by a growing prison of ice—spears falling about them faster and faster. The one-armed Algasi was among them. Ayva remembered hearing his name—Yunwa. Dalic was running for him, but Ayva was quicker. Unsure of exactly what she was doing she breathed in the sun, soaking it into her skin. It seeped into her muscle then deeper, into her bones, then she threaded it forth to her fingers. One word was loud in her head. *Hope.* She had to fill her heart with hope. She whipped her arm, watching as rope-like threads of sun strung together and lashed the descending spears of ice hurtling toward the trapped Algasi. Like a whip of sunbeams, it lashed at the ice. The spears burst into puffs of vapor. With muscles coiled, the Algasi watched where the huge spears had been in disbelief, then turned to Ayva. Their faces were still masked but she saw the awe in their eyes, particularly Yunwa.

But more ice rained down.

She dove out of their way, but each dive cost her precious time as ten more fell in the same span. Zane was suddenly at her side. "Back to back!" She pressed her spine to his. "Target the ice that falls upon the Algasi. I'll stop anything that comes towards us!"

And she nodded.

A dozen shards pelted toward the main cluster of the Algasi. Ayva shot out her hand, threading bits of sun. Her warm breath turned frosty as little buds of light formed inside the shards, looking like frozen yellow gems. The buds of light grew and the dozen shards ruptured. But a hundred more spikes fell. She cried out, breathing in the light, feeling the air grow wintry. She cast more bursts of light as the icy spears nearly reached the Algasi, but each time they exploded into smaller shards of ice, puffs of vapor or icy water. Her power was still varied, and she couldn't control how much light she poured into each threading.

Fire was hot on her face, knowing Zane was doing his best, but the spears of ice were getting closer and closer. Hannah was crying out too—and Ayva saw chunks of rock being flung to collide with the ice, redirecting their paths in the last moment.

There was a sudden, anguished shout rising above the rest, and she twisted to see one of Dalic's Mundasi. An icy spear pierced his calf. He roared like a feral beast, tugging on the shard of ice as more descended from all around, but there were too many to stop.

Dalic saw the wounded Algasi and began to run.

"No!" she cried.

But Dalic ignored her as he leapt to save his brother-in-arms.

Ayva grit her teeth and sent a concentrated beam of light. It melted the shard at the base and freed the Mundasi. Freed, the Mundasi spun, but then spotted the hundreds of descending icy spears—his eyes widening—knowing it was too late and that there were too many. *Please, no,* she thought. But Dalic didn't stop. He dove, skimming beneath a huge lance Ayva couldn't stop that smashed into the ground, nearly running him through. He rose to his feet swiftly. Dalic snatched the wounded Mundasi, throwing his arm around the man's shoulder and dragging him as the giant splinters of ice rained down.

There were too many that Ayva couldn't simply watch. She roared, throwing her hands out. *One, two, five, a dozen.* She burst them one after another—*two dozen. Three.* Ice melted, falling like rain, but still the spears came.

She screamed, tears flowing.

Hope.

The word consumed her. The pulsing sun in her mind felt like fire—searing, hot, and overwhelming, and Ayva fell to her knees, arms trembling. "Too much…" she whispered. Something trickled out of her nose, warm. *Blood,* she knew.

She felt Zane's presence as he joined in her defense, fire licking at the air—burning the ice that descended on Dalic and his man, but there were still too many. *There are too many!* he yelled through their bond as a huge lance flew past them, feeling the rush of wind on her skin. *Too close,* she knew, panicked. Then another. *Then…* Ayva blinked and heard Zane bellow in pain. She twisted and saw a finger-thin lance piercing his shoulder.

"Zane!"

Hannah leapt to his side as well and he pushed them off. "I'm *fine,*" he growled.

* * *

Dalic made it to Ayva's side. "We have to keep moving!" she called.

Wounded Algasi formed around her as she turned to Zane. "Are you all right?"

He growled, breaking off the long spike of ice and rose. Fire flashed from his fingertips and the ice melted, leaving only a blotch of blood on his red vest. "What do you take me for?" Zane asked and shrugged off their help, but Hannah persisted—and together they helped him to his feet and ran. Panic and need had consumed her thoughts, pushing fear and sorrow back, but as they moved—the ice falling about them— she saw the dead Algasi, two bodies run through by icy lances. Blood flowed across the watery ground and where it didn't run, chunks of ice made treacherous footing, her feet crunching with every step. Clinging to Zane's arm slung across her shoulders, she nearly buckled under his weight. He was surprisingly heavy for his height, but she grit her teeth and didn't slow. As she ran, the water coating the ground suddenly began to heat, and then turned to steam in their path.

"Is that you?" she asked Zane.

He shook his blond head. "Not this time."

And with Ayva's next step heat washed over her, as if stepping into a cloud of hot steam. She opened her mind to use her power, but the sun was nowhere to be seen. Fear and panic rose inside her. Even now, she felt her left arm like a block of ice at her side, dangling uselessly.

"What is it?" Zane asked.

He'd sensed her anxiety.

She shook her head. "Nothing, but we have to clear this—" Before she could finish the sentence a gust of wind blew away the mist, making her think of Gray. Those thoughts shattered as she took in the new, strange surroundings.

In place of mist or forest, she saw the land was now gray and fissured, like broken slate. In the cracks she saw a strange orange liquid. It bubbled and churned, little spouts of flame hissing petulantly. *Magma.* She'd heard of such a thing in her stories. Tales said it appeared when Farhaven's crust cracked or mountains erupted. Ayva coughed as a dry heat enveloped her, stung her eyes, and filled her nose. And a sudden smell like rotten eggs made her gag.

"What is this place?" an Algasi murmured.

"The Seven Hells," Zane replied, blade unsheathed in his good arm.

"Be careful," Dalic declared. His voice was drained, but still held its normal hard edge. She knew sorrow hid behind his blue eyes for the loss of the Mundasi. And she swallowed down her own pain, watching their surroundings. "The land is growing ever more angry. It must mean we are close to our goal—for *she* senses our presence and fears our arrival." She... The Enchantress...

"We must continue," Ayva agreed.

And they pressed onward. The Algasi twisted and turned, spears held high, though useless, walking along the scorched earth. Ayva finally saw what a terrible state they were in. Though she'd melted most of the ice before the lances had fallen, tiny shards had still left their mark. Cuts marred the Algasi's arms, legs and bodies. It left their sandy clothes shredded, drenched, or both. But as the heat worsened, steam rose from their sopping clothes. The air was like a furnace, making Ayva's eyes water, baking her inside her loose clothing. A sudden hiss and pop made Hannah yelp.

All turned towards her.

Hannah flushed red. "Sorry, I was just spooked by that thing."

Ayva saw what she was pointing at and breathed a sigh. A little orange flame danced into the air but didn't dissolve. It looked like an oversized water droplet. The lively flame zipped and zagged, squealing lightly and spitting little puffs of smoke. "That's just a firespryte," Ayva said.

"Is it evil?" Hannah asked, huddling closer.

Dalic grunted. "No. Not evil. Good sign."

"*Good*," Zane sniffed. "I don't trust anything here that moves, or doesn't move for that matter." He swatted at the firespryte when it got too close but it danced away.

Ayva reached her hand out and it zipped near, landing in her upturned palm as they moved. It emitted heat but it wasn't hot. "Sprytes are just Farhaven's spark come to life—wind, water, fire, stone, metal and sun. Though no one knows how or why it happens." As she spoke, other firesprytes joined the first, sizzling and spitting more puffs of smoke.

Abruptly, the land rocked beneath Ayva. She staggered, falling to the earth. Her hands burned at the contact and she pulled them away. She looked up to see the land stretching, being pulled apart like paper tearing. "It's moving," she shouted. The other Algasi were all spread out on different chunks of stone, but the gaps were widening. Soon they'd be too far away, each stuck on their own island amid a sea of fire. "You have to jump or you'll be stuck," she yelled at them.

Dalic leapt.

The other Algasi began to bound across the pallets of stone, but the faster they jumped, the quicker the land seemed to spread apart. Luckily, the Algasi were nimble and strong—the jumps were easy for most. But four were injured, including Yunwa who Dalic carried out of the ice storm. But still they leapt, barely skimming the gap as lava gurgled and bubbled up. Ayva realized they were caught up in it too.

"Run!" Zane shouted.

She didn't hesitate. The ground tossed beneath her and she leapt to the next slab, then the next. But the gaps widened. Her legs stretched with each leap and she felt hot flames licking at her with each bound. Her breaths grew short, Hannah and Zane running at her side. There was only one slab left between them and solid ground. A small copse of green trees hedged the final plot of land, and the earth was a darker, richer brown and absent of churning fire. The rock cracked beneath her. Hannah yelped, tripping on a protruding rock. Ayva ran back, pulling Hannah to her feet. "C'mon," she shouted, "we're almost there." Hannah gave a nod and they leapt.

Air whistled and fire burned beneath her. She landed, but felt her toes slip on the edge, stone crumbling. She reached out and felt a rock-hard grip, looking up to see Dalic. Hannah had been caught by Zane. When she glanced back she saw Algasi jumping from one stone to another, but the injured were slower than the rest.

"They're not going to make it," Zane said, holding Hannah's hand, watching as the gap between the last two slabs of stone widened to an impossible jump. Terror spiked inside of Ayva as the three Algasi sprinted. The first was a tall Algasi whose shroud had been torn, exposing curly golden hair. He leapt the divide, clipping the edge, but was grabbed by several hands and pulled to safety. The next Algasi leapt. He was too far. Ayva cried out, reaching, but there was nothing she could do. She watched in horror as the Algasi landed in the lake of fire. The Algasi shrieked, but his cry was quickly snuffed as the mulching orange liquid swallowed him whole.

Zane shielded Hannah's eyes and Ayva felt sick, turning her gaze.

Still, there was one left.

The one-armed Algasi—Yunwa.

He ran, leaping one slab, then the next at full speed. Hope burgeoned inside Ayva's chest, but in the last moment as he reached the final slab the man slid—staggering to a halt, breathless.

"Jump!" Dalic yelled, reaching out. "Jump now!"

But Ayva saw it was an impossible jump—three-dozen feet. Easily the length of five men. No one could make that. Not even Dalic. Yunwa shook his head as the pallet of stone began to float farther and farther away. He looked down and withdrew his mask. Ayva saw he had an attractive, young face. His eyes were blue, unlike the rest. Her chest felt as if it were being pressed down by a dozen heavy stones, realizing who he was for the first time.

Dalic growled, "You can make it."

Yunwa shook his head softly. "It is too far. We both know this."

The Algasi leader grabbed Ayva, a sudden fervor and fear in his eyes she wasn't used to, "Help him, please. You must do something."

"I…" she stuttered, "I can't. My power…"

Dalic turned to Zane. "You…"

"What do you want me to do, dammit? I've nothing left! And even if I did, what in the Seven Hells am I supposed to do? I thread *fire*—that's as much use here as water to a drowning man."

The Algasi leader's body shook, eyes strained. He turned back. "Jump, boy."

"It is all right, father," Yunwa said. "It is all right." His eyes were filled with tears, but he smiled.

Ayva felt her heart drop. "No…" she whispered.

Dalic shook, rage and sorrow colliding through him.

The slab of stone Yunwa sat on split, then split again, breaking into smaller and smaller pieces as the magma nibbled away at its sides. Ayva touched Dalic's arm. "Go," he answered in a strained voice, "You do not need to watch this."

Zane grabbed her but she twisted free of his grip. She couldn't leave the man. *We have to be able to do something!* she shouted in anger through their bond, watching the young Algasi as he stripped free his spear and cloth mask, placing them on the ground at his side, drifting deeper into the burning sea.

And what exactly are you going to do? Zane snapped.

She shook her head. *I don't know! Something, dammit! We can't just sit here and watch… We can't…*

Hannah touched her arm compassionately. Tears were in her big brown eyes. She saw the other Algasi standing in a ring, waiting, gesturing her to follow. "Come, lightspeaker," said a tall Algasi, steam still rising from his tan clothed-body. His black cloth mask had ripped at the top and a bloody head wound matted his curly golden hair. "We must continue."

"I…"

"Go," Dalic said again behind her, his hard voice cracking like the brittle stone. "Leave us."

With tears in her eyes, Ayva slowly ripped herself away.

She looked back over her shoulder, watching father and son—seeing the slab of stone break into smaller and smaller pieces. Her heart like a sinking stone in her chest, Ayva followed the dark crusted earth as it turned suddenly into a forest.

❊ ❊ ❊

The world felt unreal as Zane dropped his sword, sliding his back down a tree with clinging red moss. Hannah huddled close to his side, silent. *Unreal*, he thought again. That was the right word. Exhausted, he glanced up, taking in their group.

The Algasi rested on the balls of their feet, wearing more cuts and bruises than a tavern brawler. Their tan cloth hung loosely on their frames in near tatters, and what wasn't ripped was soggy from the ice or blackened by the fires of that hellish place. Four Algasi, not counting Dalic.

Four.

The number was like a dagger.

They'd started with twelve. Four scouts died during the journey from some strange evil, then two to the shards of ice and the lake of fire, now Dalic's son. Yunwa. He forced himself to remember the young Algasi's name. He had liked him from the first moment he'd met him back in Vaster—honest, brave and openhearted, qualities the world needed more of. Zane felt a growl grow in his throat. They'd lost too many and so quickly, their deaths almost felt dreamlike, just like their surroundings.

Ayva looked hollow, distant, sitting on the damp earth. Her arms hugged her legs as she stared at the ground. No, not at the ground, *through* it. He'd seen that look before. It was the look of the mind trying to wrap itself around the horror it had seen. Trying to find solid ground— to distinguish reality from dream. Zane knew it well, but his mind had long ago reconciled with such visions. His heart felt like a lump of hardened coal in his chest; it had slowly lost its warmth after viewing so much

427

tragedy like a sword that had been quenched in the blacksmith's bellows.

He realized that until now Ayva had seen Darkwalkers die and a few Darkeye bandits run though, but nothing so morbid and horrifying as watching a friend burned alive.

In short, she hadn't seen deaths like he'd seen them. Nor had Hannah. His sister had been close to them, sure, but he'd sheltered her from such things, taking the brunt of it himself. She'd never seen a man die like that Algasi.

"We have to keep moving," said the tall Algasi, rising from the group of sullen faces.

"Dalic's not returned yet," said another Algasi, clutching a bloody forearm wound where an ice shard had come too close.

"He will find us," the mountain of a man said. "It is not safe to linger in these lands long." He watched the surrounding mists as if they were about to take shape and attack.

He had his spear withdrawn—held loosely, but still at the ready. Zane noticed the single pale blue ring near the glinting tip. He was a Mundasi too. Algasi were strong, but Mundasi were a different breed altogether. The man had huge shoulders and his torso cut to a tapering waist. Zane had no delusions about his own height. He was short, slightly below average, but his broad build and hard-earned muscle had always made up for it and dissuaded much taller men from opening their mouth or raising a fist. And if they did? He made sure they didn't make the same mistake again. But this man was tall and muscular—not a scrap of fat on him, as if it had been cooked out of him by the Rehlias sun. He looked like a perfectly chiseled dark marble statue. He wasn't sure the limit of their abilities, but from the rumors, a Mundasi could easily match a Devari or a Lightguard in a contest. Or perhaps even both.

428

Dalic…

How had he not seen that the one-armed Algasi had been Dalic's son? He looked back through the mists to where the cracked, hot land had been. A vision of the boy's face and his calm expression came back to him. A look that he knew his death was imminent and accepted it. *Yunwa.* He ground his teeth, forcing himself to remember the boy's name. He wasn't just another nameless life taken too soon. *Yunwa.* Courageous, honorable, loyal. *Yunwa.* Hannah's touch on his arm made him realize he was quaking with anger. Her brown eyes were full of worry and fear. And Zane breathed a long breath, letting his tense muscles relax. He gave her a brief smile, hiding, but not subduing his anger, then looked up to the Mundasi and focused on one task at a time. "There are injured among us. We should see to them first," Zane advised tiredly, his voice sounding hoarse and gravelly. "Then we should move."

The man seemed hesitant. What was he afraid of? "See to it," said the big Mundasi, "but be quick, for we cannot linger here." He looked around and then said under his breath, "*She watches.*"

Zane shivered. *She?*

He wanted to ask but Hannah scooted closer to him. "You're hurt."

She touched his shoulder and he pulled away. "It's nothing."

She raised a brow, looking angry. *At least some things felt normal.* "Don't make me pin you to the ground to heal you. I'm sure Ayva would help. I could probably get him to as well," she said, throwing a nod to the huge Mundasi. Zane grumbled.

"See for yourself," he said tiredly, watching the woods. "It's healed."

Dubiously, she waved a hand and he grudgingly unbuttoned his red tunic and shirt, showing her. Hannah's hands gently touched where the spear of ice had pierced him. Her hands were cold on his hot skin. She made a surprised sound, seeing that instead of blood or exposed flesh and muscle, it was a little darkened spot of charred flesh. "You…"

429

"Cauterized the wound," he finished. "That's the word for it, isn't it?" He didn't know much about healing. Only death. And killing. Those two went hand-in-hand he supposed, like smoke to fire, but not all the death he'd seen was at the end of his blade. Still, he'd spent enough time around Father and the Healing Quarters to overhear a few words of those who healed rather than destroyed. The thought of Father was like another ice lance in his side. He pushed back the swell of memories and the gut-wrenching pain of his loss. He missed him, even now. Perhaps especially now. But he'd died at Darkeye's hands. Father had been his conscience, helped him distinguish right and wrong. It was Zane who drew the blood, but Father had helped him channel his boiling rage and guided his sword. Without him, Zane feared the man inside himself. But as he looked to Hannah, whose fingers were gently prodding his wound, he realized he hadn't lost his conscience. As long as he had Hannah, he could still be good.

"You could have ruined muscles," she griped, examining the wound. "I'm not a Reaver or anything, but without healing what's inside, it might—"

Zane dropped his shirt and buttoned his tunic, then rolled his shoulder as if showing off. It hurt. But he hid a tight breath of pain, displaying a toothy smile instead. "See? It's fine."

She squinted, planting her small fists on her hips, clearly not buying it. "Knowing you, I doubt it."

"Look to the others," he said plainly. "They need it more than I."

Grudgingly, she listened and moved off to heal the wounded Algasi, starting with the man with the forearm gash.

It gave Zane a chance to think. He sat on a small rock, looking ahead, breathing in the moist air. He put his chin on his fist, watching the misty green woods. He hadn't survived thinking about the problems *just* at his feet. Looking to the woods, he tried to prepare himself for what was next but it was impossible to guess what was coming. In a city, he could adjust for its hidden dangers, from men hiding in shadows to thieves posing in silks or as Farbian guards, and a thousand other hidden threats. Here? It was a damned roll of the dice. Like guessing at a gambler's hand without even knowing the *game* he was playing. Not to mention that he sucked at gambling. Still, he soaked in the landscape, appraising it like he would a blade.

430

Trees… they were strange, scraggly and brown like sinew. A red hue seemed to glow from their bark.

The ground was wet, like Father's famous sloppy porridge.

The air was neither cold nor hot—a blessing after whatever the hell they'd faced before. It was damp but not too misty. All in all, it felt *ancient*. Like breathing in the air of a coffin long closed.

And—

"What are you thinking?" Hannah asked, suddenly at his side. She was already finished? How long had he been thinking? He looked to the Algasi and saw their minor wounds had been mostly seen to, and bandages covered what didn't need the use of the spark.

"*That,*" he answered with a nod to the darkened forest ahead.

"It doesn't look so scary," said Hannah, sounding hopeful.

He didn't want to frighten her, nor did he want to delude her. But it was better to be armed with caution or fear than a false sense of safety. He grunted. "Dalic said that the Eastern Path got the runoff of the Everglade's magic."

"So?" she asked.

"So," he replied, "if that madness back there was just a hint of what we're about to face…"

Hannah made a sour face. "That's not a pleasant thought," she admitted.

Ayva joined their side, and Zane was glad to see her face was resolute. "Ready?" she asked.

He judged her eyes, but her haunted look was gone. Her brows were drawn, and her eyes looked forward, almost through him. She looked strong, standing in her golden vest. Her shirt had rips in it, and he saw flecks of blood on her arms and a cut beneath her left eye. "Welcome back," he said.

"What's wrong with your arm?" Hannah questioned.

Ayva let it go quickly, placing it behind her back. "It's nothing."

"If it's nothing why are you hiding it?" she asked.

Ayva opened her mouth but came up with nothing.

"Ugh! What's with you two? Is it a requirement to be a stubborn blockhead if you're a Ronin?" She rose and snatched Ayva's arm. "Dear spirits… It's colder than ice!" She quickly let Ayva's hand drop, placing fingers to her mouth in alarm.

"It's just temporary," Ayva insisted. "It'll thaw."

Zane stood, muscles groaning in protest. "You sure? I can help make it thaw quicker," he said, lifting his hand, little flames dancing on his fingertips like firesprytes. But even *that* drained him.

Ayva pulled her arm away fearfully. "No, *thank you*. I'll be fine."

He rolled his shoulders in a shrug. Again, it hurt. "If you insist. But how'd that even happen?"

She dropped her guarded posture, shaking her head. "I'm not sure. Just like Gray's bloodpact, or Hannah when you drew too much of the spark and got spark fever, I think Farhaven demanded a balance. I drew too much sun, too much of the flow and this happened."

Zane grunted. *Heat subtracted from her turned her limb to ice. A balance.* It made sense. But it reminded Zane of something. Something from his past, but it was a tickling memory, too distant to grasp and he shook it off.

"Are you sure it will heal?" Hannah asked, brows furrowed in concern.

Ayva nodded. "It's already feeling warmer," she said.

A decent attempt, but Zane still knew a lie when he heard one. He debated calling her on it when he heard a rustling in the woods behind.

All turned to see Dalic. If they looked on death's door, the Algasi

431

leader could've been mistaken for a walking corpse. His eyes glistened with unshed tears as he moved silently through their midst. His quiet approach held the group until he reached the edge of the glade and looked back as if puzzled. "What are you waiting for?"

"Do you…" Ayva began, "Do you need some time?"

"Time?"

"To rest, to mourn?" she asked softly.

Dalic paused, but only briefly before answering, "Death comes to us all. How we treat our lives until the end is what matters. Yunwa wished for us to retrieve the blade as much as I wish it. And so we do not stop. Besides, within these lands rest is death. To move is to live, and even that is uncertain."

Ayva opened her mouth to argue but Dalic made clear his intentions, cutting the conversation short as he pressed onward. *A hard man, indeed,* Zane thought.

And so they followed.

The Algasi leader stopped at the edge of the treeline—beyond Zane spotted more bogs and twisted trees. Dalic spoke clearly, "This is the Everglades. But it's just the start," he said. "I must warn you. Trust nothing once we enter, for the stories say anything in the Everglades can come to life. We must stick close and keep our wits about us."

* * *

Zane watched the land, as they pressed onward, keeping one hand to his sword. The Everglades were a twisted tangle of trees and bubbling bogs. Moss clung to everything in shades of blue, yellow and even red. The moss seemed to ooze in places, almost as if the land had festering wounds. As they continued, he spotted spider webs. They started small, but grew in size and frequency. Eventually the white webs were so big that they looked like hammocks made for giants.

He gave a low growl. "Spiders' nests, and yet no spiders. No creatures at all, for that matter."

The Algasi's eyes were wary as they passed beneath a huge web that brushed barely above their heads between two larger trees. Hannah ducked with a cringe. As another web approached, Ayva lifted her good hand and the spider webs burned.

"Thanks," said Hannah.

"No problem."

"Why are there no animals here?" Zane asked.

"If there are, then they are her," Dalic said.

"What does that mean?" Zane queried irritably.

"She is the land, the beast, the trees. One entity."

Zane shivered as Hannah jumped at his side as a bog to their right belched like a drunkard and bubbles formed on its surface.

"Is that?" Hannah asked.

"Gas," said Ayva at her right. "It's trapped beneath the surface of the water and bubbles forth."

"How do you know that?"

"Books," she admitted.

Zane wished he had his mount, but an icy spear during the chaos had run it through, just like Ayva's cormac. He found it odd that the death of animals somehow affected him more than humans sometimes. Gardel had been a good steed. He'd pushed hard and brought him far—all the way from Farbs to Vaster, and then from Vaster to this point. Only to be cut down so callously, so simply. Now they were all mountless, and so they walked.

But none of the surroundings touched him. His mind was plagued with other thoughts.

He saw a tree on his right… bleeding? He put a finger to it and pulled it away, fingers covered in warm liquid.

"That can't be…" said Hannah, huddling close to his side.

He put his tongue to his finger and tasted the familiar metallic bite. "Blood," he confirmed. Human blood. He wasn't sure how he knew, but he knew.

"How?" asked Hannah.

Zane remembered one story of the Eastern Path, told in a tavern long ago. It was like a bone he'd buried and hoped not to remember. It came drifting back, sinking into him with sickening realization, the hoarse voice of the Median sailor grating in his ears even after all this time, "*It's true, I tell ya. The land feeds off the fallen. If a man dies in that forsaken hellhole of a forest, he's absorbed back into the land. Eaten. That's the source of her demon powers.*"

Hannah was still looking at him, waiting for an answer. And he managed a half-hearted shrug, "I'm not sure," he lied. It was a bad lie, but Hannah bought it. As if she wanted to buy it. And he didn't have the

433

heart to tell her differently. But they wouldn't die here, and the Enchantress, whoever she was—wasn't about to consume anyone else if he could help it.

Zane felt suddenly sick, realizing the blood on his finger that he'd tasted may very well have been one of the Algasi's—perhaps even Dalic's son.

Zane felt a sudden anger toward Dalic.

How could a man continue after losing his son? Zane looked around and wondered if any of the other Algasi had been brothers or fathers or sons to one another. And yet they wore such stoic looks—and none of them talked of it. He shivered. It made him uncomfortable. It felt inhuman. Like the perfect solider. Why should he care? He'd done a thousand worse things in his dark career as Shade—the man who killed or stole to keep the Lost Ones fed and clothed. He'd been a murderer for the sake of good, but it didn't make him good. It just made him a necessity. Like an executioner's axe.

"What're you thinking?" Hannah asked again at his side, drawing him out of his thoughts.

He glanced down at her over his shoulder with a wry look. Her face was spackled with mud, her skin pale in the eerie green luminescence of the woods. Her clothes bore tears along the vest, a long rip down her right sleeve and smudges of smoke. Her good-natured face was ashen, mournful. "Why do you still ask me that? You always know what I'm thinking."

"What're you talking about? No, I don't. Those hooded eyes of yours are impossible to read."

He grunted in disagreement but simply pointed. "Them," he said under his breath. The Algasi moved in a bent-knee stalk, their footsteps making no sound on the wet mulch beneath them. In contrast, Zane's feet slopped softly, and Hannah and Ayva, despite their small statures, plodded like oblivious mules through the Farbian streets after a rare rain. The Algasi knew how to move so not to attract attention. Better than Zane. Way better than Hannah and Ayva.

"So? What about them?" she asked.

He growled, wishing she hadn't spoken so loud. She was brash. It was the only clear sign sometimes that she was his sister, other than her bold nose. He lowered his voice more as if to indicate what she should be doing. How well could they hear, he wondered. But even a Ren-tailed hawk couldn't hear his low murmur. "They unnerve me," he admitted.

"Something unnerves *you*?"

He sighed.

Ayva joined them. She'd heard the entire conversation through their bond. He was starting to realize he could turn off his thoughts at will—block her, so to speak. But he wanted her to hear. "Why?" Ayva asked adamantly. "Why do they unnerve you?"

Zane felt it was a little late for this conversation and undermining your ally at this point was… He shook his head. "They've lost seven men and they've grieved, but they move relentlessly forward—like possessed beings."

"Like we would move," said Ayva. "The sword. Thousands of lives hang in the balance, Zane."

He scratched his jaw, stepping over a particularly wet patch of ground. "I can't disagree, and I've never been the touchy-feely type but…" He rolled his shoulders and winced, remembering it still hurt.

"I saw Dalic's tears, brother. Those were real."

He nodded.

"What are you really worried about?" Ayva breathed in a bare hush, watching the men who moved a fair distance away like stalking wolves.

"I don't know," he admitted. "Something about this sword… I worry what they'll do if—*when*—we find it. I fear they would sacrifice anything for its sake." He looked at the two of them for emphasis, letting it sink in.

"Even us?" Hannah whispered, realizing his implication. *At least she'd been quiet.*

"Even *themselves*," he answered.

Hannah looked troubled by his words, but he looked to Ayva. She didn't seem to find the news terribly shocking. Her blue eyes looked wary, but a familiar wariness and something else was in them. Her thin brows were pinched, her face with its light dapple of freckles upon her smooth cheeks was scrunched up, anxious. And yet… he realized whose blue eyes they looked like and which emotion they held. Stubborness. Dalic's.

"Ayva…?" Hannah asked, seeing the direction of Zane's dark gaze.

She looked up as if spooked and let out a pent-up breath. "I don't know," she said. "It makes sense. But they haven't led us astray this far—I see no reason to think they'll suddenly betray us now. We'll just have to see." With that, Ayva left them, walking forward—toward Dalic.

Zane sifted into her thoughts but then—

Pain. He blinked, rubbing his temple. It felt as if he'd thrown his

435

brain into a solid brick wall. He watched her lithe form move, her blue cloak wavering behind her as she picked her way through the muck—tiptoeing across smooth rocks as she fell in at the big Algasi leader's side.

"What's with her?" Hannah asked.

Zane continued to rub his head. *She'd learned that surprisingly quickly,* he thought. *And at a convenient time too.* He shook his head, looking back to his sister. She looked worried. He winced inwardly, wishing he hadn't brought it up. Though it didn't hurt to be cautious, it was all merely speculation. He hated to see those fretful, big brown eyes. Then he smiled the biggest, goofiest smile he could muster. The one he used on rare occasions and gave only to her. "Dunno, I'm just the muscle." He dabbed at his throbbing head. "Strong back, weak mind, remember?"

She rolled her eyes. "Idiot," she breathed, but a smile slipped out and he gave a real smile in turn, looking ahead.

Now he just wished the sun would slip through and clear away this mist. He debated burning it all away with fire, but he was utterly drained after the madness with the raining shards of ice. His body sagged like a wet rag but he kept it upright, feigning strength for Hannah's sake. Besides, he didn't know what was ahead. He'd have to conserve his energy. Especially with the Algasi…

436

* * *

Zane spotted glowing lights in the distance like bobbing yellow lanterns. He nudged Ayva. "Do you see those?" Her eyesight had proven to be keen in their journey.

She nodded. "I do," she said warily.

"People?" he asked, reaching for his blade, feeling its smooth handle.

"Possibly. But I doubt there's anyone else in these woods." *Anyone but 'Her,' the Enchantress,* she didn't amend. She called Dalic's name softly, pointing to the bobbing lights. "Are those real?"

"Real?" he asked.

Ayva's jaw set. "Sorry, do you *see* that as well?"

"*See.*" The man grunted. "This word holds little meaning here, for what you see may not be true, and what is true you may not see."

Zane rolled his eyes. "What in the Seven Hells does that mean?"

"Trust nothing," said Dalic flatly. "Seeing, hearing, smelling. As I warned before, you cannot trust these senses. Not here."

"Then what can we trust?" he growled back, biting back more profane words.

"Nothing," he said simply. "As for those lights, Lightspeaker, yes. They are said to be her, watching at all times." The yellow lights pulsed softly, then shifted—just like thousands of eyes watching from the green beyond. "They will not harm us, nor will they aid us. Not exactly."

"Then what do they want? Why is she watching and why won't she show herself?" Hannah asked.

"She is waiting to see," said another Algasi in a low tone above the slop of muddy footfalls.

"*See?* See what?" Hannah asked more anxiously.

"If we are worthy."

"Worthy of *what?*"

"Of her presence," said Dalic, "Of saving or killing, I can only imagine."

The lights continued to pulse, in and out, in and out. Zane's gaze flickered to each new pulse as if he could track the thousands of sets of eyes. But each time he found them, they faded and more appeared.

Zane joined the stalking Algasi. "This whole place is her turf? This Enchantress?"

437

"It is one of her many names. And yes, she is ruler here. She controls all, sees all and knows all," Dalic said.

Zane scoffed. "Sounds like a god," he said dryly.

But Dalic grunted. "*Gods* do not exist."

Zane grunted in return. He was glad the man had some sense.

Ayva interjected, "I thought Algasi believed in the Diviner."

"Diviner?" Hannah asked.

"What you call the Messiah," she explained. "Or Covai calls the Lifegiver, Median the Stormbringer, Eldas the Eternal Spirit, Vaster the Lightgiver, Narim the Master of Shadows… Each land has a different name for him *or* her. Just as each Great Kingdom has their own origin stories—but in each *He* is the same, more or less."

Zane understood. He didn't pay attention to the stories, but he'd have to be deaf and dumb not to know what Ayva was talking about. The Messiah was the creator of the Ronin. And it was true Farbs had its own tale for his arrival—a thousand years ago, born from fire like a phoenix, nine men at his side. He shook his head with a growl. The story was practically ingrained in him. But Zane didn't believe in gods. He'd seen men beg a thousand times for the hand of some greater power to save them upon their hands and knees and had been struck down all the same, or others use the name of the Creator, or Holy Spirit, to justify their hideous deeds and never be punished for it. As far as Zane was concerned, if the Messiah did exist, he was either a real prick or too spineless to help those in need. He didn't know which was worse.

Dalic spoke up, "It is true. But the Diviner is more than a god. He is everything. He is us." Zane scratched his head, but the big Algasi continued, "*He* brought the Lightbringer, the Fireseer, the Windrunner and the other nine."

"You mean the Ronin," said Hannah.

"*Us*," Zane corrected.

Dalic grunted again. "Yes. He who brought the Ronin is the only true God. As I said, gods do not exist but God, or the Diviner, does." Zane sniffed. It sounded like semantics. "But you are not incorrect otherwise, Fireseer. Within these borders, if there were such things, she is much like a god, indeed."

Zane scratched his jaw, not liking the sound of that. "So is she evil?"

"Her motives are as fickle as the wind," said another Algasi. "All stories say she has killed saints and saved murderers. Her powers are vast. She can move oceans or level mountains. She can even raise the dead, so it is said."

"She sounds like an Arbiter," Ayva said, speaking up.

"Arbiters," Dalic said, musing, "yes, we know these. Much like the Reavers. They are powerful threaders of the life seed, are they not?"

Ayva nodded. "The most powerful. There are only three in existence, but each is leagues beyond an average Reaver."

"I see. Then the Enchantress is all three combined."

"You're telling me she's the Patriarch, Arbiter Ezrah, and Arbiter Fera all bound up into one? The most powerful threaders in all of Farhaven?"

"She may not be as potent with the spark outside these mists, but within? It is likely so."

Zane shivered. He had enough issues with one Reaver alone. They had nearly murdered a man who had saved him—a Devari by the name of Victasys. The man had survived and returned to safeguard them at the behest of Gray's grandfather, Ezrah, but the memory still put a sour knot in Zane's stomach, remembering Victasys's cries and the wicked etch on the Reaver's face who had done it. Zane shut down the obvious following fact. Victasys was dead—killed by Jian, the new leader of the Devari for his 'betrayal' in defending Zane and acting out against a Reaver. Jian would answer for that one day, Zane promised.

And he let out a hot breath, releasing his anger, focusing on the path ahead. "So what are we looking for anyway?" Zane asked.

"The prophecy is the map," Dalic declared.

"Right, well, does anyone remember it then? Because I recall seeing it, but for some damned reason I can't remember a word of it."

"As is the case with all prophecy," Dalic said. "It fades from memory and cannot be retained."

"Then it's a good thing I scribed it down," said Ayva, pulling out a piece of paper. It was no more than a scrap of parchment but Zane glanced over her shoulder, reading the smooth lines of her elegant writing.

THE RIDDLE OF SUN

The four will become five:
Five for the warrior of water,
Whose home he seeks - like war seeks slaughter,
But all will drown within the lakes,
If the Lady's word the Sun forsakes,
If word they heed, and cast no ear to song of *Dun*,
What's lost can still be won, that ancient treasure - a Sword of Sun.

439

"Four will become five…. That seems obvious enough. Warrior of water, though?" he asked. "That's odd. I don't even know where the Great Kingdom of Water is."

"No one does. It's a lost kingdom," Ayva said. "But that's not important. At least, not for our cause." She pointed to a thicker line, one she'd underlined, "Here. This line. '*All will drown within the lakes / if the Lady's word the Sun forsakes.*'"

"How cheerful," Hannah grumbled, shivering.

"If I'm correct," Ayva continued, "then the Sword of Sun must be near one of these lakes."

Zane scratched his jaw. "All I see is bogs and," he lifted his foot from the muck, stepping back onto the slightly drier path, "this filth. No lakes yet. Perhaps the word is used loosely?"

She shook her head. "I don't think so. From what little I know, prophecy can be misleading, but it's usually very literal."

"What do we do then?" Hannah asked.

Ayva looked hesitant for a second, but then she rolled up the parchment and stood straight-backed, her gaze firm. "We keep looking. Look for lakes, more than one. I believe we'll know it when we see it."

Zane looked back to his sister to ask a question. But she wasn't there. It was Ayva. Had she been standing on his right? He opened his mouth but nothing passed his lips. He shouted, but only a dull muffle escaped. A song sounded in the distance, coming closer.

A haunting ethereal song.

The Song of Dun.

THE SOUND OF MONSTERS

Pressing himself up on an outcropping, Helix looked back from where he'd come.

The land steadily dropped away behind him. The hills of short-cropped grass led back to a cracked plain covered with shadows from the Narim Foothills. The land looked like the shadows of grand titans. He could barely make out the watery chasm—the stone beast of Narim — from here. It was nothing but a tiny spigot while Covai was a dust cloud in the south. To the northeast, he glimpsed Cloudfell Lake. It looked like a small puddle. But he didn't like looking back on where he'd come from. He liked looking forward. Behind him was chaos and sorrow.

So with a heavy heart, he looked ahead and saw green hills. They would eventually flatten out and become a forested wetland.

The Nimue Everglades.

He should have felt elation from being so close, but he only felt tired. Bone tired. And angry too, which he wasn't entirely sure about, but, if he closed his eyes, he had a good guess at the anger's origins. Each time, he saw faces.

Gambol.

Xavvan.

Even Faye.

And his f—

He shut his eyes and pressed forward.

Helix's legs burned as he trudged the steep incline. Every muscle felt aflame with tiny embers, but still he put one leg in front of the other. Silveroot trees became scrawny things, looking like crooked witch's fingers with frost in their branches. *Frost?* Abruptly, a gust hit him and he wiped a cold flake from his cheek. *Snow.* But his hot, sweaty skin made the ice melt quickly. He passed strange ruins—stone crusted with more ice.

One looked like a huge foot.

A person?

He'd heard of such a thing—the Ronin. Back before they were exposed as killers and traitors to humanity, they had been almost holy beings. All the world had revered them and built statues as edifices, hoping to sway their affections or simply pay homage to the god-like warriors. Helix continued past the gargantuan shattered granite foot, plodding toward his goal, toward Seria.

More flurries assaulted him. Why was it so cold? It was so odd. And he trembled beneath the chilled winds, but he didn't care. Wrapping his clothes tighter to his bony frame, he set his focus ahead. Day faded to night; and night shed as the sun rose. Still Helix moved as if he were an anchor and an invisible chain was pulling him from the water's depths toward *something.* But the cold wore at him, finding a way through his thin Median attire like nibbling bites. *How in the Seven Hells could this place be so frigid? Is my home truly this awful of a land?* But Seria had been everything else the world wasn't. It was salvation. And so he continued.

Helix grew tired.

Too tired.

He fell to his knees.

He huffed short, angry breaths.

He knew death was coming, but he wasn't afraid—instead, knees buried deep into the snow, the storm raging about him, he felt angry to his bones.

Helix hated everything.

He hated how tired he was. He hated how much death he'd seen in his life. He hated that he was always at the center of it. But most of all, Helix hated his weakness. He'd never thought himself weak, not until he realized that every event up until now he'd been a victim to—not a force that could change it. All the death and pain and suffering. How many had died for him?

Words burned in his mind, feeding his determination. *Live on, my son.*

This may be my end, but it will not be yours.

How... Helix had pleaded with teary eyes. *How can I ever forgive myself?*

But his father simply smiled. Then the fear had come, and his terrifying end.

Helix rose. Slowly. But nonetheless, he rose.

He continued, one step after another—oblivious that his coat had been slashed open by the terrible winds. Oblivious that the wind cut gashes into his face and arms. Ice filled in the cracks, frosting across his brows and making his lungs burn. Oblivious even to the numbness spreading across his body. Distantly he felt it and knew it was a bad sign. His limbs would lose their strength simply so his guts could stay warm. But he plodded onward, his father's words echoing in his head.

With his next step the wind, the ice, everything stopped.

Helix stood in a world of greenery and warmth.

Dumbstruck, he twisted, looking behind. As if looking into another realm, the world behind him was one of snow and sleet and ice, raging like a thousand storms. Had he really been in that? A storm that even the intrepid ice climbers of the De'Grael would fall victim to. And he realized what it was. A blizzard. He'd survived a blizzard and in paper-thin clothes. It should have frozen him like an icicle in the first few minutes but he'd weathered it. *Barely*, but he'd done it. It was nothing short of a miracle. Or, Helix knew, perhaps it wasn't. He lifted his hand. The whole trip had felt agonizingly long, but how long had it really been? How much of what had drained him had been his slogging legs, and how much had been his mind, distracted, using magic to stave off the bitter cold? He shivered even deeper at that thought. He hated not being in control, but control or not, that pulsing sphere of water *had* saved him. Amused, he watched the snow flurries rage toward him then fall miraculously short, like icy fingers burned by the light of the sun.

"You can't kill me, storm. Do you know why?" he said and pulled back his banished mark tauntingly. "Because I'm already dead. But once I find Seria, I'll be reborn."

He turned back and saw his surroundings.

Magic and greenery—signs of water everywhere. Where life had been devoid before, now it flourished. Butterflies flitted, deer watched from a distance, insects crawled from mossy fallen logs, birds trilled and a family of squirrels scrambled up a bent tree. As Helix gazed upon a nearby

443

white-spotted deer, his stomach rumbled. How long had it been since he'd eaten? The creature's tufted ears twitched, watching him unafraid. Why was it unafraid? Unafraid creatures, a magical snowstorm that suddenly stops and an overabundance of life? And Helix realized that once more, he was standing in a Node.

Was that the trick of it all... Seria... it was a Node? It hadn't been lost...simply moved by the magic of Farhaven, shifting its location to save itself. And now it was back. It made sense. Maglock too—the story of the fabled pirate who'd seen Seria with his armada, ready to loot and pillage, but had surrendered and recanted his ways without even a fight. That must have been why he was so in awe of the Great Kingdom—Nodes were truly breathtaking.

Helix was so hungry. Had he eaten at all lately? It seemed he'd only drank water during his travel. The last things he'd ingested were those berries and nuts Gambol had given him. Even if his legs didn't give out soon, he couldn't go on much longer without sustenance. The deer continued to watch him and Helix remained frozen. His breath frosted lightly in the air. *I've nothing to kill it.* But immediately he realized he was wrong. *My power,* he thought.

He lifted his hand.

Anger surged forth, need rose...

But nothing came forth.

Who am I kidding? Then the thought of the deer covered in blood, its eyes staring lifelessly at him made his stomach turn and he let his hand drop. "Go," he said angrily, shooing the animal.

There was a much louder rustle and the deer bounded off into the brush.

Someone or something was coming.

444

The Forms of Death

Hannah was gone.

Zane's stomach lurched, calling out for her.

But Ayva grabbed his shoulders, squaring him, her blue eyes blazing defiantly. "Zane! Trust *her*. Trust Hannah. Focus on yourself. Don't let her—" Then Ayva's eyes went wide and her lips parted as if seeing something both terrifying *and* beautiful all at once. Her hands fell and she reached out to the air, gripping nothing. "Oh light, she's here… Zane—"

Zane growled, trying to grab her but as he did she turned to mist in his hands. He roared in anger. Ahead, the other Algasi continued to walk, oblivious. He cried out, but with his next step they faded too. Only Dalic remained. He stood before Zane, a statue of coiled muscle. "She comes," said the Algasi leader. Dalic looked up, his blue eyes both sad and fearful. "Beware, Fireseer. Trust nothing she says. If you let her, her song will destroy you." Then he smiled. "Good luck."

"NO!" Zane bellowed, sprinting with all his might and grabbing the Algasi's arm—as if he could save him from what he knew was coming, but his hand passed *through*. Dalic's form burst to a cloud of vapor like Ayva's, and Zane was left standing alone. He twisted, seeing only trees and mist. The land seemed to grow darker, the shroud of green encroaching like a living thing.

His heart pounded in his chest, fear rising. Not for himself but for

Hannah. He tried to think rationally. *If I'm seeing this, what are they seeing? Am I acting crazy or are they all in this world too?* His breaths grew quick, panicked. He couldn't imagine Hannah alone in her own world, shouting for help but hearing only silence. But what could he do? The sword in his iron-grip was worthless. He remembered Ayva's words.

Trust her.

Then she came.

Out of the mist, a figure in white breathed through the woods. With each step she created bursts of life—mushrooms swelled, as if puffing their chests to impress, flowers stood straighter and the grass gleamed a brighter green. Even the muddy water cleared to translucent and pure. He tried to make out her face, but she glowed so brightly it burned his eyes. He shielded his gaze, wincing in pain from the brilliant glare. He forced himself to watch her out of the corner of his gaze—seeing her silver outline—as he raised his blade. "What did you do with the others?" he growled.

A voice sifted to him, dark and primal as a rush of wind it coursed over him. It rattled his bones and made him want to drop his blade and clasp his head with both hands, but he grit his teeth and listened.

"Others?" she asked. 'What *others?*" She tilted her head, hovering above the ground, her skirts undulating.

"My friends," he breathed in anger, pointing with his blade to where they had been standing only moments before, "what did you do with them?"

"Nothing," said the voice. Then he saw pale lips amid the blinding white—a predatory grin. "*Everything.*"

His ire was rising like a beast that was breaking free of its chains. She was teasing him or, perhaps, testing him. Either way, his patience felt like frayed rope waiting to snap. "Bring them back or I will—"

"You will? You will *what?*" she breathed, and a thousand leaves suddenly plastered against him, the trees and land roaring with violent gusts. It tore at his clothes and he felt his feet lift from the ground—branches and debris clouding his vision—but he stabbed his blade into the ground, rooting himself.

The fire in his veins turned molten. "*Give them. Back. To me.*"

"They're not gone," said the voice above the winds. "They're here beside you." An arm extended from the blinding white light, gesturing to his side and Zane twisted to see a shadowy figure. Hannah. She lacked all color, looking like a shadow composed of ash, seen as if in a dream, but it was clearly his sister—features etched with fear, her eyes wide. His heart panged. He reached out to aid her, to let her know he was there, but his hand moved through her colorless form. He shouted her name, but her gaze was fixed upon something he couldn't see. She couldn't hear him.

"What's wrong with her? Why can't she hear me?"

"Wrong with her? That is a complex question, young Ronin. And also quite nearly the answer to your great *riddle.*"

Riddle? *The prophecy,* he realized. He shook his head, watching Hannah and raised his blade to the burning light. "I don't give a damn about the prophecy! Give her back to me!"

"Ah, ah, that's not very nice," said the curling mist. The sword in his hand grew hot—but he still he held it. "Speak nicely or I'll end you and your sister before you find what you seek."

Zane curbed his anger, but still he kept the blade to her translucent throat. At his side, Hannah reached out. Her fingers curled hopefully, plaintively trying to touch... something but only passing through Zane.

"*What...*" He swallowed the venom in his voice, but his chest still puffed with subdued rage. "What's she looking at?"

"Me," the Enchantress said, alighting from the air. Zane watched, feeling torn as the woman's hand stretched forth from the ambient white light. Then, with the back of her slender fingers, and almost tenderly she stroked the cheek of his shadowed sister. Zane noticed the woman's skin. It was not human, but something else. It glowed a warm translucence. The same translucence as when he put his hand to a lantern's glass case, revealing blushing red flesh. "A vision of me at least. As do you. A form that you mortals can handle, can comprehend. But her vision is more *vivid* than yours." Sudden tears rolled down Hannah's eyes and the Lady's finger scooped one up, putting it to her tongue. "Ah, but she is sweet. It only figures that her fear tastes sweet as well."

She sounded *hungry* and Zane growled, charging forward.

A sudden gust of wind blew him back again. He skidded across the wet ground, keeping his feet and he felt his arm heat. He flung his mountain of rage, taking the form of a huge bolt of fire. It seared the air, angry and loud. But as it reached the floating figure, it whisked through her form harmlessly. Like fire through smoke. "Such silly things you mortals do, don't you think?"

He lifted himself from the mud, raising his sword, teeth grinding like a whetstone.

"You bash and you rage like a blustering storm—or, in your case, an angry inferno—and yet all this gains you what?" the Enchantress asked. Zane leapt and slashed where she stood, hoping to cut her down and her nightmare along with it. The smoke sliced in two but then reformed, and she sighed. "You clearly see you have no power here. Not over me. Not over her." She pointed to Hannah who was now openly sobbing. Zane's heart cracked, seeing her face, wanting to aid and yet being worlds apart. *What was she seeing?* "You're powerless, Zane. In these lands even *legends* bow to me." She ground the words out and a huge pulse of air pounded at Zane, throwing him to his knees—it continued to bash down like a raging waterfall on his back, but slowly he felt the fire growing inside of him and he rose. His legs groaned in protest, his whole body straining under the pressure, but he locked his knees and stood straight—gazing furiously at the floating nightmare before him.

"Is that what you want? Power? *Submission?*" he roared.

His words were answered by a lilting laugh—again both feminine and strong yet oddly child-like, echoing through the now gloomy woods. "No, dear Ronin. I merely seek to correct your perspective. You believe you have power here, I will show you the opposite."

"What is it you want then? Just to torment us?"

"Truth," she said—the single word like a chime inside his head. "If you can prove to me that you can handle the truth then your nightmare shall end. And perhaps you shall find what you came here looking for…" Her words lingered on that as if the subject was sacred, and yet she continued on quickly, "…if not? You will find what you've always feared."

"I don't fear death," he snapped in reply. "Wrong again."

"Your death? Perhaps not." Then she pointed. "But hers?"

Anguish and anger tore through Zane.

"Besides," said the figure, "there are many forms of death. Death of honor," she said and pointed to another shadowy figure of ash with a spear raised threateningly at an imaginary foe. *Dalic.* He seemed to be listening too, his jaw tight and eyes watching with heavy skepticism until he vanished, like dust on the wind. "*Death of hope.*" She pointed to another. He knew who it was before he turned, seeing Ayva's short-cropped hair sway—twisting and turning, as if searching frantically for him and the others. She cried out, louder and louder. The lady cast her hand and Ayva vanished too. But he knew she wasn't really gone. She was here, but he couldn't see her. *No more than tricks*, he told himself with a sneer, trying to restrain his mounting anger. He tried reaching out through the link, through their mutual bond.

Ayva! he roared.

And he heard her voice, but it was distant—like shouting down a hallway thousands of feet long, only a faint echo. The lady turned to him. "And last but not least... Death of humanity, when a man becomes the beast he's always feared. The chained creature without a heart. But what happens when those chains break, young Ronin? What purpose does your anger have if it holds no moral bounds? What point to all the killing, all the blood you've spilled, if you have no soul?"

She smiled again through the white mist—a haunting smirk.

Zane had heard enough. He cried out, anger, rage, pain as emotions stormed through him. Blasts of fire seared the air, long flames burned and scorched, and he hacked at her form, slicing the smoke to smaller and smaller pieces as the laughter echoed in it—loud and grating, burning hotter than the blood in his veins.

But then she was gone. He panted, a film of sweat coating his hot skin, listening to the silence until her voice echoed on the winds. "Face your fears and live. Run from them and die."

And the world was lost to Zane as the forest turned to stone.

Familiar stone and a moment in time he'd always feared.

A moment more terrifying than death.

449

* * *

Zane rose slowly.

His hands were no longer wet and dirty. Why would they be? he wondered.

He was standing in a familiar room.

The walls were sheer stone, cut at odd angles as if sheared by the spark. The *Underbelly*, he knew immediately. A soft gurgle of water sounded behind him, and he twisted to see that he stood in his old chambers. His and Hannah's. Against the largest far wall empty wooden crates formed a makeshift home and pieces of their life. At the entrance to their abode, several torches flickered to give a cozy amber light and make the room seem warm and soft—even in this forlorn place.

Hannah would be home soon and...

He shook his head.

No, he was in the Everglades, under a witch's spell. He twisted, looking for a way out. Then how did he leave this place?

But it felt so familiar. And his heart warmed, feeling strangely at peace. The torch's fire crackled softly. It was strange, but part of him didn't want the dream to end. A hard life, but one he knew, one he'd grown accustomed to—with dangers that were tangible and quantifiable. Yet his fear and anger banished that small thought. *Hannah was in danger*—his mind shouted. *You must leave.* But the voice was drowned, turned to a muted, fearful squeak.

Just then, shadows danced on the wall behind him from the nearby lighted torches.

Someone was approaching.

The shadows drew long, stretching up the wall, but voices preceded them as they stopped suddenly, outside the range of sight. "And I say Shade is more than human!"

"More than human?" scoffed another echoing voice, more timid than the first. "How can he be more than human? What are you trying to say, Lucky—that he's a Reaver?"

Lost Ones, Zane realized. Lost Ones were what his people called themselves—a band of mostly young orphans, with a sampling of beggars, homeless, and most recently, refugees from the rougher parts of the world. Basically, what Farbs had tossed out as refuse, the forgotten sons and daughters of the Great Kingdom of Fire. Of course, as refuse, many had turned to a life of petty crime. But Zane, as the sword of the Lost Ones and with Father's sage counsel, had helped convert thousands of wayward souls and brought them into the fold of their ragtag family. And if he were right, the chatting voices were a special trio he'd always kept an eye on.

"Reavers *are* human, stupid." Lucky spat back.

"Nuh uh, no, they aren't!"

"Yeah huh! They just hold more of the spark than we do—that's all."

Another voiced chimed in. "Shade ain't like a Reaver, you dolts, nor is he human. How do you think he can kill like he does? He's got no heart. We filch a few coins here and there, but Shade…" The voice sounded as if it had shivered, "I've seen more blood on his hands than flows in most men's veins. That ain't human."

It seemed to still the others' arguments.

Zane felt a stab of pain, hearing those words. He wanted to turn, to walk into the shadows and shut out their voices, but the craggy voice spoke up. "Human, elf, dryad, dragon—I don't care. Shade fights for us Lost Ones and that makes 'im one of us. That's enough for me."

Something distant yelled at him. *Wake!* it called. The voice bounded off the stone all about him. It sounded like his growly voice, but wake from what? He was awake. And he shook the oddity off and moved to confront the boys, resisting the urge to vanish before they arrived.

Outside of the arched entryway to his and Hannah's hidden chambers he saw the speakers standing in a semi-circle. His shadow caught their attention and they twisted. "Shade!" said the biggest of the bunch.

Rygar, Zane knew.

He flushed red, seeing him.

This is real, something told him. *Or was real.*

"Uh… Shade… we uh… didn't expect you to be… Did you hear any-thing strange?" said the oldest of the bunch, Trevor.

Trevor.

Something burned in his gut seeing the man.

He'd been the one saying Zane wasn't human. But it was true, out of any of them—Trevor had seen Zane with bloodied hands the most. He often relayed Father's orders to Zane as third-in-command of the Lost Ones.

"*What do you want?*" he asked coldly. Something felt strange about it. Did they always know about his hideout? Sure they did.

"Father needs you. He sent us to get you."

"Go on," he told them, "tell Father I'll see him soon. I've other busi-ness to attend to this night." He remembered what he had to do: a guard, part of the his eyes and ears of the city, promised him blood money in exchange for the life of a thief who had gutted a Farbian guard and taken his purse. But as he looked at the boys, he hesitated. The description of the thief wasn't too far from these boys. He would kill a child tonight—justice some would say, vengeance, others. But still, the blood would be on his hands. The life taken, his doing. And so many more.

They were right, weren't they? But he could change, couldn't he? Father determined his kills and thus far, they were all moral. Sometimes life needed to be taken, didn't it?

He would solve it—he would stay and fix the Lost Ones, save Hannah, and Father and—

451

Father is dead.

The words were like a brick wall to Zane's thoughts. *This isn't real.* And he grabbed his skull, fingers digging into his temples. He stumbled backward. "No! This isn't right, I don't belong here."

"Zane?" said Rygar.

But when he looked up the other boys were gone.

He stood in a room of shadows. There were flickering lights of orange in the distance. Zane squinted, trying to recognize them, and then understood.

Fires…

And echoing like nightmares were faint plaintive screams.

Zane ran.

He passed two broken bodies at the entrance to Sanctuary—the den the Lost Ones called home. He spared them only a moment, checking their pulses and found both were dead, but blood still warm. He gritted his teeth and grabbed a spear from their bodies with a broken haft, anger rising. Beyond, he pressed down the bile rising in his throat passing bodies everywhere, eyes roving—then he saw them: dark cloaked figures, black lumps moving amid the bodies, checking to see if they were all dead.

Anger surged inside him as he saw a man lift his hand over a huddled figure. He yelled, charging forth and slammed his body into the attacker. They fell to the stone floor in a tangle of bodies. He lay a flurry of punches, unleashing his rage, hearing grunts as his fists thudded into the attacker's soft flesh. Harder, faster, and he realized he was bellowing. In the corner of his vision, a sword flashed out of the darkness—a bright glimmer of steel and he ducked it out of sheer instinct.

He leapt to his feet, facing his new opponent.

He couldn't distinguish the man. Too far from the fires, he was just a shrouded mass, tall, slight shoulders and shrewd blue eyes that gleamed in the darkness. But his identity didn't matter. He was a murderer—another Darkeye lackey willing to slit the throats of innocents, of women and children, for a heavier coin. The man was human refuse.

Zane saw a broken lance at his feet and reached for it, but the man was already attacking. It was a sluggish strike, but his cry seemed filled with desperation. It hacked at Zane's outreached arm, but he pulled away precisely in time. The sword shattered the lance to splinters. Zane growled and charged the man, but this one was smarter. He leapt back and slashed, creating space—the slice nearly severed Zane's throat, the blade whistling past his eyes in the darkness, a silver flash.

The man spoke, sounding… fearful? Something cried at the voice, but it was a dim, frightful yell. Besides, Zane's ears were deaf to the pleas. The fire in his veins could only be quenched by this man's blood. And he rolled, grabbing the spearhead from the ground, then sidestepped an awkward fencing blow. The figure dropped the blade out of fear, clearly, as Zane twirled, jabbing the spearhead into the man's chest.

The Darkeye brute stumbled back knocking over a brazier, sending sparks and hot coals rolling upon the ground.

Zane breathed deeply, triumphant.

Then he saw the figure in the light, clutching his chest, gasping.

Terror made Zane's heart seize.

Father…

The man's face was clear in the orange light of the coals. Father lay, blood pouring from the spearhead, his head crooked at an awkward angle, leaning against a broken pillar on the healer's terrace. Zane approached, his breaths tight and small. Numbly he knelt at the man's side. His expression. His warm fatherly face was stuck in horror, eyes split wide. His blood was everywhere. But his eyes bored into Zane, as if in silent accusation.

"I…" he staggered trying to breathe, panic rising.

Terror, read the eyes.

Murderer.

❊ ❊ ❊

Her, his voice shouted.

"This isn't real," he repeated to himself, holding his head. Then louder. "This isn't real." He lurched to his feet, staggering away from the terrace. He stumbled on a corpse, seeing Rygar's face. Zane's favorite rutted dagger protruded from Rygar's eye. *No, Rygar might still be alive… I didn't find him. I couldn't have killed him.* He realized tears were flowing down his face as he backed away, trying to flee. "It's not my fault… It's… it's not my fault!"

But as he scrambled away, his hands felt something hot and warm. More blood. More faces. Lost Ones. Cuts across their throats and daggers in their eyes, familiar attacks. Efficient and fatal—no room for en-

453

joyment. Moves he employed. The same look of betrayal etched into their terror-stricken faces. "Just a dream," he repeated, turning away from them—forcing himself not to look, as if looking would make it real. "Let me out of this damned dream," he yelled and grabbed his sword and roared, twisting in a circle, cutting at the imaginary air.

Suddenly and magically, it disappeared—the dark pit of death that had been the Lost Ones' home vanished, replaced by swamp and moss. He was back in the Everglades, stumbling to his knees and falling into the wet muck. He wiped his grimy hands on his now red tunic and brown pants and rose. Still a dream? he wondered. He breathed in the air. It coated his throat, moist—no longer dry and stale like within the Underbelly, but old. Ancient, even. And it *felt* real. But was he out? Only one way to know for sure. He withdrew his rutted dagger—the same one he'd seen sprouting from Rygar's eye—and without a second thought drew it slowly across the inside of his forearm. Sharp pain made him suck in a tight breath as flesh peeled and hot blood oozed from the fresh wound. He gave a self-satisfied grimace, dropped his arm, and let the blood continue to dribble down his wrist, falling to the wet forest floor when he heard a cry.

454

Hannah.

He ran.

He tore through brush and tree, following the direction of the voice until…

He found her.

His heart clenched and his mind reeled.

Hannah looked up upon his entrance, terror filling her brown eyes. She was pinned against a tree by a sword that had run through her stomach. She gasped, trying to suck in a breath.

Instincts flared to life. He dashed to her side, painstakingly pulled the blade from her belly. As he did, she gasped as the blade slid free. It dripped blood and he threw it angrily aside, hearing a soft splash as he did, and frantically ripped his vest and shirt free, then used the shirt—pressing it to her open wound. "You're going to be all right," he said. He realized he was saying the words over and over again. *Think!* his mind bellowed.

She pointed limply at his arm.

His arm! What about his arm?

It hit him.

Cauterize the wound!

And he reached out. The ball of fire in his mind roared with need. He pressed his hands to her stomach and the air grew cold about them, heat leaching from it and into his hands. The heat grew and a low, burning fire seared Hannah's flesh. She screamed in pain. Sweat formed on Zane's brow, working faster, panic rising. And then it was done. He pulled his hands away. Hannah collapsed in an unconscious slump. He'd drained all her energy. He felt her pulse; not dead, but weak. Too weak. She needed fluids, needed blood or she would still die. But how? There was nothing he could do!

Silveroot!

The tree's other name was 'lifeblood.' It wasn't certain, but it was his best bet.

He leapt to his feet and dashed, searching for the nearest silveroot. Eyes split in surprise and elation as he found one after ten steps. He stumbled to its base, ripping his pitted dagger from its sheath and plunged it into the tree's gray skin, digging for the sap that would heal his sister. It felt soft, cutting into it. But he dug deeper. Hannah's life depended on it. The tree's bark tugged irritatingly, then ripped and its amber juices flowed forth. Finally. But *not* silver. Red. He'd seen golden silveroots in Vaster; was this just another version?

455

It poured over his hands, strangely warm.

What an odd tree... But then the world... *fuzzed.* He shook his head and when he opened his eyes he saw a dark face. It stared at him in horror, blood pouring from his mouth. Zane looked down and saw his dagger. No... He staggered back. The blade hadn't pierced bark, but flesh and now sat embedded in the Algasi's stomach. Confusion warred on the man's features—as if he had been recently released from a dream world as well, only to find steel run through his gut. The Algasi tried to speak, but only frothing blood poured forth.

And he fell over, dead.

"No..." he breathed.

He looked about, stumbling back, but Hannah was nowhere to be seen. The spot where he'd laid her was strewn with brown leaves, untouched. No blood, no blade, nothing. As if he'd never been there, and then he realized...he hadn't. *Simply another dream.* The warmth on his hands made him shiver and want to vomit. He frantically wiped the blood from his hands on his shirt, backing away from the dead Algasi.

Not my fault. It's not my fault. The words thundered in his ears. But this time they sounded hollow. Zane twisted, tears welling in his eyes. "Where are you? You did this!"

Soft mocking laughter tittered through the trees and he twisted, bellowing his rage. Suddenly the laughter sounded inside his head and tears began to fall from his eyes.

"*Did I kill him? Whose hands are stained with his blood?*"

"You forced me to!"

"*And the boy? Who forced you to kill him?*"

Zane grabbed his head, fingers tearing into his scalp, anger and pain boring into him like a slow knife. "No! They told me he killed a guard."

"*Did you ever believe that?*"

"I did!" he seethed.

"*Was it easy?*"

He nodded, tears falling from his eyes.

"*How easy?*"

"Too easy..." *I killed him. I killed a man for no reason—just like... Just like the Algasi.* He waited for the vision to fuzz and fade but the Algasi sat there, staring at him, growing cold. His eyes now eerily vacant of the spark of life. Never to breathe or think, or *be*, again. She seemed content to let him sit in this world—the world of reality, to taunt him and let him stew in his own mounting anger. It threatened to consume him. He heaved heavy, ragged breaths as if the anger were a molten river, coursing through him. But then a sudden node of fire roared to life in his mind. His power. The flame was like a burning beacon and he reached out to it. It seared as he touched it, but as he breathed it in, he felt it fill his limbs. *I didn't do this.* The words.... Were they his? Or were they... Something else?

Slowly, Zane opened his eyes.

He still felt rage, and it wasn't fully controlled, but it was on a leash— like a fire inside a glass cage.

He saw something. His gaze was different. Moss, plants, creatures in the distance and more—each could be seen in shades of red, some deeper than others. And he understood. He could see the heat in their bodies. But that's not what he sought. On a nearby tree, he saw it: a vague outline blending with the moss. Then it shifted. *Eyes.*

Her.

He lashed his hand out and this time, rather than by simple dumb luck, he understood his power. It obeyed and he saw its intricacies. In the air he saw thousands upon thousands of tiny drops of moisture. As Zane breathed in, heat was sapped from the air and more moisture filled in the gaps. He was literally drawing the heat from Farhaven. It filled his lungs. He lashed out, pointing a finger. The threads—looking like tiny dots of orange in his mind's eye—wove together, forming a single long hot thread of orange, like a tongue of fire. It was a deeper, more powerful orange than he'd ever seen before and it almost seared his eyes. He directed it.

The tongue of fire whipped like a cord, burning a hole into the tree.

A scream cut through the air—shrill, haunting and ethereal. The figure in the moss fell. A woman. The moss decayed from her body, turning brown, then oozed off her form—showing a glowing white figure. This time Zane didn't shield his gaze.

"You cheated!" the Enchantress raged. Her voice was loud, a multi-layered shriek laced with the spark—but it didn't sound in his skull and from everywhere at once. *Powerful, but not god-like.* "You didn't face your fears! This isn't how it's done!

Through his torrential anger, Zane smiled. "I did face my fears—I just didn't have anything to say to them." And he lifted his hand to send another tongue of fire as a gust of wind rocked the glade, catching leaves and tearing at his clothes. The Enchantress cast him a hateful glare, hissing, then suddenly vanished. No, not vanished. He saw a vague shape of her face on the sudden gust of wind, fleeing on the current of air. *She can become the elements...* a voice in his head told him calmly. The spark-laden voice boomed, sounding both ancient and commanding. It was his voice, clear as day, but more—as if fed with the knowledge of his now burning power.

457

Zane realized that sweat lathered his body, soaking through his black cloth shirt and into his red leather vest. He was breathing as if he'd sprinted the length of Farhaven. The power left him, and he slumped as if ten blacksmith's aprons were thrown onto his body. He was spent. Every single part of him ached. He wanted to curl up into a ball and sleep, but he forced himself upright.

Whatever I did, I expended more energy than intended.

But I think it worked.

He looked around. The world seemed different. The Algasi still lay dead, which made his heart clench in pain, but he stuffed it down into a node where the image of the boy and his other dark fears laid, tucked away for another time. Aside from the Algasi, however, the Everglades looked different. Even the pervasive green glow remained, but not as ominous. The brown leaves were no longer just brown, but instead were rich purples, deep greens, violent reds, jarring yellows, cool blues and other shades of colors he couldn't even name. The huge cobwebs that stretched from tree to mossy tree were now no more than small little webs with thumbtack-sized spiders in their center. He laughed, and realized that ever since they'd entered this land, they'd been inside her spell—a darker, more foreboding version of the Everglades. He'd shattered her image, he knew.

Feeding his pain into his anger, Zane knelt and closed the Algasi's lids. "Sleep well, brother." Then he thought, *I'll see you one day—but not today.* Now he needed to find the others and help them escape their visions. Zane knew his power hadn't killed the Enchantress. She wouldn't die so easily. Even as he stood, he knew she was visiting horrors upon the others. But the Algasi's death was evidence enough that she would go to any length to make them face their fears, even if it meant making them face one another.

Even if it meant their deaths.

Snatching the Algasi's spear he leapt into a jog, running to find the others and shatter their trances.

LETTING GO

omeone or something was coming.

Helix listened to the crackle of leaves, of nearing footfalls. His instincts whispered. *Hide.* He trusted them and leapt behind a tree. Helix pressed his back to the mossy bark, steadying his breathing, trying to think. *What if it was someone in danger?* The footsteps grew louder, until Helix knew they were a few paces away, maybe just behind the tree. His heart thundered in his chest.

"Helix…?"

Something seized up inside him, freezing his blood.

That voice…

Every muscle went rigid and his breath was cut short.

"Helix, is that you?"

He moved from behind the tree.

His father stood in the clearing. He was exactly like he remembered him. His eyes were the clear blue of a stormless sky, set in a weathered, bearded face. Upon seeing Helix, his father let out a breath—a pent-up gasp of emotion. His whole face warmed like the sun. "It's true… I knew it…"

"How…" Helix croaked. His mind shouted, screaming a warning, but in his desperation to see his father, he shut it out. "I don't understand."

"You were searching for the Great Kingdom. And so I followed the tales, every little rumor. Hoping, praying I'd find you here." He laughed, tears forming in his eyes. "It wasn't easy... Gods, it wasn't easy, but I've found you, my son." He stepped forward to embrace Helix.

Helix's brain churned in confusion, feeling fogged. Something was wrong about this in so many ways... *Why?* But as he grasped for it, it slipped like water through his fingers. He looked back at the man, at his *father*, that warm, familiar face and felt a flood of emotions. Everything in Helix's body wanted to rush forward, to hold the man, to bury his face into his father's worn coat and never let go...

But he didn't move.

As his father neared, he retreated. His hand reached for the small letter opener Captain Xavvan had given him and he held it up. It shook, despite his best efforts to keep it still. "Stay back!" he snapped.

"Son..." his father said, eyeing the small blade, brows pinched.

"You're..." he tried to form the words, but he couldn't... *Why?* He shook his head, shaking away tears. "You're not real, are you?"

His father laughed. "Not real, am I?" He pinched his salt-and-pepper cheek, letting the skin fall. "Do you wish to feel for yourself? I'm real, boy. As real as the seas, as real as the sun above. And I've found you, my son. At last." *Why did he keep saying that?* Helix's father moved forward, but Helix pressed the dagger out more threateningly. This time his father's face looked hurt—wincing, as if confused.

"Helix, I—"

Helix interrupted him, angry. "No! Don't talk! Answer me first, *how?* How did you get through the blizzard?" He pointed behind him. His dagger was trembling now.

"I..." his father began. "I heard your voice. It guided me here. I nearly died, but I think some magic kept me alive."

Died.

The words were like a crystal bell, chiming through him.

Visions flashed.

He saw a face, and he remembered blood. Vacant eyes staring.

He shook himself as a sudden truth that he didn't want to admit came back to him. The fog that sat upon his brain was banished. His gut twisted as his memories came back with the feeling of a dagger slammed in his gut. He gasped, remembering. "You can't be here. You're not real. You're dead. I killed you."

"It was an accident, boy. But that doesn't matter. I'm here now." Again, he moved forward. Again, Helix moved back. But his 'father'

460

sounded sincere. The dagger dropped a bit, his arm growing heavy.

His father's weathered face split in a smile. "I know I'm real, but that doesn't mean I don't sense that this is… strange."

"How are you here?"

His father shook his head, gazing at the emerald mist. "I'm not certain. I… think the magic of this place brought me back."

"Following clues that led you to me, what do you mean?" he asked warily.

"I don't quite know" his father stuttered. "It *feels* real. Asking bartenders, meeting travelers and asking them questions, reading unusual books in locked away places…" He looked to his hands and gave a small, uncomfortable laugh, "I can even smell the musky scent of Sevia's parchment." He shook his head, looking up, as if realization was dawning on him. "They're fake. They have to be. The memories must be implanted. The magic of this place… It must have given me something to fill in the gaps after I died. Between then and now."

"Then… then you're not real."

"Oh, I'm real. By the Crystal Seas, I swear I'm telling the truth, boy. But that doesn't mean I didn't…" *Die*, Helix filled in. "But I'm here now." When he looked up, his father was holding his shoulders. "I'm here now, boy." He repeated the words and Helix realized he was crying—he couldn't hold it back. He didn't pretend to be tougher than he was. He just cried. And his father held him. Time seemed to stop. All that mattered was the feel of his father's cold, sturdy chest against him.

Cold?

Why… Why was his father cold? That made no sense. It was balmy here. A humid mist clung to Helix, making sweat press from his pores, coating his skin. Something sharp pricked his skin, and immediately he knew something was wrong. Very wrong.

A dagger.

As it pierced skin, Helix shifted, twisting in the man's grip, shifting his body. The dagger buried itself into his back, sinking into his flesh with a searing agony. *Deep.* He felt the sharp edge chip bone and nerve, jarring. His twist veered the blade and it clipped his spine. He gasped—trying to breathe. The world went numb with pain, but he clung to consciousness as he stumbled away from the enemy. Looking up, he saw his father—not his father—holding a kris, a curved snaking blade. Blood dripped from it, all the way up to the hilt. *His blood.*

461

He took in the man that was his father.

It was now a creature of bright white light.

In its center—it burned, brighter than the sun. A softer white lumi-nescence wreathed the creature's frame. Wispy and undulating, it moved slowly. A face, vaguely human and faintly feminine watched him. But those eyes! They were anything but human. A horrifying shade of pur-ple, arresting and perfect.

"You're a handsome creature, aren't you?" she whispered, taunting him. Her voice was haunting, quiet yet tremendously loud—crashing in his ears like waves – it could have been beautiful, but it was distasteful, horrifying. She *drifted* closer. "Water, is it? Ever has water been my fa-vored element. But you aren't very water-like, are you? Pain and sorrow you hold so tightly. It was so easy to blind you," she hissed, "so easy to deceive you. Just like the others."

The world spun and he put a hand to the ground to steady himself; with his other hand he waved his blade, feeling woefully inadequate, "Stay back!"

She neared, oblivious to his blade, "Your demon was simple, but oh, so interesting. Your father. He's a pain you've buried deep, hidden away like a secret in a box. But we can't hide from our demons forever, and if we don't conquer them... they will conquer us."

As she glided closer, he noticed her eyes changed color slowly, meld-ing from one color to the next. Blue. Green. White. Gold. Orange. Ash-en. Brown. Tan. White. As she spoke to him, they seemed to settle most often on blue, the color of the sea after a storm: a bottomless, deep blue that bordered on black, with a faint light that shone from deep within.

He didn't waste time on stupid questions. This woman was death— and Helix would kill her. He lifted his dagger then staggered, falling to one knee.

"What a shame to end such beauty. But it must be done... You should see your final fear before you die. A vision without Seria— your kingdom is gone and its people mere husks of their former grand selves. You will die here, alone, but your people are already dead."

"No..." Helix cursed, painfully dragging himself to his feet. "You lie. I will kill you, then search for it." He lifted his pitiful dirk and aimed it at her throat.

"Why? Why do you continue? What drives you so?"

Names hammered in his head.

Gambol.

Xavvan.

Faye.

But she didn't deserve to know their names. And he charged the woman of terrifying light, bellowing and knowing it was useless—but he wouldn't and he couldn't give up. She raised her bloody kris as he neared, preparing to skewer him. He kept running, blade held high.

But as he made the last step the world disappeared, and a voice sounded in his head. *"The Ronin broke us…"*

Visions of the Past

"*The Ronin broke us…*" a whisper sounded on the wind. "*You broke us.*"

The whispers took life, turning into a vision.

Helix was no longer in the forest with the terrible witch-like woman. Instead, he was in a city the likes he'd never seen before. A city of wonder and flowing water.

Helix took in where he stood. He was on a massive, round, stone platform, which sat in the center of the city surrounded by jungle. It felt like a great circular staging area to witness a world of splendor. Helix saw a small altar at the center and neared, noticing a small offering bowl of water. He leaned forward and saw his reflection, then stumbled back. Edging back to the bowl, he was confused by what he was seeing. His clothes were different. He now wore a long white haori—a sleeveless cloth vest that skimmed the ground—with blue symbols of water on the breast…

The clothes were the least of his differences. A fall of white hair brushed his strong shoulders, framing an unfamiliar face. His strange clothes, the feeling of power flowing through his veins, even his height—was he taller?—and he understood. This wasn't his vision. He was someone else.

Polished white stone and wood buildings made of white silveroot were built over the falls and tucked into the crannies of the sloping green hillside. It was a terraced city. The city itself was stuck in the middle of a jungle filled with verdant overgrown trees, mossy vines and large ferns. Everywhere waterfalls poured, some gargantuan, some tiny, trickling down to feed a misty pool that sat far below the suspended white stone platform beneath Helix. A canopy shrouded them, but it broke in the center to show a bright sun. "*Where am I?*" he wondered.

This… This was the Great Kingdom of Seria.

He could scarcely believe it—his eyes watered from the vision of it, and from the mist that hung in the air. Even as he turned, he saw more glimpses of grandeur that made his pulse beat faster. The city continued deeper into the mystical woods, showing graceful bridges made of silveroot, vines dangling from their railings, dipping into pools beneath, life abounding.

Motes of gold from a city laden with the spark floated in the misty air. In the waterfalls he glimpsed darting fish—blue, yellow, gold, red and more.

Citizens.

Blue-eyed denizens of the fair city. Blonde hair. Pale skin. Just like him. They walked the winding paths and watched from verandas, but there was… something strange in the air. A tension. A city of this size should be teeming. Where was the trade? And the faces he saw… So many women and children, and so few men. Why were so many missing? And he realized it wasn't where he was—for it was surely Seria, the Great Kingdom of Water—but *when*.

A voice sounded and Helix twisted—taken aback by its quiet gravity. It was a smooth voice, calm and soft, but with a weight behind it that reminded him of the water around Helix. It held a confidence and control that made him envious. But beneath it all he heard the unequivocal threat. He realized it was his voice. "Why have you brought me here?"

No, yelled a voice. *This is not the vision I wish for him!*

But it was drowned beneath the crashing of water.

465

He noticed new things that he wouldn't normally have noted, but these eyes were accustomed to noting the minute. The trivialities that added up to a greater threat. The great blue curtains near the eastern and western edge of the platform wavered... Fear in the eyes of the spectators who watched... Some ushered children away as if a terrible storm were coming... And Helix knew it was.

He realized a man stood in front of him on the platform. *The great Waterstone*, something inside him said, but it was hard to imagine him as simply a man. He looked like a king of kings. Decked in a deep blue cloak hemmed in lush ermine and full plate armor, the metal of which was a blinding white, almost clear—*white metal? Such a thing doesn't exist, does it?* Somehow he knew it was metal, or perhaps a gem. Light hit it and it shimmered, rainbow-like. *Everplate*, a voice in his head said. It was less malleable than the more common dragonborne armor, but it was the only thing stronger. Some said the plate was impenetrable. The everplate was molded to emphasize, or perhaps lie about, the man's well-defined musculature. Aside from the armor and cloak, the stately figure had a perfectly trimmed white beard that came to a sharp point. He was old, lines marring a pale face from a life of hard decisions—a life of rule.

466

King Orulus, said the voice. "You know why I called you here," Orulus intoned. "Are they true?"

"Are what true?" he asked, feeling oddly threatened.

"The rumors. Rumors of you killing, destroying, raping, pillaging and a thousand other dark deeds I will not put voice to."

Helix wanted to say it wasn't him. But the body he inhabited was calm. He was calm. The line between himself and this new other self began to blur.

You're losing yourself, he thought. His grip with his former reality was fading. And Helix felt a stab of fear. As much as going back was death, sorrow and a world without a home, he was afraid to be stuck. Afraid to lose himself in this vision. Still, his curiosity and the wonder of the vision were overpowering. He wanted to know more, *needed* to know more.

Helix saw guards at the rim of the Waterstone approaching, raising their blades, stalking forward. He lifted his hands, easing a calm breath from his lungs. "I don't wish this. Whatever you've heard, you're wrong. Allow me to explain—at least grant me that."

"It's too late for words," said the great King Orulus, rage burning in his blue eyes—a man who some had once called the Tranquil King. Something was wrong. Helix knew it. He knew this man, had played with his children, had given him counsel when his heart was darkest. He—*Helix*—hadn't done those things, but the man he stood inside had. And something was *off* about the Tranquil King today. King Orulus's blue eyes narrowed and then—

A darkness. Helix saw a fetid oil roiling over the white of the man's eyes. Then it was gone. "The Ronin have been a burden on us for too long. Now you've broken us."

Ronin.

And all of it slammed home with stunning clarity.

This vision was Hiron's—the Ronin of water.

At the same time a hundred, then two hundred Waterbearers—the most elite warriors of the Great Kingdom—marched out onto the great platform, streaming with fluidity, making perfect rows. Their full plate armor, holding a sapphire hue, gleamed in the bright sun. Helix's heart hardened. He squinted up at the sun high above, gazing down on the wondrous Seria—making waterfalls shimmer and the Waterbearers' blue armor glint. "Far too bright a day for such madness..." the body he inhabited whispered. "It doesn't have to be this way."

But the Tranquil King's gaze was pure ebony now as he backed away slowly. Helix noted sorrow in his face, but it was overwhelmed by the darkness, by the putrid evil.

"DROP YOUR WEAPONS!" a voice bellowed.

Helix turned.

The leader of the Waterbearers.

He stood in his brilliant sapphire plate, sun gleaming off its seamless overlapping pieces. The four perfect blue sapphires of his rank set into the plate's shoulder. Peering from his brushed steel helmet was a grizzled face he knew all too well, a face that matched the gruff voice. Alec Hasian. The words sounded almost discordant. Words yelled when Hiron had stood at Alec's side, forcing their enemies to disarm. "Alec... You too..."

Alec said nothing but raised his blade. A Yronia-worked blade that gleamed with blue bloodstones—as all Waterbearers bore. A blade that could cut the spark from the air, even the flow.

Helix felt his chest tighten. That Alec had turned against him was a wound greater than any blade could make. Both seemed to know this. Helix had visions and memories that were not his own: saving Alec's life

467

from stray arrows, from errant blades a dozen, then two dozen times; then of the man saving him as well. He saw memories of pulling Alec from a heap of dead bodies, bloody and dying, then stitching his wounds in the dead of night. They both shared the misery of the endless deaths they'd witnessed together. He gasped, back in the Ronin's body. *So much pain... How could any one man live with such sorrow?* It threatened to crack Helix's heart, robbing him of his breath. He saw tears in Alec's eyes. They both knew the extent of Alec's betrayal.

"I can handle Orulus's treachery," Helix said in that silken powerful voice that was not his own. Unable to control the words that came out of his mouth, he listened, spellbound as Hiron spoke, "He is a king. Such is the way of things. The darkness and greed of power are insatiable to all men of his position, but my own friend? How many times have I pulled you from the depths of hell? How many friends have we watched perish before our eyes? How many? You were my *friend?*"

Alec's eyes grew more pained with each word until the leader of the Waterbearers bellowed at last, "I *am* your friend!"

"Yet you believe them? You take their word over mine and allow me no chance to speak my part, to denounce the claims set against me? Truly, if even you would raise blade to me, then perhaps I deserve it. Perhaps I am mad, or this world is mad, or both..."

Alec withdrew his helmet, showing an almost handsome face, if it hadn't been broken and battered by their countless skirmishes over the many hard years. "It's you," Alec said in a hard, bitter tone, surprising him. Helix searched for the madness in his eyes. It wasn't there. "The madness of you and your Nine. The war grows, more die every day, and all because of a missing blade... All because of the sun Ronin. And now you've broken us. Your deeds have cast a shade upon this land that hath fissured our unity. Killing our own kind? Slaughtering innocent women and children? Leading the Everspawn creatures of lore upon this land? You were my councilor, my brother, my—" His voice broke, and he turned his gaze down. His face was a mask of confusion—warring with turmoil. But then he shook his head and placed his helmet back. And from within his visor his dark brows made a hard line. "It's too late... Perhaps the world has gone mad and I with it, but I will follow my duty. It's the only thing I have left in this world, and I won't let you take that from me. Now drop your blades."

Hiron sighed. He pulled two blades from their sheaths at his side—familiar blades, storied blades. One had light blue steel, the other a deep, dark azure. From the lighter blade, a faint blue aura pulsed like mist, while the other blade gave off a deeper blue glow—resembling the depths of the Kalvas Ocean. Their hilts were different too. The deep blue one had a crossguard that looked like water in motion, splashing to protect the hand, and also curling back towards the blade. The other blade's crossguard looked like jagged shards of ice, stemming in all directions. Despite their legendary beauty, the crystalline blades were sharper and harder than Yronia steel. *Calid and Ladir,* a voice whispered. And Hiron let the blades clatter to the stone platform. "You know I don't need those."

"You can't take all of us, brother. You're... you... but you can't take all of us. Not two hundred Waterbearers. You trained us too well."

Hiron's heart felt like a knot of steel, like Baro's as his lips twitched—feeling a rage that would rival Seth's that slowly burned in his ever-calm heart. His words came out, not quiet and even, but wrathful and snide. "Enough talk. If you wish my death, then come and see it done."

The battle cry of the two hundred Waterbearers was thunderous, like a crash of waves breaking upon Hiron. And they attacked.

This is not my vision! a voice bellowed, a scream of power.

The Waterbearers were nearly to him. He raised his hands, summoning water from the depths of his soul—drawing forth titanic threads from the waterfalls, from the pool below, from the nearby streams, when—the vision shattered around Helix, falling apart right before the blades pierced his body and before the tidal wave of water fell.

469

* * *

Helix stumbled forward, falling upon his hands and knees into a puddle of muddy water and soggy leaves. Looking about, he saw he was back in the cursed bog, seeing the familiar murky green surroundings. He grabbed his side, pulling his hands away. Blood still coated his fingers, warm. And fear made his blood run cold. How long had the vision been? How much blood had he lost? Judging by the spreading coin-sized blot of blood on his white shirt, it had only been moments.

He couldn't believe it...

Seria. The Great Kingdom of Water. She did exist.

And *Hiron...* He'd stood in the boots of a Ronin at the end of the Lieon, during the collapse of everything—just as the stories said. "The

Ronin were real," he whispered aloud in disbelief.

"Yes," a voice answered and he looked up to see the ethereal creature of light. "That was an unintended vision. But you're correct. The Ronin were real. Real and dead. Just as you are about to be. Come closer and I can finish it, I can end your search once and for all. After all, you've failed, dear Helix. Your search for the Great Kingdom of Water is futile, and you will die with that knowledge."

Helix raised his hand, hoping and praying... *Please.* His anger was loud, but he calmed it with a single breath. A ball of water pulsed in his mind. Water formed from the humid air and he shot it forth. It blasted against the woman's chest—sending her back a dozen feet, smacking and cracking the trunk of a nearby gnarled tree with its force. "It..." Helix breathed heavily, "it does exist."

He neared and saw the woman's face.

But it wasn't a woman at all... It was twig and vine and leaf, so intricately woven together it almost appeared human, with white moss for her face, blue flowers in the sockets of her eyes, silken strands of witherbark for hair and... Helix shook his head, befuddled. "Where did she go?" Instead of an ephemeral creature of light, the demon that had stood before him, posing as his father, now was no more than twigs and moss. He looked about, but she was gone. This place made him uneasy, nervous, uptight. He took in a deep rattling breath. He had to take care of this wound.

Helix heard the crunching of twigs. Someone was approaching. He grabbed hold of his dagger.

Before he could turn around, a deep voice spoke, "I'm not sure how she escapes, but she did the same to me, fleeing before I could deal anything more than a glancing blow." Helix twisted, seeing a figure at the edge of the woods. A red-vested, black-shirted burly young man with a spear in hand. He was a few years older than Helix, but the young man almost looked worse for wear than he did, and Helix had just been stabbed.

"Who?"

"A demon," the young man replied, as if that answered *anything.* And he neared and kicked it. The body fell apart into a simple hodgepodge pile of flora. "The Enchantress of the Woods."

Helix had heard stories... but he thought them simply that. A witch. A sorceress. A creature that could take any elemental shape. Seducing travelers in the form of a man or woman, but they were merely a child's

470

tales. Or so he thought. "Sorry… who are you?"

"Zane," the man replied. Helix clutched his wound, wavering on his feet and gulped a breath, wincing as it caused him pain. He knew he looked a sorry sight. "You're hurt."

"You think?" Helix snapped, irritably. He hated that the woman had tricked him. He… he thought it had been his father. He knew it couldn't have been, but he hated her for making him believe. He was still too vulnerable, too naïve.

Zane watched him as if reading him, but said nothing

And Helix sucked in a tight breath as the agony in his side spiked. Zane noticed this and grunted, pointing to a mossy rock. "Sit. I have to bind that wound of yours before you lose too much blood."

Helix obeyed. There was a bluntness to the man that made him agree without thinking and Helix eased himself down on the rock with a sigh. Zane grabbed Helix's hands and put them to his wound. "Apply pressure. Constant, but not too hard, and breathe evenly." Then he ripped the sleeves off his black shirt. Using his teeth and a rutted blade at his side, he cut them into long strips, then laid them end to end.

"That… doesn't look particularly clean," Helix said.

Zane didn't glance up. "You know something about wounds?"

Helix, who was easing his breaths in and out, shrugged—but it made his wound smart. He watched Zane work, tying the strips together. "I worked on a fishing vessel for a few summers as a deckhand. Lots of sailors get wicked cuts from splintered wood, or gouged by fish hooks and the like… months on the water without proper care can lead to some pretty nasty-looking wounds."

Zane grunted. He seemed to be good at that. "You're right. This is just temporary. Enough to keep you from… passing out from blood loss so I don't have to carry you. Hannah will take care of the rest."

"Hannah? There are others with you?"

Zane nodded.

"How many?"

"We started our journey with over a dozen warriors. Now?" Zane shook his head. "I fear the answer."

Helix shivered. "Why? Why are you here?"

Zane pointed. "Put your hand here," he said, indicating the bandage. "And that's a long story," he replied. He looked up, lifting a thick blonde brow. "What about you?"

471

Helix sighed. *Finding the Great Kingdom of Water, his home, his very soul...* But as he looked about he was growing less and less certain that that's what this was... Orange-speckled mushrooms oozed viscous amber goo from their caps, trees cowered, flowers wilted and even the once-blue pools of water were now more mud than water. *Where am I?* he wondered. "Same," he replied. "A long damned story. So who's this Enchantress anyway?

"A witch who shows you images, both what you wish to see and what you fear most. Lies, smoke and mirrors—petty illusions."

Helix shivered. "They seemed pretty real for petty illusions." Zane said nothing, but again Helix noted a haunted specter in his gaze. "So what then? If you don't conquer the visions and face your demons, she'll kill you?"

Zane nodded.

"She got pretty close," Helix admitted, eyeing the hot blood slipping through his fingers.

"Judging by the angle of the blade, it looks like she had you in a..." He didn't say the word, but Helix guessed it—*hug? Embrace?* "... it looks like she had the opportunity to finish it, severing your spine. But the blade veered a touch to the side of a killing blow."

"Luck," Helix mumbled.

"Or skill."

Helix winced, and tried not to sound afraid. "How bad is it?"

"Better than bad, worse than good. It missed all your vitals at least."

"How'd you know that?"

"You'd be a lot less chatty. A stab to the kidneys is excruciating."

"So I'm not going to die?" Helix tried to say it lightly, dryly but instead it felt awkward and a hint scared. He felt a stab of fear at saying the words aloud.

Zane glanced up, looking at him seriously, then glanced back to his work. "You'll be fine. It missed everything important. It's not as deep as I expected."

"It *felt* deep," Helix replied tightly.

Zane grunted. "I've had worse." He said it so off-handedly, Helix was certain his new friend was being humble or simply curt—he felt a little silly for being so afraid for a moment.

"You never answered my question. Why are you doing this? What if I'm the Enchantress, or worse, just another one of her illusions? A fear of yours come to life like you said?"

"I…" Zane hesitated. "I shattered my illusion. Dealt with my fears." He looked troubled still. A darkness shuttled across his eyes and Helix knew the look of a man with demons.

He sniffed. "I see," he said, not wanting to voice his disbelief. The man was saving his life, after all.

"Besides, I've a knack for sensing the good or bad in people. You're definitely not her."

"You're saying I'm good?"

"I'm saying you're not her, and that's enough for me."

Makes sense, Helix admitted to himself. "Right then. What's your plan?" he asked, sucking in a pained breath as Zane pulled the cloth tight, cinching the makeshift bandage.

Zane didn't answer and stepped back with a self-satisfied grunt. "How's that?"

Helix examined it. It was tight. Not tight enough that the binding's tautness exacerbated, but enough that it staunched the flow of blood. It also was tied in a way that seemed to prevent slipping, looping one of the thinner bandages over his shoulder. "I can move—that's good enough," he said, not wanting to show any weakness. Never again.

"You still look awful."

"Look who's talking," Helix snapped.

Zane smiled. "Good, you've a fire. We're going to need that. Are you ready to move? We need to find Hannah and the others before it's too late."

"Hannah and the others? Too late for what?"

"No time to explain," Zane said and rose. Now sleeveless, his arms were bare, exposing thick muscles and long scars. *So many scars…* More questions for the mysterious fiery man rose to mind, but he suppressed them.

Helix figured he was safer with Zane than alone. And if he were telling the truth—which was likely, as he'd just patched him up—then his wound did need medical attention. "Lead on."

473

A Darker Enemy

"Stay close," Zane told his new companion as they trudged deeper into the witch's lair. He'd broken his nightmare, but he still didn't trust these woods. Besides, something in the air felt dangerous, and he'd learned long ago to trust his instincts.

"*Helix...*" came a cough on his left.

"Huh?"

"That's my name, by the way." Helix paused as if expecting a response. "It's just you never asked, and I figured it'd be easier than calling me, 'guy' or 'you' or something equally cordial."

Zane grunted.

In the corner of his gaze, he saw Helix roll his eyes, limping along with sweat straining from his face as he moved—sweat more from pain than their brisk pace. Zane took in Helix quickly. *Blue lips. Pale skin. Excessive sweating.* Zane had seen it before and knew if they didn't find Hannah soon, his newfound friend would pass out from blood loss. "You do that a lot, you know?"

"Do what?"

Helix grunted in example, mimicking him.

Zane held back another grunt, scanning the woods. *Where is she?* he thought, fighting down his panic, fists clenching rhythmically at his side as he moved faster and faster. In his rush, he realized he'd left the spear behind when he'd patched up Helix.

Luckily, Helix kept up with him. "What're we looking for?"

"Anything," Zane said, fighting down the panic in his voice, replacing it with anger.

But as he searched, all he saw were dark swaying trees and the sound of distant, mocking laughter.

He cursed but moved faster until—

"—Zane," Helix said behind him. His blue-eyed companion knelt in the mud, breathing hard from their pace but staring at something. Zane's blood chilled as he followed Helix's gaze.

Footprints.

Small ones.

"Is it her? Hannah?" Helix asked.

A little flower was stamped into the mud, the one she'd engraved in the bottom of the sole. He had a sudden flashback...

"What are you doing with my dagger?"

"None of your darned business," she said, sticking her tongue out, carving something in the bottom of the new boots he'd just filched for her.

"Brand new boots, and first thing you do is carve into them," he grumbled. He shouldn't have been upset. It was almost impossible for Hannah to make him upset, but it wasn't an easy lift. The cordwainer had two guards on his store, and both had nearly spotted him—and a theft in Farbs of that scale meant a lost hand, and a lost hand would mean death. But Hannah ignored him, so he tried a different tact. "That's a waste of a good blade."

"Oh hush, it isn't hurting it—besides," she said, holding up the rutted dagger, "this thing's more scrap metal than a real dagger. Why don't you get rid of it?"

"It reminds me that killing isn't pretty," he confessed.

That made her go quiet, looking thoughtful. Until a smile cracked her round face, lighting up. "There! Done! See?" She held up her boot, showing off the tooled symbol of a flower in the center of the sole.

He scratched his head. "I don't get it. No one's going to see that," he said. "What's the point?"

She sighed, rose, and tapped him on the side of the head, then kissed him on the cheek. "Don't be silly. Everyone's going to see it. Now wherever I go I leave behind something beautiful."

Zane returned to the moment, swallowing his rage, wiping his clouding gaze.

475

"At least we know she was here…" Helix said, touching his shoulder.

It was a small consolation. "She's *still* here," Zane said, trying to keep his teeth from grinding. "She can't fly and the tracks just end. So she has to be *here*." He looked up into the knotted, twisted boughs of the nearby trees but saw nothing. He continued to rove. "Search everywhere," he instructed, and with Helix's help, they scoured the muck.

A strangled sound drew Zane to Helix's side. "I… think you should have a look at this," Helix said tightly. Zane's chest grew tight, anger and fear rising. Stamped into the mud were huge prints, round like a log but with five clawed toes.

"What in the hell kind of creature…?"

"A Verg," Zane answered. He'd heard stories of them. Ayva and Darius had told him tales of the monstrous troll-like creatures and confirmed their existence, but to see it here?

"No," Helix said, pointing, "that."

A dozen paces away were another set of prints that Zane hadn't seen. They were covered in a thin pool of murky water. He lifted a hand, letting the rage feed the swirling ball of fire in his mind. Fire seared away the water, showing the prints more clearly.

"You can thread…" Helix whispered. "You're a Reaver?"

"Something like that," Zane said, examining the footprints.

One print was human—made by a boot, not much different than Zane's, but then the other… It looked like a human foot in size, but the whole of it was too sharp, too angular. Four deep indentations where toes should be left rivet-like holes in the hard-packed mud. A *human foot… but with razor-sharp claws?*

"What is it?" Helix asked.

"I don't know," Zane admitted.

"It's not human, whatever it is," Helix said and then paused, looking up.

Zane moved to look up as well but Helix tackled him to the ground.

Before he knew what was happening, he was suddenly wrestling with the scrappy blond. He grabbed Helix's wrist, stopping him mid-strike. Zane tried to speak, to ask what in the Seven Hells was going on, but Helix kept fighting him. This time Zane twisted his companion's arm, causing Helix to cry out in pain. Fed by his rage and fear, he pinned Helix's flailing fists with one hand, then snatched the blue-eyed youth's dirty collar, lifting him up. "What the hell are you doing? We don't have time for this, we have to find Hannah."

"Fine, let's go. Just… just don't, look. Whatever you do, please don't look," Helix pleaded, tears in his eyes.

Dread tore through Zane. He threw Helix from him and—

Dangling from the tree was a small body—blood dripping from her limp arm, down onto Zane's cheeks—still warm.

There were slash marks all over the small body and a pool of blood on the ground. Her face still held a note of surprise. She was strung up, as if on display—vines coiled around her neck, tying her to a thick, arching branch that hung over the path. Now he stared at his waking nightmare, his worst fear made visible.

No, *it can't be*—his mind shouted, his whole body numb.

But even were it not for that blonde hair, and those big, brown, now vacant eyes, he spotted her boots. Imprinted onto the bottom of each sole were small, hand carved flowers. In a daze, Zane lifted a hand. A small ember sizzled the vine above her head and Hannah's body fell. He caught her easily, softly. Cradling her in his arms, he felt her warmth slowly fade. With that fading warmth, Zane felt his sanity slip—his humanity and hope crumbling along with it. His world blurred with tears; and the fear, disbelief, and denial were replaced by one thing and one thing only.

Rage.

An undeniable, burning, and unquenchable rage that promised to kill himself or burn the world to cinder.

477

THE FIПAL FEAR

Ayva continued in this madmen's realm, the mysterious forest, alone, anxious, but filled with purpose. Farhaven needed her to find the Sword of Sun. Vaster was relying on her. She saw visions of that boy who had died of the sickness, of his mother, of the whole city, and she shivered. She couldn't save those who had already passed, but she could save those who still clung to life. And so she walked.

She had a hard time grasping how long she'd been in here – the light wasn't clear enough to see the sun's movement in the sky. The leafy canopy was too thick. It made her uneasy. But somewhere in the forest, after some time, she found something worth following: a zipping sylph of light that laughed airily, dancing from tree to tree. She hoped it would lead her to the sword.

Sometimes she would lose sight of it, but it always came back. It'd led her away from the murky, oppressive bogs to a serene glade.

"Welcome, Ayva. I've been waiting for you," the voice echoed, eerily beautiful—bouncing off the mossy trees, rippling across the pools of water about her.

The glade was a flat bed of mossy earth, hundreds of little pools surrounding her—each filled with glassy water of a hundred different colors: passionate red, silver, azure, gold, white and more. It was beautiful, but she didn't let it affect her. She knew that the place *and* that voice was pure evil. She could sense it. It would kill her if she turned her back, as surely as a thief in the dark.

"You have what I want," she called, her voice sounding loud in the unearthly quiet of this place. "Where is it?"

Laughter sounded all about her, making her head flick around—on her left, then her right, then behind, and then she breathed a long, calming breath—focused on the sun in her mind, feeding her confidence—and the laughter stopped.

"Show yourself," she yelled, stopping before a giant blue lake in the center.

Ayva squinted as sudden light bloomed in the depths of the water. She tiptoed to the water's edge, leaning forward. As she did, the light burgeoned, growing. It raced from the depths like a shooting star and burst forth, breaching the water. Ayva stood her ground as a glowing transcendent creature of unearthly light floated above the pond's surface. Light nearly blinded her, but she stared into it, seeing the creature's feminine outline. Water fell from her angelic form, then burnt to mist about her before evaporating completely. Ayva clenched her hands, stilling her racing heart. The Enchantress. "Here I am, and here you are once again. How did you find my home? You are in the heart of it now—I wanted to show you and only you. Do you find it pleasing?"

479

Light trickled down, and Ayva used it to feed her voice, ignoring the woman's question. "I've come for the sword," she said again. "Where is it?"

The reply was amused. "The warbringer. It carries the seed of evil as surely as that dark-souled leader of yours… Not in its heart like that windcutter of his, but in its deeds. A thousand years of death and chaos, of sisters and brothers, of mothers and fathers slain, all for the sake of a missing blade… And that blessed City of Sun is to blame. Jewel of the north," she mocked. "Covered in blood and mired in guilt."

"It wasn't their fault," Ayva found herself saying. "It was stolen."

"Stolen?" the Enchantress questioned, sounding amused.

Her words shook Ayva's confidence. "Yes," she replied a little less soundly than she wished. "Stolen."

"And the only person who could touch the blade was your predecessor. Odd, isn't it?" Ayva knew this was a gap in the story she didn't have an answer to… "Do you really think the Windseeker, the one you call Kail, was the only one who betrayed the world?"

Ayva's mouth went dry. "I…" Stories came to mind. Kail and Omni.

Omni was his right hand — his voice, his friend above all others, his confidante.

"How — I wonder — do you think I got the blade?"

Pieces started to click in Ayva's head. Terrifyingly huge pieces that made a shiver run the length of her spine.

"I remember her, standing where you stand now. Golden, resplendent, proud... I could not harm her, for she had already laid a wound upon her heart that I could never outdo. A cut so deep that it could drown the world in her sorrow."

Ayva's blood ran cold.

"She told me little," she continued, "but even in my secluded little home I listened to the wind and heard the rumors... Burgeoning war... Treachery... A missing blade... Of course, she and I knew a crack had already formed in the world. A crack the Ronin of the time could never heal... But she believed the Ronin of the future... They could."

"And so you took it," she breathed softly in realization. "You started a war that killed tens of thousands of innocents that spread the crack in the world deeper just for the uncertain hope that we'd one day heal it?"

"Such sorrow, such empathy," said the creature of light, sounding more inhuman than ever. She floated down and Ayva moved for her dagger, but a thick tuber suddenly shot from the green covered earth, circling her wrist. At the same time the Enchantress floated nearer, gently brushing Ayva's face with her limb of light, which looked something between a tendril and a hand. Ayva saw fingers within that misty yellow and, as they neared she recoiled, expected searing heat, but instead felt an icy chill.

480

Ayva bit back her anger, but it bubbled forth despite her effort. "How could you? You helped start the Lieon..."

"You're just like her. It was quite difficult for her, if that helps."

"And for you?

"I care not for human tragedies," she laughed. "I care for the existence of my world. The darkness the Ronin faced, the darkness that you now face *will* destroy everything. Even me and everything you see. That is what I hold dear. The Lightbringer before you knew this. It will end the world if it's not stopped. That is why I took the blade. Humans, elves, dryads, dragons, sprytes, nothing will remain if it has its way..."

It? A thousand questions churned and boiled in Ayva's mind. She knew there was a darkness out there, she felt it in her heart. And she'd heard enough tales of it during their journey to validate her feeling. Something connected to the dark mantra that was taking over the land: 'Strength is life, weakness, death.' But this? Her world rocked. She felt sick. "How can you justify it? You doomed them. Vaster. So many people… Just for us… for a hope you know nothing about…"

"Yes," said the creature of light. "A decision I'd make again if I had to, and so should you. In the end, it was simple. Risk our fates on you and let a small number suffer, or let all suffer and die, dooming my existence and that of your world. Again, a fairly easy choice to make, even if I did care for the lives of mortals. And even though I agreed with her end, she still had to atone for her demons. No one leaves these woods without facing their deepest fears, that which haunts them when all else slumbers."

"And so Omni faced hers? Faced the needless deaths of countless souls?"

"Needless," she scoffed. "Your heart serves you well, but it blinds you to logic. But I suppose that is a very human thing. To feel first and think later." Then suddenly and surprisingly, the Enchantress shivered—tendrils of light shuddering—as she looked away. "Human emotions are… amusing to me. But I will never forget that woman's screams. Such terror. Pray that you never witness such fear." She quivered again, but then her gaze settled on Ayva. "And yes, she faced them. I watched as her mind nearly split, madness creeping over her, fingers clawing and tearing at her eyes to free them from her own skull just to stop the visions of what was to come… the visions of what she had wrought with her deed, but she faced them and won. Just as you will have to do if you wish to find what you seek. That is… if you still wish the blade. Do you now? Now that you know what stains its memory?"

481

"I…" Ayva hesitated. *None of that matters*, she shouted to herself. But her heart wrenched, hating both Omni for what she'd done and herself for being a part of it. *She* was the reason Omni had cast away the blade. And still, Omni had gone on to fight a war she knew she was going to lose. To watch those she loved die, almost solely because of her. How? It seemed almost impossible to comprehend. Even the idea of the ancient evil that hadn't died, that seeped into the cracks of the lands, widening the darkness of the world…. Stopping that… Was that really enough to balance the tide of Omni's heinous act? The world would die, hundreds of thousands, millions even, dead or worse… Still. Ayva couldn't stomach it. Could she have been strong enough to condemn so many in order to save the world? It's not as if Omni had killed them herself. It had simply been the catalyst. A small push of a boulder already waiting to tumble…

The Enchantress watched her, as if relishing in her torment. Ayva realized tears were falling from her eyes. She wiped them gruffly away and stood straight. "I'm here to reclaim the blade. No matter what."

"So easy a decision, is it?"

"The blade isn't evil, and even if what Omni did was… Even if… I have to stop what's coming."

"Then you'll finish what she started. A grand task, indeed. You have strength, just like her. I see it burning in your eyes. But can you truly do what your predecessor couldn't? A woman of infinitely more power, with a thousand years to hone her abilities, to learn every intricacy and she still failed."

Then Ayva sensed it. She mocked her, but the Enchantress was truly curious, and if she wasn't mistaken… "You're afraid."

She laughed again. "It's a simple rule of life, dear girl. No one wants to die. Even me."

"Then why don't you kill it? If it's such a terrible evil and you're so powerful, why don't *you* kill it?"

"I… am limited to my realm. It's a realm of the spark and the flow. As the world of magic dies, just like any other Node, my world dies and so, too, do I," she said, looking pained by the admission. Ayva sensed it in the air with a trickle of her power. *Truth.* She wasn't sure how, but it felt like a thin thread of light connected from her to the woman, without a hint of shadow or darkness. Somehow the strand seemed to represent honesty. "Besides, the evil spreads like a sickness in the form of truth."

"'*Strength is life, weakness, death,*'" Ayva quoted.

The Enchantress inclined her head. "Precisely, and an idea cannot be killed."

"Then how do we destroy it?"

"You must find a way."

"Still, there must be a head to the snake," Ayva said.

"Even if I were careful enough to lure the origin of the evil here," replied the Enchantress, lifting her hand. A sphere of water lifted from a nearby puddle, swelling as she spoke, "it grows ever more powerful, even as we speak. I fear I'm not strong enough anymore. It will take a greater force than even I…" The sphere burst and Ayva cast out her hand, threads of light filling her breath and racing outward, searing the water to mist before it touched her. Despite the glaring brilliance, Ayva thought she saw the Enchantress smile. "I've decided," she said with resounding clarity.

Ayva's brows furrowed, confused, watching as the Enchantress raised one of her ephemeral light-filled arms. And then something bubbled and churned in the water's depths. A light blossomed from within—like a golden sun, embedded in the water, then it broke the surface and Ayva's breath caught in her throat. Her limbs tingled as a thousand emotions collided in her, seeing it at last.

The sword.

It sat in the air, rotating slowly—brilliant as she'd imagined it in all her dreams. "Take it," said the Lady of the Lake. "It's yours."

Her heart raced and she reached out, but then hesitated. "Is this a trick?"

"No."

"Why then? What is this? You told me that *all* have to face their fears to get what they want. I haven't, yet now you offer me the blade?"

A sorrow entered the Lady's voice. "Yes."

"Why?" And then she understood, eyes narrowing. "What happens to you?"

"If I break my code, I lose my power. I will become mortal."

"Then why? I thought that's all you cared about."

483

From within the radiance, a soft smile appeared as if Ayva had missed the point. "My home," she answered softly and gestured. As she did, Ayva noticed all the life she'd been oblivious to—it was everywhere, birds, beasts, even bugs in every nook and cranny, branch and bush. But all hidden behind the Lady's spell. "I will live a normal life, grow old and die like any other, but my home will endure. That is enough for me." She stretched her arm out and the blade floated closer. "But you will survive. If you fail in the test of fear, then all hope for my home is lost."

Ayva moved to reach out but then clenched her fist, pulling her hand back. "Test me," she demanded.

"I'm giving you the blade, fool human. You don't have—"

"I want the blade rightfully. I want to face my fears as Omni faced hers. And as I see it, if I can't face my fears here and now, then I won't be able to handle what's to come… Especially if Omni could not. What would that say of me? I'm supposed to succeed where she failed and I can't even handle the same task?"

Ayva didn't need the ki like Gray to sense the Enchantress's surprise. The Lady's form trembled, her eyes shifting from gold to violet to black, then back to a shade of blue. "If you fail, you will die. You understand this, yes?"

Ayva nodded.

"Perhaps you mortals are not as weak as I thought," she said, sounding for the first time like something other than coldly superior. "Then consider this your first test. A sign of things to come, perhaps, and a symbol of the strength you will need to face the coming darkness."

BOOM.

The land shuddered beneath Ayva's feet and trees melted, rock crumbled and the pools turned to mist. Terror filled her as she fell, screaming as she tumbled into a black void that opened in the crack of earth.

A voice echoed in her head as the world turned to an abyssal black place... So dark it hurt Ayva's soul. "Hope. Dying hope. That is your test. That all the good you thought exists in this world was simply a lie. And all those you counted on, trusted in, are what you fear most... betrayers."

***

Ayva stood in her illusion.

484

She'd fought a thousand images already—dozens of variations of her father, or Darius, or Zane, or Hannah, or Gray. But most often, it was her father.

Sometimes her father yelled at her, screaming behind the amber windows of *The Golden Horn* as he burned alive. Sometimes the door was locked. She'd leapt through the glass only to find him a seared, blackened corpse. Other times she'd enter only to find a Kage—the dark versions of the Ronin—had run him through with a sword before turning on her. Each time she almost saved him, pulling him from the burning building or nearly stopping the Kage from killing him. Each time she failed.

Several times she'd fought her friends.

Gray had tried to run her through in her sleep with Morrowil. Darius, with tears in his eyes, tried to choke the life from her—that one had hurt the most. Even Hannah had buried a dagger in her back.

But Ayva dragged onward.

The last vision shattered.

It was another of her father.

She'd succeeded, pulled him from the fires that had burnt him to a crisp, but still he breathed.

"Don't... please don't die..."

He choked on his blood and reached a limp hand to her cheek, but it seemed to cause him excruciating pain. And he let it fall. No words came forth. No final utterance of love—just fear in his eyes, and pain. She'd held him, tears flowing as fire raged all about her... She wanted to die. But each time, the fire stopped before reaching her. The visions wouldn't let her die. They just wanted to bury her hope.

The vision shattered and she rose from his body as the flames died, snuffed as if by a gust of wind. She was left standing in a desolate Lakewood. Bodies surrounded her. The quiet before the next storm, and despite her tears, she looked up into the sky—and she saw a glimmer of yellow. The sun? *No*, she realized. It was smaller, and yellow tendrils wavered from its body. *It was her*, she figured, *the Enchantress, she's watching and waiting for me to fail*. Ayva was so tired—she wanted to lie down, to let the tears wash over her or to stop them altogether, to curl up on the cold cobblestones next to the other blackened corpses, but instead she took an even breath—focusing on that burning light, that small but vibrant radiance that burned in her chest.

"You seek to break me by giving me hope, then shattering it," she said in realization—into the dead of the night, as if speaking to the lifeless forms about her. "But you cannot break me. Not when I know this is a lie." *Is it?* a part of her whispered, remembering the dozens of times Gray had tried to end her life, or Darius or... She shut her eyes, shaking her head. The golden node pulsed.

Are you so certain? The Enchantress's voice asked—ever-present.

And Ayva breathed out, feeling the warm blood of her father dry on her hands and she smiled, finally finding her center. "I am."

Humans betray. It is in their hearts... They will turn on you—directly or indirectly in the end, for nothing lasts. Not even the Ronin.

"You were right before," she shouted into the silence. "When you asked how can you kill an ideal? I realize now you're right. You can't. But you can overpower it with an even greater ideal." She breathed. "So you can show me Gray killing me a hundred more times, or my father's death a thousand more—and all because of me—but it won't matter."

Why not? How can you be so certain that they won't betray you?

"Because," Ayva said simply. "I have hope."

* * *

Ayva broke the vision and fell forward, but caught herself.

485

The Enchantress was standing before her, looking frantic—she wasn't sure how she could tell; she was still angelic and radiant, but the edges of her luminescence seemed to buzz with frenetic energy.

Suddenly the woods shook, the ground trembled. Birds and beasts took to the air, crying out. Again the woods rattled as if a titan was stomping its way through their midst—puddles rippling. "What's happening?" Ayva asked.

"I..." the Enchantress began, sounding uncertain, afraid. "He's come..."

"Who's come?" Ayva asked, angry.

The specter of a woman's eyes focused on her, wide, terrified. "Something ancient. My home is dying... it fights, but it's losing. Something's wrong. I fear the evil is here. Your friends are in terrible danger."

"Where are they?"

The Enchantress pointed with one golden, ethereal arm to the east. "You don't have much time... Let me—"

Ayva interrupted her, extending a hand. She felt the blade—in her core, and it listened. Summoned from the depths, it burst from the pond, water falling from its gleaming golden metal. Ayva grabbed it from the air. She nearly gasped as wind suddenly rushed about her and the blade grew hot in her hand. It felt as it were fusing with her skin, but she held on. The warmth spread across her limbs, to her chest. There it grew blazing hot. Her chest felt ready to burst with molten magma, tears sprouted from her eyes—as if the blade were merging with her very soul. At last, the warmth receded and she opened her eyes, not realizing she'd closed them, and found the Enchantress's glowing, undulating appendages still in the same place, moving slowly. And Ayva understood. It had all happened in a flashing moment.

Ayva turned to go, light pulsing from her core and purpose fueling her.

The Enchantress spoke and her voice lost some of its ethereal haunt—sounding grim. "Heir of Omni."

Ayva froze.

"I feel my power weakening by the moment. I'm not sure what I can do against this evil, but I will do my best to hold it off for as long as I can." Ayva didn't need to look back to hear a note of terror in the Enchantress's voice. "One last thing.... Whatever you do—don't let that monster touch you."

Ayva nodded without turning, and with that—she ran, hearing a voice following her on the winds.

"*Fly,*" said the Enchantress. "*Save them.*"

But Ayva needed no goading. Her heart thundered as she raced, tearing through the woods, and above the crashing in her breast she heard a terrible cry. A bellow of pure suffering and rage. And she knew who it was...

Zane.

A Sea of Red

Zane knew nothing but anger. It clouded his vision until the world was nothing but a sea of red. And he bellowed from his core, making everything nearby rattle and shake. And he continued to bellow. Distantly, he was aware that he was threading. Threading enough to burn his soul. NO MORE! something shouted. His nexus? A flaming ember in his mind roared, but with each ball of raging fire he threw from his hand, the ember in his mind shrank, eating itself alive. It was dying. He was dying.

Zane bellowed louder, flinging a head-sized ball of angry fire from his hand. It collided with the trunk of a tree. The tree exploded, sending up a shower of splinters. Again he threw his anger outward, unable to contain it in his chest. More trees, bushes—everything—they ignited in a conflagration until the world about him burned red and orange, just like his vision.

ENOUGH! the voice shouted again. So loud, so angry. In his head?

Zane paused.

He looked up through the flames, his breathing ragged.

A young man stood encased in a shield of water, like a bubble waiting to pop but it didn't.

Helix. That was the young man's name.

"Enough…" Helix breathed. "No more." Helix was clutching his side, blood leaking around his fingers and dripping to the scorched earth.

Yet around Helix it was oddly wet. None of it made sense to Zane. Then the bubble around Helix burst, and the young man collapsed.

Zane registered it — confused.

I did that, something told him. Seeing Helix's unmoving form, a shrapnel of guilt made his power wane, the fires diminish, but then Zane gritted his jaw. He held onto his rage. It was all he knew and all that made sense and kept the torrent of sorrow from washing him away.

Hannah was dead.

All about the glades, fires still danced — oaks, elms, and scraggly trees all turned to torches in the darkening night and his eyes burned, tearing up from rising heat.

Then he appeared.

Seen through a film of red, a terrible figure stepped out from behind a tree. He looked like something out of a nightmare, standing amid the sea of scarlet flames at the edge of the glade. Zane's anger faltered and the flames rising from his hands sputtered and died as he took in the creature before him.

A demon.

The demon stood roughly seven feet in height, taller than an average man. His body looked stretched as if pulled by a torturing rack. It appeared half-demon, half-man, split down the middle. Both his left arm and left leg were black and full of odd, sharp angles as if cut from obsidian glass. Zane knew that terrible black. Darkwalker. Half-darkwalker. Sharp claws on his inhuman foot dug into the fetid earth as the demon stepped forward. The black glass reflected Zane.

489

He knew that face, or at least half of it.

"Sithel..."

"My, my, what a treat — name recognition," Sithel said. Immediately Zane backstepped, hearing that voice. It rumbled like dark thunder and set his teeth on edge. Sithel rested his dark clawed hand on his obsidian chest, tapping with an awful *clack* and gave a mocking bow. "I'm flattered, truly." His cruel smile widened. "And from a Ronin himself no less."

Zane was frozen for only a moment. Then he lifted his hand, calling on his nexus, the burning ball of fire in his mind.

Threads of fire formed in the air, sucking at his soul, draining the last of his power — he knew he was drawing too much, but he didn't care. He pulled more. His insides burned as he did. The threads grew, eating at the moisture in the air as it became larger and hotter still, until it was a swirling ball of fire as big as a horse cart. He lobbed the molten fire and it roared, angry and alive. Something blue pulsed in the bulging front pocket of Sithel's bloody apron, but the fire was undaunted, hurtling forth. Sithel glanced down as if noticing, but didn't flinch. The demon glanced back up. The fire collided and Sithel lifted his obsidian arm in the last moment. The molten orb ricocheted off of the black skin—crashing into a tree, sending a spray of tiny flames raining to the earth.

"Curious…" Sithel said, "the voidstone doesn't work on the flow. I wonder what makes you so different? But it doesn't matter, does it? Not when I have this." He lifted his obsidian arm where feeble little flames danced along its surface before dying.

Zane swallowed, backpedaling again as Sithel marched through the flames. Zane raised his sword, but Sithel was faster. The human hand shot out like a dart and snatched Zane's throat. Sithel's hand was cold and oily, and Zane stared into the heart of the man and saw true evil. Sithel's right eye was human, but black rot had crept in at the edges, as if trying to engulf his human side. The rest of it was bloodshot and fueled by madness. His left eye was a terrible red. Like a nugget of glowing bloodstone, set into the obsidian black socket where a human eye should be. "Hello again, Zane," Sithel said, squeezing with inhuman strength and Zane gasped, feeling as if steel worms were circling his throat, crushing him. How… how was he so strong? His eyes bulged and his vision began to blur, and slowly he relaxed his grip on his weapon.

The demon tilted his head, as if inquisitive, searching. "No fear. Not like her. She was afraid when she died. No, not afraid. *Terror.* That would be a better word." He smiled, and it was terrifying. "Funny, isn't it? Even at the very end she held out, believing that you would save her. *Hope.* How pointless of an emotion against truth, don't you agree?"

Zane choked the words free. "You goddamn bastard… You killed her… you killed… Hannah." His voice was hoarse from bellowing.

Sithel threw Zane to the ground.

Zane tried to catch himself but his body was exhausted. He crumpled. Still he shook himself, and scrambled for his blade in the muck, but he couldn't find it. Where is it? WHERE IS IT? he raged inwardly, frantic.

"Pathetic. This is it, isn't it? Look at you," Sithel said as Zane scrambled desperately. "In your veins runs the blood of a legend, the strength of a *god*, but one simple act and you're reduced to this… Weak, small, lost and *pathetic.* Just like your sister."

Zane finally found his blade beneath the muck and, shaking with anger, he lifted his sword arm, crying out.

Sithel dodged the first strike. The second collided with his arm, sending sparks. The demon struck. Zane saw it coming, but he was so tired. His rage was drowned by a torrent of sorrow, his heart dragging dully in his chest. And the strike came. A black knee, like a hewn chunk of obsidian slammed into his chest. He sucked in his breath to absorb the blow, but still it took the air from him. Zane staggered back then charged forward, lifting his blade to cut Sithel's head free. Sithel leaned back just enough and the sword's tip whipped past his throat. The demon struck, lightning quick, raking across Zane's left arm with his claws. Jagged gashes, angry and red rent down Zane's arm and pain exploded. His training kicked in, and Zane continued the attack. He blinked the tears away, and heaving the blade overhead with his good arm, he made to cut Sithel in half, to end it all, crying out. Certain Sithel couldn't block this attack, he put all his strength into the blow. He would sever the demon's arm and his body with it.

Sithel was quicker. He lunged forward, using the speed of a darkwalker, and snatched Zane's sword hand with his dark clawed hand.

491

Pain shot through Zane, feeling as if he were held by glowing metal tongs that had sat too long in the bellow's fire. He dropped his sword with a shriek of pain. He forced his muscles to move, gripping Sithel's throat with his other hand. He squeezed with everything in him, but the dark black tendons in the demon's neck felt like steel cords beneath his grasp. Sithel's demonic face was half twisted human skin, oddly attached, as if stretched like leather upon a tanning bed and sewn at the edges to that black flesh, half hard, with black unnatural angles. The monstrosity sneered and his dark glassy orbs for eyes widened as he tossed Zane like a sack of meat to the ground once more. Zane gasped, breathing sweet air back into his lungs as the pain abated.

"Is that it? Is that truly all you have?" the predator sounded angry. His demonic voice reverberated through the woods.

Zane groped at the ground once more, trying to rise, but his arms trembled as he pressed himself up. He staggered to his knees only to see a huge boot slam into his chest, knocking him back down hard. He felt ribs crack beneath the blow and he spat blood. He blinked, tiredly, angrily and through his blurred vision, on the ground beside him he saw a figure.

Sithel knelt next to it and gripped a fistful of the boy's blonde hair. The demon prodded a wound on the boy's back that now looked seared like burnt meat. The demon sniffed at the boy, then dropped him. His head slumped back to the earth, lifeless. "Who's this? Another weakling?"

No... Zane thought in rising dread, remembering. *Oh gods, Helix. I killed him... I killed Helix.* The remaining ire that still burned in his chest was suddenly doused by a wave of overwhelming sorrow as Zane stared vacantly at Helix in shock and disbelief. *No. No. No...*

Monster... the words echoed through his head.

Demon.

A beast without a leash, without a soul.

The nightmare—his greatest fear slammed into him again as Zane lay in the mud, but he was too sick, too terrified to even move.

Sithel stalked nearer, looming over him, dark claws mulching the wet earth. He placed his dark clawed hoof on Zane's chest, pressing down—slowly, excruciatingly pressing the air out of Zane's lungs as he struggled to rise. "This was too easy! Had I known you would be this weak, this wretched, I wouldn't have gone through all that trouble of planting the seed in Vaster."

Vaster... Realization dawned on Zane.

"Ah, you didn't know, did you? Yes, it was I that destroyed the Macambriel. Granted, it was my master's idea. She knows where the prophecy leads and that the previous Ronin of sun cast away that ill-famed blade into the witch's lair, and so with the Sunroad broken, you fools would be forced to chase after it... I needed to draw you away, to make you desperate. Only then could I pick you off with ease." Sithel knelt and scratched his dark claw into Zane's cheek, creating lines, drawing a sharp breath of agony from Zane. "One... by... one. And believe me, it's been almost too easy."

Zane remembered their screams, the terror in the eyes of a little boy who'd died to the plague in Vaster. "You're a monster. How many are dying or dead, all because you're a madman?" He tried to rise, but the black claw upon his chest was weighted like an anvil.

Sithel looked down at him, unsympathetic. "Mad? Perhaps. But brilliance and madness hold a fine line, don't they? For in your urgency to find the sword, you've risked all—left the dead in your tracks and were careless at every turn. Those Algasi were a real treat. Cold, hard to the marrow, aren't they? Killing off their brothers barely seemed to slow them!

492

Speaking of which…" He turned to the woods. "Come out, my pets."

At his words, three nightmarish creatures trundled out of the woods, shaking the earth beneath Zane. *Vergs.* Zane had heard stories of these horrible creatures with thick necks and trunk-like arms and legs—trolls, some versions called them. Gray and the others had told them they were more than stories. But these looked nothing like those stories or his friend's descriptions. Their thick, leathery hides were fused in places with a terrible black plate, somewhere between metal and carapace, mostly upon their chest, shoulders, legs and neck. The plate was full of thorns, curling wickedly. The largest of the three had a gray hide, another was shorter with dark skin and a spiked chain coiled about its thick torso, resting on the black plate, and the last was a mottled gray-black who wielded a huge scimitar.

Towering over him, Zane felt small, weak and afraid for one of the first times in his life.

The demon that was Sithel turned to the Verg with mottled black and gray skin, the smallest of the three—its heavy blade twice the size any human could ever wield and spoke. "Find the other Algasi. With our appearance and the voidstone Soul-Draining the spark of this place, their nightmares should be fading. Whatever you do, don't let them interrupt our little… party." He held up a dark clawed finger. "But be wary of their leader. He's not an easy meal like the others."

The beast grunted in understanding, steam flaring from his nostrils and lumbered off, leaving its brothers—its earth rattling steps sounded into the depths of the dark woods.

"Why?" Zane asked still a breath away from Sithel's clawed foot.

"Why else? To live. You see, you and your friends ruined me. The battle upon the sands… I lost everything. Everything I'd worked so hard for. I was going to remake the world—make it stronger. Make it so no one would ever suffer again like I suffered."

"You mean you planned to kill the weak and defenseless as your putrid mantra commands… 'Strength is life, weakness, death.'"

Sithel's claws buried a little deeper into Zane's chest, scorching his red tunic, inching into flesh. Agony flared as the red-hot spines burrowed deeper, as if searching for his heart. Sithel continued, "You mock those words… I don't understand this. You of all people know the horrors of this world. Farbs is your home, isn't it? It's no more than a cesspit. A den of depravity where children go hungry, where smirking thieves spill each

493

other's blood in dark alleys, for what? A bit of coin? To fill their bellies? If only the strong survived, then all suffering would vanish. Without the weak, there'd be no one to weigh society down. No one in need of protection. The strong would protect themselves. And if anyone does break the law, well… With true strength on our side, we could enforce stability, law, justice. Peace. Everlasting peace throughout Farhaven, just as the Lieon was intended for and as the Ronin were meant to do… but failed. A perfect world."

The pain suddenly abated.

Sithel still stood over him, but his face was a thunderhead. "Why're you doing that?"

Zane was confused, but then he realized. He'd laughed. In the face of impending death, in the face of terrible, heartbreaking sorrow and unfathomable anger—Zane had laughed. Lying on his back, Zane realized he was *still* laughing. A low soft chuckle that emanated from deep within that he couldn't stop. It hurt to laugh, the claws digging deeper, but he couldn't help it. "You."

Sithel cocked his head. "Me?"

"You don't get it." Zane continued to laugh, the sound growing in his throat.

"Get what? *What don't I get?*"

"How weak you truly are." Zane laughed again, even louder, and Sithel's rage grew with each mounting word. "You feed upon the weak and helpless. You kill without mercy. And all the while, you're a slave to a master whom you can't escape. The truth, and the great irony to your little world, Sithel, is that you're too weak yourself. You're a sad, pathetic nothing. And in this great world of yours, a world without the weak?" Zane snorted and his cocky sneer grew. "You'd be the first to die."

"Zane, Zane, Zane…" Sithel's whole body shook with rage, but then he took a slow even breath. "You don't get it, do you? I've *changed*. I will show you what true strength is…"

Then he smashed his clawed hand into Zane's face. It felt like being hit with a brick of metal. He tried to catch his breath, to regain his vision and stand, but it was hard. The world spun and Sithel *was* strong. Slowly, his blurred vision cleared. Though his head throbbed powerfully, he put fingers to his cheeks and felt a sting… The blood was strange upon his fingertips. Red but bubbling, as if the mere touch of Sithel had made his blood boil.

Zane moved to rise. But Sithel was quicker. He slammed his clawed foot into Zane's ribcage and more ribs *popped*. "No! Stop pretending to be this weak. Get up and fight me!" Again he hammered his foot into Zane's side and ribs turned, stabbing into vital flesh and organs. Agony exploded. The world turned silent, save a terrible ringing in his ears. Zane gasped, sucking, trying vainly to pull a desperate breath, but breath was nowhere to be found. Again the foot slammed, digging into his belly, into his broken ribs. Zane gasped louder, choking, frantic for air. Tears flowed freely from his eyes and a familiar blackness crept around his vision, but he held onto consciousness—he wouldn't pass out. He couldn't. He knew if he did, all was lost. He would die and all of it would be for nothing. Hannah. Helix. All of it—his fault. With the rage fueling him, the darkness crept back, slowly but surely. Still the terrible pain remained unabated. Sithel was screaming, but Zane's world was still ringing numbness—deaf to all things.

Zane knew he was going to die. But he wouldn't die on his back. He'd fight until the very end. For Hannah. For Helix. For everyone and everything he'd failed. He'd kill Sithel if it was the last thing he did.

Sithel's foot kept slamming into his side until—

Zane felt it. This time, it was the human boot. It was warm. As if he could feel the blood pumping inside the man's human leg. He could feel it parting the air—the air that grew colder as Zane pulled at his power, heat enveloping him. And despite the agony in his side and his sorrow, Zane felt life return to his limbs. The boot rushed forth, not toward his side, but toward his head, to crush him where he lay. Zane moved. Not fast, but deliberately, twisting his muscles and catching the leg before even seeing *it*. He felt oiled leather in his grip and looked up to see Sithel's boot caught in his hands. He looked higher and saw the madman's surprise and confusion.

And rage exploded through Zane. He roared and lifted with all his might. The demon that was Sithel was heavy—it felt like upturning a horse cart laden with bricks and his muscles groaned against the weight, but he let his ire surge through him and Sithel catapulted through the air, landing against the far tree with a shattering crack. Zane rose. He hoped it'd killed the madman, but he knew better. There was a hopeful silence…. Until the madman shook his head. His wet hair was strung across his face as he stared up at Zane with pure hatred. The half-man rose sluggishly.

495

The Vergs just watched as Sithel roared, staggering, trying to rise to his feet... Now it was Zane's moment. He moved to grab his blade, to cut Sithel down as he regained his senses. But everything Zane had just done was too much. He'd used too much power. On top of that, the pain of broken ribs and of shattered insides came slamming home. It all hit at once. Zane gasped for air, clutching at the ground, trying to pull life back into his bones.

The atrocity staggered forward and put his claw to Zane's head. The black claw was like a hot needle on his brain. He tried to pull away but he couldn't. "If you beg me to stop, I'll end your pitiful life quickly."

Zane spat at Sithel.

"So be it." Sithel lifted his black claw and the pain abated. Zane dragged in a full breath only to see the black claw high above as the demon prepared to plunge it into Zane's skull. And he grinned into it, readying himself for the death he knew he deserved—the death he had spared for so long by sheer luck and skill. But now Hannah was dead and all was lost. He didn't care anymore. It just hurt too much.

The claw descended.

Light blossomed in the corner of Zane's vision. Glowing. Almost a pure gold. Zane squinted against the light, seeing a figure bathed in resplendent gold. And he saw it. Threads of yellow flowing over her body.

Ayva.

496

A Long-Awaited Meeting

*L*ight and color and pain—that's what Faye felt.

Death was already pretty awful. In fact, it felt a lot like life. Worse even.

Suddenly, a bright light blossomed over her and she felt stinging pain radiate throughout her body. It was warm, like hot coals hovering a breath away from her many wounds. She opened her crusted lids and saw a face. It hovered over her. Bulbous eyes strained with fear, and then sudden elation. *Odaren.* "You're alive."

"Barely," said another, the voice of a woman.

"*Where am…*" Faye tried to sit up and groaned loudly, clenching her eyes against the agonizing pain, blackness swimming in her vision.

"If you try that again, you'll surely die. Flesh and bone is hard enough to heal without you flailing about like a floundering fish," griped the woman. Then she turned inward, as if talking to herself. "How on earth you've survived till now is a blasted mystery. She's suffered no shock?"

"Shock?" asked Odaren.

"Paralysis, freezing. Loss of consciousness."

Faye, her lids squeezed shut against the pain, could *feel* Odaren's pudgy face shake, scratching his oily hair. She tried to respond, to open her eyes, but the blinding pain came again—this time in her stomach.

"No," Odaren said. "But she's tougher than dirt."

"Dirt doesn't have nerve endings," said the woman with a soft snort.

"Truly, the pain alone should have caused her to go unconscious several times over again."

"Will she live?" he asked anxiously.

She could feel him hover closer.

The woman cleared her throat. "Dimitri, would you mind restraining our little friend here who is averse to the concept of soap?" Faye opened her eyes and caught a glimpse of a man with hard eyes, watching from a distance with arms crossed. *Pain. Sorrow.* Even from here, Faye saw his anguish buried deep. Her sun sword was in his hand. She reached for it like a child reaching for a sweetcake, but the woman pressed her arm down and then snapped her fingers. The man's haunted eyes snapped up. "*Dimitri!* Help me!"

Dimitri obeyed, pulling Odaren back, who squawked in protest.

Faye closed her eyes again, exhausted.

"A Devari who daydreams, and quite the time to do it too," she chided the man. "Really, saving a life has become more raucous than a Cloudfell Playhouse."

"Can you do it?" Odaren asked. "Can you save her?"

"Oh, she'll live. But be the same? Not likely. I doubt she'll be able to feel anything in half her extremities but…" The woman paused as something deep stabbed into Faye's guts. Despite her best efforts, Faye cried out from the pain. The woman took a deliberate breath, as if silencing her next words. "The depths of her problems can be discussed another time." She clicked her tongue. "So much blood. If only an Arbiter were here. They'd be able to form the necessary amounts of water, proteins, and trace minerals to—oh, I'm speaking nonsense again aloud."

"Meira too," said a huskier voice.

Above Faye, she heard the woman let out a sad sigh. "Yes, Meira was a true prodigy of the spark."

Faye opened her eyes, groaning. "Who… are… you people…"

The woman's head was bent over Faye's abdomen working, doing something, but apparently she saw the direction of her gaze. "That's Dimitri. He found you. Placed in the warrens of the lower halls. You'd never had been found if it weren't for him." *Warrens of… What?* She realized now that she lay on a cold slab of stone. "Perhaps your dour nature had a purpose after all, Dimitri. It brought us quite a specimen."

"I'm not dour for dour's sake, Ethelwin."

"Yes, I know, I know. But nothing will bring your brother back again.

498

Perhaps this life is a trade for his, a sort of redemption for your loss, if you will." Faye knew deception well, and the woman, though smooth of tongue, was clearly lying.

"You don't believe that," said Dimitri.

"Not wise to use the *ki* on a Reaver, Dimitri. Especially not when that Reaver is trying to save a life. Now quiet, both of you, so I can work." Agony flared anew and Faye was lost to a dream world. *Unconsciousness, si'tu'ah* told her rationally. But she ignored her ever-present voice of perception and let the visions engulf her.

Wind raged about her, lashing at her hair and clothes. She pulled a scarlet strand of her hair from her face to see Gray standing at the ledge gazing down. It loomed over Farhaven, like standing on a cloud.

She grabbed her head, feeling dizzy. "Where are we?" Gray said nothing. She grabbed his arm, turning him and was taken aback, her breath stolen. He looked... stunning.

Layered, dark brown leather shoulder pads made him seem imposing and even more broad of shoulder than usual. The leather bore scrawled runes of white in a language she couldn't read. It layered his upper arms, leading down to clean white vambraces. At his waist and at the hinge of his elbows, was glorious silver mail. A sleeveless cloth haori, long and flowing, fell to the ground in place of a cloak. It still bore the crossed-swords of the Devari, but it was a brilliant snow-white. His thick hair was pulled back into a komai braid to show off the fine cut of his clean-shaven features. He looked almost holy. *Kingly.* But his eyes. They were stunning orbs of white. They seemed pure, like slow-moving clouds. Totally unlike the dreaded Shadow King's eyes. Beautiful.

499

She swallowed her surprise, annoyed by the fluttering of her heart. *Really, Faye?* she growled to herself. *You're no better than a simpering Cloud-fell barmaid.* Faye sighed, coming back to herself. "The clean-shaven look doesn't suit you," she said at last. "Too young and innocent-looking. I'm more a fan of a little scruff, personally."

"That's... all you have to say?" Gray asked.

She raised a brow in question. "Hmm?"

"My outfit," he said. "My eyes. None of it?"

"Oh, are you wearing something different?" she asked. "I can never keep up with the trends, really—they come and go so quickly."

Gray sighed and turned.

And Faye smirked inwardly, glad she'd gotten a rise out of him, even if he was just a figment of Farhaven and her imagination. "So what's this place?"

"My legacy," said Gray, gesturing to the arid cracked land around him. "My home." *Wind*. They stood on the windy cliffs of Ren Nar. Morrow.

"Then it's true. You are the betrayer of men?"

"You waste so much time on such pointless questions," he said. It sounded like something she would say. "Besides, it doesn't matter much, does it?" Gray asked. "I suppose this is my real legacy now," he said, wiping blood from the corner of his mouth, but more issued forth immediately. He laughed coldly, wiping the blood on his snowy haori.

"What questions should I be asking?"

"My true self was quite clever. He used clues to deduce where you were."

"And that turned out swimmingly."

Gray snorted. "Yes. He judged wrongly, used the wrong clues. But you're cleverer than he is, than I am, aren't you, Mistress of Shadows? There's something you've never taught me. Something you've held onto all this time. *Si'tu'ah*. Use it now and deduce where I truly am."

"I'll play your game, but it won't matter. I'm being healed as we speak."

"We both know that won't work. The healing will only cover your surface wounds." He pointed and Faye looked behind her. She gazed through a strange portal. The dusty cliffs warped and a gaping hole with frayed. Blurry edges showed a stone chamber where she lay on her back, covered in blood. A woman squatted over her, working feverishly. "You will seem healed to an outside observer, even to a keen-eyed Reaver. But you will still be dying on the inside."

She looked back. She'd known that... but part of her had hoped. A *small* part. "That's depressing. What's the point then?"

"What's the point of anything? You enjoy a game, don't you?"

Faye sighed. "I suppose. I've nothing better to do." She took in Gray. His armor was truly imposing. His stern features and handsome face... He could have been a high-ranking general from the Lieon. She supposed he, or *Kail*, had been. But there were other oddities to his attire. Oddities that were somehow from the present, in real time. He had sand on his boots, but not the dusty sand that surrounded them currently. It was dark and grainy. She knew that sand. "You're in Farbs, aren't you?"

"Brilliant as ever."

"Don't make me blush," she said flatly. "Really though, how was that hard? We both spent a lot of time on those sands, though I suppose my memories are a tad more stained with blood." Then she shook her head. "How is it possible? Are you truly in Farbs? Did you not leave?"

Gray smiled. "No, I left—but I returned hoping you hadn't."

She grunted. "A good but utterly *incorrect* guess."

"I had nothing else to go on."

"And now you're dead. As am I," she announced, then yawned. At least the game had been fun. More or less. She awaited an answer from the Gray that wasn't Gray, but he said nothing, merely gave a toothy grin. "What a waste. I failed to save Leah, I killed for nothing, let a dark madman get away…" She laughed. "I don't think I could have botched this up anymore if I'd *tried*."

"At least you tried," Gray said at last.

"That's not comforting," Faye replied. "But thank you."

"Goodbye, Faye," Gray said, and began to turn to dust, fading into the raging winds. "Until next we meet in this life or the next."

She felt a stab to her heart at his words—remembering they were the same words she'd told Ayva and Darius when she'd abandoned them in that pit of Darkeye's. Now she was abandoned in this dream world, left to die.

Alone.

She supposed that's how all people died.

Alone.

501

* * *

Faye groaned again, opening her eyes.

Still alive.

It wasn't a particularly comforting thought.

A woman stood over her, hands upon her hips wearing a wry look. She was matronly with faint lines at her mouth, as if she were very familiar with the act of scowling. Her eyes were brown and sharp like an owl's and she was bulky for a woman, but not fat—at least, judging her lean, tan face. The woman folded her arms in front of her, and, on the cuffs of her scarlet robes, were four distinctive black stripes. A *four-stripe Reaver?* How many of those had she seen recently? They were supposed to be rarer than a chivalrous bandit, but they seemed to be sprouting like weeds in the summertime.

"Who are you?"

"You're welcome," said the woman tersely. *Reaver Ethelwin*, she recalled the Devari saying.

Faye groaned, sitting up higher, examining her wounds. Pink flesh, smooth and taut. No scars. She sniffed. Too bad; she kind of liked scars. They reminded her of who she'd killed or still needed *to* kill. Faye replied offhandedly, "I didn't say thank you."

"No, you didn't. You show an odd lack of respect to someone who just saved your life."

Faye felt her body twitch in annoyance. "And if I didn't want my life saved?" *And if it isn't actually saved?* she thought to herself.

"I can change that right quick," Ethelwin said. "Though with all the severing of nerves, I doubt you'd feel it much." Faye's head still drummed in pain, her wits feeling sluggish as if she were dragging them through mud. "How did I…"

"Get here?" Ethelwin asked. "A good question. One I was prepared to ask you."

Faye groaned, sitting up groggily and looking to her pudgy thief.

Odaren rubbed his arms nervously.

Ethelwin raised a hand. "You need not look like a fish waiting to be gutted, my odoriferous friend. I've already deduced how you arrived in this location." Faye smiled through her wooziness. *Odoriferous Odaren.* She'd have to remember that when she was more cognizant. Ethelwin pointed to a square block on the wall. "It seems transporters were stowed away here. Nine of them." And Faye saw what Ethelwin meant. Nine colored stones. They circled the room, set into the stone wall. They would have looked like just another stone if it weren't for their odd hues — blue, green, orange, brown, tan, white, gold, dark gray and black. The black stone had less dust and spiderwebs clinging to it than the others, she noticed. "Ancient by the looks of them, nothing Reavers of this age would know how to construct, surely. Might I ask what was on the other side?"

Faye's mind flashed back. Pain seared her mind. Guilt wracked her soul. Leah. She'd failed her sister, failed to kill the Shadow King and left Leah to wither and die in the hands of the madman. Then the image of that boy with the cold blue eyes, his expressionless face and… blood. So much blood.

She returned. "I…"

Odaren stepped up to her side protectively, grumbling. "Can't you see she's not fit to jabber on with your prying questions, Reaver?"

Faye put a hand to her head and answered absently, putting her other hand on Odaren's arm—letting him know it was all right, "The city of moon. That's what lies beyond that stone." *And a man who deserves a thousand deaths.*

Faye finally took in the room.

It was huge and round. Intricately spun tapestries covered the walls—a gossamer cloth that looked ages old, yet held no tatters. Same as before, the wall hangings depicted the figures. Nine of them. The Ronin, with one tapestry for each. Their gazes were unnerving, even in cloth. The blazing eyes of Seth, the cool gaze of Hiron, the apathetic cold stare of Dared, the blazing red of Kail, like Gray, just like her dream, and so forth—each bearing their blades in grand poses. She was surprised she remembered her childhood memories in this haze, but all knew the names of the Ronin.

Beside the Ronin's grand figures, carved into the walls, were the nine symbols.

Suddenly she squinted. When she looked again, the tapestries were in tatters, the figures unrecognizable, the colorful threads now muted to a uniform gray from a thousand years, and the seamless stitching was frayed and mouse-eaten. *I was... imagining it?*

503

The rest of the room was barren. She shook her head. It didn't matter. The Reaver was talking, Faye realized, "—other Reavers with more time than I have spent their lives trying to ascertain the purpose of this and other ancient parts of Farbs. The Underbelly is another. Some believe that each of these dusty old reliquaries is a piece to a great puzzle that was forgotten with time, something that will play a great role in the coming events of Farhaven." She wiped a finger along the dusty wall. "I had viewed it as a waste of time. But now?" She gave a breath. "I might have a change of heart. Truly astonishing, to say the least. Still, how did you get the transporter to work? I tried briefly, as have many others, but brute force was useless, and the spark had no effect either."

Faye shook her head. "I'm not sure."

Odaren spoke, "A boy did it."

"A boy?" Ethelwin said, eyes churning. "Who was this 'boy?'"

Odaren shrugged. "He didn't say."

"And you didn't ask? A boy with the power to use an ancient device comes and saves your mistress's life and you didn't even ask his name?"

Odaren's lips flapped and he grew red-faced. "She was on death's door!" he exclaimed. "What was I supposed to do? Invite him to dinner?"

Ethelwin waved the matter aside. "No matter. The greater piece of the puzzle has been unearthed. The other Reavers will be quite thrilled with this find. They've all but given it up in the last few years. No one else comes down here anymore besides chastised Neophytes who are delegated to dust the lower rungs of the Citadel. Them and dour Devari."

Faye rose with the Devari's aid—though she grimaced the whole way, while the woman stared into her soul. "I remember your face now," Ethelwin said. "You were the one who aided us in retaking the Citadel, aren't you?"

"No," she said. "You're mistaken."

The woman exhaled, bemused. "The boy, he called you Faye, didn't he?"

It was Faye's turn to grimace. The shrewd-faced woman was too astute for her own good. She sighed. "What do you want from me?"

"Want? Nothing," she said at last, but her eyes said differently. Faye felt like a piece of hot metal waiting for the forge before the woman's gaze—as if she were waiting to see how to bend her to her purpose. If so, she would surely be disappointed. "Your Darkeye brand tells differently, but if you're a friend of the Arbiter and that boy, I suppose saving your life was the right choice. Just don't make me regret it," she said sharply. "But now you will need rest, and plenty of it." She looked to Dimitri, his fall of black hair nearly obscuring his brooding gray-blue gaze. Faye saw why his gaze was so curious now. One eye blue, the other a light gray. Faye had heard of such a thing. Inhabitants of Morrow—the lost ones, were said to have that gaze. "What are you waiting for? Take her to the Healer's Quarters and see she gets adequate rest."

Rest? Faye scoffed. Rest meant death. She didn't need to rest—she needed to find Gray. She staggered to her feet, making her way to the door. All watched her as if she were mad. But then she stumbled and her muscles suddenly tensed—as if by command. Spark. Dimitri was there too, catching her.

"You wish to undo all the good I did by acting like a stubborn fool?" Ethelwin asked. "Now I've no more time to waste here. Take her to her quarters. Put a guard on her if necessary to ensure she doesn't jump about like a floundering sunfish."

"Wait," she called as Ethelwin neared the door.

504

The Reaver paused.

"Where are we?" she asked, propping herself up.

"Isn't it obvious?" Ethelwin asked, her face an annoyingly smooth mask. "Farbs."

505

Ayva's Redemption

"Let him go." Ayva's voice thundered. She looked down on the glade below, feeling a fire raging through her veins. A fire of hope.

Zane knelt in the mud. His short blonde hair was now red, matted with blood, his lip fat and split, and his hand trembled upon his ribs. Sorrow wanted to overwhelm her at her friend's wretched state, but she pushed it down.

Standing over Zane was a nightmare.

Sithel.

He was nothing like the Sithel she remembered from Farbs. He was no longer human. His body, half of it, running from head to toe, was hard angles of what looked like black glass. But it wasn't glass. *Darkwalker,* Ayva knew. The other half of Sithel was more or less human. The right side of his face was the same pale, sneering face she remembered. A human brown eye peered at her with amusement, disgust, triumph and a tad of… uncertainty. His human right arm was sinewy and black-veined, and his right leg in that ratty boot must've been human as well. Though he'd been tall as a human, he was now lopsided—his human leg still shorter than his demonic leg. Dangling from him were the shredded remains of human clothes and a disgusting, oversized butcher's apron with splotches of old, dried blood and some newer, brighter spots.

Zane looked up wearily at her entrance and his copper eyes gained a light of recognition. Ayva sent a message through the bond, trying to instill hope. *Sorry, I'm late,* she sent, heart panging at the sight of so much blood.

Ayva... Zane sent through their bond, sounding afraid.

Ayva smiled. *It's all right, Zane—I'm here to save you.*

"No..." Zane groaned, this time aloud. *"Run, Ayva... Save your—"*

The demon at his side moved with inhuman speed, curling his black claws into a fist and ramming it into Zane's gut. Zane retched, letting out a gust of air and spitting bile before slumping over as if lifeless. "Pathetic," the demon growled, kicking Zane's limp form in disgust.

Ayva's anger spiked. Every muscle in her flared to life, wanting to dash forward, but she stopped herself.

She noticed the creatures behind Sithel.

Two Vergs. Two nightmares come to life.

The gray-skinned Verg'ss head skimmed even the tallest boughs. The other had a hide as black as night with a thick, oiled chain coiled about its chest. Terrifying and unlike any Verg she had ever seen, these two had metal carapaces covering their chests, backs and arms. It was as if sheets of steel were fused to their skin, most of it curling wickedly, ready to impale any who ventured too close.

The armor seemed strange. A glint of red. Bloodstone. From what Faye had told her, uncut bloodstone would absorb and explode upon contact with the spark. Bloodstone that was cut and fashioned into blades, like the Devari or the Vergs' armor, however, could deflect the spark and flow. It was magic-resistant armor. Avva had to think this through. The blade in her hands beckoned to be used, her arm trembling with restrained power.

Sithel wore his familiar, terrible grin, but it was now accentuated by sharpened teeth and a half glassy-black mouth. "You're late," he announced, looking up from Zane. Ayva took in his eyes. Human and demon, both full of madness. A madness and... *fear?* She doubted it but stowed it away, gripping the Sword of Sun tighter. "You're alone, aren't you? Where's that pathetic witch that rules these woods? Hiding, I assume?" He put an ear to the air as if waiting for her song, and then looked back at Ayva with a cruel grin. "Do you hear that? Nothing. Not a bird, not even a rustling branch, and all because of this. Amazing, isn't it?" He extracted the voidstone from his bulging front pocket and lifted it in the air, marveling at the crackling blue orb. "Such a simple thing, yet with it, even the strongest are made to scrape and grovel. Your friend and leader, Gray, knew this well. I made my mark deep on him, didn't I? But deeper

507

on his grandfather. *Arbiter.*" He laughed. It was dark and menacing. "Gods of the spark, some say. But to me, no more than a sniveling pile of flesh, trembling and weak before the power of the voidstone. Before *my* strength. Just like all the rest. Just like you will be. *Ronin of sun.*"

He knew her identity. But it didn't matter. Ayva was busy assessing the situation. Judging the distance between Sithel and Zane, she knew she couldn't reach Zane before Sithel reached him. She'd have to fight. Besides, she didn't want to flee with Zane in hand. She wanted to fight.

Distantly she was aware of the canopy's gaps, the little holes that allowed the light to flow from above and sink into her, filling her with power. She quickly noted the spots of light about the glade, saving the information for later. She knew that hope gave her power, but she'd have to keep herself to the patches of light for her power to be at its upmost in her spent state.

She started forward.

Sithel snorted. "What, no grand speech? Not going to tell me how I'm wrong or how I deserve justice at the end of your sword?"

"You know what you deserve," Ayva said, not willing to bandy words with a monster. "Anything else will be a waste of breath. So come now. Meet your end."

"Well, my pets, don't just stand there. Can't you see she's begging for a proper greeting?" Sithel's grin deepened, showing rows of sharpened black teeth. "Kill her."

The Vergs obeyed. The hulking beasts shambled forward, attacking. Ayva lifted her hand sending a beam of light, but their dark-plated carapaces reflected it. The black Verg unwrapped its chain and attacked. The chain whipped through the air. Ayva raised the sun blade, and the chain wrapped itself about the sword. She tried to cut, but the Verg was quicker. The black Verg pulled and the Sword of Sun was ripped from her grip, tumbling into the shadows. She cursed as the gray-skinned Verg, and bigger of the two barreled forward. Ayva ducked its strike to her head, feeling the wind part with the force of the monstrous fist.

As she gained her balance, the black Verg swung its leg-thick chain with both hands. The chain snapped with surprising speed. Ayva couldn't dodge it. Panicked, she raised a hand and a glowing shield of light formed in her hands. The chain clashed with the shield and a loud crack sounded. The force of it shuddered through Ayva, sending her to the ground and knocking the air from her lungs. She opened her eyes to see the black

Verg heave the chain over its head once more, smashing down. Seeking to end her. She couldn't form anything in time. *Hope*, she pleaded. A few desperate ideas sprung to mind. Ayva didn't let the shield die. Instead, she tied the threads off, leaving the shield of light suspended in the air, and scrambled back just as the two—chain and shield—collided. The shield shattered like brittle glass. In its place, a splotch of darkness remained, hanging in the air, as if to balance the light's sudden absence. As the shield shattered, the beast's chain smashed into the ground where she had lay, spraying a fountain of mud and water.

Ayva clambered to her feet, breathing hard. Up until now, she moved by purpose, by need. Now terror wormed its way into her thoughts as both huge beasts stormed toward her. She wanted to use the flow, but the golden sun in her mind—the nexus—felt awkward and unfamiliar, the voidstone was making its mark, weakening her power. Ayva's teeth chattered as the Vergs took earth-rattling steps.

Zane, Hannah, Gray, Darius. They all counted on her.

She wouldn't fail.

"Hope," she whispered.

They still came.

Louder. "Hope," she said, still scared, but wanting to believe.

They barreled forth, nearly on her.

No, it can't end this way.

They were almost on her.

"HOPE!" she yelled.

Like a dam bursting, light filled her breast.

Lightbonds.

Threads came to her mind. Complicated golden threads of light seen in the black field of her mind. Each layered and braided a thousand times over again in a mindboggling pattern. But it was too late. The Vergs were upon her. Still she obeyed, tracing their patterns in real life as fast as she could and then thrust them outward. A single dense bar of light raced forward curving in the air, stretching as it flew. It slammed into the beast in a U-shape, right as the gray Verg fell upon her, his foot racing down. The light's force was strong enough to stop the momentum of the creature, blowing it back and against a giant oak. The light bond wrapped around the tree and the Verg's neck, locking him in place.

The beast bellowed, raging against his lightbonds but Ayva put it out of her mind. The black Verg attacked. Again, she sidestepped the huge

509

chain as it tried to slice her in half. The chain didn't stop its momentum as the Verg yanked it back with a snarling grunt, trying to cut her legs from beneath her. Ayva leapt but it caught her boot. She fell to the earth, hard. Blinding pain shot through her heel and up her leg, making her vision become blurred tears. Distantly, she heard the Verg approaching. Its huge chain rattled, feet shuddering the earth. She fought to see straight. The Verg lifted its enormous foot, preparing to flatten her. Ayva rolled to the side as its foot slammed down, barely missing her, and the Verg raised its chain once again.

As it did, Ayva realized her roll had put her in a patch of shadows. The nexus in her mind was dim and hard to touch. She tried to grasp it but it felt slick and the threads in her mind were frail. Too frail to stop the impending chain. Her chest grew tight as if the beast were standing upon it. Hope started to dwindle, to crack. As it did, the threads unraveled even more. The chain descended. Ayva grew frantic, seeing the barbed metal headed towards her and —

She felt light.

On her skin. Warmth crept across her flesh from above. Not a ton, but enough that in that flickering moment she felt it and its energy, and knew what she had to do. As the chain descended, she sent a feeble ray of her last burning light upward. It scorched the canopy above. And light fell. The Verg's thorny chain closed the last bit of distance. The beast's face hungered with delight, knowing it had won and she would be impaled. Sithel's face reflected that same delight and Ayva merely let the warmth fill her, a smile faint upon her lips. It happened in an instant. Her nexus burned like a sun in her mind. Her limbs roared with power. She didn't raise her hands — that would take too long. But she looked up. As she did, the hurtling, wicked chain *stopped*.

Frozen in air, girded by thick threads of gold. Threads so thick and pure they nearly made Ayva squint. She held the chain, and better yet, she still had control of it — she felt it like a rope in her hand. The Verg stared at her confused, still holding the chain. And Ayva felt her power surge inside her. She swung the chain with all her might — using the force from the light above. The Verg realized what was happening. It released the chain, but it didn't matter. The rest of the chain was still wrapped about the Verg's black body. Ayva demanded and the light obeyed. The Verg was flung to the side, its weight colliding with a tree, cracking it in half. It shook its head, stupefied, but Ayva wasn't done. She lobbed the chain like a lasso, wrapping it around the Verg's body, again and again, tighter and tighter—winding it until the carapace on the Verg's body threatened to crack, and it groaned in pain. At last, she let the chain drop. The black-skinned Verg struggled uselessly, but the spiked chains dug into its thick hide with every useless squirm, and she looked away, casting the creature from her mind.

As she did, the larger Verg gave a spittle-inducing bellow and the tree it was bound to groaned—its roots ripped from the earth.

It charged.

Ayva waited, still staring at the ground, seeing the monster barreling forth in the upper field of her vision. The ground rattled. Her body shook. Its bellow grew. Still she waited. At the last moment, she sprayed a tiny bit of light into the beast's eyes and dove.

Temporarily blinded, the Verg howled, stumbling. Its head collided with the boulder behind her. A fissure ran up the center of the stone, and the gray-skinned Verg slumped, unconscious or dead. Either way, it was over.

Ayva looked up, slowly, coolly.

Her hand quaked with power and she lost herself to it. *Hope.* The word pulsed in her chest. Ayva's lungs felt like fire in her chest, but her gaze felt peculiar. She felt as if she looked out from two glowing lanterns on the scene before her—all things—trees, bushes, figures, seemed bathed in light.

Sithel stared at her in disbelief, and in his glassy body she saw her reflection.

Golden.

It was still her, but she glowed now—light seemed to saturate the air about her and her eyes shone like burnished gold.

"Enough," she declared in a voice that almost surprised her—strong, loud, throaty. She knew whom it sounded like. But she didn't waste time thinking on it as she lifted a hand, seeing threads come to life. "You've sowed enough darkness to last a lifetime. No more." She loosed the threads. They snapped rigidly, coming to life. A *solarflare.* The word, the description came unbidden. A whip of light flared to life and she gripped it, letting its long shaft coil on the ground.

Sithel smiled cruelly, showing his black teeth again as he lifted the crackling blue voidstone. "You pitiful fool, don't you realize by now? Spark, flow, all of it is worthless beneath the power of the voidst—"

511

Ayva struck. The solarflare's tip flicked the voidstone from Sithel's grip and the stone flew, landing in a shallow puddle where it hissed, then fell dormant. There was an eerie silence. Sithel's grin faltered and he snarled, charging. Ayva flung the whip and it lashed around Sithel's neck. His thick black tendons strained as he clawed at it but his fingers burned beneath its touch. Steam rose where it burned his neck, and his eyes bulged.

"No... wait..." Sithel said, reaching out. Ayva released a breath and used her whole body, yanking on the whip, sending the demon smashing into a nearby tree trunk with a shower of bark and splinters. Sithel staggered to his feet. "You don't—" And Ayva pulled, hard, smashing him back into the ground before he could spew his filth. This time he was slower to rise. Again, she wrenched on the solarflare in her hands, slinging the demon into another trunk, making the thick trunk crack and shudder beneath the impact. Sithel groaned, then gave a terrible guttural roar and slashed at the tether about his neck. The solarflare snapped and Sithel rose, panting.

His eyes flickered from Ayva to the voidstone and he dove. She let him. He grabbed it and scrambled back to his feet. Turning to her, the half-man cackled, chest rattling and boughs shaking with the sound of his horrible laughter. "You simple stupid girl... Now you're mine. You and your Ronin will fall here before ever seeing the tide of darkness that will consume the land. Be grateful. Consider this a merciful death to what's in store for the others." Spittle dribbled from Sithel's foaming mouth as his eyes frothed with rage, but Ayva felt calm as she lifted her hand. The sword that was embedded in the nearby tree flew and slapped into her waiting palm. It was warm, glowing. She stepped forward when her legs trembled, wanting to buckle. Why?

Sithel saw this and his eyes grew craven, his lips peeling back to show his sharpened teeth. "You're drained, aren't you? Powerful but still untrained in the ways of the flow. If you continue to fight you'll die." The demon stepped forward. "You've lost."

He   was   right.
No, she thought inwardly. *Not now.*

Sithel took another step, lifting the stone. Darkness pulsed from it, eating at her and one knee bowed. She looked up through bared teeth—her smooth face cracking. Her power started to wane as hope fled her. Light leaked from her body, until... Ayva remembered the blade.

The demon's black claw stepped forward again, only paces away, looming over her.

Help me, she pleaded. Silence. She asked again, louder. Still silence.

Sithel was almost upon her, voidstone approaching, and she felt her heart twist like a wet rag as he pressed the crackling stone forward. "This is how it ends, it seems. How sad, don't you think? You die before the world even knows you were ever alive."

She closed her eyes, feeling the golden steel as an entity.

At last, it listened. She gasped, closing her eyes in shock as a fire burned through her veins, starting at her wrist and shooting up her arm. As it reached her chest it made her heart thunder. Sweat flushed from her skin and Ayva opened her eyes. The world burst with color. Fear rose at the power inside her. She felt it leaking from her pores, her eyes, even her mouth, like steam from a kettle, but Ayva gripped it and snapped her mouth shut, holding the power within. She forced her fear down, focusing on the single word *Hope,* and the leaking stopped.

Sithel was upon her, slashing. She sidestepped the strike and brought her blade down. He slipped away from it, diving in closer and Ayva grabbed the dagger in her back belt with her other hand, twisting in a full circle. She slammed it into his black chest. The blade's tip found its mark, then shattered beneath Sithel's obsidian skin, but it bought her all the time she needed. Sithel staggered, frozen for a moment, and Ayva dropped both blades and dove. Her fingertips felt its smooth glassy surface and she clung to it, prying it free from Sithel's grip as she skidded across the mud-slicked ground.

513

When she looked up, the voidstone was clutched to her chest and Sithel was laughing, standing over her. "You think the voidstone will save you?" He raised his dark claw in the air. "You are a foolish little girl after all. You forget I don't need a stone to finish what I started."

"Now!" Ayva yelled.

The Enchantress wriggled free of the tree she'd been hiding in, moss and bark dropping from her form.

Sithel backpedaled.

Ayva rose. "Merciful? To kill you as you stand now would be merciful. But I hear a lie on your tongue every time you speak. You're afraid of something. Something buried deep. Whatever you fear is worse than the death I can give you, Sithel." Ayva said. "So consider this my gift to you. Your greatest fear."

***

Sithel twisted and saw her.

The Enchantress gave a predatory grin from within her gleaming aura of gold as her head swiveled to look at the crackling blue orb in Ayva's hands... The voidstone... Too far from his grip. Too far to use and stop her power. The witch opened her mouth. He lunged, reaching for the voidstone before her terrible song hit him.

But he was too slow.

The layered song smashed into him—sounding like a reedy cry and a dreadful bellow—and the memory returned, slamming home freezing him in place.

He was small, maybe ten or twelve. Standing in the dusty, bloody shop—

"NOOO!" he bellowed, ripping himself back to the present moment. He snatched his head with his clawed and human hand, screaming, trying to cover his ears and shake the memory free. But again it came, creeping across his vision, slowly, painfully. Sithel cast a hateful glare to the Enchantress who floated above him through his darkening vision. "I won't let you. I won't let you take me back there." He staggered forward. "I won't go back. You don't know the first thing about what—" But his words fell short as her eyes flared with anger and power, issuing a golden stream of light, her song growing. Sithel scrambled for Ayva, but she was too far away. Her face was not one of gloating or anger, but of pity. It was the last thing he saw before the memory consumed him.

A rage-filled roar sounded from the back of the butcher's shop.

Sithel was rooted in his ratty brown rags. He busied himself by rubbing the greasy rag across the wood chopping block, marred by thousands of cuts. The roar continued, growing louder and Sithel scrubbed harder, fear rising in his chest like a balloon. The door crashed open, pounding steps nearing Sithel.

"Where is it?" a deep voice asked, standing behind him.

"Where is what?" he asked, voice trembling, not turning.

"Turn and face me, you rat."

And Sithel did.

He faced the most vile, putrid looking man he'd ever met. He thought he'd met the worst of them. Over the last three years since being orphans, he and his brother had been apprenticed to nearly two dozen artisans. It was easy to explain how he'd got here, standing before this vile creature. Sithel had a knack for 'messing up.' When he would, and he always did, he and his brother were dragged back, often by their ears, to the city registry, which administered Covian slaves. With a sigh upon seeing him and his brother, those quill-wielding mouth-breathers would turn around and coldly pawn them off onto some even meaner, nastier and often more incompetent artisan with all the care of trading bushels of wheat. Until they'd ended up here. Sithel still wasn't sure if he messed up on purpose, hoping against hope that anywhere was better than before, but each time he was wrong. Each time was worse. The Butcher, Agron Maleus, was the worst of them all.

With missing teeth, a lazy eye, a pudgy, almost baby face and a lumpy body — as if he'd grown boils about his body that had formed into layers of fat, the butcher looked scary, almost not human. 'Birth-defects,' his brother explained to him. 'An inbred piece of garbage,' Sithel had sneered in reply. Sithel refused to call him a human name out loud, or at least, he tried his best. Butcher or Sunha was all he deserved. He doubted the butcher's soiled dark clothes were ever washed. The only thing that he kept clean was a white apron that he made Sithel or his brother wash daily. It bulged against his bulk as the butcher loomed over Sithel.

"I... I don't know what you're talking about," Sithel said.

"You lie. I saw you. You were eyeing my hiding spot just the other day and now it's gone. Where is it? Where's the silver purse from this morning's market earnings?"

Sithel had taken it. He'd stashed it and the bastard would never find it. He'd already decided about this moment. He'd rather die than let the man have that silver. He wouldn't spend another day living this pathetic life. If that meant death, so be it. If not, he'd take the silver and he and his brother could leave this awful, stinking heap of a city. Covai could burn behind him for all he cared. But he'd never tell the Butcher a peep. Sithel opened his mouth to lie again and —

A hard smack that jarred his brain and rattled his teeth — harder than he'd ever felt sent him sprawling. Agron was strong. Muscle sat beneath those layers of fat. And Sithel was small. It felt like ages until his head cleared. He felt his lip. It was split and bleeding and he felt a tooth loose in his mouth. His head still rung painfully and he realized his whole body was trembling. In all his life, he'd never been hit that hard. "Sunha..." he began.

Again, the fist struck. This time in the gut. Agron's meaty fist rammed

515

him in the stomach and he gagged, feeling his small, brittle ribs cracking beneath the butcher's ruthless strike.

"I won't stand for a single lie from your stinking lips," Agron said, his fat lips slurring the words. "You'll tell me where it is, or I'll slit you from ear to ear right here, right now and leave your corpse for the buzzards."

Sithel knew he couldn't lie his way out of this one. He was going to die. Unless... Unless... The words came, almost unbidden. "Calid. Calid took it. I swear. I told him not to, I told him it was too much, but he couldn't..." He had to stop to swallow blood that was filling his mouth. "I couldn't stop him. It was Calid."

The butcher's ugly face twisted, looking both confused and mollified. It's working... Sithel thought. "I don't believe you. He's the better of you two. Don't you lie to me. Only thing worse than a worthless apprentice is a lying one. I won't stand for either, but I'll gut you right here if you're the latter."

Sithel shook his head, trying to hold back his trembling. But he couldn't. He couldn't stop his tears. Tears of fear. He didn't want to die. He'd seen death—it was terrifying. "I swear, Sunha. I swear it was Calid. I swear it on my life."

"On your life, is it?" Agron gave an awful laugh—the same condescending rumble that made his whole mouth twist repulsively. "An apt phrase if ever there were one," said his sweaty, foul-smelling Sunha. "Let's put that to the test, shall we?" Sithel shook his head. The man had threatened him before, beat him, but had never actually threatened death. But Agron had madness in his eyes as he stomped forward and snatched a fistful of the boy's hair, dragging him kicking and screaming, the sharp pain making his eyes water.

"You... you can't kill me. You won't!" Sithel screamed. "The guards, they'll—"

The reply was dark, coarse, cutting him off. "—they'll hear nothing. You're just a worthless scrap of meat that a few coppers in the right hands will see to the depths of the Boneyard. In a few days, you'll be mixed in with the rest of the pathetic creatures that couldn't pull their weight. How do you find that, hmm? Your bones indistinguishable from those of a cerabul or hogs for slaughter."

True terror entered Sithel and he scrambled to grab anything to stop or defend himself. Pans, knives, hammers, but his fingers only clipped the well-notched chopping block. Sithel wasn't strong enough to hold on as he was dragged like a sack of meat by his master's brute strength. Finally, the big butcher stopped, throwing him to the dusty ground. "Calid!" Agron called.

Calid entered the dusky shop, ducking out of the lighted back alley where he'd been scrubbing down the killing block. Sithel twisted, looking up at Calid's entrance. His brother was named after one of the Ronin Hiron's twin daggers. The smaller of the two. A worthy name. Whereas Sithel's whore of a mother had hated him more upon birth, giving him the old tongue name for "snake." True to his name, Calid was small for his age, smaller even than Sithel. But where Sithel was lanky and sunken-chested, Calid had muscle to his bones. Not much, of course. No Diaon could eat enough to build anything more than a lean frame, but Calid had the muscle to chop the meat into smaller portions in one stroke, and to lift himself up to the loft without groaning. Sithel hated how simple things seemed for Calid. Worse than that, he looked nothing like his brother. Calid was chestnut-haired, green-eyed and tan skinned. Sithel had skin paler than a Narim dweller, dark brown eyes and stringy black hair. He clearly looked out of place in a City of Sun and dust.

Calid took off the wool cap that he always wore as he entered the butcher's hut. Upon seeing Sithel, his brother's smile wilted. "Brother, what's going on?"

517

"What an excellent question! Why don't you enlighten your better half, my worthless Diaon, hmm?" His master glared down at Sithel, waiting for him to answer, but his tongue felt swollen in his mouth. He tried to speak, to tell Sunha his lies and explain it was his fault, that he'd stolen the silver from the pouch this morning, but he remained silent. Coward.

"No?" Agron asked and barked a terrible laugh. "Silence. Perhaps incriminating, or perhaps trying to save the skin of your dear brother. So be it. Calid, do you care to hear what your brother has said about you?"

Calid still looked to Sithel, questioning. "Brother..."

The fat butcher spoke, this time his voice devoid of laughter, "Your dear brother here accused you of filching the silvers from this morning's market. Is he telling the truth? Was it you?"

Calid said nothing.

"Then it was you."

Still, his brother remained silent. A stoic silence, watching, his eyes burning into Sithel. And Sithel felt anger. Anger for his brother's strength, anger for the accusation in his eyes and anger for the sympathy in them too. He felt rage at his weakness. He was always false, weak and groveling.

He worked just as hard as Calid, who was rewarded with praise, while he was always beaten. He hated Calid, but even more than he hated Calid, he hated himself. And Sithel stood, shakily. It still hurt to breathe, his ribs aching, but he ignored it and continued. "Well? What are you waiting for?" he asked, impatient. "You know if you tell the truth it'll go easier on you and on me. Just tell Sunha that you did it and it'll all be over. Tell him it was your fault and not mine."

"Tell him… it was my fault…" his brother repeated.

Sithel nodded. Hearing his brother's voice made a strain of fear, of hesitancy rise inside his body, but he pushed it down.

"Is he lying?" the fat butcher asked. "I don't like liars. I can't stand 'em." Agron Maleus put the sharp edge of the meat clever to Sithel's throat, and Sithel felt his skin break as it cut closer—the butcher slowly applied pressure.

"You did it," Sithel stammered. "Just tell him you did it!"

Silence.

Heartbeats sounded, pounding loudly. Until…

"I did it," his brother said at last.

Sithel felt all his fear flee, but then—

The butcher roared. His cleaver cut the air and hacked into his brother's skull, and stuck. His brother's eyes were wide, staring at Sithel, blood leaking from the ghastly wound in his head, and dripping down his mouth. He tried to speak, but nothing came. Fear and confusion held Sithel. Then Calid crumpled to the ground. The butcher's animal-like bellow continued to rise and fall as he fell to the floor, taking sickening, sloppy hacks into Calid's corpse. Blood splashed in the air.

Out of breath, the butcher rose.

Sithel was frozen in shock and terror. He wanted to run, to cry, anything, but he was simply mute, staring at his brother's lifeless body.

Agron took off his apron and threw it to the bloody ground, then raised his meaty forearm, pointing to it as it soaked in his brother's blood. "Put it on."

Sithel shook his head.

"Do it or I'll gut you right here, just like I did him." And he raised his meat cleaver, still dripping with Calid's blood.

Trembling, Sithel picked it up, putting the butcher's apron around his neck, his numb fingers tying it, fumbling. He clenched his eyes, trying not to think about why the apron felt warm. Warm from Calid's blood.

518

"You'll wear that from now on. Wear that and know that it was your hand that killed your brother."

"But I—" And his Sunha smiled. And Sithel knew true evil, understanding. "You knew… You knew the whole time that I was lying, that it wasn't Calid's fault, but mine."

"Now live with the knowledge. Live with your brother's blood on your hands because you were too weak, too cowardly and too pathetic to admit the truth." Agron paused at the door, a cruel smile lighting his hideous face from the Covian sun outside. "And Sithel? Don't forget. Put the coin back where you found it—or the hogs will feast twice tonight."

And the vision broke.

* * *

Ayva looked down upon Sithel as he returned to the world. If a monster could look ashamed, he looked it. "You didn't see it, did you?"

Ayva's silence seemed enough of a testimony. Somehow she had—as if granted the vision by the Enchantress seen through a gray haze. The vision would give her nightmares. But the truth was even worse for the creature before her… he had killed his own brother.

Words started to tumble from Sithel's mouth, "Don't you understand, you damn fools? *I* bear the hatred my brother's heart couldn't. The hatred that is needed to survive in this godforsaken world." He laughed, looking around, nodding to himself. "In the end, he was simply too soft. Too weak to do what was necessary… *That's* why I still live and he doesn't."

Ayva said nothing.

Sithel changed tact. "You're too late to stop the darkness that will consume you."

"Why? Why did you do it?" she asked.

"Vaster, you mean? Vaster was just a cleansing fire—a plague that will rid one Great Kingdom of its weak and feeble, and leave the strong in its place—those who have the will to survive. Can you see it?" he asked and a crazed light entered his dark eyes. "No more suffering, Ayva. No more famine. No wars, no begging, no slaves, no kings, no peasants. A world filled with only the strong. *That* is my master's image." His grin widened. "The start of it at least."

Ayva stood over him, sword point to his throat, gazing down at the creature before her. He was mad. Crazed. She couldn't begin to tell

519

him how insane that was. There would always be weakness. Killing off thousands of people wouldn't solve that. And weakness wasn't bad; it was relative and a necessary part of life. For instance, she was weaker than Darius in strength-of-arms, but stronger in knowledge of Farhaven. What was strength and weakness after all? If he weighed it by the ability to simply survive, then insects should rule the world, for she'd known bugs with a surprising ability to continue to exist, while great men and women had died before their time. Even if one could determine 'true' strength and then weed the strong from the weak, killing only meant a world without humanity. A world she didn't want to live in. Still, Ayva couldn't help herself from asking, "With no kings or queens, who would rule in this world of yours?"

"No one would. For once, men and women would be in charge of their own lives."

"And your master in charge of theirs?"

Sithel debated this for a moment, lying on the ground, then grinned. "Naturally—gods don't mingle with mortals."

She held back a shiver. She wanted to hate the man and his twisted ideals. But she only felt pity. She abstained from philosophy and delved to the heart of the matter. "Your master, who is he?"

Sithel writhed on the ground like a worm, pushing himself back, scrambling away from the tip of her gleaming blade. "You fool. My master is not a who, but a *what*. It's an idea. A man or woman can die, but an idea? An idea is immortal, unassailable. And this idea is truth *itself*. 'Strength is life, weakness, death,'" he crooned, then began to cackle as he pushed himself up, back against a tree.

Ayva sighed. "How pathetic. You think I don't see through you? That sad attempt to hide the truth? You don't know anything, do you?" She snorted. "You're still just a pawn being played to die. I bet you don't even know the name of your pitiful master."

Sithel's black eyes flared with rage and then… recognition. He smiled, showing rows of black teeth. "Clever, girl. But you won't incite me to tell you anything. All you need to know before you die is that what you fear is already in motion. Whole towns swayed to the truth of our mantra. Good people, people who stand in the light, turned to darkness… brothers betraying brothers… small cities reverting to terrible laws in order to 'protect' themselves. Aberton? Aster Plains? More men die in Aster in a day than fell upon the battle of the sands. You see, the bloodshed grows every day, and with it, our idea thrives. An idea that will consume Farhaven slowly but surely, until you find yourself looking behind you, watching the shadows. And then you will fall. Killed not by a creature, but by the very people you seek to protect."

Ayva pressed the gleaming Sword of Sun harder against Sithel's dark throat, drawing both black and red blood. "Fall to your knees, beg forgiveness right here and now, and I'll consider simply putting you in shackles and dragging you back to Vaster for justice."

Sithel sniffed, eyeing the blade before him. "And if I decline?"

"Thousands are suffering, dying for what you did, for destroying the Macambriel," she said, rage wanting to snuff her hope. *So many*, she thought. But she took a deep breath, embracing hope. "I suppose I'll have to find what justice I can, here and now."

"Justice at the end of a blade," Sithel replied. "My, how amusing when our truths collide. Show me then, holy Ronin. Kill me and prove me right, that there's only justice if you're the one holding the blade. That strength means everything." He had tears forming in his eyes. "That there's no morality in this world. No justice. No good or evil. That even the most horrid of deeds holds no meaning in the end... None of it matters. Only strength." He grabbed the blade and his dark claw hissed with steam. Sithel cried out in pain, but he held on. "Do it! Kill me and prove me right! KILL ME!" He bellowed the final words, and Ayva pulled her blade sharply, causing a gush of black blood to fountain into the air.

Sithel's dark claws fell to the ground—each of his jagged, black digits burning in the soil, severed from his demonic hand. Crying out, Sithel gripped his bleeding stump, trying to stem the flow of terrible black liquid. It continued to ooze and his haunting cry continued as he staggered to his feet, stumbling about the glade, grabbing anything he could for balance.

As his human hand leaned on the boulder in the center of the glade, Ayva took a deep breath. Bonds of light came to life and encircled Sithel's hand. One layer and then the next, over and over, until his human arm was lashed by a thousand cords of gold to the immovable boulder behind him. He seemed unaware of this as he reached to grab his black digits. But they were too far away. Sticks and leaves stuck to his black nub as it bled more, burning and hissing at the air. Tears leaked down his inhuman face as he slumped in his strange, demonic form.

Ayva let the mantle of light drop and rushed to Zane's side.

Was he alive?

521

His chest didn't rise. Panicked, she put her fingers before his nose, when there was an agonizing cry and an awful ripping sound from behind her.

Still bound to the boulder was his human arm, shreds of flesh hanging from where he'd used inhuman strength to rip it free. Ayva launched to her feet, sprinting. There was a sound in the distance, rushing and loud, but she ignored it and prepared bonds of light. Sithel was fast. He wove through trees, moving faster than should be possible but she wouldn't let him out of her sight. The rushing sound grew louder with every step. Two bonds of light flew through the air and wrapped around a tree's trunk, just shy of Sithel. She shot another. It hit Sithel square in the back and he stumbled. But as Ayva let the light bond fly, sharp pain stabbed in her heart. She gripped her chest as her nexus stuttered—the ball of light in her mind, winking in and out, like a fluttering candle. *Too much power.* She pushed it down. Sithel saw her, fumbled to his feet with curses and growls. Ayva raised her hand. Light formed in her hand and he froze, but as it did, she watched ice trail along her arm, freezing it in place. The light in her mind stuttered.

Sithel's maw split in a jagged, bloody smile.

He stepped behind the trunk of a huge tree. Ayva ran after him, gripping the Sword of Sun and burst out of a stand of trees and lifted her hand, not caring about the consequences—even if it killed her, she would end his half-life—preparing to level all her courage.

She found herself staring at a wide, torrential river filled with jagged rocks. She followed the trail of blood, seeing it end at the river's edge. Jumping into that river meant death. Rocks, both seen and unseen, could split her head. And the gushing speed all but promised to drown her in seconds if the rocks didn't crack her skull open first. Her arm was frozen, limp, useless. And she had failed.

Sithel was gone.

※ ※ ※

Helix came to and pain flared. He lie unmoving, but saw leaf litter move before his face. He was alive… and in a forest? Forest? Wait, Seria. The Great Kingdom of Water. Had he made it?

No… Memories sifted back.

Zane. Then… His sister—a girl swinging from tree branches, dead.

The pain and awful fire from Zane. Distantly he remembered fending off the torrent of flames and a bubble of water? But it was a vague image in his mind. He came back to his body and the moment.

His skin burned. He knew he wasn't on fire anymore, but his skin felt oddly hot. He'd gotten a sunburn a few times when working the ships back home in Median. This felt worse than a sunburn and it was all over his body. He winced, feeling tears run down his cheeks from the pain—not crying, just his body's reaction. He breathed shallow breaths, watching the leaf litter move before his mouth, as he tried to look around and gain his bearings. Slowly he twisted, feeling his neck crack. Movement made his hot skin flare with agony anew. He saw a woman... or a girl? She turned, showing half of her features. Light blue eyes, blonde hair, freckles across the bridge of her small nose and cheeks. Despite his pain, Helix felt more blood rush to his limbs and the pain increased. He cursed his young, hormonal self. She was utterly beautiful.

The young woman, he deduced, for she was perhaps several years older than him, was standing, talking to...

What in the...

He blinked, trying to make sense of what he saw. It was her. The Enchantress. But seeing her like this, his anger seemed to dissolve. The Enchantress stood before the girl. For all practical purposes, she looked like a woman in her prime. Facing him, he could see her full figure, and what he saw made him question if he was still dreaming. Instead of hair, the Enchantress had trailing autumnal and green leaves. Her skin was beautiful on her face, almost translucent, but the skin on her arms, and legs were strange and familiar. He squinted. *Bark!* That's what it was. Intricate bark with an almost human skin tone, if a little more brown. As before, the Enchantress was encased in a glow, but instead of gold, it was a bright bluish-green which reminded him of the encrustation that sometimes formed on copper spyglasses. Her cloak was breathtaking. Thousands upon thousands of multicolored leaves interlocked together, trailing to the ground, like a suit of nature's scalemail. It left her shoulders and upper chest bare, revealing much of her ample... He blushed. Blushing made blood rush to his skin, and blood rushing to his skin made pain flare in his already skin-burnt cheeks. He cursed silently. *Really, Helix? Her bark skin is making you blush?* But she was terribly beautiful in a strange, inhuman way.

They both stood over Zane.

523

"Is he going to die?" the girl asked. He was surprised by the calmness in her voice, but Helix could hear the lump she swallowed afterward, even from here.

"He'll live. I've healed what I can with what little power I've left, but I must warn you. He won't be the same Zane when he wakes."

"Why not?" There was an edge to the girl's voice. She gripped the sword tighter, as if preparing to use it. "What did you do?"

"It's not what I did, but what that demon did." The Enchantress neared, touching Zane's head sweetly, caressing his cheek. "Reading a person's fears gives you a unique insight into their psyche. I fear Hannah's death will leave a rift your friend may not recover from. You have to be ready for that, Ayva."

Ayva nodded reluctantly as if she understood. Helix listened, confused, but deeply interested. He didn't want to move. It hurt to move.

"I forgot to mention that this is yours," the Enchantress said. Helix couldn't see what the woman handed over, but he thought it was a... sheath?

"What do we do next?" Ayva asked.

"A battle has been won, but the war is still to come."

524

"War," Ayva repeated. "I don't want a war. I just wanted to stop the sickness of Vaster and find the blade..." She fell silent and knelt at Zane's side, gently cupping her friend's cheek. "Hannah's dead. Dead." She repeated it again, as if trying to make it real. "Gods, Zane, will you ever forgive me? If I had only been quicker, if I'd just stayed near you none of this would've ever happened." She shook her head, shaking away tears.

"The 'if' game is a dangerous one, child. But two can play it. Let us 'if,' shall we? *If* you hadn't left them, then you would never have faced me. And in so doing, never have faced your fears and retrieved the blade, and you would have fallen to Sithel, just like Hannah and Zane."

Helix saw Ayva nod reluctantly. "Zane," she whispered. "He's never going to be the same is he?"

"No," the Enchantress answered bluntly.

Helix felt a lump form in his throat.

Ayva continued, softly—barely loud enough for Helix to hear. She looked up to the canopy above, brows pinching as she whispered, "Where are you two light-blinded fools? If only you were here. But you're not. You're gone. A thousand miles away from here." She laughed. It sounded crazed. "Light, I don't even know if you're alive or dead, or if you even made it to Farbs." Helix swallowed for her, feeling the weight of her sorrow even from here. Ayva scrubbed away her tears roughly then said confidently, taking a deep breath, "No, I know you made it. But wherever you are, come back soon."

The Enchantress put a hand on her shoulder, a golden glow surrounding her.

"I never expected it to be this way." She was silent for a long moment as she looked down to something that she'd laid in the dirt.

Helix gasped. He couldn't help it.

The two twisted, looking at him.

"He's awake," the Enchantress said.

Ayva rose, wiping away tears and approached. "You're alive," she said with a sad smile. "But how? I felt Zane's fire from nearly a mile away. You should be dead."

He felt awkward. He'd been eavesdropping and here she was pouring her heart out for *him*, a stranger, even after he'd found out her friends were all dead or missing. *'Should be' a Great Kingdom here. 'Should be' uninjured, without burns from some random guy I just met. 'Should be'... *He growled inwardly. *'Should be' can make a boat and sail it into the Abyss for all I care,* is what he thought. But Helix's tongue was thick in his throat. Ayva seemed to note his silence and helped him to his feet. Pain radiated across his body, every inch of skin burning anew, and more tears leaked from the corner of his eyes. His skin felt as if it were going to crack and burst like one big boil. But he didn't stop and he didn't groan in pain. Granted, he did stumble. *Once.* And Ayva reached out an arm, supporting him.

"Thanks," he mumbled, standing straight.

She nodded.

Once he caught his breath from the pain, he looked down at the blade in her hand. "That sword. Sepharis take me," he cursed, using the god of water's name in vain, "that's a Ronin's blade, isn't it?"

The pommel was simple, like a perfect golden bauble. The blade itself started wide, then tapered at its center, then broadened again to a diamond-like head. Beneath the steel, light churned as if a golden sun were embedded just below its surface. How did a girl have a blade like that? Surprisingly, she held it with confidence. Her slender grip on the blade seemed right. The girl's blue eyes would occasionally dart to the blade. Each time a wave of elation, hope and disgust would flash across

525

her features.

"Who are you?" Ayva asked, sheathing the blade with a click into a white and gold sheath. All her sorrow and hesitancy from earlier seemed to be washed away like a strong tide.

"Who are *you* is a better question," he replied, arching a single brow. Hells, even *that* hurt! "And what're you doing with a Ronin's blade? And not just a Ronin's blade, that's the missing the blade of sun, isn't it?"

"I..." she almost answered, then her eyes fanned wide. "Dalic, the Algasi—"

"Ask and receive," the Enchantress said.

The woods rustled to Helix's left and men marched out of the woods, bloodied and half-dead. Five in total. Helix stiffened. He'd heard stories of the Algasi. All had. Tan-clothed warriors who had originally hailed from the City of Sun, Vaster, but were now considered nomads who left a trail of bodies wherever they went. Of course, something about the rumors always seemed *off* to Helix, but he couldn't put a finger on why. Still the rumors must've been ingrained in his bones because he couldn't help but shy a few steps back, readying himself to run if need be. Even bloody and injured, they looked fearsome.

The tallest one drew Helix's gaze.

Each of the men looked like serpents with a blade—muscled and lean—but this man was clearly born to wield a weapon. As he stalked forward out of the shadows of the woods, he held a dark grace. Helix could only see his piercing blue eyes as a white-cloth mask, unlike his brother's black shrouds, covered the rest of his face. Those eyes looked tired. So tired.

There was a slight rush of wind. Helix peeked over his shoulder and saw that the Enchantress was gone. Ayva seemed to notice too, but her surprise only lasted moments as she looked back to the Algasi.

"Welcome back," Ayva said, smiling at last.

A Reunion

Faye's heart pounded… Farbs.

Was he truly here? She knew she didn't have long. The woman had healed her, but it was only temporary. The bloodpact was still killing her, eating her alive. She could still make it if he were truly here. Faye brushed herself off and moved to Odaren, grabbing the dagger from the pudgy man's belt. "What are you planning to do?" he asked her in a low voice so the Devari wouldn't hear.

She cupped his face almost sweetly. "This isn't done. Not yet." He saw her look and she turned, but then paused at the Devari's side, looking back, "Are you coming?"

Odaren's face split with a grin, and for the first time she didn't see his mismatched rows of yellowed teeth, or the balls of dough he had for cheeks or the black pebbles he had for eyes. She did notice all that. But she also thought that if Odaren hadn't been placed in a den of evil, he might have been just a simple farmer in the Narim Foothills—making some stocky Narim farmwoman, if not happy, at least content. As it were, she knew the pudgy thief was now hers for life. Part of her chafed at that thought. Part of her didn't.

At an intersection, Faye stopped short and Odaren nearly crashed into her.

"What is it?" Dimitri asked.

Several one-striped Reavers and a pair of Devari passed around them, and she waited until they moved down another corridor and the three of them were alone. "Which way to the nearest courtyards?"

Dimitri hesitated, then inclined his head west. "Just beyond there, past Wayfarer's Hall."

"And to the Healer's Quarters?"

"In the eastern end of the Citadel. Why?"

Opposite directions. She nodded. "I see. Then this is where we part, dear Devari."

He looked at her, confused. "I'm afraid I can't allow that. Reaver Ethelwin gave me strict orders to see you to the healer's quarters and I'm certain Arbiter Ezrah will wish to see you and cure your ailment."

"Unfortunately, that would be a grand waste of the Arbiter's time."

Dimtri's thick brows knit in puzzlement.

"Even the high-and-mighty Arbiter Ezrah won't be able to do anything for me. That is, nothing but watch me die. *Slowly and painfully,* I might add." That'd be just her luck, having Gray's grandfather, one of the most powerful men in the world, watch her die, helpless to stop it. Then short-ly after, he would discover that his grandson had died—because of her.

Dimitri gave her a hard stare, clearly trying to deduce if she was lying or not. She stared back, unflinchingly. "I'm sorry, my lady," Dimitri said at last, shaking his head. "He's a good man, the Arbiter. He helped me when I was… sick. Trust me, he'll know what to do." *My lady?* When she said nothing he added, "You will come willingly, won't you?"

Faye gave a tight-lipped smile. "Oh, of course. Orders are orders, after all."

"I'm glad you understand." Dimtri started forward, yanking on her arm.

But Faye didn't budge.

Dimitri looked back, eyes widening in comprehension. "Don't—"

Faye didn't let him finish his sentence. She moved. She circled her arm, pulling against the weakness of his thumb, the weakest part of his grip. Despite Dimitri's considerable strength, her whole body against his thumb ripped his grip free. He reached out to snatch her arm again but she slammed her elbow into his nose, making him fountain blood. Stunned only for a moment, Dimitri reached for his blade. He moved quickly and she was tired and sluggish, but determined—not willing to stop. She knew his draw would kill her. Faye didn't slow. She'd rather die by the blade than waste away in some healer's quarter. Dimitri drew, steel ringing, and then… he seemed to hesitate. His hand stalled on his blade, a look in his eyes. And Faye head-butted him—hard. The Devari collapsed in a heap. Faye winced, feeling sorry for the man.

She grabbed his feet and glanced up to Odaren who stared slack-jawed. "Mind helping me?"

Odaren's trance broke. And together they lugged his heavy body, propping him against the wall. Now asleep, she noticed he had no sorrow on his features. He looked almost peaceful. He had let her get away, she knew. Faye didn't know why, but something in her felt for this man and for his sorrow. He'd lost something, just like her, she knew.

"Thank you," she said.

Odaren pretended not to watch. "What's the plan now?"

Faye rose. The hallway was empty, but it wouldn't be for long. She wasn't sure how much longer she had to live, or if she'd even make it to the courtyard of the Citadel, but she stumbled onward. If she died, at least she would die on her feet in the sun. "Come on, we're almost done." Then Faye muttered to herself, *Gray, you better be here.*

And Odaren followed.

Ayva's Last Hope

Ayva let a tired smile slip through. Seeing Dalic amble out of the woods, his men flanking him, made something in her break and she had to fight back tears. She realized her heart had been hardening up until now. Now it softened. Despite all the death and suffering, he'd made it. "You're truly a sight for sore eyes, sunla," she said, using the Sand Tongue word for friend.

But Dalic didn't look pleased. He paused at the edge of the glade with his warriors at his side. His eyes roved the woods, his muscles tense. "Back?" Dalic asked slowly, doubtfully. "How are you so certain? Are we truly back, or are we still in the witch's nightmare? And if this is not our dream, how are you so certain it's not yours?"

The question made Ayva waver. She hadn't thought of that. Could he be right? Could this all have been one long prolonged vision from the Enchantress? The sword in her hands, Zane's rage, even Hannah's death? Everything from the moment they entered the woods until now—all of it could be a dream. A dream she might never escape. She shook her head. No, it was too much. The Enchantress' appearance and her words. Ayva could read the truth in them.

The Enchantress wished Ayva to have the blade and stop the evil that was coming. Ayva could only do so if she were set free. Besides, what possible reason could the Enchantress have to torment her so? But if it *were* a dream, that meant Hannah could still be alive. Zane may still be whole.

A part of her hoped it was. She could do it all again and do it better. She could save Hannah, save Zane. Yet she was so tired, and part of her knew something she didn't want to admit.

If she did it all again, she doubted she'd live.

"It's not a dream," Ayva said firmly. She'd found the sword, Zane was still alive and she would stop Vaster's sickness. It was worth it. The Enchantress's words echoed in her head: *In real life, evil destroys, and there will always be a cost to stop it.*

Dalic nodded, taking a breath as if allowing himself to come back to the moment, to believe this wasn't a dream. For a moment, Ayva wondered what Dalic's visions had been. What darkness did the Algasi leader run from? And what could set a man like Dalic on edge?

But her questions were blown away as Dalic's eyes fell to the blade at her side. "Is it true..." he ventured. "Could it really be?"

Ayva gave him his answer. She took the sheathed blade and drew it forth, clearing it from its scabbard with a crystalline ring. The woods seemed to still at that. She felt her heart beating in her chest loudly as Dalic's eyes fell to the blade of light, shining like a second sun. He strode forward, eyes locked. His men followed. She held the blade out in both hands, feeling the warm steel in her upturned palms. A foot away from the blade Dalic fell to one knee, as did his men, drawing his weapon free and ramming it into the wet earth. Words issued from his lips, too fast and low for Ayva to understand, but she gathered their intent when he rose.

531

Tears glistened in Dalic's eyes. "At last. You've found your second heart."

"And the salvation of Vaster," she said. Ayva waited, half-expecting and half-fearing Dalic's next move. Would he try to take the blade? His men looked ready, their hands moving to their spears planted in the ground.

But the Algasi leader gave only a bare dip of his head. "So it seems."

Ayva surprised herself. She heaved a huge breath, sheathed the blade, and embraced the Algasi leader. He didn't hug back, but it didn't matter. She felt his muscles relax beneath her embrace. Pulling away, she found her heart buoyant.

Dalic glanced around, taking in the scene, seeing the scorched black ground from Zane's rage and the small fires that still burned. The two enormous Vergs. The black Verg in chains, huffing angry hot snorts, but sullen otherwise. And the unconscious beast lay beside the cracked boulder. Then he saw Sithel's bloody vestige still bound to the boulder. "It seems I've missed a great battle," he said. Ayva told him briefly what happened, retelling her fight in a bare bones fashion. But with each subsequent word, from defeating the Vergs, first with the *lightbonds*, then with the boulder, to finally her fight with Sithel, Dalic's eyes widened. At last, he nodded, proud. "I named you Lightspeaker before. I name you again. Lightbringer. You are she. For that was a feat only the Lightbringer herself could accomplish." Ayva felt her cheeks grow hot.

"But Sithel got away," she said, guilt and anger warring inside her. "We failed. *I* failed."

"You didn't fail. The sword was our goal and you have it."

"But those we've lost..." She shut her eyes to prevent tears, then opened them, holding Dalic's gaze. "Sithel mercilessly ended their lives and now he's gone, escaped, and it's my fault."

Dalic placed his hand upon her shoulder. "A man's death does not bring back the lives of those we loved, even one as wicked as Sithel. Besides, that demon tasted defeat this day because of you. He has been proven weak, and he *will* find his end, this day or another."

Ayva felt pure hatred wanting to burst inside her, but Dalic's words calmed her.

Then Dalic gave a brief glance to Helix.

"A newcomer," Ayva explained.

"Helix," said the boy. "That's my name. You all aren't very good at introductions, are you?"

"Median?" Dalic asked, taking in the man's apparel.

Ayva noticed the subtle signs too. A long white shirt and a light, ill-fitting blue jacket. Upon closer inspection, the jacket looked like it at one time had been a blue haori—what most Medians still wore and the traditional garb of the Ronin and many other kingdoms of old. But it had been fashioned into a more modern jacket by adding a flaring collar and sleeves. The stitching at the seams wasn't so bad, actually, but she noticed it. Helix also wore white fingerless gloves and heavy brown boots whose tops were folded over, like many sailors or pirates of the Frizzian Coast. A dirty red sash circled his narrow waist.

The youth had blue eyes, dry, windswept hair that stuck on end from Median's constant salty breezes, pale skin and thin lips—all of which were common traits of a citizen of the Great Kingdom of Water. Then she saw a mark on the boy's forearm. *Scars?* But before she could examine them further, Helix quickly tugged his sleeve down, hiding them. She saw his look. Shame and fear. "I…" Helix began. "Maybe once," he admitted softly, then took in his surroundings with a sigh. "But no longer. I have no home now." Then he looked away. To the south. And Ayva assumed he was embarrassed. Dalic asked no more.

The Algasi leader turned, taking in Zane on the ground. "The fire-speaker… is he?"

"Alive," Ayva said. Then her throat grew tight. "But Hannah's dead. Sithel killed her."

Dalic nodded solemnly. "He will be alright. The fire in him was strong."

But Ayva wasn't so sure. She nodded but kept silent, unsure of what to expect from her friend now. The Enchantress's words held truth, she knew. What would happen to Zane without his moral compass? She feared for him to wake and face his demons. But whatever his demons were, she swore he wouldn't face them alone.

A cool and soothing light rain began to fall. Little fires that had dappled the glade hissed, steamed, and then were extinguished. Even to Ayva it felt like a washing away of sorrow. She felt their eyes on her.

"What's next, Lightbringer?" Dalic asked.

And Ayva looked up through her plastered hair, returning Dalic's cold blue gaze and hefting the Sword of Sun. "We go home."

533

Gray's End

ray kicked open the door with a crash and quickly took in the
dark room. Melted candles littered every table, chair, and over-
turned book, but they did nothing to press back the depressing
gloom. The rest of the room was a jumbled mess in Gray's frantic mind.
Cork-stopped bottles. Strange, shiny metal instruments. Dried herbs,
tree bark, and fungi hung from the cramped rafters. And hundreds of
books, most musty and ancient looking, rimmed the walls on an array
of shelves, stands, tables, and were piled from floor to ceiling. Dust was
everywhere. Only the table in the center of the room seemed clean, if
cluttered. A smell permeated the air. The same overpowering one that
he'd followed.

The cloying smell of death.

Two people inhabited the dark room.

One huge hulking figure sat in a chair, which strained beneath his
massive muscled frame. He wore a bearskin shirt and rugged leather pants
that still sported bits of fur on them. His hands cradled a leather-bound
book, almost ludicrously small for his frame. He'd been obviously reading
until Gray's entrance. Now he stared at Gray with a hooded expression
of wariness.

The other person was a gaunt-faced old man, the centerpiece to the
room. He stood working over a bundle of fur and blood. The old man
twisted at his entrance. He was short and nebbish-looking and had a

stooped back, accentuating his short stature. But those eyes: brown and hard. Not piercing, but like dirt hardened into clay, pounded over and over again into little nearly black stones. Those deep brown eyes quickly assessed the crashing door, the limp body in his arms and the blood.

"Please... Help me..." And the last of Gray's energy fled him. His legs gave. Suddenly, hands were there to help him. "Put him down here, Walsh. Yes, facedown, just like that. Quickly now, watch his head and for god's sake, don't torque his spine!"

A woman rushed out from a side room, wiping her hands on a cloth apron, rushing to help. "By the gods, be gentle you two lummoxes—he's just a boy." She was breathless as she helped Walsh lay him on the table. "Wash your hands thoroughly this time, Drowsy. Simple mistakes cause for simple deaths."

"I'm not going to kill him, woman. Not unless you kill me first with your incessant badgering."

"Badgering? I'm not badgering! Badgers badger. I'm helping!"

Clearly, Drowsy, the old man scoffing in disgust, was the healer Gray was looking for. The healer waved his hands, ushering the two back as he bent over Darius, examining his injuries. Drowsy mumbled as he worked. "The last time you helped me was when you left the room to let me do my business. And I can't remember when that was..." He interrupted his sentence to prod his fingers slowly up and down Darius' spine to the left and right of the bloody wound. He *tsked*, shaking his head, his wrinkled face crinkling in disappointment.

"What?" Gray asked worriedly. "What is it? Is he... he's going to live, right?" The words sounded so... weak. He clutched his stomach. The chair behind him looked inviting, but he wouldn't sit.

"Live? He's not going to die yet, if that's what you're asking. Living, on the other hand? That will require swift hands, perfect silence, and on your friend's part, a strong will and a light heart. Does he have that?"

Gray nodded.

Drowsy smiled, but his eyes held a worried but determined gleam as he twisted back to Darius. He quickly washed his hands in the nearby soapy basin as he spoke in a clipped tone. "Bernie—get me the gut and needle, will you?"

"If you call me that name again, you'll need to be watchful of your missing shears and your manhood to follow." But the woman quickly did as he instructed, an anxious look on her face. Gray's whole body felt

535

clammy, and not just from the sickness.

As Bernie, or whatever her real name was, pulled away and the old man dove into work, the woman looked to Gray at last. "My gods, child… You look worse than Drowsy's experiments gone awry. Sit, sit, you poor thing…here." She grabbed his arm, leading him to a chair. Gray staggered, his muscles going wet and weak and he fell. "Help me, you big lump of muscle!" the woman shouted. The big man, Walsh, had been standing, watching the whole exchange until now, and together they guided him to a nearby seat. "What ails you, young one?" she asked as Gray sat.

"It's nothing," Gray said. "Darius, he—"

She ignored him though, primping and prodding, two fingers to the inside of his wrist, lifting his lids, and—

As she lifted his lids her breath caught in her throat. She staggered back.

Walsh caught her as she tumbled, knocking over corked-stopped bottles and a stack of musty tomes. "Bernice!" Walsh rumbled. He shot a dark glare toward Gray, as if Gray had mysteriously backhanded the woman without him seeing. Walsh's chest heaved and he glanced to a huge cudgel that rested near the hut's entrance.

"I… I didn't do anything," Gray said. "It wasn't me."

Bernice waved off Walsh and slowly rose on aging limbs. "I'm fine, Walsh! Lay off. It wasn't the boy, you silly oaf. You would see that if you used your brain for once and not just your muscles." Somehow she said the words sweetly. Walsh grunted as if unsure, but the big man helped her to her feet and she hobbled to Gray again. Gray felt her gaze to his heart. Deep, penetrating, knowing.

She knelt back in front of him and looked deep into his eyes. "By the gods… It's true… What drove you to this, child? You enacted a bloodpact more binding than the Messiah's and the Great Kingdoms' *Three Rules*."

Gray swallowed. "I…" He felt nervous and afraid beneath her look. He delved her with the ki. Fear. Knowing. Compassion. *Sorrow*. "How long do I have?" He kept his voice low; he didn't want to distract the old man from his work, from saving Darius. But he had to know.

His pulse raced as Bernice read his eyes. "Only two people in all this green land know Farhaven's maladies this well, and neither is me, child." She looked over her shoulder. As if on cue, Drowsy looked up from his work. Gray wasn't sure when he'd donned it or how long he'd had it on, but Drowsy now wore a strange apparatus on his head with leather straps and hooks. All designed to hold a thick looking glass that made his right eye appear bug-eyed as his head swiveled to Gray. He handed the needle and gut to Walsh as he limped over.

"Darius?" Gray asked worriedly.

Drowsy's hands were covered in blood. So much blood... The aged healer looked weary, making him appear even older. "He lives. I've done all I can."

"That's all? You've done all you can?" Gray realized he sounded angry. He didn't care. He staggered to his feet, gripping the old man. "Please, do more! Heal him! You have to... you have to promise me he's going to be alright."

Drowgard, not Drowsy, stared back at him. Hard. That small frame seemed suddenly tougher than old oak, and Gray's power and anger seemed so childish in the wake of all that happened. Drowsy gave his answer with a steely gaze. "No." Gray's heart dropped. "I'm sorry, but life has no guarantees, boy." The old man took a deep breath. "All I can promise is that he's crossed through the worst of it. That's as much hope and promise as I can muster for you."

Gray slowly sat back down, his anger dying. "And... the Sungarsi? My sickness?"

Drowsy scrubbed his chin in thought. "Radament, my Sunha, might be able to cure it... He was working on a cure, a way to heal the spark in those deprived. That is, until that bastard Marlan stole most of his life's work."

Gray looked to Bernice, sensing he was missing something. "Marlan," the woman said tersely. "He's Drowsy's brother. Marlan was Radament's Diaon too, until the day he filched from his own Sunha. An unspeakable act of treachery."

Then Drowsy shook his head as if angry, but moved forward. "Forget it. Ancient history and useless to us now. 'Cure the sick, leave the dead.' The worst and best advice I've ever received, and you may lean to the latter, my boy, but you still have a chance at life. But only if you leave. And now."

"Do you know where your other half is? Your bloodpact partner?" Bernice asked.

Gray looked to the bent floorboards. "I hope, but I don't know... "

"Sometimes hope is all we have, boy," said Drowsy. "My wife is

537

right..." He gripped the hand that still held his lapel, examining the pulsing black veins beneath Gray's paper-thin skin. "You're dying, boy. You should be dead. I've never seen a man with that much sparkrot about their eyes still with breath in their lungs. Whatever drives you onward is truly something. But it won't last. You'll die and soon, unless you find your other half and fulfill the bloodpact's oath. That's the only way."

Bernice hobbled forward and touched Gray's arm warmly. "Go, child. Please... Your friend is safe with us. I promise." Something in her eyes held a fear, a memory and Gray quickly delved her with the ki, unable to help himself.

He felt her tired bones. Not nearly as tired and achy as his head, and not with sickness, but of age. Beneath those tired bones, pounding in her heart was a simple emotion...

Love.

Compassion.

And a protective grip to her weathered hand. Motherhood. Gray trusted her. He unslung his sword. "In payment."

They hesitated. Bernice shook her head. "Child, we've no use for—"

"Please, take it," he said. "I've no coin or anything else to barter with, and you saved my friend's life. Hold onto it for now, and when I return I'll return with coin to repay you for what you've done."

Something in Drowsy's eyes swirled as he looked at Morrowil. And he simply nodded for the two of them before Bernice could refuse again. "So be it," the old man said.

Gray placed the sheathed blade on the table beside Darius as he knelt at his friend's side. "I..." Gray was afraid to leave, but it wasn't just that. He was terrified if he did... And he left Darius... Faye may not be there, and when he met his end, he'd die alone. Alone, cold and afraid. Like those days so long ago in the Lost Woods, running without an identity and stumbling upon Mura's hut. Now he'd found family and friends. *I don't want it to end this way. It won't end this way.*

"I'll return for you," he said, then pressed his forehead to Darius's. "Goodbye, my friend." Darius gave a rattled, soft breath in reply and Gray turned, stalking toward the door. As he opened it, he paused. "Whatever you do, don't touch the blade. And if I don't make it back, find the queen of the elves. Give the blade to her. She'll know what to do with it. And if not, tell her to bury it. Bury it so deep that no one will ever find it."

With that, Gray left the three and entered the light of day. He would head towards the Citadel.

To find Faye and save his life. Hopefully.

* * *

Gray moved. He found the Node quickly enough, but as he entered the stand of tall frawn-filled dola trees he saw no sign of the archwolf or the lordling. Fear, like ice, made his blood colder than it already was. He stumbled about the glade until he heard laughter. Puzzled, he followed it and found a scene that made him question his remaining sanity.

Cid had stripped himself of his fancy coat and shirt and now stood bare-chested waist deep in the Node's turquoise pond. In his hands, the boy had a plank of fallen dola bark and was now using it to scoop and toss water at the archwolf. As he did, the archwolf leapt onto its heavy hind haunches, batting its golden wings. Gray felt a surge of fear for the lordling, only for the fear to be instantly replaced by bewilderment. The archwolf lunged forward then stopped, batting its light-woven wings to create a spray that doused Cid in turn. Both turned at his entrance. Gray must have looked a sorry state for Cid's mirthful face suddenly darkened, laughter dying.

"Gray..." Cid paused and looked around. "Where's Darius?"

Gray barely heard him though. He was already dismounting, and he didn't stop moving as he tied the cormac to a nearby dola and reached for Morrowil, only to realize it wasn't there. Slowly he moved to the pile of clothes near the water and with one hand grabbed a cloth shirt, and with the other withdrew Cid's ceremonial dagger that the lordling had unbuckled in the midst of his frivolity. It made a clear ring and as he neared the cormac's side he checked the blade's keenness. Sure enough, it drew a thin line of blood across his thumb. Satisfied, Gray moved to the cormac, aware that the lordling was watching him in confusion, but he was in his own world. A world of burning focus and anger.

Only as Gray put one hand to the cormac's warm flank, whispering an apology did the boy shout, leaping from the water, "What're you doing?" Cid cried and Gray lifted one hand as Cid charged forth. The last trickle of his power came, bidden by his anger and serenity, and he blew the lordling back into the water. Casually he glanced over his shoulder, seeing Cid sputtering water, and then looked back to the cormac.

"What I have to," he said and cut. Not a large cut, but a clean, smooth

539

incision about two fingers in width several hands in length—he wouldn't fail because he was too shy and gave too little for the archwolf to eat. He continued to usher apologies as he cut, keeping his eyes clenched tight and feeling the blade's path until it was over. He opened his eyes and saw a flank of meat on the sandy ground. He noticed its color—less red and more a strange pink hue. The cormac hadn't even moved. Blood dripped down his hands and down the cormac's silken hair. It covered Gray's hands, hot and sticky. He felt sick to his stomach and he vomited, but it was only a dry-heave as there was nothing left in his guts. Somehow it hurt worse. He gagged and retched, feeling as if he was trying to free his stomach from its lining. At last, he stopped, and Gray wiped his mouth and rose, feeling eyes on him. When he looked up the cormac was look-ing to him. Its pure silver eyes held a strangeness in them, and Gray was certain he would never be able to ride the beast again.

The archwolf had watched as well.

Gray growled, kicking the slab of meat. "This is what you wanted, isn't it? This is why Darius got a dagger in the back and I sit on the edge of death, one breath from either ledge, for *this*." The archwolf just watched him. "What are you waiting for?" he said. "Go on, eat it!" At last its huge wolf paws tramped the divide and it wolfed up the hunk of meat.

Revulsion rose inside Gray. He wanted to be sick, but he took an angry breath and suppressed it all as images flashed through his mind.

Open blue skies. The rush of wind.

"So be it." And they rode.

* * *

Gray's world was a blur as he moved relentlessly, riding the archwolf toward Farbs to find Faye.

"I won't die—not lying down," he growled into the wind as he gripped the archwolf's feathered fur tighter. Those words were a repeating man-tra, giving him life, as minutes rushed by like hours. His fingers grew weak but he held on. Wind rushed about him, which was normally re-assuring, but he now felt as if the wind were trying to rip him from the saddle. Gray's hands began to tremble, growing sweaty, slipping inch by inch. He was sliding from the saddle. *I'm going to fall*, he realized with a calm clarity. He almost shouted for the archwolf to slow, but the cry died in his throat. Slowing down would spell his death. He spotted the long leather reins circled about the pommel that he'd forgotten in his haste. Quickly he wrapped the reins about his waist, then bound them around his wrists and tied it to the leather saddle's pommel. His muscles failed him as he did and he became limp in the saddle. Luckily, his makeshift leather bonds held him.

Fly, he pleaded to the archwolf, and the beast understood and increased its pace, racing faster over the desert plains.

Then he saw it. In the distance. He feared it was a mirage again but he didn't stop. His eyes opened and closed in long intervals. *Black keep.* Then the darkness of his mind. *Tan walls nearing.* Then darkness. Each time the darkness lasted longer and longer, until he feared it would last forever. At last, he saw silver specks... Farbian guards walking the walls of Farbs.

Gray's arms began to shake and he saw black veins beneath his pale skin pulsing. His lids grew terribly heavy, wanting to close but he forced his eyes to stay open. *No. I have to see this.* He rushed over the city's gates, and, even in his numb state of mind he heard the gasps of the city guards. Crowds saw him and they pointed to the sky, murmurs rushing over the thousands of citizens preparing for their day, garbed colorfully. He must have looked a sight. A golden winged beast from legend and its death-like rider. But Gray's eyes were only for the Citadel. The black castle sat in the heart of the city, drawing nearer. The archwolf flew faster than it ever had. Gray felt something dreadful and yet paradoxically *peaceful* rise up inside him. His chest swelled with the feeling as the archwolf soared over the black gate with its tall black spikes—the entrance to the Citadel. Gray knew what that feeling was…

The end of all things.

Death had finally come.

Gray's eyes began to close, too tired to fight despite the burning anger inside him. Distantly, so distantly, he was aware of contact. Huge paws landed on soft earth. And Gray's last image of this world as the leather straps unwound from his wrists and waist, as if by threads of silken air, was a figure. Across the long dirt courtyard she stood in menacing armor with a spiked pauldron and kohl-blackened eyes.

She watched him, wavering on her feet, a thousand and one emotions flashing across her face that he could scarcely register. But he noticed one emotion amid them all.

Disbelief.

They had actually found each other. The crystal white sand on her clothes—picked up from the famous white dunes of the Rehlias Desert and carried on the constant Farbian winds. Farbs. Her skin too had a deeper tan, as if from the Farbian sun, just like he'd seen in his visions. And he realized they had led him here, to this moment.

Si'tu'ah had worked.

As Gray fell to the earth and to eternal darkness, his last word was soft on his lips.

"Faye."

A Cold Hearth

It had been two days since Hannah's death. They were back in Vaster, and despite being hailed as a hero, Zane was a cauldron of wrath and despair.

He retreated from the celebrations to their quarters high in the Apex, turned the glass walls to their darkest tint to block out the sun and closed out the world. Laughter echoed in the corridors beyond. Zane growled and waved a hand. At his gesture, the fire in the hearth flared to life. The hot flames ate at the wood until cracks and snaps overcame the sounds of merriment.

He was sick of celebrations—they felt jarring in light of the darkness in his heart. Zane had grieved fallen friends and loved ones before. He'd mourned for Father, the gentle, ancient-seeming caretaker of the Lost Ones who had all but raised him. When Father died, it felt like a chunk of his heart had been excised and then thrown away. This was different. Hannah's death felt like the rest of his still beating heart had been ripped completely free. The anger never seemed to abate. All he wanted was for the pain to end.

Only his anger consoled him. And to help fuel his ire, Hannah's death replayed in his mind. He imagined step-by-step the horrors Sithel had visited upon his sister. Alone and afraid, she'd likely waited for him. She might've even taunted Sithel, telling him Zane would come. But he hadn't. Cold and alone, Sithel had wrung her throat. She would have fought, but it would've been useless against the demon's strength. Then the terror would have set in. The fight would have turned to panic, to a sudden dark realization that... She was all alone, that Zane wasn't coming and that she was going to die.

The fire continued to roar, growing until it burned beyond the hearth's confines. Zane debated letting it consume him, but instead closed his eyes. As he did, the darkness came. It was only in the darkness that Zane could see her, and hear her voice.

"*Don't die.*"

The words were so soft, a faint echo in his head, but he knew it was her voice.

Hannah. "Why not?" Zane asked. He spoke the words in his mind. He knew his eyes were still closed, but his mind painted a picture. He was inside the room in Vaster. But instead of a room that was orange and cozy, he saw one that was black and menacing. And in place of the fireplace before him, there was a rocky, dark ledge. His feet scraped the edge and little rocks tumbled away—into death and madness. He lifted one foot, hovering it over the fall, contemplating that black chasm. How comforting it looked. To end it all, to not feel this weight upon his chest, this crushing sorrow and unquenchable anger that was Hannah's death. Somewhere back in his own body, the heat of the fire grew on his skin. "This is a deserving end. Without you I've nothing left."

"Oh, stop it. You're putting a Resah bull to shame with words like that. In fact, I'd wager there's not enough Resah bulls in the world to dish up such a load of crap." The voice came from everywhere in his mind, all around the room.

"That language," Zane growled. "Where did you even hear something like that?"

"From you."

He sighed. "I really should have watched my tongue."

"You watched my back, my front, and even my soul. That's enough watching for any one man. Even you."

Zane sighed again, staring into the abyss.

"Stop sighing!" she said, appearing at his side, materializing from thin air. She wore her white dress with blue flowers. She had her hair in braids again. Hannah scowled at him and smacked him on the arm—but the fist passed right through, as if made of cloud. "You're beginning to sound like a gust of wind. Ronin of fire, my fat—"

He shot her a glare and she smiled. He opened his mouth to sigh again, but suppressed it and simply asked, "What am I supposed to do?"

But she faded. He waited, teeth gnawing, praying for her to return. But he saw only the darkness of his closed lids. Zane opened his eyes. The fire had died down, sinking back into the hearth. Zane's hand gripped the smooth, white marble mantelpiece. He bore Hannah's cloak around his bare shoulders as he stared into the flames, watching, thinking.

He hadn't slept in days—he wondered if that was the reason for the visions when he closed his eyes. Hallucinations. But he wouldn't lie down. Sleep was the last thing he wanted.

It had been two days since they'd returned. Gray and Darius were still gone, but Zane, Ayva and Helix had found a triumphant city. Ayva and Helix were nowhere to be seen—gone to Lord Nolan to discuss the future of the sword or something. It didn't matter and he didn't care.

Outside, despite the height of the Apex and the thick glass walls, with the fire dampened—he heard muffled cheers again. The celebration continued. It seemed it would never end. The mirth in the hallways returned once again.

It reminded Zane of their homecoming.

Trumpets and horns and pink flowers. He'd seen Lord Nolan too. The Steward's face had been lined and worn, aged a hundred years in the span of two weeks. But upon seeing the sword, relief and joy had washed over Nolan's tired visage. Zane knew the man's great and terrible burden had been lifted.

It didn't start so cheery and bright.

The day they returned, entering the gates, they'd been greeted by a surprising sight. Vaster was a graveyard. The streets had been empty on their arrival, and dark shadows skulked in all corners. Shops shuttered. Doors locked and barred. They'd rushed to return the sword to its rightful place, putting it back in its hold beneath Vaster, where the Macambriel had been shattered. As soon as Ayva slid it home, there had been a dazzling burst of light, blinding all, followed by a torrent of air. They'd walked out to see that the Sunroad, which had been blackened, was changing... From his place on the city's highest rise, Zane had watched it flow like a river of molten gold, snaking through Vaster once more, alive. And as the Sunroad returned to its former glory, so did Vaster. The shadows slunk back, retreating. Even the sun came out to greet them. So had the people.

People had stumbled out of their abodes—men and women, children, the elderly, blinking in the bright light. They moved slowly, their eyes wide, as if surprised to see the outside world still existed, still intact. They whispered curses and blessings and hugged those that still lived. But so many fewer people, Zane had noted. He could see the missing ones. Mothers without children or without husbands—or men all alone. Some were stone faced and still in shock, whereas others wore gutted expressions of heartbreak. The sickness had struck them all. He guessed a third of the populace had survived, but it was only a bleak guess from his very dark heart. No one spoke of the sickness. Instead, their darkness and despair turned to hope and smiles.

And in a whirlwind, the largest celebration Zane had ever seen sprung from nothing. Not thrown by the city or Council or any ruling establishment, but by the people themselves. Thousands flocked, preparing foods, giving gifts, lighting streamers and twirling great long colorful bands of ribbons. From somewhere, thousands of pink blossoms from hame trees were gathered—children and adults alike went to the city rooftops to rain them upon their heads. Ayva, Zane and the Algasi had trotted back to the center of the city in a flurry of flowers.

Zane was dimly aware of the claps on his back from jubilant Vasterians. Ayva, and he, along with Dalic and the last Algasi, were heralded as heroes, gifted with anything they wanted. Citizens had tried to approach them in droves, but thankfully Nolan had kept most at bay. Zane even listened to the hollow words of approval from the Council of Sun. But it all felt like a dream. Even drawing his sword on one of the lords and nearly cutting the man's throat for his ignorant words was a vague memory. Still, thousands rejoiced, alive, because of them and the return of the sword. Part of him had even felt content at that. The rest had felt empty, dead. Like a cold fireplace, devoid of all warmth.

Zane looked to the fireplace. Sitting on the mantle was a long, spindly branch with pink blossoms and flickering candles that smelled of cinnamon—decorations the servants recently brought for the celebrations. On the mantelpiece was something else. Something that *he* had placed, fished out of Ayva's pack. A glass bottle, its murky black contents swirling and alive. Brisbane. Zane stuffed down the memory of him, Ayva and Hannah receiving it from the strange woman in her apothecary shop. He snatched the bottle, feeling its warmth in his hand.

"What am I supposed to do, Hannah?" he asked again, watching the fire die and the hearth grow colder.

But there was no answer.

Until…

A knock.

Zane stared at the door, puzzled, but didn't reply. Helix or Ayva wouldn't knock, and a servant or maid would introduce themselves, so maybe it was just his imagination, like the voice of Hannah. Maybe he was going crazy. Then the knock sounded again, almost timidly, and the door opened.

She looked different. On her shoulder rested her thick brown braid. She had white ribbons in it this time instead of gold. He was surprised to notice that. Those perceptive, benevolent eyes—he could almost hear her thoughts churning as she stared at him. *What was she thinking?* Her dress was different, too, than the night he'd knocked on her door. The white and green silk was a tad less…. *less.* It covered her fair skin from head to toe and wasn't see-through, but it fit her like water.

The real distinction, however, was her expression.

Evangeline stood in the doorway wearing a small, mischievous smile, "I figured since you knocked on my door in the middle of the night, I'd return the favor." He said nothing, and her smile wilted slightly, and she clutched her arm as if a cold wind had blown through the open door. "Well? Are you going to let me in?"

A silence stretched until—

Zane lifted his hand, letting the fire in the hearth grow to a cozy crackle.

Evangeline's smile returned and she entered, closing the door.

547

Another Life

Ayva kicked off her shoes and wriggled her toes with a luxuriant sigh, feeling the plush carpet beneath. Standing and serving all day in the inn could be exhausting and her shoes were too tight for her feet—her father said she'd get new ones soon but she was still growing fast and he was afraid she'd replace those twice as—

She shook her head, confused. *New shoes? What am I thinking? I don't need new shoes.*

But the thought slipped away as she laid eyes on her small cot and the little lantern nearby, and the stack of tomes more precious than a pile of glimmering gems.

She practically giggled—*giggled?*—as she leapt into her hard bed, belly first, landing and making the covers flop. She reached over and snatched the nearest tome stacked haphazardly on her nearby bedside stand and dove into a world of magic and intrigue, a world from long ago and faraway.

"Farhaven..."

She cracked the spine with a smile on her face.

The pages were smudged with dirt. Her fingers had fanned over the well-loved pages more times than she could count. She wasn't sure how much time went by as she read, her mind spinning with distant lands and magical places like Covai—the city of flesh where man and beast toiled beneath the harsh sun like a glaring yellow eye. Or Drymaus, a forest where it was said the primordial creatures of the world rested, magical beings like Dryads and elemental Dragons—even the Great Dragon, composed of all the nine elements—entities that had existed since the dawn of time, since *before* the Lieon and the Great Kingdoms' formation even! Of Sprytes, balls of pure energy, each comprised of wind or water, fire or stone, and so much more. Her head spun with it all, and though her eyes grew tired, the rest of her only grew more breathless with each adventure. Finally, she set down *Fables of Farhaven* and gripped her favorite tome with pages falling from it like a brittle branch with cracked autumn leaves.

Tales of the Ronin.

Delicately she pulled it close to her chest and started to read when she heard a small creak behind her.

"I figured that's what mischief I'd find," a voice said from behind her. "Why couldn't you steal pies, or play in Sophie's pig pen or even throw eggs at grumpy ole' Shamus' house like the other kids? No, not my girl. Instead, you forget that thing called *sleep* and drive your old man up the wall with twice as much worry."

Ayva froze guiltily, hands on the pages. She looked around. He stood, a dark silhouette in the doorway, thick arms folded across his broad chest. He had wild blond hair, both from his head and a hairy chest that was partly exposed due to his wide-neck tunic. The combination made him look like a great owl, and she a mouse. Behind him the rest of the inn was perfectly quiet—tables and chairs now empty and cold, waiting for the warmth of a new night, for the sounds of Sophie's harp, and for the laughter and life only a common room could possess.

"Do you know what time it is? How late it is?" he asked her sharply.

She peered up. A tiny window outside was dark, but faint rays of light showed that it was almost dawn. Soon Parker, the blacksmith, would be up to clang away on his hammer and anvil and the tendrils of life would seep back into a waking Lakewood.

Her heart clenched.

Lakewood... Lakewood is gone. She wanted to say this, to ask where she was, but instead spoke as if another were controlling her, as if she'd said it all before—her mind in a track like a cart down a Menalas mine rail. "Sorry, Da. If it helps my case anyway, it's not *technically* late anymore. It's really more early than anything." She made her best attempt at cute, not sassy, smiling and wincing.

549

His stern face broke at last and a grin split his gruff features. "I can't stop you, can I?"

"Probably not," she admitted. "It's not your parenting, really. I'd find a way to read if the Ronin themselves were ushering me to bed." *That was true. But the Ronin?* That comment felt so odd now for some reason. *But why?* It escaped her brain like fingers grasping at mist.

He clicked his tongue. "You say that word so freely, and you know I don't mind, but others do."

She sighed. "Because they're superstitious and dumb—"

He arched a brow, looking at her sharply.

"I mean, *'gifted with less between their ears.'*"

His expression darkened even more till the points of his brows touched, then he broke out into a laugh despite himself. "I don't know what to do with you sometimes, my little bookworm. And worse yet, the smarter you get, the harder it is to parent you."

"Then don't?" she said, wincing. He rolled his eyes and she filled in quickly, "I'm teasing. You're a great parent, Da. Really. You know it, I know it. Just... don't worry so much."

He scratched his head, at a loss, then pointed to his disheveled blond hair. "Gray hair. Soon. Because of you."

"You're welcome," she said, smiling, "because I think you'll look distinguished as ever. The ladies of Lakewood will chase you all the more."

He only grunted in reply. He hadn't taken a wife since Ayva's mother had passed and she knew it was because he loved her so—he said his heart was still torn in two and another woman wouldn't bridge the gap. He said no one could ever fill her mother's shoes. But sometimes she wished he were wrong. She wanted to see her dad happy, even if it was with another woman, but she felt a small bit of satisfaction that he hadn't, either. He was hers and she liked it that way.

He sighed again. "If I can't stop you, at least I can keep you from going blind as a bat."

"Bats aren't blind," she replied.

"Sure they are," he said, nearing with his second lantern, bobbing in her dark room and lighting his broad nose and casting shadows across his tan face. He placed it at her side. "I'm baffled you can read at all in this darkness," he said, squinting at the page. It was a page on Omni and her foray with a Menalas king and Esterian king who had attempted to unite to form a Great Kingdom. It was her favorite. Of course, she knew the way it ended—she could practically recite the words from memory, but she liked pretending the words were new each time. This story in particular always did seem to have a freshness.

"You know the page is only for show," she admitted. "Besides, it's not that dark."

He squinted over her shoulder than shook his head with a laugh. "If you say so," then turned. At the door he looked back. "Bed soon," he instructed, wagging a thick finger, finally serious.

"Soon," she promised sincerely and smiled.

"Good night, sunshine."

She warmed at the name—her nickname since she was a little girl. "Goodnight, Da." And he shut the door, and with it the memory shut as well, the dream fading as little Ayva turned back into the world of the Ronin.

* * *

Ayva awoke, sitting up sharply.

The dream was pleasant, or should have been—a sharp contrast to the horrid visions given by the Enchantress—but somehow it had given her shivers.

They were back in Vaster.

It'd been two long days of travel. Zane had woken up the first night in a cold sweat. Ayva had sat at his side, comforting him, but he hadn't said a word. She'd wanted to say something, to console her friend, but she honestly didn't know what to say. When she finally opened her mouth, saying his name, he'd gotten up and walked away into the night. Staring at the darkness, she'd feared he wouldn't return. At last, when he did, she silently swore she'd hold her tongue—afraid a single misplaced word would make him leave once more and he might not return. She told herself she'd give him some time, at least a week. And so they rode.

Upon reaching Vaster, they were greeted with darkness and sorrow. After they'd returned the blade, however, Vaster came alive. She'd feared the city had become a cemetery, but she was proven wrong. Thousands of Vasterians slunk from their abodes as the Sunroad had been relit, returning to life. As soon as it did, Vaster transformed. They were hailed as heroes, flower petals rained from the buildings, the sounds of trumpets blasted from all corners of the city and the sound of cheering continued

551

for what felt like days. Food, drink and laughter were plentiful. They rejoiced as if they had won the Lieon, and perhaps in a way, they had. The Lieon and so many who had died were redeemed.

Redeemed, but at what cost?

Now back in her room, Ayva's fist curled, gripping the covers. She looked around the room, seeing the dark outline of Helix, but no Zane. There were still flower petals on her pack. She kept her blanket wrapped around her shoulders and rose. She touched the fog-glassed window and it turned clear. Outside the moon still shone, but it was light as well. The sun always rose early in Vaster, she knew.

Ayva looked to Helix who slept with a thin blanket over him—blond hair covering most of his face. The youth was a curious one… He told her he'd survived the Western Pass to the Everglades, the path with the blizzard. No one survived the Western Pass. He was—

There was a soft knock, disrupting her thoughts. "Come in," she offered quietly, still lost in a trance, staring at Helix. She looked up to see Lord Nolan standing in the dark doorway. He wasn't wearing his gold pauldrons of phoenixes in midflight, or his other fancy regalia, but he still looked grand. She was taken aback. Ayva wasn't sure who she expected, but his presence still surprised her.

"Might I… have a word with you?" he asked softly, glancing to the sleeping form of Helix.

She nodded, and motioned to the door that led to the balcony.

He followed her, and together they moved to the terrace, then she closed the glass door so as not to disturb Helix. Standing on the balcony, far above Vaster, the morning had a chill wind and she wrapped her blanket tighter around her like a shawl.

Thoughts assailed her.

This was the same balcony that Gray and Darius had stood on, one of the last moments she'd seen them before they'd left. Standing here now felt like standing in their shoes, but so much had changed. Hadn't it? She hoped that they were okay, that they were still alive, that she would see them again soon. She needed them to.

Nolan stood for a long moment, his hands on the smooth railing, staring out over his city. He seemed content with silence and she was too. "It's a hobby of mine," he began, nodding down to a series of ramparts that connected a set of tall towers that surrounded the Apex. They were stone, not glass, and not nearly as tall as the central tower, but still awe-inspiring.

A year ago, Ayva would have thought she were dreaming to see just a glimmer of this city. The Steward of Sun continued in a casual, pleasant tone, "I used to walk those ramparts. Used to, and still do, I suppose. They help me think. Formulate my troubled thoughts and give me hope." He paused for a long time until she thought that was the end of his thought. "That seems unnecessary now."

Now that you are here, she knew he was thinking. Hope. The word returned to her once again, a beacon she couldn't avoid. She looked to him. He was older than her, and yet he looked to her for salvation. She supposed that would happen more and more soon. She gave a small smile, then looked away, turning from his bright gaze to the city. To beyond the city.

Nolan continued, his voice graver. "The Ronin won't be a secret for long after this—stories of the returned Sword of Sun have already traveled across Farhaven. The girl who is responsible will follow shortly after. It'll only be a matter of time until they know your name, your face and who you are."

"Some might think it's simply gossip or rumor," she replied finally. "The Ronin are legends, thousand year-old heroes with the power to level cities and ravage armies. Not a seventeen-year-old girl and her friends."

"Some will doubt," he admitted. "I myself was… skeptical at first." He'd attacked her, Zane and Hannah with his Lightguards to prove their status and worth. She thought that act was more than just 'skeptical.' But she didn't belabor his point with semantics. "But enough will still wonder."

She jumped to the heart of his point. "The Ronin won't stay secret for much longer."

"I'm afraid not."

"What do we do?" she whispered. Not so much to Nolan, but to herself, to her friends that weren't at her side.

"I know I might be stating the obvious, and forgive me for doing so, but not all the world will treat you as I do—as Vaster does." Ayva knew that was a grand understatement bordering on just plain ludicrousness. Vaster now regaled them as heroes, whilst most of the world loathed the Ronin. Nolan continued, "You have a long road ahead of you. Convincing the world you're Ronin will be your first difficult act. The second and harder task, will be to prove that you're here to save them." Both those tasks sounded impossible, but Ayva didn't interrupt him. "And with this dark

553

trend of 'strength is life, weakness death'—it's growing. I fear the will of Farhaven and its peoples' minds are more polluted than ever. Your presence and the dreaded 'Return' might very well start another war, another Lieon."

Ayva shivered, gripping her blanket tighter around her as if to stave off his words, but they had the ring of truth. *Gray, Darius—where are you dammit? I need you—now more than ever.* And she replied, staring out on Vaster, "You know, for a moment when you arrived, I thought you were coming to tell me that breakfast was ready, or that we're to be awarded some sort of metal for our efforts. I wish I'd been right."

He put a hand on her shoulder. It felt fatherly, warm. She needed it in that moment. "I'm just trying to help."

She looked up into his eyes. They crinkled, apologetic but resolute and she nodded. "We will do what's necessary."

Nolan looked hopeful. "I know you will. And so you know, you'll always have a home in Vaster. We will help you in any way we can. The council may not agree with me, but with your recent deed, well… let's just say they won't have their way for a while. You have the peoples' hearts, Ayva."

554

She smiled in return, and nodded solemnly. Then a silence formed between them and she asked, watching the rising sun as it lit the great city in shades of gold, "Is that all?" She meant it as a joke, but Nolan shook his head. She glowered. "What else is there?"

And Lord Nolan, Steward of Vaster, smiled and answered, "Breakfast is ready."

THE BEGINNING OF THE END

The Shadow King was growing soft. The feeling made a vein throb in his forehead and his muscles twitch with the urge to use the great Yronia blade on his back. Since he was young, he'd sworn to carve a path of truth and unite the world, but all that he'd worked for, all his well-laid plans were now threatening to collapse.

555

One thing was certain.

Blood would flow.

After all, his rule depended on it. One ruled by strength, or died by it. And after his little… disaster with Faye, he needed to prove his might. If his men thought him weak, or smelled blood, like the serpents off the Frizzian Coast, they would tear him apart. He wouldn't even blame them for it. He could take dozens, maybe a score or two… but all of them? So Halvos stalked his way deeper into the Black Hive's warrens towards Leah's quarters.

Everything depended on her now—she would spell his success or ruin.

The Shadow King passed into the smoky blue caverns and saw it was empty.

His cloudy white eyes surveyed his surroundings—dripping water, little pools that gathered in craggy recesses, and archways of natural stone. Water dripped from stalactites meeting with their pointed stalagmite pairs. Thick candles flickered, resting on rock shelves scattered along walls, and on little plateaus of stone jutting from the rock floor.

Leah had requested the candles. He'd refused—he preferred the dim blue light—but she'd insisted for a whole year. At last, he'd granted her wish. At the far end, the vaulted chamber narrowed like a funnel, continuing in a winding series of tunnels that hadn't been fully explored. His men feared the eerie tunnels, and Halvos saw no reason to pursue the knowledge within. His battle was for the surface of Farhaven, not its depths.

Everywhere hung the blue vapor of Narim.

To most, the blue vapor was simply an attribute of Narim, the Great Kingdom of Moon. To Halvos it was much more. It was alive. And as is the case with all living things, the blue vapor exuded a subtle emotion. It was hard to describe the emotion—something akin to melancholy.

Halvos had his guess why the vapor was 'morose.' While it kept the city of moon alive and fulfilled its duty, perhaps the magical entity hoped for more—to be the guardian of life over a city of death was a paradox he doubted it wished for. Tales told that Narim had once been something grand, much more than a dark hold for the pitiless.

It would be much more again. He would see to that.

It would be a kingdom to dwarf all others.

But because the blue fog had an emotion, all that the blue touched shone for Halvos. He could see. It still rankled that Faye, the red-haired bitch, had found a way to hide from him. She had somehow learned to hide her emotions completely from him, and he'd been blinded because of it. But it was his fault. He was not so blind as to blame others. His confidence in his nearly faultless plan had been his downfall. All things had a weakness—he hadn't seen his own.

"Where are you?" he asked, voice booming off the craggy walls, shuddering the small dark pools, causing ripples that he couldn't see.

A splash sounded. On the far right wall, there was a prison—a cave he'd fashioned into a wall to hold her. From the dark depths of the prison, she walked forth. Leah held the bars with slender fingers, looking at him. "Here, my king."

Halvos soaked in her emotions, giving him a vision of her. She was thin, malnourished. A paper-thin dress that was once white clung to her bony form. Now it was a drab brown from the dust of the caverns. Scars laced her arms, ankles, and even a few shining white lines peeked from her dress's neckline, slashed across her collarbone. The rest were concealed—he'd made sure of that. He wanted to leave his mark, but not to ruin her beauty. Each was shiny and a few were raised like white welts—he'd preferred his own hands when doing such things, but occasionally a whip and other devices, had been called for to break her spirit. Fortunately, the pale lines were difficult to see against her porcelain skin.

Narim's blue light touched Leah's face. The face…. Those same perceptive, almond-shaped eyes with that same slight, exotic, and alluring tilt. But she was thinner than Faye, which made her features sharper, her cheeks more sunken, her eyes more hollow. Although it lessened her beauty, it gave her a haunting appeal. She was beauty stripped of all its niceness, of all its softness, like a blade without any polish or embellishment—only an edge fine enough to cut through flesh and bone. However, with a bit more fat on her bones, Leah and Faye could have been twins. Their emotions, however, were opposite.

"What're you playing at?" he asked—his voice a dark rasp that made most people unconsciously take a step back in fear.

Leah didn't back away, but she did flinch. It was minor and she regained her composure quickly as her bony hands caressed the prison's bars. "What? You don't approve? Come, my king, don't be so dull. After all, you built this for me, and I'm just…" She smiled. "Reminiscing."

Halvos watched her as she casually lifted the latch—which no longer bore its tarnished, heavy iron lock—and opened the door. It screeched in grievance due to its ill-use—yet another sign that he was softening. She strolled out of the prison, her hips swaying with each step. Each time, her ripped skirt exposed her shapely leg and that… delicious curve at her hip. Halvos' lip curled in pleasure, amusement and interest. More than anything, she fascinated him. Leah watched him as she approached—holding his eerie gaze—quite aware of what she was doing. She drifted over a puddle, letting her dress drag across it, as if oblivious or uncaring and reached him.

He loomed over her.

Leah gently placed her hand on his chest. He'd removed his dragon-borne armor and now his broad chest took deep breaths, and she put her ear to his stomach as if listening to something. "Have you ever listened to your own heartbeat? I like to listen to my own sometimes in the dark of night as it thrums, pumping lifeblood to every part of my body, over and over again without fail." She inhaled a big breath, listening. A smile grew as she looked up at him. "Yours beats like a drum," she remarked with all the wonder of a child. He watched her, curious. She did this from

557

time to time, reverted into a childish reverie. She would cry and squeal as if she were about to be attacked. She would cry 'daddy' when he'd beat her—a time that felt ages ago now.

Looking back, the act had been base, disgusting even. Torture was primitive. Brutish idiots tortured and bullied to make themselves feel superior. Halvos had no need for that. He knew was superior. The torture had been for a greater purpose—yet never had he imagined it—she—would turn out quite like this. He had tried to break her, to make her a puppet, and instead found something else entirely.

But now Leah's eyes weren't full of fear seeing the demons of her past. They glittered with intelligence. She continued, "Some might find the fact that you have a beating heart a weakness. A soft spot." She jabbed where his heart was, accentuating each word, then looked up at him with pure adoration. "I find it lovely."

Halvos' eyes tightened. This was the side that had him baffled, entranced, and… afraid. What had his beatings done? What had he broken inside her? She wasn't a sycophant. He had those. This was different. Could it be real? Worse still, her eyes didn't hold the doe-eyed glaze of a love-struck fool. Instead, intelligence and fire burned in her eyes, and he saw gears turning in her head. She was thinking, calculating even now. Halvos suppressed a shiver and pushed her away, but he didn't give the shove enough force and she held onto his arm. "You know that lovesick gaze of yours turns my stomach," he snarled, a low growl. But there was no real threat in his voice, and that wasn't why he pushed her away. Sometimes it felt as if she were peering into his soul.

Leah ignored him. Her hand that had been caressing his muscular chest had found a nick where a falling stone had cut deeply—a mark from her sister.

Leah's eyes danced with amusement and her childish grin became wolfish. "My my, look what she did to you… Perhaps I had good cause to be hiding in my cell. It seems it might be the only safe place now."

"Faye will die."

"Will she? That was the plan before, was it not? She was gift-wrapped for the butcher, for you, and you failed."

"Failed?" Anger rose inside him. She knew it wasn't wise to taunt him too far. But she always skirted the limits, fingers dancing right above the fire's flames.

She continued, "She only came because of me. I brought her to you—I gave you all that you needed. She was bloody and ruined, and you failed. She beat you."

He moved fast. His hand came across her jaw, laying her low. It felt like hitting brittle timber, seeing it crack beneath his monstrous blow. Wisely, he didn't use his fist. She might die from that, but his open palm still left a growing red blemish on her pale, sunken cheek. Leah rose to her feet, gingerly touching her face. "You forget your place," he boomed.

"And yet you lost to a half-dead woman," she said with smile, blood leaking from the corner of her mouth.

Halvos felt an admiration for the fire in Leah's eyes, overpowering his anger. He reached out his hand. She took it and rose shakily. Looking at her, he felt a strange mix of emotions warring inside him. Her eyes showed nothing—a strange hollow void where love should be. Reaching out with the ki, he felt even more cold. He sifted into her body and felt little tendrils of emotion: rage, sorrow, despair, and a dozen others. But each felt faint, as if they were not locked away, but dried up. Leah was a void of emotion—a chasm that made him uncomfortable. He pulled away quickly, as if he would be infected by her complete lack of human emotion.

Before him, contrast to what he'd just felt, Leah touched him tender-ly. "She'll come again," she said, almost sweetly. If he knew better, he'd think her tone sincere and comforting. "It's in her nature. She never gives up, and she won't give up on me."

"Then we wait." He hated that it sounded like a question, as if he need-ed her advice. But he did.

Leah shook her head. "We were lucky this time. Faye's determined, not stupid. She won't make the same mistake. *Si'tu'ah* runs in her blood. By instinct, she'll have seen our layout and its every weakness. Now she'll sit back and like a spider, she'll spin her web. Next time, she'll be ready - with an army of her own, and a plan to bring us to our knees."

Many things stood out in Leah's words. Not in the least how well she knew her sister. Darkeye had been a formidable enemy. Having no male heir, Darkeye had imparted his viciousness, his lethality, and stratagems to Faye. It had been a beautiful realization that Faye hadn't been the only benefactor of Darkeye's wisdom.

More than that, Leah had been right about everything so far. She had said her sister would arrive alone. She'd been right. That she would come with rage in her eyes, clouding her vision and making her forgo any

559

rational plan. Again, right. With Leah's help, Faye was delivered on a platter. It irked him that it had been *him* that had failed. And the question thundered in his head, *why? Why was she helping him?*

"And then?" he asked.

"We will be ready for her."

"How? She won't simply go away and if she lives, she'll return to Farbs. Darkeye's forces are bigger than ours as we stand. The other thiefdoms will not join us now—not as we stand." Unfortunately, although Halvos ruled all of Narim, the Great Kingdom was still a pittance compared to the other kingdoms. It had fractured over centuries. All the good inhabitants had left as the city grew ever darker, dwindling their population. The inhabitants who remained preferred to kill, and destroy, rather than live and reproduce. It left him with a hollowed out, ever-dwindling city. The other thiefdoms seemed to have a constant pool of talent to draw from—their cities on the surface swelling and nearly bursting, so unlike Narim.

Leah held up a finger. "If she can unite the clans. If she decides to build an army. If she survives. If she decides to march on us, which she won't until she knows it's a fight worth taking. And that's more ifs than weeds in a garden."

"Then what's your plan? Faye isn't the merciful sort, and I won't leave this to chance. I won't fall to her again."

"You're not seeing the bigger picture, my love. Our army *is* growing."

He narrowed his gaze at her, not understanding.

"Farhaven's sisters, brothers, mothers, fathers… they will come, seeking us—seeking a home that will succor their belief of strength over weakness. We must promise them that if they serve and show their might, that they will live and be rewarded for it."

"Where are these supposed followers?" he asked with a snort.

"Everywhere," she said with a smile. "From the Aster Plains bloodshed, from the Seria's inner turmoil and their royal war, to even Dryan and Karil, the misplaced princess of Eldas, and their growing war."

Halvos smiled in understanding.

She clung to him tighter, her fingers curling only part way around his thick arms. "You see, don't you my love? The world is our crop. We have planted the seed, and soon we will sow it. Soon we will be too big to catch for the spider. Very soon. But for now? We must be the wasp. And the wasp is clever. Once it lays its venom inside the spider, it waits for its prey to burst from the inside out. I know her. Give me a few of your best men and I'll teach them how to close the distance, to climb her web, to plant the dagger in her back. If she doesn't die from that, then our swelling armies will eat the remains. In the end, her web will be her demise. They'll be no hiding from us."

"Us…" he repeated the word, testing it in the air.

Leah smiled, a vulpine grin. "We're in this together now, my love."

That look in her eye meant one thing.

Blood would flow.

561

562

"The Shadow"

The Final Age will come to play,
When darkness, like the end of day,
Worms its way to make us pay.

In the robes of truth, it holds its sway.
Until the Ronin, like the dawning sun,
Rise and make the darkness run.

- Inscription seen carved into the Black Hive, and inscribed in the codex of 'Lost Songs' by Atheria Alasi, a two-stripe Reaver, 952 A.L.

564

ACKNOWLEDGMENTS

To my amazing Kickstarter supporters, especially David Telles, Jason D Kobylarz, Paul Muller, Gerald P. McDaniel, and last but not least Joshua Gray – an Omni Level backer. These are huge and incredibly generous individuals who have done so much for The Ronin Saga. I appreciate you and your support more than you know.

To Victoria – my beautiful, kind and tirelessly supportive girlfriend who has worked beside me, both at conventions in the thick and amazing mire of signing books, or just day-to-day - where the true stress and hard work occurs. Whether it's listening to me blab about characters, or debate editors, she's there for me. The Saga is so close to my heart and each decision is weighty, important, and on occasion onerous. However, with her help, I take the next lumbering step to make a better series.

To Flavio Bolla for more amazing cover art that blows my mind – his hand depicts the world of Farhaven with stunning clarity and brought Vaster to life. To Logan Uber for tireless edits and when I stumbled, he picked me up. And he always has believed in the Saga's potential. That meant everything.

To Vanessa Carlson, for her amazing edits out of the goodness of her heart and a love of the story. With an incredibly astute eye you poured over the book and helped me bring out a better reiteration. Then I thought I was done, and yet again, we found a deeper cord, a stronger scene, and a better story. If the book was good, then you helped make it great.

To my Beta Readers - thank you! Including you Maddy - thanks for your keen proofreading eye - you deserved the award that day. And thank you Emily for your amazing design work, yet again, and putting up with my endless "Can we include this?"

Lastly, to all the fans I've ever met at conventions, libraries, bookstores, and more. You pushed me, inspired me, gave me such heartfelt words of encouragement - to make something better, to not settle. I only hope I've not disappointed, and I hope you enjoy what's to come. The Saga has so much room for growth and such an amazing foundation because of you. Thank you.

GLOSSARY

The terms within are not equal with regards to the timeline of the Saga. Lastly, what you see below are terms mostly pertaining to the Ronin and their legacy, for a detailed background on the history of the Ronin and the war of the Lieon see www.roninsaga.com.

Algasi (ALL-gah-si) – Nomadic warriors who originally hail from Vaster. They are dark-skinned with light, curly hair and are often short. They are considered "as hard as stone," with every moment spent training their bodies to be weapons. They value light, truth, and courage.

Apex – The majestic center building of Vaster where the Chamber of Sun is located.

Arbiter – A supreme threader of magic, whose home is the Citadel. The title of arbiter is reserved for only the three most powerful threaders of spark in Farhaven. To become an Arbiter one of the mandatory requirements is a "Grand Creation"—to create and object, artifact, or device that will help mankind; and will exist for all time.

Arbiter Fera (Ar-be-ter Fairuh) – The third most powerful threader of the spark. Enigmatic and playing behind the scenes her nature and ultimate plans are hidden to almost all. She is also one of the few spark users who attempts to understand the flow, and researches and experiments with magical creatures. Her half Darkwalker half phox pet is always at her side.

Archwolf – rare mythical mount of Sun.

Aurelious (Oh-RAIL-ee-US) – A Ronin, also known as the Confessor for his ability to pull the truth from his enemies. His element is that of flesh and his home is Covai, the Great Kingdom of Flesh. He is brother to Aundevoriä and known for having a small temper, but a fierce love for his brother, and loyalty for his Ronin brothers.

Aundevoriä (ON-de-voria) – A Ronin, also known as the Protector. He wields Durendil, the stone blade and his home is the Great Kingdom of Lander, a fortress of stone, its walls thicker than most cities. He is known for his willingness to sacrifice all for the sake of humanity.

Ayva (AY-va) – Ayva is the tomboyish, intelligent friend of Gray and Darius. She and her father ran The Golden Horn in Lakewood. Ayva is an avid reader of the world that lies outside Lakewood.

Balder – A man who claims to be the leader of the Stonemason Guild.

Baro (bah-ro) – A Ronin, also called the Bull and Slayer of Giants. His element is that of Metal, and his home is Yronia, Great Kingdom of Metal—a city that is a mass of steel and billowing steam. Its forges were once lit with undying fires but now it is one of the "forgotten kingdoms". Baro wields the blade Iridal, a giant sword made of unbreakable steel. In all the stories, he is larger than any man known, described as having a waist like an oak trunk, and shoulders as broad as an ox, often known as the one who led the vanguard of the Ronin into battle.

Bloodpact – a pact made by two or more people in blood that is sealed by the magic of Farhaven. Both parties must fulfill the whole of the bargain or Farhaven will demand payment.

Burai Mountains (boo-rai) – Endlessly tall mountains that reach towards the heavens, and are often called the spine, or back of the world. Death's Gate is nestled between these impassible peaks.

Calad (Kah-lahd) – One of Hiron's famous twin swords.

Citadel – A great keep of black stone within the Kingdom of Fire, and home to both Devari and Reavers.

Cloudfell Lake – Lake beside Cloudfell Town, turquoise waters and low-lying mist make the lake look like it hovers just beneath the clouds.

Cloudfell Town – A lively series of towns linked together—a common rest stop for wayward travelers full of taverns and inns.

Shining City – The great city in the mountains. It is a part of a massive kingdom, and the last remnant of the Kingdom of Ice.

Cormacs – Cormacs are elvin steeds. They have long legs and broad, powerful chests which makes them formidable sprinters. They have shorter muzzles than a horse, long silken tails, and slopping backs. Karil also mentions they are attuned to the spark.

569

Covai – Kingdom of Flesh, the city of men, women and beast, land of the Mortal Being, one the largest spiritual sects of all the lands.

Covai Riders – A vast horse tribe from the Kingdom of Flesh that controls much of the plains of Farhaven.

Curtana – Dared's twin daggers, thin with broken tips.

Cyn (KIN) – A game played with small, carved figurines, consisting of followers and a mark.

Daerval (dare-vahl)– A land without magic, on the other side of Death's Gate.

Dalic (DALL-ick) – The leader of the Algasi tribe—a two-stripe Mundasi warrior.

Dared (DARE-ED) – A Ronin, also known as the Shadow. His element is that of moon and his home is the Great Kingdom of Narim—a vast sub-terranean gem located in the dark hills, half above the land, half below. The least is known about Dared. He is said to never have spoken. Rumors of his powers include the ability to turn completely invisible in the night even under the brightest moon.

Dared [the statue] – Dared the silent Ronin in statue form.

Darius (dare-ee-us)– Darius is a wiry young man of seventeen who is from Lakewood, and we learn very little of his parentage; he appears to be an orphan. Darius is perhaps most well-known for his love of gambling, a skill he holds no modesty about.

Darkeye – Leader of the Darkeye clan whose hold is called Lairof the Beast. He is famed for his brutality and malevolent deeds. He wears a cloak that flaunts these skills, showing the patches of slain Devari.

Darkwalkers – Creatures that are neither living nor dead. They are im-mune to the spark and most weapons save for a Devari's blade. They are described as black beasts with many forms, like a "hundred-limbed spider" or even walking on two legs. Most, however,
are faceless with black prism like bodies that shine like obsidian and knife-sharp limbs and beady dark eyes.

Death's Gate – The infamous gates that divide the two lands. The origin of the name is said to come from all those that died during the Great War, specifically during the final battle that stained the White Plains red.

Desiccating – To remove one forever from their innate spark. It is a dread-ed occurrence that is often worse than death to any threader of the spark.

Devari (duh-var-ii) – An elite group of warriors who live within the Cita-del, and they are masters of the blade. Using "Ki" they hold certain powers, including inhabiting another's body and feeling their sensations. They have two ranks, apprentices and "Sword-Forged", Devari who wield powerful soulwed blades.

Diaon (die-on) – Translates to "knows nothing". It is title given to ap-

prentices and slaves of Farhaven.

Dipping Tsugi – Mistress Hitomi's inn in the Shining City.

Drowsy – Healer who helps Gray and Darius.

Dryads – Fabled magical creatures of the forest of Drymaus, a great mythical forest to the north of Eldas.

Dryan – High Councilor and elf who takes the throne after Karil's father, King Gias dies.

Drymaus (dry-moss) – A magical forest where the spark hangs thick in the air. Home of the mythical dryads, baalrots, dragons, and more.

Dun Varis – An offshoot and fragment of Lander, the Great Kingdom of Stone, rumored to exist again within Daerval, and Aundevoriä's homeland.

Durendil – Aundevoriä's famed sword. It has a wire-wrapped handle, and turns to stone.

571

Eldas – Home of the Elves, also one of the nine Great Kingdoms—the Great Kingdom of Leaf.

Elders of Eldas – Also known as the sages or High Council of the City of Eldas. They are the ruling council of the Great Kingdom of Leaf.

Elementals – Magical creatures of Farhaven. More commonly known as "Sprytes". See: Sprytes. [Also commonly confused with "The Elementals."]

Elementals, The – Also called "The Guardians." Fabled myths about magical beings the size of cities that are the essence or embodiment of each of the nine elements. Stories claim they look like sprytes. According to most fables, "sprytes" are the elementals' children.

Elements – A game involving the different elements, wind, water, moon, sun, fire, stone, leaf, metal, and flesh. Each figurine is called a "shard" and is often made of glass. There are nine clear pieces that can be raised to elements, and each element varies on how many paces it can move on the board. Certain elements work better in conjunction.

Eminas – The name for Gray used by the elves, and literally means eminent one, but its variant meaning is harbinger.

Ester – A rich mining city once bound together with Menalas, once considered a "false kingdom". They are known for their gems. Often referred by its nickname "Emerald Ester".

Ethelwin – A powerful Reaver and lecturer who is only a few below in rank and prestige of the female Arbiter.

Ezrah – Arbiter of the second rank who lives in the Citadel, and Gray's grandfather.

Farbs – The sprawling desert city wherein the Citadel resides.

Farhaven – A land full of magic, on the opposite side of Death's Gate.

Faye – Enthralling and unpredictable, Faye is a woman of many talents. A skilled fighter and a Farhaven-versed individual, she aids Gray, Ayva, and Darius on their journey to Farbs. Though with strange ties to Darkeye and his clan, she finds a way to be both a
curse and a blessing in disguise.

Fendary – Also called the Stormbreaker, or the Sentinel. Fendary Aquius was a high general during the Lieon who supposedly fought the Ronin.

Fisher in the Shallows – An advanced technique where one flows through Low Moon stances, and makes several sweeping horizontal slashes directed at the attacker's legs.

Fisher in the Shallows to Dipping Moon – A snaking thrust to an upward strike, from which its power is derived from the bending and swift upward lift of the legs

Flow – *What is often called the source of all magic, or the "essence." It is what the Ronin thread.*

Frizzian Coast – *Located in Farhaven, full of peaceful towns and villages along the coast and in the Northern provinces.*

Full Moon – *A defensive stance where one's blade is above the head and their knees are heavily bent in order to absorb and redirect coming blows. It mimics the pattern of the arcing moon in the sky or a sphere, where water flows off the perfectly round surface, unable to find solid contact.*

Fusing – *A bond between magic threaders that threads even greater power. It is said hundreds of Reavers were used in ancient times to forge epic creations, including the transporters.*

Heartgard – *The name for Seth's famed sword; meaning brave, enclosed.*

Godfrey – *councilor of Vaster.*

Great Tree – *The tree that is at the center of Eldas, and bears the Spire; the great buildings where all nobility reside.*

573

Gryphons – *Mounts of Farbs that are half eagle and half lion.*

Hall of Wind – *Within the legendary Morrow, Great Kingdom of Wind. Mura claims Kail stashed his most precious of weapons in the "Hall of Wind."*

Hando Cloak – *A black and forest green cloak Rydel wears. It signifies that he is one of the Hidden, the highest rank of warriors among elves.*

Haori (Ha-o-ri) – *Colored vests, each matches the powers the Ronin hold, and the color of the Kingdom they represent.*

Heartwood – *Harder than most human metals, most of Eldas is constructed out of it, including the Gates of Eldas.*

Heron in the Reeds – *A powerful and agile strike from above—most of-*

ten where one baits with the front leg, then pulls it into a "Heron" (a stance upon one leg), and strikes down at the now lunging and exposed attacker.

Herbwort – An herb that aids with shivers and insomnia.

High Council – The council of elves in Eldas that oversee affairs; see also Elders of Eldas.

High Moon – A Devari stance where the back leg is heavily bent, and holding the majority of the weight, while the other foot rests lightly upon the ground. The fighter's shoulders are angled, just enough to minimize a target, but enough to engage their upperbody,
turning for powerful strikes if need be. It is a stance few ever master.

Hitomi – Often called "Mistress" Hitomi. Hitomi is the proprietor of the Dipping Tsugi in the Shining City.

Hiron (He-row-nn) – A Ronin, also known as the Kingslayer. His element is that of water, and the Great Kingdom of Seria. He is known as the peacekeeper, and the Ronin of wisdom and serenity.

Iridal – Baro's famed sword, rumored to be impossible to shatter.

Jiryn (Jiro) – A High Elf healer from Eldas.

Kage (KAH-gey) – The nine nameless evils that pose as the Ronin and have similar powers.

Kagehass – The saeroks and verg's name for what others refer to as the Nameless (the Shadow's Hand).

Kail – The once leader of the fabled Ronin. He is known by many names, from many eras including the blight seeker, betrayer of men, and the wanderer. He is rumored to have survived the Lieon, and still exists, told in fearful tales for the past two thousand years.

Karil – Karil is the queen of Eldas, home and kingdom of the Elves. She is half-human and half-elf. Karil is tall and beautiful, with silver eyes, and *white-blonde hair. Her beauty is only equaled by her intelligence.*

Ki – The source and power of a Devari. It is equated to intense "empathy"—the ability so sense another emotions and react to them. The stronger the ki of a Devari, the more nuanced emotions they can read within a person.

Kin – Dark men and women who are agents of the "shadow", specifically the Kage. Gray runs into one in Lakewood when trying to retrieve the sword.

King Gias – Karil's father and the King of Eldas.

King Katsu – King of the Shining City.

King Owen Garian – King of Median, the rebuilt Great Kingdom of Water—said to be a righteous man of conviction with a blue tinted beard.

King Orulus Garian – The ancient King of Seria—the lost Great Kingdom of Water. He is the first in the line who ruled during the Lieon. Often called "The Tranquil King",Orulus is the great ancestor to King Owen Garian.

Koru Village – A small town just north of Lakewood.

Laidir – The second of Hiron's famous twin swords.

Lair of the Beast – The home of the Darkeye clan within the Underbelly, the world beneath Farbs, Great Kingdom of Fire.

Lakewood – A peaceful town. It resides close to the ill-famed Lost Woods. It is the home of Ayva and Darius.

Lander – One of the "forgotten kingdoms". Lander was the Great Kingdom of Stone. It was a city that had walls purported to be the size of a small village.

Lando – Translates as "redeemers" or "liberators" in the common tongue. They are the group that saves Karil in the woods of Eldas.

Lieon –The war in which the Ronin supposedly nearly destroyed the world.

Limfuns – very tart, almost bitter citrus fruits.

Lokai/Lokei – The god Darius evokes; the god of "luck".

Lopping the Branch – A slashing strike, twisting the torso and attacking the opponent's head.

Lord Nolan – Steward of Vaster, Great Kingdom of Sun.

Lost Woods – The infamous dark forest where Gray and Mura live, and said to be full of direbears and other nefarious beasts. Villagers say the woods come alive at night, and travelers who venture in are rarely ever seen again.

Low Moon – A Devari stance where one leg is heavily slanted for a low center of gravity for balance and stability, and the other is heavily bent and holds the majority of the swordsman's weight.

Malik – Leader of the Kage. He has a spiked pauldron and is bigger than his brethren. He speaks to Vera and is the voice of the dark army.

Maris (mare-is) – A Ronin, also called the Trickster, a Ronin of many names and faces. He wields Masamune, the leaf blade—its powers unknown. His element is that of leaf, and his homeland is the Great Kingdom of Eldas.

Maris' Luck – The most dangerous inn in Farbs and perhaps all of Farhaven.

Masamune – The Ronin of Leaf's blade.

Mashiro – Guard captain of the Shining City.

Matriarch – Leader of the phoxes.

Menalas – A southern city of Farhaven that was once joined with Ester under a single banner long ago. However, they were deemed a 'false kingdom' at the end of the great war and forced to split and divide up their power, becoming Menalas and Ester. To this day, many of their citizens and rulers still lust for a powerful throne that no longer exists, to return to their former glory. During the Lieon they tried to unite once more, but failed. Menalas shares a single, great iron mine with Ester that produces much of the metal for Farhaven—almost a complete monopoly after the fall of Yronia. The city of Menalas is known for gold, silver and platinum; as opposed to their gem savvy sister city, Estar, they are known as "Mining Menalas" for the metallurgic opulence.

Mirkal – Darius' cormac.

Mistress Sophi – She owns an inn in Lakewood, and taught Darius how to dance.

Morrow – A city upon the windy high cliffs of Ren Nar that oversaw the world. It is the Great Kingdom of Wind. It is one of the three lost Great Kingdoms and the most famous. It is Kail's homeland. It contains the Hall of Wind, the famous meeting place for the great kings, queens, and generals who fought for the armies of Sanctity and against the Alliance of Righteous in the Great War of the Lieon; and according to stories, housed some of the rarest weapons and relics of all time.

Morrowil – The infamous sword that Gray inherits from Kail.

Mortal Being – A religion of Covai that often encourages self inflicted bodily harm to achieve a higher spiritual state.

Motri (moh-tree) – Gray's hawk and companion, who also seems to have a mysterious alliance with Karil.

Mundasi – The elite warriors of the Algasi tribe.

Mura – Mura is a charming, but irascible hermit. He is Karil's uncle

577

and close friend to Gray.

Nameless – Created from Reavers, a horrible evil that mists from thin air, and is rumored to be invincible to "mortal blades." Their armor is made from overlapping dark plates. Gray and Darius fight them in the back alleys of Lakewood, behind the Golden Horn.

Narim (NAIR-im) – The Great Kingdom of Moon in the dark hills, half above, half beneath the land, and is a vast subterranean gem.

Nell Atwood – Shopkeeper of Apothecary's Attic.

Neophyte – A threader of the spark, the newest initiates to the Citadel, and the rank below a Reaver. They reside in the Neophyte Palace and wear gray robes.

Nexus – The source of Gray's power. It is a swirling ball of air that he focuses on to tap into his power.

Niux – A unit of twelve, that consists of vergs and saeroks.

Nodes – A magical oasis and a safe haven for all living creatures of Farbs especially in times of dire need.

Nolan – Steward of Vaster. His daughter is Evangeline.

Omni – A Ronin, also known as the Deceiver. Omni's element is that of Sun, and from the Great Kingdom of Vaster. Omni was the right hand and second-in-command to Kail, leader of the Ronin.

Oval Hall – Where the Seven Trials takes place in the Citadel. It is beautiful and ancient.

Phoxes – Angelic white creatures with long snow-white fur, sharp elongated teeth, and huge silver eyes. They are wind creatures, and mounts of the city of Morrow, Great Kingdom of Wind. They are led by the Matriarch.

Patriarch – The well-known benevolent ruler of Farbs, the Great King-

dom of Fire; as well as the most powerful threader of the spark and first rank
Arbiter.

Quenching the Fire – A Devari stance.

Reaver – A powerful threader of magic trained in the Citadel, in the City
of Farbs.

Rekdala Forhas – "Honor and duty" in the Yorin tongue.

Reliahs Desert – A vast desert in southern Farhaven that surrounds
Farbs, sometimes called the Farbian desert.

Relnas Forest – The forest of Eldas, home of the elves.

Ren – Close friend of Kirin's and leader of the Devari. He wears a graying Komai tail, a long braid, and is described as ageless. Most characteristi-
cally, he is a man hardened from years of training and battle, both mentally
and physically. Descendent of Renald Trinaden.

579

Renald Trinaden – Warden and Keeper of the Silver, and author of The
Lost Covenant.

Rimdel – Trader's paradise or jewel of the Eastern Kingdoms–capital
with no central rule, inhabited by only thieves, ruffians and traders as hard
as stone, destroyed by the Kage.

Ronin – The legends of the Lieon, nine warriors who each holds a supreme power. According to the stories, they are dreaded and the bane of
mankind.

Rydel – An elf of the rank of Hidden, the most elite of guards that protect
the royal family of Eldas, the Great Kingdom and home of the elves. He
is Karil's ever-present companion and guard. He has shoulder-length dark
hair and piercing eyes.

Sa Hira – "I see", in Yorin.

Saeroks – Creatures in the Kage's dark army. They are tall beasts with thin, patchy fur, sinewy muscled frames, and long gangly arms and legs with long claws. They walk on two legs, but can run on all fours for greater speed.

Salamander – A powerful lackey of Darkeye who can thread the spark.

Sanctuary – The home of the Lost Ones within the Underbelly.

Seth – A Ronin, also called the Firebrand. Seth's element is fire, and his home is the Great Kingdom of the Citadel, a dark keep whose fires light the night sky. He wields the sword Heartgard. Seth is known for his fiery temper, and proud spirit.

Sevia (seh-vee-ah) – Green lands known for their wine, silk, and, unfortunately, bandits.

Shifting – Kail's rumored ability to transport great lengths of space in a short amount of time.

Si'tu'ah (sih-too-ah) – 'Way of the sword' literally translated from the Sand tongue; but more generally, it is a vast philosophy attributed to tribes dating as far back as the First Age, before even the Lieon. Its principles include both fighting and everyday life. Its core tenants revolve around using all facets of yourself (mind, body, spirit) and your enemy in order to succeed.

Silveroot – A tree of both Farhaven and Daerval. Within Farhaven it is described as having veins of glowing silver that flow visibly beneath its bark, and bark that shimmers like a fish's scaled belly. Within Daerval, where there is no magic, it is simply a large evergreen, producing nut-sized fruits.

Silvias River – A magnificent river that flows south and divides much of Daerval.

Simulacrum – A statue that holds the spark and can be used to convey messages over long distances. The young boy Lucky has one named Dared.

Sithel – The madman who takes over the Citadel. Possessed by a fear of his own weakness Sithel strives to be powerful. Though deprived of the spark, he uses others and finds power through servitude to a higher, darker cause and individual. He is described as oily in every manner, possessing a white robe that looks like a butcher's apron.

Spark – The magic that all but the Ronin thread, including Reavers, Neophytes and Arbiters, and the majority of Farhaven's magical beings. It is said to be derived from the Flow.

Sparkstorm - Storms fueled by the magic of Farhaven,

Spark fever – A potentially deadly fever induced by threading too much of the spark.

Spire – The highest building of Eldas where the council, king, queen and their family reside.

Sprytes – Magical creatures that are "pure" spark of a particular element; e.g. firesprytes, leafsprytes, watersprytes are just a few. They are seen as symbols of good luck.

581

Star of Magha - The famous insignia that symbolizes the eight recognized kingdoms.

Stice – Aurelious' famed sword.

Sungarsi - translates to "the black void." It is the antithesis to life, to the spark and the resulting sickness from the bloodpact's lack of fulfillment.

Sunha – translates to "the learned".

Sunroad – A Grand Creation of Vaster, the Great Kingdom of Sun—it sustains life, grows whole crops, provides energy, produces light, and gives vitality to all its citizens.

Taer (tay-err) – A northeastern land within Farhaven.

Tales of the Great Schism – Stories about the end of the Lieon and the

Devari's split from old alliances to new ones, including their origin in the Citadel.

Tales of the Ronin – One of most famous books about the deeds of the Ronin.

Temian – An elf with long golden hair, and strange golden eyes. Gray befriends the elf in the encampment beyond the Gates at the border of the woods.

Terus – A game where one flips a dagger in the air and attempts to catch it by the handle or blade.

The Great Kingdoms –The legendary cities. There were nine. Stone, Water, Leaf, Fire, Flesh, Moon, Sun, Metal, and Wind. Each kingdom was home to one of the Ronin, and coincides with their powers.

The Red Moon – A mythical event that is said to occur with "The Return" of the Ronin.

The Return – The fated return of the Ronin, an event the world fears. It is said they will finish the destruction of the lands they were rumored to nearly destroy during the Lieon.

The Rift – A rumored chasm where the world split thousands of years ago, before the Lieon and the Ronin even existed.

The Seven Trials – The trials that a Neophyte must pass to become a Reaver.

The Sodden Tunnels – The tunnels that lead out of the Shining City; a dark and dismal place with no light, full of thousands of misleading paths. At one point, Mura says darkness called his name within the Tunnels. Karil also refers to them as the "Endless Tunnels".

The Terma – Elite elvin warriors, the second highest rank in the armies of Eldas.

The Wasteland – A vile land where vergs and saeroks are rumored to be born. It is east of the Lost Woods.

Tir Re' Dol (teer-reh-dol) – Often called The First City. Appropriately named as it was the first city to rise from the ashes of the Lieon, and soon became the capital of Daerval for millennia.

Transporter – A device that transports a person to a specific place by use of magic. They are hidden around the Citadel. Ren says they were created by a hundred Reavers working as one through the use of a "fusing." See: Fusing.

Trimming the Stalks – A move that uses the rotation of the upper body and shoulders to lash at lower extremities, arms and sword moving in a figure-eight fashion.

Underbelly – The halls and tunnels beneath the Citadel and Farbs, including The Lair of the Beast, and Sanctuary. Some parts are said to have existed since the beginning of all the lands, created by unknown creatures.

583

Untamed – A threader of the spark who is untrained by the Citadel (neither Neophyte, Reaver, or Arbiter). They are often considered dangerous to themselves and others and a bounty is sometimes rewarded for their capture.

Vaster – The Great Kingdom of the rising Sun, named for the shining keeps that gleam like alabaster jewels, always in the dawn's light. Omni's homeland.

Vera – Kirin's sister. Gray's sister.

Vergs – Brutish, behemoth like creatures.

Victasys (vic-tay-sis) – A powerful scarred Devari who Gray and Zane befriend.

Void – the opposite of a Node, a dark place where no magic – spark or flow can be threaded.

Yorin – The old human tongue for all of Farhaven.

Yronia (YOR-own-ee-uh) – Great Kingdom of Metal once known for their gleaming steel and mountainous walls of iron, and home to the Ronin Baro. Also home of the Great Forge and the Deep Mines. However, its "unbreakable" walls were shattered during the Lieon and it now lies as one of the forgotten kingdoms.

Zane (ZAY-nn) – An orphan from the Underbelly, the refuge for all misfits and reformed thieves of Farbs. Zane is a hard-bitten young man. However, his rough, fiery exterior softens as he befriends the Devari Victasys and Gray. His sister is Hannah.

CPSIA information can be obtained
at www.ICGtesting.com
Printed in the USA
LVOW08*2244090217

523657LV00002B/2/P